MAN'S BOOK

THE VULTURE
IS A PATIENT BIRD

James Hadley Chase

*

ENQUIRY

Dick Francis

*

THE INNOCENT
BYSTANDERS

James Munro

ODHAMS BOOKS
LONDON

MADE AND PRINTED IN GREAT BRITAIN
BY ODHAMS (WATFORD) LTD.
SBN600778843
11.70

CONTENTS

THE VULTURE
IS A PATIENT BIRD

James Hadley Chase

'The Vulture is a Patient Bird' is published
by Robert Hale and Company

The Author

Born in London, James Hadley Chase was first
intended for a banking career, but preferring
freedom and the world of books he started selling Arthur Mee's *Children's Encyclopaedia*. He
says in two years he knocked on 100,000 doors.
It was always raining: now he hates rain—and
walking. At 20 he joined the biggest book
wholesalers in Britain, kept his finger on the
public pulse and worked out for himself what
it was the public wanted in fiction—he came up
with *No Orchids for Miss Blandish* (despite
never having visited the U.S.A.) and since then
has not looked back. He gets up each morning
at 5.20 precisely, and reckons to type two and
a half thousand words before one o'clock.

CHAPTER ONE

•

HIS BUILT-IN INSTINCT for danger brought Fennel instantly
awake. He raised his head from the pillow and listened. Black
darkness surrounded him: the darkness of the blind. Listening,
he could hear the gentle slap-slap of water against the side of
the moored barge. He could hear Mimi's light breathing. There
was also a slight rhythmetic creaking as the barge heaved in the
swell of the river. He could also hear rain falling lightly on the
upper deck. All these sounds were reassuring. So why then, he
asked himself, had he come so abruptly awake?

For the past month he had lived under the constant threat of
death, and his instincts had sharpened. Danger was near: he felt
it. He imagined he could even smell it.

Silently, he reached down and groped under the bed until his
fingers closed around the handle of a police baton. Attached to
the end of the baton was a short length of bicycle chain. This
chain turned the baton into a deadly, vicious weapon.

Gently, so as not to disturb the sleeping woman at his side,
Fennel raised the sheet and blanket and slid out of bed.

He was always meticulously careful to place his clothes on a
chair by the bed: no matter where he stayed. To find his clothes,
to dress quickly in the dark was vitally important when living
under the threat of death.

He slid into his trousers and into rubber soled shoes. The
woman in the bed moaned softly and turned over. Holding the
flail in his right hand, he moved silently to the door. He had
learned the geography of the barge and the solid darkness didn't
bother him. He found the well-greased bolt and drew it back,
then his fingers found the door handle and turned it. Gently, he
eased open the door a few inches. He peered out into the rain and
darkness. The slapping sound of water against the side of the
barge, the increased sound of the rain blotted out all other
sounds, but this didn't deceive Fennel. There was danger out
there in the darkness. He could feel the short hairs on the nape
of his neck bristling.

Cautiously, he opened the door wider so that he could see the
full length of the deck faintly outlined by the street lights of the
embankment. To his left, he could see the glow of light from

London's West End. Again he listened; again he heard nothing to alarm him. But the danger was there . . . he was sure of it. He crouched, lay flat and slid out on to the cold, wet deck. Rain pattered down on his naked, powerful shoulders. He edged forward, then his lips came off his even white teeth in a snarl.

Some fifty metres from the moored barge, he could see a rowing boat drifting towards him. There were four powerfully built men crouching in the boat. He could see the outline of their heads and their shoulders against the glow of the distant lights. One of the men was using an oar to direct the boat towards the barge: his movements were careful and silent.

Fennel slid further onto the deck. His fingers tightened on the handle of the flail. He waited.

It would be wrong to describe Fennel as courageous as it would be wrong to describe a leopard as courageous. The leopard will run when it can, but when cornered, it becomes one of the most dangerous and vicious of all jungle beasts. Fennel was like the leopard. If he saw a way out, he ran, but if he were trapped, he turned into a nerveless animal determined only . . . no matter the means . . . on self preservation.

Fennel had known sooner or later they would find him. Well, they were here, drifting silently towards him. Their approach left him only with a vicious determination to protect himself. He was not frightened. He had been purged of fear once he knew for certain that Moroni had decreed that he should die.

He watched the boat as it drifted closer. They knew he was dangerous, and they were taking no risks. They wanted to get aboard, make a quick dash down into the bedroom and then the four of them would smother him while their knives carved him.

He waited, feeling the rain cold on his naked shoulders. The man with the oar dipped the blade and made a gentle stroke. The boat heaved over the wind-swept water at a faster rate.

Fennel was invisible in the shadows. He decided he had judged his position accurately. They would board the barge about four metres from where he was lying.

The rower shipped the oar and laid it gently as if it were made of spun sugar along the three seats of the boat. He now had enough way to bring the boat to the side of the barge.

The man sitting on the front seat stood up and leaned forward. He eased the boat against the side of the barge, then with an athletic spring, he came aboard. He turned and caught the hand of the second man who moved forward. As he was helping him onto the deck, Fennel made his move.

He rose up out of the darkness, slid across the slippery deck and slashed with the flail.

The chain caught the first man across his face. He gave a wild yell, staggered, then pitched into the river.

The second man, his reflexes swift, spun around, knife in hand to face Fennel, but the chain slashed him around the neck, tearing his skin and sending him reeling back. He clutched at nothing, then went into the water, flat on his back.

Fennel darted into the shadows. His grin was vicious and evil. He knew the other two men in the boat couldn't see him. The light was behind them.

There was a moment of confusion. Then frantically, the man who had used the oar, grabbed it and began to pull away from the barge. The other man was trying to get his companions out of the river into the boat.

Fennel lay watching. His heart was hammering, and his breathing came in jerky snorts through his wide nostrils.

The two men were dragged aboard. The rower had the second oar now in the rowlock and was pulling away from the barge. Fennel remained where he was. If they saw him, they might risk a shot. He waited, shivering in the cold, until the boat disappeared into the darkness, then he got to his feet.

He leaned over the side of the barge to wash the blood off the chain. He felt the icy rain sliding down inside his trousers. He thought they might come back later, and if they did, the odds would be stacked against him. They would no longer be taken by surprise.

He shook the rain out of his eyes. He must get out, and get out fast.

He went down the eight steps into the big living and bedroom and flicked on the light. The woman in bed sat up.

'What is it, Lew?'

He paid no attention to her. He stripped off his sodden trousers and walked naked into the small bathroom. God! He was cold! He turned on the hot shower tap, waited a moment, then stepped under the healing hot spray.

Mimi came into the bathroom. Her eyes were drugged with sleep, her long black hair tousled, her big breasts escaping from her nightdress.

'Lew! What is it?'

Fennel ignored her. He stood, thick, massive and short, under the hot spray of water, letting the water soak the thick hairs on his chest, belly and loins.

'Lew!'

He waved her away, then turned off the shower and took up a towel.

But she wouldn't go away. She stood outside the bathroom, staring at him, her green, dark ringed eyes alight with fear.

'Get me a shirt . . . don't stand there like a goddam dummy!' He threw aside the towel.

'What happened? I want to know. Lew! What's going on?'

He pushed past her and walked into the inner room. He jerked open the closet door, found a shirt and struggled into it, found a pair of trousers and slid into them. He pulled on a black turtle neck sweater, then shrugged himself into a black jacket with leather patches on the elbows. His movements were swift and final.

She stood in the doorway, watching.

'Why don't you say something?' Her voice was shrill. 'What's happening?'

He paused for a brief moment to look at her and he grimaced. Well, she had been convenient, he told himself, but no man in his right mind could call her an oil painting. Still, she had provided him with a hideout on this crummy barge for the past four weeks. Right now, without her plaster of make-up, she looked like hell. She was too fat. Those sagging breasts sickened him. Her anxious terror aged her. What was she . . . forty? But she had been convenient. It had taken Moroni four weeks to find him, but now it was time to leave. In three hours, Fennel thought, probably less, she would not even be a memory to him.

'A little trouble,' he said. 'Nothing. Don't get excited. Go back to bed.'

She moved into the room. The barge lifted slightly as the wind moved the river.

'Why are you dressing? What were you . . .'

'Just shut up, will you? I'm leaving.'

Her face sagged.

'Leaving? Why? Where are you going?'

He took a cigarette from the box on the table. He was feeling fine now after the hot shower and more assured, but he knew she was going to be a nuisance. She was horribly possessive. She needed his brutal love-making . . . the reason why she had kept him there. She wasn't going to be shaken off easily.

'Get into bed,' he said. 'You'll catch cold.' Thinking: as if I give a damn. 'I have a phone call to make.'

She knew he was lying and she grabbed hold of his arm.

'You can't leave me! I've done everything for you. You're not to go!'

'For God's sake, shut up!' Fennel snarled and shoving her aside, he crossed the room to the telephone. As he dialled the number, he looked at his wrist-watch. The time was 03.50 hrs. He waited, listening to the steady burr-burr-burr of the ringing tone. There was a click and a sleepy voice demanded, 'W'o the 'ell is this?'

'Jacey? This is Lew.'

'Gawd! I was asleep!'

'This earns you twenty nicker,' Fennel said, speaking slowly and distinctly. 'Get your car. Meet me at the Crown pub, King's Road in twenty minutes, and I mean twenty minutes.'

'You crackers? Look at the time! W'ot's up? I'm not coming out. It's raining fit to drown a duck.'

'Twenty nickers . . . twenty minutes,' Fennel said quietly.

There was a long pause. He could hear Jacey breathing heavily and imagined he could hear his greedy brain creaking.

'The Crown?'

'Yes.'

'The things I do! Well, okay. I'm on my way.'

Fennel replaced the receiver.

'You're not leaving!' Mimi's face blotched with red and her eyes were glaring. 'I won't let you leave!'

He ignored her and went swiftly to the dressing-table, jerked open a drawer and snatched up the essential articles he always kept there: a safety razor, a tube of brushless cream, a toothbrush, three packs of Players cigarettes and a haircomb. These he stowed away in his jacket pocket.

She again grabbed hold of his arm.

'I've done everything for you!' she wailed. 'You blasted jail-bird! Without me, you would have starved!'

He shoved her away and crossed the room to the mantelpiece that framed a phony fireplace in which stood an electric stove. He took down a big Chinese teapot. The moment he touched it, she sprang forward and tried to take the teapot from him. Her eyes were wild, her long black hair hung over her face making her look like a demented witch.

'Take your hands off that!' she screamed.

The flickering evil in his washed out grey eyes should have warned her, but she was too frantic to stop him taking her savings to be warned.

'Take it easy, Mimi,' he said. 'I have to have it. I'll let you have it back . . . promise.'

'No!'

She hooked her fingers and slashed at his face as her left hand wrenched at the teapot. Fennel jerked his head back, released the teapot and then savagely struck her on the side of the jaw. The force of the blow flung her backwards. She fell, her eyes rolling up and her head thudding on the floor. The teapot smashed to pieces as her grip was released and money spewed from it.

Fennel poked aside the pile of silver and picked up the small roll of ten pound notes. He didn't look at the unconscious woman. He put the money in his hip pocket, picked up his flail and went up on deck. As far as he was concerned his thirty days with Mimi were chalk marks on a blackboard now erased.

Rain was falling heavily, and the wind felt bleak against his face. He stood for some seconds looking at the embankment, letting his eyes become accustomed to the darkness. Nothing moved. He would have to take a chance, he thought, and ran the landing plank, from the barge, down to the wet tarmac. He slid down the plank, gained the dark shadows and again paused to listen. Again he heard nothing to alarm him. His fingers tightened on the flail and keeping close to the embankment wall, he walked silently to the distant steps that led to the upper embankment.

If Jacey was late, he could be sunk, he thought. They would have to stop the bleeding: the one who had been hit on the neck would bleed like a stuck pig. Then they would telephone Moroni and report failure. Moroni would get four or five men down there fast. Fennel decided he had a possible half-hour of freedom: certainly not more.

But he had no need to worry. As he reached the darkened Crown public house, he saw Jacey's battered Morris pull up. He sprinted across the road, opened the car door and slid in.

'Back to your place, Jacey.'

'Wait a mo',' Jacey said. The street light lit up his aged, rat face. 'W'ot's on the move?'

Fennel gripped Jacey's thin wrist.

'Back to your place!' he snarled.

Jacey caught a glimpse of the vicious twist of the mouth and the half mad expression of contained rage. He grunted, engaged gear and set the Morris in motion.

Ten minutes later, the two men were in a small, shabbily furnished room, lit by a dusty, shadeless lamp that hung precariously from the dirty ceiling.

Jacey put a bottle of Black & White on the table and two

glasses. He poured two stiff drinks and cradled his glass in his dirty hands while he regarded Fennel uneasily.

Jacey was a bookie's clerk and did any odd job for the lesser tearaways to earn extra money. He knew Fennel to be a major tearaway. He had met him in Parkhurst jail when they were serving sentences: Fennel for robbery with violence: Jacey for trying to pass badly forged ten shilling notes. When they had been released, they had kept in touch and Jacey had been flattered to have a big man like Fennel interested in him. But now he was sorry he had had anything to do with Fennel. He had heard through the underworld grapevine that Fennel had talked and five of Moroni's men had walked into a police trap. He knew Moroni had put the death sign on Fennel, but he was too greedy to pass up the chance of earning twenty pounds.

Fennel took out Mimi's roll of ten pound notes. He pulled off two and tossed them on the table.

'Freeze onto those, Jacey,' he said. 'I'm staying here for a couple of days.'

Jacey's ferret-like eyes widened. He didn't touch the money on the table.

'Can't 'ave you 'ere for two days, Lew. Ain't safe. They'll carve me if they find out you've been 'ere.'

'I can carve you too,' Fennel said softly. 'And I'm here.'

Jacey scratched his unshaven chin. His eyes darted about the room while he considered the situation and the risks. Moroni was probably in bed, asleep, but Fennel was here. Fennel could be as dangerous as Moroni.

'Okay, then . . . two days . . . not an 'our more,' he said finally.

'In two days, I'll be out of the country,' Fennel said. 'I've got a job. Maybe, I won't be coming back.' He finished his whisky and then walked into the inner room and over to the battered couch that served Jacey as a bed. He kicked off his shoes and lay down.

'You sleep on the floor, and turn that goddam light off.'

'Go a'ead,' Jacey said bitterly. 'Make yourself at 'ome.'

He reached up and turned off the light.

A week previously, Garry Edwards had seen in the *Daily Telegraph* the following advertisement:

Experienced helicopter pilot required for a three week unusual assignment. Exceptionally high remuneration. Send career details and photograph. Box. S. 1012.

He had re-read the advertisement and had brooded over it.

He liked the two words *unusual* and *exceptional*. He was looking for unusual work and badly needed exceptional money, so without telling Toni, he had written a letter to Box S.1012, setting out the details of his past career which was as full of lies as a colander is full of holes. He had enclosed a passport photograph and had mailed the letter.

A week had passed, and he now had given up all hope of any exceptional remuneration and any unusual job. On this cold, wet February morning, he sat in Toni's small, untidy sitting-room with a cup of Nescafé by his side while he searched the *Situations Vacant* columns in the *Daily Telegraph*.

Garry Edwards was a tall, powerfully-built man of twenty-nine years of age. He was handsome in a rugged way, with humorous brown eyes and dark-brown hair worn fashionably long to his collar. His mouth could laugh easily or tighten to a dangerous thinness. As he sat on Toni's broken down settee, dressed in a white beach wrap, his long narrow feet bare, the wall clock showed the time was 08.45 hrs.

Having searched the *Situations Vacant* columns carefully, he dropped the newspaper to the floor in disgust. Well, he would have to do something pretty soon, he told himself. He had exactly one hundred and thirty pounds, five shillings and seven pence before he had to ask Toni to support him, and this, he told himself without much conviction, he would never do.

He had run into Toni White on the Calais-Dover channel boat. Happily, she had been in the bar when he had embarked with two tough-looking French detectives who remained with him until the vessel was about to sail. When they had gone, and after Garry had waved cheerfully to them as they stood on the rain-swept quay to see the vessel leave the harbour—a wave they had stonily ignored—he had gone down to the first class bar for his first drink in three years.

Toni had been sitting on a bar stool, her micro-mini skirt scarcely covering her crotch, sipping a Cinzano bitter on the rocks. He had ordered a double Vat 69 with a dash and then had saluted her. She seemed the kind of girl a man could salute if the man had a way with him, and Garry certainly had a way with him.

Toni was twenty-two years of age, blonde, elfin-like with big blue eyes with dark, heavy eyelashes a cow would envy. Also, she was very, very chic.

She regarded Garry thoughtfully and with penetration. She decided he was the most sexy-looking man she had ever seen, and she had a hot rush of blood through her body. She wanted to have him: to be laid by him as she had never been laid before in her short, sensual life.

She smiled.

Garry knew women. He knew all the signs, and realized that here was an invitation that needed little or no finesse.

He had in his wallet the sum of two hundred and ninety pounds: what remained of the sale of his aircraft before the French police had caught up with him. He was full of confidence and rearing to go.

He finished his drink, then smiling, he said, 'I would love to know you better. We have over an hour before we land. May I get a cabin?'

She liked this direct approach. She wanted him. His suggestion made everything simple. She laughed, then nodded.

It was easy to get a cabin, draw the curtains and lock themselves in. The steward had to rap a dozen times to remind them they had reached Dover and if they didn't make haste, they would miss the boat train.

While sitting by his side in an otherwise empty first class compartment on their way to London, Toni had told him she was a successful model, had plenty of work, had a two room apartment in Chelsea and if he wanted a roof . . . 'well, honey-love, why not move in?'

Garry had been planning on a cheap room in some modest hotel off the Cromwell Road until he could take stock and find himself lucrative employment. He didn't hesitate.

He had been living now with Toni for some three weeks, spending his remaining capital but not finding any lucrative employment. Now, with no prospects, he was getting slightly anxious. Toni, however, thought it all a huge joke.

'Why worry, you big gorgeous animal?' she had demanded the previous evening, jumping on to his lap and nibbling his ear. 'I have all the money in the world! Let's make hectic love!'

Garry finished his half-cold coffee, grimaced and then went to the window to stare down at the slow-moving traffic and at the stream of men and women, sheltering under umbrellas, hurrying to work.

He heard a sound at the front door: letters being dropped into the box.

Toni received many letters each morning from gibbering young men who adored her, but Garry hoped there just might be a letter for him. He collected fifteen letters from the box, flicked through them quickly and found one for himself. The deckled edge, handmade paper of the envelope was impressive. He ripped it open and extracted a sheet of paper.

The Royal Towers Hotel
London. W.1
Would Mr. Garry Edwards please call at the above address on February 11th at 11.30 hrs. and ask for Mr. Armo Shalik. (*Ref* Daily Telegraph. *Box. S.1012.*)

Well, yes, Garry thought, he would certainly call on Mr. Armo Shalik. With a name like that and with such an address there had to be a smell of money.

He took the letter into the small bedroom.

Toni was sleeping heavily. She lay on her stomach, her shortie nightdress rucked up, her long, lovely legs spread wide.

Garry sat on the edge of the bed and admired her. She really was delightfully beautiful. He lifted his hand and smacked her sharply on her bare rump. She squirmed, closed her legs, blinked and looked over her shoulder at him. He smacked her again and she hurriedly spun around and sat up.

'That's assault!' she declared. 'Where are my pants?'

He found them for her at the end of the bed and offered them. She regarded him, smiling.

'Do I need them?'

'I shouldn't have thought so,' Garry said with a grin. 'I've had a letter. Could you turn your indecent mind to business for a moment?'

She looked questioningly at him.

'What's cooking?'

He told her about the advertisement in the *Daily Telegraph*, that he had answered it, and now he had a reply. He gave her the letter.

'The Royal Towers! The newest and the best! What a lovely name! Armo Shalik! I smell bags and bags of gold and diamonds.' She tossed the letter into the air and threw her arms around Garry's neck.

Around 11.00 hrs. Garry detached himself from Toni's clutch, took a shower and then dressed in a blue blazer and dark-blue Daks. He surveyed himself in the mirror.

'A little dark under the eyes,' he said, straightening his tie, 'But that is to be expected. Still, I think I look healthy, handsome and handmade . . . what do you think, you beautiful doll?'

Completely naked, Toni was sitting in the armchair, sipping coffee. She regarded him affectionately.

'You look absolutely gorgeous.'

Garry picked her out of the armchair and fondled her. Having kissed her, he dumped her back in the chair and left the apartment.

At exactly 11.30 hrs. he approached the hall porter of the *Royal Towers Hotel* and asked for Mr. Armo Shalik.

The hall porter surveyed him with that blank expression all hall porters wear when they neither approve nor disapprove. He called a number, spoke quietly, then replaced the receiver.

'Tenth floor, sir. Suite 27.'

Garry was whisked up by the express lift to the tenth floor. He was conducted by the lift-man to the door of Suite 27. He was obviously too important and too fragile to knock on the door. The lift-man did this service, bowed and retired.

The smell of money, as far as Garry was concerned, was now overpowering.

He entered a small distinguished room where a girl sat behind a desk on which stood three telephones, an I.B.M. golf ball typewriter, an intercom and a tape-recorder.

The girl puzzled Garry because although she had a nice figure, was dressed in a stylish black frock, was beautifully groomed, her hair immaculate, she was nothing to him but a sexless photograph of a woman long since dead. Her blank face, her immaculately plucked eyebrows, her pale lipstick merely emphasized her lack of charm: a robot that made him feel slightly uncomfortable.

'Mr. Edwards?'

Even her voice was metallic: a tape-recording badly reproduced.

'That's me,' Garry said, and because he never liked to be defeated by any woman, he gave her his charming smile.

It had no effect. The girl touched a button, paused, then said, 'Mr. Edwards is here, sir.'

A green light flashed up on the intercom. Obviously, Mr. Shalik didn't care to waste his breath. He preferred to press buttons than to talk.

The girl got up, walked gracefully to a far door, opened it and stood aside.

Impressed by all this, Garry again tried his smile which again bounced off her the way a golf ball bounces off a brick wall.

He moved past her into a large sunny room, luxuriously furnished with period pieces and impressive looking paintings that could have been by the great masters but probably weren't.

At a vast desk sat a small, fat man, smoking a cigar, his chubby hands resting on the desk blotter. Garry judged him to be around forty-six years of age. He was dark-complexioned with close cut black hair, beady black eyes and a mouth that he used for food but not for smiles. Garry decided he was either an Armenian or an Egyptian. He had the stillness and the probing stare of power. As Garry walked slowly to the desk, the beady black eyes examined him. They were X-ray eyes, and by the time Garry had reached the desk, he had an uncomfortable feeling this fat little man knew him rather better than he knew himself.

'Sit down, Mr. Edwards.' The accent was a little thick. A chubby hand waved to a chair.

Garry sat down. He now regretted laying Toni an hour ago. He felt a little depleted and he had an idea that this fat little man wouldn't have much time for depleted applicants for the job he was offering. Garry sat upright and tried to look intelligent.

Shalik sucked in rich smelling smoke and allowed it to drift from his mouth like the smoke from a small, but active volcano. He picked up a sheet of paper which Garry recognized as his letter of application and he studied it for several moments, then he tore it up and dropped it into a hidden wastepaper basket.

'You are a helicopter pilot, Mr. Edwards?' he asked, resting his hands on the blotter and regarding the ash of his cigar with more interest than he regarded Garry.

'That's correct. I saw your ad and I thought . . .'

The chubby hand lifted, cutting Garry off.

'This nonsense you have written about yourself . . . at least it proves you have imagination.'

Garry stiffened.

'I don't get that. What do you mean?'

Shalik touched off his cigar ash into a gold bowl at his elbow.

'I found your lies amusing,' he said. 'I have had you investigated. You are Garry Edwards, aged twenty-nine, and you were born in Ohio, U.S.A. Your father ran a reasonably successful service station. When you were sufficiently educated, you worked with your father and you came to know about motor cars. You and your father didn't get along. Probably faults on both sides, but that is of no interest to me. You had the opportunity to learn to fly: you took it. You have talent with machines. You got a job as an air chauffeur to a Texas oilman who paid you well. You saved your money. The job didn't interest you. You met a wetback smuggler who persuaded you to smuggle Mexicans into the States. The pay was good, and when the operation was over, you decided to go into the smuggling business. You went to Tangiers, bought your own aircraft and flew consignments of various contrabands into France. You prospered as smugglers do for a time. However, you became greedy as smugglers do and you made a mistake. You were arrested. Your co-pilot managed to get your plane in the air while you were struggling with the police. He sold your plane and banked the money for you to have when you came out of the French prison after serving a three year sentence. You were deported from France and you are here.' Shalik stubbed out his cigar and looked at Garry. 'Would you say my information is correct?'

Garry laughed.

'Dead on the nail.' He got to his feet. 'Well, it was a try. I won't take up any more of your time.'

Shalik waved him back to his chair.

'Sit down. I think you are the man I am looking for. You can satisfy me that you have a pilot's licence and that you can handle a helicopter?'

'Of course,' Garry returned and lugged out a plastic folder which he had brought along and laid it on the desk. Then he sat down again.

Shalik examined the papers which the folder contained. He took his time, then he returned the folder.

'Satisfactory.' He took another cigar from his desk drawer, regarded it carefully, then cut the end with a gold cutter. 'Mr. Edwards, am I right in thinking you would be prepared to handle a job that is not entirely honest so long as the money is right?'

Garry smiled.

'I'd like that qualified. What do you mean . . . not entirely honest?'

'Difficult, unethical work that does not involve the police in any way, but pays handsomely.'

'Can you make it clearer than that?'

'I am offering three thousand dollars a week for a three-week assignment. At the end of the assignment you will be nine thousand dollars better off. There are certain risks, but I can promise you the police won't come into it.'

Garry sat upright. Nine thousand dollars!

'What are the risks?'

'Opposition.' Shalik regarded his cigar with indifferent, beady eyes. 'But life is made up of opposition, isn't it, Mr. Edwards?'

'Just what do I have to do to earn this money?'

'That will be explained to you tonight. You will not be alone. The risks and responsibilities will be shared. What I want to know now is if you are willing to do three weeks work for nine thousand dollars.'

Garry didn't hesitate.

'Yes . . . I am.'

Shalik nodded.

'Good. Then you will come here at 21.00 hrs. tonight when I will introduce you to the other members of the team and I will explain the operation.' The chubby hand made a slight signal of dismissal.

Garry got to his feet.

'Please don't talk about this assignment to anyone, Mr. Edwards,' Shalik went on. 'You must regard it as top secret.'

'Sure . . . I'll say nothing.'

Garry left the room.

The girl at the desk got up and opened the door for him. He didn't bother to smile at her. His mind was too preoccupied. Nine thousand dollars! Wow!

The girl watched him enter the lift and then she returned to her desk. She sat for some moments, listening. Then hearing nothing from the inner room, she softly opened a drawer in her desk and turned off a small tape-recorder whose spools were conveying tape through the recording head.

Precisely at 21.00 hrs. Garry was shown into Shalik's office by the dark-haired girl who he knew now by the name-plate on her desk to be Natalie Norman.

There were two men sitting uneasily in chairs, smoking and waiting. They both looked closely at Garry as he took a chair. In his turn, he looked closely at them.

The man on his left was short and heavily built. He reminded Garry a little of Rod Steiger, the Oscar-winning movie star. His close cut woolly hair was white, his washed out grey eyes shifty. His thin lips and square chin hinted at viciousness.

The other man was some ten years younger: around Garry's age. He was of middle height, thin, his hair bleached almost white by the sun and his skin burnt to a dark mahogany. He wore a straggly moustache and long sideboards. Garry liked the look of him immediately, but disliked the look of the other man.

As he settled himself in the chair, a door at the far end of the room opened and Shalik entered.

'So you have all arrived,' he said, coming to his desk. He sat down and went through the ritual of lighting a cigar while he looked at each man in turn with intent, probing eyes. 'Let me introduce you to each other.' He pointed his cigar at Garry. 'This is Mr. Garry Edwards. He is a helicopter pilot and a car expert. He has spent three years in a French prison on smuggling charges.' The other two men looked sharply at Garry who stared back at them. The cigar then pointed to the younger man. 'This is Mr. Kennedy Jones who has flown from Johannesburg to attend this meeting,' Shalik went on. 'Mr. Jones is a safari expert. There is nothing he can't tell you about wild animals, South Africa in general and the fitting out of an expedition into the African bush. I might add Mr. Jones has had the misfortune to spend a few years in a Pretoria jail.' Jones stared up at the ceiling, a grin hovering around his humorous mouth. There was a pause, then Shalik went on, 'Finally, this is Mr. Lew Fennel who is an expert safe breaker . . . I believe that is the term. He is regarded by the police and the underworld as the top man in his so-called profession. He too has served a number of years in prison.' Shalik paused and looked at the three men. 'So, gentlemen, you have something in common.'

None of them said anything: they waited.

Shalik opened a drawer in his desk and took out a folder.

'The introductions concluded, let us get down to business.' He opened the folder and took from it a large glossy photograph. This he handed to Fennel who stared with puzzled eyes at the medieval diamond ring shown in the photograph. He shrugged and passed the photograph to Garry who in turn passed it to Jones.

'You are looking at a ring,' Shalik said, 'designed by Caesar Borgia.' He looked at the three men. 'I take it you all know of Caesar Borgia?'

'He's the guy who poisoned people, wasn't he?' Fennel said.

'I think that is a fair description. Yes, among many other things, he poisoned or caused to be poisoned a number of people. This ring you see in the photograph was designed by Borgia and made by an unknown goldsmith in 1501. To look at the ring, it would be hard to believe that it is a lethal weapon, but that is what it is . . . a very lethal weapon. It works in this way. There is a tiny reservoir under the cluster of diamonds and this reservoir was filled with a deadly poison. In the cluster of diamonds is a microscopic hollow needle of exceptional sharpness. When Borgia wished to get rid of an enemy, he had only to turn the ring so the diamonds and needle were worn inside and he had only to clasp the hand of his enemy to inflict a small scratch. The enemy would be dead in a few hours.

'The ring was lost for four centuries. It turned up in the effects of a Florentine banker who died with his wife and family in a car crash a couple of years ago. His effects were sold. Fortunately, an expert recognized the ring and bought it for a song. It was offered to me.' Shalik paused to tap ash off his cigar. 'Among my various activities, I buy *objets d'art* and sell them to wealthy collectors. I knew of a client who specialized in Borgia treasures. I sold him the ring. Six months later, the ring was stolen. It has taken me a long time to find out where it is. It was stolen by agents working for another collector who has acquired, through these agents, probably the finest collection of art treasures in the world. This operation, Gentlemen, which I am asking you to handle, is for you three to recover the ring.'

There was a long pause, then Fennel, sitting forward, said, 'You mean we steal it?'

Shalik looked at Fennel with distaste.

'Putting it crudely, you could say that,' he said. 'I have already pointed out there is no question of police interference. This collector has stolen the ring from my client. You take it from him. He is in no position to complain to the police.'

Fennel let his cigarette ash drop on the rich Persian carpet as he asked, 'How valuable is this ring?'

'That doesn't concern you. It is, of course, valuable, but it has a specialized market.' Shalik paused, then went on, 'I will tell you a few details about the man who now has the ring. He is enormously rich. He has a compulsive urge to own the finest art treasures he can lay his hands on. He is utterly unscrupulous. He has a network of expert art thieves working for him. They have stolen many *objets d'art* from the world's greatest museums, and even from the Vatican, to fill his museum which is without doubt the finest in the world.'

Feeling he should make a contribution to this discussion, Garry asked, 'And where is this museum?'

'On the borders of Basutoland and Natal . . . somewhere in the Drakensberg mountains.'

Kennedy Jones leaned forward.

'Would you be talking about Max Kahlenberg?' he asked sharply.

Shalik paused to touch off his cigar ash.

'You know of him?'

'Who doesn't, who has lived in South Africa?'

'Then suppose you tell these two gentlemen what you know about him.'

'He's the man who has the ring?'

Shalik nodded.

Jones drew in a long, slow breath. He rubbed his jaw, frowning, then lit a cigarette. As he exhaled smoke, he said, 'I only know what is common knowledge. Kahlenberg is a bit of a mythical figure on which all kinds of weird rumours stick. I do know his father, a German refugee from the First World War, struck it rich, finding one of the biggest gold mines just outside Jo'burg. Old Karl Kahlenberg was shrewd and no fool. He invested well and milked his mine dry. From what I hear, he ended up with millions. He married a local girl when he was over sixty years old. He married because he wanted a son to carry on his name. He got his son: Max Kahlenberg. There was a real mystery about the birth. No one except the doctor and the nurse saw the baby. There was a rumour it was a freak . . . some even said it was a monster. Anyway, no one ever set eyes on the baby. The old man died in a hunting accident. Mrs. Kahlenberg moved from Jo'burg and built house in the heart of the Drakensberg range. She continued to keep her son hidden, cutting herself off from all social contacts. She died some twenty years ago. Max Kahlenberg remains a recluse. He is supposed to be as clever as his father. He has enlarged the house his mother built. He has around one hundred square miles of jungle surrounding the house and he employs a number of trained Zulus to keep hikers, tourists and gapers away from the house.' Jones paused, then leaning forward, stabbing his finger into the palm of his hand, he went on, 'From what I've heard, getting near Kahlenberg's place would be like trying to open an oyster with your fingers.'

Again there was a long pause, then Fennel crushed out his cigarette and looked at Shalik, his eyes narrowed.

'Is what he says right?'

Shalik lifted his fat shoulders.

'A fairly accurate statement,' he said. 'I have never said that this is an easy assignment. After all, I am paying very well. The approach to Kahlenberg's house is not easy, but not impossible. I have a considerable amount of information which will help you.'

'That's fine,' Fennel said with a little sneer, 'but suppose we get to the house . . . how do we get in?'

'Although Mr. Jones has a fair knowledge of Kahlenberg's background,' Shalik said, 'He has omitted—or perhaps he doesn't know—the fact that although Kahlenberg is a cripple, he is fond of beautiful women.' He leaned back in his chair. 'Every fortress has its soft underbelly if you know where to look for it. I have a woman who will act as your Trojan Horse. If she can't get you into Kahlenberg's house, no one can.'

He pressed a button on his desk.

There was a long pause, then the door behind Shalik opened and the most sensational, beautiful woman any of the three men, gaping at her, had ever seen, came slowly into the room and paused by Shalik's desk.

CHAPTER TWO

SOME TEN YEARS AGO, Armo Shalik, sick of his small way of life, let it be known by a discreet advertisement in an Egyptian newspaper that he was prepared to undertake for a reasonable fee any assignment that presented difficulties. He received only one answer to his advertisement, but it was enough, since his client was an Arabian Prince who wished to have inside information concerning a future oil deal between a rival of his and an American oil company. By using the Prince's money and his own brains, Shalik obtained the information. The deal netted him $10,000, a modest enough fee, but the Prince was grateful, and he passed the word around that if you were in difficulties, if you wished for inside information, Shalik was the man to consult.

The following year with the capital he had saved, Shalik moved to London. He acquired a small list of extremely wealthy clients who continually consulted him. Money, of course, was no object. Shalik's fees rose sharply, but he always delivered. Among his clients were three Texas oil millionaires, four Arabian princes, two enormously wealthy American women, a Greek shipping tycoon and a number of British, French and German industrialists.

He was often to say, 'Nothing is impossible with unlimited money and brains.' He would pause to stare at his client. 'You will supply the money . . . I the brains.'

Armo Shalik prospered. In the early days, he considered whether to have a permanent staff to work under him, but he decided this was economically unsound. Shalik never wasted a dime. To keep a staff of experts on his payroll would mean half of them most of the time would be drawing on his money and doing nothing. He decided to fit men and women to the job when the job arrived. He discovered a not too scrupulous Detective Agency who were prepared not only to recommend likely applicants without asking awkward questions, but also to screen them, giving him intimate details of their background. It was in this way that he had found Lew Fennel, Kennedy Jones and Garry Edwards.

His permanent staff was small: consisting of Natalie Norman who acted as his receptionist and personal assistant, and George Sherborn who was his private secretary and valet.

But Shalik soon found that his assignments became more complicated and therefore more lucrative, he needed a woman in the field to be permanently at his disposal: a woman who had to be trained to work with and for him: a woman of exceptional talents and exceptional looks. Such a woman could be more useful to him than a dozen male experts. During the past years, he had hired a number of women to work with his experts, but more often than not they had failed him: either losing their nerve at a crucial moment or becoming sentimentally attached to the men they were working with, and this was something Shalik abominated.

So he set out to find a woman he could train to become his ideal woman operator. She had to be beautiful, perfectly built, talented and to be prepared to dedicate herself to his work.

Shalik travelled extensivly, and while visiting the major cities of the world, he was constantly on the look-out for the woman he needed. He came across several likely applicants, but when he approached them, they either would have nothing to do with his proposition or proved to be beautiful but brainless. After some six months, he began to despair, wondering if he had set his sights too high.

Then one day he had a letter from one of his rich, spoilt women clients, living in Tokyo, who asked him to buy her a leopard skin coat, a mink stole and a broadtail coat for evening wear. He was to get these furs from Finn Larson, a Copenhagen furrier who had her measurements and knew exactly what she required. Since the woman paid Shalek $21,000 a year as a retaining fee and since he charged fifteen per cent on all purchases made on her behalf and since he was in need of a brief vacation, he was happy to oblige.

Natalie Norman telephoned Finn Larson in Copenhagen to alert him that Shalik was coming and what he wanted. She was told that there was to be a lunch held at L'Angleterre Hotel for a number of Larson's special clients when models would display his furs and the clients would eat interesting Danish food. Larson hoped Mr. Shalik would attend.

Shalik arrived at the hotel the following day and went to the private room that Larson used for his excellent lunches and was welcomed by Larson, a balding, heavily-built Dane who gripped his hand and led him to a table before hurrying away to welcome yet another of his clients.

While Shalik was eating his lunch, girls came in to display Larson's beautiful furs.

Then suddenly, as a girl swept in, wearing a magnificent leopard skin coat, Shalik paused in his eating. After six months of searching, this was his moment of truth. He was certain this time this was the girl he was looking for.

Above average height, with tawny hair, hanging in silken waves to her shoulder blades, this girl—possibly twenty-six or so years of age—was the most sensationally, sensually beautiful feminine creation he had ever seen. Her jade green eyes, her full lips that gave promise of sexual excitement, her long tapering legs, her slim lovely hands made a picture of a male dream of desirability.

Shalik lost interest in his lunch as he watched her move with the arrogant walk of a trained model to the end of the room. She turned and walked back past him. He scarcely glanced at the leopard skin coat. When she had gone, to be replaced by another girl, wearing a seal skin coat, Shalik beckoned to Larson who came over.

'I'll take the leopard skin coat,' Shalik said. 'It is for Mrs. Van Ryan.' He paused, then looked up and asked, 'Who is the girl who modelled the coat?'

Larson smiled.

'Almost as magnificent as my coat, don't you think? She is Gaye Desmond . . . An American freelance model who comes here from time to time. I use her for my leopard skins . . . no other girl has such flair to show off leopard.'

Shalik took out his wallet, extracted his card and handed it to Larson.

'Would you be so kind as to give her my card?' he asked. 'I believe I can employ her should she need employment. You might mention to her who I am.' Shalik regarded Larson. 'You know, Mr. Larson, I am always serious. This is strictly business. You will be doing the girl a favour.'

Larson, who knew Shalik, had no hesitation.

Later, while Shalik was sitting in his suite, reading a complicated legal document, the telephone bell rang.

He lifted the receiver.

'This is Gaye Desmond.' He liked her rich contralto voice. 'You sent me your card.'

'Thank you for ringing, Miss Desmond. I have a proposition I would like to discuss with you. Could we have dinner together at the Belle Terresse, Tivoli, at 21.00 hrs?'

She said yes, and hung up.

She arrived punctually which pleased Shalik, and together they went to a table on the terrace that overlooked the lighted pool and the flowers that make Tivoli famous.

'It is a pity we didn't meet in Paris, Miss Desmond,' Shalik said as he began to examine the menu. 'The food here is indifferent. In Paris I could have offered you a meal worthy of your beauty.'

She was wearing a simple blue dress with a mink stole. Diamonds glittered at her ears as she tossed her tawny coloured hair back from her shoulders.

'I believe in eating what a country offers,' she said. 'Why yearn for better food in Paris when you are in Copenhagen?'

Shalik liked that. He nodded.

'So what will you have?'

She had no hesitation, and this also pleased Shalik. Women who stare vacantly at a menu and can't make up their minds bored him.

She chose Danish shrimps and the breast of duck in wine sauce. Having taken a little longer to examine the menu, Shalik decided her choice was not only safe, but sound. He ordered the same.

'Miss Desmond,' Shalik said when the waiter had gone. 'I am looking for a woman to help me in my work. I am a rather special agent who looks after extremely wealthy, spoilt people, clever business men and even princes. I boast that nothing is impossible. Nothing is impossible if you have money and brains.' He paused, regarding her. 'However, I believe my work would be made easier if I had a woman like yourself working for me permanently. I must warn you it would be exacting work: sometimes dangerous, but always within the law of the country in which I operate.' This statement was untrue. Recently, Shalik had pulled off a number of illegal currency deals in London that could have landed him in jail had they been discovered, but Shalik's philosophy was that so long as he wasn't found out, any deal was within the law. 'The pay will be good. You will have your own apartment at the Royal Towers Hotel in London, paid by me. You will have many opportunities to travel.' He regarded her with his black, beady eyes. 'And I assure you, Miss Desmond, this will be a strictly business association.'

The tiny, pink, delicious shrimps now arrived with slices of toast, and there was a pause.

While Gaye buttered her toast, she asked, 'What makes you imagine I am suitable for such a post, Mr. Shalik?'

Shalik nibbled at his shrimps. He regretfully avoided the toast. He was four kilos overweight and was determined to make a sacrifice.

'Instinct, I suppose. I think you are just the woman I am looking for.'

'You say the pay will be good . . . just what does that mean?'

He ate another three shrimps before saying, 'Suppose you tell me about yourself. I can then make a valuation.'

She sipped the chilled Hock and regarded him with her green eyes: thoughtful, shrewd, calculating eyes that pleased him.

'Well . . ' She suddenly smiled and her smile lit up her face, making it gay and charming. 'As you can see, I am beautiful. I am intelligent. You will discover this. I speak French, Italian and Spanish fluently. I can get along in German. I was practically born on a horse. My father bred horses in Kentucky. I ski well. I can handle a sailing boat and, of course, any kind of motorboat. I have been a racing driver and there is nothing I don't know about cars. I understand men and what they want. Sex doesn't frighten me. I know how to please men if . . . and only if . . . I have to. I earn a comfortable living modelling specialized clothes, but I like money and want to make more.'

Shalik finished his shrimps and then stroked his thick nose.

'Is that all?'

She laughed.

'Isn't it enough?'

'Yes, I think so. Can you handle firearms?'

She lifted her eyebrows.

'Why should I need to?'

'Since you are otherwise so well equipped, I think you should have weapon training and also training in self-defence. This I can arrange. When a woman is as beautiful as you and when she may have to mix with dubious types of men, it is sound for her to understand the art of self-defence.'

They paused while the waiter served the duck and poured a

Margaux '59 which Shalik had ordered in a moment of recklessness. The price was outrageous, but the wine excellent.

'Now it is your turn,' she said. She cut into the duck and grimaced. 'It's tough.'

'Of course. What did you expect? This is Copenhagen, not Paris.' He looked at her across the candle-lit table. 'My turn . . . for what?'

'Your turn to make a valuation. I've told you about myself. Value me.'

Shalik liked her direct approach.

'If you are prepared to do exactly what I tell you, Miss Desmond,' he said as he began to cut the duck into small pieces. 'If you are prepared to be at my beck and call for eleven months in each year . . . the remaining month will be yours to do as you wish. If you are prepared to take a course in self-defence, then I will play you $10,000 a year with a one per cent cut on whatever I make on assignments you help me with. At a rough guess this should net you $25,000 a year."

She drank a little of the Margaux.

'At least the wine is good, isn't it?'

'It should be, at the price they charge for it,' Shalik said sourly. He hated wasting his money. 'What do you say?'

She toyed with her glass as she considered his proposal, then she shook her head.

'No . . . I am not interested. I could become an old man's mistress for twice that sum. You are asking me to hand myself over to you as a slave for eleven months, leading no life of my own during those months, to be entirely at your beck and call." She laughed. 'No, Mr. Shalik, that is no kind of a price for what you are offering.'

Shalik would have been disappointed if she had said otherwise.

'So . . . suppose you tell me under what conditions you will work for me?'

He was pleased she told him without hesitation.

'$30,000 a year whether I work or not, and five per cent of whatever you make in the deals in which I am concerned.'

Shalik shook his head slowly and sadly.

'Then I am sorry, Miss Desmond. I must look elsewhere.'

They looked at each other and she gave him a charming smile, but he saw there was a jeering light in her eyes.

'Then I'm sorry too. So I must also look elsewhere.'

Shalik now knew she was the woman he was looking for and he settled down to bargain, but here he found his master and this pleased him. He hated to be defeated, but he realized if she could defeat him, the men she would have to mix with at his bidding would be as pawns in her hands.

At the end of the meal, and after Shalik had paid the outrageous bill, they had come to an agreement. A basic salary of $30,000 a year, plus four per cent of Shalik's earnings which involved her co-operation, to be paid into a Swiss bank, tax free, which Shalik decided ruefully would net her at least seven per cent of his take.

Once this was agreed, she came to London and went through a self-defence course that Shalik arranged for her. Her instructors were delighted with her.

'This woman is now highly proficient in defending herself,' they told Shalik. 'She can cope with any emergency.'

Completely satisfied with his find, Shalik installed her in a small suite on the floor below his at the Royal Towers Hotel, and within two months she had quickly proved her worth.

She handled two assignments not only successfully, but with a polish that delighted Shalik. The first assignment was to obtain a chemical formula required by a rival company. The second assignment was to obtain advance information about a big shipping merger which netted the client a considerable profit on the Stock Market: a part of which he handed to Shalik. In both cases, Gaye had had to sleep with the two men who supplied the information required. Shalik asked for no details. He was only too pleased to turn the information she gave him into cash.

Now, she had worked for him for six months and she had more than earned her basic salary.

Delighted with her, he had sent her off on a skiing vacation. He was sure she hadn't gone alone, but what was left of her private life was no concern of his. Then the Borgia ring affair came up and he had sent a telegram to Gstaad telling her to return immediately.

She returned by the first available aircraft and when she walked into his office, burned golden brown by the Swiss sun, her tawny hair around her shoulders, Shalik thought she looked magnificent.

He explained about the Borgia ring and was pleased by her interest.

'You will like Natal,' he said. 'The country is splendid. The three men who will work with you are all experts and should present no difficulties for you.' He stared at his evenly burning cigar. 'I think I should warn you that there are risks. Kahlenberg is dangerous.'

She shrugged her beautiful shoulders. Her smile was confident. 'Many men are dangerous,' she said quietly, 'so are many women.'

As Gaye Desmond paused beside Shalik, the three men got to their feet. While Shalik introduced them, Gaye regarded them searchingly. She liked the look of Kennedy Jones. She decided he was harmless and would be easy to handle and could be fun. Her green eyes swept over Fennel. This man was not only dangerous but he could be tricky to handle. Her experience of men and the expression in his washed out grey eyes as he looked at her, told her sooner or later, there would have to be a show-down with him. The she took in Garry Edwards who was looking at her with an appreciative expression that she found flattering and pleasing. He was all right, she decided. Well, they were a mixed bunch to travel with, but at least two of them could be handled. The fat one was bound to be a nuisance.

'This is Miss Gaye Desmond . . . our Trojan Horse,' Shalik said.

'That I love,' Gaye laughed. 'I would rather be Helen than the horse.'

'Sit down, please.' Shalik drew up a chair for Gaye. 'Miss Desmond will travel with you. You will be flying to Johannesburg on Tuesday. I have arranged for your rooms at the Rand International Hotel. You will stay there until Mr. Jones has organized the expedition. I have also arranged for the hire of a helicopter which Miss Desmond and Mr. Edwards will use.' He touched ash off his cigar, then went on, 'I have managed to obtain a certain amount of information about Kahlenberg's place, but none of this information is completely reliable. Before you can hope to get at the ring, it is essential for Miss Desmond to get into Kahlenberg's house and check the information I have obtained: this information is to do with various security measures and where the museum is located. Miss Desmond will pose as a professional photographer after wild game. I have arranged that she is credited to Animal World which is a sound, small American magazine for whom I have done past favours. It is possible that Kahlenberg might check, and it would be stupid not to be covered. Mr. Edwards will be her professional pilot. A helicopter is the ideal machine from which to get photographs of wild animals. Kahlenberg has an airfield. You two'—here Shalik looked at Gaye and Garry—'will land on the airfield. Your story will be that you saw the house from the air and can you take photographs? You will be refused, of course, but I am certain Kahlenberg will want to meet Miss Desmond.'

'But suppose he doesn't?' Garry said.

Shalik frowned at him.

'I said I was certain, and that means he will. I don't use words lightly.' The snub administered, Shalik went on, 'I have no idea where the museum is. I imagine it must be somewhere in the house which is a vast one-storey building. As the museum contains many stolen treasures, it will be well hidden and well guarded. One of my agents in Durban, some eight years ago, happened to be watching a ship unload and noticed a considerable number of crates coming ashore with Kahlenberg's name on them. Knowing I was interested in Kahlenberg, he investigated. The crates came from Bahlstrom of Sweden who you may know are the best safe makers and security experts in the world.' He glanced at Fennel. 'Am I telling you anything new?'

Fennel grinned.

'I know all about Bahlstrom. Years ago, I worked for them. They are good.'

'Yes, Mr. Fennel,' Shalik said. 'This is the main reason why I am hiring you.' He again touched off his cigar ash and continued. 'Fortunately, my agent was intelligent. He obtained a copy of the invoices from the shipping agent at some cost and sent it to me. I give it to you now to examine. It is possible with your knowledge of Bahlstrom's security system and with these invoices, you may get some idea of Kahlenberg's security set-up.' He handed a plastic envelope to Fennel who glanced at it and then shoved it in his hip pocket. 'You have until Monday morning to let me know what you think.'

'Okay,' Fennel said, crossing one fat leg over the other. 'I'll tell you.'

Shalik turned to Garry.

'Mr. Edwards, I have aerial maps of the Drakensberg range and of Kahlenberg's estate.' Again another plastic envelope passed across the desk. 'I will want you to tell me if you can land the helicopter from a place chosen by Mr. Jones on the Kahlenberg airfield. This we will also discuss on Monday.'

Garry nodded, taking the envelope.

Shalik now turned to Kennedy Jones.

'You will be responsible for fitting out the expedition and for transport. You and Mr. Fennel will go by road while Miss Desmond and Mr. Edwards fly. You can spend what you like but you must insure against the many difficulties which you could meet on the way in. The route to Kahlenberg's estate is exceptionally difficult at this season when the rains can be expected. But this is your affair. You will also have to find a way through the circle of Zulus who guard the approaches. You are the expert, so I don't propose making any suggestions.'

'I'll take care of it,' Jones said.

'Well then, we will have our final meeting on Monday,' Shalik said. 'We will then clear up the final details. Any questions?'

Fennel leaned forward.

'How about some money? We are being paid nine thousand each for this caper, but how about something in advance?'

Shalik made a grimace that could pass for a smile.

'I was expecting that request from you.' He took from a drawer four envelopes and handing one to Gaye, he passed the other three across his desk. 'You'll find in each envelope blank Travellers' Cheques to the total of $3,000. When you have successfully completed your mission, you will get the balance.' He glanced at his gold Omega. 'Then we meet here at 09.30 hrs. on Monday.'

Gaye left the room by the door behind Shalik. Garry and Ken Jones watched her going with regret. They started towards the far door as Fennel got to his feet.

'Mr. Fennel . . .'

Fennel looked at Shalik.

'There are a few additional things to discuss without wasting the time of these other gentlemen,' Shalik said quietly.

Fennel shrugged and sat down again. Shalik waved to the other two, dismissing them.

When they had gone, Shalik selected another cigar, clipped the end and lit it while he looked stonily at Fennel.

'It is necessary, Mr. Fennel, to have a straight talk with you. Your two companions have both served jail sentences, but you can hardly describe them as criminals. However, you are not only a criminal, but a dangerous and vicious one. I have selected you for this operation because of your expertise, but don't imagine I am ignorant of your criminal background. I know you are on the run and anxious to get out of England. You betrayed five criminals in order to reduce your own sentence and the leader of this gang—a man called Moroni—has sworn to kill you. An attempt was made last night, but failed. The second attempt might not fail.' Shalik paused to stare at Fennel who was now sitting up straight, his eyes glittering. 'So from what I am telling you, Mr. Fennel, you will see I keep myself well informed about the people I employ. Now I have received additional information about you. You are wanted for three vicious murders in Hong Kong, Cairo and Istanbul. Two of your victims were females: the third was a male prostitute. I have evidence of these crimes that Interpol would gladly receive. Does all this that I am telling you, Mr. Fennel, interest you?"

Fennel moistened his lips with his tongue.

'Are you threatening me? I got the idea we are working together.'

'Yes . . . we are working together, but that doesn't mean I can't threaten you. There are two things you are to keep constantly in mind.' Shalik pointed his cigar at Fennel. 'The first point is you will leave Gaye Desmond strictly alone. As soon as she came into this room, your disgusting mind began to wonder about her. You were thinking that in the African bush you would have opportunities to behave in the animal way that comes naturally to you. So I am warning you: try something like that with Miss Desmond, and I promise you Interpol will have your dossier from me. Is that clear?'

Fennel forced an uneasy grin.

'You hold the aces,' he said with an attempt at bravado. 'You are reading me wrong, but okay, so she is like my mother.'

Shalik grimaced.

'If you will excuse the personal remark . . . I feel sorry for your mother.'

Fennel gave a hard, barking laugh.

'You don't have to. She was one of the smartest thieves in the racket. If you want to be sorry for anyone, be sorry for my old man. He cut his throat when they put my mother away for ten years.'

'I am not interested in your family history,' Shalik said curtly. 'My second point is this. I want this ring. The operation won't be easy, but a man of your experience and ruthlessness should be able to handle it. However, if you fail, I see no reason why I shouldn't pass your dossier to Interpol . . . so you must understand that I will not tolerate failure.'

Fennel bared his teeth in a snarling grin.

'I'll get the goddam ring for you, but if so much depends on me, how about some extra money?'

'I will consider that when I have the ring. Now get out!'

Fennel stared at him, but Shalik was reaching for the telephone. As he began to dial a number, Fennel got up and went into the inner room where Natalie Norman was typing. He didn't look at her, but went out into the corridor and to the lift.

When he had gone, and when she was satisfied she could hear Shalik talking on the telephone, she turned off the hidden tape-recorder and removed the spool.

Garry shut himself in a telephone booth and called Toni who answered immediately.

'We're celebrating, chicken,' he said. 'I'm hungry. Meet me at the Rib Room, Carlton Towers in exactly one hour from this minute,' and he hung up, cutting off her squeal of excitement.

He knew he had to give her at least an hour to get ready. Toni was a languid and slow dresser. By the time he reached the Rib Room he was pleasantly high, having drunk four vodka martinis in the bar of the Royal Towers Hotel.

Ken Jones had left him, saying he had a date with a girl friend. They had paused in the crowded lobby of the hotel and Jones had asked, 'What do you think of it all?'

'It's a job and the money's nice,' Garry returned. 'You and I will get along. I feel that. It's Fennel . . .'

Jones grinned.

'What are you worrying about? You have Gorgeous and a chopper. I have Fennel.'

'Well, watch him.'

'You bet . . . so long, see you Monday. Happy bed bouncing,' and Jones went off into the cold, wet night.

Toni, looking ravishing, turned up at the Rib Room just when Garry was losing patience.

'I'm damn well starving,' he complained. 'You're late!'

'I know, sweetie, but I just can't help it.' She flicked her long eyelashes at him. 'Like me?'

But now Garry had met Gaye Desmond, Toni White seemed suddenly a little young, trying a little too hard, and less exciting.

'You're wonderful.' The four martinis gave his voice conviction.

They moved into the restaurant. As they sat down, Toni asked, 'So you got the job?'

'You don't imagine we would be here if I hadn't?'

'Let's order and then you tell me, huh?'

'Don't say huh . . . only American businessmen say that.'

Toni giggled.

'God! I'm starving too! Let's order quickly.'

The maitre d'hôtel came over. Garry ordered a dozen oysters each with a half bottle of Chablis, followed by the Scotch beef with a baked potato in its jacket and a bottle of Batailley 1961. The dessert, it was decided, should be a lemon sorbet.

'Mmmmmm!'' Toni purred. 'This job must be marvellous. You do realize this is going to cost a f-o-r-t-u-n-e?'

'So what? I'm worth a fortune.' Under the cover of the table, Garry slid his hand up Toni's mini skirt, but she clamped her legs together.

'Mr. Edwards! I'm surprised at you!' she said.

Garry disengaged his hand.

'I'm continually surprising myself, Miss White.'

The oysters arrived.

'Well, tell me . . what is the job?' Toni asked as she cut a fat oyster from its shell. 'God! I adore oysters!'

'Don't be greedy,' Garry said, forking an oyster into his mouth. 'It's never becoming for a young and sexy girl to sound greedy.'

'Shut up! Tell me about the job.'

'Well, it's a dilly. I go to Natal, and as your geography is as dodgy as mine, Natal is somewhere in South Africa. I lug an American photographer around in a helicopter so she can take photos of wild animals. It is a three week assignment and the money is very acceptable.'

Toni's oyster hovered before her mouth. She looked searchingly at Garry who avoided her eyes.

'She? You mean you are flying a *woman* around jungles for three weeks?'

'That's it,' Garry said carelessly. 'Now don't start getting into a state. I've met her. She's around forty-five, looks pregnant, and is the type who slaps you on the back and picks her teeth immediately after a meal.'

Toni stared at him.

'But that sounds horrible.'

'Doesn't it? Still the money is good and after all she could have had a beard and a wooden leg, couldn't she?'

Toni nodded and attacked another oyster. 'Yes, I suppose so.'

There was a long silence while the waiter removed the debris and a longer silence while the beef was served.

Garry stole a look at her face and then grimaced. Hell! he thought, she knows I'm lying. Now what am I going to do?

He said gently, 'Toni, darling, have you got something on your mind?'

'Should I have?' She didn't look at him but concentrated on her beef. 'They have here the most marvellous beef in the world.'

'I wouldn't say in the world. I remember in Hong Kong . . .'

'Never mind Hong Kong. Please tell me how much you are being paid to convey a pregnant woman around the jungle.'

'I didn't say she was pregnant, I said she looks pregnant. Not quite the same thing.'

'How much?'

'Three thousand dollars,' Garry lied.

'Well, that's very nice. So you will be away for three weeks?'

'Yes.'

Toni continued to eat. There was a dazed expression in her eyes that began to bother Garry.

'I hear Natal is pretty interesting,' he said. 'It could be quite a trip.'

'Shall we try to enjoy our dinner, Garry? This is the first time I've been to the Rib Room.'

'I thought we were enjoying it. Are you trying to be dramatic?'

Her long lashes flickered at him, then she dug into her baked potato.

'Please let us enjoy something even if we can't enjoy each other.'

That spoilt his meal. Impatiently he pushed aside his plate and lit a cigarette. Toni ate slowly, obviously enjoying the beef. They said nothing until she had finished, then when the waiter had removed the plates, Garry said, 'Just what the hell has suddenly bit you, Toni? This is supposed to be a celebration.'

'I love sorbets. Queen Victoria used to stuff sorbets down the throats of all her over-stuffed guests half-way through the menu. The sorbets allowed them to go on stuffing.'

'I didn't know you were so well educated, darling. I asked what is biting you.'

The lemon sorbets arrived. Garry, in a fit of frustrated rage, crushed his cigarette in the ice.

'Is that how you feel, Mr. Oxfam?' Toni asked, spooning ice into her pretty mouth.

'Look, Toni, I don't know what's come over you, but this has turned into a drag.'

'Has it?' She put down her spoon. 'Garry, dear, I am always asking myself how it is I land up with a lover who lies to me. It is beginning to bore me.'

They stared at each other.

'Women who are able to spot my lies bore me too,' Garry said quietly.

'There it is.' Toni lifted her hands helplessly. 'Damn you, I love you. Let's get out of here and go home and have sex.'

He paid the bill without shuddering with one of the $50 Travellers' Cheques Shalik had given him.

In the taxi, Toni sat away from him, putting her feet up on the tip-up seat.

'This photographer . . . she's marvellous, isn't she?' she asked. 'Darling Garry, don't lie to me . . tell me.'

He watched the street lights and the rain beating on the pavement, and he sighed. 'Okay . . . yes . . . she's marvellous.'

Toni's small, pretty face tightened with misery.

'Will you be coming back, Garry?'

'Now look, Toni . . .'

'I'm asking you . . will you be coming back to me?'

He hesitated, thinking of the tawny-haired woman who now filled his mind.

'I don't know.'

'Well, thanks for being truthful.' She moved closer to him and slid into his arms.

Fennel told the taxi driver to take him to the end of Hornsey Road where Jacey had his shabby flat. As the taxi passed Jacey's building, Fennel peered through the rain-splashed window, looking for trouble, but saw nothing to alarm him. At the end of the long road, he paid off the taxi and walked back, keeping in the shadows, his eyes alert for trouble.

He reached the entrance of the block, stepped inside and looked at the steep stairs leading to the upper floor of the building, lit by a yellow electric light bulb.

Instinct warned him he could be walking into danger. He hesitated, then, moving silently into the smelly lobby, he stepped into the telephone booth behind the stairs. He dialled Jacey's number. He listened to the steady ringing for some minutes, then he hung up. It was unlikely Jacey would be out in this cold rain at this hour . . . it was after 22.00 hrs. Jacey got up early and went to bed early. Fennel hesitated. His equipment which he had to have for the Natal trip was up there. He had to get it. It was securely hidden in the rafters of Jacey's attic. It would want some finding if they searched for it. He hadn't told Jacey where he had hidden it so they would have no success if they had put pressure on Jacey.

He grinned suddenly as an idea came into his mind. He lifted the receiver and dialled 999. To the answering police voice, he said, 'There's bad trouble at 332 Hornsey Road . . . top flat . . . could be murder,' and he hung up.

He then moved cautiously out of the booth, listened, then walked into the darkness and the rain. Keeping in the shadows, he crossed the road and stood in the entrance of a dark alley to wait.

He didn't have to wait long.

Two police cars came swiftly out of the night, pulled up outside the building and four policemen ran up the steps.

Fennel looked up at Jacey's darkened windows. After a few moments a light flashed up. He waited, leaning against the damp wall of the alley, shivering slightly in the bleak cold. After some twenty minutes, three of the policemen came out, shoving two powerfully built men into the police cars. The two men were handcuffed. They drove away. That left one policeman up there.

What had happened to Jacey? Fennel wondered. Well, he couldn't wait. He had to get his equipment. He took his handkerchief from his pocket and tied it across his face, making a mask, then he crossed the street and entered the building and ran silently up the stairs. When he reached Jacey's floor, he paused to listen. Jacey's front door stood open. He could hear the policeman moving around in the room.

Fennel crept like a ghost to the door and glanced in. The far wall was splashed with blood. His back turned to him, the policeman was kneeling by Jacey's body.

Fennel grimaced. So Jacey, the poor stupid sod, had been carved. He didn't hesitate. Moving swiftly, he was on the policeman before the man realized he was being attacked. With laced fingers, Fennel smashed his hands down on the man's bent neck with one shattering, terrible blow. The policeman spread out over Jacey's blood-stained body.

Fennel darted into the tiny, evil smelling bedroom and up the ladder that led to the attic. In seconds, he had got the bag containing his equipment, then slid down the ladder, out on to the landing. He paused to listen, then went down the stairs to the ground floor, three at the time. Panting, he reached the front door where he paused again, hearing the distant sound of a police siren. He slid out into the rain, ran across the road and backed against the wall of the alley as an ambulance and two police cars came roaring to a standstill.

Fennel grunted . . . well timed, he thought, then set off by the back alleys until he reached a main road. He saw a cruising taxi and waved. The taxi pulled up and he told the driver to take him to the Royal Towers Hotel.

He arrived outside Shalik's suite and rapped on the door.

There was a delay, then the door opened. George Sherborn, a portly, elderly man who acted as Shalik's confidential secretary and valet regarded Fennel with startled disapproval. He knew all about Fennel and, after hesitating, stood aside and let him in.

'Mr. Shalik is away for the weekend,' he said. 'What is it?'

'I've got to get the hell out of the country fast,' Fennel said wiping his sweating face with the back of his hand. 'I'm in dead trouble. The creeps after me found my pal and carved him. The cops are there now. It won't take them long to find my finger-prints all over the goddamn place, and when they do I'm blown.'

Sherborn was never flustered. He could rise to any emergency with the calmness of a bishop presiding over a tea party. He knew without Fennel the Borgia ring operation couldn't succeed. He told Fennel to wait and went into the inner room, shutting the door. Half an hour later, he returned.

'A car is waiting for you downstairs, to take you to Lydd,' he said. 'You fly by air taxi to Le Touquet. There will be another car at Le Touquet to take you to the Normandy hotel, Paris, where you will stay until the Johannesburg plane leaves. Your ticket will be at Orly, waiting for you.' Sherborn's round goose-berry eyes regarded Fennel impersonally. 'You understand the cost of all this will be deducted from your fee?'

'Who says so, fatty?' Fennel snarled.

Sherborn looked at him with contempt.

'Don't be impertinent. Mr. Shalik will be most displeased by what has happened. Now get off.' He handed Fennel a sheet of paper. 'All the necessary details are here for you. You have your passport?'

'Oh, get stuffed!' Fennel snapped and, snatching the paper, hurried to the lift.

Five minutes later, seated in a hired Jaguar, he was being whisked down to Lydd.

CHAPTER THREE

TEN MINUTES after the meeting between Gaye, Garry, Jones and Fennel had broken up, Shalik had come into Natalie's office, an overcoat over his arm and a week-end case in his hand. She paused in her work and looked up.

To Shalik, Natalie Norman was part of his background: useful, exceedingly efficient: a dedicated, colourless woman who had been with him for three years. He had chosen her to be his personal assistant from a short list of highly qualified women an agency had submitted to him.

Natalie Norman was thirty-eight years of age. She spoke fluent French and German, and she had an impressive degree in Economics. With no apparent interests outside Shalik's office she was, to him, a machine who worked efficiently and who was essential to him.

Shalik liked sensual, beautiful women. To him, Natalie Norman with her plain looks, her pallid complexion, was merely a robot. When he spoke to her, he seldom looked at her.

'I shall be away for the week-end, Miss Norman,' he said, pausing at her desk. 'I will ask you to come in tomorrow for an hour to see to the mail, then take the week-end off. I have a meeting on Monday morning at 09.00 hrs.,' and he was gone.

There was no look, no smile and not even a 'nice week-end.'

The following morning, she arrived at her usual time, dealt with the mail and was beginning to clear her desk as George Sherborn came in.

She loathed Sherborn as he loathed her. To her thinking, he was a boot-licking, sensual, fat old horror. On the day she began to work for Shalik, Sherborn, his fat face flushed, had run his hand over her corseted buttocks as she was sealing a large envelope full of legal documents. His touch revolted her. She had spun around and slashed his fat face with the side of the envelope, making his nose bleed.

From then on they hated each other, but had worked together, both ably serving Shalik.

'Have you finished?' Sherborn asked pompously. 'If you have, get off. I'm staying here.'

'I'll be going in a few minutes,' she returned, not looking at him.

Sherborn nodded, regarded her contemptuously and returned to Shalik's office.

Natalie sat for a long moment listening, then when she heard Sherborn dialling a number, she took from a drawer a big plastic shopping bag. From another drawer she took out the tiny tape recorder and three reels of tape. These she hurriedly put in the shopping bag and zipped it shut. She could hear Sherborn talking on the telephone. She moved silently to the door and listened.

'I've got the place to myself, baby,' Sherborn was saying. 'Yes . . . the whole week-end. Suppose you come over? We could have fun.'

Natalie grimaced with disgust and moved away. She put on her coat, tied a black scarf around her head and, taking the shopping bag, she crossed to the lift and pressed the call button.

As she waited, Sherborn appeared in the doorway.

'You off?'

'Yes.'

She stared bleakly as she saw him looking curiously at the shopping bag.

'Taking all the secrets with you?'

'Yes.'

The lift doors swung open and she entered. As the doors closed, Sherborn smiled sneeringly at her.

Natalie took a taxi back to her two room flat in Church Street, Kensington. She had slept very little the previous night, tossing and turning, trying to make up her mind whether to betray Shalik or not. Even now as she unlocked the front door and entered the small but pleasant living-room which she had furnished with care, she still hadn't made up her mind.

She put down the shopping bag, took off her head scarf and coat and then dropped into an armchair. She sat there for some minutes, knowing she would do it and loathing herself. She looked at her watch. The time was 11.10 hrs. There was always the chance that Burnett wouldn't be at the bank on this Saturday morning. If he wasn't, then it would be a sign for her not to do what she was planning to do. For a brief moment, she hesitated, then crossed to the telephone and dialled a number.

She sat on the arm of the chair as she listened to the ringing tone.

An impersonal voice said, 'This is the National Bank of Natal.'

'Could I speak to Mr. Charles Burnett, please?'

'Who is calling?'

'Miss Norman . . . Mr. Burnett knows me.'

'One moment.'

There was a brief delay, then a rich, fruity baritone voice came over the line.

'Miss Norman? Delighted . . . how are you?'

She shivered, hesitated, then forced herself to say, 'I would like to see you, Mr. Burnett . . . it's urgent.'

'Of course. If you could come at once . . . I am leaving in an hour for the country.'

'No!' Hysterical self-loathing now had her in its grip. 'In half an hour . . . here . . . at my flat! 35a Church Street, fourth floor. I said it was urgent!'

There was a pause, then the rich baritone voice, sounding slightly shocked, said, 'I'm afraid that is not convenient, Miss Norman.'

'Here! In half an hour!' Natalie cried, her voice going shrill and she slammed down the receiver.

She slid down into the seat of the chair, resting her head against the cushion. Her body shuddered and jerked as she began to sob hysterically. For some minutes she allowed herself the luxury of crying. The hot tears finally ran no more. Trembling, she went into the bathroom and bathed her face, then spent some minutes repairing her make-up.

She returned to the sitting-room, opened a cupboard and took out the bottle of whisky she kept for Daz. She poured herself a stiff drink and swallowed it neat, shuddering.

She sat down to wait.

Thirty-five minutes later, the front door bell rang. At the sound of the bell, blood rushed into her face and then receded leaving her face chalk white. For a long moment, she sat motionless, then when the bell rang again, she forced herself to her feet and opened the door.

Charles Burnett, Chairman of the National Bank of Natal, swept into the room like a galleon in full sail. He was a large, heavily-built man with a purple red face, shrewd hard eyes and his bald head, fringed by glossy white hair, was glistening pink. Immaculately dressed in a Savile Row grey lounge suit with a blood red carnation in his button hole, he looked a movie version of what a rich, influential banker should be.

'My dear Miss Norman,' he said, 'what is all the urgency about?'

He regarded her, his mind registering distaste, but he was far too shrewd and experienced to show it. What a dreadful hag! he was thinking: nice figure, good legs, of course, but that pallid face, the plainness of it, those depressing black eyes and the dark overshadowed face.

Natalie had control of herself now. The whisky had given her false confidence.

'Sit down, please, Mr. Burnett. I won't be wasting your time. I have information regarding Mr. Kahlenberg that you will wish to hear.'

Burnett lowered his bulk into an armchair. His expression showed mild interest, but his shrewd mind was thinking: So it has paid off. One drops a seed here and there, and sometimes it germinates.

As Chairman of the National Bank of Natal which was owned by Max Kahlenberg, Burnett was under instructions from his Chief to collect every scrap of information circulating in London that could affect Kahlenberg's kingdom in Natal.

Some twelve days ago, Kahlenberg had sent him a brief cable: *Need information regarding activities of Armo Shalik. K.*

Burnett knew all about Armo Shalik, but nothing of his business activities. The cable dismayed him. To get information about Shalik . . . the kind of information that would interest Kahlenberg . . . would be as difficult as getting information from the Sphinx.

However, Burnett knew he had to do something about this request. When Kahlenberg asked for information, he expected to get it no matter the difficulties or the cost.

It so happened that, two days later, Shalik threw a cocktail party in his suite to which Burnett was invited. Here he met Natalie Norman.

Burnett believed in being pleasant to the underlings. Didn't George Bernard Shaw say once: you may kick an old man: you know what he is, but never kick a young man: you don't know what he will become?

Seeing Natalie supervising the drinks and being ignored by the chattering guests, he had detached himself from his tiresome wife and cornered her. He had charm, and was an easy conversationalist and he quickly learned that this pale-faced, plain-looking woman was Shalik's personal assistant, and he could see that she was sexually starved.

He easily won her confidence and chatted with her for some minutes while his mind worked swiftly. She could be vitally important to him and he knew he couldn't remain with her for long as Shalik was already glancing in their direction with lifted eyebrows.

'Miss Norman,' he said quietly, 'I am in the position to help people like yourself should you need help. Please remember my name; Charles Burnett, the National Bank of Natal. Should you ever get dissatisfied with your job here, should you wish to earn more money, do please contact me.'

As her expression became bewildered, he smiled and left her.

After returning home, he sat in his study and considered his next move. He hoped he hadn't rushed his fences with this pale-faced woman. She could be the spy he needed. Obviously, she needed physical contact with a virile man. Burnett knew all the signs: her thinness, her dark ringed eyes, her depressed expression. What she needed was a lusty bedmate: he decided this must be the first move to ensnare her.

Burnett had many useful contacts and among them was ex-Inspector Tom Parkins of the C.I.D. He telephoned him.

Parkins . . . I am looking for a young rogue who could do a special job for me. He must be completely unscrupulous and good looking with personality and around twenty-five, not older. Do you know of anyone like that?'

The cop voice said, 'Shouldn't be too difficult, sir. Would the pay be interesting?'

'Very.'

'I'll turn it over in my mind, sir. Suppose I call you after lunch?'

Do that,' Burnett said, satisfied he would get what he wanted.

Around 15.00 hrs., Parkins telephoned.

I've got your man, sir,' he said. 'Daz Jackson: twenty-four years of age, excellent appearance, plays a guitar in a fifth rate Soho club and needs money. He served two years for petty larceny three years ago.'

Burnett hesitated.

'This might be a little tricky, Parkins. I'm not letting myself in for blackmail?'

'Oh no, sir. Anything like that . . . and it won't happen, I assure you . . . I could handle for you. I have quite a lot on this young tearaway. You don't have to worry about that angle.'

'Very well. Send him here at 17.00 hrs. I'll arrange to have ten pounds credited to your account with us, Parkins.'

'That's very kind of you, sir. You will be quite satisfied with Jackson.'

Daz Jackson arrived ten minutes after the hour. He was ushered into Burnett's vast office by Burnett's secretary. She had worked so long for Burnett that nothing surprised her . . . not even Daz Jackson.

Burnett regarded the young man as he lounged into the big room, a supercilious grin on his face. He wore mustard-coloured hipsters, a dark-blue frilled shirt and a gilt chain around his neck from which hung a small bell that tinkled as he moved.

What a specimen Burnett thought, but, at least, he is clean.

Without being asked, Jackson lowered his lean frame into a chair, crossed one leg over the other and regarded Burnett with an insolent lift of his eyebrow.

'The ex-bogey said you had a job. What's the pay?' he asked. And listen, I don't dig to work in this graveyard. Catch?'

Burnett was used to dealing with all kinds of people and he was adaptable. Although he would have liked to have kicked this young beatnik out, he saw he could be the man he was looking for.

'I'm not asking you to work here, Mr. Jackson,' he said. 'I have a special job which you could handle and which pays well.'

Jackson raised a languid hand in mock protest.

'Skip the mister and all that jazz,' he said. 'Call me Daz.'

Burnett's insincere smile became a little stiff.

'Certainly . . . but why Daz?'

'The chicks call me that . . . I dazzle them.'

'Splendid.' Burnett leaned back in his executive chair. 'What I want you to do is this . . .' He explained.

Daz Jackson lolled in his chair and listened. His ice grey eyes searched Burnett's face while Burnett talked. Finally, when Burnett said, 'Well, that's it . . . do you think you can handle it for me?' Daz grimaced.

'Let's get it nice and straight,' he said, stretching out his long legs. 'This piece wants to be laid . . . right?' When Burnett nodded, he went on, 'Once I've given it to her, she'll want more . . . right?' Again Burnett nodded. 'Then she has to pay for it . . . you want me to squeeze her dry . . . right?'

'Yes . . . that is the situation.'

'You will pay me a hundred nicker for doing the job and what I get out of her I keep . . . right?'

Burnett inclined his head. Dealing with a man like this made him feel slightly soiled.

Jackson leaned back in his chair and stared at Burnett.

'Well, for God's sake, and they call me a delinquent!'

Burnett's eyes turned frosty.

'Do you want the job or don't you?'

They stared at each other for a long moment, then Daz shrugged.

'Oh sure . . . what have I to lose? What's this piece like?'

'Plain but adequate,' Burnett returned, unconsciously using the phrase in the Michelin Guide to France to describe a third rate hotel.

'Okay, so where do I find her?'

Burnett gave him Natalie's home and business address typed on a blank card.

'I want quick action.'

Daz grinned.

'If you say she's thirsting for it, she'll have it and once she has had it from me, she'll want it again and again.' Daz regarded Burnett, his eyes calculating. 'The cops won't come into this?'

'There's no question of that.'

'Well, if they do, I'll squeal. I'm not mad about this job.'

Burnett stared coldly at him.

'But you will do it?'

Daz shrugged.

'I said I would, didn't I?'

'Get as much money out of her as you can. I want her to be in an impossible financial position. I want her to be up to her eyes in debt.'

Daz dragged himself to his feet.

'How about some money now . . . I'm skint.'

'When you deliver,' Burnett said curtly and waved a dismissal.

In the bitter cold of a January night, Natalie Norman found her rear off-side tyre was flat. She had been working late, and was now looking forward to getting home and into a hot bath. She had parked her Austin-Mini, as she always did, in a cul-de-sac off Park Lane. She stood shivering in the biting wind while she looked helplessly at the flat tyre, when out of the shadows came a tall, lean young man, wearing a lamb skin lined short coat, his hands thrust deeply into the pockets of his black hipsters.

Daz had learned where Natalie parked her car, and he had let the air out of the tyre some fifty minutes ago. He had stood in a nearby doorway, freezing and cursing until he saw her come to the car. This was his first glimpse of her. He brightened considerably as the street light lit up her long, slim legs. The least he had expected was some woman with legs that could support a grand piano.

He waited, watching her. She moved into the full light and he grimaced. Good body, but so obviously a plain, sex-starved spinster with as much personality as a drowned cat.

Boy; he thought. Will I have to use my imagination to get her laid!

'You in trouble, miss?' he said. 'Can I give you a hand?'

Natalie was startled by his sudden appearance. She looked helplessly to right and left, but there was no one in the cul-de-sac except themselves.

'I have a puncture,' she said nervously. 'It's all right. I'll get a taxi . . . thank you.'

He moved under the street light so she could see him. They regarded each other, and she felt her heart beat quicken. He was lean and tall and like a beautiful young animal, she thought. His hair, curling to his collar, excited her. She felt a rush of blood through her: something that often happened when she saw really masculine men on the street, but her pale, expressionless face revealed nothing of the feeling that was moving through her body.

'I'll fix it,' Daz said. 'You get in the car, miss. Get out of the cold. Phew! It's cold, isn't it?'

'Yes . . . but please don't bother. I'll take a taxi.'

'Hop in . . . I'll fix it . . . won't take me a jiff.'

She unlocked the car door and got gratefully into the little car, closing the door. She watched his movements. He was very quick. Under ten minutes, he came to the car window, wiping his hands on the seat of his hipsters.

'All fixed, miss . . . you can get off.'

She looked up at him through the open car window. He leaned forward, staring down at her. Was there something of promise in his young eyes? she wondered. Her heart was jumping about like a freshly landed trout.

'Can't I give you a lift?'

She smiled and when she smiled, he decided she wasn't all that bad to look at.

'You wouldn't be going near Knightsbridge?' he asked, knowing that was where she lived.

'Oh yes . . . Church Street.'

'Well, a lift would be nice.'

He went around the car and slid in beside her. His shoulder touched her and she felt as if she had received an electric shock.

She was furious with herself because her hand was shaking so violently she couldn't get the key into the ignition lock.

'You're cold. Like me to drive, miss?'

Silently, she handed him the keys and he slid out of the car as she moved over to the passenger's seat. Her skirt got rucked up on the gear lever. She hesitated, then knowing her legs and slim thighs were her only attractive features, she let her skirt remain as it was.

'I'm frozen,' she forced herself to say as Daz got under the driving wheel.

'Me too . . . it's perishing.'

She expected him to drive fast and flashily, but he didn't. He drove well, keeping just under the 30 m.p.h. limit and with expert confidence that surprised her.

'Do you live in Knightsbridge?' she ventured.

'Who . . . me?' He laughed. 'Nothing so posh. I live in a rat hole in Parsons Green. I'm out of work. Whenever I get down to my last quid I like to walk around Knightsbridge and window shop. I imagine what I would buy from Harrods if I had a mass of lolly.'

She looked at his handsome profile, and again she experienced this devastating pang of desire.

'But why are you out of work?' she asked. 'People need never be out of work these days.'

'I've been ill. I've got a weak lung . . . plays up sometimes . . . then I get laid off. I've been laid off now for two weeks.' Daz thought: The lies I can tell. I almost believe this myself. Then feeling he was laying it on a little too thick, he added, 'I'll get something next week, I'm feeling fine now.'

Natalie digested all this.

'I'm glad.'

He turned and gave her a smile that had earned him his nick name. She felt sloppily weak as her desire for him mounted.

'You don't have to worry about me, miss. No one, including me, worries about me.' He paused, then went on, 'You're out late, aren't you?'

'I often work late.'

'Church Street you said?'

They were now driving by Knightsbridge Underground Station. 'Yes.'

'You live on your own?'

Oh yes, Natalie thought bitterly. Alone . . . always alone.

'Yes.'

Daz's eyes moved to her legs, exposed to above the knee. Poor cow! he thought. This is going to be easy.

'Well, lots of people live on their own,' he said. 'When they get back from work, they shut themselves in their dreary rooms and that's it until they go out to work the next morning. That's why I like to walk the streets at night. Staying in my room on my own gives me the horrors.'

'I can understand that.' Then as he began to drive up Church Street, she went on, 'This is the place . . . on the right.'

Well, here's the crunch, he thought. Is she going to invite me in?

'You mean this big block here?'

'Yes. You go down the ramp to the garage.' She hesitated then said in a small voice, 'I expect you would like a wash after changing that tyre. I think you deserve a drink, too.'

He hid a grin. He had felt it would be easy, but not quite this easy.

'Yes. I could do with a wash,' and he drove the car down into the big lighted garage.

They went up in the lift to the fourth floor. Neither of them looked at each other on the way up nor spoke.

She unlocked her front door and led him into the small, bright sitting-room.

'Do take your coat off.' Her voice was very unsteady.

He looked around.

'This is real nice.'

She came to know *nice* was his favourite word.

'The bathroom's through there.'

She left him in the bathroom and she took off her coat and scarf, feeling desire for him raging through her. She was still standing in the middle of the room, white and shaking, when he came out of the bathroom. He knew at once there would be trouble.

'We don't know each other. I'm Daz Jackson.'

'I'm Natalie Norman.'

'Nice name . . . Natalie . . . I dig for that.'

They stared at each other, then he moved close to her and slid his arms around her.

She shivered as his hands moved down her thin back. For one brief moment, her subconscious mechanism fought to repulse him, but her need was too strong.

She was only dimly aware of being carried into the bedroom. She relaxed on the bed, moving a little from side to side as he stripped off her clothes. Then she gave herself up to his animal lust.

Daz Jackson opened his eyes and let out a long, slow sigh. Well, for shouting aloud! he thought as he looked up at the white ceiling. Who would have believed it. It's the best I've ever had!

He turned on his side and looked at Natalie who lay on her back, her hands covering her small breasts, sleeping. He regarded her body. Good, pity about that face. He gave her a gentle prod in the ribs.

'Wake up! I'm hungry. You got any food?'

She stirred and looked up at him, her eyes glazed with a satisfaction she had never known before. She felt as if a hidden door she had long been searching for had suddenly opened and the sun and the breeze and the sound of the sea had come into the barren, dark cave in which she had lived for so long.

'Food . . . of course.' She sat up, swung her legs off the bed and snatched up a wrap. 'Stay there . . .I'll get you something. Would you like a drink . . . I have only gin.'

He regarded her. Her anxiety to please, the soft look in her eyes and her eager trembling made her a bore.

'Just grub.'

She ran into the kitchen. He waited a moment, then got off the bed and struggled into his clothes. He saw by the bedside clock that the time was 02.25 hrs. He listened, smelling bacon frying, then he looked around the small neat room. He looked beyond the doorway, across the sitting-room and saw her standing by the stove in the kitchen, her back to him. Working quickly, he went through her chest of drawers. In the top drawer he found a gold cigarette case, a gold lighter and a small jewel box which contained a string of pearls and two rings of little value, but he took all of them, dropping them into his pocket. Then he lounged into the sitting-room and stood in the kitchen doorway.

'Smells nice,' he said.

She turned and smiled at him.

'Can you eat more than four eggs?'

'That'll be fine.'

She hurried past him and quickly laid the table.

'Aren't you eating?' he asked, seeing she had set only one place.

'No . . . it's ready. Sit down.'

He ate hungrily. Well, she certainly could cook eggs and bacon, he thought as he sipped the tea she had poured him. Pity there weren't chips and tomato ketchup, but you can't expect everything.

He was aware of her, sitting on the settee, watching him. There was that soft look in her eyes that told him she was hooked. When he had finished, he sat back, wiping his mouth on the paper serviette she had provided.

'Nice,' he said. 'Really nice.'

'You were hungry, weren't you?'

He stared directly at her.

'Yes . . . and so were you.'

Blood stained her face and she looked away.

'Nothing to turn hot about.' He smiled his dazzling smile. 'It's nature. You liked it, didn't you? I'll tell you something: you were good . . . really good.'

'Please don't talk about it. I've never done it before.'

'So what? You have to start sometime.' He got to his feet.

'Well, I must be taking off.' He paused. 'Thanks for everything. It was real nice . . . all of it.'

He watched her hands turn into fists.

'Wouldn't you like to—to stay?' she said breathlessly. 'It's such a horrid night. You can stay if you like.'

He shook his head.

'Got to get back to my pad.' He began to move slowly to the front door.

'I suppose we—we could see each other again,' she said, her dark eyes desperate.

Here it is, he thought. The hook.

'You never know. Things happen, don't they? So long,' and before she realized he was really going, he had gone.

The front door slammed. The sound was like a disastrous clap of thunder inside her head.

It wasn't until the following evening that she discovered the loss of her cigarette case and lighter, given to her by Shalik as a birthday present, and her pieces of jewellery. The discovery shocked her and she knew at once who had taken them. Her first reaction was to rush to the telephone to inform the police, but then she controlled her anger and sat down to think. He was out of work. He had been hungry. What did she need with a gold cigarette case or the lighter? She didn't smoke anyway. Thinking of him, she decided that he could have everything she owned so long as he came back to her.

For five long, shattering days she waited with growing desperation to hear from him again until finally a slow horror began to build up inside her that she would have to face the crushing fact that he had made use of her, stolen her things and had forgotten her.

Then on the fifth night, as she sat miserably alone in her flat, facing yet another long night of loneliness, the telephone bell rang. Her heart gave a great leap as she sprang to her feet and ran across the room to snatch up the receiver.

'Yes?'

'This is Daz . . . remember me?'

Her legs felt so weak she had to sit down.

'Of course.'

'Look, I'm sorry I took your things. You mad at me?'

'No . . . of course not.'

'Well, it wasn't nice. I pawned them. I had to have money

fast . . . bit of trouble. I'll let you have the tickets . . . Shall I bring them round now?'

'Yes.'

'Okay, then,' and the line went dead.

He didn't arrive until 22.05 hrs., giving her a frantic wait of an hour and a half. She thought he looked thinner and he wore a scowling frown that gave him a dark, sullen look.

'Here you are,' he said, dropping three pawn tickets on the table. 'I shouldn't have done it . . . but I was in trouble . . . I had to raise money fast.'

'It's all right. I understand. Are you hungry?'

'No . . . I can't stay. I've got to go,' and he turned to the front door.

She gazed at him in panic.

'But you—please stay. I want you to stay.'

He turned on her, his eyes suddenly savage.

'I've go to raise more money,' he said. 'I can't fool around here. There's a girl living near my pad who is trying to raise something for me. I've got to see her tonight.'

'A girl?' Natalie turned cold. 'Daz . . . won't you explain what this is all about? Won't you sit down? I could help you if you would explain.'

'I've had enough out of you.' Daz shook his head. 'Anyway, Lola has practically promised . . .'

'Please sit down and tell me.'

He sat down. It was easy to lie to her. The horse that was a cinch. The bet he couldn't cover, and now the bookie was after him. 'They are a tough lot,' he concluded. 'If I don't raise fifty pounds by tomorrow they are going to do me.'

'*Do* you?' Natalie looked at him in horror. 'What does that mean?'

'Carve me, of course,' he said impatiently. 'Slash me with a razor . . . what do you think?'

She imagined that handsome face bleeding. The thought made her feel faint.

'I can let you have fifty pounds, Daz . . . of course.'

'I can't take it from you . . . no, I'll see Lola.'

'Don't be silly. I'll give you a cheque now.'

An hour later, they were lying side by side on the bed. Natalie was relaxed and happy for the first time since last she had seen Daz. It had been wonderful, she was thinking, better even than the first time. She turned to look at Daz and her heart contracted to see that sullen dark look back on his face again.

'What is it, Daz?'

'Just thinking . . . can't a man think, for God's sake?'

She flinched at the harsh note in his voice.

'Wasn't it good for you? Did I disappoint you?'

'I wasn't thinking about that.' He looked impatiently at her in the shaded light of the bedside lamp. 'That's over. I'm thinking ahead. Just shut up a minute, will you?'

She remained still, waiting and watching his hard young face and the way his eyes shifted, reminding her of an animal in a trap.

'Yes,' he said finally as if speaking his thoughts aloud. 'That's what I'll do. I'll get out. I'll go to Dublin. That's it! Danny will get me a job.'

Natalie sat up, clutching the sheet to her breasts.

'Dublin? What do you mean?'

He frowned at her as if just aware she was with him.

'What I say. I have to get out. That fifty quid you've given me will keep Isaacs off my neck for a couple of days. By then, I'll be out of his reach.'

She felt as if she were going to faint again. Watching her, Daz saw he had played a trump card.

'But you said if I gave you the money it would be all right,' she gasped. 'Daz! Tell me! What do you mean?'

He looked scornfully at her.

'You don't imagine a bookie would carve anyone for fifty quid, do you? I'm in the hole for twelve hundred.'

Once she had absorbed the shock, her trained mind searched for ways and means. Twelve hundred pounds! It was an impossible sum! She had taken an expensive autumn vacation, and she had only two hundred pounds to her credit at her bank. But the idea of Daz leaving England and going to Ireland was unthinkable.

She slid off the bed and put on her wrap while Daz watched her. He saw there was a change of expression on her face. He saw her mind was working, and he lay still, waiting results. He wondered uneasily if he had put the price too high, but Burnett had told him to clean her out. Just suppose she hadn't the money?

She walked around the room while she thought, then she came and sat on the bed, looking straight at him.

'Daz . . . if I give you twelve hundred pounds, could you remain in London?'

'Of course, but you can't give me that amount . . . so why talk about it?'

'I can try. How long can you wait?'

'Why talk about it?' He lay on his back, staring up at the ceiling. 'I must get out. I'll go tomorrow.'

'How long can you wait?' Her voice was now as harsh as his.

'Ten days . . . not more.'

'If I give you this money, Daz, will you come and live here?'

How easy it was to lie to this poor cow, Daz thought.

'You mean move in? You want me here?'

'Yes.' She tried to control her voice. 'I want you here.'

'It would be nice . . . yes, of course. I could get a job, and we could be together. But why talk about it?'

'I think I can manage,' Natalie threw off her wrap. She dropped down beside him on the bed. 'You love me, don't you, Daz?'

That old jazz he thought and pulled her to him.

'You know I do. I'm crazy about you.'

'Then love me!'

While Daz slept by her side, Natalie lay staring into the darkness, her mind busy. She knew it would be hopeless to ask Shalik to lend her a thousand pounds. Even as she was telling Daz that she thought she could get the money for him, she had been thinking of Charles Burnett of the National Bank of Natal.

Natalie was well aware of the espionage and counter-espionage that goes on in present day big business. She knew Burnett had been hinting that he would pay for information and she had treated the hint with the contempt it had deserved, but now under pressure, with the real risk of losing Daz forever, she found she was much less scrupulous.

Before dozing off, she made up her mind to contact Burnett.

Leaving Daz sleeping, she had gone to the Royal Towers hotel the following morning.

She quickly arranged Shalik's mail on his desk, left a note to remind him of his various engagements for the day and then returned to her office.

At this hour, she knew Shalik was being shaved and dressed by the hateful Sherborn. She hesitated only briefly, then called the National Bank of Natal.

She was put through immediately to Charles Burnett who had already been alerted by Daz by telephone what to expect.

'Of course, Miss Norman. I will be delighted to meet you again. When would it be convenient?'

'At your office at 13.15 hrs.,' Natalie told him.

'Then I will expect you.'

When she arrived, Burnett greeted her like a benign uncle. Natalie told him abruptly that she needed one thousand pounds.

'It is a large sum,' Burnett said, studying his pink finger nails, 'but not impossible.' He looked up, his eyes no longer benign. 'You are an intelligent woman, Miss Norman. I don't have to spell it out to you. You want money: I want information concerning Mr. Shalik's activities that might have the remotest reference to Mr. Max Kahlenberg of Natal.

Natalie stiffened.

During the past few days she had learned from scribbled notes on Shalik's desk and from overhearing him talk to Sherborn that something important was being planned that concerned a man named Max Kahlenberg who until this moment had meant nothing to her.

All Shalik's private correspondence was typed by Sherborn. Natalie's job was to arrange Shalik's appointments, his lunches and dinners and to act as hostess at his cocktail parties as well as taking care of the hundred and one personal matters that made his life smooth and easy.

'I don't think I can help there,' she said, dismay in her voice. 'I'm excluded from Mr. Shalik's business life, but I do know something is going on to do with a man called Kahlenberg.'

Burnett smiled. 'I can help you, Miss Norman. Your task will be absurdly easy. Let me explain . . .'

Twenty minutes later, she accepted a plastic shopping bag he had ready which contained a miniature tape-recorder, six reels of tape and a very special eavesdropping microphone.

'The quality of the recordings, Miss Norman, will naturally influence the amount of money I will pay you. However, if you are urgently in need of a thousand pounds and providing you give me something of interest, the money will be available.'

Now, after eight days, he was here in her flat, his fat, purple face creased in a smile, his blood red carnation a status symbol.

'My dear Miss Norman, what is all the urgency about?'

During the past three days, Burnett's microphone had eavesdropped. During the past eight days Daz had slept with her, sweeping her into a world of technicolour eroticism. She had promised him the money and he was prepared to service her, telling himself that in the dark, all cats were grey.

'I have information regarding Mr. Kahlenberg which you will wish to hear,' Natalie said. The whisky she had drunk made her feel reckless and light headed.

'Splendid.' Burnett crossed one fat leg over the other. 'Let me hear it.'

'Mr. Shalik is arranging to steal the Caesar Borgia ring from Mr. Kahlenberg,' Natalie said. 'I have three tapes, recording the details of the operation and who are involved.'

'The Borgia ring?' Burnett was surprised. 'So he is after that? My congratulations, Miss Norman. Play me the tapes.'

She shook her head.

'I want one thousand pounds in ten pound notes before you hear the tapes, Mr. Burnett.'

His smile became fixed.

'Now, Miss Norman, that won't do. How do I know you even have the tapes? I must hear them . . . let us be reasonable.'

She had the tape-recorder already loaded and she let him listen to three minutes' conversation between Shalik and Garry Edwards, then as Shalik was saying, 'All that will be explained tonight. You will not be alone. The risks and responsibilities will be shared,' she pressed the stop button.

'But nothing so far has been said about Mr. Kahlenberg,' Burnett pointed out, looking hungrily at the tape recorder.

'When you have brought me the money, you will hear the rest, but not before.'

They regarded each other and Burnett saw it would be useless to try to persuade her. He got to his feet, reminding himself that one thousand pounds meant as much to Max Kahlenberg as one penny meant to the Prime Minister of England.

Two hours later, his Saturday afternoon ruined, Burnett was back with the money. He listened to the tapes, his fat, purple face becoming more and more startled. He realized as he listened that he was getting these tapes cheaply.

'Splendid, Miss Norman,' he said as she wound off the last tape. 'Really splendid. You have certainly earned your fee. Any further information you can get like that I will, of course, pay you as handsomely.'

'There won't be a next time,' Natalie said. Her face was white and her expression of self-loathing startled Burnett. She thrust the tiny tape recorder at him. 'Take it away!'

'Now, Miss Norman . . .'

'Take it! Take it!' she screamed and fearing a scene, Burnett grabbed the recorder and the three tapes and hurriedly left. It was only on his way down in the lift that he realized she hadn't returned the expensive eavesdropping microphone. He wondered if he should go back for it, but her distraught face and the wild look in her eyes warned him not to. He would pick up the microphone after the week-end when she would be calmer.

Some three hours later, Daz returned to the flat. He had already checked with Burnett who had told him the money was waiting for him.

Elated that he was going to lay his hands on such a sum, he had dated a chick to meet him at Billy Walker's Boozer that was once an elegant restaurant, and from there they would go to a club in King's Road and from there into her bed.

He was through with Natalie. With a thousand pounds in hand and with his know-how, Dublin would be the place for him.

He was slightly startled when he entered the flat to find Natalie sitting on the settee, white faced, trembling and crying.

'What the hell's up?' he demanded, thinking how ugly she looked.

She dabbed her eyes and straightened.

'I have the money, Daz.'

He moved further into the room.

'You have? What are you so miserable about? You oughta be pleased.'

'Judas wasn't pleased . . . he hanged himself.'

Daz had vaguely heard of Judas. He wasn't sure who he was, but he had an idea he was a baddie and not a goodie.

'What are you talking about? Who's hanging who?'

'Nothing . . . you wouldn't understand. Are you hungry?'

He wiped his mouth with the back of his hand.

'Where's the money?'

'You're not hungry? I've bought you a steak.'

'To hell with the steak. Where's the money?'

Looking at him, she was shocked to see the greed on the lean, handsome face.

She got unsteadily to her feet and went to a cupboard. She brought the money to him in neat stacks.

It made her heart contract to watch him fondle the money. This couldn't be the man she loved so desperately who had opened the hidden door in her life: this was a greedy, vicious young animal who mauled the money as he had mauled her body.

'Are you pleased?'

He ignored her and began stuffing the money into his various pockets.

'What are you doing?' Her voice went shrill.

He stowed away the last packet of money and then regarded her.

'Getting the hell out of here . . . that's what I'm doing.'

'You mean now you have the money, you—you don't want me?'

'Who the hell would want you?' He pointed a finger at her. 'I'm going to give you some advice. From now on, baby, keep your legs tightly crossed. That's your trouble. You dig your own grave,' and he was gone.

Natalie stood motionless, her hand against her slow thumping heart. She listened to the lift descend, taking him out of her life forever.

Then she walked slowly to a chair and sat down. She remained there as the hands of the clock on the wall moved around its face, marking the hours. Then, when the light began to fade, she eased her stiffness by stretching out her long, slim legs. Her mind began to work again. After all, she told herself, why should he care? I could have guessed what was going to happen. She closed her eyes. Now her lack of charm and her plainness was underlined as it had never before been so underlined. She realized all along she had been praying, waiting, hoping for a miracle, but this wasn't the year of miracles.

She thought of the long, lonely nights ahead of her. She knew too that her conscience would be burdened by the guilt of her betrayal. She had done this disgusting act of disloyalty only to keep Daz for herself. Why go on? She asked herself. You can't hope to live with yourself . . . so why go on?

She went into the kitchen, moving slowly like a sleepwalker, and found a small, sharp vegetable knife. Taking this with her, she paused to put the front door on the latch, then she went into the bathroom. She turned on the bath taps and stood in a black daze until the bath was half full of tepid water. She kicked off her shoes and stepped into the bath. Her pleated skirt ballooned out and she pressed it down. She felt the comforting water soak through her clothes to her despairing body.

She lay still. Would it hurt? They said it was the easiest way to die. Gritting her teeth, she drew the sharp blade across her left wrist. She cut deeply and she fought back a cry of pain. The knife slipped from her hand. For a brief moment, she looked at the water surrounding her, now turning pink and darkening, then she closed her eyes.

She lay there, thinking of Daz with his handsome face and his long black curly hair and his beautiful strong body until she quietly slid away from a life she no longer had use for.

CHAPTER FOUR

ARMO SHALIK returned to his suite at 08.30 hrs. on Monday morning. He was met by Sherborn who reported that Fennel was in Paris. He explained the circumstances while Shalik sat at his desk, glowering at him.

'I hope I did right, sir. Had I known where to contact you, I would, of course, have consulted you.'

The fact that Shalik had had an unsatisfactory week-end with a call girl somewhere in the country, and he had no intention of advertising this fact to Sherborn, increased his rage.

'Well, he's gone. He said nothing about what he thought of the Kahlenberg set-up?'

'No, sir. He was in and out like a rocket.'

Shalik had a feeling this was going to be a black Monday. Had he known that the three tapes, recording the details of his plan to steal the Borgia ring, had already arrived on Max Kahlenberg's desk, he would have considered this Monday to be a disaster, but he didn't know.

Irritated and short tempered, he presided over the 09.30 hr. meeting, explaining to Gaye, Garry and Ken Jones that Fennel had had to leave and was now in Paris.

'There is no need to go into details,' he said. 'Mr. Fennel left so hurriedly he was unable to tell me his opinion about Kahlenberg's security measures. I trust he will be able to tell you when you all meet at the Rand International hotel. As I have a busy morning, there is no useful purpose served in prolonging this meeting.' He looked at Garry. 'You have studied the maps I gave you?'

'Yes . . . no trouble,' Garry said. 'I'll get there.'

'Well, then, the operation is now in your hands. I have done my best to make it easy for you. It is now up to you. You will be leaving tonight, and you will arrive at Johannesburg tomorrow morning.' He paused, hesitated, then went on, 'It is only fair to warn you that Fennel is a dangerous criminal, but absolutely necessary if this operation is to succeed.' He looked directly at Garry. 'You appear able to take care of yourself, so I will ask you also to take care of Miss Desmond.'

'That will be my pleasure,' Garry said quietly.

'Oh, Armo!' Gaye said impatiently. 'You know I can well look after myself. What are you fussing about?'

'Men fuss over beautiful women. I am no exception,' Shalik said, lifting his fat shoulders. Again he looked directly at Garry, who nodded. 'Well, bon voyage and success. Sherborn will give you your tickets and all the necessary details.'

When the three had gone, Shalik looked for his list of appointments which Natalie always left on his desk. He couldn't find it. Again, he had a feeling that this Monday was going to be more than tiresome. Angrily, he went into her room. That she was not sitting at her desk as she had always sat for the past three years startled him. He looked at his watch. The time was 10.00 hrs. Returning to his office, he rang for Sherborn.

'Where is Miss Norman?'

'I have no idea, sir,' Sherborn returned indifferently.

Shalilk glared at him.

'Then find out! She may be ill. Call her flat!'

The buzzer of the telephone sounded. Impatiently, Shalik waved to Sherborn to take the call.

Sherborn picked up the receiver and said in his pompous voice, 'Mr. Shalik's residence.' There was a pause, then in a voice suddenly off-key, he said, 'Who? What did you say?'

Shalik looked angrily at him, then stiffened for Sherborn had lost colour and there was alarm in his eyes.

'Hold on.'

'What is it?'

'Sergeant Goodyard of the Special Branch is asking to speak to you, sir.'

The two men looked at each other. Shalik's mind flew to those three dangerous currency transactions he had recently made when he had moved some nine hundred thousand pounds out of England. Could Scotland Yard have possibly got on to that? He felt his hands turn moist.

Steadying his voice and not looking at Sherborn, he said, 'Tell him to come up.'

Three minutes later, Sherborn opened the door of the suite to be confronted by a large, heavily-built man with probing eyes, a mouth like a fly trap and a jaw like the prow of a ship.

'Come in, sir,' Sherborn said, stepping aside. 'Mr. Shalik will see you immediately.'

Sergeant Goodyard moved into the room. He stared at Sherborn, then lifted heavy eyebrows.

'Why, hello George . . . I thought you were dead.'

'No, sir,' Sherborn said, sweat on his face.

'A pity. You keeping out of trouble?'

'Yes, sir.'

Sergeant Goodyard surveyed the outer room with a critical eye.

'You've found a nice little nest here, haven't you, George? Better than Pentonville I dare say.'

'Yes, sir.'

Sherborn opened the door to Shalik's office.

After staring at him for a long moment, Goodyard walked into the impressively luxurious room.

Shalik glanced up. He regarded the police officer as he came slowly to the desk.

'Sergeant Goodyard?'

'Yes, sir.'

Shalik waved him to a chair.

'Sit down, sergeant. What is it?'

Goodyard settled himself in the chair and looked stonily at Shalik, who felt the unease that all guilty people feel when under police scrutiny, although his face remained expressionless.

'I believe Miss Natalie Norman works for you?'

Surprised, Shalik nodded.

'That is right. She hasn't come in this morning. Has something happened to her?'

'She died Saturday night,' Goodyard told him in his flat, cop voice. 'Suicide.'

Shalik flinched. He had a horror of death. For some moments he remained motionless, then his quick, callous mind became alive. Who was he going to find to replace her? Who was now going to look after him? The fact that she was dead meant nothing to him. The fact that he had relied on her for the past three years to arrange his social and business life meant a lot.

'I'm sorry to hear that.' He reached for a cigar and paused to clip the end. 'Was there any reason?'

What a bastard! Goodyard thought, but his cop face revealed none of his disgust.

'That is why I am here, sir. I hoped you could tell me.'

Shalik lit the cigar and let the rich smelling smoke roll out of his mouth. He shook his head.

'I'm sorry, but I know nothing about Miss Norman . . . nothing at all. I have always found her an efficient worker. She has been with me for three years.' He leaned back in his executive chair and looked directly at Goodyard. 'I am a busy man, Sergeant. It is impossible for me to take much—if any—interest in the people who work for me.'

Goodyard felt in his overcoat pocket and produced a small object which he laid in front of Shalik on the white blotter.

'Would you know what that is, sir?'

Shalik frowned at the thick paper clip: the kind that is used to clip together heavy legal documents. 'Obviously a paper clip,' he said, curtly. 'I hope you have reason for asking me such a question, Sergeant. You are taking up my valuable time.'

'Oh, yes, I have a reason.' Goodyard was unperturbed by Shalik's sharp note. 'I understand, Mr. Shalik, that you are engaged in many transactions about which rival companies could be interested.'

Shalik's face hardened.

'Surely that is no business of yours?'

'No, sir, but it could explain this object here,' and Goodyard tapped the paper clip.

'Just what do you mean?'

'This apparent paper clip is a highly sensitive microphone which is illegal to possess and which is used only by authorized bodies. In other words, sir, this gadget is only used in espionage work.'

Shalik stared at the paper clip, feeling a sudden rush of cold blood up his spine.

'I don't understand,' he said.

'This paper clip was found in Miss Norman's flat,' Goodyard explained. 'Fortunately, the district detective investigating her death was smart enough to recognize what it was. It was passed to the special branch. That is why I am here.'

Shalik licked his dry lips as he said, 'I know nothing about it.'

'Have you seen it before?'

'I don't think so . . . how can I tell?' Controlling a feeling of panic, Shalik waved to a pile of documents on his desk, each held together with big paper clips, but none quite as big as the clip lying on his blotter. 'It is possible . . . I don't know.'

'To use this microphone successfully,' Goodyard said, picking up the microphone and putting it in his pocket, 'a special tape-recorder is required. Could I examine Miss Norman's desk?'

'Of course.' Shalik got to his feet and led the way into Natalie's office. 'That is her desk.'

Goodyard's search was quick and thorough. He also looked into the many filing cabinets and into the closet where Natalie used to hang her coat.

'No . . .' He turned to Shalik. 'Have you any reason to believe that Miss Norman was spying on you?'

'Certainly not.'

'You know nothing about her private life? I understand she had a young man living with her. Several people in her building have seen him entering her flat. Would you know who he is?'

Shalik's face showed his astonishment.

'I can scarcely believe that . . . still, if you say so. No, I know nothing about her.'

'Further inquiries will be made, sir. I shall want to see you again.'

'I am usually here.'

Goodyard made for the door, then paused.

'I don't know if you are aware that your servant is George Sherborn who has served six years for forgery.'

Shalik's face was expressionless.

'Yes, I know. Sherborn is a reformed character. I am very satisfied with him.'

Goodyard's bleak, cop eyes stared at him.

'Do they ever reform?' he asked and left.

Shalik sat down at his desk. He took out his handkerchief and wiped his damp hands while he thought.

Had the microphone ever been on his desk?

Suppose it had? Had that white-faced bitch been recording his transactions? He thought of the dangerous currency deals. Then there was the information given him by the P.A. to the Chancellor of the Exchequer which had netted four of his clients' fortunes. There was the merger leak he had got from a typist frantic for money. The list was endless. If she had planted the microphone on his desk, how many of his deals had been taped? There was also the Kahlenberg affair. Had she recorded that? He screwed his handkerchief into a ball, his face vicious. Where was the tape-recorder? Maybe, he thought, someone had got at her and she had only been half-convinced. Maybe, he thought, she had taken the microphone and had second thoughts about taking the tape-recorder. She could have felt soiled. She was a neurotic type. Maybe she had decided to kill herself rather than to betray him. But suppose she had recorded the conversation he had had with the four who were going after the Borgia ring? Suppose the tapes were already on their way to Kahlenberg?

He leaned back in his chair, staring at the opposite wall while his mind worked swiftly.

Should he warn them?

He considered the risk. The three men were expendable. He would be sorry to lose Gaye Desmond. He had taken a lot of trouble to find her, but, after all, he told himself, Gaye wasn't the only woman in the world. If he did warn them that the operation might already be blown, wouldn't they back out? His fee for regaining the ring was to be $500,000 plus expenses. He grimaced. It was too large a sum to give up because of four people. In a situation like this, he told himself, he must keep his nerve and gamble that this dead bitch hadn't recorded what was said.

After more thought, he decided to say nothing and to wait.

He reached for his mail and, because he had a trained mind, a few minutes later he had completely dismissed Goodyard's visit and had dismissed the thought that Kahlenberg could know that he was to lose the Borgia ring.

Charles Burnett sailed majestically into his office. He had lunched well on smoked salmon and duck in orange sauce and was feeling well fed and satisfied with himself.

His secretary handed him a coded cable, telling him it had arrived a few minutes ago.

'Thank you, Miss Morris,' Burnett said, stifling a small belch. 'I'll attend to it.'

He sat down at his desk and unlocked a drawer. From it he took Kahlenberg's code book. A few minutes later, he was reading:

Pleased. Visitors will receive exceptionally warm welcome. Have bought 20,000 Honeywell for your Swiss account. K

Burnett asked Miss Morris to give him the day's quotation on Honeywell. She told him the share had moved up three points.

Burnett was feeling extremely satisfied when ex-Inspector Parkins came on the line.

'I thought you should know, sir, that Mr. Shalik's secretary, Natalie Norman, was found dead in her flat this morning . . . suicide.'

Burnett was unable to speak for some seconds.

'Are you there, sir?'

He pulled himself together. So he had been right: she had looked mental: he had been sure of it.

'Why should you imagine, Parkins, that I could be interested?' he asked, trying to keep the quaver out of his voice.

'Well, sir, this young tearaway, Daz Jackson, was seeing a lot of her. I thought possibly you should be told, but if I have made a mistake, then I apologize.'

Burnett drew in a deep, slow breath.

'So Jackson visited her . . . very odd. Will he be involved?'

'I doubt it. Jackson left for Dublin on Saturday night. The police do have his description. Still, Dublin is a good place for him to be.'

'Yes. Well, thank you, Parkins . . . interesting.' Burnett could almost see Parkins's foxy face and the expectant hope in his little eyes. 'There will be an additional credit in your account,' and he hung up.

He sat for a long moment, thinking. He remembered the expensive microphone left in Natalie's flat. For some seconds, he worried about it, then he assured himself no one would recognize it and it would be thrown away with her other rubbish.

Parkins's call, however, had spoilt his afternoon.

The lobby of the Rand International hotel was crowded with large, noisy American tourists who had just arrived off a bus from which assorted luggage was already spewing.

Wrapped in transparent raincovers, they milled around, shouting to each other, completely oblivious to the uproar they were creating.

The lobby was shattered by cries of: 'Joe . . . you seen my bag?' 'Goddamn this rain . . . where's the sun?' 'For God's sake, Martha, you're only exciting yourself. The luggage isn't all out yet.' 'Hey, Momma . . . the guy wants our passports!' and so on and so on. America had taken over the Rand International for some ear splitting moments while the white and the coloured staff coped with the invasion.

Sitting near the breakfast-room with a view of all this commotion, Lew Fennel watched sourly.

Rain fell steadily. The Bantus, sheltering under umbrellas, paused to stare through the glass doors of the hotel at the confusion going on in the lobby. Having stared, they grinned and moved on, splay footed, the men in shabby European dress, the women wearing bright scarves over their heads and bright dresses that set off their colour.

Fennel sucked at his cigarette and watched the last of the American party, still screaming to each other, whisked away in the lifts. He had been in Johannesburg now for thirty-six hours. He had had a nervous half day in Paris before catching the plane to South Africa. Now for the first time for over a month, he felt relaxed and safe. Moroni and the police were far away.

He looked at his watch, then shifted his heavy body more comfortably in the chair.

A black Cadillac drew up outside the hotel and Fennel got to his feet as he saw Gaye's tawny head emerge as she ran under the cover of the hotel's canopy.

Ten minutes later, the three were with him in the small sitting-room of his suite on the eighth floor of the hotel.

Fennel was in an amiable and expansive mood.

'I guess you all want to rest,' he said as he served drinks from the refrigerator, 'but before you go, I'd like to fill you in with what we can expect . . . okay?'

Garry eased his heavy shoulders. The fourteen hour flight had cramped his muscles. He looked at Gaye.

'Do you want to listen or do we take a bath first?'

'We listen,' Gaye said, leaning back on the settee. She took a sip of the gin and tonic Fennel had given her. 'I'm not all that dead.'

Fennel's eyes narrowed. So Edwards was already taking a proprietary interest in the woman he had mentally reserved for himself.

'Well, make up your minds!' he said, his temper rising. 'Do you or don't you want to hear?'

'I said yes,' Gaye said, her cool eyes surveying him. 'What is it?'

'Those invoices Shalik gave me. It puts us right in the photo.' Fennel drank a little of his whisky and water. 'I now know the museum must be underground. A lift complete with all the works was delivered to Kahlenberg's place and as the house is on one floor, the answer to the lift is the museum is under the house. Get it?'

'Keep going,' Garry said.

'Listed in the invoices are six television close-circuit sets and one monitor. That tells me there are six rooms in the museum and there is one guard watching the monitor, probably some-where in the house. By pressing buttons, the guard can survey each of the six rooms, but only one at the time.' Fennel lit a cigarette, then went on, 'I know this system. The weakness is that the guard could fall asleep, he could read a book without watch-ing the monitor or he could leave to go to the toilet. But we must find out if he does all or any of these things and if he is on duty at night. That's your job to find out,' and Fennel pointed his stubby finger at Garry.

Garry nodded.

'The door to the museum is listed on the invoice. It is of massive steel. I worked for Bahlstrom so I know about their equipment. The door has a time lock on it. You set it at a certain time and set the counter dial at another time and no one on earth except Bahlstroms can open the door between these two times.' Fennel grinned. 'Except me. I know how to handle that time lock. I helped to build it. Now we come to something you will have to take care of.' He was talking directly at Garry.

'The lift . . . this is a tricky one. We will do the job at night. What I want to know is if the lift is out of action during the night. By that, I mean is the electricity cut. If the lift doesn't work at night I don't see how the hell we are getting to the museum.'

'Let's be pessimistic,' Garry said. 'Suppose the juice is cut off?'

'It's up to you to turn it on or we're sunk.'

Garry grimaced.

'There's always the chance there could be stairs as well as the lift.'

'Could be.' Fennel nodded. 'That too you have to find out. It's your job to find out as much as you can once you're in. Another thing you will have to tell me is how I get in . . . door or window? Again this is up to you. All the dope you collect you give to me over the two-way radio so I'll know what to be ready for.'

'If the dope can be got, I'll get it.'

Fennel finished his drink.

'If you don't get it, we don't do the job . . . it's as simple as that.'

Gaye got to her feet. She looked sensationally lovely in the sky blue cotton dress she was wearing: a dress that clung to her figure. The three men watched her.

'Well, I'll leave you and take a tub. I want some sleep. I didn't sleep a wink on the plane.'

She nodded to them and left the room. Garry stretched and yawned.

'Me, too . . . unless you want me for anything else?'

'No.' Fennel looked at Ken. 'How about the equipment? Have you got that lined up?'

'I think so. I'll take a bath and go check. A friend of mine is organizing it for me. I sent him a cable from London telling him what we want. I'll go over there and see how far he's got. Do you want to come with me?'

'Why not? Okay, I'll wait here for you.'

Garry and Ken went along the corridor to their rooms. They were all on the eighth floor: each had a small suite with an air conditioner and a view of the city.

'Well, see you,' Garry said, pausing at his door. 'This could be a tricky one.'

Ken grinned. Garry had now learned that Ken was an incurable optimist.

'You never know . . . could work out fine. Me for the tub,' and he went off whistling to his room.

An hour later, he returned to Fennel's room. Fennel had been punishing the whisky and looked a little flushed.

'Shall we go?' Ken asked, leaning against the doorway.

'Yeah.' Fennel got to his feet and the two men walked along the corridor to the lifts.

'This pal of mine runs a garage on Plein Street,' Ken said as the lift descended. 'It's just across the way We can walk.'

They pushed their way through another consignment of American tourists who had just arrived. The noise they were making made both men wince.

'What makes an American so noisy?' Ken asked good humouredly. 'Do they imagine everyone around is stone deaf?'

Fennel grunted.

'I wouldn't know. Maybe they weren't taught as kids to keep their goddamn traps shut.'

They paused under the canopy of the hotel and surveyed the rain sweeping Bree Street.

'If it's going to rain like this in the Drakensberg Range we're in for a hell of a time,' Ken said, turning up his jacket collar. 'Come on . . . may as well start getting wet . . . it'll be good practice.'

Their heads bent against the driving rain, the two men walked briskly across to Plein Street.

Sam Jefferson, the owner of the garage, a tall, thin elderly man with a pleasant, freckled face, greeted them.

'Hi, Ken! Had a good trip?'

Ken said the trip was fine and introduced Fennel. Jefferson lost some of his sunny smile as he shook hands. He was obviously a little startled at the cold, hard expression on Fennel's face. Fennel wasn't his kind of people.

'I got all the stuff and it's there laid out for you,' he went on turning to Ken. 'Take a look. If there's anything I've forgotten, let me know. Excuse me now. I've got a gearbox in my hair.' Nodding, he went off across the big garage to where two Bantus were staring vacantly at a jacked up Pontiac.

Ken led the way to a smaller, inner garage where a Land Rover was parked. A Bantu, sitting on his haunches and scratching his ankle got slowly to his feet and gave Ken a wide, white toothy grin.

'All okay, boss,' he said and Ken shook hands with him.

'This is Joe,' he said to Fennel. 'Sam and he have collected all the stuff we need.'

Fennel had no time for coloured people. He glowered at the smiling Bantu, grunted and turned away. There was an awkward pause, then Ken said, 'Well, Joe, let's see what you've got.'

The Bantu crossed to the Land Rover and pulled off the tarpaulin that covered the bonnet. 'I got it fixed like you said, boss.'

Welded to the front of the radiator was a drum between two steel supports. Around the drum was wound a long length of thin steel cable. Ken examined it, then nodded his satisfaction.

'What the hell's that for?' Fennel demanded, regarding the drum.

'It's a winch,' Ken explained. 'We're going over some very sticky roads and we could easily get bogged down. When there's heavy rain, the roads over the Drakensberg can be hell. This winch will drag us out without us breaking our backs.' He found a small yacht anchor lying on the floor of the Land Rover. "See this? We get stuck, and all we have to do is to slam this anchor into a tree root and winch ourselves out.'

'The roads going to be that bad?'

'Brother! You have no idea. We have quite a trip ahead of us.'

Fennel scowled.

'Those other two have it the easy way . . . flying in, huh?'

"I don't know so much about that. If one of the fans falls off, they land in the jungle and that will be that. I'd rather drive than fly in this country.'

'Boss . . .' Joe, still smiling, but uncomfortable in Fennel's presence, pulled off a tarpaulin that covered a long trestle table standing away from the Land Rover. 'You want to check this stuff?'

The two men moved over to the equipment laid out. There were four jerrycans for water, another five for gas, four sleeping bags, four powerful electric torches with spare batteries, two six foot steel perforated strips for getting out of mud, a collapsible tent, two wooden cases and a large carton.

'With luck, I reckon we'll take five days in and four days out to do the job," Ken said, patting the two wooden cases. 'We have enough canned food to last us that time.' He tapped the carton. 'That's booze: four Scotch, two gin and twenty-four quarts of beer. I have a Springfield, a 12 bore and a .22. There's plenty of game where we are going. You like guinea-fowl? Impala? Ever tried a saddle of impala done over a slow fire and served with chilli sauce?' He grinned and rolled his eyes. 'It's marvellous!'

'How about medical supplies?' Fennel asked.

'In the Land Rover . . . complete medical chest. I took a safari first-aid course awhile ago. I can handle anything from a snake bite to a broken leg.'

'Looks like you've taken care of it all.' Fennel lit a cigarette and let smoke drift down his nostrils. 'Then all we have to take is our own personal kit?'

'That's it . . . we travel light . . . just a change.'

'I've got my tool bag.' Fennel rested his fat back against the Land Rover. 'It's heavy, but I can't do without it.'

'Well, so long as you can haul it.'

Fennel cocked his head on one side.

'We drive, don't we?'

'We might have to walk some of the way. Even with this winch the road up to Kahlenberg's place could sink us and if it does, we walk.'

'How about taking the nigger along?'

'Look, friend, drop that.' Ken's face had hardened. 'We don't talk about niggers here. We talk about natives, Bantus or non-Europeans but not niggers.'

'Who the hell cares?'

'I do, and if we're going to get along, you will care too.'

Fennel hesitated then shrugged.

'Okay, okay, so what? What's wrong with taking the native, the Bantu, the non-European bastard along with us to carry the goddamn bag?'

Ken regarded him, his dislike plain.

'No. He could talk his head off when he gets back. I've a friend of mine who's joining us at our camp at Mainville. He worked with me when I was on a game reserve. He's coming with us. He is a Kikuyu and a marvellous tracker. Without him, we would never get there. He's out at Kahlenberg's estate now finding a way through the guards and let me tell you there are around three hundred Zulus guarding the estate, but I'll bet when we meet at Mainville, he'll have found a way through them, but he doesn't carry anyone's stuff but his own. Just get that into your skull.'

Fennel squinted at him through his cigarette smoke.

'What is he . . . black?'

'He is a Kikuyu . . . that makes him coloured.'

'A friend?'

'One of my best friends.' Ken stared hard at Fennel. 'If that's so difficult for you to believe let me tell you the Bantus out here are damn good friends when you get to know them and damn good people.'

Fennel shrugged.

'This is your country . . . not mine. Suppose we go back to the hotel? This goddamn rain is giving me a thirst.'

'You go on. I've got to settle up for all this stuff and get it loaded. Suppose we all have dinner together? There's a good restaurant next to the hotel. We can iron out anything that needs ironing out. We could get off tomorrow.'

'Okay . . . see you,' and Fennel left the garage and headed for the hotel.

Ken watched him go, frowning. Then shrugging, he moved over to where Sam Jefferson was working on the Pontiac.

They all met at the Checkmate restaurant which is part of the Rand International Hotel a little after 20.30 hrs. As was her privilege, Gaye was the last to arrive, wearing a lemon-coloured cotton dress and making every male eye in the restaurant stare at her with that hungry look males have for really beautiful women.

Fennel eyed her as she slid into her chair and felt sweat break out down his fat back. He had known many women in his life, but none to compare with her. He felt a white hot surge of desire go through him and it so shook him that he purposely dropped his serviette so he could bend, grope for it while he forced the desire out of his face.

'Well, what are we going to eat?' Garry asked.

They were all hungry and chose sea food on the broche and breaded veal with french fry.

'How's it been going?' Garry asked Ken. He was aware of Fennel's tenseness and glanced at his flushed face, then looked away.

'All under control. We have everything organized now. We could leave tomorrow if that suits you two.'

'Why not?' Garry looked at Gaye for confirmation and she nodded.

'The sooner we're off, the easier for us it will be. The rains have started. There is a chance the rain hasn't reached Drakensberg yet, but if it has, Fennel and I will have quite a trip. So, if it's all right with you, we will leave at 08.00 hrs. tomorrow morning. We drive in the Land Rover . . . it won't be too comfortable as we're pretty loaded. We have around three hundred kilometres to our camp at Mainville.' The sea food was served and when the waiter had gone away, Ken went on, 'Mainville is about four hundred kilometres from Kahlenberg's place. The chopper will be at Mainville. The airlift won't take long unless anything goes wrong. You two will stay in camp for a day while Fennel and I go on by road. Then you take off. We'll be in touch with you on the two-way radio. I've tested them . . . they're good. We'll reach Mainville just after noon with luck. Fennel and I will start around 05.00 hrs. the following morning. You will take off around 10.00 hrs. the following morning. You should arrive at Kahlenberg's place in an hour or so. You don't want to be too early. How does it sound?'

'Sounds fine,' Garry said. 'And the chopper? How about service and gas?'

'All that's taken care of. You'll have enough gas to take her in and bring her out. I have a guarantee she will be fully serviced. It's up to you to satisfy yourself she is okay, of course, but from what I've been told, she'll be there waiting for you and ready to go.'

'What's Mainville like?' Gaye asked, laying down her knife and fork.

Ken grinned. 'A horse and buggy town. I have the camp organized five miles out of town in the bush.'

They began eating the veal which they enjoyed. They discussed further details of the operation. Both Gaye and Garry were aware that Fennel had little to say except to grunt over his food and keep looking at Gaye. At the end of the meal, they had coffee while Ken talked. He was an easy and interesting talker and he amused them.

'You'll have fun driving to Mainville,' he said. 'I won't be going on the highway on the last lap and you'll see game . . . warthogs, impala, waterbuck, vervet monkeys and so on. I'll give you the dope on them when we see them if you're interested. I was once a game warden on a swank reserve . . . taking people around in a Land Rover to spot game.'

'What made you give it up?' Gaye asked. 'I should have thought it was a lovely life.'

Ken laughed.

'You would, wouldn't you? Nothing the matter with the animals, but the clients finally got me down. You can't expect to go into the bush and just find animals waiting for you. You have to be patient. There are days, especially in this season, when you can drive for miles without seeing a thing. The clients always gripe . . . blaming me. After a couple of years I got fed up with it. There was one client who really bore down on me. Okay, he had no luck. It was the rainy season, and he wanted to photograph a buffalo. He had a thousand dollar bet with a pal back in the States that he would bring the photo back . . . no buffaloes. We drove for hours hunting for them, but no luck, so he took it out on me.' Ken grinned. 'I hauled off and busted his jaw . . . got eighteen months in jail for it so when I came out, I quit.'

Fennel who had been listening impatiently, broke in, 'Well, I don't know what you two guys are going to do, but I'm inviting Miss Desmond to come along with me and take a look at the nightspots.' He stared directly at Gaye, his face set. 'How about it?'

There was a slight pause. Garry looked quickly at Fennel's flushed face and then at Gaye who smiled, completely relaxed.

'That is nice of you, Mr. Fennel, but excuse me. If I'm going to get up so early, I need my sleep.' She got to her feet. 'Good night. See you all in the morning,' and she made her way followed by male stares, out of the restaurant.

Fennel sat back in his chair, his face pale, his eyes burning.

'Some brush-off,' he snarled. 'Who the hell does she think she is?'

Ken got to his feet.

'I'll fix the bill and then I'm going to bed,' and he walked over to the cash desk.

Garry said quietly, 'Take it easy. The girl's tired. If you want to go somewhere I'll come with you.'

Fennel didn't appear to hear. He sat there, his eyes slightly mad, his face now getting back some colour. He got heavily to his feet and walked out of the restaurant and to the lift. He was shaking with frustrated rage.

All right, you bitch, he was thinking as the lift doors swung open. I'll fix you! Just let me get you alone for ten minutes and I'll fix you so goddamn fast you won't know what's hit you.

He reached his room, slammed the door shut and tore off his clothes. He threw himself down on the bed, his nails biting into the palms of his hands, sweat running down his heavy jowls.

For more than an hour, his lewd mind enacted the things he would do to her when he had her alone, but after a while, the erotic thoughts became exhausted and his mind began to return to normal.

He suddenly remembered what Shalik had said: *You will leave Gaye Desmond strictly alone . . . try something like that with Miss Desmond and I promise you Interpol will receive your dossier from me.*

How had Shalik found out about the three killings?

Fennel moved uneasily on the bed. He reached for a cigarette, lit it and stared across the room, lit by the revolving sign across the way.

He was suddenly back in Hong Kong, coming off a junk at Wanchai's Fenwick Street pier. He had been on a smuggling trip with three of his Chinese friends. They had unloaded a cargo of opium at Chu Lu Kok Island without any trouble and Fennel had $3000 in his hip pocket. He was due to fly back to England in ten hours. After being cooped up in the stinking junk for six days, he was in need of a woman.

His Chinese friends had told him where to go. He had walked along Gloucester Road amid rickshaws, the fast moving traffic, the fruit vendors and the crowds of noisy Chinese until he had come to the brothel, recommended.

The Chinese girl was small, compact with heavy buttocks which Fennel liked, but she was as animated as a side of beef. She acted merely as a receptacle for his lust and when the unsatisfactory union was over, Fennel, with half a bottle of whisky inside him, dulling his senses, slept, but Fennel only ever slept slightly below the level of unconsciousness. He had always led a dangerous life and had trained himself never to become entirely unconscious, no matter how much he drank. He came awake to find the girl, still naked, her ivory skin lighted by the street light coming through the uncurtained window, helping herself from his well stuffed wallet.

Fennel was off the bed and had hit her before he was fully awake. His fist smashed into her face, snapping her head back and she went down, his money falling from her small hand, her eyes rolling back.

Fennel snarled at her, then began to collect the money. It was only when he had thrown on his clothes and had stuffed his wallet into his hip pocket that he realized something was wrong. He bent over the still body and a chill crawled up his spine. He lifted her head by her thick hair and grimaced as the head rolled horribly on the shoulders. His savage, violent blow had broken her neck.

He looked at his watch. He had two hours before he took off for London. He left the room, shutting the door and walked down the stairs to where an old Chinaman was seated at the desk to check clients in and out. He knew he would have to pay for his freedom.

'I'm leaving by junk in twenty minutes,' he lied. 'The whore's dead. What's it going to cost?'

The yellow wrinkled face showed nothing: a parchment map of old age.

'One thousand dollars,' the old man said. 'I have to call the police in an hour.'

Fennel showed his teeth in a savage snarl.

'Old man, I could wring your neck . . . that's too much.'

The Chinaman lifted his shoulders.

'Then five hundred dollars and I call the police in half an hour.'

Fennel gave him the thousand dollars. He had been in Hong Kong long enough to know a bargain was a bargain. He had to have at least an hour to get clear and he had got clear.

Lying in his bed, watching the reflected light making patterns on the opposite wall, he remembered the girl. If she had been more responsive, he wouldn't have hit her so hard. Well, he told himself without conviction, she had deserved what she had got.

The male prostitute he had been unlucky enough to run into in a dirty, evil smelling alley in Istanbul, also got what he deserved. Fennel had come off a ship to spend a few hours in the city before going on to Marseilles. He had brought three kilos of gold from India for a man who was paying well: a fat, elderly Turk who wanted the gold as a bribe. Fennel had done the deal, collected the money and then found a girl to spend the night with. Thinking about her now, Fennel realized she had been smart. She had got him drunk and when the time came for them to share the hotel bed, he had been too drunk to bother with her. He had slept three hours, waking to find her gone, but at least she hadn't been a thief. Livid with frustrated rage, and nearly sober, Fennel had started back to his ship. Here, in this sleazy alley, he had met a perfumed boy: handsome with liquid black eyes and a sly, insinuating smile, who had importuned him. Fennel had vented his rage on him, smashing his head against the wall, leaving a big red stain where the wall had been dirty white.

A woman, peering out of her window, had seen the act of brutal violence and had begun to scream. Fennel got back to his ship, but it was only when the ship sailed that he considered himself safe.

Fennel often lived with his ghosts. He kept telling himself that the dead had no part in his life, but they persisted in his mind. In moments like this, when he was sexually frustrated, and alone, his past violence kept on intruding.

This third murder haunted him more than the other two. He had been hired by a wealthy Egyptian to open a safe belonging to a merchant to whom the Egyptian had given bonds as security for a big loan. Fennel understood these bonds were forgeries and they could be discovered at any moment: the job was urgent.

He had got into the palatial house easily enough and had settled down in front of the safe to open it. The time was 02.45 hrs. and the household was asleep.

The safe was old-fashioned and Fennel had trouble in opening it. As he finally got the safe door open, his tools scattered around him, the door leading into the room where he was pushed open.

Fennel snapped off his torch, grabbed up a short steel bar with which he had been working and spun around.

A shadowy figure stood in the doorway, then the light went on.

A girl stood in front of Fennel in a nightdress and dressing-gown. She was small, dark with large black eyes and an olive complexion. She could not have been older than ten years of age—in fact she was nine. She stared at Fennel in terror and her mouth began to open to scream. He reached her in two swift strides and slammed the steel bar down on her head.

In that moment of panic, he had had no hesitation about killing her. The blow, as he well knew, was lethal. She had seen him, and if he had merely stunned her, she could have given the police a description of him.

He had snatched the bonds from the safe, bundled his tools together and had left. It was only when he got into his car that he saw blood on one of his hands and became fully aware of what he had done.

Those big, terrified dark eyes often appeared in his dreams. From the newspapers the following day, he learned the child was a deaf-mute. He had tried to convince himself that she was better dead, but when he was alone and in bed, the picture of the child in her nightdress and the look of terror on her face as she tried to scream pricked at what remained of his conscience.

He lay watching the red and blue light from the sign across the way, reflected on the ceiling until finally, he drifted off into an uneasy sleep.

CHAPTER FIVE

MAX KAHLENBERG always woke at 05.00 hrs. It was as if he had an alarm clock inside his head. During the seven hours in which he slept, he might have died. He had no dreams nor did he stir until he opened his eyes to watch the sun rise over the magnificent range of mountains that lay beyond the huge picture window opposite his bed. ,

The bed was enormous, set on a dais with a shell-shaped head-board done over in lemon-coloured silk. Within his reach was a set of push-buttons set in fumed oak. Each button controlled his method of rising. The red button opened and closed the lemon-coloured window drapes. The yellow button lowered the bed to the floor level so he could swing himself into his electrically pro-pelled wheel chair. The blue button opened a hatch by his bedside through which his coffee tray came. The black button filled his bath automatically and at exactly the right temperature. The green button operated the TV monitor at the end of his bed, putting him in direct contact with one of his secretaries.

Max Kahlenberg came awake and touched the red button. The window drapes swung open and he viewed the sky, seeing the scurrying clouds and he decided rain couldn't be far off. He switched on the defused light concealed behind the headboard and thumbed the red button. He shifted himself higher in the bed as the hatch at his side slid up and a tray containing a silver coffee pot, a jug of milk, a container of sugar and a cup and saucer slid within his reach and the hatch closed.

Lying in the enormous bed, Max Kahlenberg looked like a handsome movie star. His head was completely shaved. He had wide set, blue-grey eyes, a well-shaped nose and a big, humourless mouth with a thin upper lip. He always slept naked, and as he hoisted himself up, he revealed a deeply tanned, magnificently developed torso.

He drank his coffee, lit a cigarette and then pressed the green button that connected him with one of his secretaries. The TV screen lit up and he saw Miah, an Indian girl, who did the early morning shift, reach for a pencil and pad. He regarded her with pleasure. He liked beautiful women, and made a point only of employing women who pleased his eyes. The girl, her thin dark face classically beautiful, her big eyes looking directly at him although she couldn't see him, said, 'Good morning, sir.'

Kahlenberg studied her, then said, 'Good morning, Miah. Has the mail arrived?'

'It is being sorted now, sir.'

'I'll be ready to dictate in an hour. Have your breakfast,' and he snapped off the set. He then pressed the black button which would fill his bath and lowered the bed to floor level. He threw off the sheet covering him.

At that moment Kahlenberg turned from a fine looking, handsome athlete into a grotesque freak. No one except his mother and his doctor had ever seen his legs. They had never grown from the time he had been born. In comparison to his well developed torso, they were two ghastly looking appendages, perfectly formed, unable to support his weight and which he loathed with a bitterness and revulsion that not only completely spoilt his life but had made him dangerously mentally disturbed.

No one was ever allowed into his bedroom while he was in it himself. It was only when he was dressed and in his chair which had a snap-on cover over his legs that he felt safe from prying eyes.

He hoisted himself into the chair and ran it into the vast bathroom.

An hour later, he emerged, bathed and shaved and having had a thorough work-out in the well-equipped gymnasium that led off the bathroom. He wrapped the lower part of his body in a cotton loin cloth, put on a white open neck shirt, snapped the cover over the chair and steered the chair into the long corridor that led to his office.

Coming towards him was a fully grown cheetah. This was Hindenburg, Kahlenberg's constant companion. He stopped the chair and waited for the big cat to approach him. He rubbed the thick fur while the cat made a deep, throaty sound, then with a final pat, Kahlenberg sent the chair on its way, with Hindenburg following behind, and reaching a pair of double doors which opened automatically, he propelled himself into the room. Kahlenberg's office was vast with a window that ran the length of the view side of the room.

From his big desk, he had an uninterrupted view of his lawns, the banks of flowers, the distant jungle, the undulating grass covered hills dotted by the scattered rondavels of his Zulus to the Drakensberg Range.

His mail was on his desk marked with various coloured stickers, denoting its priority.

Before going to bed, he had made notes of various affairs that needed attention. He pressed the green button on his desk and when the TV monitor lit up and he saw Miah seated at her desk, he began to dictate.

An hour later, he had finished the previous day's notes.

'That is all, Miah. Is Ho-Lu there?'

'She is waiting now, sir.'

'I'll be ready for her in half an hour,' and he switched off the set.

He went rapidly through the mail of some fifty letters, made quick decisions that would add to his already vast fortune, then lit up the monitor screen again.

This time a flower-like Vietnamese girl was at the desk, patiently waiting. He greeted her and began dictating.

By 10.00 hrs. he had cleared his desk. He sat for some moments, relaxing, his fingers caressing Hindenburg's head, then he flicked down a switch on the intercom and said, 'Come in, please.'

There was a moment's delay, then a tap sounded on the door which swung open.

Guilo Tak, Kahlenberg's personal assistant came in, shut the door and approached the desk.

Guilo Tak was a tall, thin man with a mop of jet black hair that emphasized his cadaverous complexion. His black eyes were sunk deep and burned feverishly in his skull-like face. Born of an Italian mother and a Czech father, he had shown astonishing talent for figures at an early age. He had obtained a job in a Swiss bank and quickly proved himself a financial genius. When Kahlenberg had asked one of the directors of the bank if he knew of a man suitable to be his P.A., the director had no hesitation in recommending Tak.

Kahlenberg found him not only a financial genius but utterly ruthless, utterly efficient and utterly loyal. For some considerable time, Kahlenberg had been hiring expert art thieves to supply his museum. Considerable organization and discussions were needed and Kahlenberg begrudged the time. He had hesitated whether to hand these machinations over to Tak, and finally decided after some eighteen months, that Tak could be trusted. Tak was now not only in charge of the museum, but also handled Kahlenberg's portfolio, often making suggestions and pointing to opportunities which Kahlenberg with his other occupations might have missed.

'Good morning, sir,' Tak said with a stiff little bow.

'Sit down,' Kahlenberg said, resting his elbows on his desk and staring at Tak, thinking what an extraordinary looking man this was. 'Any news of the Borgia ring affair?'

'Yes, sir. The three thieves concerned arrived at the Rand International Hotel a few minutes ago. Fennel arrived the day before yesterday. He came from Paris. A garage owner, Sam Jefferson, has been buying their equipment. I have a list of it here if you wish to see it. I have also photographs of these people taken as they arrived at the airport.' He paused to give Kahlenberg a quick glance before laying a large envelope he had brought with him on the desk. 'You may find the woman attractive.'

Kahlenberg glanced at the blown-up photographs of the three men and laid them on the blotter but he sat for some moments studying Gaye's photograph. Then he glanced up. 'What do you know about her?'

'All their dossiers are in the envelope, sir.'

'Thank you, Tak. I'll see you later.'

When Tak had gone, Kahlenberg picked up Gaye's photograph and again studied it for several minutes, then he opened a drawer and put the photograph away. He read the four dossiers, studied the list of equipment, read that the camp was situated near Mainville and a helicopter had arrived there the previous day. He put all the papers back into the envelope and locked it away.

He sat staring with hooded eyes down at his blotter for a long time, then with a slight nod of satisfaction at the decision he had reached, he set his chair in motion and snapping his fingers at Hindenburg, he propelled himself out into the garden and along the broad path for a half hour's break. The big cat wandered by his side.

Back at his desk at 11.00 hrs., Kahlenberg dealt until lunch time with more papers that had arrived. He lunched on a smoked trout with horseradish sauce and a coffee, then returning to his office, sent for Tak again.

'How much did I pay for the Borgia ring?' he asked.

'Sixty thousand dollars. Mercial paid a quarter of a million. We got it very cheaply. Now Mercial is paying Shalik half a million to recover it. Absurd, but without it, his Borgia collection is spoilt.'

'I am inclined to let him have it back,' Kahlenberg said, staring at Tak who said nothing. He knew by now the way Kahlenberg's mind worked. 'It might be amusing, but it wouldn't do to let these four have it without working for it, would it?'

Tak inclined his head and continued to wait.

'So why not let them arrive here? As you say the woman is attractive. It will be interesting to see if Fennel who is supposed to be such an expert can break into the museum. Let us encourage them. I can leave the details to you.'

'You want them to walk away with the ring, sir?'

'We will make their entrance easy and their exit difficult, but if they can get it off the estate, then I think they would be entitled to keep it, but only if they can get it off the estate.' Kahlenberg's eyes searched Tak's face. 'You understand?'

'Yes sir.'

'So we let them in and make it difficult for them to get out. If anything should happen to them, I suppose the crocodiles would welcome extra food.'

Tak's eyes narrowed.

'Is it your wish something should happen to them, sir?'

'Well, it would be awkward if they got into the museum and then got away to talk. We wouldn't want Interpol here making enquiries. The Vatican was particularly incensed at losing the bust of Jupiter. How that rogue ever got it out of the Vatican has always puzzled me. No, it wouldn't do for Interpol to know the museum is below ground.'

'But there was some suggestion, sir, that you were returning the ring to Mercial.'

'Yes . . . I will return the ring but not his operators.'

Tak didn't follow this, but he waited.

'Our Zulus would welcome a man hunt for a change, I think?'

'They can be relied on, sir.'

'Yes . . . they are very close still to the savage. That may not be necessary, of course. Our enterprising four could get lost. Still, let them be alerted. Arrange some sort of reward and insist on proof.'

'Yes, sir.'

'I must admit such a hunt would amuse me.' Kahlenberg's thin-lipped mouth tightened. 'When they have been hunted down and the ring returned to me, I will mail it to Mercial.' He rubbed his jaw as he stared at Tak. 'We mustn't make a mistake. It would be dangerous if even one of them got away. What chances do you think they have against a hundred of my Zulus and the jungle?'

Tak considered the problem, then shook his head.

'No chance at all, sir.'

'That's what I think.' Kahlenberg paused, thinking of the photograph locked in his desk. 'Pity about the woman.'

Tak got to his feet.

'Is there anything else, sir?'

'Yes . . . let me have the Borgia ring.'

When Tak had gone, Kahlenberg flicked down a switch on the intercom and said, 'Send Kemosa to me.'

A few minutes later an old, bent Bantu, wearing immaculate white drill came into the office. Kemosa had served Kahlenberg's father and was now in charge of the native staff, ruling them with a rod of iron. He stood before Kahlenberg, waiting.

'Is the old witch doctor still on the estate?' Kahlenberg asked.

'Yes, master.'

'I never see him. I thought he was dead.'

Kemosa said nothing.

'My father told me this man has great experience with poisons,' Kahlenberg went on. 'Is that correct?'

'Yes, master.'

'Go to him and say I want a slow working poison that will kill a man in twelve hours. Do you think he could supply a poison like that?'

Kemosa nodded.

'Very well. I want it by tomorrow morning. See he is suitably rewarded.'

'Yes, master.' Kemosa inclined his head and went away.

Kahlenberg pulled a legal document towards him and began to study it. A few minutes later Tak came in carrying a small glass box in which, set on a blue velvet support, was the Caesar Borgia ring.

'Leave it with me,' Kahlenberg said without looking up.

Tak placed the box on the desk and withdrew.

After reading the document and laying it down, Kahlenberg picked up the glass box and leaning back in his chair, he slid off the lid and took out the ring.

He took from a drawer a watchmaker's glass and screwed it into his eye. He spent some moments examining the ring before he found the minute sliding trap, covered by a diamond that gave access to the tiny reservoir that held the poison.

They left the Rand International Hotel a little after 08.00 hrs. and headed for Harrismith on the N.16 highway.

They were all wearing bush shirts, shorts, knee stockings, stout soled shoes and bush hats around which was a band of cheetah skin. The men all eyed Gaye as she climbed into the front seat of the Land Rover. The outfit set off her figure and suited her. Again Fennel felt a stab of frustrated desire go through him.

Ken Jones took the wheel and Garry and Fennel sat on the

rear bench seat. It was a tight squeeze for the four of them and their equipment. Each had brought along a rucksack containing their personal essentials and these were piled on the rear seat between the two men.

The sky was grey and the atmosphere was close and steamy and they were glad when they had left the city and had got onto the open road.

'This is going to be a pretty dull run,' Ken said. 'Two hundred kilometres to Harrismith, then we turn off the National road and head down for Bergville. We'll get to Mainville for lunch, pick up our guide and then we have thirty kilometres through jungle to the camp. That'll be fun: we're certain to see some game.'

'Who's looking after the chopper?' Garry asked, leaning forward. 'You haven't just left it in the jungle, have you?'

Ken laughed.

'I hired four Bantus to guard it. I know them . . . they're okay. It only arrived yesterday. You've nothing to worry about.'

Gaye said she was glad to leave Johannesburg.

'I didn't like it.'

'I don't know anyone who does,' Ken returned. 'But you'd like Cape Town and go crazy about Durban.'

The three chatted together as the Land Rover ate up the miles. Garry noticed that Fennel was sullenly silent. He sat forward with his heavy bag of tools between his feet and his little eyes continually eyeing Gaye's back and the view he could get of the side of her face.

Every so often they came upon a series of beehive shaped huts where they could see the Bantus moving aimlessly about, and tiny boys guarding lean, depressed looking cattle and herds of goats.

Gaye asked a stream of questions which Ken answered. Fennel paid no attention to the chatter. All he could think of was to get Gaye alone. He was confident, once he did get her alone, she would submit to him. He had no interest in black people and he wished Ken would stop yakking.

It was after 14.00 hrs. when they drove into Mainville's town centre that consisted of an untidy square, shaded by magnificent flamboyant trees in full flower. To the left of the square was the post office. Next to it was a native store and across the way was a shop run by a Dutchman who seemed to sell everything from a pair of boots to a bottle of cough mixture. The Bantus, sitting under the trees, watched them curiously, and two or three of them waved languidly to Ken who waved back.

'You seem to be a known character around here,' Gaye said.

'Oh, sure. I get around. I like these guys and they remember me.' Ken drove around the square and headed for a large dilapidated garage. He drove straight in.

Two Bantus came over and shook hands with him as he left the Land Rover. Ken spoke to them in Afrikaans and they nodded, beaming.

'Okay, folks,' he said turning to the others. 'We can leave it all here and go to the hotel for lunch. I could eat a buffalo.'

'You mean they won't steal any of this stuff?' Fennel asked.

Ken regarded him, his mouth tightening.

'They're friends of mine . . . so they won't steal any of the stuff.'

Fennel climbed down from the Land Rover .

'Well, if you're sure about that.'

The other three walked out into the blinding sunshine. Since leaving Johannesburg the sun had come out and it was hot.

The hotel was plain but decent and Ken got a good welcome from a fat, sweating Indian who beamed at the other three.

'Seen Themba?' Ken asked as they walked into the big diningroom.

'Yes, Mr. Jones. He's around. Said he would be here in half an hour.'

They all had a good chicken curry lunch, washed down with beer. From their table, they could see across the square to the garage and Fennel kept looking suspiciously at the garage.

'They're not stealing anything!' Ken said sharply. He had become exasperated by Fennel's suspicion. 'Can't you enjoy your lunch, for God's sake?'

Fennel squinted at him.

'The stuff in that tool bag is worth a lot of lolly,' he said. 'It's taken me years to collect. Some of those tools I've made myself. I'm making sure no goddamn blackie steals it.'

Seeing Ken's face flush with anger, Gaye broke in to ask about the hotel. The tension eased a little, then Ken got to his feet.

'I'll fix the bill, then go look for Themba.'

'Is he our guide?' Gaye asked.

'That's right.'

'And another black friend of his,' Fennel said with a sneer.

Ken hesitated, then walked away.

Garry said, 'Wouldn't it be an idea if you tried to be pleasant for a change? Right now, you act as if you have a boil on your ass.'

Fennel glowered at him.

'I act the way I like, and no one stops me!'

'Plenty of time to squabble when the job's done,' Gaye said quietly. 'Be nice, Mr. Fennel.'

He glowered at her, got up and walked out of the restaurant. Gaye and Garry paused to congratulate the fat Indian on his curry, and then followed Fennel across the square to the garage.

'He's sweet, isn't he?' Gaye said softly.

'He's a fat slob. If he goes on like this, he'll get a poke in his snout!'

'Remember what Armo said . . . he's dangerous.'

Garry scowled.

'So am I. It bothers me that Ken has to travel with him.'

But he was less bothered when he saw a tall, magnificent built Bantu, wearing bush clothes with a bush hat pinned up Australian fashion on one side, shaking hands with Ken.

'That must be Themba. Well, Ken and he can take care of Fennel; that's for sure.'

Ken made the introductions. Whereas Garry and Gaye shook hands, Fennel just stared at the big Bantu and then walked over to the Land Rover to make sure his bag of tools was still there.

'Themba only talks Afrikaans,' Ken explained. 'So conversationally he's a dead loss to you two.'

'I think he looks wonderful,' Gaye said admiringly.

'He's great. We've worked together for five years . . . no better tracker in Natal.'

They climbed into the Land Rover. Themba occupied a small swing-out seat at the rear, placing him above the others and giving him a good view of the country.

'Now, we go into the jungle,' Ken said. 'If there's any game to spot, Themba will find it.'

Another ten minutes of driving brought them off the main road to a grit road and the drive became bumpy.

'It gets worse as it goes on,' Ken said cheerfully, 'but you'll get used to it.'

It did get worse, and Ken had to cut down speed. Pot holes began to appear in the road and the Land Rover banged and bumped, making everyone hold on, with Fennel cursing under his breath.

A mile or so farther on, Themba said something to Ken, and Ken slowed and steered the Land Rover off the road into the bush. They were moving slowly now and they all had to look out for thorny bushes and low hanging branches which became hazardous as they went on.

Suddenly before them was a big waterbuck with its majestic antlers, looking towards them. It turned and was away with high leaping steps, displaying a perfect ring of white fur around its rump.

'Oh, I love him!' Gaye explained. 'And that white ring . . . it's marvellous!'

'Do you know how he got that?' Ken asked, grinning. 'I'll tell you. When the waterbuck arrived at the Ark, he rushed up to Noah and said, "Mr. Noah, please where is the nearest toilet?" Noah said, "You'll have to wait. All the toilets have just been painted." The waterbuck said, "I can't wait." It's had that ring ever since.'

'Why don't you look where you're driving and stop the yak?' Fennel growled while the others laughed.

'Can't please everyone all the time,' Ken said, shrugging, and continued on.

Gaye was noticing that many of the trees were broken and dead, giving the bush a stricken look.

'Did lightning do all this damage?' she asked.

'What, those trees—No . . . elephants. Must have had a big herd through here at one time. The elephant is the most destructive beast of any wild game. They strip the trees and smash them as they move. Wherever an elephant has been, you'll find dead trees.'

A little later they came upon five giraffes and Ken stopped within fifty metres of them. The animals stood motionless, staring.

'I wish I hadn't packed my camera,' Gaye sighed. 'They seem completely tame.'

'They're not tame . . . they're eaten up with curiosity,' Ken explained, and even as he spoke the gigantic animals turned and lolloped away, covering the ground at high speed although seeming to move like a slow motion film.

'Lions dig for them, but they seldom catch them,' Ken went on, setting the Land Rover moving again.

'Are there any lions in this district?' Gaye asked. 'I'd love to see one.'

'You will, and hear them too.'

Themba from his perch above them was continually calling to Ken, giving him directions.

'Without this guy,' Ken confided to Gaye, 'I'd never find the camp. He has a compass built inside his head.'

After half an hour's drive, during which time they disturbed a large herd of zebras which went crashing away into the thick bush almost before they could be seen, they came out of the bush onto a wide flat clearing where the helicopter was parked.

Squatting before the helicopter were four Bantus who rose to their feet with wide grins as the Land Rover pulled up.

'Here we are,' Ken said getting out of the truck. 'I'll pay these guys off. We don't want them hanging around. Themba and I can get the tent up.'

Garry went at once to the helicopter. Gaye slid to the ground and stretched. It had been a bumpy ride and she felt stiff and hot. Fennel got down and lit a cigarette. He showed no inclination to help Themba unload the equipment, but stood with his hands in his shorts pockets, eyeing Gaye as she stood with her back to him, her legs wide apart, her hands on her hips.

Ken got rid of the Bantus and came back to the Land Rover. 'There's a big pool beyond those trees and a waterfall,' he said to Gaye, pointing. 'It's safe swimming . . . no crocs.'

'Can I help?'

'No thanks . . . Themba and I can handle it.'

He joined Themba, and together the two men unloaded the tent. Breathing unsteadily, Fennel moved over to Gaye.

'A waterfall, huh? Suppose we go take a look at it?'

He was expecting her to refuse, and already his vicious temper began to rise. She regarded him, her face expressionless, then to his surprise, she said, 'Yes . . . let's look at it, 'and turning, she walked ahead, making for the thick line of trees and high elephant grass that surrounded the clearing.

Fennel felt a hot rush of blood through his body. Was this an invitation? He looked quickly towards the helicopter. Garry was busy stripping off the engine tarpaulin. Ken and Themba were occupied with unfolding the tent. Shaking a little, Fennel strode after Gaye who had now disappeared into the bush.

He caught up with her as she moved along a narrow track and he slowed his pace, his eyes on her slim back and long beautiful legs. Some twenty metres farther on they came to a small waterfall that fell some ten metres into a big basin of water which flowed at its far end into a broad stream. The basin formed a perfect, artificial bathing pool.

She turned as he reached her.

'Isn't it lovely?'

The sun beat down on them. They were surrounded by trees. They could have been the only two people on earth.

'Let's have a swim,' Fennel said and stripped off his shirt. 'Come on, baby, strip off.'

She looked at his hairy, muscular torso, her eyes watchful as she shook her head. 'I swim in private, Mr. Fennel.'

'Aw, come on! You don't imagine I've never seen a naked woman before, and I bet you've seen a naked man.' He grinned fixedly, his face flushed with desire for her. 'You don't have to be coy with me. Strip off, or I'll have to help you.'

Her cool, unafraid gaze disconcerted him.

'You swim . . . I'm going back.'

As she turned away, he caught hold of her wrist.

'You're staying here,' he said, his voice low and unsteady, 'and you're stripping off. You want some loving, baby, and I'm the guy to give it to you.'

'Take your hand off me,' she said quietly.

'Come on, baby, don't act coy . . . a little loving and then a swim.'

She moved towards him, and for a brief moment, he thought she was going to submit to him. Grinning he released his grip to encircle her waist. Her hand gripped his wrist and an excruciating pain shot up his arm, forcing him to cry out. Her foot slapped against his chest as she fell flat on her back. Fennel felt himself shooting into the air and then he splashed into the pool. The cool water closed over him, and when he bobbed to the surface and had dashed the water out of his eyes, he found her standing on the bank, looking down at him. Choking with rage, his arm aching, he glared murderously at her, seeing she was holding a large chunk of rock in her hands.

'Stay where you are unless you want your skull cracked,' she said.

Her stillness and her cold eyes warned him she wasn't bluffing.

'You bitch!' he snarled. 'I'll fix you for this!'

'You don't frighten me, you fat animal,' she said scornfully. 'From now on, you leave me alone. If you ever try to touch me again, I'll break your arm. If you weren't so important to this operation, I would have done it just now. Remember that! Now have a swim and cool off, you revolting ape.' She tossed the rock into the water just in front of him, and by the time he had cleared his eyes, she had gone.

Kahlenberg was signing a batch of letters when his office door opened silently and Kemosa came in. He waited patiently in the doorway until Kahlenberg had finished and when Kahlenberg looked up inquiringly he shuffled forward. He put a small glass bottle on the blotter.

'There it is, master.'

Kahlenberg regarded the bottle.

'What is it?'

'The poison you ordered, master.'

'I know that . . . what is the poison?'

Kemosa looked blank.

'That I don't know, master.'

Kahlenberg made an impatient movement.

'Did you tell the witch doctor exactly what I wanted?'

'Yes, master.'

'A poison that would kill a man in twelve hours?'

'Yes, master.'

'Is he to be trusted?'

'Yes, master.'

'What did you pay him?'

'Twenty goats.'

'Did you tell him if the poison doesn't work, he will lose all his goats and I will burn his hut and turn him off my estate?'

'I told him that if the poison doesn't work, two men would come in the night and throw him in the crocodile pool.'

'Does he believe that?'

'Yes, master.'

Kahlenberg nodded, satisfied.

'Go to the medical chest, Kemosa, and bring me a syringe and a pair of rubber gloves.'

When Kemosa had left, Kahlenberg sat back, looking at the small bottle. His mind went back four hundred years. Caesar Borgia might also have contemplated a similar phial of poison, planning the end of an enemy, feeling the same pleasure that Kahlenberg was experiencing.

He was still sitting motionless when Kemosa returned with the syringe and gloves.

'Thank you,' and Kahlenberg waved him away.

When the door had closed, he opened a drawer and took out the glass box containing the ring. He took out the ring and put it on the fourth finger of his right hand. He studied the flashing diamonds thoughtfully, then he turned the ring so the diamonds were worn inside. The plain silver band now showing looked very innocent. He took off the ring and laid it on the blotter. Then he put on the surgical gloves. Screwing the watchmaker's glass into his eye, he slid open the trap in the ring. Then laying the ring down again, he uncorked the bottle and drew some of the colourless liquid into the syringe. Very carefully he inserted the needle of the syringe into the reservoir of the ring and equally carefully pressed the plunger. When, through the watchmaker's glass, he saw the liquid was level with the top of the reservoir, he withdrew the needle and slid the diamond trap into place. Laying down the syringe, he wiped the ring on his handkerchief, taking time over the operation. Still without removing his gloves, he began shaking the ring sharply over the blotter, looking for any signs of a leak in the reservoir. Finally satisfied, he put the ring in a drawer, put his handkerchief in an envelope and sent for Kemosa again. When the old man came in, he told him to destroy the syringe, the poison, the gloves and the handkerchief.

'Make certain they are all destroyed,' he said. 'You understand? Be very careful not to touch the needle of the syringe.'

'Yes, master.'

When he had gone, Kahlenberg took out the ring and regarded it. Was this now a lethal weapon? he asked himself. The witch doctor must be over eighty years of age. Had he lost his cunning? Could he be trusted? If the poison were lethal, could the tiny hollow needle, hidden in the cluster of diamonds, have become blocked with dust? If it had he would be wasting his time, and this was something Kahlenberg never tolerated. He had to know for certain. He sat thinking, then making up his mind, he put the ring on the fourth finger of his right hand and turned the ring the wrong way round. He propelled himself into the garden, followed by Hindenburg.

It took him a little time to find Zwide, a Bantu about whom Kemosa had often complained, saying this man was not only incurably lazy but also ill-treated his wife. He was due to be dismissed at the end of the month, and to Kahlenberg's callous thinking no loss to anyone.

He found him squatting in the shade, half asleep. When he saw Kahlenberg, he rose hurriedly to his feet, grabbed up a hoe and began feverishly weeding a nearby rose bed.

Kahlenberg stopped his chair beside him. Hindenburg sat, his eyes watchful.

'I hear you are leaving at the end of the month, Zwide,' Kahlenberg said quietly.

The man nodded dumbly, stiff with fear.

Kahlenberg stretched out the ringed hand.

'I wish you good fortune. Shake my hand.'

Zwide hesitated, his eyes rolling with embarrassment, then

reluctantly stretched out his hand. Kahlenberg caught the dirty pink palmed hand in a hard, firm grip, his eyes intent on the man's face. He saw him give a little start. Then Kahlenberg released the hand and set the chair in motion. When he had gone a few metres, he looked back.

Zwide was staring with a bewildered expression at his hand and as Kahlenberg watched, Zwide raised a finger to his mouth and licked it.

Kahlenberg went on his way. At least the needle had scratched, he thought. In twelve hours' time he would know if the ring was lethal.

As Gaye reached the clearing, she heard the engine of the helicopter start up. She came to a standstill watching the propellers churning. She could see Garry at the controls.

She cried, 'Hey! Wait for me!'

But he didn't hear her. The machine took off, climbing steeply and then went out of sight behind the trees.

Ken and Themba had got the tent up. They had been also watching the take-off. Now they continued to unload the Land Rover. She joined them.

'Why didn't he wait for me?' she asked. 'That was mean!'

Ken grinned.

'You ask him when he comes back. Where's our lovely boy friend?'

'Having a swim.'

There was a note in her voice that made him look sharply at her.

'Trouble?'

'The usual, but I settled it.'

'You're quite a girl.' His look of admiration pleased her.

'Be careful of him . . . he's vicious.'

'Themba and I can take care of him.' He dragged out the four sleeping bags. 'I'm putting yours between Garry's and mine. Themba sleeps next to me . . . then Fennel.'

She nodded.

'It's only for one night, isn't it?'

'Yes . . . for him and me, but two nights for Garry and you.' He looked up at the clouds moving across the sky. 'The sooner we get off the better. If it rains the road will be a real mess. You'll be all right on your own with Garry . . . he's a good guy.'

'I know.'

He took the sleeping bags into the tent and laid them out.

Themba was building a fire some little way from the tent. Ken collected the .22 rifle and pocketed some ammunition.

'I'm going after guinea-fowl. Want to come?'

'Of course.'

They set off together into the bush.

Fennel came out of the trees, moving slowly. His arm still ached. He looked around, then seeing only Themba busy with the fire, he went to the Land Rover, got out his rucksack and went into the tent. He changed out of his wet shorts and put on a dry pair. He came out into the dying sunshine and sat on one of the wooden cases. His mind was smouldering. Well, he would fix her, he told himself as he lit a cigarette. There was time. Get the operation over. On the way back, he'd teach her.

He was still sitting there, brooding, when the helicopter came in to land. After a while Garry came over.

'A beauty,' he said enthusiastically. 'Goes like a bird.'

Fennel looked up and grunted.

'Where are the others?'

Fennel shrugged.

'I wouldn't know.'

'How about a beer?'

'Yeah.'

Garry opened the carton. Themba came over with glasses and a Thermos of ice. As Garry was opening the bottles, Gaye and Ken came out of the bush. Ken had four guinea-fowl hanging from a string to his belt.

'Why didn't you wait for me?' Gaye demanded.

Garry shook his head.

'Trial flight. First time I've handled her. Cockeyed for both of us to get killed.'

Gaye's eyes opened wide. She took the beer Themba offered her with a smile. Ken drank from the bottle, sighed, then handed the birds to Themba who took them away.

'We'll eat well tonight,' Ken said and squatted down on the grass. 'Let's talk business, Lew. We two and Themba leave at first light . . . around 04.00 hrs. We'll take the rifle and the shot-gun, our sleeping bags, rucksacks and food.' He looked over at Garry. 'You any good with a .22?'

Garry grimaced. 'Never tried.'

'I am,' Gaye said. 'I'll get you a guinea-fowl, Garry.'

'That's fine.'

Fennel glanced up, looked at Gaye, then at Garry, then looked away.

'Okay . . . anyway, you have only one more day here. The day after tomorrow you take off for Kahlenberg's place.' Ken took a pencil from his pocket and drew a rough circle in the sand. 'I've been talking to Themba. He's been up to Kahlenberg's estate for the past two days.' He glanced over at Lew who was lighting a cigarette. 'You listening, Lew?'

'You think I'm goddamn deaf?'

'This circle represents Kahlenberg's estate. Themba tells me it is guarded by a lot of Zulus south, west and east, but not on the north side. The road into the estate on the north side is reckoned impassable, but Themba has been over it. He says there's one really tricky bit, but if we can't get over it, we can walk. It's our only safe way in.'

'How far do we walk if we can't drive?' Fennel asked, leaning forward as Ken marked a spot on the north side of the circle.

'Twenty kilometres as near as damn it.'

Fennel thought of his heavy tool bag.

'But there's a chance we can get through in the truck?'

'Themba thinks so, so long as it doesn't rain too hard. If it really rains then we are in trouble.'

'Well, some people have all the luck,' Fennel said, looking over at Garry, but Garry wasn't to be drawn. He got up and walked over to watch Themba cooking the birds. He wished he could speak Afrikaans. There was something about the big Bantu's face that appealed to him. As if reading his thoughts, Themba looked up and grinned cheerfully and then continued to turn the spit.

Gaye joined Garry.

'Hmmmm, smells good . . . I'm starving.'

Themba raised a finger and crossed it with a finger of his left hand.

'That means you have to wait half an hour,' Garry said. 'Come over to the chopper. I'll tell you about it.'

They walked over to the helicopter.

Fennel watched them, his eyes glittering. Ken had no desire to talk to him. He went over and joined Themba. They spoke together in Afrikaans.

'Looks like rain soon?' Ken said, squatting beside the Bantu.

'Could come tonight.'

Ken grimaced.

'Well, we've got the winch. If that doesn't pull us out, nothing will.'

'Yes.'

They talked on. Half an hour later, the birds were cooked. It was dark now and the air heavy and close. They all sat around the fire, eating with their fingers. Without Fennel, the party could have been gay, but his dour expression and his silence killed any light-hearted atmosphere.

When they had finished and Themba had cleared up, Ken said, 'I'm turning in. We have to be up early tomorrow.'

'Yes . . . I'm dying to sleep.' Gaye got to her feet.

'Give you five minutes to get into your bag,' Ken said, 'then I'm coming in.'

Gaye disappeared into the tent.

'I guess I'll join you,' Garry said, stretching. 'That was some meal.' He looked at Fennel. 'You turning in?'

'Is the smoke sleeping in there?'

'If you mean is Themba sleeping in there . . . he is.'

Fennel spat in the fire.

'I don't dig breathing the same air as a black man.'

'Okay . . . take your sleeping bag out then.'

Fennel got swiftly to his feet and advanced on Ken, his fists clenched. He was much more powerfully built than Ken who wouldn't have stood a chance against him, Garry stepped between them, facing Fennel.

'I'm getting fed up with you,' he said evenly. 'If you're aching to hit someone, hit me.'

Fennel eyed him, hesitated, then backed away.

'Go to hell,' he growled and sat down. He sat by the dying fire long after the others were sleeping, then finally realizing he must get some sleep, he entered the tent and crawled into his sleeping bag.

Towards 02.00 hrs. the sound of rain drumming on the roof of the tent woke them all.

Above the sound of the rain came the choked roar of a lion.

CHAPTER SIX

FENNEL CAME AWAKE as someone turned on a powerful flashlight. He could see Ken wriggling out of his sleeping bag. Themba held the flashlight and was leaving the tent.

'Time to go?' Fennel asked with a yawn.

'Just about. Themba's getting the breakfast. I'm going down for a swim . . . coming?'

Fennel grunted, slipped on his shoes and shorts and grabbed

up a towel. He followed Ken out into the damp half light. It had stopped raining, but the clouds were heavy and swollen.

'Going to be sticky,' Ken said as the two men trotted down to the pool, 'but with the winch, and if we're lucky, we'll make it.'

Reaching the pool, they dived in, swam across, turned and swam back and came out. They towelled themselves vigorously, slipped into their shorts, then trotted back to the camp.

Both Gaye and Garry were up and squatting by the fire watching Themba frying a batch of eggs and bacon.

By the time they had finished breakfast and Themba had cleared up, it was light enough to move.

'Well, let's go,' Ken said. Turning to Garry, he went on, 'Do you think you can get the tent down and fold it?'

'Sure. I'll pack it in the chopper . . . right?'

'If you leave it here, it'll disappear for sure.' Ken looked at Themba. 'All okay?'

Themba nodded.

'Let's synchronize our watches. We'll call you on radio at 11.00 hrs. just to report progress. After that we'll call you every two hours . . . okay?'

They checked their watches, then Garry offered his hand.

'Good luck . . . watch that bastard.'

Fennel was putting his tool kit in the Land Rover. He got in at the back and sat on the bench seat, staring moodily ahead.

'Sweet type, isn't he?' Ken grinned. He turned to Gaye and shook hands. They watched him slide into the driving seat. Themba waved a cheerful hand and got in the front seat beside Ken.

Ken drove into the jungle where it was dark enough for him to put on the headlights. He drove slowly, and Fennel wondered how the hell anyone could know where he was going in this dense jungle. Themba was continually directing Ken. Maybe this blackie wasn't all that of a monkey, Fennel thought. He knew he himself would be helpless on his own, and this thought riled him.

As they progressed the sun began to come up and Ken switched off the headlights. He was able to increase speed slightly. It was a nagging, bumpy ride and Fennel had to hang on.

Themba suddenly pointed and Ken slowed.

'To your right . . . a rhino!'

Fennel swivelled his head.

Standing not more than twenty metres away was a huge

rhinoceros. The ungainly animal slowly turned its head to stare at them. Fennel eyed the big horn and he reached for the Springfield, aware his heart was beginning to thump.

'They're dangerous, aren't they?' he asked, his voice low.

'That's the white rhino. He's docile,' Ken told him. 'It's the black one you have to watch out for.'

He drove on, increasing speed. At this hour the bush seemed alive with game. Herds of impala scattered at the approach of the Land Rover. Two warthogs went crashing into the shrubs, their tails up like periscopes. Black bellied storks watched them from the tree tops. It was as they were nearing the edge of the bush that Themba pointed, and Ken said, 'Lions!'

Lying by the side of the track were two full grown male lions. Fennel calculated they would pass within four metres of them.

'You're not passing those bastards?' he demanded.

'Nothing to worry about,' Ken said cheerfully. 'You leave a lion alone and he'll leave you alone.'

But Fennel wasn't convinced. He picked up the Springfield, his finger curling around the trigger.

They were nearly on the lions now. Both beasts raised their heads and regarded the on-coming Land Rover with sleepy indifference. Fennel felt sweat on his face. As they passed, they were so close he could have touched the lions with the end of the rifle.

'See?' Ken said. 'You don't have to worry about lions, but you wound one and go in after him and you'll have a hell of a lot to worry about.'

Fennel put down the rifle and wiped his sweating face with the back of his hand.

'That was too damn close.'

They came out of the jungle on to a dirt road. Themba indicated that Ken should turn to the right.

'This is the road leading to Kahlenberg's estate . . . the whole sixty kilometres of it,' Ken said after he had talked with Themba. He looked at his watch. The time was 08.00 hrs. 'Themba reckons we'll get to the edge of the estate in three hours. We'll radio back to Garry when we get there.'

'Three hours to do sixty kilometres. You nuts?'

'The road's bad. It could take us longer.'

The road was bad, and gradually deteriorated. It was climbing gently all the time. The night's rain had softened the surface and the Land Rover began to slide a little. Ahead of them was a very sharp rise and as Ken increased speed for the run up, the back wheels slid and Ken hurriedly steered into the skid just as it seemed they were about to leave the road.

'Watch what you're doing!' Fennel snarled, startled.

'I can do without a back seat driver,' Ken returned. 'Just shut up, will you?'

The Land Rover crawled up the rise and Ken slammed on his brakes when he saw the dip below was full of water and there was another sharp rise to get out of the dip.

'We're not going through that,' he said and put the truck into reverse, slowly sliding back down the rise. He then drove off the road and on to the tangle of dead branches, shrubs and coarse, rain soaked grass. They hadn't gone more than ten metres when the rear wheels spun and Fennel felt the truck sink.

Ken gave the engine more gas, resulting only in producing a shower of wet, sticky mud that sprinkled them as the wheels spun.

Themba sprang out and went around to the back. Ken engaged gear while Themba pushed, but they only sank deeper.

Ken turned, and as he disengaged gear, he looked straight at Fennel.

'Let's get this straight, Lew. Are you with us or are you just a goddamn passenger?'

Fennel hesitated, then got down from the Land Rover. His bull strength combined with Themba's weight began to tell. There was more splattering of mud, then the tyres got a new purchase and the Land Rover came out of the two holes it had dug. Walking beside it, ready to go into action again, Fennel and Themba, watched warily. Twice the Land Rover skidded but righted itself. They were past the dip now and Ken steered back on the road.

'See what I mean?' he said. 'Twenty minutes wasted.'

Fennel grunted and climbed on board. He was breathing heavily. By now the sun was hot and beat down on them. Ken increased speed and they continued to climb, banging and bumping over the stony road, avoiding the water filled pot-holes where he could, and when he couldn't, banging into them, jolting them all and making Fennel curse.

The road narrowed suddenly and became nothing better than a rough track, strewn with fair-sized boulders. Three times during the next hundred metres, Themba had to jump down and heave the rocks out of the way. They were now crawling at around ten kilometres an hour.

It didn't look to Fennel as if any vehicle had ever come along this narrow track which kept climbing. Branches of trees hung low, causing both men to keep ducking. Themba was walking ahead now as the Land Rover's speed was even more reduced.

'You mean we've got another fifty kilometres of this bitching road to drive on?' Fennel exclaimed as he ducked under another branch.

'That's about it. According to Themba it gets worse as we go on, but at least we are moving.'

That appeared to be a rash thing to have said for almost immediately they struck a soft patch of ground and before Ken could control the skid, they had slid off the narrow track and the off-side wheels slammed down into a gutter.

They stopped.

Themba came running back as Ken got out of the Land Rover. The two men surveyed the position of the wheels and discussed it together while Fennel got down and lit a cigarette. He felt irritatingly useless. To him, they looked stuck for good.

'Only thing to do is to lift her out,' Ken said.

He began to unload the truck, handing the jerry cans of water and gas to Themba. Fennel got the rucksacks, sleeping bags and his heavy tool bag out.

'Back wheels first,' Ken said.

The three men got grips and at Ken's shout, heaved up. Their combined strength lifted the wheel and the next heave got the tail of the truck back on to the road.

'I can pull her out now,' Ken said. 'You two shove against the side in case she slides in again.'

Three minutes later, the Land Rover was once more on the road. They hastily reloaded, then Fennel said, 'I'm having a drink.'

Ken nodded and Themba opened two bottles of beer and a bottle of tonic water for himself.

Fennel looked at Themba. 'You say it's going to get worse?'

'So he says,' Ken broke in. 'No use talking to him, he doesn't understand English.

Fennel emptied his bottle of beer.

'Looks like we three have picked the crappy end of the stick, doesn't it?' he said.

'That's the way the cookie crumbles.' Ken finished his beer, tossed the bottle into the gutter and climbed under the driving wheel. 'Let's go.'

At least the two incidents seemed to have made Fennel more human, he thought as he engaged gear. He had spoken to Themba and he had shown a spark of comradeship.

They now came to a series of steep hairpin bends. Using the four wheel drive, Ken continued the climb but at not much more than twelve kilometres an hour. The exertion of dragging the wheel around as he came into the bends and then straightening was making him sweat. The bends seemed to go on and on and they climbed higher and higher.

Fennel leaned forward.

'Want me to take a turn? I can handle this crate.'

Ken shook his head.

'Thanks . . . I can cope.' He spoke to Themba in Afrikaans and Themba replied.

Feeling out of it, Fennel demanded, 'What are you talking about?'

'At the top is the bad place. Themba says this is where we could get stuck for good.'

'That's fine! Bad place! What the hell does he call this?'

Ken laughed.

'From what he says, this is like driving down Piccadilly to what we're coming to.'

Then from nowhere grey sluggish clouds crossed the sun, shutting it out and it turned cold. As Ken left the last hairpin bend and started up a long narrow, rocky rise, the rain came down in solid warm sheets.

The three men were soaked to the skin in seconds and Ken, blinded, stopped the Land Rover. They all crouched forward, shielding their faces with their arms while the rain slammed down on their bowed backs. They remained like that for some minutes. Water was in the Land Rover and sloshing around Fennel's shoes, and water lay inches deep on the tarpaulin covering their equipment.

Abruptly as it began, the rain ceased, the clouds moved away and the sun came out. In a very few minutes their clothes began to steam.

'This is one hell of a picnic,' Fennel said. 'My goddamn cigarettes are soaked!'

Ken took a pack from the glove compartment and offered it. 'Take these.'

'I'll take one . . . keep the rest in there. If the bitch is going to start again, we don't want to run short.'

They both lit up and then got back into the truck. Themba had walked on ahead. By now he was at the top of the rise and stood waiting.

As they reached him, he motioned Ken to stop. Both men

looked beyond him at the road ahead. They appeared to be on the top of a mountain and the track abruptly narrowed. One side was a sloping bank of coarse grass and shrubs: the other side was a sheer drop into the valley.

Fennel stood up in the Land Rover and stared at the track. He was never sure of himself when in high places, and the sight of the distant valley far below and the narrowness of the rough track brought him out in a sweat.

'We're bitched!' he said, his voice unsteady. 'We can't hope to get through there!'

Ken turned and looked sharply at him. Seeing his ashen face and how his hands were shaking, he realized this was a man with no head for heights and felt sorry for him.

'Look, Lew, you get out. I think I can get through. It'll be a tight squeeze, but it can be done.'

'Don't be a fool! You'll kill your goddamn self!'

Ken shouted to Themba, 'Can I do it?'

The Bantu stood in the middle of the track and regarded the Land Rover, then he nodded.

'Just,' he said.

'What's he say?' Fennel demanded.

'He thinks it's all right.'

'All right? Hell! You'll go over!'

'You get out.'

Fennel hesitated, then picking up his tool bag, he got down on to the track.

'Wait a minute,' he said, sweat pouring down his face. 'If you're going to kill yourself, I'm going to get all the equipment off first. If she goes over, we'll be stuck without food or drink.'

'Maybe you have something there,' Ken said with a wide grin. He climbed over the back and Themba, realizing what they were doing, joined them. The three men carefully lifted off the tarpaulin, draining the rain water on to the track, then they hastily unloaded all the equipment.

Fennel glanced at his watch. It was 10.55 hrs.

'We'll have a beer,' he said. 'In five minutes you have to contact Edwards. How much further have we to go?'

Ken consulted Themba as he opened two beer bottles.

'About twenty kilometres. Then another ten kilometres to the big house,' Themba told him.

Ken translated.

'Rough going?'

Themba said once over this bit the going was good.

They finished the beer and then Ken picked up the two-way radio.

'Ken to Garry . . . are you receiving me?'

Immediately: 'Garry to Ken . . . loud and clear. How goes it?'

Briefly Ken explained the situation.

'Sounds dicey. Look, Ken, why not use the winch? Anchor ahead and wind yourself in. If the truck slips you have a chance to jump.'

'Idea. Roger. Call you back. Out.'

'I bet he feels smug,' Fennel growled. 'Did he say if he's laid that bitch yet?'

'Skip it, Lew,' Ken said impatiently. He talked to Themba, who nodded and, taking the tarpaulin cover off the winch, he ran the cable out until he was beyond the narrowest part of the track. Ken gave Fennel the drag.

'You any good at splicing? It's got to be secure.'

'I'll fix it.'

Averting his eyes from the drop on his right, Fennel joined Themba, anchor in hand, his tool bag slung over his shoulder. It took him a little over half an hour before he was satisfied. While he worked, Ken sat behind the wheel and smoked. He had steady nerves and was quite cool. He knew there was a risk, but he was also confident that he could get through.

Finally, Fennel stood up.

'It's okay.'

He had fixed the drag firmly in a root of a massive tree growing nearby, and, using a club hammer, he hammered the drag well home.

He walked back to the Land Rover.

'That won't come out. The cable won't burst. Depends now if the winch gets torn out of its casing.'

'Cheer up,' Ken said, grinning. 'Well, let's try. Will you stay behind me, Lew? If the back begins to slide either correct it or yell to me if you can't. I want Themba ahead to watch the off-side wheels.'

'I'll tell you something,' Fennel said, breathing heavily. 'You've got more bloody guts than I have.'

The two men looked at each other, then Ken turned, set the engine going, released the handbrake and moved the lever operating the winch forward. The drum began to revolve. He quickly cut the speed of the drum and the Land Rover began to inch forward.

Fennel walked behind, both his hands on the tailboard of the truck, his eyes on Themba, who was squatting down, his eyes glued to the front wheels, beckoning Ken on.

The truck covered ten metres before Themba raised his hand sharply to stop.

Ken flicked the winch lever to neutral.

'What's the matter now?' Fennel growled from behind.

Themba had gone to the drag and was looking at it.

'Does that black ape think I would let it pull loose?' Fennel snarled. 'That's in, and it'll stay in!'

'Don't get so worked up,' Ken said, taking out a soiled handkerchief and wiping his face.

Satisfied, Themba went back to the middle of the track.

'Four more metres and you're on the narrow bit,' he called.

Ken set the drum revolving again.

The Land Rover began to crawl forward again. Then the unpredictable happened, three metres before the narrows. The road, sodden by the rain, crumbled under the weight of the truck. Fennel felt the back sliding towards the drop and he threw his weight desperately against the tailboard, trying to steer the truck back, yelling to Ken to jump. He felt himself being dragged to the edge and, shuddering, he let go and rolled on his back towards the grass slope. He was on his feet in an instant, but the Land Rover had gone.

He looked wildly up the road. Themba, on the edge of the drop, was staring down, his big eyes rolling. Cursing, Fennel saw the taut cable was vibrating, and, steeling himself, he went to the edge, feeling sick and dizzy, and looked over.

Four metres below, dangling by the cable, was the Land Rover. Ken was standing on the back of the seat, his hands gripping the wind shield. Far, far below, spread out like an aerial map, was the valley.

Even as he looked, Fennel saw the drum was slowly parting from the casing.

'Get to the drum!' he bawled. 'Ken . . . it's coming away! Get to the drum!'

Ken balanced himself, stepped over the wind shield and flattened himself upright on the perpendicular bonnet. He caught hold of one of the steel stanchions supporting the drum, heaved forward, his hands around the cable of the drum. Even as he got a grip, the drum parted from the truck and the truck went hurtling down into the void.

Ken swung on the end of the cable. Themba had the cable in his hands and was trying to haul him in. Shaking from head to foot, Fennel joined him. Ken swung hard against the side of the mountain and his feet got a purchase. As the two men hauled, he began to walk up the slightly sloping side and, moments later, he rolled on to the track.

He sat up and forced a grin.

'Now, we will damn well have to walk,' he said.

As the Land Rover drove into the bush, Gaye sighed with relief.

'Well, thank goodness, he's out of the way,' she said. 'He was really beginning to get on my nerves.'

'Mine too.' Garry lit a cigarette. 'Do you want some more coffee?'

She shook her head.

'When it gets lighter, I'll have a swim. The pool looks marvellous.' She wandered over to the fire and knelt before it.

Garry watched her, thinking how lovely she looked, the flames of the fire lighting up her face. Then he went into the tent, found his cordless electric razor and shaved in the light of the flashlamp. As he shaved, he thought of the hours ahead of them before they took off. He was sharply aware that they were alone together. Firmly, he put the thought out of his mind. Picking up a towel, he left the tent. The light was brighter now. In another hour the sun would be up, but he felt in need of cold water and was too impatient to wait.

'I'll take my swim first,' he called to her. 'Are you all right alone here?'

She laughed.

'Yes, unless a lion turns up. It'll be cold.'

'That's how I like it.'

She watched him move off into the shadows and she fed the fire with more sticks collected in a big heap by Themba. She also thought of the hours ahead. She admitted to herself that Fennel in his brutish way had stirred a dormant desire in her for a man. How long, she pondered, had it been since she had had a satisfactory lover? Her mind went back over the number of men who had shared her bed. She could remember only two who had really pleased and satisfied her. The first had been a little like Garry, not so tall and more handsome . . . an American on vacation. She had been in Paris, modelling clothes. On one hot July night, she had been sitting alone at Fouquet's café which had been crowded. He had come up and asked if he could share her table. They had looked at each other, and she knew immediately that she would be sleeping with him within a few hours as he too seemed to know. Again, the second man, also an American and also who had looked a little like Garry, had come out of the dimness of a bar where she had been waiting for friends and had invited her to drink with him. They had left the bar together before her friends arrived. She decided this Garry type of man had sexual attraction for her that sparked with her instantly as two flints struck together will cause a spark.

She had only met these two men once and only knew their Christian names, but the few hours she had spent with them were etched on her mind, and now, after that ape Fennel had aroused her after so long, she knew that sometime during the day Garry would become her lover.

The sun was rising, and already she could feel its warmth. She moved away from the fire and went into the tent to straighten up. By the time she had finished, she could feel the heat of the sun coming through the canvas of the tent and she went out, taking a towel with her.

She saw Garry coming towards her, wearing shorts and shoes, his towel over his shoulder.

She smiled at him.

'Was it good?'

'Marvellous, but cold. It'll be fine now.'

'See you later.' She was aware that he was looking at her as the two Americans had looked at her, then he looked away.

She nodded and ran off, swinging her towel, towards the pool.

She seldom had the opportunity of swimming naked and this she loved to do. She stripped off and dived in. The sun was fully on the pool by now the chill was off the water. She swam for some time, then turned on her back, closed her eyes and let herself float.

Two grey, black-faced monkeys high up in a tree watched her. Then, as if by agreement, they slid down the tree, moved swiftly to where she had left her shorts, shirt and towel, snatched them up and shinned up the tree again. Having examined the clothes and finding them of no interest, they left them hanging on a high branch and went swinging from tree to tree further into the forest.

As they went, Gaye opened her eyes and saw them. She watched them, thinking how cute they looked, but she didn't think them cute when, on climbing out of the pool, she found only her shoes on the bank.

Looking up, she caught sight of her towel hanging on a branch. She hesitated, knowing she could never climb up there, then shrugging, she put on her shoes and walked back to the camp. Garry, sitting in the shade of the tent, was examining the aerial map Shalik had given him. He glanced up as she came out of the line of trees and, startled, he dropped the map. For a moment he couldn't believe his eyes, then he got to his feet.

Quite unconcerned, naked as she was born, Gaye came on.

'Monkeys have stolen my clothes . . . the little devils. They are up a tree by the pool. Could you get them for me, Garry?' she called as she was half-way across the plain. She made no attempt to hide her nakedness. Her arms swung loosely at her sides as she moved. She behaved as if she were fully dressed.

'Sure . . .'

He started towards her, then deliberately made a wide half circle so he wouldn't pass close to her and she liked him for that.

They passed and she went into the tent. She was quite sure he hadn't looked back at her. Her heart was beating fast. She went to her rucksack to get her duplicate shirt and shorts. She got them out, looked at them, hesitated, then dropped them to the ground and stretched herself out on top of her sleeping bag. With her legs crossed and her hands covering her breasts, she waited his return.

'It's nearly 11.00 hrs., Garry said. 'They will be coming through on the radio.'

She was loath to let him go, but as he moved away from her, she let her arms slide away from his body. She watched him stand up and put on his shorts, then she closed her eyes.

She had been right about him. It had been even better than it had been with the other two Americans, and also, she did know his surname. The tensions that had been building up inside her for the past year had been released by the explosive coupling, and now she felt as if she had had a shot of some hard drug. She didn't wish to be disturbed, but to be allowed to remain still and to do nothing. She drifted off into semi-sleep which was all the more relaxing and pleasant in the heat of the tent.

She was startled awake by Garry coming to the opening of the tent and calling her name sharply.

She half sat up and immediately became fully alert at the sight of his worried expression.

'What is it?'

'Those three are in trouble. Put your things on and come out. It's too damn hot in here.'

There was a hard note in his voice and she could see he was

impatient with her lying there like a cat before a fire. She slipped into her clothes and came out to join him in the shade.

'The road collapsed and they've lost the Land Rover,' Garry told her. 'Ken was nearly killed.'

'Is he hurt?'

'No . . . shaken, but all right, now they'll have to walk and it's a hell of a walk.'

'But they'll get there?'

'They think so. They'll be contacting me again in two hours.'

'And the equipment?'

'That's all right. They unloaded before attempting to get over the worst part of the track.'

'How will they get back?'

'We'll all have to fly out . . . nothing else for it. It'll be a load, but it can be done.'

She relaxed, resting her back against the tree.

'So it really isn't so bad . . . they'll just have to walk.'

'In this heat, it won't be so good.'

'Oh, well . . . get some of that ape's fat off. Do you know how to pluck and draw a bird, Garry?'

'No . . . do you?'

'No. So we won't bother to hunt guinea-fowl. We'll have beans and bacon for lunch.' She got to her feet. 'I'm going to have another swim . . . coming?'

He hesitated. 'Those three are worrying me, Gaye.'

'Then a swim with me will put them out of your mind. There's nothing we can do for them . . . so come on and swim.'

She went into the tent for the towels and then together they walked in the burning sun towards the pool.

Fennel wished now he hadn't drunk so much beer in the past. The rough, stony track, the hot sun and the pace that Ken was setting all reminded him of how out of condition he was. The strap of his tool bag was rubbing his shoulder raw. Sweat streamed down his face and blackened his shirt. He was breathing heavily.

At a guess, he thought, they had covered only six kilometres. Ken had talked of thirty kilometres before they reached Kahlenberg place. Twenty-four kilometres! Fennel gritted his teeth. He was certain he couldn't do it with this tool kit: it got heavier and heavier with every step he took. Apart from his tool kit, he was also carrying his rucksack.

Before setting off, they had decided to leave the sleeping bags and the shotgun. Ken carried the Springfield and his own ruck-sack, Themba was carrying a rucksack stuffed with provisions and a five litre jerrycan of water.

Fennel plodded on, dragging one foot after the other. He longed for some shade, but there was none on this narrow track. He badly wanted a drink and thought regretfully of the beer they had left behind them. He had wanted it along with them, but when Ken said it was okay with him if Fennel would carry it, Fennel decided against the idea.

He paused to wipe the sweat out of his eyes and was stung with mortification to see the other two walking and chatting together, well ahead of him.

Ken glanced back and then stopped. Themba continued on for a few steps and then he stopped.

Fennel felt a spurt of rage go through him. He came plodding up to them. One look at his exhausted face told Ken that he was going to be a liability. Themba thought so too, and putting down the jerrycan he said something to Fennel who didn't understand.

'He says he'll carry your tool bag if you'll carry the jerrycan,' Ken translated.

Fennel hesitated, but he knew the bag now was too much for him.

'What makes him think *he* can carry it?' he demanded, lower-ing the bag thankfully to the ground.

'He wouldn't make the offer if he didn't,' Ken pointed out as Themba hoisted up the bag and slung it on his shoulder.

Fennel hesitated, then said, 'Well, tell him . . . thanks. It's a bitch of a thing to carry.' He caught hold of the jerrycan and the three men continued on their way: the other two slowing down to keep pace with Fennel.

The next hour was a hellish up-hill grind for Fennel, but he kept plodding on, breathing heavily, furious with himself to see how easily the other two were taking the ordeal.

'How about a drink?' he gasped, coming to a halt.

But the drink gave him no satisfaction as the water was warm and, anyway, Fennel loathed drinking water.

Ken looked at his watch.

'In another ten minutes, we'll call Garry. Then we'll have a rest.'

'That guy must have been born lucky,' Fennel growled, pick-ing up the jerrycan. 'He doesn't know how well off he is.'

They continued on, and at 13.00 hrs. they left the track and sat down in the shade of the jungle. Ken contacted Garry and reported progress.

'We should be in position by 18.00 hrs., he said, and added the going was rough.

Garry made sympathetic noises, said he would be standing by at 15.00 hrs. and switched off.

After a half an hour's rest, they continued on for another hour, then Ken said it was time to eat. They left the sun soaked track and sat down in the shade of the trees. Themba opened cans of steak pie and baked beans.

'How much farther?' Fennel asked, his mouth full.

Ken consulted Themba.

'About six kilometres and then we'll be in the jungle.'

'Ask him if he wants me to carry the bag again.'

'He's okay . . . don't bother about it.'

'Ask him! That bag's goddamn heavy!'

Ken spoke to Themba who grinned and shook his head.

'Black people are used to carrying white men's burdens,' Ken said, keeping his face straight.

Fennel eyed him.

'Okay, I'll take that . . . so he's a better man than I am.'

'Skip it or I'll burst into tears.'

Fennel smiled sourly.

'My time's coming. You two may be pretty hot with this jungle and walking crap, but you wait until you see me in action.'

Ken offered his pack of cigarettes and the two men lit up.

'Do you think he's giving it to her?' Fennel asked abruptly. When not on his discomforts, his mind kept returning to Gaye.

'Who's giving what to whom?' Ken asked blandly.

Fennel hesitated, then shrugged. 'Forget it!'

An hour later, they again contacted Garry and again reported progress, then they left the mountain track and entered the jungle. Although it was steamy hot, the relief of constant shade helped them to quicken their pace.

Themba led the way with Ken and Fennel following. A narrow track through the dense undergrowth forced them to walk in single file. Overhead, Vervet monkeys swung from tree to tree, watching them. A big sable buck that was standing in the middle of the track as they rounded a high shrub went crashing away into the jungle, startling Fennel.

They had to keep a watch-out for shrubs with long, sharp thorns, and they all concentrated on the ground ahead of them. None of them suspected that they were being watched. High on a branch of a tree sat a giant Zulu, wearing only a leopard skin. In his right hand, he held a two-way radio. He waited until the three men had passed, then spoke rapidly into the mouthpiece of the radio, his message being picked up by Miah, Kahlenberg's secretary, who had been detailed to keep in touch with the twenty watching Zulus positioned to report the movements of strangers on the estate.

From the moment the three men entered the jungle, they were never out of sight from the watchful eyes of the Zulus, hidden in the undergrowth or concealed in the tree tops.

Miah took down the Zulus' reports in rapid shorthand, passed them to Ho-Lu, who rapidly transcribed them on a typewriter and then had them sent immediately to Kahlenberg.

Kahlenberg was enjoying this. The drama of the Land Rover had been observed and reported to him, and now he knew these three men were actually on his estate.

He turned to Tak.

'The Bantu is expendable,' he said. 'Give the order that, if the occasion presents itself, he is to be got rid of. As he seems to be acting as a guide, it is unlikely the others will be able to find their way out without him.'

Tak picked up a two-way radio and spoke softly into it.

While he was speaking, Ken called a brief rest as they reached a clearing in the jungle. The three men sat down in the shade and all took a drink of water.

Ken talked to Themba for a few minutes. Themba pointed. Ahead of them was a narrow track that led into dense undergrowth.

'That's the track that leads directly to Kahlenberg's place,' Ken explained to Fennel. 'We can't miss it. We'll leave Themba here, and we'll go on. If we come unstuck, I don't want him involved. When we have done the job, we'll pick him up here and he'll guide us out. Okay?'

'You're sure we can find our way without him?'

'We follow the track. It leads directly to the house.'

'Well, okay.' Fennel looked at his watch. 'How long will it take to get to the house?'

'About two hours. We'll go now. We'll get near enough to the house before dark.'

Fennel grunted and got to his feet.

Ken talked again to Themba, who grinned, nodding his head.

'We'll take some food with us. I've got a water bottle,' Ken said, turning to Fennel. 'You'll have to carry your kit again.'

'Okay, okay, I'm not a cripple.'

Themba put some canned food into Ken's rucksack.

'We'll leave our other stuff here,' Ken went on, shouldering the rucksack, 'and the rifle.' He shook hands with Themba. Speaking in Afrikaans, he said, 'We'll be back the day after tomorrow night. If we are not back in four days, go home.'

Fennel came up to Themba. He looked slightly embarrassed as he pointed to his bag of tools, then, grinning sheepishly, he offered his hand. Themba was delighted and, grinning widely, he gripped the offered hand.

As he fell into step beside Ken, Fennel said, 'I was wrong about him . . . he's a good man.'

'We all make mistakes.' Ken looked at Fennel with a sly grin. 'I seemed to have been wrong about you.'

Themba watched them walk into the jungle and disappear. He set about collecting sticks for the fire he would light at dusk. He liked being on his own and was always at home in the jungle. He was slightly curious why the two white men had gone off on their own, but decided it was no business of his. He was being well paid for acting as a guide, and already Ken had given him enough money to enable him to buy a small car when he returned to Durban where he rented a bungalow in which his wife and son lived. He didn't see much of them as he was constantly on various game reserves in the district, but every other week-end, he would come home . . . something he always looked forward to.

He made a neat pile of sticks near the tree where the equipment was stacked, then moved into the jungle to find a few dead branches to give guts to the fire.

Suddenly he paused to listen. Something had moved not far from him. His keen ears had distinctly heard the rustle of leaves. A baboon? he wondered. He stood motionless, looking in the direction of the sound.

Out of a thicket behind him rose a Zulu, wearing a leopard skin across his broad muscular shoulders. The sun glittered on the broad blade of his assegai. For a brief moment, he balanced the heavy stabbing spear in his huge black hand, then threw it with unerring aim and with tremendous force at Themba's unprotected back.

High in the evening sky, six vultures began to circle patiently.

CHAPTER SEVEN

'THERE IT IS on your right,' Garry said suddenly.

Gaye peered through the helicopter's window. They were flying over dense jungle and, as Garry banked, the jungle abruptly terminated and she could see acres of rich green lawns, green cement paths and vast beds of flowers that would have done credit to a botanical garden. Beyond the lawns she saw the one storey house which was built in a slight curve and, from this height, seemed to her to be at least seventy metres long. Behind the house, some two hundred metres away were numerous small bungalows with thatched roofs and white painted walls in which she supposed the staff lived.

'It's enormous!' she exclaimed. 'What an extraordinary shape! Imagine walking from one end to the other several times a day.'

'Perhaps they use skates,' Garry said. 'It's certainly big.' He circled the house again. They could see a swimming-pool, terraces, sun umbrellas and lounging chairs. 'We'd better get down. Are you nervous?'

She shook her head, smiling.

'Not a bit . . . excited. I wonder if we'll get in.'

'You've got to get us in,' Garry said.

He spotted the airfield and a hangar. As he came lower, he saw three Zulus in white drill, staring up at the helicopter.

He landed not far from them and, as he slid back the door, he saw a jeep coming along the road from the house, driven by a Zulu with a white man in a grey city-suit sitting at his side.

'Here comes the welcoming committee,' he said, and dropped to the ground.

Gaye handed him down the Rolleiflex camera and her camera bag, and then joined him on the runway as the jeep pulled up.

Tak got out of the jeep and came towards them. Leaving Garry, Gaye advanced to meet him.

'I am Gaye Desmond of Animal World magazine,' she said and held out her hand.

Tak regarded her, thinking she was even more lovely than her photograph. He took her hand briefly and gave her a little bow.

'I apologize for landing like this,' Gaye went on. There was something about this tall man that she instantly distrusted and disliked. 'I'm on my way to Wannock Game Reserve, and I saw this lovely house and just couldn't resist calling. If I shouldn't have, please tell me, and I will leave at once.'

'Not at all, Miss Desmond,' Tak said silkily. 'We seldom have such a beautiful visitor. Now you are here, I hope you will stay to lunch.'

'How nice of you! We would love to, Mr. . . .' She looked inquiringly at him.

'Guilio Tak.'

She turned to Garry, who joined them.

'Mr. Tak, this is Garry Edwards, my pilot.'

Again Tak bowed.

'Mr. Tak has kindly invited us to lunch.'

Garry shook hands with Tak. He too didn't like the look of him.

Gaye went on, 'The house is marvellous and so isolated! I couldn't believe my eyes when I saw it. Have you had it long, Mr. Tak?'

'This is not my residence, Miss Desmond. It belongs to Mr. Max Kahlenberg.'

Gaye stared at him, her eyes widening.

'You mean the millionaire? *The* Mr. Max Kahlenberg?'

The expression in his black eyes was slightly sardonic as Tak said, 'That is correct.'

'But I have heard he is a recluse!' Gaye said. Watching her, Garry thought she was putting over the act well. 'We'd better go. We mustn't disturb him.'

'You won't do that. Mr. Kahlenberg is not a recluse. I am sure he will be pleased to meet you.'

'Would it be possible to photograph the house. I also freelance for *Life*. It would be a marvellous scoop for me.'

'That you must ask Mr. Kahlenberg. But don't let us stand here in the sun.' Tak moved to the jeep. 'I will take you to the house.'

Gaye and Garry got in the back seat and Tak beside the driver. The Zulu turned the jeep and sped back down the road.

A few minutes later, Gaye and Garry were being ushered into a huge lounge which led through wide french windows to a flower laden terrace with a big swimming-pool. The luxury of the room stunned Garry, who had never seen anything to compare with it, and even impressed Gaye, who had been in many luxurious homes in her time.

'If you would wait here, I will tell Mr. Kahlenberg of your arrival.'

A Zulu in white drill came in silently.

'Have a drink please while you are waiting,' Tak continued and then went away.

The Zulu went behind the bar and stood waiting.

They asked for two gins and tonics and then moved out on to the terrace.

'I don't like the look of that guy,' Garry said in a low whisper. 'There's something about him . . .'

'Yes. He gives me the creeps. He looks as if he sleeps in a coffin.'

'Don't you think we got in very easily?' Garry went on, pulling up a basket chair for Gaye and then sitting down himself.

'It's my charm.' Gaye smiled. 'I'm irresistible to spooks. The chances are we will be thrown out as soon as Mr. K. hears we have arrived. Tak must be his major-domo or secretary, I suppose.'

The Zulu brought the drinks with two plates of delicious looking canapés and silently withdrew.

'What a gorgeous way to live!' Gaye sighed. 'I adore this place. Wouldn't you love to own it?'

Garry sipped his drink, then shook his head.

'Not for me. I like something a bit more rugged. This is too lush.'

'Oh, no!' She helped herself to a cracker covered with caviar. 'I think it is marvellous.'

They had eaten most of the canapés and had finished their drinks before Tak appeared again.

'Mr. Kahlenberg is happy to have you here, Miss Desmond,' he said. 'Unfortunately, he is tied up with a series of long distance calls and other business and won't be free to meet you until tonight. Is it possible for you to stay?'

'You mean . . . stay the night?' Gaye asked, looking up at the pale face.

'Certainly. That is what Mr. Kahlenberg suggests.'

'But I have no clothes with me.'

'That is no problem. We have a number of women secretaries here. One of them will gladly lend you something.'

'How nice! Did you ask him if I could take photographs?'

Tak shook his head.

'I thought it would come better if the request came from you, Miss Desmond.'

'Well, then, we will stay the night. It is very kind of Mr. Kahlenberg.'

'It will be his pleasure.' Tak glanced at his watch. 'Lunch will be served in an hour. Perhaps you would care to change?'

As they got to their feet, Tak turned to Garry.

'You too, of course, have no clothes with you, Mr. Edwards?'

'Only what I've got on.'

'That can be arranged.' Tak turned as Miah came out on to the terrace. 'This is Miss Das. She will take care of you both. If you will excuse me now,' and with a stiff little bow, Tak left them.

Miah came forward.

'Please follow me.'

She led them across the lounge into a wide corridor that stretched away into the far distance. What looked like an electric golf cart stood nearby and she slid under the driving wheel while the other two took the rear seats.

'This corridor is so long,' she said, turning to smile at them, 'we have to use this to save our legs.'

'I was wondering how you managed,' Gaye returned. 'When I saw the house from the air, I thought of the tremendous amount of walking it must make.'

Silently, the trolley took them quickly past many closed doors until they reached the far end.

'This is the guest wing,' Miah said, stopping the car. She walked to a door and opened it. 'Please come in.'

They entered a long narrow luxuriously furnished room which led on to a small terrace, also with a swimming-pool and a bar.

'You will find everything you want here,' Miah said. 'Your lunch will be served on the terrace at 13.00 hrs. This is your bedroom, Miss Desmond.' She crossed the room and opened a door. 'I will send a maid to help you dress. I thought it would be the easiest thing for you to wear one of my saris. Would that be all right?'

'It would be perfect.' Gaye stood in the doorway looking into the bedroom. It was a delightful room, decorated in pale-blue with a king's size bed, closets, a big dressing-table on which stood a variety of face creams, lotions, perfumes and a make-up kit in a flat, silver box. Moving around the room, Gaye saw on the opposite wall, facing the bed a huge mirror which made the room seem to be twice its size. The bathroom was equipped with every luxury, including a sun lamp, a cabinet equipped with nozzles from which hot air could be released thus saving the fatigue of drying oneself on a towel, and a vibro-massage machine.

While Gaye was exclaiming over the room, Garry was moving around the sitting-room, making a careful examination of the doors and windows.

Miah came to show him his bedroom and bathroom, both of them as luxurious as Gaye's.

A tall Zulu maid came in carrying the sari. Gaye said she didn't need her help and could manage on her own. A Zulu manservant brought Garry a pair of white slacks, heelless slippers and a white shirt.

'Mr. Kahlenberg is quite informal,' Miah said. 'Dinner tonight will be on the main terrace. Please make yourselves at home. If you wish to swim, there are swim suits in the changing-room. Do explore the garden. If there is anything you wish for, please use the telephone.' With a nod of her head and a smile, she left the room.

Gaye and Garry looked at each other and Garry whistled.

'Talk about living it up . . .'

There came a tap on the door and a Zulu came in with their rucksacks. These he set on the floor and withdrew.

Garry went quickly to his rucksack and satisfied himself the two-way radio hadn't been removed. He looked at Gaye.

'I wonder if they spotted this?'

'It doesn't matter if they did, does it?' Gaye's mind was occupied with the luxury surrounding her. Her eyes shining, she went on, 'Isn't it really marvellous! I'm taking a bath. See you later.' Picking up her rucksack, she went into her bedroom and shut the door.

She quickly undressed. Naked, she stood for a moment admiring herself in the big mirror, then she went into the bathroom and turned on the bath taps. Again while waiting for the bath to fill, she regarded herself in the mirror, striking poses and laughing happily to herself.

What she didn't realize was that both the big mirrors were two-way: anyone behind the mirrors could see her as if the mirrors were plain glass, whereas from the front she imagined the mirrors were genuine and not trick ones.

His affairs forgotten, his desk neglected, Kahlenberg sat in his wheelchair in a narrow passage which was air conditioned and took his fill of Gaye's naked beauty.

From the edge of the jungle, Fennel watched the helicopter land. He and Ken had found a vantage point on a big balancing rock, formed by soil erosion, surrounded by trees and bushes, yet giving them an excellent view of Kahlenberg's house, garden and airfield far below them.

Fennel had powerful field glasses to his eyes. He saw Tak arrive in the jeep and Gaye meet him. He watched Gaye and Garry get into the jeep and drive to the house. He saw them enter and the front door close.

'Good for them! They're in!' he said, lowering the glasses.

'That was pretty easy, wasn't it?' Ken asked, puzzled. 'From what I hear of Kahlenberg, he doesn't welcome strangers.'

'Shalik said he was a sucker for a glamour puss. Looks like Shalik knew what he was talking about.'

'Yes . . . but I didn't think it would be that easy.' Ken picked up the two-way radio. 'I'll keep this switched on. Garry may be coming through any time now.'

Fennel lit a cigarette and stretched out on the rock. He was feeling tired after the long walk, carrying his tool bag. He dozed while Ken kept watch. After some little time, Fennel sat up, lit a cigarette, yawned, then asked, 'When you've got the money, what are you going to do with it?'

'A pal of mine in Jo'burg is starting a travel agency,' Ken told him. 'He needs more capital. I'm going into partnership with him.'

'Travel agency? Is that so hot?'

'It's good. We plan a de luxe service. Personally conducted tours around the game reserves. That's where I'll score. There's a lot of money in it. The Americans are heavy spenders if you give them real personal service. I've been dealing with them for some years. I know what they want, and I plan to give it to them.'

Fennel grunted.

'Sounds like hard work to me. I don't believe in work. Only suckers work.'

'So what are you going to do with your share?'

'Spend it . . . that's what money is for. I've got no time for the punks who save their money. What happens? They kick off and some other punk gets it.'

'Maybe that's what they want.'

'To hell with that! There's always money around. When I've spent what I get from Shalik, I'll do another little job. I've got plenty of contacts. They know I'm good so I'm never short of a job.'

Ken held up his hand, cutting him short. He had heard a crackle on the two-way radio and he put the set to his ear.

'Ken . . . hi, Garry . . . hearing you loud and clear . . . over.' He listened for some moments while Fennel watched him intently. 'Roger. Good luck. Out,' and he switched off.

'Well?'

'They're staying the night,' Ken told him. 'Kahlenberg seems pleased they dropped in. I must say that surprises me. Anyway, they are meeting him at 21.00 hrs. Garry says he'll call back at 23.00 hrs., and for us to stand by.'

Fennel grunted. He looked at his watch. It was just after midday.

'You mean we stay on this goddam rock for twelve hours?'

'I guess so. We don't want to walk into any of the guards. I reckon it is safe up here. Let's eat.' He brought out the inevitable can of beans.

'Goddam it! Isn't there anything else to eat except beans?'

'Steak pie . . . want that?'

'That's better than beans.' Fennel brooded as Ken searched in the rucksack for the can. 'I bet those two are doing themselves well.' His mind dwelt on Gaye and a vicious spurt of rage ran through him. Get this job over, he told himself, and then you fix her and you fix her good.

'What's bitten you?' Ken asked seeing the savage expression on Fennel's face.

'Nothing . . . how much longer are you going to take to open that can?'

'I wish I knew we weren't going to be disturbed,' Garry said.

Gaye and he were sitting on the terrace after an excellent lunch served by two Zulu waiters.

Gaye was stretched out on a reclining chair, a cigarette between her fingers. Garry thought she looked lovely in the red and gold sari. It was the type of costume that suited her, and which he admired.

'Why?' Gaye asked, looking at him.

'Obvious reasons,' Garry returned with a grin. 'I would take you into the bedroom.'

She laughed.

'Then I too wish we knew we weren't going to be disturbed.'

'Could be embarrassing if Mr. Tak arrived on the scene.'

'It could. So instead, we had better do some work.' She sat up, crushing out her cigarette. 'Have you thought about how Fennel is to get in?'

'Through here.' Garry waved his hand to the big lounge. 'With us here, he has only to walk in.'

'Would it be as easy as that?'

'I think so. There could be guards patrolling the house at night. I don't see any of them around now.'

'Perhaps Kahlenberg is so sure no one could get through the jungle, the house isn't guarded.'

'Want to take a look at the garden?'

'Not now. It will be terribly hot out there.'

'Then you take a nap . . . I'm going.' Garry got to his feet.

'You have more energy than I have. You'll be roasted.'

'See you,' and with a wave of his hand, Garry wandered off down the green cement path.

She watched him go, then she closed her eyes and thought about him. When the job was done, they would all separate. She wondered what he would do. She would have liked to have had a long week-end with him in Paris, and then say goodbye. She was twenty-six years of age, and she was sure Shalik would continue to make use of her for at least five more years before he began to look around for a younger woman. She had no illusions about Shalik. In those five years she would have made and saved enough money to give her complete independence and that was what she wanted more than anything else. To be financially free to live well, to travel and possibly to get married.

She considered the possibility of marrying Garry, but decided it wouldn't work out. Although he attracted her physically, she knew she wasn't in love with him and also he hadn't her need for gracious living. Luxury was essential to her whereas it wasn't to him. No . . . he was a good bed companion, but nothing else. If she were to marry, she must find a man who was wealthy, intelligent, cultured and luxury loving. She knew this was a pipe dream for she had met many men in her life, had many proposals of marriage, but there was always some snag, or was it that she valued her freedom too much?

Anyway, pipe dreams were pleasant when lying in a comfortable chair in the shade, surrounded by luxury.

She dozed off, and it was more than an hour later that Garry, returning, awakened her.

'Want a drink, lazybones?' he asked, moving to the bar.

She nodded, stretched and sat up.

'Find anything interesting?'

'Yes and no. There's no access to the far end of the house. Garry brought over two Tom Collins and sat down. 'The path leading to it is guarded by a Zulu who looks as if he's stepped right out of a movie. He was wearing a leopard skin, ostrich plumes and carried a shield and an assegai. He turned me back without trying to be polite.'

'Kahlenberg's quarters, I suppose.'

'Yes. Another thing: there's a big pool full of enormous crocodiles at the far end of the garden and sitting on surrounding
trees are about ten well fed looking vultures. That corner of the
garden gave me the creeps.

Gaye laughed. 'But why?'

'Just struck me it would be a marvellous place to dispose of
a body.'

She looked at him and seeing he was serious, she asked, 'Why
should Kahlenberg want to dispose of a body?'

Garry sipped his drink, then cradling the glass in his hand,
shaking it slightly so the ice cubes tinkled, he shrugged.

'The atmosphere of the place made me think of it, but I'm
uneasy about all this, Gaye. I think we were invited in too easily.
I don't like the look of Tak. Once or twice while you were talking
to him, I got the idea he was laughing at you. Particularly when
you asked if this place was his. It struck me he knew you knew
it belonged to Kahlenberg.'

'Do you think he suspects us?'

'I think he could.'

'You don't think he guesses we are after the ring?'

'I don't know, but I'm pretty sure he thinks we are phonies.'

'So what do we do?'

As if in answer to this question, Garry saw Tak coming along
the path towards them.

'Here he is now,' he said, getting to his feet.

'Please don't let me disturb you,' Tak said approaching. There
was a thin smile on his lips and his glittering eyes moved from
Garry to Gaye. 'Did you enjoy your lunch?'

'It was wonderful, thank you.' Gaye gave him her most charming smile. 'It really is lovely here.'

'Yes . . . it is very pleasant.' He paused, then went on, 'Miss
Desmond, would you be interested to see Mr. Kahlenberg's
museum?'

Although her heart skipped a beat, Gaye kept her face mildly
interested.

'Has Mr. Kahlenberg a museum?'

'Mr. Kahlenberg is one of the most famous collectors in the
world.'

'I knew that, but I didn't know he had a museum. I thought . . .'

'He has a museum, and he wondered if it would interest you
to see it.'

'Very much. I would love to see it.'

'And you, Mr. Edwards?'

'Sure . . . thanks.' Garry kept his expression dead-pan, but like Gaye, he had been startled.

Gaye got to her feet. 'Is it far from here?'

Again Garry caught a jeering expression come into the dark eyes. It came and went so quickly unless he had been watching closely he wouldn't have seen it.

'You are standing on it,' Tak said.

'You mean it is underground?'

'That is correct.'

'May I bring my camera, Mr. Tak?'

He shook his head.

'I regret not.' He turned. 'Will you follow me, please?'

He entered the lounge and walked into the corridor.

Gaye and Garry exchanged swift glances as they followed him. They all got into the electric trolley and Tak drove down the long corridor, past the big lobby and front door of the house and on down the corridor.

'Here is where Mr. Kahlenberg has his quarters,' he explained as they drove past several doors. He stopped the trolley by what appeared to be a blank wall and got out. Watching him closely, Garry saw him put his fingers under the ledge of one of the big windows. The wall he was facing slid back to reveal double doors. As he approached these doors, they slid open.

'Mr. Kahlenberg is a cripple,' Tak explained, regarding Gaye. 'All doors in his quarters are electronically controlled. This is the elevator that takes us down to the museum.'

The three entered the green satin lined cage. There were four different coloured buttons on the control panel. Garry watched Tak press the green button and the elevator descended smoothly and silently. While it descended, Tak pressed the red button, paused, then pressed the yellow button.

'What are all those buttons for, Mr. Tak?' Gaye asked innocently.

'The green button controls the elevator. The yellow button turns on the lights in the museum and the red button turns off the alarm,' Tak told her.

'Thank you . . . you're marvellously well equipped.'

The doors slid back and they entered a cool, vaulted chamber.

'Would you wait here for a moment?' Tak said and he crossed to a grey painted door. He spent a minute or so at the door, his hands busy, his body concealing what he was doing.

Again Garry looked at Gaye, lifted his eyebrows, then looked away as Tak turned.

'The museum contains many priceless treasures,' he said. 'We have taken every precaution against theft. This door that leads into the museum is armour plated and specially treated to make it impossible to cut into. The walls either side are five feet thick. The lock to the door is controlled by a time switch which is set every night at 22.00 hrs. and no one can open the door until 10.00 hrs. the following day. Please come in.'

They followed him into a vast domed ceiling room, lit by diffused lighting. On the walls hung many pictures. Gaye recognized a Rembrandt, several Picassos and a number of Renaissance masterpieces which she was sure she had seen in the Uffizi, the Vatican museum and the Louvre.

'These aren't the originals, Mr. Tak?' she asked.

'Of course they are the originals.' Tak frowned as if annoyed by such a question. 'I told you Mr. Kahlenberg has the finest private museum in the world. The inner room will amuse you more I think.' He led the way through the picture gallery and entered another vast room. In the middle of the room stood a four metre high Buddha in shining gold.

'This is an interesting piece,' Tak went on. 'It comes from Bangkok. During the last war, the Japanese, knowing it was in the City, searched for it, but the priests were too clever for them. They moved it to a lesser temple and covered it with dirty cement. Although the Japanese visited this temple they failed to recognize what they were looking for.'

'You mean this is solid gold?' Garry said, gaping at the glittering figure.

'Yes, it is solid gold.'

He led them around the room, pausing to explain various objets d'art. Garry had no knowledge of art treasures, but even he was impressed by what he saw.

'But surely that is one of the panels of Ghiberti's Gates to Paradise,' Gaye said, pausing before a beautifully carved panel on the wall. 'What a wonderful copy!'

'The copy is in Florence, Miss Desmond. This is the original,' Tak said, an acid note in his voice. 'And this statue of David by Bernini is also the original. The copy is in the Bargello in Florence.'

Gaye was so startled by the effrontery of this remark, that she turned away. It was then she caught sight of the Caesar Borgia ring in a small glass box on a pedestal in the lighted alcove. 'And what is this?' she asked, moving to the glass box and peering at the ring.

'The Caesar Borgia ring,' Tak said. 'It was made by an unknown goldsmith at Borgia's request. It is a poison ring and so the story goes, the goldsmith was its first victim. To test its efficiency and to stop the man from talking, Borgia gave him his fatal handshake while wearing the ring. There is a needle hidden in the cluster of diamonds and this scratched the victim's hand while he was shaking hands with Borgia. Ingenious, don't you think?'

'Those were cruel, horrible times,' Gaye said with a little grimace. 'Is it dangerous now?'

'Oh no, Miss Desmond. It would have to be recharged with poison before it could be dangerous, and I doubt if the needle is now sharp enough to scratch.'

He led them on, showing them a beautiful alabaster unguent jar which he told them came from the tomb of Tutankhamen. They spent a further half-hour in the museum and then Tak, looking at his watch, suggested they might like a drink before dinner. He led them from the museum, closed the door and Garry watched him spin the dial, scrambling the combination, then they took the elevator up to the corridor. He drove them back to their suite and after accepting their thanks, said a servant would conduct them to the main terrace in an hour and a half and left them.

The time now was 19.30 hrs. and they both went out on to the terrace.

'I want something short and strong,' Gaye said sitting down. 'A vodka martini on the rocks.'

'I'll dig for that too.' Garry began to mix the drink. He filled two cocktail glasses and carried them over to the table and sat down. 'Did you spot the TV snoopers in both rooms?'

'No . . . did you?'

'Yes. Fennel said there were six monitors and therefore six rooms in the museum. Tak only showed us two of the rooms. You know, Gaye I'm liking this less and less. I have an idea we could have walked into a trap.'

Gaye looked startled.

'Surely not! He wouldn't have shown us what he did if he is really suspicious of us.'

'That's what puzzles me. He must realize we have guessed most of those exhibits have been stolen. Then why did he let us see them? Why did he tell us how the elevator works and about the time lock? He must know we will talk about this visit when we leave unless . . .' He paused, frowning, then shook his head.

'Unless . . . what?'

'Unless he's not going to let us leave.'

Gaye stiffened.

'He can't keep us forever, Garry, do talk sense.'

Garry sipped his drink.

'All right, but I don't like it. If Fennel and Ken weren't out there, I'd be worried. I'm going to talk to them.' He got up and went into his bedroom.

Gaye waited. She was also puzzled that Tak had taken them into the museum, but she wasn't worried. She told herself that Kahlenberg was so confident about his safety precautions, he didn't mind strangers seeing his museum.

Garry returned after some twenty minutes.

'Fennel agrees it looks suspicious. Themba has been left guarding the equipment. Fennel is coming here on his own, leaving Ken to keep watch. If Kahlenberg starts trouble, at least Ken can do something to help us. When we get the ring, we'll signal Ken and we'll all meet at the airfield and take off. We'll pick up Themba and get back to Mainville.'

'Do you think Kahlenberg will start trouble?'

'I'll tell you when I've met him,' Garry returned. 'How about another drink?'

At exactly 21.00 hrs., a Zulu servant came to take them to the main terrace.

Seated in his chair, Kahlenberg was waiting for them. He greeted them pleasantly and waved them to chairs near him.

'Tak tells me you are from *Animal World,* Miss Desmond,' he said, after Gaye had thanked him for receiving them. 'Have you been with them long?'

'Not very . . . six months.'

'It is a magazine I take regularly. I am interested in animals. Why don't they give you a credit line, Miss Desmond?'

Watching, Garry was relieved to see Gaye was cool and seemed quite at ease. She laughed a little ruefully.

'I am one of the small fry, Mr. Kahlenberg. I do the routine work. I was hoping you would allow me to photograph this lovely house. I would get a credit for that.'

He studied her. 'I am afraid then you will have to wait a little longer for your credit. Photography is forbidden here.'

She met his blue-grey eyes, smiling.

'Even to me? I promise I will be most discreet and photograph only the house and the garden.'

'I am sorry.' He changed the subject by asking if she found his museum interesting.

'It is magnificent. I congratulate you.'

Three Zulus came silently on to the terrace and stood waiting before a beautifully laid table. At the same time, Hindenburg who had just finished his dinner, came slowly across the terrace to Kahlenberg.

'What a beauty!' Gaye exclaimed. 'May I stroke him?'

'It would be unwise,' Kahlenberg said, rubbing the cheetah's ear. 'My pet is a little uncertain with strangers . . . even beautiful strangers, Miss Desmond.' He set his chair in motion and drove up to the table. 'Let us have dinner.'

When they were seated, Kahlenberg turned to Garry.

'And you, Mr. Edwards, have you been a professional pilot for long?'

Garry shook his head.

'Just started,' he said easily. 'Miss Desmond is my first client. Of course I've done a lot of chopper flying in the States, but I like a change, so I've set up business in Durban.'

'I see.'

Ice melons were served.

'You are after big game, Miss Desmond?'

'Yes. We were on our way to Wannock Game Reserve when I saw this wonderful house and I felt I had to see more of it. I do hope you don't think I was presumptuous.'

'Not at all. If I didn't wish you to be here, Tak would have sent you away. No, it is a pleasure to have such unexpected guests.'

'You are certainly out in the wilds . . . don't you find it lonely?' she asked.

'When one is as busy as I am, one hasn't time to feel lonely. It surprises me that you are a photographer.' Kahlenberg looked directly at her. 'I should have thought by the way you walk and by your appearance that you would have been a model.'

'I have done modelling, but I find photography more interesting.'

'I too am interested in photography in an amateurish sort of way. I suppose you work entirely in colour?'

Gaye who had only the haziest knowledge of photography, realized they were getting on to dangerous ground.

'Yes, I work in colour.'

'Tell me, Miss Desmond . . .' Kahlenberg began when the second course of blue trout was served.

Gaye immediately began to enthuse about the fish, hoping to change the subject. 'It's my favourite fish,' she told him.

'How fortunate, but I was . . .'

Garry too had seen the red light and he tried to steer the conversation into another channel.

'Mr. Kahlenberg, I took a walk in your wonderful garden and came across a Zulu in full war dress . . . at least, I think it is war dress from what I've seen on the movies . . . a magnificent specimen.'

'Yes. I have over a hundred of these men,' Kahlenberg said. 'I like them to dress in their traditional costume. They are great hunters of beasts . . . and of men. They are the guardians of my estate. No one approaches here without being seen and turned back. They patrol the surrounding jungle day and night in shifts.'

'Not the garden?' Garry asked casually as he could as he removed the back bone of the fish.

There was such a long pause that he glanced up to find Kahlenberg's eyes on him. The amused contempt in those eyes made Garry look quickly down at his fish.

'No, Mr. Edwards, they don't patrol the garden at night, but I have a few of them in the garden during the day when there are strangers here.'

'Well, they are certainly impressive,' Garry said, laying down his knife and fork. 'That was excellent.'

'Yes.' Kahlenberg absently reached out his hand and began to stroke Hindenberg's rough fur. The cheetah began to purr.

'What a marvellous sound,' Gaye exclaimed. 'Have you had him long?'

'A little over three years. We are inseparable.' Kahlenberg looked over at Garry. 'He is a magnificent watch-dog or I suppose I should say watch-cat. I had good proof of this a few months ago. One of my servants went mad and tried to attack me. He came into my office with a knife, but before he could even reach me, Hindenberg had literally torn him to pieces. The cheetah is the fastest moving animal on earth. Did you know that, Mr. Edwards?'

Garry eyed the cheetah and shook his head.

'He looks as if he could give a good account of himself.'

'He can.'

One of the waiters presented the main course which was a chicken browned in a casserole, the rib cage removed and the bird stuffed with diced lobster in a cream sauce, coloured by the coral of the lobster.

'Ah! This is something out of the ordinary,' Kahlenberg said. 'I got the recipe from one of the great Paris chefs. I think you will find it excellent.'

While the waiter was carving the chicken, Kahlenberg chatted agreeably, but both Gaye and Garry could see his mind was only half with them. He was obviously occupied with some business problem and wasn't giving them his entire attention.

The chicken was excellent as Kahlenberg had said it would be, and both of them expressed their appreciation.

Although the food was delicious, Gaye was relieved when the meal was over. She found she had to work hard to hold Kahlenberg's interest. She was used to mixing with difficult people, but she mentally decided Kahlenberg was the stickiest host she had ever met. He was polite, but distant and she knew she had only half his attention. But she kept the conversation going, avoiding dangerous topics, asked questions about himself, discussed New York, Paris and London with him while Garry kept more or less silent, admiring her persistence.

As they were drinking coffee, Tak came out on to the terrace. He went up to Kahlenberg.

'Excuse me, sir, Mr. Vorster is on the telephone.'

Kahlenberg frowned.

'Oh, yes, I had forgotten. Tell him I will call back in five minutes.'

Tak bowed and went away.

'I must apologize, Miss Desmond, but I regret I will now have to leave you to your own devices. I have work to do. I doubt if we will meet again before you leave. I am sorry about the photographs. I hope you enjoyed your dinner.'

They got to their feet and both thanked him for his hospitality. He looked at them with an odd expression in his eyes, nodded, then set his chair in motion and drove off the terrace, followed by Hindenburg.

Reaching his office, he found Tak waiting for him.

'Thank you, Tak, those two were beginning to bore me. Lovely looking woman, of course, but a play thing.' He manoeuvred himself behind his desk. 'They are being watched?'

'Yes, sir.'

'Good. And the other three?'

'The guide no longer exists. Fennel and Jones are on the balancing rock watching through field glasses. They have been in contact with Edwards by two-way radio. Their conversation was intercepted. Fennel is coming here on his own, leaving Jones where he is. Edwards thinks we suspect him and is taking precautions.'

'Very wise of him. All right, Tak, you can go to your bungalow. I have some work to do, but intend to retire at my usual time. The rest of the staff can go.'

Tak hesitated.

'Is it wise, sir?'

'The guards will be here and Hindenburg. Yes, it is all right.' Kahlenberg looked thoughtfully at Tak. 'It is much wiser that you don't have anything to do with this little affair. Good night.'

'Good night, sir,' and Tak went away.

Kahlenberg settled down to read a mass of papers that had come by the afternoon air delivery.

A little after half past ten, there came a soft tap on the door. Frowning, he called, 'Come in.'

Kemosa entered.

'What is it?'

'Zwide, one of the gardeners, master, is dead.'

Kahlenberg raised his eyebrows.

'Dead? How did it happen? An accident?'

'I do not know, master. He complained of a headache and pains in his muscles. As he is always complaining, no one took any notice. Later he said his throat was on fire. A few minutes later, he fell down and died.'

'Extraordinary thing. Well, bury him, Kemosa. I dare say his wife will be pleased. He is no loss.'

Kemosa eyed his master, then bowed.

'I will have it done, master,' and he went out, closing the door softly behind him.

Kahlenberg sat back in his chair. A little smile that gave him a devilish expression lit up his face.

So the Borgia ring was lethal.

CHAPTER EIGHT

WHEN GAYE AND GARRY returned to their suite, they found all the windows and the doors leading to the terrace closed and the air conditioner in operation.

Garry went immediately to the terrace doors and tried to open them, but they were securely locked and the key had been removed. When he tried to open one of the windows, he found it immovable.

'Battened down for the night,' he said, scratching his head. 'Now, how the hell is Fennel going to get in?'

'I thought you were being over optimistic. Is it likely they would leave all this open at night?' Gaye asked, sitting on the arm of a lounging chair. 'What are you going to do?'

'Alert Fennel. It's his job to get in. Maybe he can cope with this lock.' Garry looked at his watch. The time was 22.00 hrs. He sat down and looked across at Gaye. 'We have an hour to wait. What did you think of Kahlenberg?'

Gaye grimaced.

'I didn't like him. I think he was bored with me and a man who finds me boring can't expect to be my favourite person.' She laughed. 'What did you think of him?'

'He's dangerous,' Garry said soberly. 'I'll go further than that. I get the feeling, watching him, he isn't quite sane. I still have the idea we have walked into a trap. But as we're here, we'd be nuts not to have a go at the ring. I wonder if he was lying when he said the grounds weren't patrolled at night. I'll have to warn Fennel to be careful as he comes.'

'You don't think he's sane . . . what do you mean?'

'There's something about his eyes . . . I'm not saying he is mad, but off balance.'

'I'm sure you're imagining all this, Garry. I can't believe he could have let us see the museum if he really suspected us. I think he is soured by being a cripple, and if he was distant, then it was probably due to that . . . for all you know, he may be in pain.'

'You could be right,' Garry shrugged. 'But the whole set-up seems to me too easy.'

'Are you going to check on the elevator?'

'Of course. If it isn't working, I don't see how we can get at the door of the museum. I'll wait half an hour, then I'll go out and see.' He got up, crossed to the door and opened it. He looked down the deserted corridor. It was lighted, and in the far distance he could see the end of it terminating in double doors. 'No one about.' He returned to the lounge, closing the door. 'Could be tricky. If Tak or one of the servants come out of any of those rooms while I'm out there, I'm fixed. A fly couldn't hide out there.'

'You can always say you're walking in your sleep.'

Garry frowned at her.

'I wish you would take this more seriously. You don't seem to realize if we're caught we could be in a very nasty situation.'

'Let's worry about that if and when it happens.'

Garry suddenly grinned.

'I guess you're right. Come here and be kissed.'

She shook her head.

'Not now . . . we're working.'

He hesitated, then lighting a cigarette, he dropped into a chair.

'If we get away with this, what are you going to do with the money, Gaye?' he asked.

'Save it. I save all my money and invest it at six per cent in a Swiss bank. Soon, I'll have a nice income and then Shalik can look for another slave.'

'You don't like him?'

'Who would? He's useful, but that's all. And you, what are you going to do with your share?'

'Take a course in electronics,' Garry said promptly. 'I've always wanted to have an education, and up to now, I've never had the chance. With Shalik's money, I'll study, and then get myself a decent paying job. There are lots of opportunities in the electronics field.'

'You surprise me . . . you don't strike me as the studious type. Do you plan to get married?'

'Yes, but not until I've qualified. Then I will.'

'Got the girl lined up yet?'

He smiled at her.

'Yes, I think so.'

'Who is she?'

'No one you know . . . just a girl. We get along okay.'

'I rather thought you were going to say me.'

He laughed.

'You would have said no anyway.'

'Why are you so sure?'

'You would, wouldn't you?'

Gaye smiled at him.

'Yes. I wouldn't want to marry an electronic engineer. When I marry it will be a man who thinks big, lives big and is rich.'

'I know that. That's why I'm picking Toni.'

'Is that her name?'

Garry nodded.

'I wish you luck, Garry, and I hope you will be very happy with her.'

'Thanks. I hope you will be happy too, but don't pin too much on money.

Gaye looked thoughtful.

'Life can be pretty rough without it.'

'Yes.' He stubbed out his cigarette and stared up at the ceiling. 'One's got to have enough, of course, but all this . . .' he waved his hand around the luxuriously furnished room. 'This isn't necessary.'

'It is to me.'

'That's where we differ.' He glanced at his watch. 'I guess I'll take a look at the elevator.'

Gaye got to her feet.

'I'll come with you. If we run into anyone, we can say we felt like a walk in the garden and as we couldn't get out through the terrace way we were going to try the front door.'

'A bit thin . . . but it'll have to do. Let's go.'

They moved silently out into the long corridor, paused to listen, heard nothing and then they walked fast down the corridor, passing the front door and on towards the hidden lift. Garry went to the window ledge and felt under it. His fingers found a button which he pressed. The wall slid back. They looked at each other, then motioning her to stay where she was, he approached the lift doors which swished silently open. He entered the cage, then first pressing the red button which Tak had told him turned off the alarm, he then pressed the green button. The doors closed and then the lift descended. When it reached ground level, Garry pressed the green button again and the lift ascended. He stepped into the corridor and reclosed the sliding wall.

Taking Gaye's hand in his, he ran silently down the corridor and back to their suite.

'Well, it works,' he said, closing the door. 'Now everything depends on whether Fennel can get in and then, of course, if he can open the door to the museum.'

After waiting a quarter of an hour, Garry picked up the two-way radio.

Fennel answered immediately.

Garry explained the situation and told Fennel the elevator was working. Fennel said there were still lights showing in the windows of the two extreme wings of the house.

'The light on the right is mine,' Garry said. 'The other light is from Kahlenberg's quarters.'

'The left wing light has gone out,' Fennel reported. 'The only light now showing is where you are.'

'Kahlenberg told me the grounds aren't patrolled, Lew,' Garry said, 'but I don't trust him. Take your time and use every scrap of cover as you come. There could be some of the Zulu guards around.'

'I'll watch it. I'll start now. It'll take me a good half-hour to get to you. Ken will remain here until we signal him.'

'Roger . . . out,' and Garry switched off. Turning to Gaye, he went on, 'He's on his way now. All the other lights have gone out.' He crossed to the bedside lamps and turned them on, then he turned off the ceiling lights. Going to the window, he peered into the darkness. The big moon was partially hidden by clouds, but after a few moments, his eyes became used to the darkness and he could make out the terrace furniture and beyond the beds of flowers.

'We could be flying back to Mainville in a couple of hours,' Gaye said. 'I'm going to change.'

She went into the bedroom, took off the sari and put on her shirt and shorts. When she returned to the lounge, she found Garry had also changed. They sat on the bed, looking through the window, waiting for Fennel. The minutes dragged by. Both of them were keyed up as they sat waiting. After what seemed an age, Garry put his hand on Gaye's arm.

'He's here.' He got to his feet and went to the window.

Fennel came out of the darkness and paused at the window and nodded. He lowered his tool kit to the ground and came to the terrace doors. With the aid of a pencil flash light, he examined the lock. Looking at Garry, he jerked up his thumb, then reached for his tool kit.

In a few minutes, the terrace doors swung open. Picking up his tool kit, Fennel moved into the lounge. He ignored Gaye as if she wasn't in the room. Turning to Garry, he said, 'Been doing yourself well, huh?' He looked around the room. 'Ken and I certainly caught the crappy end of this stick, didn't we?'

'Tough,' Garry said, smiling. 'Never mind. You'll recover.'

Fennel gave him an evil look, then turned away. Seeing the mood he was in, Gaye watched him, but didn't speak.

'Where's the lift?' Fennel asked. 'This job could take me three or four hours.'

Garry turned to Gaye.

'You'd better stay here if it's going to take that long.'

She nodded.

'All right.'

'How about the TV snoopers?' Fennel asked.

'They're there in the museum, but I've no idea where the monitor-room is or if anyone keeps watch at night.'

Fennel flushed with rage. 'Your job was to find out!' he snarled.

Garry went to the door, opened it and beckoned to Fennel.

'Take a look . . . there are about thirty-five doors down that corridor. It could be behind any one of them. We can't walk in and check. Did you see any Zulus as you came through the garden?'

'No. What's that to do with it?'

'The chances are if they aren't patrolling the grounds, they don't keep watch at night on the TV monitor.'

'If they do, we're sunk.'

'There it is. Have you any ideas how we can check?'

Fennel thought, then shrugged.

'It could be anywhere . . . could be in one of the huts away from the house.' He hesitated. 'It's taking a hell of a chance.'

'We either take the chance or we leave without the ring.'

'Will you take the chance?' Fennel demanded.

'Sure, if you will.'

'Then let's go.'

They moved silently into the corridor, leaving Gaye still sitting on the bed. A few minutes later, they were descending in the lift. When they reached the vaulted chamber, Garry pointed to the TV lenses in the ceiling.

'There it is.'

Fennel moved under the lens and peered at it. Then he sucked in a deep breath.

'It's not operating.'

'Sure?'

'Yeah.'

Garry wiped his sweating hands on the seat of his shorts.

'There's the door to the museum. Do you want me to do anything?'

Fennel went to the door and examined the dial and the lock.

'No . . . just leave it to me. It's going to take time, but I can get it open.' He opened his tool kit and laid out a selection of tools on the floor. Garry went over to a high-backed leather chair and sat down. He lit a cigarette and tried to contain his impatience.

Fennel worked carefully, whistling softly under his breath. His body concealed what he was doing, and after a while, Garry got bored watching his broad back, and getting up, he began to pace up and down. He smoked one cigarette after another and continually looked at his watch. After an hour had dragged by, he paused in his pacing to ask, 'How's it coming?'

'I've neutralized the time switch,' Fennel said, sitting back on his heels and wiping his forehead with his arm. 'That's the worst part of the job behind us. Now, I've got to tackle the lock itself.'

Garry sat down and waited.

Another hour dragged by, then Fennel gave a little grunt.

'I've done it!' he exclaimed.

Garry joined him at the door.

'Quicker than you thought.'

'Just luck. I've been five hours on one of these goddamn locks before now.' He stood up and pulled the door open. 'Do you know where the ring is?'

'I'll take you to it.'

Fennel hastily repacked his tool bag and together the two men moved into the picture gallery. Going ahead, Garry entered the second room and made for the lighted alcove. Then he paused, experiencing a sense of shock. The pedestal was there, but the glass box and the ring were missing.

'What is it?' Fennel demanded.

'It's gone!' Garry licked his dry lips. 'That's where it was . . . it's gone! I thought . . .'

He stopped short as he saw Fennel, his face twitching, was staring at the wide archway through which they had come into this room from the picture gallery.

Standing in the archway, wearing only leopard skins, were four giant Zulus, each holding a broad-bladed stabbing spear, their cruel, fierce black eyes fixed on the two startled men.

One of them said in guttural English, 'You come with us.'

'What they call a fair cop,' Garry said and moved towards the Zulus. Fennel hesitated, but he knew they hadn't a chance against these four giants. Cursing softly, he picked up his tool bag and moved after Garry.

As the minutes crawled by, Gaye became more and more uneasy and restless. She prowled around the luxurious lounge wondering how Fennel was getting on. It was now nearly two hours since they had left the lounge. She kept telling herself Fennel had said it might be a four hour job. She wished now she had gone with them. This long wait was getting on her nerves.

Then she heard a gentle tap on the door. Thinking it was Garry, she hastened across the lounge and opened the door. She was confronted by a Zulu who towered above her, the overhead light making his black skin glisten and the blade of his assegai flash.

She stifled a scream and stepped hurriedly back, her hand going to her mouth. The Zulu glared at her, his eyes like wet stones.

'You come with me,' he growled and stepped aside.

'What do you want?' Gaye asked, her voice husky with shock.

'The Master wants you . . . come!'

She hesitated. So Garry had been right after all, she thought, they had walked into a trap. By now she was recovering from her shock. There was nothing else to do but to obey, and lifting her head high, she walked out into the corridor.

The Zulu pointed to the double doors at the far end of the corridor with his assegai. She knew it was useless to try to escape so she walked down the corridor, followed by the Zulu.

When she finally reached the double doors, they swung open automatically. Without looking at the Zulu, she walked into Kahlenberg's office, her heart thumping and her mouth dry.

At the far end of the vast room, Kahlenberg was sitting at his desk, a cigarette between his fingers, Hindenburg at his side.

'Ah, Miss Desmond,' he said, looking up. 'Please come and join me. I am watching something of great interest.'

As she moved around the desk, she saw the small TV set was on. Kahlenberg waved to a chair near his, away from Hindenburg who hadn't taken his eyes off her since she had entered the room.

'Sit down and look at this.'

She sat down, folding her hands in her lap and looked at the lighted screen. Her heart skipped a beat as she saw Fennel kneeling in front of the door leading to the museum.

'I believe he is actually defeating my beautiful lock,' Kahlenberg said. 'The makers assured me no one could do it.'

Fennel suddenly sat back on his heels.

'I've done it!' he exclaimed. His voice, slightly muffled, came through the speaker well enough.

Then Garry moved into the picture.

'Your friend is clever,' Kahlenberg said. Although he spoke mildly, his eyes glittered angrily. 'I didn't believe he could do it, but as you see, he has done it.'

Gaye said nothing.

'Usually, we immobilize the lift,' Kahlenberg went on, leaning back in his chair, his eyes still on the screen. 'But I was interested to see if this expert could break in. I will have to talk seriously with the makers. This won't do at all.'

They watched Fennel and Garry enter the museum. The picture changed to another angle as Kahlenberg reached forward and pressed a button on the set.

'I didn't want to alarm your friends so I didn't operate this set until they were satisfied it wasn't operating,' Kahlenberg went on. 'Now I fear they are in for a disappointment and a surprise.'

The picture showed the two men staring at the pedestal in the lighted alcove.

Gaye heard Fennel say, 'What is it?'

Leaning forward, Kahlenberg turned off the set.

'They will be here in a few minutes, Miss Desmond,' he said. He reached for a gold cigarette box and offered it. 'A cigarette?'

'Thank you.' Gaye took a cigarette and accepted a light.

'By the way, how is Mr. Shalik?'

If he had expected to startle her, he was disappointed. Her face was expressionless as she said, 'Last time I saw him, he seemed very well.'

'He continues to concoct his miserable little swindles?'

'I really don't know. He always seems to be busy, but just what he does I have no idea.'

'It is time he was stopped for good.' The flash of fire in Kahlenberg's eyes made her remember that Garry had thought this man was unbalanced. 'He is developing into a nuisance.'

'Do you think so? I should have thought he is no more of a nuisance than others,' Gaye said coolly. 'After all, Mr. Kahlenberg, surely you are birds of a feather?'

Kahlenberg's eyes narrowed slightly.

'What makes you say that, Miss Desmond?'

'Mr. Tak tells me everything in your museum is an original. I don't imagine the authorities of Florence would have sold you the Ghiberti panel or the Bernini David. I do know you stole the Borgia ring. Surely you are just as much a nuisance to the curators of various museums as Mr. Shalik is to you.'

Kahlenberg smiled.

'Yes, I admit everything in my museum has been stolen, but there is a reason. I appreciate beautiful things. I need beauty. I am too busy to visit Europe so I prefer to have my beauty here where I can see it when I have the inclination. But Shalik only plots for money, not beauty. He lives for money as I live for beauty. I intend to stop him.'

'Perhaps he needs the money,' Gaye said. 'You have more than enough. Perhaps you would be like Mr. Shalik if you had no money.'

Kahlenberg crushed out his cigarette. She could see he was controlling his temper only with an effort.

'You are a spirited woman, Miss Desmond. I am sure Mr. Shalik would be flattered to hear you defending him.'

'I am not defending him. I am just saying I see no difference between you and him,' Gaye said quietly.

At this moment the double doors swung open and Garry and Fennel walked in.

The four Zulus paused in the doorway, looking towards Kahlenberg who dismissed them with a wave of his hand. They stepped back and the doors closed.

'Come in, gentlemen and sit down,' Kahlenberg said, waving to chairs opposite his desk. 'As you see, Miss Desmond has already joined me.'

Garry went to a chair and folded himself down into it, but Fennel remained standing, glaring at Kahlenberg.

'Please sit down, Mr. Fennel,' Kahlenberg said quietly. 'Let me congratulate you. I didn't believe it was possible for anyone to open the door to my museum and yet you have done it. It is an achievement.'

'You can cut out the soft soap!' Fennel snarled. 'We came for the ring and we haven't got it so now we're getting the hell out of here and you're not stopping us!'

'Certainly you shall leave,' Kahlenberg said, 'but we have something to discuss first.'

'I'm not discussing anything with you!' Fennel snapped. He was livid with rage and disappointment. He looked at Gaye and Garry. 'Come on . . . he daren't stop us.' And he started towards the door, grabbed the handle but found the door locked. He spun around, glaring at Kahlenberg. 'Open this door or I'll break your goddamn neck!'

Kahlenberg raised his eyebrows.

'That could be dangerous for you, Mr. Fennel,' he said and made a soft clicking sound with his tongue against his teeth. Immediately, Hindenburg stood up and began to move slowly forward, his eyes on Fennel, his lips drawn off his teeth in a ferocious snarl that made Fennel back away. 'I assure you,' Kahlenberg went on, 'my pet would tear you to pieces if I give him another signal. Sit down!'

Cowed by the cheetah, Fennel sat down abruptly by Garry.

'Thank you,' Kahlenberg said, then went on, 'I don't want the effort you three have made to get the Borgia ring to be wasted. As Miss Desmond has rightly pointed out, the ring doesn't legally belong to me. Since you all have shown so much initiative in getting as far as you have, I have decided to give you the ring on certain conditions.' He opened the drawer in his desk and took out the glass box, containing the ring. He placed the box on his desk where the three could see it.

Fennel glared at the ring and then looked at Garry.

'Is that it?' and when Garry nodded, Fennel turned to Kahlenberg. 'What do you mean . . . conditions?'

Kahlenberg addressed himself to Gaye.

'Miss Desmond, although I live in considerable luxury, although I am an exceedingly busy man, there are times when I get very bored with myself. As you see, I am a cripple. I am chained to this chair. One of my ambitions when young was to be a hunter. Nothing would have given me more satisfaction than to go on safari. But being a cripple, this has been impossible and I admit to a certain frustration. Any form of frustration to a man of my power and wealth is intolerable.'

'What the hell is this?' Fennel demanded impatiently. 'What are these conditions you are talking about?'

Kahlenberg ignored him.

'Here is the Borgia ring.' He picked up the glass box and handed it to Gaye. 'I understand each of you will be paid nine thousand dollars when you hand the ring to Shalik.' He smiled bleakly. 'You see, I have an excellent spy system. Nine thousand dollars to you is important money and naturally it will give you incentive to deliver the ring to Shalik.'

'You mean you are giving us the ring?' Fennel demanded.

'Miss Desmond already has it. I am now going to give you a further incentive . . . a much more important one . . . to deliver the ring to Shalik. But in spite of these two incentives, you still have to get the ring out of my estate.'

'So that's it.' Fennel's eyes narrowed. 'Your savages are going to stop us . . . is that it?'

'If they can they will. I am going to arrange a hunt. You three and Mr. Jones who is waiting for you will be the hunted and my Zulus will be the hunters. You must regard it as exciting a game as I shall. You will have a reasonable chance to escape the hunters because I am going to give you a three hour start. You will leave here at 04.00 hrs. when it will be light enough for you to make good speed and you will need good speed. At 07.00 hrs. my Zulus will come after you. It will be entirely up to your speed and ingenuity to avoid them.'

'Are you serious?' Garry asked.

'Certainly I am very serious as you will discover should you be unfortunate to be captured.'

'Suppose we are captured? What happens?'

Kahlenberg inclined his head.

'A sensible question, Mr. Edwards. If you are captured, you will be cruelly put to death. My men are extremely primitive. In the days of Shaka, the famous Zulu chief, when he caught his enemies, he had them impaled. This is done by hammering a sharpened skewer into the lower intestine and leaving the victim to die slowly and in extreme agony.'

Garry's face tightened.

'And your savages would do that to us if they caught us?' he asked.

'Yes, they would.'

There was a long pause, then Garry said, 'So you are staging this hunt to pander to your perverted, sadistic frustration. Is that it?'

Kahlenberg's face changed: from a courteous, mild spoken man he turned suddenly into a cruel, vicious looking lunatic.

'I am going to teach you not to trespass on my estate,' he said, leaning forward and glaring at Garry. 'You have dared to come here with your ridiculous tale and now you will pay for it!' He gained control of himself and sat back, his mouth working and he remained motionless until his rage died down. 'It is necessary to get rid of you all since you have seen my museum. It is essential that you don't escape to talk.'

A little shaken to realize that his idea that Kahlenberg was mentally unbalanced was now confirmed, Garry said, 'Then why give us the ring? Why not call your men in and kill us now?'

'The hunt will amuse me. You have the ring because if you do happen to escape, you deserve to keep it . . . but I assure you, it is unlikely you will escape.'

'Suppose we give you our word not to talk and leave the ring with you?' Garry said. 'Would you allow us to use the helicopter and fly out?'

'No, and in case you are hoping to use your helicopter, I will tell you at once that it is under guard. Ten of my Zulus surround it and tomorrow early, one of my pilots will fly it back to the company you hired it from.' He pressed a button on his desk and a panel slid back on the opposite wall revealing a relief map of the estate and the house. 'I will give you a reasonable chance and I would be disappointed if the hunt were over in a few hours. I would like it to last several days. So please look at the map and study it. You will see the exit from the east is blocked by a range of mountains. Unless you are all expert rock climbers, I wouldn't advise you to go that way. I will warn you my Zulus think nothing of scrambling down the mountainside of these dangerous heights and they would quickly catch up with you. Nor would I recommend the exit to the south. As you can see from the map there is a river there, but what isn't shown is that the approaches to the river is swamp land and infested by crocodiles and some of the most deadly snakes in Natal. The north exit is straightforward. That is the way you came in. However, twenty of my Zulus are always guarding that approach. You didn't see them as you came in, Mr. Fennel, but they saw you and Mr. Jones and were continually reporting your progress. So I would advise you not to leave that way as although they let you in on my instructions, you may be sure they won't let you out. So this leaves only the west. It is not easy, but possible. You will find no water there, but there is a good jungle track that leads finally to the main highway to Mainville. It is some hundred and twenty kilometres and you would need to hurry. A Zulu can easily keep pace with a fast moving horse, but you do have a three hour start.' Kahlenberg looked at his watch. 'It is past my bed time. Please return to the guest suite and get a little rest. At 04.00 hrs. you will be released. Again I advise you to move as quickly as you can.' He pressed a button on his desk and the doors opened. The four waiting Zulus came in.

'Please go with these men,' Kahlenberg continued. 'There is an old African saying which you will all do well to remember. It is that the vulture is a patient bird. Personally, I would prefer a vulture to one of my Zulus. Good night.'

Back in the guest suite and when Fennel closed the door, Garry said, 'He's a pathological case. I had a feeling about him the moment I saw him. Do you think he's bluffing about the Zulus?'

'No.' Gaye suppressed a shiver. 'He is a sadistic pervert. That expression on his face when he let the mask drop! Let's go now, Garry. They think the terrace doors are locked. We might gain seven hours if we leave at once.'

Garry went to the terrace doors and opened them. He paused, then stepped back, closing the doors.

'They are out there already . . . waiting.'

Gaye joined him and peered through the glass. She could see a half-circle of squatting Zulus, facing her: the moonlight glittered on their spears, their ostrich plumes moved in the slight breeze. Feeling frightened, she moved away from the doors and sat down.

'What are we going to do, Garry?'

'Are you any good on a mountain?' Garry asked, coming over to sit by her side.

'I don't think so .. I've never tried.'

'You can cut the mountains out,' Fennel said, wiping his face with the back of his arm. 'I've no head for heights.'

'We'll have to consult Ken. We have to start north to pick Themba up. Without him, we're not going to get out.'

'That's right,' Fennel said. 'Ken says that the guy has a compass in his head. He'll get us out.'

'Let's have a drink.' Garry got to his feet and went over to the bar. 'What will you have, Gaye?'

'Nothing at this hour.'

'Lew?'

'Scotch.'

As Garry mixed the drinks, he asked, 'Has Ken got the Springfield with him?'

'No. We left it with Themba.'

'We could need it.'

'Yeah. We'll pick up Ken, and then go straight to where we left Themba. He's not only got the rifle, but extra water and most of the food. If we have to walk all the goddamn way, we could be at it for three or even four days.'

Garry saw Gaye was examining the ring through the glass of the box. He joined her and peered over her shoulder.

'Take it out and wear it,' he said. 'That box is awkward to carry and could get smashed. The ring will be a lot safer on your hand than in the box.'

'If anyone's going to wear it, it'll be me,' Fennel said, putting down his drink.

'She's wearing it,' Garry said quietly. 'I trust her, but I can't say I trust you.'

Fennel glared at him, but Garry's steady stare made him hesitate. Finally, he sat down with bad grace and picking up his glass, he drained it. Okay, you sonofabitch, he thought. I'll fix you, when I fix her.

Gaye took the ring out of the box.

'The diamonds are lovely, but the ring isn't very beautiful, is it?' She tried the ring on the third finger of her right hand, but found it much too loose. 'Of course, I was forgetting . . . it's a man's ring.' She slid it on her thumb. 'This is all right. It's a little awkward, but it won't come off.'

Garry looked at his watch. The time was 02.00 hrs.

'Go and lie down, Gaye. I'm going to my room. We want all the rest we can get. We don't know when we'll get our next sleep.'

He watched her go to her room, then he went to his, ignoring Fennel.

Fennel stretched out on the settee. He knew he wouldn't sleep. All his desire and frustration came back to him as he thought of Gaye. If he had to follow her back to England, he told himself, he would get even with her. He had hoped to have found a chance of fixing her on the way back to Mainville, but they would have to keep moving if they were to shake off the Zulus. Fennel shifted uneasily. The thought of being hunted by a pack of Zulus dried his mouth.

A little before 04.00 hrs., Gaye was awakened by the sound of the beating of a drum. She sat up, swung her feet to the floor and listened.

Not far away, she could hear the rhythmic sound of the drum like a pulse beat. She looked hastily at her watch and saw it was two minutes to the hour. She snatched up her rucksack and went into the lounge.

Garry and Fennel were standing by the terrace doors.

A giant Zulu came across the terrace and beckoned to them. He was a magnificent specimen of a man in his leopard skin and ostrich plumes.

'Here we go,' Garry said and opened the terrace doors.

The drum beat now was very loud. A row of some thirty Zulus made a wall of glistening black bodies, covered with leopard skins. The ostrich plume head-dresses bobbed as they shuffled and stamped to the drum beat. They carried long narrow shields of buffalo hide and held in their left hands six throwing spears as they bent, straightened, shuffled and stamped. They made a frightening, awe-inspiring sight.

The lone Zulu made a savage gesture, jerking his assegai first at the three and then towards the distant jungle.

The two men slung their rucksacks on their shoulders and, with Gaye between them, moved out on to the terrace.

At the sight of them the dancing men uttered a loud, savage growl that set Gaye's heart racing. The drum beat increased.

They walked quickly across the lawn, looking ahead and not at the Zulus. Gaye had to control herself not to run. They kept on, and in a few minutes they were in the jungle.

'Nice looking lot,' Garry said. 'They are the boys who are coming after us. Where's Ken?'

Fennel pointed.

'See that balancing rock up there? That's where he is.' He cupped his hand to his mouth and bawled, 'Ken! Come on down, pronto!' Then, taking out his flashlight, he turned it on and began waving it. A light signalled back from the rock and they heard Ken shout, 'I'm coming. Keep your light on.'

Five minutes later he joined them.

'Did you get it? I thought you were going to the airfield.'

'We got it!' Fennel said. 'We've got to get to Themba fast. The chopper's out. Come on, I'll tell you as we go.'

Ken peered at him.

'Trouble?'

'I'll say . . . get going!'

Ken started off with Fennel, talking, by his side. Garry and Gaye kept together.

When Ken understood the situation, he increased his pace.

'You really think they're coming after us?'

'Damn sure of it. I won't worry so much once I've got the rifle,' Fennel said. 'If they look like overtaking us, we can ambush them, but without the rifle we're in dead trouble.'

As they hurried along the jungle track, Garry was thinking of the best way to evade the Zulus. If they took the exit from the west which Kahlenberg had said was relatively easy, it would develop into a race between them and the Zulus who could move with the speed of a galloping horse. The east exit was out. None of them had any experience of mountain climbing whereas, according to Kahlenberg, the Zulus had. The north exit was too dangerous. Garry felt sure Kahlenberg had been speaking the truth when he had said he had men already posted there. That left the south exit . . . swamps and crocodiles and possibly the last exit the Zulus would imagine they would try.

In around forty minutes, they reached the open space where they had left Themba. Twenty minutes less than it had taken Ken and Fennel to reach the balancing rock. They were all a little breathless and all jumpy.

'It's that tree over there,' Ken said pointing.

'You sure? He's not there.' Fennel stared across the open space in the dim light of the approaching dawn.

'Themba!' Ken shouted. 'Themba!'

The silence that greeted them sent a chill through them. Ken broke into a run. The others followed him.

Reaching the tree, Ken stopped. He knew it was the tree under which they had left Themba. Not only did he recognize the stunted thorn bush he had noticed when he had left with Fennel, but there was a heap of firewood piled by the tree. Under this tree had been their jerry can of water, the bag of food and the Springfield rifle. There was no sign of any of these things.

'The bastard's skipped with our stuff!' Fennel snarled.

'He wouldn't do that. Something's happened to him.'

It was Garry who spotted the grave away to his right.

'What's that?'

They looked at the mound of freshly turned earth and moving together, they approached it.

So there should be no mistake as to what lay under the soil, placed on top of it was Themba's Australian bush hat.

Ken was the first to realize what had happened.

'They killed him, and they've taken the food, the water and the rifle,' he said huskily.

For a long moment they all stood staring down at the grave.

Pulling himself together, Garry said, 'Well, we now know what to expect. We've got to get moving. Look, Ken, Fennel's told you about the four exits. I'm opting to go south. They'll expect us to go by the west exit. With luck, by going south and through the swamps, they may not be able to track us. What do you think?'

'It depends how bad the swamps are. They can be sheer hell, and that's crocodile country.'

'All the same, I think it's our best bet. Have you a compass?'

Ken produced a small compass from his pocket.

'I'm a qualified navigator,' Garry went on. 'Do you want me to lead the way or will you do it?'

'You do it. I've always relied on Themba.'

'Then we go south.' Garry steadied the compass and got a bearing. 'Let's go.'

He started along a track with Gaye at his heels. Fennel and Ken followed behind.

None of them said anything. Themba's death had shocked them all. The danger that was threatening them had been sharply brought home to them.

They moved at a fast pace. The time was now 04.50 hrs. In a little more than two hours the Zulus would be after them.

They had been walking for some twenty minutes when Garry stopped and checked the compass.

'This track's beginning to curve to the west,' he said as the other two came up. 'We'll have to leave it and cut through the jungle.'

They looked at the high tangled grass and the thorny shrubs and the trees.

'That's going to slow us up like hell,' Fennel complained.

'Can't be helped. We've got to go south and that's the way to the south.'

'I don't want to scare you,' Ken said quietly, 'but this is snake country. Keep your eyes skinned.'

Gaye clutched hold of Garry's arm.

'Don't worry,' he said, forcing a grin. 'I'll look after you. Let's go.'

They began to toil through the thick matted grass, zigzagging around the trees, aware of the chattering monkeys overhead.

Garry kept checking the compass. While Kahlenberg had been talking, Garry had been studying the wall map. He had realized that the river could be their salvation for he remembered as he flew over the estate, seeing the river in the distance and also seeing a small town to the south of it. The river was now vitally important to them as they had no water with them.

But he was also aware that since entering the jungle, their pace had slackened and he felt pretty sure the Zulus would have much less difficulty in covering this kind of ground than they were having.

After some three kilometres, they came out onto another jungle track which headed due south.

'How are you making out?' Garry asked, as he quickened his pace, catching hold of Gaye's hand and pulling her along with him.

'I'm all right, but I wish we knew how far we have to go.'

'I don't think it's too far . . . around twenty kilometres before we get off the estate. I studied that wall map. This is the nearest exit to Kahlenberg's boundary.'

Plodding along behind, Fennel was being handicapped by the weight of his tool bag.

'I'll carry it for a bit,' Ken said, seeing Fennel was tiring.

Fennel stopped and regarded the bag angrily.

'No, you won't! I've had enough of this bloody thing. We'll never get anywhere if we go on carrying it. So okay, it cost me money, but if we get out of here I can buy a new kit. If we don't get out, then I won't need one. To hell with it.' He heaved the tool bag far into the jungle.

'I would have carried it,' Ken said.

Fennel grinned crookedly at him.

'I know and thanks. I'm glad to be rid of it.'

They stepped out and soon caught up with the other two. Then suddenly the track petered out into a large puddle of oozing mud.

'This is where the swamp starts,' Ken said. 'With the rain we've had, it could be bad.'

They left the track and moved into the jungle. The ground felt soft under their feet, but they pushed on. Later, the ground began to squelch under their weight and the going became harder.

By now the sun was up and they could feel the steamy heat. Garry kept checking the compass. When the ground got too sodden, they had to find a way around it and then get back on the compass bearing. The smell of rotting humus, the steamy heat that steadily increased as the sun climbed above the trees, the slippery boggy ground made progress slow and unpleasant.

They kept moving, their eyes searching the ground for snakes.

Ken said suddenly, 'They're on their way.'

Garry looked at his watch. The time was exactly 07.00 hrs. They all increased their pace with a feeling of slight panic, but the increase didn't last long: the going was too hard.

Ken said suddenly, 'I can smell water. The river's not far off.'

Ten minutes later, they came out of the shade of the trees to a broad, slippery bank leading down to a brownish stream, not more than twenty metres wide.

'That's our direction if we can get across,' Garry said. 'Think it's deep?'

'Could be.' Ken joined him and surveyed the water. 'It's no distance . . . just the curse of getting wet in that foul water. I'll see.' He took off his shoes and shirt, padded across the oozing mud and grabbing hold of a branch of a tree, he lowered himself into the stagnant water while he groped to find bottom with his foot.

'It's deep. We'll have to swim.' He let himself go, then started across the stream to the other side of the bank with a strong, over-arm stroke.

It happened so quickly none of the other three watching him believed what they were seeing. There was a sudden rush from the thick jungle grass on the opposite bank. Something that looked like a green and brown tree trunk flashed into the water near Ken. An evil looking scaly snout revealed itself for a brief moment. Ken screamed and threw up his arms.

Then he and the crocodile vanished under the water which became agitated and rapidly turned into a foaming vortex of stinking, brown water, horribly tinged with red.

CHAPTER NINE

AT MIDDAY IT RAINED. For the past two hours, swollen, black clouds had slowly built up, darkening the sky and blotting out the burning sun. The heat, by the placidly flowing stream, had become more and more oppressive. Then abruptly the rain came as if the sky had opened, releasing a deluge of warm water that soaked the three to the skin in seconds. So heavy was the rain, they were blinded by the water smashing down on them and were enveloped in steaming mist.

Catching hold of Gaye's hand, Garry ran into the jungle and paused under the cover of a vast baobab tree, its thick foliage offering a leaky shelter.

Cursing and muttering, Fennel joined them. They squatted down, their backs against the tree, and stared at the now raging river in silence.

None of them had spoken for four hours. The shock of Ken's horrible end had reduced them to a numbed silence. Although they hadn't known him for long, they had all liked him for there had been nothing to dislike about him. What shocked them more than anything was the swiftness and the way of his going.

Gaye was sure that the terrible scene was now indelibly printed on her mind. Ken's terrified expression, his wild scream as the crocodile's teeth had crunched down on his leg and the brief sight of the evil, scaly snout were the ingredients of future nightmares.

Garry too had been violently shocked, but he was mentally much more resilient than either Gaye or Fennel. When he had seen Ken disappear and had seen the blood on the foaming water, he knew there was nothing he could do to help him. His duty to the others and himself was to keep moving, for he knew they dare not waste a moment, even aware of Kahlenberg's threat that if caught they would be impaled, and he had enough imagination to know such a death would be far more horrible than Ken's death. So, catching hold of Gaye's hand, ignoring her hysterical sobbing, he dragged her away from the scene and back into the jungle. He kept moving until finally she steadied herself, stopped sobbing and continued with him, walking like a zombie.

Perhaps of the three of them, Fennel was the most affected. He had come to admire Ken. The episode with the Land Rover on the narrow track had enormously impressed him. He knew he hadn't the guts to have done such a thing. Ken's coolness when he was dangling at the end of the cable had completely wiped out Fennel's hostility. Ken's death now left him viciously angry, and in a brooding, homicidal state of mind. Why hadn't this sonofabitch Edwards gone into the stream first? He and his whore weren't worth a tenth of what Ken had been worth. He looked at them out of the corners of his small, glittering eyes. Garry had his arm around Gaye and Fennel felt a hot, furious rush of blood to his head. Well, I'll fix them, he thought. No one shoves me around as that bitch did without paying for it.

Garry was speaking quietly to Gaye.

'This rain's lucky. It'll wash out our tracks. This was the one thing I was praying for. They can't track us after this storm.'

Gaye clutched his hand. She was still too shocked to speak.

After some ten minutes, the rain began to slacken.

'We must get on,' Garry said, getting to his feet. 'We've got to cross the river.' He turned to Fennel. 'Think we could build a raft?'

'I've thrown my goddamn tool kit away,' Fennel told him. 'How the hell can we build a raft without tools?'

Garry walked to the edge of the river. The opposite bank was thick with high grass and shrubs. Were more crocodiles lurking on the bank, hidden from sight, waiting for them? After what had happened to Ken, he decided the risk was too great to attempt a crossing. He decided to push on down the river in the hope that they would come to a clearing where crocodiles couldn't conceal themselves.

'Before we go further, let's eat,' he said, and, opening Ken's rucksack, he produced a can of stewed beef. 'We'll split this between the three of us.'

'I'm not hungry . . . I don't want any,' Gaye said listlessly.

'You've got to eat!' Garry said sharply. 'Now, come on.'

'No . . . leave me alone.'

Garry looked closely at her. Her white drawn face, her eyes that had become sunken, began to worry him.

'Are you all right?'

'I have a headache. The thought of food makes me feel ill . . . just leave me alone.'

Turning from her, he opened the can and shared the contents with Fennel. From time to time, he looked at Gaye, who was resting against the tree trunk, her eyes closed.

Was it shock? he asked himself. Or was she ill? He flinched at the thought. To fall sick now would be a disaster.

The meal finished, the two men got to their feet. Garry went over to Gaye and touched her lightly on her shoulder. She opened her eyes, and again he felt a pang of alarm at the heavy, dull look in her eyes. She dragged herself to her feet.

'You're not ill, Gaye ' he asked.

'No.'

'Come on!' Fennel barked. 'I want to get going if you don't!'

Garry walked by Gaye's side. She moved listlessly and had lost the spring in her step. He took her arm.

'Don't fuss!' She tried to pull away. 'I'm all right. It's just this awful headache.'

He kept hold of her and walked on, but they weren't making the speed they had made earlier on.

'Keep moving for God's sake!' Fennel barked suddenly. 'What the hell are you two loitering for?'

Gaye made an effort and quickened her pace. They kept on, but after a couple of kilometres she again began to lag and Garry found he had to force her on. He was seriously worried now. She seemed to be walking in her sleep, dragging one foot after the other.

'You're feeling rotten, aren't you?' he said at last. 'What is it?'

'My head feels as if it is going to burst . . . I suppose it's the sun.'

'Let's rest for a moment.'

'No . . . I'll manage. Just don't fuss.'

Another three kilometres brought them to a place Garry was hoping to find. The jungle fell away either side of the river and mud flats with no cover spread out before them.

'This is where we cross,' Garry said. He eyed the swift moving river. 'Do you think you can manage, Gaye?'

'Yes, if you keep near me.'

Fennel came to the edge of the bank and surveyed the water suspiciously.

'Are you going first?' he asked Garry.

'Don't get excited . . . it's safe enough and it's not far across,' Garry said curtly. He led Gaye to some shade. 'Sit down. I want to find a branch of a tree to get our stuff over dry.'

She sank down as Garry went off into the jungle.

Fennel eyed her, thinking all the glamour had gone out of her now.

'What the hell's the matter with you?' he demanded, standing over her.

She put her head in her hands.

'Leave me alone.'

'Are you sick?'

'I have a headache . . . leave me alone.'

The sunlight reflected on the diamonds of the Borgia ring, making them sparkle. Fennel eyed the ring.

'You better give me the ring to carry. I don't want it lost. Come on, give it to me!'

'No!'

Garry came out of the jungle dragging a long branch covered with foliage behind him.

Muttering under his breath, Fennel moved away from Gaye.

It took Garry very few minutes to tie the rucksacks and their shoes to the branch.

'Let's go,' he said to Gaye. 'Hang on to the branch. I'll push it over.'

Uneasily, Fennel watched them enter the water. He looked up and down the opposite bank, expecting to see a crocodile appear, but saw nothing. They were across in a few minutes, and his eyes narrowed when he saw Gaye had collapsed on the mud bank and lay face down. He entered the water and swam fast and in panic to the other side.

Garry had turned Gaye and was kneeling over her, looking anxiously down at her white face. She seemed unconscious.

Water streaming from him, Fennel came up.

'What's the matter?' he demanded roughly.

'She's ill.' Garry picked up the unconscious girl and carried her across the mud flat into the shade of a tree. He laid her down on a carpet of rotting leaves. 'Get the rucksacks and the shoes,' he went on.

Fennel did as he was told, put on his shoes and came back to where Garry was anxiously watching Gaye.

'I guess she's picked up some bug,' Fennel said indifferently. 'Well, come on, Edwards, let's go. Those black bastards may be right behind us.'

'Look around and see if you can find two straight branches. We could make a stretcher with our shirts.'

Fennel stared at him.

'You out of your head? Do you imagine I'm going to help

carry that bitch through this goddamn jungle and in this heat when those blacks are racing after us? You carry her if you want to, but I'm not.'

Garry looked up at him, his face hardening.

'Are you saying we should leave her here?'

'Why not? What's she to us? You're wasting time. Leave her and get going.'

Garry stood up.

'You go. I'm staying with her. Go on . . . get out!'

Fennel licked his lips as he stared at Garry.

'I want the compass and the ring,' he said softly.

'You get neither! Get out!'

For a man of his bulk, Fennel could move very quickly. His fist flashed out as he jumped forward, but Garry was expecting just this move. He ducked under the fist and hooked Fennel to the jaw: a crushing punch that flattened Fennel.

'I said get out!' Garry snapped.

Fennel had landed on his back, his arms flung wide. His groping fingers closed on a rock, half-hidden in the grass. He gripped it and, with a violent movement, hurled it at Garry. The rock smashed against the side of Garry's head and he went down as if he had been pole-axed.

His jaw throbbing, Fennel struggled to his feet. He approached Garry cautiously and bent over him. Satisfied that Garry was unconscious, Fennel slipped his fingers into Garry's shirt pocket and found the compass. He crossed over to where Gaye was lying. Catching hold of her right wrist, he pulled the Borgia ring off her thumb. As he did so, she opened her eyes and, seeing his face close to hers, she struck at him with her left hand. It was such a feeble blow Fennel scarcely felt it. He grinned viciously.

'Good-bye, baby,' he said, bending over her. 'I hope you suffer. I'm taking the compass and the ring. You two will never get out of here alive. If you had been nice to me, I would have been nice to you. You asked for it and you're getting it.' He stood up. 'If the Zulus don't find you, the vultures will. So long, and have a wonderful time while it lasts.'

Gaye closed her eyes. He doubted if she had understood half what he had said, but it gave him a lot of satisfaction to have said it.

He picked up the rucksack containing the last of the food and the water bottle, checked the compass for his bearing, then set off fast into the dark steamy heat of the jungle.

Garry stirred and opened his eyes. A shadow passed over his face, then another. He looked up at the tree. He could see through the foliage, heavy grey clouds moving sluggishly westward. Then he saw two vultures settling heavily on the topmost branch of the tree, bearing it down under their combined weight. Their bald, obscene looking heads, the cruel, hooked beaks and their hunched shoulders sent a chill of fear through him.

His head throbbed, and when he touched the side of his face he felt encrusted blood. He was still dazed, but, after resting a few minutes, his mind began to clear. His hand went to his shirt pocket and he found the compass gone. He struggled to his feet and went unsteadily over to where Gaye was lying. She now looked flushed and her forehead was covered with beads of sweat. She seemed to be either sleeping or unconscious. He looked at her right hand. It was no surprise to see the ring was missing.

He squatted down beside her and considered his position. He had possibly fifteen kilometres of jungle swamp ahead of him before he reached the boundary exit. He glanced towards the rucksacks and saw the rucksack containing the food was also missing. Without food or water, he couldn't hope to last long. His watch told him it was 16.00 hrs. The Zulus had been searching for them now for nine hours. Had the rain washed out their tracks? If it hadn't, he could expect the Zulus to appear any time now.

Had he been alone, he would have gone off at once in the hope of overtaking Fennel, but he couldn't leave Gaye.

He looked down at her. Maybe Fennel had been right about her picking up a bug. She looked very ill and was obviously running a high temperature. As he watched her, she slowly opened her eyes. It took her a few moments to get him into focus, then she frowned, moving as if in pain.

'You're hurt,' she said huskily.

'It's all right.' He took her hot hand in his. 'Don't worry about that.'

'He's taken the compass and the ring.'

'I know. Take it easy. Don't worry about anything.'

The sudden crashing of branches overhead startled them and both looked up. One of the vultures had dropped from the upper branch to a lower one and was stretching its mangy neck, peering down at them.

Getting to his feet, Garry picked up the blood-stained rock and heaved it up into the tree. The rock whistled by the vulture. It flew off with a great flapping of wings and rustling of leaves.

'It knows I am dying,' Gaye said, her voice breaking. 'Garry! I'm so frightened.'

'You're not dying! You've caught a bug of some sort. In a day or so, you'll be fine.'

She looked at him, and his heart sank at the fear and hopelessness he saw in her eyes.

'There's nothing you can do for me,' she said. 'Leave me. You must think of yourself, Garry. It won't be long for me. I don't know what it is, but it's as if something is creeping up inside me, killing me piecemeal. My feet are so cold, yet the rest of me burns.'

Garry felt her naked feet. They were ice cold.

'Of course I'm not leaving you. Are you thirsty?'

'No. I have no feeling in my throat.' She closed her eyes, shivering. 'You must go, Garry. If they caught you . . .'

It dawned on him then that she could be dying. With her by his side, the attempt to get through the jungle wouldn't have daunted him, but realizing he might have to do it alone sent a prickle of panic through him.

'Do you believe in God?' she asked.

He hesitated.

'Sometimes.'

'For both of us this is really the time to believe, isn't it?'

'You're going to be all right.'

'Isn't it?'

'I guess so.'

There was a sudden disturbance in the tree above them as the vultures settled again.

She caught hold of his hand.

'You really mean you are going to stay with me?'

'Yes, darling. I'm staying.'

'Thank you, Garry, you're sweet. I won't keep you long.' She looked up at the vultures who were looking down at her. 'Promise me something.'

'Anything.'

'You won't be able to bury me. You can't dig with your bare hands, darling, can you? Put me in the river, please. I don't mind the crocodiles, but the vultures . . .'

'It's not coming to that. You rest now. By tomorrow, you'll be fine.'

'Promise, Garry.'

'All right, I promise, but . . .'

She interrupted him.

'You were right when you told me not to pin everything on money. If money hadn't meant so much to me, I wouldn't be here now. Garry, have you a piece of paper and a pen? I want to make my will.'

'Now, look, Gaye, you've got to stop being morbid.'

She began to cry helplessly.

'Garry . . . please . . . you don't know what an effort it is even to talk. I hurt so inside. Please let me make my will.'

He went to his rucksack and found a notebook and a biro.

'I must do it myself,' she said. 'The manager of the Swiss bank knows my handwriting. Prop me up, Garry.'

As he raised her and supported her, she caught her breath in a sobbing moan of pain. It took her a long time to write the letter, but finally it was done.

'Everything I have, Garry darling, is for you. There's over $100,000 in securities in my numbered account in Bern. Go and see Dr. Kirst. He's the director there. Tell him what has happened . . . tell him everything and especially tell him about Kahlenberg's museum. He'll know what to do and keep you clear. Give him this will and he will arrange everything for you.'

'All right . . . you're going to be all right, Gaye. Rest now,' and Garry kissed her.

Three hours later, as the sun, a red burning ball in the sky, sank behind the trees, Gaye drifted out of life into death. With the deadly scratch she hadn't noticed, the Borgia ring claimed yet another victim.

Fennel had been walking fast now for the past two hours. From time to time, swamp land had made him take a wide detour, wasting time and energy. Once he had floundered up to his knees in stinking wet mud when the ground had given under his feet. He had had a desperate struggle to extricate himself: a struggle that left him exhausted. The silence in the jungle, the loneliness and the heat all bothered him, but he kept reassuring himself that he couldn't now be far from the boundary exit and then his troubles would be over.

He kept thinking of the triumphant moment when he would walk into Shalik's office and tell him he had the ring. If Shalik imagined he was going to get the ring for nine thousand dollars, he was in for a surprise. Fennel had already made up his mind he wouldn't part with the ring unless Shalik paid him the full amount the other three and he would have shared . . . thirty-six thousand dollars. With any luck, in another four or five days, he would be back in London. He would collect the money and leave immediately for Nice. He was due a damn good vacation after this caper, he told himself. When he was tired of Nice, he would hire a yacht, find some bird and do a cruise along the Med., stopping in at the harbours along the coast for a meal and a look around: an ideal vacation and safe from Moroni.

He had now dismissed Gaye and Garry from his mind, never doubting he had seen the last of them. The stupid, stuck-up bitch had asked for trouble. No bird ever turned him down without regretting it. He wished Ken were with him. He frowned as he thought of the way Ken had died. With Ken, he would have felt much more sure of himself. Now, the sun was going down and the jungle was getting unpleasantly dark. He decided it was time to stop for the night. He hurried forward, looking for a clearing where he could get off the narrow track. After some searching, he found what he was looking for: a patch of coarse grass, clear of shrubs with a tree under which he could shelter if it rained.

He put down his rucksack and paused to wonder if he dare light a fire. He decided the risk was negligible and set about gathering sticks and kindling. When he had collected a large heap by the tree, he got the fire going, then sat down, his back resting against the tree. He was hungry and he opened the rucksack and took stock. There were three cans of stewed steak, two cans of beans and a can of steak pie. Nodding his satisfaction, he opened the can of steak pie. When he had finished the meal, he lit a cigarette, threw more sticks on the fire and relaxed.

Now he was sitting still, he became aware of the noises in the jungle: soft, disturbing and distracting sounds: leaves rustled, some animal growled faintly in the distance: Fennel wondered if it were a leopard. In the trees he could hear a sudden chatter of hidden monkeys start up and immediately cease. Some big bird flapped overhead.

He finished his cigarette, added more sticks to the fire and stretched out. The dampness had penetrated his clothes and he wondered if he would sleep. He closed his eyes. Immediately, the distracting sounds of the jungle became amplified and alarming. He sat up, his eyes searching beyond the light of the fire into the outer darkness.

Suppose the Zulus had spotted the fire and were creeping up on him? he thought.

They hammer a skewer into your lower intestine, Kahlenberg had said.

Fennel felt cold sweat break out on his face.

He had been crazy to have lit the fire. It could be spotted from a long distance away by the sharp-eyed savages. He grabbed up a big stick and scattered the fire. Then, getting to his feet, he stamped out the burning embers until the sparks had died in the wet grass. Then it was even worse because the darkness descended on him like a hot, smothering, black cloak. He groped for the tree, sat down, resting his back against it, and peered fearfully forward, but now it was as if he were blind. He could see nothing.

He remained like that for more than an hour, listening and starting with every sound. But finally he began to nod to sleep. He was suddenly too exhausted to care.

How long he slept, he didn't know, but he woke with a start, his heart racing. He was sure he was no longer alone. His built-in instinct for danger had sounded an emergency alarm in his mind. He groped in the darkness and found the thick stick with which he had scattered the fire. He gripped it while he listened.

Quite close . . . not more than five metres from him, there was a distinct sound of something moving through the carpet of leaves. He had his flashlight by him and, picking it up, his racing heart half suffocating him, he pointed the torch in the direction of the sound, then pressed the button.

The powerful beam lit up a big crouching animal that Fennel recognized by its fox-like head and its filthy fawn and black spotted fur to be a fully grown dog hyena.

He had only a brief glimpse of the animal before it disappeared into the thicket on the far side of the track, but that glimpse was enough to bring Fennel to his feet, panic stricken.

He remembered a conversation he had had with Ken while they were in the Land Rover on the first easy leg of the journey to Kahlenberg's estate.

'I get along with all the animals out here except the hyena,' Ken had said. 'He is a filthy brute. Not many people know this scavenger has the most powerful teeth and jaws of any animal. He can crack the thigh of a domestic cow the way you crack a nut. Besides being dangerous, he is an abject coward. He seldom moves except by night, and he will go miles following a scent and has infinite patience to wait to catch his prey unawares.'

With his eyes bolting out of his head, his hand shaking, Fennel played the beam of the flashlight into the thicket. For a brief moment he saw eyes gleaming like rubies caught by the light, and then vanish.

He has infinite patience to wait to catch his prey unawares.

Fennel knew there was no further sleep for him that night, and he looked at his wristwatch. The time was 03.00 hrs. Another hour before it began to get light and he could move. Not daring to waste the battery, he turned off the flashlight. Sitting down, he leaned against the tree and listened.

From out of the darkness came a horrifying, maniacal laugh that chilled his blood and raised the hairs on the nape of his neck. The horrible, indescribably frightening sound was repeated . . . the howl of a starving hyena.

Fennel longed for Ken's company. He even longed for Garry's company. Sitting in total darkness, knowing the stinking beast might be creeping slowly on its mangy belly, his powerful jaws slavering, towards him, he remained motionless, tense and straining to hear the slightest sound. He remained like that, his body aching for sleep, his mind feverish with panic for the next hour.

Whenever he dozed off, the howl of the hyena brought him awake and cursing. If only he had the Springfield or even an assegai, he thought, but he had nothing with which to defend himself except the thick stick which he was sure would be useless if the beast sprang at him.

When dawn finally came, Fennel was almost a wreck. His legs were stiff and his muscles ached. His body cried out for rest. He dragged himself upright, picked up his rucksack, and after assuring himself there was no sign of the hyena, he set off along the jungle track, again heading south. Although he forced himself along, his speed had slowed and he wasn't covering the ground as he had the previous day. He wished he knew how much further he had to go before he reached the boundary exit. The jungle was as dense as it had been yesterday and showed no sign of clearing. He walked for two hours, then decided to rest and eat. Sitting on a fallen tree, he opened a can of beans and ate them slowly, then he took a small drink from the water bottle. He smoked a cigarette, reluctant to move, but he knew he was dangerously wasting time. With an effort he got to his feet and set off again. Having walked for some five kilometres, he paused to check the compass. From the reading, he realized with dismay that he was now walking south-west instead of due south. The track had been curving slightly, taking him away from his direction, and he hadn't noticed it.

Cursing, he fixed his bearing and saw that to move in the right direction he would have to leave the path and force his way through the thick, evil smelling undergrowth. He hesitated, remembering what Ken had said about snakes.

It would be a hell of a thing, he thought, to have got this far and then to get bitten by a snake. Gripping his stick, he moved into the long, matted grass, feeling the sharp blades of the grass scratching at his bare legs. The sun was coming up, and already the heat was oppressive. The going was deadly slow now, and sweat began to stream off him as he slashed his way through the grass and tangled undergrowth with his stick, cursing aloud. Ahead of him, after a kilometre of exhausting struggle, he saw a wide open plain and he gasped with relief. He broke through to it, but almost immediately his feet sank up to his ankles in wet, clinging mud and he backed away, returning to the undergrowth. The plain he had imagined would be so easy to cross was nothing more than a dangerous swamp. He was now forced to go around the swamp, making an exhaustive detour, feeling his strength slowly ebbing from him as he struggled on in the breathless heat.

He now began to wonder if he would ever get out of this hellish place. He would have to rest again, he told himself. That was the trouble. He was worn out after a sleepless night. Maybe if he could sleep for three or four hours, he would get back his strength which he had always taken for granted and relied on.

It was a risk, he thought, but a risk that had to be taken if he was to conserve his strength for the last lap through the swamp. He remembered Ken had said hyenas only hunted at night. The beast was probably miles away by now. He would have to find somewhere to hide before he dare have the sleep his body was aching for. He dragged himself on until he saw a big fallen tree some way from the track and surrounded by shrubs. This seemed as good a place as any, and when he reached it he found the ground on the far side of the trunk reasonably dry. Thankfully, he lay down. He made a pillow of his rucksack, placed the rucksack of food near at hand and the thick stick by his side. He lowered his head on the rucksack, stretched out, and in a few moments he was asleep.

He hadn't been sleeping for more than a few minutes when out of the jungle came the hyena. It sniffed the ground, paused, then cocked its head on one side as it eyed the fallen tree. Making a silent, wide detour, it slunk around to the other side of the tree where Fennel was sleeping.

The hyena hadn't eaten for two days and it was half mad with hunger, but, although there was a meal before it for the taking, it was too cowardly as yet to attack. It sank down, its muzzle resting on its paws and stared with gleaming red eyes at the sleeping man.

Unhappily for Fennel, he was so exhausted, he slept the sleep of the dead, neither making a sound nor moving. After half an hour of watching, the hyena finally convinced itself that there was no danger for a hit and run attack.

It hunched its hind legs, lifted itself and struck.

Fennel was awakened by such intense pain that he was screaming out as he opened his eyes. He half started up, but the pain raging in his legs absorbed all his strength and he fell back, his fists pounding the sides of his head as the rising pain drove him frantic. Looking down, he was horrified to see that where his right calf had been there was now only a mess of blood and splintered bone. He could even see the white of his shin bone where the fleshy part of his calf had been ripped away.

Sobbing and moaning, he looked frantically around and he saw the hyena some ten metres from him, its muzzle bloodstained as it chewed the lump of flesh.

Blood was pouring from the terrible wound and Fennel realized if someone didn't come to his help at once, he would be dead in a few minutes. Already faintness was gripping him. Gathering his remaining strength, he yelled, 'Help!' at the top of his voice.

The shout echoed through the jungle. Startled, the hyena dashed into the undergrowth and released its horrible laughing howl.

Fennel tried to shout again, but only succeeded in making a croaking sound that carried no distance. The agony raving through his body brought unconsciousness near. The blood pouring from his wound attracted a swarm of flies which were now excitedly buzzing around the fast growing pool of blood.

Fennel was now too weak to do anything but lie flat, shuddering and moaning with pain. He could see, outlined against the grey clouds, a number of vultures circling overhead. He watched them drop into a nearby tree one by one and peer down at him speculatively.

He didn't see the hyena creeping on its belly towards him. He was only aware of it when he felt a sudden rush, smelt decay as the beast pounced on him, then a blinding pain as the sharp, powerful jaws and teeth bit through the top of his shorts and disembowelled him.

Ngomane, a magnificently built Zulu, had once worked on the

Kahlenberg estate, but there had been woman trouble and he had been dismissed.

Before his dismissal, Ngomane had been one of the forty guards patrolling the jungle on the look-out for unwelcomed visitors and poachers. He knew the jungle as he knew the back of his hand, and after his dismissal he pondered how he could earn a living. He decided that as there were many crocodiles on Kahlenberg's estate, and as he knew where to find them, and as the other guards were sympathetic about his dismissal, it would be safe and profitable, from time to time, to kill a few of the reptiles and sell their skins to the white storekeeper in Mainville who never asked questions and paid well.

Ngomane was trotting silently along the jungle track, having just entered from the south boundary, and was heading for the river, when he heard Fennel's frantic cry for help. He stopped abruptly, fingering his ancient rifle, looking uneasily in the direction of the sound. Then, curiosity getting the better of caution, he moved into the jungle and in a few moments he had found what was left of Fennel.

Garry walked slowly along the river bank, keeping in the shade where possible, his eyes searching the ground before him for snakes and signs of hidden crocodiles.

He had decided that without a compass it would be inviting disaster to attempt to reach the boundary exit through the jungle. He remembered that the relief map in Kahlenberg's office had shown that, after the river had passed the boundary of the estate, it continued on for some twenty kilometres to pass through a small town. Although he would be faced with a walk at least twice as long as the direct south route through the jungle, he knew if he could keep going he could not lose his way, and with any luck would not encounter swamp land and be forced to make exhausting detours.

On the other hand he exposed himself to attack from crocodiles and he could be more easily spotted if the Zulus had got this far up the river. But weighing the pros and cons, he finally opted for the river route.

He was feeling depressed and weary. He had committed Gaye's body to the river and had watched it float away into the darkness. He had hated the task, but he had no tool to dig a grave. Having seen her on her way, he had gone into the jungle and laid down. He had slept badly, dreaming of her, and had started his walk soon after 05.00 hrs.

He had been walking now for four hours, not moving quickly, but steadily, carefully pacing himself to conserve his strength. He was hungry and thirsty. From time to time, he moistened his lips with the foul river water, but refrained from drinking it. He had four packs of cigarettes in his rucksack, and, by continually smoking, he took the edge off his hunger and kept the mosquitoes at bay.

As he walked, he wondered how far Fennel had got by now. By the time he himself reached Mainville—if he ever reached it —Fennel would be on his way to Johannesburg. Garry was sure Fennel would immediately fly to London, hand over the ring, collect his share and then disappear. Garry wondered if Shalik would pay him his share once Shalik had the ring: he probably wouldn't. It didn't matter, Garry told himself. Thanks to Gaye, he was now worth $100,000. With such a sum, he could take the course in electronics and then buy himself a partnership. But first he had to get back to England.

He rested at midday for an hour and then continued on. By dusk, he had covered twenty-five kilometres. By keeping to the river, the walk, except for the gnawing pangs of hunger and a raging thirst, had been far less arduous than if he had taken to the jungle, but he knew he had at least another thirty kilometres to face the following morning and he, like Fennel, began to wonder if he would make it.

He moved into the jungle when it became too dark to see where he was going and laid down under a tree and slept. He woke soon after 05.00 hrs. as the sun was beginning to rise. Going down to the edge of the river, he scooped the brown dirty water over his face and head and moistened his lips without swallowing. The temptation was great, but he resisted it, sure that the water could contain a host of deadly bacteria.

He started off, keeping his pace steady, heading for an elbow bend in the river and wondering what he would find around the corner. With luck, he told himself, he could be at the exit of the estate.

It took him an hour to reach the bend and to get a clear view of the river which was now wide and straight. As he paused to examine both banks of the river, he suddenly stiffened. Could that be a boat pulled up on the mud flat some sixty metres ahead of him or was it a fallen tree?

He started forward, peering into the half light, and in a few minutes he decided that it was a flat bottom canoe.

His hunger and thirst forgotten, his heart pounding, he broke into a stumbling run. He reached the canoe and then stopped abruptly.

Lying in the bottom of the canoe was a dead Zulu. By his side were two rucksacks which Garry recognized as belonging to Ken and Fennel, and, more welcome still, Ken's water bottle.

On the Zulu's forefinger of his right hand, flashing in the sunlight, was the Caesar Borgia ring.

As soon as Garry had cleared the customs at London Airport, he hurried to a telephone box and dialled Toni's number. The time was 10.25 hrs. and he was pretty sure she would be still sleeping. After the bell had rung for some minutes, he heard a click, then a sleepy voice said, 'Miss White is away.'

Knowing she was about to hang up, Garry shouted, 'Toni! It's me!'

There was a pause, then Toni, now very much awake, released a squeal of excitement. 'Garry! Is that really you, darling?'

'Yes. I've just got in from Jo'burg.'

'And you're calling *me*? Oh, darling! So she isn't so marvellous after all?'

'Don't let's talk about her.' Garry's voice went down a note. 'Listen, Toni, how are you fixed? I'm flying to Bern tomorrow morning and I want you to come with me.'

'Bern? Where's Bern?'

'It's in Switzerland. Didn't you learn anything at school?'

'I learned to make love. Who cares where Bern is anyway? You want me to come with you? Why, darling, of course! I'd go with you to Vierwaldstattersee if you wanted me to.'

'That's nice. Where's that?'

She giggled.

'It's in Switzerland too. How long will we be staying?'

'A day or so, then I thought we would go down to Capri for two weeks and really live it up. You know where Capri is, don' you?'

'Yes, of course. I'd love to, Garry, but I simply can't. I have to work. I can manage three days, but not two weeks.'

'Wives shouldn't work, Toni.'

There was silence. He could hear her breathing over the line and he imagined her kneeling on the bed in her shortie night dress, her big blue eyes very round and astonished, and he grinned.

'Did you say *wives* shouldn't work?' she asked, her voice husky

'That's what the man said.'

'But I'm not married, Garry.'

'You soon will be. See you in two hours from now,' and he hurriedly hung up.

He piled his luggage into a taxi and told the driver to take him to the Royal Towers Hotel.

Arriving at the hotel, he had his luggage put in the baggage room and then asked the hall porter to call Shalik's suite and announce him.

There was a brief delay, then the hall porter told him to go up.

Arriving at the suite, he tapped and entered the outer room. A blonde girl sat at the desk, busily typing. She surveyed him as she paused in her work and got to her feet. Dressed in black, she was tall and willowy and exactly the type of girl Garry went out of his way to avoid: hard, shrewd, intelligent and very efficient.

'Mr. Edwards?'

'Correct.'

'Mr. Shalik will see you now.' She opened the door to Shalik's office and motioned him forward as if she were shooing in a nervous chicken.

Garry smiled at her more from force of habit than to be friendly. He need not have bothered. She wasn't looking at him and her indifference irritated him.

He found Shalik sitting at his desk, smoking a cigar, his plump hands resting on the blotter.

As Garry walked towards him, he said, 'Good morning, Mr. Edwards. Have you the ring?'

'Yes, I have it.' Garry sat down in the lounging chair opposite Shalik. He crossed his long legs and regarded Shalik.

'You have? My congratulations. I take it the other three will be coming to join us in a moment or so?'

Garry shook his head.

'No, they won't be coming to join us.'

Shalik frowned.

'But surely they want their fee?'

'They won't be coming and they won't be collecting their fee.'

Shalik sat back, studied the end of his cigar, then looked hard at Garry.

'And why not, Mr. Edwards?'

'Because they are dead.'

Shalik stiffened and his eyes narrowed.

'Are you telling me Miss Desmond is dead?'

'Yes, and so are the other two.

Shalik made an impatient movement which conveyed he wasn't interested in the other two.

'But what happened?'

'She caught a bug . . . lots of dangerous bugs in the jungle, and she died.'

Shalik got to his feet and walked over to the window, turning his back to Garry. The news shocked him. He disliked strangers knowing that he was capable of being shocked.

After a few moments, he turned and asked, 'How do I know you are telling me the truth, Mr. Edwards? How did the other two die?'

'Jones was eaten by a crocodile. I don't know what happened to Fennel. He was probably killed by a Zulu. I found the Zulu dead with Fennel's rucksack and the ring. Fennel had stolen the ring and my compass and left Gaye and me to find our way out of the jungle. I succeeded: Gaye didn't.'

'Are you quite sure she is dead?'

'I'm sure.'

Shalik sat down. He wiped his damp hands on his handkerchief. He had an important assignment involving a million dollars lined up for Gaye when she returned. Now, what was he to do? He felt a bitter rage seize him. He would have to start another long and difficult search for a woman to replace her, and in the meantime the assignment would fall through.

'And the ring?' he said, controlling his rage.

Garry took a matchbox from his pocket and pushed it across the desk to Shalik, who picked it up, shook the ring out on to the blotter and regarded it. Well, at least, this assignment hadn't failed. He was suddenly very pleased with himself. By using his brains and these four people as his pawns, he had made half a million dollars within the space of a few days.

He examined the ring closely, then nodded his satisfaction. As he put the ring down, he said, 'I am sure the operation wasn't easy, Mr. Edwards. I am very pleased. In fairness to you, I will double your fee. Let me see . . . it was nine thousand dollars. I will make it eighteen thousand. Is that satisfactory to you?'

Garry shook his head.

'Nine is enough,' he said curtly. 'The less I have of your money, the cleaner I will feel.'

Shalik's eyes snapped, but he shrugged. He opened his desk drawer and took out a long envelope which he tossed across the desk.

Garry picked up the envelope. He didn't bother to check the

contents. Putting the envelope in his breast pocket, he got up and walked to the door.

'Mr. Edwards . . .'

Garry paused.

'What is it?'

'I would be glad if you would dictate a full report of what happened during the operation. I would like to have all the details. My secretary will supply you with a tape-recorder.'

'What do you want it for . . . to give to the police?' Garry said. 'You have the ring . . . that's all you're getting from me,' and he went out, walked past the blonde secretary without looking at her and hurried to the elevator, his one thought now being to get back to Toni.

Shalik stared at the closed door, thought for a moment, then shrugged. Perhaps, after all, it was better not to know too much about what happened, he decided. Pity about Gaye. He knew she had no relations. There would be no awkward questions asked. She had come into his life, served a useful purpose, and now she had gone. It was a nuisance, but no woman was irreplaceable.

He picked up the ring and examined it. Holding it in his left hand, he reached for his telephone and dialled a number.

The diamonds were nice, he thought, and ran his forefinger over the cluster, then started as something of needle sharpness cut his finger. He dropped the ring, frowning, and conveyed his bleeding finger to his mouth.

So the Borgia ring still scratched, he thought. The poison, of course, would have long dried up: after all, the ring was nearly four hundred years old. He looked at his finger. Quite a nasty scratch. He continued to suck his finger as he listened to the burr-burr-burr of the telephone bell, thinking how pleased his client would be to get the ring back.

ENQUIRY

Dick Francis

*'Enquiry' is published by
Michael Joseph Ltd.*

The Author

Dick Francis can't remember learning to ride. It came to him as early and as naturally as walking. And from child star at horse shows to champion steeplechase jockey, his skill in the saddle took him always to the top of his game. Six wartime years in the R.A.F. (rising from A.C.2 to Flying Officer) marked the break with showing and hunting and the entry into racing, which led him to become the Queen Mother's jockey, and to partner her horse Devon Loch in his tragic collapse while looking the certain winner of the 1956 Grand National. Retiring in 1957, Dick Francis had a pen practically thrust into his hand. The result, an autobiography, THE SPORT OF QUEENS, a job as racing correspondent on the *Sunday Express,* and an ever-lengthening list of thrillers. He says he found race-riding much easier than writing, but brings to both the same thorough preparation. He used to 'walk the course' to know which way to go. Now he goes to equal lengths to get his background facts right for the novels. With his wife Mary, who helps with the research, he lives on the edge of the Berkshire Downs and still rides racehorses regularly, besides judging hunters at shows.

PART ONE

FEBRUARY

CHAPTER ONE

YESTERDAY I lost my licence.

To a professional steeplechase jockey, losing his licence and being warned off Newmarket Heath is like being chucked off the medical register, only more so.

Barred from race riding, barred from racecourses. Barred moreover from racing stables. Which poses me quite a problem, as I live in one.

No livelihood and maybe no home.

Last night was a right so-and-so, and I prefer to forget those grisly sleepless hours. Shock and bewilderment, the feeling that it couldn't have happened, it was all a mistake . . . this lasted until after midnight. And at least the disbelieving stage had had some built-in comfort. The full thudding realization which followed had none at all. My life was lying around like the untidy bits of a smashed teacup, and I was altogether out of glue and rivets.

This morning I got up and percolated some coffee and looked out of the window at the lads bustling around in the yard and mounting and cloppeting away up the road to the downs, and I got my first real taste of being an outcast.

Fred didn't bellow up at my window as he usually did. 'Going to stay there all day, then?'

This time, I was.

None of the lads looked up . . . they more or less kept their eyes studiously right down. They were quiet, too. Dead quiet. I watched Bouncing Bernie heave his ten stone seven on to the gelding I'd been riding lately, and there was something apologetic about the way he lowered his fat bum into the saddle.

And he, too, kept his eyes down.

Tomorrow, I guessed, they'd be themselves again. Tomorrow they'd be curious and ask questions. I understood that they weren't despising me. They were sympathetic. Probably too sympathetic for their own comfort. And embarrassed: that too.

And instinctively delicate about looking too soon at the face of total disaster.

When they'd gone I drank my coffee slowly and wondered what to do next. A nasty, very nasty, feeling of emptiness and loss.

The papers had been stuck as usual through my letterbox. I wondered what the boy had thought, knowing what he was delivering. I shrugged. Might as well read what they'd said, the Goddamned pressmen, God bless them.

The *Sporting Life*, short on news, had given us the headlines and the full treatment.

'Cranfield and Hughes Disqualified.'

There was a picture of Cranfield at the top of the page, and half way down one of me, all smiles, taken the day I won the Hennessy Gold Cup. Some little sub-editor letting his irony loose, I thought sourly, and printing the most cheerful picture he could dig out of the files.

The close-printed inches north and south of my happy face were unrelieved gloom.

'The Stewards said they were not satisfied with my explanation,' Cranfield said. 'They have withdrawn my licence. I have no further comment to make.'

Hughes, it was reported, had said almost exactly the same. Hughes, if I remembered correctly, had in fact said nothing whatsoever. Hughes had been too stunned to put one word collectedly after another, and if he had said anything at all it would have been unprintable.

I didn't read all of it. I'd read it all before, about other people. For 'Cranfield and Hughes' one could substitute any other trainer and jockey who had been warned off. The newspaper reports on these occasions were always the same; totally uninformed. As a racing enquiry was a private trial the ruling authorities were not obliged to open the proceedings to the public or the press, and as they were not obliged to, they never did. In fact like many another inward-looking concern they seemed to be permanently engaged in trying to stop too many people from finding out what was really going on.

The *Daily Witness* was equally fog-bound, except that Daddy Leeman had suffered his usual rush of purple prose to the head. According to him:

'Kelly Hughes, until now a leading contender for this season's jump-jockeys' crown, and fifth on the list last year, was sentenced to an indefinite suspension of his licence. Hughes, thirty, left the hearing ten minutes after Cranfield. Looking pale and grim, he confirmed that he had lost his licence, and added, "I have no further comment." '

They had remarkable ears, those pressmen.

I put down the paper with a sigh and went into the bedroom to exchange my dressing-gown for trousers and a jersey, and after that I made my bed, and after that I sat on it, staring into space. I had nothing else to do. I had nothing to do for as far ahead as the eye could see. Unfortunately I also had nothing to think about except the Enquiry.

Put baldly, I had lost my licence for losing a race. More precisely, I had ridden a red-hot favourite into second place in the Lemonfizz Crystal Cup at Oxford in the last week of January, and the winner had been an unconsidered outsider. This would have been merely unfortunate, had it not been that both horses were trained by Dexter Cranfield.

The finishing order at the winning post had been greeted with roars of disgust from the stands, and I had been booed all the way to the unsaddling enclosure. Dexter Cranfield had looked worried more than delighted to have taken first and second places in one of the season's big sponsored steeplechases, and the Stewards of the meeting had called us both in to explain. They were not, they announced, satisfied with the explanations. They would refer the matter to the Disciplinary Committee of the Jockey Club.

The Disciplinary Committee, two weeks later, were equally sceptical that the freak result had been an accident. Deliberate fraud on the betting public, they said. Disgraceful, dishonest, disgusting, they said. Racing must keep its good name clean. Not the first time that either of you have been suspected. Severe penalties must be inflicted, as a deterrent to others.

Off, they said. Warned off. And good riddance.

It wouldn't have happened in America, I thought in depression. There, all runners from one stable, or one owner, for that matter, were covered by a bet on any of them. So if the stable's outsider won instead of its favourite, the backers still collected their money. High time the same system crossed the Atlantic. Correction, more than high time; long, long overdue.

The truth of the matter was that Squelch, my red-hot favourite, had been dying under me all the way up the straight, and it was in the miracle class that I'd finished as close as second, and not fifth or sixth. If he hadn't carried so many people's shirts, in fact, I wouldn't have exhausted him as I had. That it had been Cranfield's other runner Cherry Pie who had passed me ten yards from the finish was just the worst sort of luck.

Armed by innocence, and with reason to believe that even if the Oxford Stewards had been swayed by the crowd's hostile reception, the Disciplinary Committee were going to consider the matter in an atmosphere of cool common sense, I had gone to the Enquiry without a twinge of apprehension.

The atmosphere was cool, all right. Glacial. Their own common sense was taken for granted by the Stewards. They didn't appear to think that either Cranfield or I had any.

The first faint indication that the sky was about to fall came when they read out a list of nine previous races in which I had ridden a beaten favourite for Cranfield. In six of them, another of Cranfield's runners had won. Cranfield had also had other runners in the other three.

'That means,' said Lord Gowery, 'That this case before us is by no means the first. It has happened again and again. These results seem to have been unnoticed in the past, but this time you have clearly overstepped the mark.'

I must have stood there looking stupid with my mouth falling open in astonishment, and the trouble was that they obviously thought I was astonished at how much they had dug up to prove my guilt.

'Some of those races were years ago,' I protested. 'Six or seven, some of them.'

'What difference does that make?' asked Lord Gowery. 'They happened.'

'That sort of thing happens to every trainer now and then,' Cranfield said hotly. 'You must know it does.'

Lord Gowery gave him an emotionless stare. It stirred some primeval reaction in my glands, and I could feel the ripple of goose pimples up my spine. He really believes, I thought wildly, he really believes us guilty. It was only then that I realized we had to make a fight of it; and it was already far too late.

I said to Cranfield, 'We should have had that lawyer,' and he gave me an almost frightened glance of agreement.

Shortly before the Lemonfizz the Jockey Club had finally thrown an old autocratic tradition out of the twentieth century and agreed that people in danger of losing their livelihood could be legally represented at their trials, if they wished. The concession was so new that there was no accepted custom to be guided by.

One or two people had been acquitted with lawyers' help who would presumably have been acquitted anyway; and if an accused person engaged a lawyer to defend him, he had in all cases to pay the fees himself. The Jockey Club did not award costs to anyone they accused, whether or not they managed to prove themselves innocent.

At first Cranfield had agreed with me that we should find a lawyer, though both of us had been annoyed at having to shell out. Then Cranfield had by chance met at a party the newly elected Disciplinary Steward who was a friend of his, and had reported to me afterwards, 'There's no need for us to go to the expense of a lawyer. Monty Midgely told me in confidence that the Disciplinary Committee think the Oxford stewards were off their heads reporting us, that he knows the Lemonfizz result was just one of those things, and not to worry, the Enquiry will only be a formality. Ten minutes or so, and it will be over.'

That assurance had been good enough for both of us. We hadn't even seen any cause for alarm when three or four days later Colonel Sir Montague Midgely had turned yellow with jaundice and taken to his bed, and it had been announced that one of the Committee, Lord Gowery, would deputize for him in any Enquiries which might be held in the next few weeks.

Monty Midgely's liver had a lot to answer for. Whatever he had intended, it now seemed all too appallingly clear that Gowery didn't agree.

The Enquiry was held in a large lavishly furnished room in the Portman Square headquarters of the Jockey Club. Four Stewards sat in comfortable armchairs along one side of a polished table with a pile of papers in front of each of them, and a shorthand writer was stationed at a smaller table a little to their right. When Cranfield and I went into the room the shorthand writer was fussing with a tape-recorder, unwinding a lead from the machine which stood on his own table and trailing it across the floor towards the Stewards. He set up a microphone on a stand in front of Lord Gowery, switched it on, blew into it a couple of times, went back to his machine, flicked a few switches, and announced that everything was in order.

Behind the Stewards, across a few yards of plushy dark red carpet, were several more armchairs. Their occupants included the three Stewards who had been unconvinced at Oxford, the Clerk of the Course, the Handicapper who had allotted the Lemonfizz weights, and a pair of Stipendiary Stewards, officials paid by the Jockey Club and acting at meetings as an odd mixture of messenger boys for the Stewards and the industry's private police. It was they who, if they thought there had been an infringement of the rules, brought it to the notice of the Stewards of the meeting concerned, and advised them to hold an Enquiry.

As in any other job, some Stipendiaries were reasonable men and some were not. The Stipe who had been acting at Oxford on Lemonfizz day was notoriously the most difficult of them all.

Cranfield and I were to sit facing the Stewards' table, but several feet from it. For us, too, there were the same luxurious armchairs. Very civilized. Not a hatchet in sight. We sat down, and Cranfield casually crossed his legs, looking confident and relaxed.

We were far from soul-mates, Cranfield and I. He had inherited a fortune from his father, an ex-soap manufacturer who had somehow failed to acquire a coveted peerage in spite of donating madly to every fashionable cause in sight, and the combination of wealth and disappointed social ambition had turned Cranfield *fils* into a roaring snob. To him, since he employed me, I was a servant; and he didn't know how to treat servants.

He was, however, a pretty good trainer. Better still, he had rich friends who could afford good horses. I had ridden for him semi-regularly for nearly eight years, and although at first I had resented his snobbish little ways, I had eventually grown up enough to find them amusing. We operated strictly as a business team, even after all that time. Not a flicker of friendship. He would have been outraged at the very idea, and I didn't like him enough to think it a pity.

He was twenty years older than me, a tallish, thin Anglo-Saxon type with thin fine mousy hair, greyish-blue eyes with short fair lashes, a well developed straight nose and aggressively perfect teeth. His bone structure was of the type acceptable to the social circle in which he tried to move, but the lines his outlook on life had etched in his skin were a warning to anyone looking for tolerance or generosity. Cranfield was mean-minded by habit and open handed only to those who could lug him upwards. In all his dealings with those he considered his inferiors he left behind a turbulent wake of dislike and resentment. He was charming to his friends, polite in public to his wife, and his three teenage children echoed his delusions of superiority with pitiful faithfulness.

Cranfield had remarked to me some days before the Enquiry that the Oxford Stewards were all good chaps and that two of them had personally apologized to him for having to send the case on to the Disciplinary Committee. I nodded without answering. Cranfield must have known as well as I did that all three of the Oxford Stewards had been elected for social reasons only; that one of them couldn't read a number board at five paces, that another had inherited his late uncle's string of racehorses but not his expert knowledge, and that the third had been heard to ask his trainer which his own horse was, during the course of a race. Not one of the three could read a race at anything approaching the standard of a racecourse commentator. Good chaps they might well be, but as judges, frightening.

'We will show the film of the race,' Lord Gowery said.

They showed it, projecting from the back of the room on to a screen on the wall behind Cranfield and me. We turned our armchairs round to watch it. The Stipendiary Steward from Oxford, a fat pompous bully, stood by the screen, pointing out Squelch with a long baton.

'This is the horse in question,' he said, as the horses lined up for the start. I reflected mildly that if the Stewards knew their job they would have seen the film several times already, and would know which was Squelch without needing to have him pointed out.

The Stipe more or less indicated Squelch all the way round. It was an unremarkable race, run to a well tried pattern: hold back at the start, letting someone else make the pace; ease forwards to fourth place and settle there for two miles or more; move smoothly to the front coming towards the second last fence, and press on home regardless. If the horse liked that sort of race, and if he were good enough, he would win.

Squelch hated to be ridden any other way. Squelch was, on his day, good enough. It just hadn't been his day.

The film showed Squelch taking the lead coming into the second last fence. He rolled a bit on landing, a sure sign of tiredness. I'd had to pick him up and urge him into the last, and it was obvious on the film. Away from the last, towards the winning post, he'd floundered about beneath me and if I hadn't been ruthless he'd have slowed to a trot. Cherry Pie, at the finish, came up surprisingly fast and passed him as if he'd been standing still.

The film flicked off abruptly and someone put the lights on again. I thought that the film was conclusive and that that would be the end of it.

'You didn't use your whip,' Lord Gowery said accusingly.

'No, sir,' I agreed. 'Squelch shies away from the whip. He has to be ridden with the hands.'

'You were making no effort to ride him out.'

'Indeed I was, sir. He was dead tired, you can see on the film.'

'All I can see on the film is that you were making absolutely no effort to win. You were sitting there with your arms still, making no effort whatsoever.'

I stared at him. 'Squelch isn't an easy horse to ride, sir. He'll always do his best but only if he isn't upset. He has to be ridden quietly. He stops if he's hit. He'll only respond to being squeezed, and to small flicks on the reins, and to his jockey's voice.'

'That's quite right,' said Cranfield piously. 'I always give Hughes orders not to treat the horse roughly.'

As if he hadn't heard a word, Lord Gowery said, 'Hughes didn't pick up his whip.'

He looked inquiringly at the two Stewards flanking him, as if to collect their opinions. The one on his left, a youngish man who had ridden as an amateur, nodded non-committally. The other one was asleep.

I suspected Gowery kicked him under the table. He woke up with a jerk, said 'Eh? Yes, definitely,' and eyed me suspiciously.

It's a farce, I thought incredulously. The whole thing's a bloody farce.

Gowery nodded, satisfied. 'Hughes never picked up his whip.'

The fat bullying Stipe was oozing smugness. 'I am sure you will find this next film relevant, sir.'

'Quite,' agreed Gowery. 'Show it now.'

'Which film is this?' Cranfield inquired.

Gowery said, 'This film shows Squelch winning at Reading on 3rd January.'

Cranfield reflected. 'I was not at Reading on that day.'

'No,' agreed Gowery. 'We understand you went to the Worcester meeting instead.' He made it sound suspicious instead of perfectly normal. Cranfield had run a hot young hurdler at Worcester and had wanted to see how he shaped. Squelch, the established star, needed no supervision.

The lights went out again. The Stipe used his baton to point out Kelly Hughes riding a race in Squelch's distinctive colours of black and white chevrons and a black cap. Not at all the same sort of race as the Lemonfizz Crystal Cup. I'd gone to the front early to give myself a clear view of the fences, pulled back to about third place for a breather at midway, and forced to the front again only after the last fence, swinging my whip energetically down the horse's shoulder and urging him vigorously with my arms.

The film stopped, the lights went on, and there was a heavy accusing silence. Cranfield turned towards me, frowning.

'You will agree,' said Gowery ironically, 'That you used your whip, Hughes.'

'Yes, sir,' I said. 'Which race did you say that was?'

'The last race at Reading,' he said irritably. 'Don't pretend you don't know.'

'I agree that the film you've just shown was the last race at Reading, sir. But Squelch didn't run in the last race at Reading. The horse in that film is Wanderlust. He belongs to Mr Kessel, like Squelch does, so the colours are the same, and both horses are by the same sire, which accounts for them looking similar, but the horse you've just shown is Wanderlust. Who does, as you saw, respond well if you wave a whip at him.'

There was dead silence. It was Cranfield who broke it, clearing his throat.

'Hughes is quite right. That is Wanderlust.'

He hadn't realized it, I thought in amusement, until I'd pointed it out. It's all too easy for people to believe what they're told.

There was a certain amount of hurried whispering going on. I didn't help them. They could sort it out for themselves.

Eventually Lord Gowery said, 'Has anyone got a form book?' and an official near the door went out to fetch one. Gowery opened it and took a long look at the Reading results.

'It seems,' he said heavily, 'That we have the wrong film. Squelch ran in the sixth race at Reading, which is of course usually the last. However, it now appears that on that day there were seven races, the Novice Chase having been divided and run in two halves, at the beginning and end of the day. Wanderlust won the *seventh* race. A perfectly understandable mix-up, I am afraid.'

I didn't think I would help my cause by saying that I thought it a disgraceful mix-up, if not criminal.

'Could we now, sir,' I asked politely, 'See the right film? The one that Squelch won.'

Lord Gowery cleared his throat. 'I don't think we have it here. However,' he recovered fast, 'we don't need it. It is immaterial. We are not considering the Reading result, but that at Oxford.'

I gasped. I was truly astounded. 'But sir, if you watch Squelch's race, you will see that I rode him at Reading exactly as I did at Oxford, without using the whip.'

'That is beside the point, Hughes, because Squelch may not have needed the whip at Reading, but at Oxford he did.'

'Sir, it *is* the point,' I protested. 'I rode Squelch at Oxford in exactly the same manner as when he won at Reading, only at Oxford he tired.'

Lord Gowery absolutely ignored this. Instead he looked left and right to his Stewards alongside and remarked, 'We must waste no more time. We have three or four witnesses to call before lunch.'

The sleepy eldest Steward nodded and looked at his watch. The younger one nodded and avoided meeting my eyes. I knew him quite well from his amateur jockey days, and had often ridden against him. We had all been pleased when he had been made a Steward, because he knew at first-hand the sort of odd circumstances which cropped up in racing to make a fool of the brightest, and we had thought that he would always put forward or explain our point of view. From his downcast semi-apologetic face I now gathered that we had hoped too much. He had not so far contributed one single word to the proceedings, and he looked, though it seemed extraordinary, intimidated.

As plain Andrew Tring he had been lighthearted, amusing, and almost reckless over fences. His recently inherited baronetcy and his even more recently acquired Stewardship seemed on the present showing to have hammered him into the ground.

Of Lord Plimborne, the elderly sleepyhead, I knew very little except his name. He seemed to be in his seventies and there was a faint tremble about many of his movements as if old age were shaking at his foundations and would soon have him down. He had not, I thought, clearly heard or understood more than a quarter of what had been said.

An Enquiry was usually conducted by three Stewards, but on this day there were four. The fourth, who sat on the left of Andrew Tring, was not, as far as I knew, even on the Disciplinary Committee, let alone a Disciplinary Steward. But he had in front of him a pile of notes as large if not larger than the others, and he was following every word with sharp hot eyes. Exactly where his involvement lay I couldn't work out, but there was no doubt that Wykeham, second Baron Ferth, cared about the outcome.

He alone of the four seemed really disturbed that they should have shown the wrong film, and he said quietly but forcefully enough for it to carry across to Cranfield and me, 'I did advise against showing the Reading race, if you remember.'

Gowery gave him an icelance of a look which would have slaughtered thinner skinned men, but against Ferth's inner furnace it melted impotently.

'You agreed to say nothing,' Gowery said in the same piercing undertone. 'I would be obliged if you would keep to that.'

Cranfield had stirred beside me in astonishment, and now, thinking about it on the following day, the venomous little exchange seemed even more incredible. What, I now wondered, had Ferth been doing there, where he didn't really belong and was clearly not appreciated.

The telephone bell broke up my thoughts. I went into the sitting-room to answer it and found it was a jockey colleague ringing up to commiserate. He himself, he reminded me, had had his licence suspended for a while three or four years back, and he knew how I must be feeling.

'It's good of you, Jim, to take the trouble.'

'No trouble, mate. Stick together, and all that. How did it go?'

'Lousy,' I said. 'They didn't listen to a word either Cranfield or I said. They'd made up their minds we were guilty before we ever went there.'

Jim Enders laughed. 'I'm not surprised. You know what happened to me?'

'No. What?'

'Well, when they gave me my licence back, they'd called the Enquiry for the Tuesday, see, and then for some reason they had to postpone it until the Thursday afternoon. So along I went on Thursday afternoon and they hummed and hahed and warned me as to my future conduct and kept me in suspense for a bit before they said I could have my licence back. Well, I thought I might as well collect a Racing Calendar and take it home with me, to keep abreast of the times and all that, so, anyway, I collected my Racing Calendar which is published at twelve o'clock on Thursdays, twelve o'clock mind you, and I opened it, and what is the first thing I see but the notice saying my licence has been restored. So how about *that*? They'd published the result of that meeting two hours before it had even begun.'

'I don't believe it,' I said.

'Quite true,' he said. 'Mind you, that time they were giving my licence back, not taking it away. But even so, it shows they'd made up their minds. I've always wondered why they bothered to hold that second enquiry at all. Waste of everyone's time, mate.'

'It's incredible,' I said. But I did believe him: which before my own Enquiry I would not have done.

'When are they giving you your licence back?' Jim asked.

'They didn't say.'

'Didn't they tell you when you could apply?'

'No.'

Jim shoved one very rude word down the wires. 'And that's another thing, mate, you want to pick your moment right when you *do* apply.'

'How do you mean?'

'When I applied for mine, on the dot of when they told me I could, they said the only Steward who had authority to give it back had gone on a cruise to Madeira and I would have to wait until he turned up again.'

CHAPTER TWO

WHEN THE HORSES came back from second exercise at midday my cousin Tony stomped up the stairs and trod muck and straw into my carpet. It was his stable, not Cranfield's, that I lived in. He had thirty boxes, thirty-two horses, one house, one wife, four children and an overdraft. Ten more boxes were being built, the fifth child was four months off and the overdraft was turning puce. I lived alone in the flat over the yard and rode everything which came along.

All very normal. And, in the three years since we had moved in, increasingly successful. My suspension meant that Tony and the owners were going to have to find another jockey.

He flopped down gloomily in a green velvet armchair.

'You all right?'

'Yes,' I said.

'Give me a drink, for God's sake.'

I poured half a cupful of J and B into a chunky tumbler.

'Ice?'

'As it is.'

I handed him the glass and he made inroads. Restoration began to take place.

Our mothers had been Welsh girls, sisters. Mine had married a local boy, so that I had come out wholly Celt, shortish, dark, compact. My aunt had hightailed off with a six foot four languid blond giant from Wyoming who had endowed Tony with most of his physique and double his brain. Out of U.S.A.A.F. uniform, Tony's father had reverted to ranch-hand, not ranch owner, as he had led his in-laws to believe, and he'd considered it more important for his only child to get to ride well than to acquire any of that there fancy book learning.

Tony therefore played truant for years with enthusiasm, and had never regretted it. I met him for the first time when he was twenty-five, when his Pa's heart had packed up and he had escorted his sincerely weeping Mum back to Wales. In the seven years since then he had acquired with some speed an English wife, a semi-English accent, an unimpassioned knowledge of English racing, a job as assistant trainer, and a stable of his own. And also, somewhere along the way, an unquenchable English thirst. For Scotch.

He said, looking down at the diminished drink, 'What are you going to do?'

'I don't know, exactly.'

"Will you go back home?'

'Not to live,' I said. 'I've come too far.'

He raised his head a little and looked round the room, smiling. Plain white walls, thick brown carpet, velvet chairs in two or three greens, antique furniture, pink and orange striped curtains, heavy and rich. 'I'll say you have,' he agreed. 'A big long way from Coedlant Farm, boyo.'

'No further than your prairie.'

He shook his head. 'I still have grass roots. You've pulled yours up.'

Penetrating fellow, Tony. An extraordinary mixture of raw intelligence and straws in the hair. He was right; I'd shaken the straws out of mine. We got on very well.

'I want to talk to someone who has been to a recent Enquiry,' I said, abruptly.

'You want to just put it behind you and forget it,' he advised. 'No percentage in comparing hysterectomies.'

I laughed, which was truly something in the circumstances. 'Not on a pain for pain basis,' I explained. 'It's just that I want to know if what happened yesterday was . . . well, unusual. The procedure, that is. The form of the thing. Quite apart from the fact that most of the evidence was rigged.'

'Is that what you were mumbling about on the way home? Those few words you uttered in a wilderness of silence?'

'Those,' I said, 'were mostly "they didn't believe a word we said".'

'So who rigged what?'

'That's the question.'

He held out his empty glass and I poured some more into it.

'Are you serious?'

'Yes. Starting from point A, which is that I rode Squelch to win, we arrive at point B, which is that the Stewards are convinced I didn't. Along the way were three or four little birdies all twittering their heads off and lying in their bloody teeth.'

'I detect,' he said, 'That something is stirring in yesterday's ruins.'

'What ruins?'

'You.'

'Oh.'

'You should drink more,' he said. 'Make an effort. Start now.'

'I'll think about it.'

'Do that.' He wallowed to his feet. 'Time for lunch. Time to go back to the little nestlings with their mouths wide open for worms'.

'Is it worms, today?'

'God knows. Poppy said to come, if you want.'

I shook my head.

'You must eat,' he protested.

'Yes.'

He looked at me consideringly. 'I guess,' he said, 'that you'll manage.' He put down his empty glass. 'We're here, you know, if you want anything. Company. Food. Dancing girls. Trifles like that.'

I nodded my thanks, and he clomped away down the stairs. He hadn't mentioned his horses, their races, or the other jockeys he would have to engage. He hadn't said that my staying in the flat would be an embarrassment to him.

I didn't know what to do about that. The flat was my home. My only home. Designed, converted, furnished by me. I liked it, and I didn't want to leave.

I wandered into the bedroom.

A double bed, but pillows for one.

On the dressing chest, in a silver frame, a photograph of Rosalind. We had been married for two years when she went to spend a routine week-end with her parents. I'd been busy riding five races at Market Rasen on the Saturday, and a policeman had come into the weighing-room at the end of the afternoon and told me unemotionally that my father-in-law had set off with his wife and mine to visit friends and had misjudged his overtaking distance in heavy rain and had driven head on into a lorry and killed all three of them instantly.

It was four years since it had happened. Quite often I could no longer remember her voice. Other times she seemed to be in the next room. I had loved her passionately, but she no longer hurt. Four years was a long time.

I wished she had been there, with her tempestuous nature and fierce loyalty, so that I could have told her about the Enquiry, and shared the wretchedness, and been comforted.

That Enquiry . . .

Gowery's first witness had been the jockey who had finished third in the Lemonfizz, two or three lengths behind Squelch. About twenty, round faced and immature, Master Charlie West was a boy with a lot of natural talent but too little self-discipline. He had a great opinion of himself, and was in danger of throwing away his future through an apparent belief that rules only applied to everyone else.

The grandeur of Portman Square and the trappings of the Enquiry seemed to have subdued him. He came into the room nervously and stood where he was told, at one end of the Stewards' table: on their left, and to our right. He looked down at the table and raised his eyes only once or twice during his whole testimony. He didn't look across to Cranfield and me at all.

Gowery asked him if he remembered the race.

'Yes, sir.' It was a low mumble, barely audible.

'Speak up,' said Gowery irritably.

The shorthand writer came across from his table and moved the microphone so that it was nearer Charlie West. Charlie West cleared his throat.

'What happened during the race?'

'Well sir . . . Shall I start from the beginning, sir?'

'There's no need for unnecessary detail, West,' Gowery said impatiently. 'Just tell us what happened on the far side of the course on the second circuit.'

'I see, sir. Well . . . Kelly, that is, I mean, Hughes, sir . . . Hughes . . . Well . . . Like . . .'

'West, come to the point.' Gowery's voice would have left a laser standing. A heavy flush showed in patches on Charlie West's neck. He swallowed.

'Round the far side, sir, where the stands go out of sight, like, for a few seconds, well, there sir . . . Hughes gives this hefty pull back on the reins, sir . . .'

'And what did he say, West?'

'He said, sir, "O.K. Brakes on, chaps." Sir.'

Gowery said meaningfully, though everyone had heard the first time and a pin would have crashed on the Wilton, 'Repeat that, please, West.'

'Hughes, sir, said "O.K. Brakes on, chaps".'

'And what did you take him to mean by that, West?'

'Well sir, that he wasn't trying, like. He always says that when he's pulling one back and not trying.'

'*Always?*'

'Well, something like that, sir.'

There was a considerable silence.

Gowery said formally, 'Mr Cranfield . . . Hughes . . . You may ask this witness questions, if you wish.'

I got slowly to my feet.

'Are you seriously saying,' I asked bitterly, 'That at any time during the Lemonfizz Cup I pulled Squelch back and said "O.K., brakes on, chaps?'

He nodded. He had begun to sweat.

'Please answer aloud,' I said.

'Yes. You said it.'

'I did not.'

'I heard you.'

'You couldn't have done.'

'I heard you.'

I was silent. I simply had no idea what to say next. It was too like a playground exchange: you did, I didn't, you did, I didn't . . .

I sat down. All the Stewards and all the officials ranked behind them were looking at me. I could see that all, to a man, believed West.

'Hughes, are you in the habit of using this phrase?' Gowery's voice was dry acid.

'No, sir.'

'Have you *ever* used it?'

'Not in the Lemonfizz Cup, sir.'

'I said, Hughes, have you *ever* used it?'

To lie or not to lie . . . 'Yes, sir, I have used it, once or twice. But not on Squelch in the Lemonfizz Cup.'

'It is sufficient that you said it at all, Hughes. We will draw our own conclusions as to *when* you said it.'

He shuffled one paper to the bottom of his pack and picked up another. Consulting it with the unseeing token glance of those who know their subject by heart, he continued, 'And now, West, tell us what Hughes did after he had said those words.'

'Sir, he pulled his horse back, sir.'

'How do you know this?' The question was a formality. He asked with the tone of one already aware of the answer.

'I was just beside Hughes, sir, when he said that about brakes. Then he sort of hunched his shoulders, sir, and give a pull, sir, and, well, then he was behind me, having dropped out, like.'

Cranfield said angrily. 'But he finished in front of you.'

'Yes, sir,' Charlie West flicked his eyes upwards to Lord

Gowery, and spoke only to him. 'My old horse couldn't act on the going, sir, and Hughes came past me again going into the second last, like.'

'And how did Squelch jump that fence?'

'Easy, sir. Met it just right. Stood back proper, sir.'

'Hughes maintains that Squelch was extremely tired at that point.'

Charlie West left a small pause. Finally he said, 'I don't know about that, sir. I thought as how Squelch would win, myself, sir. I still think as how he ought to have won, sir, being the horse he is, sir.'

Gowery glanced left and right, to make sure that his colleagues had taken the point. 'From your position during the last stages of the race, West, could you see whether or not Hughes was making every effort to win?'

'Well he didn't look like it, sir, which was surprising, like.'

'Surprising?'

'Yes sir. See, Hughes is such an artist at it, sir.'

'An artist at what?'

'Well, at riding what looks from the stands one hell of a finish, sir, while all the time he's smothering it like mad.'

'Hughes is in the habit of not riding to win?'

Charlie West worked it out. 'Yes, sir.'

'Thank you, West,' Lord Gowery said with insincere politeness. 'You may go and sit over there at the back of the room.'

Charlie West made a rabbit's scurry towards the row of chairs reserved for those who had finished giving evidence. Cranfield turned fiercely to me and said, 'Why didn't you deny it more vehemently, for God's sake? Why the Hell didn't you insist he was making the whole thing up?'

'Do you think they'd believe me?'

He looked uneasily at the accusing ranks opposite, and found his answer in their implacable stares. All the same, he stood up and did his best.

'Lord Gowery, the film of the Lemonfizz Cup does not bear out West's accusation. At no point does Hughes pull back his horse.'

I lifted my hand too late to stop him. Gowery's and Lord Ferth's intent faces both registered satisfaction. They knew as well as I did that what West had said was borne out on the film. Sensing that Squelch was going to run out of steam, I'd given him a short breather a mile from home, and this normal everyday little act was now wide open to misinterpretation.

Cranfield looked down at me, surprised by my reaction.

'I gave him a breather,' I said apologetically. 'It shows.'

He sat down heavily, frowning in worry.

Gowery was saying to an official, 'Show in Mr Newtonnards' as if Cranfield hadn't spoken. There was a pause before Mr Newtonnards, whoever he was, materialized. Lord Gowery was looking slightly over his left shoulder, towards the door, giving me the benefit of his patrician profile. I realized with almost a sense of shock that I knew nothing about him as a person, and that he most probably knew nothing about me. He had been, to me, a figure of authority with a capital A. I hadn't questioned his right to rule over me. I had assumed naively that he would do so with integrity, wisdom and justice.

So much for illusions. He was leading his witnesses in a way that would make the Old Bailey reel. He heard truth in Charlie West's lies and lies in my truth. He was prosecutor as well as judge, and was only admitting evidence if it fitted his case.

He was dispersing the accepting awe I had held him in like candyfloss in a thunderstorm, and I could feel an unforgiving cynicism growing in its stead. Also I was ashamed of my former state of trust. With the sort of education I'd had, I ought to have known better.

Mr Newtonnards emerged from the waiting-room and made his way to the witnesses' end of the Stewards' table, sporting a red rosebud in his lapel and carrying a large blue ledger. Unlike Charlie West he was confident, not nervous. Seeing that everyone else was seated he looked around for a chair for himself, and not finding one, asked.

After a fractional pause Gowery nodded, and the official-of-all-work near the door pushed one forward. Mr Newtonnards deposited into it his well-cared-for pearl-grey-suited bulk.

'Who is he?' I said to Cranfield. Cranfield shook his head and didn't answer, but he knew, because his air of worry had if anything deepened.

Andrew Tring flipped through his pile of papers, found what he was looking for, and drew it out. Lord Plimborne had his eyes shut again. I was beginning to expect that: and in any case I could see that it didn't matter, since the power lay somewhere between Gowery and Ferth, and Andy Tring and Plimborne were so much window-dressing.

Lord Gowery too picked up a paper, and again I had the impression that he knew its contents by heart.

'Mr Newtonnards?'

'Yes, my Lord.' He had a faint cockney accent overlaid by years of cigars and champagne. Mid-fifties, I guessed; no fool, knew the world, and had friends in show business. Not too far out: Mr Newtonnards, it transpired, was a bookmaker.

Gowery said, 'Mr Newtonnards, will you be so good as to tell us about a certain bet you struck on the afternoon of the Lemonfizz Cup?'

'Yes, my Lord. I was standing on my pitch in Tattersall's when this customer come up and asked me for five tenners on Cherry Pie.' He stopped there, as if that was all he thought necessary.

Gowery did some prompting. 'Please describe this man, and also tell us what you did about his request.'

'Describe him? Let's see, then. He was nothing special. A biggish man in a fawn coat, wearing a brown trilby and carrying race glasses over his shoulder. Middle-aged, I suppose. Perhaps he had a moustache. Can't remember, really.'

The description fitted half the men on the racecourse.

'He asked me what price I'd give him about Cherry Pie,' Newtonnards went on. 'I didn't have any price chalked on my board, seeing Cherry Pie was such an outsider. I offered him tens, but he said it wasn't enough, and he looked like moving off down the line. Well . . .' Newtonnards waved an expressive pudgy hand . . . 'business wasn't too brisk, so I offered him a hundred to six. Couldn't say fairer than that now, could I, seeing as there were only eight runners in the race? Worse decision I made in a long time.' Gloom mixed with stoicism settled on his well covered features.

'So when Cherry Pie won, you paid out?'

'That's right. He put down fifty smackers. I paid him nine hundred.'

'Nine hundred pounds?'

'That's right, my Lord,' Newtonnards confirmed easily, 'Nine hundred pounds.'

'And we may see the record of this bet?'

'Certainly.' He opened the big blue ledger at a marked page. 'On the left, my lord, just over half way down. Marked with a red cross. Nine hundred and fifty, ticket number nine seven two.'

The ledger was passed along the Stewards' table. Plimborne woke up for the occasion and all four of them peered at the page. The ledger returned to Newtonnards, who shut it and let it lie in front of him.

'Wasn't that a very large bet on an outsider?' Gowery asked.

'Yes it was, my Lord. But then, there are a lot of mugs about. Except, of course, that once in a while they go and win.'

'So you had no qualms about risking such a large amount?'

'Not really, my lord. Not with Squelch in the race. And anyway, I laid a bit of it off. A quarter of it, in fact, at thirty-threes. So my actual losses were in the region of four hundred and eighty-seven pounds ten. Then I took three hundred and two-ten on Squelch and the others, which left a net loss on the race of one eight five.'

Cranfield and I received a glare in which every unit of the one eight five rankled.

Gowery said, 'We are not enquiring into how much you lost Mr Newtonnards, but into the identity of the client who won nine hundred pounds on Cherry Pie.'

I shivered. If West could lie, so could others.

'As I said in my statement, my Lord, I don't know his name. When he came up to me I thought I knew him from somewhere, but you see a lot of folks in my game, so I didn't think much of it. You know. So it wasn't until after I paid him off. After the last race, in fact. Not until I was driving home. Then it came to me, and I went spare, I can tell you.'

'Please explain more clearly,' Gowery said patiently. The patience of a cat at a mousehole. Anticipation making the waiting sweet.

'It wasn't him, so much, as who I saw him talking to. Standing by the parade ring rails before the first race. Don't know why I should remember it, but I do.'

'And who did you see this client talking to?'

'Him.' He jerked his head in our direction. 'Mr Cranfield.'

Cranfield was immediately on his feet.

'Are you suggesting that I advised this client of yours to back Cherry Pie?' His voice shook with indignation.

'No, Mr Cranfield,' said Gowery like the North Wind, 'The suggestion is that the client was acting on your behalf, and that it was you yourself that backed Cherry Pie.'

'That's an absolute lie.'

His hot denial fell on a lot of cold ears.

'Where is this mysterious man?' he demanded. 'This un-identified, unidentifiable nobody? How can you possibly trump up such a story and present it as serious evidence? It is ridiculous. Utterly, utterly ridiculous.'

'The bet was struck,' Gowery said plonkingly, pointing to the ledger.

'And I saw you talking to the client,' confirmed Newtonnards.

Cranfield's fury left him gasping for words, and in the end he too sat down again, finding like me nothing to say that could dent the preconceptions ranged against us.

'Mr Newtonnards,' I said. 'Would you know this client again?'

He hesitated only a fraction. 'Yes, I would.'

'Have you seen him at the races since Lemonfizz day?'

'No. I haven't.'

'If you see him again, will you point him out to Lord Gowery?'

'If Lord Gowery's at the races.' Several of the back ranks of officials smiled at this, but Newtonnards, to give him his due, did not.

I couldn't think of anything else to ask him, and I knew I had made no headway at all. It was infuriating. By our own choice we had thrust ourselves back into the bad old days when people accused at racing trials were not allowed a legal defendant. If they didn't know how to defend themselves: if they didn't know what sort of questions to ask or in what form to ask them, that was just too bad. Just their hard luck. But this wasn't hard luck. This was our own stupid fault. A lawyer would have been able to rip Newtonnards' testimony to bits, but neither Cranfield nor I knew how.

Cranfield tried. He was back on his feet.

'Far from backing Cherry Pie, I backed Squelch. You can check up with my own bookmaker.'

Gowery simply didn't reply. Cranfield repeated it.

Gowery said, 'Yes, yes. No doubt you did. It is quite beside the point.'

Cranfield sat down again with his mouth hanging open. I knew exactly how he felt. Not so much banging the head against a brick wall as being actively attacked by a cliff.

They waved Newtonnards away and he ambled easily off to take his place beside Charlie West. What he had said stayed behind him, stuck fast in the officials' minds. Not one of them had asked for corroboration. Not one had suggested that there might have been a loophole in identity. The belief was written plain on their faces: if someone had backed Cherry Pie to win nine hundred pounds, it must have been Cranfield.

Gowery hadn't finished. With a calm satisfaction he picked up another paper and said, 'Mr Cranfield, I have here an affidavit from a Mrs Joan Jones, who handled the five pound selling window on the Totalizator in the paddock on Lemonfizz Cup day, that she sold ten win-only tickets for horse number eight to a man in a fawn raincoat, middle aged, wearing a trilby. I also have here a similar testimony from a Mr Leonard Roberts, who was paying out at the five pound window in the same building, on the same occasion. Both of these Tote employees remember the client well, as these were almost the only five pound tickets sold on Cherry Pie, and certainly the only large block. The Tote paid out to this man more than eleven hundred pounds in cash. Mr Roberts advised him not to carry so much on his person, but the man declined to take his advice.'

There was another accusing silence. Cranfield looked totally nonplussed and came up with nothing to say. This time, I tried for him. 'Sir, did this man back any other horses in the race, on the Tote? Did he back all, or two or three or four, and just hit the jackpot by accident?'

'There was no accident about this, Hughes.'

'But did he, in fact, back any other horses?'

Dead silence.

'Surely you asked?' I said reasonably.

Whether anyone had asked or not, Gowery didn't know. All he knew was what was on the affidavit. He gave me a stony stare, and said, 'No one puts fifty pounds on an outsider without good grounds for believing it will win.'

'But sir . . .'

'However,' he said, 'We will find out.' He wrote a note on the bottom of one of the affidavits. 'It seems to me extremely unlikely. But we will have the question asked.'

There was no suggestion that he would wait for the answer before giving his judgement. And in fact he did not.

CHAPTER THREE

I WANDERED AIMLESSLY round the flat, lost and restless. Reheated the coffee. Drank it. Tried to write to my parents, and gave it up after half a page. Tried to make some sort of decision about my future, and couldn't.

Felt too battered. Too pulped. Too crushed.

Yet I had done nothing.

Nothing.

Late afternoon. The lads were bustling round the yard setting the horses fair for the night, and whistling and calling to each other as usual. I kept away from the windows and eventually went back to the bedroom and lay down on the bed. The day began to fade. The dusk closed in.

After Newtonnards they had called Tommy Timpson, who had ridden Cherry Pie.

Tommy Timpson 'did his two' for Cranfield and rode such of the stable's second strings as Cranfield cared to give him. Cranfield rang the changes on three jockeys: me, Chris Smith (at present taking his time over a fractured skull) and Tommy. Tommy got the crumbs and deserved better. Like many trainers, Cranfield couldn't spot talent when it was under his nose, and it wasn't until several small local trainers had asked for his services that Cranfield woke up to the fact that he had a useful emerging rider in his own yard.

Raw, nineteen years old, a stutterer, Tommy was at his worst at the Enquiry. He looked as scared as a two year old colt at his first starting gate, and although he couldn't help being jittery it was worse than useless for Cranfield and me.

Lord Gowery made no attempt to put him at ease but simply asked questions and let him get on with the answers as best he could.

'What orders did Mr Cranfield give you before the race? How did he tell you to ride Cherry Pie? Did he instruct you to ride to win?'

Tommy stuttered and stumbled and said Mr Cranfield had told him to keep just behind Squelch all the way round and try to pass him after the last fence.

Cranfield said indignantly: 'That's what he *did*. Not what I told him to do.'

Gowery listened, turned his head to Tommy, and said again, 'Will you tell us what instructions Mr Cranfield gave you *before* the race? Please think carefully.'

Tommy swallowed, gave Cranfield an agonized glance, and tried again. 'M . . M . . M . . Mr Cranfield s . . s . . said to take my p . . p . . pace from S . . S . . Squelch and s . . s . . stay with him as long as I c . . c . . could.'

'And did he tell you to win?'

'He s . . s . . said of course g . . g . . go on and w . . w . . win if you c . . c . . can, sir.'

These were impeccable instructions. Only the most suspicious or biased mind could have read any villainy into them. If these Stewards' minds were not suspicious and biased, snow would fall in the Sahara.

'Did you hear Mr Cranfield giving Hughes instructions as to how he should ride Squelch?'

'N .. No, sir. M .. Mr Cranfield did .. didn't g .. give Hughes any orders at all, sir.'

'Why not?'

Tommy ducked it and said he didn't know. Cranfield remarked furiously that Hughes had ridden the horse twenty times and knew what was needed.

'Or you had discussed it with him privately, beforehand?'

Cranfield had no explosive answer to that because of course we *had* discussed it beforehand. In general terms. In an assessment of the opposition. As a matter of general strategy.

'I discussed the race with him, yes. But I gave him no specific orders.'

'So according to you,' Lord Gowery said, 'you intended both of your jockeys to try to win?'

'Yes. I did. My horses are always doing their best.'

Gowery shook his head. 'Your statement is not borne out by the facts.'

'Are you calling me a liar?' Cranfield demanded.

Gowery didn't answer. But yes, he was.

They shooed a willing Tommy Timpson away and Cranfield went on simmering at boiling point beside me. For myself, I was growing cold, and no amount of central heating could stop it. I thought we must now have heard everything, but I was wrong. They had saved the worst until last, building up the pyramid of damning statements until they could put the final cap on it and stand back and admire their four square structure; their solid, unanswerable edifice of guilt.

The worst, at first, had looked so harmless. A quiet slender man in his early thirties, endowed with an utterly forgettable face. After twenty-four hours I couldn't recall his features or remember his voice, and yet I couldn't think about him without shaking with sick impotent fury.

His name was David Oakley. His business, enquiry agent. His address, Birmingham.

He stood without fidgeting at the end of the Stewards' table holding a spiral bound notebook which he consulted continually, and from beginning to end not a shade of emotion affected his face or his behaviour or even his eyes.

'Acting upon instructions, I paid a visit to the flat of Kelly Hughes, jockey, of Corrie House training stables, Corrie, Berkshire, two days after the Lemonfizz Crystal Cup.'

I sat up with a jerk and opened my mouth to deny it, but before I could say a word he went smoothly on.

'Mr Hughes was not there, but the door was open, so I went in to wait for him. While I was there I made certain observations.' He paused.

Cranfield said to me, 'What is all this about?'

'I don't know. I've never seen him before.'

Gowery steamrollered on. 'You found certain objects.'

'Yes, my Lord.'

Gowery sorted out three large envelopes, and passed one each to Tring and Plimborne. Ferth was before them. He had removed the contents from a similar envelope as soon as Oakley had appeared, and was now, I saw, watching me with what I took to be contempt.

The envelopes each held a photograph.

Oakley said, 'The photograph is of objects I found on a chest of drawers in Hughes's bedroom.'

Andy Tring looked, looked again, and raised a horrified face, meeting my eyes accidentally and for the first and only time. He glanced away hurriedly, embarrassed and disgusted.

'I want to see that photograph,' I said hoarsely.

'Certainly.' Lord Gowery turned his copy round and pushed it across the table. I got up, walked the three dividing steps, and looked down at it.

For several seconds I couldn't take it in, and when I did, I was breathless with disbelief. The photograph had been taken from above the dressing chest, and was sparkling clear. There was the edge of the silver frame and half of Rosalind's face, and from under the frame, as if it had been used as a paperweight, protruded a sheet of paper dated the day after the Lemonfizz Cup. There were three words written on it, and two initials.

'As agreed. Thanks. D.C.'

Slanted across the bottom of the paper, and spread out like a pack of cards, were a large number of ten pound notes.

I looked up, and met Lord Gowery's eyes, and almost flinched away from the utter certainty I read there.

'It's a fake,' I said. My voice sounded odd. 'It's a complete fake.'

'What is it?' Cranfield said from behind me, and in his voice too everyone could hear the awareness of disaster.

I picked up the photograph and took it across to him, and I couldn't feel my feet on the carpet. When he had grasped what it meant he stood up slowly and in a low biting voice said formally, 'My Lords, if you believe this, you will believe anything.'

It had not the slightest effect.

Gowery said merely, 'That is your handwriting, I believe.'

Cranfield shook his head. 'I didn't write it.'

'Please be so good as to write those exact words on this sheet of paper.' Gowery pushed a plain piece of paper across the table, and after a second Cranfield went across and wrote on it. Everyone knew that the two samples would look the same, and they did. Gowery passed the sheet of paper significantly to the other Stewards, and they all compared and nodded.

'It's a fake,' I said again. 'I never had a letter like that.'

Gowery ignored me. To Oakley he said, 'Please tell us where you found the money.'

Oakley unnecessarily consulted his notebook. 'The money was folded inside this note, fastened with a rubber band, and both were tucked behind the photo of Hughes's girl friend, which you see in the picture.'

'It's not true,' I said. I might as well not have bothered. No one listened.

'You counted the money, I believe?'

'Yes my Lord. There was five hundred pounds.'

'There was no money,' I protested. Useless. 'And anyway,' I added desperately, 'Why would I take five hundred for losing the race when I would get about as much as that for winning?'

I thought for a moment that I might have scored a hit. Might have made them pause. A pipe dream. There was an answer to that, too.

'We understand from Mr Kessel, Squelch's owner,' Gowery said flatly, 'That he pays you ten per cent of the winning stake money through official channels by cheque. This means that all presents received by you from Mr Kessel are taxed; and we understand that as you pay a high rate of tax your ten per cent from Mr Kessel would have in effect amounted to half, or less than half, of five hundred pounds.'

They seemed to have enquired into my affairs down to the last penny. Dug around in all directions. Certainly I had never tried to hide anything, but this behind-my-back tin-opening made me feel naked. Also, revolted. Also, finally, hopeless. And it wasn't until then that I realized I had been subconsciously clinging to a fairy tale faith that it would all finally come all right, that because I was telling the truth I was bound to be believed in the end.

I stared across at Lord Gowery, and he looked briefly back. His face was expressionless, his manner entirely calm. He had reached his conclusions and nothing could overthrow them.

Lord Ferth, beside him, was less bolted down, but a great deal of his earlier heat seemed to have evaporated. The power he had generated no longer troubled Gowery at all, and all I could interpret from his expression was some kind of resigned acceptance.

There was little left to be said. Lord Gowery briefly summed up the evidence against us. The list of former races. The non use of the whip. The testimony of Charlie West. The bets struck on Cherry Pie. The riding orders given in private. The photographic proof of a pay-off from Cranfield to Hughes.

'There can be no doubt that this was a most flagrant fraud on the racing public . . . No alternative but to suspend your licences . . . And you, Dexter Cranfield, and you, Kelly Hughes, will be warned off Newmarket Heath until further notice.'

Cranfield, pale and shaking, said, 'I protest that this has not been a fair hearing. Neither Hughes nor I are guilty. The sentence is outrageous.'

No response from Lord Gowery. Lord Ferth, however, spoke for the second time in the proceedings.

'Hughes?'

'I rode Squelch to win,' I said. 'The witnesses were lying.'

Gowery shook his head impatiently. 'The Enquiry is closed. You may go.'

Cranfield and I both hesitated, still unable to accept that that was all. But the official near the door opened it, and all the ranks opposite began to talk quietly to each other and ignore us, and in the end we walked out. Stiff legged. Feeling as if my head were a floating football and my body a chunk of ice. Unreal.

There were several people in the waiting-room outside, but I didn't see them clearly. Cranfield, tight lipped, strode away from me, straight across the room and out of the far door, shaking off a hand or two laid on his sleeve. Dazed I started to follow him, but was less purposeful, and was effectively stopped by a large man who planted himself in my way.

I looked at him vaguely. Mr Kessel. The owner of Squelch.

'Well?' he said challengingly.

'They didn't believe us. We've both been warned off.'

He hissed a sharp breath out between his teeth. 'After what I've been hearing, I'm not surprised. And I'll tell you this, Hughes, even if you get your licence back, you won't be riding for me again.'

I looked at him blankly and didn't answer. It seemed a small thing after what had already happened. He had been talking to the witnesses, in the waiting-room. They would convince anyone, it seemed. Some owners were unpredictable anyway, even in normal times. One day they had all the faith in the world in their jockey, and the next day, none at all. Faith with slender foundations. Mr Kessel had forgotten all the races I had won for him because of the one I had lost.

I turned blindly away from his hostility and found a more welcome hand on my arm. Tony, who had driven up with me instead of seeing his horses work.

'Come on,' he said. 'Let's get out of here.'

I nodded and went down with him in the lift, out into the hall, and towards the front door. Outside there we could see a bunch of newspaper reporters waylaying Cranfield with their notebooks at the ready, and I stopped dead at the sight.

'Let's wait till they've gone,' I said.

'They won't go. Not before they've chewed you up too.'

We waited, hesitating, and a voice called behind me, 'Hughes.'

I didn't turn round. I felt I owed no one the slightest politeness. The footsteps came up behind me and he finally came to a halt in front.

Lord Ferth. Looking tired.

'Hughes. Tell me. Why in God's name did you do it?'

I looked at him stonily. 'I didn't.'

He shook his head. 'All the evidence . . .'

'You tell me,' I said, rudely, 'Why decent men like Stewards so easily believe a lot of lies.'

I turned away from him, too. Twitched my head at Tony and made for the front door. To hell with the press. To hell with the Stewards and Mr Kessel. And to everything to do with racing. The upsurge of fury took me out of the building and fifty yards along the pavement in Portman Square and only evaporated into grinding misery when we had climbed into the taxi Tony whistled for.

Tony thumped up the stairs to the darkened flat. I heard him calling.

'Are you there, Kelly?'

I unrolled myself from the bed, stood up, stretched, went out into the sitting-room and switched on the lights. He was standing in the far doorway, blinking, his hands full of tray.

'Poppy insisted,' he explained.

He put the tray down on the table and lifted off the covering cloth. She'd sent hot chicken pie, a tomato, and about half a pound of Brie.

'She says you haven't eaten for two days.'

'I suppose not.'

'Get on with it, then.' He made an instinctive line for the whisky bottle and poured generously into two tumblers.

'And here. For once, drink this.'

I took the glass and a mouthful and felt the fire trickle down inside my chest. The first taste was always the best. Tony tossed his off and ordered himself a refill.

I ate the pie, the tomato, and the cheese. Hunger I hadn't consciously felt rolled contentedly over and slept.

'Can you stay a bit?' I asked.

'Natch.'

'I'd like to tell you about the Enquiry.'

'Shoot,' he said with satisfaction. 'I've been waiting.'

I told him all that had happened, almost word for word. Every detail had been cut razor sharp into my memory in the way that only happens in disasters.

Tony's astonishment was plain. 'You were framed!'

'That's right.'

'But surely no one can get away with that?'

'Someone seems to be doing all right.'

'But was there *nothing* you could say to prove . . .'

'I couldn't think of anything yesterday, which is all that matters. It's always easy to think of all the smart clever things one *could* have said, afterwards, when it's too late.'

'What would you have said, then?'

'I suppose for a start I should have asked who had **given** that so called enquiry agent instructions to search my flat. Acting on instructions, he said. Well, *whose* instructions? I didn't think of asking, yesterday. Now I can see that it could be the whole answer.'

'You assumed the Stewards had instructed him?'

'I suppose so. I didn't really think. Most of the time I was so shattered that I couldn't think clearly at all.'

'Maybe it *was* the Stewards.'

'Well, no. I suppose it's barely possible they might have sent an investigator, though when you look at it in cold blood it wouldn't really seem likely, but it's a tear drop to the Atlantic that they wouldn't have supplied him with five hundred quid and a forged note and told him to photograph them somewhere distinctive in my flat. But that's what he did. Who instructed him?'

'Even if you'd asked, he wouldn't have said.'

'I guess not. But at least it might have made the Stewards think a bit too.'

Tony shook his head. 'He would still have said he found the money behind Rosalind's picture. His word against yours. Nothing different.'

He looked gloomily into his glass. I looked gloomily into mine.

'That bloody little Charlie West,' I said. 'Someone got at him, too.'

'I presume you didn't in fact say "Brakes on, chaps"?'

'I did say it, you see. Not in the Lemonfizz, of course, but a couple of weeks before, in that frightful novice 'chase at Oxford, the day they abandoned the last two races because it was snowing. I was hitting every fence on that deadly bad jumper that old Almond hadn't bothered to school properly, and half the other runners were just as green, and a whole bunch of us had got left about twenty lengths behind the four who were any use, and sleet was falling, and I didn't relish ending up with a broken bone at nought degrees centigrade, so as we were handily out of sight of the stands at that point I shouted "O.K., brakes on, chaps," and a whole lot of us eased up thankfully and finished the race a good deal slower than we could have done. It didn't affect the result, of course. But there you are. I did say it. What's more, Charlie West heard me. He just shifted it from one race to another.'

'The bastard.'

'I agree.'

'Maybe no one got at him. Maybe he just thought he'd get a few more rides if you were out of the way.'

I considered it and shook my head. 'I wouldn't have thought he was *that* much of a bastard.'

'You never know.' Tony finished his drink and absentmindedly replaced it. 'What about the bookmaker?'

'Newtonnards? I don't know. Same thing, I suppose. Someone has it in for Cranfield too. Both of us, it was. The Stewards couldn't possibly have warned off one of us without the other. We were knitted together so neatly.'

'It makes me livid,' Tony said violently. 'It's wicked.'

I nodded. 'There was something else, too, about that Enquiry. Some undercurrent, running strong. At least, it was strong at the beginning. Something between Lord Gowery and Lord Ferth. And then Andy Tring, he was sitting there looking like a wilted lettuce.' I shook my head in puzzlement. 'It was like a couple of heavy animals lurking in the undergrowth, shaping up to fight each other. You couldn't see them, but there was a sort of quiver in the air. At least, that's how it seemed at one point . . .'

'Stewards are men,' Tony said with bubble-bursting matter-of-factness. 'Show me any organization which doesn't have some sort of power struggle going on under its gentlemanly surface. All you caught was a whiff of the old brimstone. State of nature. Nothing to do with whether you and Cranfield were guilty or not.'

He half convinced me. He polished off the rest of the whisky and told me not to forget to get some more.

Money. That was another thing. As from yesterday I had no income. The Welfare State didn't pay unemployment benefits to the self-employed, as all jockeys remembered every snow-bound winter.

'I'm going to find out,' I said abruptly.

'Find out what?'

'Who framed us.'

'Up the Marines,' Tony said unsteadily. 'Over the top, boys, Up and at 'em.' He picked up the empty bottle and looked at it regretfully. 'Time for bed, I guess. If you need any help with the campaign, count on my Welsh blood to the last clot.'

He made an unswerving line to the door, turned, and gave me a grimace of friendship worth having.

'Don't fall down the stairs,' I said.

PART TWO

MARCH

CHAPTER FOUR

ROBERTA CRANFIELD looked magnificent in my sitting-room.
I came back from buying whisky in the village and found her
gracefully draped all over my restored Chippendale. The green
velvet supported a lot of leg and a deep purple size ten wool
dress; and her thick long hair the colour of dead beech leaves
clashed dramatically with the curtains. Under the hair she had
white skin, incredible eyebrows, amber eyes, photogenic cheek-
bones and a petulant mouth.

She was nineteen, and I didn't like her.

'Good morning.' I said.

'Your door was open.'

'It's a habit I'll have to break.'

I peeled the tissue wrapping off the bottle and put it with the
two chunky glasses on the small silver tray I had once won in a
race sponsored by some sweet manufacturers. Troy weight, twenty-
four ounces: but ruined by the inscription, K. HUGHES, WINNING
JOCKEY, STARCHOCS SILVER STEEPLECHASE. Starchocs indeed. And
I never ate chocolates. Couldn't afford to, from the weight point
of view.

She flapped her hand from a relaxed wrist, indicating the
room.

'This is all pretty lush.'

I wondered what she had come for. I said, 'Would you like some
coffee?'

'Coffee and cannabis.'

'You'll have to go somewhere else.'

'You're very prickly.'

'As a cactus,' I agreed.

She gave me a half minute unblinking stare with her liquid
eyes. Then she said, 'I only said cannabis to jolt you.'

'I'm not jolted.'

'No. I can see that. Waste of effort.'

'Coffee, then?'

'Yes.'

I went into the kitchen and fixed up the percolator. The kitchen was white and brown and copper and yellow. The colours pleased me. Colours gave me the sort of mental food I imagined others got from music. I disliked too much music, loathed the type of stuff you couldn't escape in restaurants and airliners, didn't own a record player, and much preferred silence.

She followed me in from the sitting-room and looked around her with mild surprise.

'Do all jockeys live like this?'

'Naturally.'

'I don't believe it.'

She peered into the pine fronted cupboard I'd taken the coffee from.

'Do you cook for yourself?'

'Mostly.'

'Recherché things like shashlik?' An undercurrent of mockery.

'Steaks.'

I poured the bubbling coffee into two mugs and offered her cream and sugar. She took the cream, generously, but not the sugar, and perched on a yellow topped stool. Her copper hair fitted the kitchen, too.

'You seem to be taking it all right,' she said.

'What?'

'Being warned off.'

I didn't answer.

'A cactus,' she said, 'Isn't in the same class.'

She drank the coffee slowly, in separate mouthfuls, watching me thoughtfully over the mug's rim. I watched her back. Nearly my height, utterly selfpossessed, as cool as the stratosphere. I had seen her grow from a demanding child into a selfish fourteen-year-old, and from there into a difficult-to-please debutante and from there to a glossy imitation model girl heavily tinged with boredom. Over the eight years I had ridden for her father we had met briefly and spoken seldom, usually in parade rings and outside the weighing room, and on the occasions when she did speak to me she seemed to be aiming just over the top of my head.

'You're making it difficult,' she said.

'For you to say why you came?'

She nodded. 'I thought I knew you. Now it seems I don't.'

'What did you expect?'

'Well . . . Father said you came from a farm cottage with pigs running in and out of the door.'

'Father exaggerates.'

She lifted her chin to ward off the familiarity, a gesture I'd seen a hundred times in her and her brothers. A gesture copied from her parents.

'Hens,' I said, 'Not pigs.'

She gave me an up-stage stare. I smiled at her faintly and refused to be reduced to the ranks. I watched the wheels tick over while she worked out how to approach a cactus, and gradually the chin came down.

'Actual hens?'

Not bad at all. I could feel my own smile grow genuine.

'Now and then.'

'You don't look like . . . I mean . . .'

'I know exactly what you mean,' I agreed. 'And it's high time you got rid of those chains.'

'Chains? What are you talking about?'

'The fetters in your mind. The iron bars in your soul.'

'My mind is all right.'

'You must be joking. It's chock-a-block with ideas half a century out of date.'

'I didn't come here to . . .' she began explosively, and then stopped.

'You didn't come here to be insulted,' I said ironically.

'Well, as you put it in that well worn hackneyed phrase, no, I didn't. But I wasn't going to say that.'

'What did you come for?'

She hesitated. 'I wanted you to help me.'

'To do what?'

'To . . . to *cope* with Father.'

I was surprised, first that Father needed coping with, and second that she needed help to do it.

'What sort of help?'

'He's . . . he's so *shattered*.' Unexpectedly there were tears standing in her eyes. They embarrassed and angered her, and she blinked furiously so that I shouldn't see. I admired the tears but not her reason for trying to hide them.

'Here are you,' she said in a rush, 'Walking about as cool as you please and buying whisky and making coffee as if no screaming avalanche had poured down on you and smothered your life and made every thought an absolute bloody Hell, and maybe you don't understand how anyone in that state needs help, and come to that I don't understand why *you* don't need help, but anyway, Father *does*.'

'Not from me,' I said mildly. 'He doesn't think enough of me to give it any value.'

She opened her mouth angrily and shut it again and took two deep controlling breaths. 'And it looks as though he's right.'

'Ouch,' I said ruefully. 'What sort of help, then?'

'I want you to come and talk to him.'

My talking to Cranfield seemed likely to be as therapeutic as applying itching powder to a baby. However she hadn't left me much room for kidding myself that fruitlessness was a good reason for not trying.

'When?'

'Now . . . Unless you have anything else to do.'

'No,' I said carefully. 'I haven't.'

She made a face and an odd little gesture with her hands. 'Will you come now, then . . . please?'

She herself seemed surprised about the real supplication in that 'please'. I imagined that she had come expecting to instruct, not to ask.

'All right.'

'Great.' She was suddenly very cool, very employer's daughter again. She put her coffee mug on the draining board and started towards the door. 'You had better follow me, in your car. It's no good me taking you, you'll need your own car to come back in.'

'That is so,' I agreed.

She looked at me suspiciously, but decided not to pursue it. 'My coat is in your bedroom.'

'I'll fetch it for you.'

'Thank you.'

I walked across the sitting-room and into the bedroom. Her coat was lying on my bed in a heap. Black and white fur, in stripes going round. I picked it up and turned, and found she had followed me.

'Thank you so much.' She presented her back to me and put her arms in the coat-putting-on position. On went the coat. She swivelled slowly, buttoning up the front with shiny black saucers. 'This flat really is fantastic. Who is your decorator?'

'Chap called Kelly Hughes.'

She raised her eyebrows. 'I know the professional touch when I see it.'

'Thank you.'

She raised the chin. 'Oh well, if you won't say . . .'

'I would say. I did say. I did the flat myself. I've been white-washing pigsties since I was six.'

She wasn't quite sure whether to be amused or offended, and evaded it by changing the subject.

'That picture . . . that's your wife, isn't it?'

I nodded.

'I remember her,' she said. 'She was always so sweet to me. She seemed to know what I was feeling. I was really awfully sorry when she was killed.'

I looked at her in surprise. The people Rosalind had been sweetest to had invariably been unhappy. She had had a knack of sensing it, and of giving succour without being asked. I would not have thought of Roberta Cranfield as being unhappy, though I supposed from twelve to fifteen, when she had known Rosalind, she could have had her troubles.

'She wasn't bad, as wives go,' I said flippantly, and Miss Cranfield disapproved of that, too.

We left the flat and this time I locked the door, though such horses as I'd had had already bolted. Roberta had parked her Sunbeam Alpine behind the stables and across the doors of the garage where I kept my Lotus. She backed and turned her car with aggressive poise, and I left a leisurely interval before I followed her through the gates, to avoid a competition all the eighteen miles to her home.

Cranfield lived in an early Victorian house in a hamlet four miles out of Lambourn. A country gentleman's residence, estate agents would have called it: built before the Industrial Revolution had invaded Berkshire and equally impervious to the social revolution a hundred years later. Elegant, charming, timeless, it was a house I liked very much. Pity about the occupants.

I drove up the back drive as usual and parked alongside the stable yard. A horsebox was standing there with its ramp down, and one of the lads was leading a horse into it. Archie, the head lad, who had been helping, came across as soon as I climbed out of the car.

'This is a God awful bloody business,' he said. 'It's wicked, that's what it is. Downright bloody wicked.'

'The horses are going?'

'Some owners have sent boxes already. All of them will be gone by the day after tomorrow.' His weather-beaten face was a mixture of fury, frustration, and anxiety. 'All the lads have got the sack. Even me. And the missus and I have just taken a mortgage on one of the new houses up the road. Chalet bungalow, just what she'd always set her heart on. Worked for years, she has, saving for it. Now she won't stop crying.

We moved in only a month ago, see? How do you think we're going to keep up the payments? Took every pound we had, what with the deposit and the solicitors, and curtains and all. Nice little place, too, she's got it looking real nice. And it isn't as if the Guvnor really fiddled the blasted race. That Cherry Pie, anyone could see with half an eye he was going to be good some day. I mean, if the Guvnor had done it, like, somehow all this wouldn't be so bad. I mean, if he deserved it, well serve him right, and I'd try and get a bit of compensation from him because we're going to have a right job selling the house again, I'll tell you, because there's still two of them empty, they weren't so easy to sell in the first place, being so far out of Lambourn . . . I'll tell you straight, I wish to God we'd never moved out of the Guvnor's cottage, dark and damp though it may be . . . George,' he suddenly shouted at a lad swearing and tugging at a reluctant animal, 'Don't take it out on the horse, it isn't *his* fault . . .' He bustled across the yard and took the horse himself, immediately quietening it and leading it without trouble into the horsebox.

He was an excellent head lad, better than most, and a lot of Cranfield's success was his doing. If he sold his house and got settled in another job, Cranfield wouldn't get him back. The training licence might not be lost for ever, but the stable's main prop would be.

I watched another lad lead a horse round to the waiting box. He too looked worried. His wife, I knew, was on the point of producing their first child.

Some of the lads wouldn't care, of course. There were plenty of jobs going in racing stables, and one lot of digs were much the same as another. But they too would not come back. Nor would most of the horses, nor many of the owners. The stable wasn't being suspended for a few months. It was being smashed.

Sick and seething with other people's fury as well as my own, I walked down the short stretch of drive to the house. Roberta's Alpine was parked outside the front door and she was standing beside it looking cross.

'So there you are. I thought you'd ratted.'

'I parked down by the yard.'

'I can't bear to go down there. Nor can Father. In fact, he won't move out of his dressing-room. You'll have to come upstairs to see him.'

She led the way through the front door and across thirty square yards of Persian rug. When we had reached the foot of

the stairs the door of the library was flung open and Mrs
Cranfield came through it. Mrs Cranfield always flung doors
open, rather as if she suspected something reprehensible was going
on behind them and she was intent on catching the sinners in
the act. She was a plain woman who wore no makeup and
dressed in droopy woollies. To me she had never talked about
anything except horses, and I didn't know whether she could.
Her father was an Irish baron, which may have accounted for
the marriage.

'My father-in-law, Lord Coolihan . . .' Cranfield was wont
to say: and he was wont to say it far too often. I wondered
whether, after Gowery, he was the tiniest bit discontented with
the aristocracy.

'Ah, there you are, Hughes,' Mrs Cranfield said. 'Roberta
told me she was going to fetch you. Though what good you
can do I cannot understand. After all, it was you who got us
into the mess.'

'I what?'

'If you'd ridden a better race on Squelch, none of this would
have happened.'

I bit back six answers and said nothing. If you were hurt
enough you lashed out at the nearest object. Mrs Cranfield
continued to lash.

'Dexter was thoroughly shocked to hear that you had been
in the habit of deliberately losing races.'

'So was I,' I said dryly.

Roberta moved impatiently. 'Mother, do stop it. Come along,
Hughes. This way.'

I didn't move. She went up three steps, paused, and looked
back. 'Come on, what are you waiting for?'

I shrugged. Whatever I was waiting for, I wouldn't get it in
that house. I followed her up the stairs, along a wide passage,
and into her father's dressing-room.

There was too much heavy mahogany furniture of a later
period than the house, a faded-plum-coloured carpet, faded plum
plush curtains, and a bed with an Indian cover.

On one side of the bed sat Dexter Cranfield, his back bent
into a bow and his shoulders hunched round his ears. His hands
rolled loosely on his knees, fingers curling, and he was staring
immovably at the floor.

'He sits like that for hours,' Roberta said in a breath beside
me. And, looking at him, I understood why she had needed
help.

'Father,' she said, going over and touching his shoulder. 'Kelly Hughes is here.'

Cranfield said, 'Tell him to go and shoot himself.'

She saw the twitch in my face, and from her expression thought that I minded, that I believed Cranfield too thought me the cause of all his troubles. On the whole I decided not to crystallize her fears by saying I thought Cranfield had said shoot because shoot was in his mind.

'Hop it,' I said, and jerked my head towards the door.

The chin went up like a reflex. Then she looked at the husk of her father, and back to me, whom she'd been to some trouble to bring, and most of the starch dissolved.

'All right. I'll be down in the library. Don't go without . . . telling me.'

I shook my head, and she went collectedly out of the room, shutting the door behind her.

I walked to the window and looked at the view. Small fields trickling down into the valley. Trees all bent one way by the wind off the Downs. A row of pylons, a cluster of council house roofs. Not a horse in sight. The dressing-room was on the opposite side of the house to the stables.

'Have you a gun?' I asked.

No answer from the bed. I went over and sat down beside him.

'Where is it?'

His eyes slid a fraction in my direction and then back. He had been looking past me. I got up and went to the table beside his bed, but there was nothing lethal on it, and nothing in the drawer.

I found it behind the high mahogany bedhead. A finely wrought Purdey more suitable for pheasants. Both barrels were loaded. I unloaded them.

'Very messy,' I remarked. 'Very inconsiderate. And anyway, you didn't mean to do it.'

I wasn't at all sure about that, but there was no harm in trying to convince him.

'What are you doing here?' he said indifferently.

'Telling you to snap out of it. There's work to be done.'

'Don't speak to me like that.'

'How, then?'

His head came up a little, just like Roberta's. If I made him angry, he'd be half way back to his normal self. And I could go home.

'It's useless sitting up here sulking. It won't achieve anything at all.'

'*Sulking?*' He was annoyed, but not enough.

'Someone took our toys away. Very unfair. But nothing to be gained by grizzling in corners.'

'*Toys* . . . You're talking nonsense.'

'Toys, licences, what's the difference. The things we prized most. Someone's snatched them away. Tricked us out of them. And nobody except us can get them back. Nobody else will bother.'

'We can apply,' he said without conviction.

'Oh, we can apply. In six months' time, I suppose. But there's no guarantee we'd get them. The only sensible thing to do is to start fighting back right now and find out who fixed us. Who, and why. And after that I'll wring his bloody neck.'

He was still staring at the floor, still hunched. He couldn't even look me in the face yet, let alone the world. If he hadn't been such a climbing snob, I thought uncharitably, his present troubles wouldn't have produced such a complete cave-in. He was on the verge of literally not being able to bear the public disgrace of being warned off.

Well, I wasn't so sure I much cared for it myself. It was all very well knowing that one was not guilty, and even having one's closest friends believe it, but one could hardly walk around everywhere wearing a notice proclaiming 'I am innocent. I never done it. It were all a stinking frame-up.'

'It's not so bad for you,' he said.

'That's perfectly true.' I paused 'I came in through the yard.' He made a low sound of protest.

'Archie seems to be seeing to everything himself. And he's worried about his house.'

Cranfield made a waving movement of his hand as much as to ask how did I think he could be bothered with Archie's problems on top of his own.

'It wouldn't hurt you to pay Archie's mortgage for a bit.'

'*What?*' That finally reached him. His head came up at least six inches.

'It's only a few pounds a week. Peanuts to you. Life or death to him. And if you lose him, you'll never get so many winners again.'

'You . . . you . . .' He spluttered. But he still didn't look up.

'A trainer is as good as his lads.'

'That's stupid.'

'You've got good lads just now. You've chucked out the duds, the rough and lazy ones. It takes time to weed out and build up a good team, but you can't get a high ratio of winners without one. You might get your licence back but you won't get these lads back and it'll take years for the stable to recover. If it ever does. And I hear you have already given them all the sack.'

'What else was there to do?'

'You could try keeping them on for a month.'

His head came up a little more. 'You haven't the slightest idea what that would cost me. The wages come to more than four hundred pounds a week.'

'There must still be quite a lot to come in in training fees. Owners seldom pay in advance. You won't have to dig very deep into your own pocket. Not for a month, anyway, and it might not take as long as that.'

'What might not?'

'Getting our licences back.'

'Don't be so bloody ridiculous.'

'I mean it. What is it worth to you? Four weeks' wages for your lads? Would you pay that much if there was a chance you'd be back in racing in a month? The owners would send their horses back, if it was as quick as that. Particularly if you tell them you confidently expect to be back in business almost immediately.'

'They wouldn't believe it.'

'They'd be uncertain. That should be enough.'

'There isn't a chance of getting back.'

'Oh yes there damn well is,' I said forcefully. 'But only if you're willing to take it. Tell the lads you're keeping them on for a bit. Especially Archie. Go down to the yard and tell them now.'

'*Now.*'

'Of course,' I said impatiently. 'Probably half of them have already read the Situations Vacant columns and written to other trainers.'

'There isn't any point.' He seemed sunk in fresh gloom. 'It's all hopeless. And it couldn't have happened, it simply could *not* have happened at a worse time. Edwin Byler was going to send me his horses. It was all fixed up. Now of course he's telephoned to say it's all off, his horses are staying where they are, at Jack Roxford's.'

To train Edwin Byler's horses was to be presented with a pot of gold. He was a north country business man who had made a million or two out of mail order, and had used a little of it to fulfil a long held ambition to own the best string of steeplechasers in Britain. Four of his present horses had in turn cost more than anyone had paid before. When he wanted, he bid. He only wanted the best, and he had bought enough of them to put him for the two previous seasons at the top of the Winning Owners' list. To have been going to train Edwin Byler's horses, and now not to be going to, was a refined cruelty to pile on top of everything else.

To have been going to *ride* Edwin Byler's horses . . . as I would no doubt have done . . . that too was a thrust where it hurt.

'There's all the more point, then,' I said. 'What more do you want in the way of incentive? You're throwing away without a struggle not only what you've got but what you might have . . . Why in the Hell don't you get off your bed and behave like a gentleman and show some spirit?'

'Hughes!' He was outraged. But he still sat. He still wouldn't look at me.

I paused, considering him. Then, slowly, I said, 'All right, then. I'll tell you why you won't. You won't because . . . to some degree . . . you are in fact guilty. You made sure Squelch wouldn't win. And you backed Cherry Pie.'

That got him. Not just his head up, but up, trembling, on to his feet.

CHAPTER FIVE

'HOW DARE YOU?'

'Frankly, just now I'd dare practically anything.'

'You said we were framed.'

'So we were.'

Some of his alarm subsided. I stoked it up again.

'You handed us away on a plate.'

He swallowed, his eyes flicking from side to side, looking everywhere except at me.

'I don't know what you mean.'

'Don't be so weak,' I said impatiently. 'I rode Squelch, remember? Was he his usual self? He was not.'

'If you're suggesting,' he began explosively, 'That I doped . . .'

'Oh of course not. Anyway, they tested him, didn't they?

Negative result. Naturally. No trainer needs to dope a horse he doesn't want to win. It's like swatting a fly with a bulldozer. There are much more subtle methods. Undetectable. Even innocent. Maybe you should be kinder to yourself and admit that you quite innocently stopped Squelch. Maybe you even did it subconsciously, wanting Cherry Pie to win.'

'Bull,' he said.

'The mind plays tricks,' I said. 'People often believe they are doing something for one good reason, while they are subconsciously doing it for another.'

'Twaddle.'

'The trouble comes sometimes when the real reason rears its ugly head and slaps you in the kisser.'

'Shut up.' His teeth and jaw were clenched tight.

I drew a deep breath. I'd been guessing, partly. And I'd guessed right.

'I said, 'You gave Squelch too much work too soon before the race. He lost the Lemonfizz on the gallops at home.'

He looked at me at last. His eyes were dark, as if the pupils had expanded to take up all the iris. There was a desperate sort of hopelessness in his expression.

'It wouldn't have been so bad,' I said, 'If you had admitted it to yourself. Because then you would never have risked not engaging a lawyer to defend us.'

'I didn't mean to over-train Squelch,' he said wretchedly. 'I didn't realize it until afterwards. I did back him, just as I said at the Enquiry.'

I nodded. 'I imagined you must have done. But you backed Cherry Pie as well.'

He explained quite simply, without any of his usual superiority. 'Trainers are often caught out, as you know, when one of their horses suddenly develops his true form. Well, I thought Cherry Pie might just be one of those. So I backed him, on the off chance.'

Some off chance. Fifty pounds with Newtonnards and fifty pounds on the Tote. Gross profit, two thousand.

'How much did you have on Squelch?'

'Two hundred and fifty.'

'Whew.' I said. 'Was that your usual sort of bet?'

'He was odds on . . . I suppose a hundred is my most usual bet.'

I had come to the key question, and I wasn't sure I wanted to ask it, let alone have to judge whether the answer was true. However . . .

'Why,' I said matter-of-factly, 'Didn't you back Cherry Pie with your own usual bookmaker?'

He answered without effort. 'Because I didn't want Kessel knowing I'd backed Cherry Pie, if he won instead of Squelch. Kessel's a funny man, he takes everything personally, he'd as like as not have whisked Squelch away . . .' He trailed off, remembering afresh that Squelch was indeed being whisked.

'Why should Kessel have known?'

'Eh? Oh, because he bets with my bookmaker too, and the pair of them are as thick as thieves.'

Fair enough.

'Well, who was the middle-aged man who put the bets on for you?'

'Just a friend. There's no need to involve him. I want to keep him out of it.'

'Could Newtonnards have seen you talking to him by the parade ring before the first race?'

'Yes,' he said with depression. 'I did talk to him. I gave him the money to bet with.'

And he still hadn't seen any danger signals. Had taken Monty Midgley's assurance at its face value. Hadn't revealed the danger to me. I could have throttled him.

'What did you do with the winnings?'

'They're in the safe downstairs.'

'And you haven't been able to admit to anyone that you've got them.'

'No.'

I thought back. 'You lied about it at the Enquiry.'

'What else was there to do?'

By then, what indeed. Telling the truth hadn't done much for me.

'Let's see, then.' I moved over to the window again, sorting things out. 'Cherry Pie won on his merits. You backed him because he looked like coming into form rather suddenly. Squelch had had four hard races in two months, and a possibly over zealous training gallop. These are the straight facts.'

'Yes . . . I suppose so.'

'No trainer should lose his licence because he didn't tell the world he might just possibly have a flier. I never see why the people who put in all the work shouldn't have the first dip into the well.'

Owners, too, were entitled. Cherry Pie's owner, however, had died three weeks before the Lemonfizz, and Cherry Pie had

run for the executors. Someone was going to have a fine time
deciding his precise value at the moment of his owner's death.

'It means, anyway, that you do have a fighting fund,' I pointed
out.

'There's no point in fighting.'

'You,' I said exasperatedly, 'Are so soft that you'd make a
marshmallow look like granite.'

His mouth slowly opened. Before that morning I had never
given him anything but politeness. He was looking at me as if
he'd never really noticed me, and it occurred to me that if we did
indeed get our licences back he would remember that I'd seen him
in pieces, and maybe find me uncomfortable to have around. He
paid me a retainer, but only on an annual contract. Easy enough
to chuck me out, and retain someone else. Expediently, and not
too pleased with myself for it, I took the worst crags out of my
tone.

'I presume,' I said, 'That you do want your licence back?'

'There isn't a chance.'

'If you'll keep the lads for a month, I'll get it back for you.'

Defeatism still showed in every sagging muscle, and he didn't
answer.

I shrugged. 'Well, I'm going to try. And if I give you your
licence back on a plate it will be just too bad if Archie and the
lads have gone.' I walked towards the door and put my hand on
the knob. 'I'll let you know how I get on.'

Twisted the knob. Opened the door.

'Wait,' he said.

I turned round. A vestige of starch had returned, mostly in the
shape of the reappearance of the mean lines round his mouth.
Not so good.

'I don't believe you can do it. But as you're so cocksure, I'll make
a bargain with you. I'll pay the lads for two weeks. If you want me
to keep them on for another two weeks after that, you can pay
them yourself.'

Charming. He'd made two thousand pounds out of Cherry
Pie and had overtrained Squelch and was the direct cause of my
being warned off. I stamped on a violent inner tremble of anger
and gave him a cold answer.

'Very well. I agree to that. But you must make a bargain with
me, too. A bargain that you'll keep your mouth tight shut about
your guilt feelings. I don't want to be sabotaged by you hairshirt-
ing it all over the place and confessing your theoretical sins at
awkward moments.'

'I am unlikely to do that,' he said stiffly.

I wasn't so sure. 'I want your word on it,' I said.

He drew himself up, offended. It at least had the effect of straightening his backbone.

'You have it.'

'Fine.' I held the door open for him. 'Let's go down to the yard, then.'

He still hesitated, but finally made up his mind to it, and went before me through the door and down the stairs.

Roberta and her mother were standing in the hall, looking as if they were waiting for news at a pithead after a disaster. They watched the reappearance of the head of the family in mixture of relief and apprehension, and Mrs Cranfield said tentatively, 'Dexter . . . ?'

He answered irritably, as if he saw no cause for anxiety in his having shut himself away with a shotgun for thirty-six hours. 'We're going down to the yard.'

'Great,' said Roberta practically smothering any tendency to emotion from her mother, 'I'll come too.'

Archie hurried to meet us and launched into a detailed account of which horses had gone and which were about to go next. Cranfield hardly listened and certainly didn't take it in. He waited for a gap in the flow, and when he'd waited long enough, impatiently interrupted.

'Yes, yes, Archie, I'm sure you have everything in hand. That is not what I've come down for, however. I want you to tell the lads at once that their notice to leave is withdrawn for one month.'

Archie looked at me, not entirely understanding.

'The sack,' I said, 'Is postponed. Pending attempts to get wrongs righted.'

'Mine too?'

'Absolutely.' I agreed. 'Especially, in fact.'

'Hughes thinks there is a chance we can prove ourselves innocent and recover our licences,' Cranfield said formally, his own disbelief showing like two heads. 'In order to help me keep the stable together while he makes enquiries, Hughes has agreed to contribute one half towards your wages for one month.' I looked at him sharply. That was not at all what I had agreed. He showed no sign of acknowledging his reinterpretation (to put it charitably) of the offer I had accepted, and went authoritatively on. 'Therefore, as your present week's notice still has five days to run, none of you will be required to leave here for five weeks. In fact,' he added grudgingly, 'I would be obliged if you would all stay.'

Archie said to me, 'You really mean it?' and I watched the hope suddenly spring up in his face and thought that maybe it wasn't only my own chance of a future that was worth eight hundred quid.

'That's right,' I agreed. 'As long as you don't all spend the month busily fixing up to go somewhere else at the end of it.'

'What do you take us for?' Archie protested.

'Cynics,' I said, and Archie actually laughed.

I left Cranfield and Archie talking together with most of the desperation evaporating from both of them, and walked away to my aerodynamic burnt orange car. I didn't hear Roberta following me until she spoke in my ear as I opened the door.

'Can you really do it?' she said.

'Do what?'

'Get your licences back.'

'It's going to cost me too much not to. So I guess I'll have to or . . .'

'Oh what?'

I smiled. 'Or die in the attempt.'

It took me an hour to cross into Gloucestershire and almost half as long to sort out the geography of the village of Downsfield, which mostly seemed to consist of cul-de-sacs.

The cottage I eventually found after six misdirections from local inhabitants was old but not beautiful, well painted but in dreary colours, and a good deal more trustworthy than its owner.

When Mrs Charlie West saw who it was, she tried to shut the front door in my face. I put out a hand that was used to dealing with strong horses and pulled her by the wrist, so that if she slammed the door she would be squashing her own arm.

She screeched loudly. An inner door at the back of the hall opened all of six inches, and Charlie's round face appeared through the crack. A distinct lack of confidence was discernible in that area.

'He's hurting me,' Mrs West shouted.

'I want to talk to you,' I said to Charlie over her shoulder.

Charlie West was less than willing. Abandoning his teenage wife, long straight hair, Dusty Springfield eyelashes, beige lipstick and all, he retreated a pace and quite firmly shut his door. Mrs West put up a loud and energetic defence to my attempt to establish further contact with Master Charlie, and I went through the hall fending off her toes and fists.

Charlie had wedged a chair under the door handle.

I shouted through the wood. 'Much as you deserve it, I haven't come here to beat you up. Come out and talk.'

No response of any sort. I rattled the door. Repeated my request. No results. With Mrs West still stabbing around like an agitated hornet I went out of the front door and round the outside to try to talk to him through the window. The window was open, and the sitting-room inside was empty.

I turned round in time to see Charlie's distant backview disappearing across a field and into the next parish. Mrs West saw him too, and gave me a nasty smile.

'So there,' she said triumphantly.

'Yes,' I said. 'I'm sure you must be very proud of him.'

The smile wobbled. I walked back down their garden path, climbed into the car, and drove away.

Round one slightly farcically to the opposition.

Two miles away from the village I stopped the car in a farm gateway and thought it over. Charlie West had been a great deal more scared of me than I would have supposed, even allowing for the fact that I was a couple of sizes bigger and a fair amount stronger. Maybe Charlie was as much afraid of my fury as of my fists. He almost seemed to have been expecting that I would attempt some sort of retaliation, and certainly after what he had done he had a right to. All the same, he still represented my quickest and easiest route to who, if not to why.

After a while I started up again and drove on into the nearest town. Remembered I hadn't eaten all day, put away some rather good cold beef at three-thirty in a homemade café geared more to cake and scones, dozed in the car, waited until dark, and finally drove back again to Charlie's village.

There were lights on in several rooms of his cottage. The Wests were at home. I turned the car and retracked about a hundred yards, stopping half on and half off a grassy verge. Climbed out. Stood up.

Plan of attack: vague. I had had some idea of ringing the front door bell, disappearing, and waiting for either Charlie or his dolly wife to take one incautious step outside to investigate. Instead, unexpected allies materialized in the shape of one small boy and one large dog.

The boy had a torch, and was talking to his dog, who paused to dirty up the roadside five yards ahead.

'What the hell d'you think you were at, you bloody great nit, scoffing our Mum's stewing steak? Gor blimey mate, don't you ever learn nothing? Tomorrow's dinner gone down your useless big gullet and our Dad will give us both a belting this time I shouldn't wonder, not just you, you senseless rotten idiot. Time you knew the bloody difference between me Mum's stewing steak and dog meat, it is straight, though come to think of it there isn't all that difference, 'specially as maybe your eyes don't look at things the same. Do they? I damn well wish you could talk, mate.'

I clicked shut the door of the car and startled him, and he swung round with the torch searching wildly. The beam caught me and steadied on my face.

The boy said, 'You come near me and I'll set my dog on you.' The dog, however, was still squatting and showed no enthusiasm.

'I'll stay right here,' then,' I said amicably, leaning back against the car. 'I only want to know who lives in that cottage over there, where the lights are.'

'How do I know? We only come to live here the day before yesterday.'

'Great . . . I mean, that must be great for you, moving.'

'Yeah. Sure. You stay there, then. I'm going now.' He beckoned to the dog. The dog was still busy.

'How would it be if you could offer your Mum the price of the stewing steak? Maybe she wouldn't tell your Dad, then, and neither you nor the dog would get a belting.'

'Our Mum says we mustn't talk to strange men.'

'Hm. Well, never mind then. Off you go.'

'I'll go when I'm ready,' he said belligerently. A natural born rebel. About nine years old, I guessed.

'What would I have to do for it?' he said, after a pause.

'Nothing much. Just ring the front door bell of that cottage and tell whoever answers that you can't stop your dog eating the crocuses they've got growing all along the front there. Then when they come out to see, just nip off home as fast as your dog can stagger.'

It appealed to him. 'Steak probably costs a good bit,' he said.

'Probably.' I dug into my pocket and came up with a small fistful of pennies and silver. 'This should leave a bit over.'

'He doesn't really have to eat the crocuses, does he?'

'No.'

'O.K. then.' Once his mind was made up he was jaunty and efficient. He shovelled my small change into his pocket, marched up to Charlie's front door, and told Mrs West, who cautiously answered it, that she was losing her crocuses. She scolded him all the way down the path, and while she was bending down to search for the damage, my accomplice quietly vanished. Before Mrs West exactly realized she had been misled I had stepped briskly through her front door and shut her out of her own house.

When I opened the sitting-room door Charlie said, without lifting his eyes from a racing paper, 'It wasn't him again, then.'

'Yes,' I said, 'It was.'

Charlie's immature face crumpled into a revolting state of fear and Mrs West leaned on the door bell. I shut the sitting-room door behind me to cut out some of the din.

'What are you so afraid of?' I said loudly.

'Well . . . you . . .'

'And so you damn well ought to be,' I agreed. I took a step towards him and he shrank back into his armchair. He was brave enough on a horse, which made this abject cringing all the more unexpected, and all the more unpleasant. I took another step. He fought his way into the upholstery.

Mrs West gave the door bell a rest.

'Why did you do it?' I said.

He shook his head dumbly, and pulled his feet up on to the chair seat in the classic womb position. Wishful regression to the first and only place where the world couldn't reach him.

'Charlie I came here for some answers, and you're going to give them to me.'

Mrs West's furious face appeared at the window and she started rapping hard enough to break the glass. With one eye on her husband to prevent him making another bolt for it, I stepped over and undid the latch.

'Get out of here,' she shouted. 'Go on, get out.'

'You get in. Through here, I'm not opening the door.'

'I'll fetch the police.'

'Do what you like. I only want to talk to your worm of a husband. Get in or stay out, but shut up.'

She did anything but. Once she was in the room it took another twenty minutes of fruitless slanging before I could ask Charlie a single question without her loud voice obliterating any chance of an answer.

Charlie himself tired of it first and told her to stop, but at least her belligerence had given him a breathing space. He put his feet down on the floor again and said it was no use asking those questions, he didn't know the answers.

'You must do. Unless you told those lies about me out of sheer personal spite.'

'No.'

'Then why?'

'I'm not telling you.'

'Then I'll tell you something, you little louse. I'm going to find out who put you up to it. I'm going to stir everything up until I find out, and then I'm going to raise such a stink about being framed that sulphur will smell like sweet peas by comparison, and you, Master Charlie West, *you* will find yourself without a licence, not me, and even if you get it back you'll never live down the contempt everyone will feel for you.'

'Don't you talk to my Charlie like that!'

'Your Charlie is a vicious little liar who would sell you too for fifty pounds.'

'It wasn't fifty,' she snapped triumphantly. 'It was five hundred.'

Charlie yelled at her and I came as near to hitting him as the distance between my clenched teeth. Five hundred pounds. He'd lied my licence away for a handout that would have insulted a tout.

'That does it,' I said. 'And now you tell me who paid you.'

The girl wife started to look as frightened as Charlie, and it didn't occur to me then that my anger had flooded through that little room like a tidal wave.

Charlie stuttered, 'I d . . d . . don't know.'

I took a pace towards him and he scrambled out of his chair and took refuge behind it.

'K . . k . . keep away from me. I don't know. I don't know.'

'That isn't good enough.'

'He really doesn't know,' the girl wailed. 'He really doesn't.'

'He does,' I repeated furiously.

The girl began to cry. Charlie seemed to be on the verge of copying her.

'I never saw . . . never saw the bloke. He telephoned.'

'And how did he pay you?'

'In two . . . in two packages. In one pound notes. A hundred of them came the day before the Enquiry, and I was to get . . .' His voice trailed away.

'You were to get the other four hundred if I was warned off?'

He nodded, a fractional jerk. His head was tucked into his shoulders, as if to avoid a blow.

'And have you?'

'What?'

'Have you had it? The other four hundred?'

His eyes widened, and he spoke in jerks. 'No . . . but . . . of course . . . it . . . will . . . come.'

'Of course it won't,' I said brutally. 'You stupid treacherous little ninny.' My voice sounded thick, and each word came out separately and loaded with fury.

Both of the Wests were trembling, and the girl's eye make-up was beginning to run down her cheeks.

'What did he sound like, this man on the telephone?'

'Just . . . just a man,' Charlie said.

'And did it occur to you to ask *why* he wanted me warned off?'

'I said . . . you hadn't done anything to harm me . . . and he said . . . you never know . . . supposing one day he does . . ."

Charlie shrank still further under my astounded glare.

'Anyway . . . five hundred quid . . . I don't earn as much as you, you know.' For the first time there was a tinge of spite in his voice, and I knew that in truth jealousy had been a factor, that he hadn't in fact done it entirely for the money. He'd got his kicks, too.

'You're only twenty,' I said. 'What exactly do you expect?'

But Charlie expected everything, always, to be run entirely for the best interests of Charlie West.

I said, 'And you'll be wise to spend that money carefully, because, believe me, it's going to be the most expensive hundred quid you've ever earned.'

'Kelly . . .' He was half way to entreaty. Jealous, greedy, dishonest and afraid. I felt not the remotest flicker of compassion for him, only a widening anger that the motives behind his lies were so small.

'And when you lose your licence for this, and I'll see that you do, you'll have plenty of time to understand that it *serves you right*.'

The raw revenge in my voice made a desert of their little home. They both stood there dumbly with wide miserable eyes, too broken up to raise another word. The girl's beige mouth hung slackly open, mascara half way to her chin, long hair straggling in wisps across her face and round her shoulders. She looked sixteen. A child. So did Charlie. The worst vandals are always childish.

I turned away from them and walked out of their cottage, and my anger changed into immense depression on the drive home.

CHAPTER SIX

AT TWO O'CLOCK in the morning the rage I'd unleashed on the Wests looked worse and worse.

To start with, it had achieved nothing helpful. I'd known before I went there that Charlie must have had a reason for lying about me at the Enquiry. I now knew the reason to be five hundred pounds. Marvellous. A useless scrap of information out of a blizzard of emotion. Lash out when you're hurt . . . I'd done that, all right. Poured out on them the roaring bitterness I'd smothered under a civilized front ever since Monday.

Nor had I given Charlie any reason to do me any good in future. Very much the reverse. He wasn't going to be contrite and eager to make amends. When he'd recovered himself he'd be sullen and vindictive.

I'd been taught the pattern over and over. Country A plays an isolated shabby trick. Country B is outraged and exacts revenge. Country A is forced to express apologies and meekly back down but thoroughly resents it. Country A now holds a permanent grudge, and harms Country B whenever possible. One of the classic variations in the history of politics and aggression. Also applicable to individuals.

To have known about the pitfalls and jumped in regardless was a mite galling. It just showed how easily good sense lost out to anger. It also showed me that I wasn't going to get results that way. A crash course in detection would have been handy. Failing that, I'd have to start taking stock of things coolly, instead of charging straight off again towards the easiest looking target, and making another mess of it.

Cool stocktaking . . .

Charlie West hadn't wanted to see me because he had a guilty conscience. It followed that everyone else who had a guilty conscience wouldn't want to see me. Even if they didn't actually sprint off across the fields, they would all do their best to avoid my reaching them. I was going to have to become adept—and fast—at entering their lives when their backs were turned.

If Charlie West didn't know who had paid him, and I believed that he didn't, it followed that perhaps no one else who had lied knew who had persuaded them to. Perhaps it had all been done on the telephone. Long distance leverage. Impersonal and undiscoverable.

Perhaps I had set myself an impossible task and I should give up the whole idea and emigrate to Australia.

Except that they had racing in Australia, and I wouldn't be able to go. The banishment covered the world. Warned off. Warned off.

Oh God.

All right, so maybe I did let the self pity catch up with me for a while. But I was privately alone in my bed in the dark, and I'd jeered myself out of it by morning.

Looking about as ragged as I felt, I got up at six and pointed the Lotus's smooth nose towards London, N.W.7, Mill Hill.

Since I could see no one at the races I had to catch them at home, and in the case of George Newtonnards, bookmaker, home proved to be a sprawling pink-washed ranch-type bungalow in a prosperous suburban road. At eight-thirty a.m. I hoped to find him at breakfast, but in fact he was opening his garage door when I arrived. I parked squarely across the entrance to his drive, which was hardly likely to make me popular, and he came striding down towards me to tell me to move.

I climbed out of the car. When he saw who it was, he stopped dead. I walked up the drive to meet him, shivering a little in the raw east wind and regretting I wasn't snug inside a fur collared jacket like his.

'What are you doing here?' he said sharply.

'I would be very grateful if you would just tell me one or two things . . .'

'I haven't time.' He was easy, self assured, dealing with a small sized nuisance. 'And nothing I can say will help you. Move your car, please.'

'Certainly . . . Could you tell me how it was that you came to be asked to give evidence against Mr Cranfield?'

'How it was . . . ? He looked slightly surprised. 'I received an official letter, requiring me to attend.'

'Well, why? I mean, how did the Stewards know about Mr. Cranfield's bet on Cherry Pie? Did you write and tell them?'

He gave me a cool stare. 'I hear,' he said, 'that you are maintaining you were framed.'

'News travels.'

A faint smile. 'News always travels—towards me. An accurate information service is the basis of good bookmaking.'

'How did the Stewards know about Mr Cranfield's bet?'

'Mm. Well, yes, that I don't know.'

'Who, besides you, knew that you believed that Cranfield had backed Cherry Pie?'

'He did back him.'

'Well, who besides you knew that he had?'

'I haven't time for this.'

'I'll be happy to move my car . . . in a minute or two.'

His annoyed glare gradually softened round the edges into a half amused acceptance. A very smooth civilized man, George Newtonnards.

'Very well. I told a few of the lads . . . other bookmakers, that is. I was angry about it, see? Letting myself be taken to the cleaners like that. Me, at my age, I should know better. So maybe one of them passed on the word to the Stewards, knowing the Enquiry was coming up. But no, I didn't do it myself.'

'Could you guess which one might have done? I mean, do you know of anyone who has a grudge against Cranfield?'

'Can't think of one.' He shrugged. 'No more than against any other trainer who tries it on.'

'Tries it on?' I echoed, surprised. 'But he doesn't.'

'Oh yeah?'

'I ride them,' I protested. 'I should know.'

'Yes,' he said sarcastically. 'You should. Don't come the naïve bit with me, chum. Your friend Chris Smith, him with the cracked skull, he's a proper artist at strangulation, wouldn't you say? Same as you are. A fine pair, the two of you.'

'You believe I pulled Squelch, then?'

'Stands to reason.'

'All the same, I didn't.'

'Tell it to the Marines.' A thought struck him. 'I don't know any bookmakers who have a grudge against Cranfield, but I sure know one who has a grudge against *you*. A whopping great life-sized grudge. One time, he was almost coming after you with a chopper. You got in his way proper, mate, you did indeed.'

'How? And who?'

'You and Chris Smith, you were riding two for Cranfield . . . about six months ago, it was . . . right at the beginning of the season anyway . . . in a novice 'chase at Fontwell. Remember? There was a big holiday crowd in from the south coast because it was a bit chilly that day for lying on the beach . . . anyway, there was a big crowd all primed with holiday money . . . and there were you and Chris Smith on these two horses, and the public fancying both of them, and Pelican Jobberson asked you which was off, and you said you hadn't an earthly on yours, so he rakes in the cash on you and doesn't bother to balance his book, and then you go and ride a hell of a finish and win by a neck, when you could have lost without the slightest trouble. Pelican went spare and swore he'd be even with you when he got the chance.'

'I believed what I told him,' I said. 'It was that horse's first attempt over fences. No one could have predicted he'd have been good enough to win.'

'Then why did you?'

'The owner wanted to, if possible.'

'Did he bet on it?'

'The owner? No. It was a woman. She never bets much. She just likes to see her horses win.'

'Pelican swore you'd backed it yourself, and put him off so that you could get a better price.'

'You bookmakers are too suspicious for your own good.'

'Hard experience proves us right.'

'Well, he's wrong this time,' I insisted. 'This bird friend of yours. If he asked me . . . and I don't remember him asking . . . then I told him the truth. And anyway, any bookmaker who asks jockeys questions like that is asking for trouble. Jockeys are the worst tipsters in the world.'

'Some aren't,' he said flatly. 'Some are good at it.'

I skipped that. 'Is he still angry after all these months? And if so, would he be angry enough not just to tell the Stewards that Cranfield backed Cherry Pie, but to bribe other people to invent lies about us?'

His eyes narrowed while he thought about it. He pursed his mouth, undecided. 'You'd better ask him yourself.'

'Thanks.' Hardly an easy question.

'Move your car now?' he suggested.

'Yes.' I walked two steps towards it, then stopped and turned back. 'Mr Newtonnards, if you see the man who put the money on for Mr Cranfield, will you find out who he is . . . and let me know?'

'Why don't you ask Cranfield?'

'He said he didn't want to involve him.'

'But you do?'

'I suppose I'm grasping at anything,' I said. 'But yes, I think I do.'

'Why don't you just quieten down and take it?' he said reasonably. 'All this thrashing about . . . you got copped. So, you got copped. Fair enough. Sit it out, then. You'll get your licence back, eventually.'

'Thank you for your advice,' I said politely, and went and moved my car out of his gateway.

It was Thursday. I should have been going to Warwick to ride in four races. Instead, I drove aimlessly back round the North Circular Road wondering whether or not to pay a call on David Oakley, enquiry agent and imaginative photographer. If Charlie West didn't know who had framed me, it seemed possible that Oakley might be the only one who did. But even if he did, he was highly unlikely to tell me. There seemed no point in confronting him, and yet nothing could be gained if I made no attempt.

In the end I stopped at a telephone box and found his number via enquiries.

A girl answered. 'Mr Oakley isn't in yet.'

'Can I make an appointment?'

She asked me what about.

'A divorce.'

She said Mr Oakley could see me at 11.30 and asked me my name.'

'Charles Crisp.'

'Very well, Mr Crisp. Mr Oakley will be expecting you.'

I doubted it. On the other hand, he, like Charlie West, might in general be expecting some form of protest.

From the North Circular Road I drove ninety miles up the M1 Motorway to Birmingham and found Oakley's office above a bicycle and radio shop half a mile from the town centre.

His street door, shabby black, bore a neat small nameplate stating, simply, 'Oakley'. There were two keyholes, Yale and Chubb, and a discreetly situated peephole. I tried the handle of this apparent fortress, and the door opened easily under my touch. Inside, there was a narrow passage with pale blue walls leading to an uncarpeted staircase stretching upwards.

I walked up, my feet sounding loud on the boards. At the top there was a small landing with another shabby black door, again and similarly fortified. On this door, another neat notice said, 'Please ring'. There was a bell push. I gave it three seconds work.

The door was opened by a tall strong looking girl dressed in a dark coloured leather trouser suit. Under the jacket she wore a black sweater, and under the trouser legs, black leather boots. Black eyes returned my scrutiny, black hair held back by a tortoiseshell band fell straight to her shoulders before curving inwards. She seemed at first sight to be about twenty-four but there were already wrinkle lines round her eyes, and the deadness in

their expression indicated too much familiarity with dirty washing.

'I have an appointment,' I said. 'Crisp.'

'Come in.' She opened the door wider and left it for me to close.

I followed her into the room, a small square office furnished
with a desk, typewriter, telephone. and four tall filing cabinets.
On the far side of the room there was another door. Not black;
modern flat hardboard, painted grey. More keyholes. I eyed them
thoughtfully.

The girl opened the door, said through it, 'It's Mr Crisp,' and
stood back for me to pass her.

'Thank you,' I said. Took three steps forward, and shut myself
in with David Oakley.

His office was not a great deal larger than the ante-room, and
no thrift had been spared with the furniture. There was dim
brown linoleum, a bentwood coat stand, a small cheap armchair
facing a grey metal desk, and over the grimy window, in place of
curtains, a tough looking fixed frame covered with chicken wire.
Outside the window there were the heavy bars and supports of a
fire escape. The Birmingham sun, doing its best against odds,
struggled through and fell in wrinkled honeycomb shadows on
the surface of an ancient safe. In the wall on my right, another
door, firmly closed. With yet more keyholes.

Behind the desk in a swivel chair sat the proprietor of all this
glory, the totally unmemorable Mr Oakley. Youngish. Slender.
Mouse coloured hair. And this time, sunglasses.

'Sit down, Mr Crisp,' he said. Accentless voice, entirely emotionless, as before. 'Divorce, I believe? Give me the details of your
requirements, and we can arrive at a fee.' He looked at his watch.
'I can give you just ten minutes, I'm afraid. Shall we get on?'

He hadn't recognized me. I thought I might as well take advantage of it.

'I understand you would be prepared to fake some evidence for
me . . . photographs?'

He began to nod, and then grew exceptionally still. The un-
revealing dark glasses were motionless. The pale straight mouth
didn't twitch. The hand lying on the desk remained loose and
relaxed.

Finally he said, without any change of inflection, 'Get out.'

'How much do you charge for faking evidence?'

'Get out.'

I smiled. 'I'd like to know how much I was worth.'

'Dust.' he said. His foot moved under the desk.

'I'll pay you in gold dust, if you'll tell me who gave you the job.'

He considered it. Then he said, 'No.'

The door to the outer office opened quietly behind me.

Oakley said calmly, 'This is not a Mr Crisp, Didi. This is a Mr Kelly Hughes. Mr Hughes will be leaving.'

'Mr Hughes is not ready,' I said.

'I think Mr Hughes will find he is,' she said.

I looked at her over my shoulder. She was carrying a large black looking pistol with a very large black looking silencer. The whole works were pointing steadily my way.

'How dramatic,' I said. 'Can you readily dispose of bodies in the centre of Birmingham?'

'Yes,' Oakley said.

'For a fee, of course, usually,' Didi added.

I struggled not to believe them, and lost. All the same . . .

'Should you decide after all to sell the information I need, you know where to find me.' I relaxed against the back of the chair.

'I may have a liking for gold dust,' he said calmly. 'But I am not a fool.'

'Opinions differ,' I remarked lightly.

There was no reaction. 'It is not in my interest that you should prove you were . . . shall we say . . . set up.'

'I understand that. Eventually, however, you will wish that you hadn't helped to do it.'

He said smoothly, 'A number of other people have said much the same, though few, I must confess, as quietly as you.'

It occurred to me suddenly that he must be quite used to the sort of enraged onslaught I'd thrown at the Wests, and that perhaps that was why his office . . . Didi caught my wandering glance and cynically nodded.

'That's right. Too many people tried to smash the place up. So we keep the damage to a minimum.'

'How wise.'

'I'm afraid I really do have another appointment now,' Oakley said. 'So if you'll excuse me . . . ?'

I stood up. There was nothing to stay for.

'It surprises me,' I remarked, 'That you're not in jail.'

'I am clever,' he said matter-of-factly. 'My clients are satisfied, and people like you . . . impotent.'

'Someone will kill you, one day.'

'Will you?'

I shook my head. 'Not worth it.'

'Exactly,' he said calmly. 'The jobs I accept are never what the victims would actually kill me for. I really am not a fool.'

'No,' I said.

I walked across to the door and Didi made room for me to pass. She put the pistol down on her desk in the outer office and switched off a red bulb which glowed brightly in a small switchboard.

'Emergency signal?' I enquired. 'Under his desk.'

'You could say so.'

'Is that gun loaded?'

Her eyebrows rose. 'Naturally.'

'I see.'

I opened the outer door. She walked over to close it behind me as I went towards the stairs.

'Nice to have met you, Mr Hughes,' she said unemotionally. 'Don't come back.'

I walked along to my car in some depression. From none of the three damaging witnesses at the Enquiry had I got any change at all, and what David Oakley had said about me being impotent looked all too true.

There seemed to be no way of proving that he had simply brought with him the money he had photographed in my flat. No one at Corrie had seen him come or go: Tony had asked all the lads, and none of them had seen him. And Oakley would have found it easy enough to be unobserved. He had only had to arrive early, while everyone was out riding on the Downs at morning exercise. From seven thirty to eight thirty the stable yard would be deserted. Letting himself in through my unlocked door, setting up his props, loosing off a flash or two, and quietly retreating . . . The whole process would have taken him no more than ten minutes.

It was possible he had kept a record of his shady transactions. Possible, not probable. He might need to keep some hold over his clients, to prevent their later denouncing him in fits of resurgent civic conscience. If he did keep such records, it might account for the multiplicity of locks. Or maybe the locks were simply to discourage people from breaking in to search for records, as they were certainly discouraging me.

Would Oakley, I wondered, have done what Charlie West had done, and produced his lying testimony for a voice on the telephone? On the whole, I decided not. Oakley had brains where Charlie had vanity, and Oakley would not involve himself without tying his clients up tight too. Oakley had to know who had done the engineering.

But stealing that information . . . or beating it out of him . . . or tricking him into giving it . . . as well as buying it from him . . . every course looked as hopeless as the next. I could only ride horses. I couldn't pick locks, fights or pockets. Certainly not Oakley's.

Oakley and Didi. They were old at the game. They'd invented the rules. Oakley and Didi were senior league.

How did anyone get in touch with Oakley, if they needed his brand of service?

He could scarcely advertise.

Someone had to know about him.

I thought it over for a while, sitting in my car in the car park wondering what to do next. There was only one person I knew who could put his finger on the pulse of Birmingham if he wanted to, and the likelihood was that in my present circumstances he wouldn't want to.

However . . .

I started the car, threaded a way through the one way streets, and found a slot in the crowded park behind the Great Stag Hotel. Inside, the ritual of Business Lunch was warming up, the atmosphere thickening nicely with the smell of alcohol, the resonance of fruity voices, the haze of cigars. The Great Stag Hotel attracted almost exclusively a certain grade of wary, prosperous, level-headed businessmen needing a soft background for hard options, and it attracted them because the landlord, Teddy Dewar, was the sort of man himself.

I found him in the bar, talking to two others almost indistinguishable from him in their dark grey suits, white shirts, neat maroon ties, seventeen-inch necks and thirty-eight-inch waists.

A faint glaze came over his professionally noncommittal expression when he caught sight of me over their shoulders. A warned off jockey didn't rate too high with him. Lowered the tone of the place, no doubt.

I edged through to the bar on one side of him and ordered whisky.

'I'd be grateful for a word with you,' I said.

He turned his head a fraction in my direction, and without looking at me directly answered, 'Very well. In a few minutes.'

No warmth in the words. No ducking of the unwelcome situation, either. He went on talking to the two men about the dicky state of oil shares, and eventually smoothly disengaged himself and turned to me.

'Well, Kelly . . .' His eyes were cool and distant, waiting to see what I wanted before showing any real feeling.

'Will you lunch with me?' I made it casual.

His surprise was controlled. 'I thought . . .'

'I may be banned,' I said, 'But I still eat.'

He studied my face. 'You mind.'

'What do you expect . . . ? I'm sorry it shows.'

He said neutrally, 'There's a muscle in your jaw . . . Very well: if you don't mind going in straightaway.'

We sat against the wall at an inconspicuous table and chose beef cut from a roast on a trolley. While he ate his eyes checked the running of the dining-room, missing nothing. I waited until he was satisfied that all was well and then came briefly to the point.

'Do you know anything about a man called David Oakley? He's an enquiry agent. Operates from an office about half a mile from here.'

'David Oakley? I can't say I've ever heard of him.'

'He manufactured some evidence which swung things against me at the Stewards' Enquiry on Monday.'

'Manufactured?' There was delicate doubt in his voice.

'Oh, yes,' I sighed. 'I suppose it sounds corny, but I really was not guilty as charged. But someone made sure it looked like it.' I told him about the photograph of money in my bedroom.

'And you never had this money?'

'I did not. And the note supposed to be from Cranfield was a forgery. But how could we prove it?'

He thought it over.

'You can't.'

'Exactly,' I agreed.

'This David Oakley who took the photograph . . . I suppose you got no joy from him.'

'No joy is right.'

'I don't understand precisely why you've come to me.' He finished his beef and laid his knife and fork tidily together. Waiters appeared like genii to clear the table and bring coffee. He waited still noncommittally while I paid the bill.

'I expect it is too much to ask,' I said finally. 'After all, I've only stayed here three or four times, I have no claim on you personally for friendship or help . . . and yet, there's no one else I know who could even begin to do what you could . . . if you will.'

'What?' he said succinctly.

'I want to know how people are steered towards David Oakley, if they want some evidence faked. He as good as told me he is quite accustomed to do it. Well . . . how does he get his clients? Who recommends him? I thought that among all the people you know, you might think of someone who could perhaps pretend he wanted a job done . . . or pretend he had a friend who wanted a job done . . . and throw out feelers, and see if anyone finally recommended Oakley. And if so, who.'

He considered it. 'Because if you found one contact you might work back from there to another . . . and eventually perhaps to a name which meant something to you . . . ?'

'I suppose it sounds feeble,' I said resignedly.

'It's a very outside chance,' he agreed. There was a long pause. Then he added, 'All the same, I do know of someone who might agree to try.' He smiled briefly, for the first time.

'That's . . .' I swallowed. 'That's marvellous.'

'Can't promise results.'

CHAPTER SEVEN

TONY came clomping up my stairs on Friday morning after first exercise and poured half an inch of Scotch into the coffee I gave him. He drank the scalding mixture and shuddered as the liquor bit.

'God,' he said. 'It's cold on the Downs.'

'Rather you than me,' I said.

'Liar,' he said amicably. 'It must feel odd to you, not riding.'

'Yes.'

He sprawled in the green armchair. 'Poppy's got the morning ickies again. I'll be glad when this lousy pregnancy is over. She's been ill half the time.'

'Poor Poppy.'

'Yeah . . . Anyway, what it means is that we ain't going to that dance tonight. She says she can't face it.'

'Dance . . . ?'

'The Jockeys' Fund dance. You know. You've got the tickets on your mantel over there.'

'Oh . . . yes. I'd forgotten about it. We were going together.'

'That's right. But now, as I was saying, you'll have to go without us.'

'I'm not going at all.'

'I thought you might not.' He sighed and drank deeply. 'Where did you get to yesterday?'

'I called on people who didn't want to see me.'

'Any results?'

'Not many.' I told him briefly about Newtonnards and David Oakley, and about the hour I'd spent with Andrew Tring.

It was because the road home from Birmingham led near his village that I'd thought of Andrew Tring, and my first instinct anyway was to shy away from even the thought of him. Certainly visiting one of the stewards who had helped to warn him off was not regulation behaviour for a disbarred jockey. If I hadn't been fairly strongly annoyed with him I would have driven straight on.

He was disgusted with me for calling. He opened the door of his prosperous sprawling old manor house himself and had no chance of saying he was out.

'Kelly! What are you doing here?'

'Asking for some explanation.'

'I've nothing to say to you.'

'You have indeed.'

He frowned. Natural good manners were only just preventing him from retreating and shutting the door in my face. 'Come in then. Just for a few minutes.'

'Thank you,' I said without irony, and followed him into a nearby small room lined with books and containing a vast desk, three deep armchairs and a colour television set.

'Now,' he said, shutting the door and not offering the armchairs, 'Why have you come?'

He was four years older than me, and about the same size. Still as trim as when he rode races, still outwardly the same man. Only the casual, long established changing-room friendliness seemed to have withered somewhere along the upward path from amateurship to Authority.

'Andy,' I said, 'Do you really and honestly believe that that Squelch race was rigged?'

'You were warned off,' he said coldly.

'That's far from being the same thing as guilty.'

'I don't agree.'

'Then you're stupid,' I said bluntly. 'As well as scared out of your tiny wits.'

'That's enough, Kelly. I don't have to listen to this.' He opened the door again and waited for me to leave. I didn't. Short of throwing me out bodily he was going to have to put up with me a little longer. He gave me a furious stare and shut the door again.

I said more reasonably, 'I'm sorry, really, I'm sorry. It's just that you rode against me for at least five years . . . I'd have thought you wouldn't so easily believe I'd deliberately lose a race. I've never yet lost a race I could win.'

He was silent. He knew that I didn't throw races. Anyone who rode regularly knew who would and who wouldn't, and in spite of what Charlie West had said at the Enquiry, I was not an artist at stopping one because I hadn't given it the practice.

'There was that money,' he said at last. He sounded disillusioned and discouraged.

'I never had it. Oakley took it with him into my flat and photographed it there. All that so called evidence, the whole bloody Enquiry in fact, was as genuine as a lead sixpence.'

He gave me a long doubtful look. Then he said, 'There's nothing I can do about it.'

'What are you afraid of?'

'Stop saying I'm afraid,' he said irritably. 'I'm not afraid. I just can't do anything about it, even if what you say is true.'

'It is true . . . and maybe you don't think you are afraid, but that's definitely the impression you give. Or maybe . . . are you simply overawed? The new boy among the old powerful prefects. Is that it? Afraid of putting a foot wrong with them?'

'Kelly!' he protested; but it was the protest of a touched nerve.

I said unkindly, 'You're a gutless disappointment,' and took a step towards his door. He didn't move to open it for me. Instead he put up a hand to stop me, looking as angry as he had every right to.

'That's not fair. Just because I can't help you . . .'

'You could have done. At the Enquiry.'

'You don't understand.'

'I do indeed. You found it easier to believe me guilty than to tell Gowery you had any doubts.'

'It wasn't as easy as you think.'

'Thanks,' I said ironically.

'I don't mean . . .' he shook his head impatiently. 'I mean, it wasn't all as simple as you make out. When Gowery asked me to sit with him at the Enquiry I believed it was only going to be a formality, that both you and Cranfield had run the Lemonfizz genuinely and were surprised yourselves by the result. Colonel Midgley told me it was ridiculous having to hold the

Enquiry at all, really. I never expected to be caught up in having to warn you off.'

'Did you say,' I said, 'that Lord Gowery asked you to sit with him?'

'Of course. That's the normal procedure. The Stewards sitting at an Enquiry aren't picked out of a hat . . .'

'There isn't any sort of rota?'

'No. The Disciplinary Steward asks two colleagues to officiate with him . . . and that's what put me on the spot, if you must know, because I didn't want to say no to Lord Gowery . . .' He stopped.

'Go on,' I urged without heat. 'Why not?'

'Well, because . . .' He hesitated, then said slowly, 'I suppose in a way I owe it to you . . . I'm sorry, Kelly, desperately sorry, I do know you don't usually rig races . . . I'm in an odd position with Gowery and it's vitally important I keep in with him.'

I stifled my indignation. Andrew Tring's eyes were looking inward and from his expression he didn't very much like what he could see.

'He owns the freehold of the land just north of Manchester where our main pottery is.' Andrew Tring's family fortunes were based not on fine porcelain but on smashable tea cups for institutions. His products were dropped by washers-up in schools and hospitals from Waterloo to Hongkong, and the pieces in the world's dustbins were his perennial licence to print money.

He said, 'There's been some redevelopment round there and that land is suddenly worth about a quarter of a million. And our lease runs out in three years . . . We have been negotiating a new one, but the old one was for ninety-nine years and no one is keen to renew for that long . . . The ground rent is in any case going to be raised considerably, but if Gowery changes his mind and wants to sell that land for development, there's nothing we can do about it. We only own the buildings . . . We'd lose the entire factory if he didn't renew the lease. And we can only make cups and saucers so cheaply because our overheads are small . . . If we have to build or rent a new factory our prices will be less competitive and our world trade figures will slump. Gowery himself has the final say as to whether our lease will be renewed or not, and on what terms . . . so you see, Kelly, it's not that I'm afraid of him . . . there's so much more at stake . . . and he's always a man to hold it against you if you argue with him.'

He stopped and looked at me gloomily. I looked gloomily back. The facts of life stared us stonily in the face.

'So that's that,' I agreed. 'You are quite right. You can't help me. You couldn't, right from the start. I'm glad you explained . . .' I smiled at him twistedly, facing another dead end, the last of a profitless day.

'I'm sorry, Kelly . . .'

'Sure,' I said.

Tony finished his fortified breakfast and said, 'So there wasn't anything sinister in Andy Tring's lily-livered bit on Monday.'

'It depends what you call sinister. But no, I suppose not.'

'What's left, then?'

'Damn all,' I said in depression.

'You can't give up,' he protested.

'Oh no. But I've learned one thing in learning nothing, and that is that I'm getting nowhere because I'm me. First thing Monday morning I'm going to hire me my own David Oakley.'

'Attaboy,' he said. He stood up. 'Time for second lot, I hear.' Down in the yards the lads were bringing out the horses, their hooves scrunching hollowly on the packed gravel.

'How are they doing?' I asked.

'Oh . . . so so. I sure hate having to put up other jocks. Given me a bellyful of the whole game, this business has.'

When he'd gone down to ride I cleaned up my already clean flat and made some more coffee. The day stretched emptily ahead. So did the next day and the one after that, and every day for an indefinite age.

Ten minutes of this prospect was enough. I searched around and found another straw to cling to: telephone to a man I knew slightly at the B.B.C. A cool secretary said he was out, and to try again at eleven.

I tried again at eleven. Still out. I tried at twelve. He was in then, but sounded as if he wished he weren't.

'Not Kelly Hughes, the . . .' His voice trailed off while he failed to find a tactful way of putting it.

'That's right.'

'Well . . . er . . . I don't think . . .'

'I don't want anything much,' I assured him resignedly. 'I just want to know the name of the outfit who make the films of races. The camera patrol people.'

'Oh.' He sounded relieved. 'That's the Racecourse Technical Services. Run by the Levy Board. They've a virtual monopoly, though there's one other small firm operating sometimes under licence. Then there are the television companies, of course. Did

you want any particular race? Oh . . . the Lemonfizz Crystal Cup,
I suppose.'

'No,' I said. 'The meeting at Reading two weeks earlier.'

'Reading . . . Reading . . . Let's see, then. Which lot would
that be?' He hummed a few out of tune bars while he thought
it over. 'I should think . . . yes, definitely the small firm, the
Cannot Lie people. Cannot Lie, Ltd. Offices at Woking, Surrey.
Do you want their number?'

'Yes please.'

He read it to me.

'Thank you very much,' I said.

'Any time . . . er . . . well . . . I mean . . .'

'I know what you mean,' I agreed. 'But thanks anyway.'

I put down the receiver with a grimace. It was still no fun
being everyone's idea of a villain.

The B.B.C. man's reaction made me decide that the telephone
might get me nil results from the Cannot Lie brigade. Maybe
they couldn't lie, but they would certainly evade. And anyway,
I had the whole day to waste.

The Cannot Lie office was a rung or two up the luxury ladder
from David Oakley's, which wasn't saying a great deal. A large
rather bare room on the second floor of an Edwardian house in
a side street. A rickety lift large enough for one slim man or two
starving children. A well worn desk with a well worn blonde
painting her toe nails on top of it.

'Yes?' she said, when I walked in.

She had lilac panties on, with lace. She made no move to
prevent me seeing a lot of them.

'No one in?' I asked.

'Only us chickens,' she agreed. She had a South London accent
and the smart back-chatting intelligence that often goes with it.
'Which do you want, the old man or our Alfie?'

'You'll do nicely,' I said.

'Ta.' She took it as her due, with a practised come-on-so-far-
but-no-further smile. One foot was finished. She stretched out
her leg and wiggled it up and down to help with the drying.

'Going to a dance tonight,' she explained. 'In me peep-toes.'

I didn't think anyone would concentrate on the toes. Apart
from the legs she had a sharp pointed little bosom under a white
cotton sweater and a bright pink patent leather belt clasping a
bikini sized waist. Her body looked about twenty years old. Her
face looked as if she'd spent the last six of them bed hopping.

'Paint the other one,' I suggested.

'You're not in a hurry?'

'I'm enjoying the scenery.'

She gave a knowing giggle and started on the other foot. The view was even more hair-raising than before. She watched me watching, and enjoyed it.

'What's your name?' I asked.

'Carol. What's yours?'

'Kelly.'

'From the Isle of Man?'

'No. The land of our fathers.'

She gave me a bright glance. 'You catch on quick, don't you?'

I wished I did. I said regretfully, 'How long do you keep ordinary routine race films?'

'Huh? For ever, I suppose.' She changed mental gear effortlessly, carrying straight on with her uninhibited painting. 'We haven't destroyed any so far, that's to say. 'Course, we've only been in the racing business eighteen months. No telling what they'll do when the big storeroom's full. We're up to the eyebrows in all the others with films of motor races, golf matches, three day events, any old things like that.'

'Where's the big storeroom?'

'Through there.' She waved the small pink enamelling brush in the general direction of a scratched once cream door. 'Want to see?'

'If you don't mind.'

'Go right ahead.'

She had finished the second foot. The show was over. With a sigh I removed my gaze and walked over to the door in question. There was only a round hole where most doors have a handle. I pushed against the wood and the door swung inwards into another large high room, furnished this time with rows of free standing bookshelves, like a public library. The shelves, however, were of bare functional wood, and there was no covering on the planked floor.

Well over half the shelves were empty. On the others were rows of short wide box files, their backs labelled with neat type strips explaining what was to be found within. Each box proved to contain all the films from one day's racing, and they were all efficiently arranged in chronological order. I pulled out the box for the day I rode Squelch and Wanderlust at Reading, and looked inside. There were six round cans of sixteen millimetre film, numbered one to six, and space enough for another one, number seven.

I took the box out to Carol. She was still sitting on top of the desk, dangling the drying toes and reading through a woman's magazine.

'What have you found then?'

'Do you lend these films to anyone who wants them?'

'Hire, not lend. Sure.'

'Who to?'

'Anyone who asks. Usually it's the owners of the horses. Often they want prints made to keep, so we make them.'

'Do the Stewards often want them?'

'Stewards? Well, see, if there's any doubt about a race the Stewards see the film on the racecourse. That van the old man and our Alfie's got develops it on the spot as soon as it's collected from the cameras.'

'But sometimes they send for them afterwards?'

'Sometimes, yeah. When they want to compare the running of some horse or other.' Her legs suddenly stopped swinging. She put down the magazine and gave me a straight stare.

'Kelly . . . Kelly *Hughes*?'

I didn't answer.

'Hey, you're not a bit like I thought.' She put her blonde head on one side, assessing me. 'None of those sports writers ever said anything about you being smashing looking and dead sexy.'

I laughed. I had a crooked nose and a scar down one cheek from where a horse's hoof had cut my face open, and among jockeys I was an also-ran as a bird-attracter.

'It's your eyes,' she said. 'Dark and sort of smiley and sad and a bit withdrawn. Give me the happy shivers, your eyes do.'

'You read all that in a magazine,' I said.

'I never!' But she laughed.

'Who asked for the film that's missing from the box?' I said. 'And what exactly did they ask for?'

She sighed exaggeratedly and edged herself off the desk into a pair of bright pink sandals.

'Which film is that?' She looked at the box and its reference number, and did a Marilyn Monroe sway over to a filing cabinet against the wall. 'Here we are. One official letter from the Stewards' secretary saying please send film of last race at Reading . . .'

I took the letter from her and read it myself. The words were quite clear: 'the last race at Reading.' Not the sixth race. The last race. And there had been seven races. It hadn't been Carol or the Cannot Lie Co. who had made the mistake.

'So you sent it?'

'Of course. Off to the authorities, as per instructions.' She put the letter back in the files. 'Did you in, did it?'

'Not that film, no.'

'Alfie and the old man say you must have made a packet out of the Lemonfizz, to lose your licence over it.'

'Do you think so too?'

'Stands to reason. Everyone thinks so.'

'Man in the street?'

'Him too.'

'Not a cent.'

'You're a nit, then,' she said frankly. 'Whatever did you do it for?'

'I didn't.'

'Oh yeah?' She gave me a knowing wink. 'I suppose you have to say that, don't you?'

'Well,' I said, handing her the Reading box to put back in the storeroom, 'thanks anyway.' I gave her half a smile and went away across the expanse of mottled linoleum to the door out.

I drove home slowly, trying to think. Not a very profitable exercise. Brains seemed to have deteriorated into a mushy blankness.

There were several letters for me in the mailbox on my front door, including one from my parents. I unfolded it walking up the stairs, feeling as usual a million miles away from them on every level.

My mother had written the first half in her round regular handwriting on one side of a large piece of lined paper. As usual there wasn't a full stop to be seen. She punctuated entirely with commas.

Dear Kelly,

Thanks for your note, we got it yesterday, we don't like reading about you in the papers, I know you said you hadn't done it son but no smoke without fire is what Mrs Jones the post office says, and it is not nice for us what people are saying about you round here, all airs and graces they say you are and pride goes before a fall and all that, well the pullets have started laying at last, we are painting your old room for Auntie Myfanwy who is coming to live here her arthritis is too bad for those stairs she has, well Kelly, I wish I could say we want you to come home but your Da is that angry and now Auntie Myfanwy needs the room any-way, well son, we never wanted you to go for a jockey, there was that nice job at the Townhall in Tenby you could have had, I don't like to say it but you have disgraced us son, there's horrid it is going into the village now, everyone whispering, your loving Mother.

I took a deep breath and turned the page over to receive the blast from my father. His writing was much like my mother's as they had learned from the same teacher, but he had pressed so hard with his ballpoint that he had almost dug through the paper.

Kelly,

You're a damned disgrace boy. It's soft saying you didn't do it. They wouldn't of warned you off if you didn't do it. Not lords and such. They know what's right. You're lucky you're not here I would give you a proper belting. After all that scrimping your Ma did to let you go off to the University. And people said you would get too ladidah to speak to us, they were right. Still, this is worse, being a cheat. Don't you come back here, your Ma's that upset, what with that cat Mrs Jones saying things. It would be best to say don't send us any more money into the bank. I asked the manager but he said only you can cancel a banker's order so you'd better do it. Your Ma says it's as bad as you being in prison, the disgrace and all.'

He hadn't signed it. He wouldn't know how to, we had so little affection for each other. He had despised me from childhood for liking school, and had mocked me unmercifully all the way to college. He showed his jolly side only to my two older brothers, who had had what he considered a healthy contempt for education: one of them had gone into the Merchant Navy and the other lived next door and worked alongside my father for the farmer who owned the cottages.

When in the end I had turned my back on all the years of learning and taken to racing my family had again all disapproved of me, though I guessed they would have been pleased enough if I'd chosen it all along. I'd wasted the country's money, my father said; I wouldn't have been given all those grants if they'd known that as soon as I was out I'd go racing. That was probably true. It was also true that since I'd been racing I'd paid enough in taxes to send several other farm boys through college on grants.

I put my parents' letter under Rosalind's photograph. Even she had been unable to reach their approval, because they thought I should have married a nice girl from my own sort of background, not the student daughter of a colonel.

They had rigid minds. It was doubtful now if they would ever be pleased with me, whatever I did. And if I got my licence back, as like as not they would think I had somehow cheated again.

You couldn't take aspirins for that sort of pain. It stayed there, sticking in knives. Trying to escape it I went into the kitchen, to see if there was anything to eat. A tin of sardines, one egg, the dried up remains of some port salut.

Wrinkling my nose at that lot I transferred to the sitting-room and looked at the television programmes.

Nothing I wanted to see.

I slouched in the green velvet armchair and watched the evening slowly fade the colours into subtle greys. A certain amount of pace edged its way past the dragging gloom of the last four days. I wondered almost academically whether I would get my licence back before or after I stopped wincing at the way people looked at me, or spoke to me, or wrote about me. Probably the easiest course would be to stay out of sight, hiding myself away.

Like I was hiding away at that minute, by not going to the Jockeys' Fund dance.

The tickets were on the mantel. Tickets for Tony and Poppy, and for me and the partner I hadn't got around to inviting. Tickets which were not going to be used, which I had paid twelve fund raising guineas for.

I sat in the dark for half an hour thinking about the people who would be at the Jockeys' Fund dance.

Then I put on my black tie and went to it.

CHAPTER EIGHT

I WENT PREPARED to be stared at.

I was stared at.

Also pointed out and commented on. Discreetly, however, for the most part. And only two people decisively turned their backs.

The Jockeys' Fund dance glittered as usual with titles, diamonds, champagne and talent. Later it might curl round the edges into spilled drinks, glassy eyes, raddled make-up and slurring voices, but the gloss wouldn't entirely disappear. It never did. The Jockeys' Fund dance was one of the great social events of the steeplechasing year.

I handed over my ticket and walked along the wide passage to where the lights were low, the music hot, and the air thick with smoke and scent. The opulent ballroom of the Royal County Hotel, along the road from Ascot racecourse.

Around the dancing area there were numbers of large circular tables with chairs for ten or twelve round each, most of them occupied already. According to the chart in the hall, at table number thirty-two I would find the places reserved for Tony and me, if in fact they were still reserved. I gave up looking for table thirty-two less than half way down the room because whenever I moved a new battery of curious eyes swivelled my way. A lot of people raised a hello but none of them could hide their slightly shocked surprise. It was every bit as bad as I'd feared.

A voice behind me said incredulously, 'Hughes!'

I knew the voice. I turned round with an equal sense of the unexpected. Roberta Cranfield. Wearing a honey-coloured silk dress with the top smothered in pearls and gold thread and her copper hair drawn high with a trickle of ringlets down the back of her neck.

'You look beautiful,' I said.

Her mouth opened. 'Hughes!'

'Is your father here?'

'No,' she said disgustedly. 'He wouldn't face it. Nor would Mother. I came with a party of neighbours but I can't say I was enjoying it much until you turned up.'

'Why not?'

'You must be joking. Just look around. At a rough guess fifty people are rubber-necking at you. Doesn't it make you cringe inside? Anyway, I've had quite enough of it myself this evening, and I didn't even *see* the damned race, let alone get myself warned off.'

She stopped. 'Come and dance with me. If we're hoisting the flag we may as well do it thoroughly.'

'On one condition,' I said.

'What's that?'

'You stop calling me Hughes.'

'What?'

'Cranfield, I'm tired of being called Hughes.'

'Oh!' It had obviously never occurred to her. 'Then . . . Kelly . . . how about dancing?'

'Enchanted, Roberta.'

She gave me an uncertain look. 'I still feel I don't know you.'

'You've never bothered.'

'Nor have you.'

That jolted me. It was true. I'd disliked the idea of her. And I didn't really know her at all.

'How do you do?' I said politely. 'Come and dance.'

We shuffled around in one of those affairs which look like formalized jungle rituals, swaying in rhythm but never touching. Her face was quite calm, remotely smiling. From her composure one would have guessed her to be entirely at ease, not the target of turned heads, assessing glances, half hidden whispers.

'I don't know how you do it,' she said.

'Do what?'

'Look so . . . so matter of fact.'

'I was thinking exactly the same about you.'

She smiled, eyes crinkling and teeth gleaming, and incredibly in the circumstances she looked happy.

We stuck it for a good ten minutes. Then she said we would go back to her table, and made straight off to it without waiting for me to agree. I didn't think her party would be pleased to have me join them, and half of them weren't.

'Sit down and have a drink, my dear fellow,' drawled her host, reaching for a champagne bottle with a languid hand. 'And tell me all about the bring-back-Cranfield campaign. Roberta tells me you are working on a spot of reinstatement.'

'I haven't managed it yet,' I said deprecatingly.

'My dear chap . . .' He gave me an inspecting stare down his nose. He'd been in the Guards, I thought. So many ex-Guards officers looked at the world down the sides of their noses: it came of wearing those blinding hats.

He was blond, in his forties, not unfriendly. Roberta called him Bobbie.

The woman the other side of him leaned over and drooped a heavy pink satin bosom perilously near her brimming glass.

'Do tell me,' she said, giving me a thorough gaze from heavily made up eyes, 'What made you come?'

'Natural cussedness,' I said pleasantly.

'Oh.' She looked taken aback. 'How extraordinary.'

'Joined to the fact that there was no reason why I shouldn't.'

'And are you enjoying it?' Bobbie said. 'I mean to say, my dear chap, you are somewhat in the position of a rather messily struck off doctor turning up four days later at the British Medical Association's grandest function.'

I smiled. 'Quite a parallel.'

'Don't needle him, Bobbie,' Roberta protested.

Bobbie removed his stare from me and gave it to her instead.

'My dear Roberta, this cookie needs no little girls rushing to his defence. He's as tough as old oak.'

A disapproving elderly man on the far side of the pink bosom said under his breath, 'Thick skinned, you mean.'

Bobbie heard, and shook his head. 'Vertebral,' he said. 'Different altogether.' He stood up. 'Roberta, my dear girl, would you care to dance?'

I stood up with him.

'No need to go, my dear chap. Stay. Finish your drink.'

'You are most kind,' I said truthfully. 'But I really came tonight to have a word with one or two people . . . if you'll excuse me, I'll try to find them.'

He gave me an odd formal little inclination of the head, halfway to a bow. 'Come back later, if you'd care to.'

'Thank you,' I said. 'Very much.'

He took Roberta away to dance and I went up the stairs to the balcony which encircled the room. There were tables all round up there too, but in places one could get a good clear view of most people below. I spent some length of time identifying them from the tops of their heads.

There must have been about six hundred there, of whom I knew personally about a quarter. Owners, trainers, jockeys, Stewards, pressmen, two or three of the bigger bookmakers, starters, judges, Clerks of Courses and all the others, all with their wives and friends and chattering guests.

Kessel was there, hosting a party of twelve almost exactly beneath where I stood. I wondered if his anger had cooled since Monday, and decided if possible not to put it to the test. He had reputedly sent Squelch off to Pat Nikita, a trainer who was a bitter rival of Cranfield's, which had been rubbing it in a bit. The report looked likely to be true, as Pat Nikita was among the party below me.

Cranfield and Nikita regularly claimed each other's horses in selling races and were apt to bid each other up spitefully at auctions. It was a public joke. So in choosing Nikita as his trainer, Kessel was unmistakably announcing worldwise that he believed Cranfield and I had stopped his horse. Hardly likely to help convince anyone that we hadn't.

At one of the most prominent tables, near the dancing space, sat Lord Ferth, talking earnestly to a large lady in pale blue ostrich feathers. All the other chairs round the table were askew and unoccupied, but while I watched the music changed to a Latin rhythm, and most of the party drifted back. I knew one or two of them slightly, but not well. The man I was chiefly looking for was not among them.

Two tables away from Lord Ferth sat Edwin Byler, gravely beckoning to the waiter to fill his guests' glasses, too proud of his home-made wealth to lift the bottle himself. His cuddly little wife on the far side of the table was loaded with half the stock of Hatton Garden and was rather touchingly revelling in it.

Not to be going to ride Edwin Byler's string of super horses . . . The wry thrust of regret went deeper than I liked.

There was a rustle behind me and the smell of Roberta's fresh flower scent. I turned towards her.

'Kelly . . . ?'

She really looked extraordinarily beautiful.

'Kelly . . . Bobbie suggested that you should take me in to supper.'

'That's generous of him.'

'He seems to approve of you. He said . . .' She stopped abruptly.

'Well, never mind what he said.'

We went down the stairs and through an archway to the supper room. The light there was of a heartier wattage. It didn't do any damage to Roberta.

Along one wall stretched a buffet table laden with aspic-shining cold meats and oozing cream gateaux. Roberta said she had dined at Bobbie's before coming on to the dance and wasn't hungry, but we both collected some salmon and sat down at one of the twenty or so small tables clustered into half of the room.

Six feet away sat three fellow jockeys resting their elbows among a debris of empty plates and coffee cups.

'Kelly!' One of them exclaimed in a broad northern voice. 'My God. Kelly. Come over here, you old so and so. Bring the talent with you.'

The talent's chin began its familiar upward tilt.

'Concentrate on the character, not the accent,' I said.

She gave me a raw look of surprise, but when I stood up and picked up her plate, she came with me. They made room for us, admired Roberta's appearance, and didn't refer to anyone being warned off. Their girls, they exclaimed, were powdering their noses, and when the noses reappeared, immaculate, they all smiled goodbye and went back to the ballroom.

'They were kind.' She sounded surprised.

'They would be.'

She fiddled with her fork, not looking at me. 'You said the other day that my mind was in chains. Was that what you meant

. . . that I'm inclined to judge people by their voices . . . and that it's wrong?'

'Eton's bred its rogues,' I said. 'Yes.'

'Cactus. You're all prickles.'

'Original sin exists,' I said mildly. 'So does original virtue. They both crop up regardless. No respecters of birth.'

'Where did you go to school?'

'In Wales.'

'You haven't a Welsh accent. You haven't any accent at all. And that's odd really, considering you are only . . .' Her voice trailed away and she looked aghast at her self-betrayal. 'Oh dear . . . I'm sorry.'

'It's not surprising,' I pointed out. 'Considering your father. And anyway, in my own way I'm just as bad. I smothered my Welsh accent quite deliberately. I used to practise in secret, while I was still at school, copying the B.B.C. news announcers. I wanted to be a Civil Servant, and I was ambitious, and I knew I wouldn't get far if I sounded like the son of a Welsh farm labourer. So in time this became my natural way of talking. And my parents despise me for it.'

'Parents!' she said despairingly. 'Why can we never escape them? Whatever we are, it is because of *them*. I want to be *me*.' She looked astonished at herself. 'I've never felt like this before. I don't understand . . .'

'Well I do,' I said, smiling. 'Only it happens to most people around fifteen or sixteen. Rebellion, it's called.'

'You're mocking me.' But the chin stayed down.

'No.'

We finished the salmon and drank coffee. A large loudly chattering party collected food from the buffet and pushed the two tables next to us together so that they could all sit at one. They were well away on a tide of alcohol and bonhomie, loosened and expansive. I watched them idly. I knew four of them, two trainers, one wife, one owner.

One of the trainers caught sight of me and literally dropped his knife.

'That's Kelly Hughes,' he said disbelievingly. The whole party turned round and stared. Roberta drew a breath in distress. I sat without moving.

'What are you doing here?'

'Drinking coffee,' I said politely.

His eyes narrowed. Trevor Norse was not amused. I sighed inwardly. It was never good to antagonize trainers, it simply meant one less possible source of income: but I'd ridden for Trevor Norse several times already, and knew that it was practically impossible to please him anyway.

A heavy man, six feet plus, labouring under the misapprehension that size could substitute for ability. He was much better with owners than with horses, tireless at cultivating the one and lazy with the other.

His brainless wife said brightly, 'I hear you're paying Dexter's lads' wages, because you're sure you'll get your licence back in a day or two.'

'What's all that?' Norse said sharply. 'Where did you hear all that nonsense?'

'Everyone's talking about it, darling,' she said protestingly.

'Who's everyone?'

She giggled weakly. 'I heard it in the ladies, if you must know. But it's quite true, I'm sure it is. Dexter's lads told Daphne's lads in the local pub, and Daphne told Miriam, and Miriam was telling us in the ladies . . .'

'Is it true?' Norse demanded.

'Well, more or less,' I agreed.

'Good Lord.'

'Miriam said Kelly Hughes says he and Dexter were framed, and that he's finding out who did it.' Mrs. Norse giggled at me. 'My *dear*, isn't it all such fun.'

'Great,' I said dryly. I stood up, and Roberta also.

'Do you know Roberta Cranfield?' I said formally, and they all exclaimed over her, and she scattered on them a bright artificial smile, and we went back and tried another dance.

It wasn't altogether a great idea because we were stopped half way round by Daddy Leeman of the *Daily Witness* who raked me over with avid eyes and yelled above music was it true I was claiming I'd been framed. He had a piercing voice. All the nearby couples turned and stared. Some of them raised sceptical eyebrows at each other.

'I really can't stand a great deal more of this,' Roberta said in my ear. 'How can you? Why don't you go home now?'

'I'm sorry,' I said contritely. 'You've been splendid. I'll take you back to Bobbie.'

'But you . . . ?'

'I haven't done what I came for. I'll stay a bit longer.'

She compressed her mouth and started to dance again. 'All right. So will I.'

We danced without smiling.

'Do you want a tombola ticket?' I asked.

'No.' She was astonished.

'You might as well. I want to go down that end of the room.'

'Whatever for?'

'Looking for someone. Haven't been down that end at all.'

'Oh. All right, then.'

She stepped off the polished wood on to the thick dark carpet, and threaded her way to the clear aisle which led down to the gaily decorated tombola stall at the far end of the ballroom.

I looked for the man I wanted, but I didn't see him. I met too many other eyes, most of which hastily looked away.

'I hate them,' Roberta said fiercely. 'I hate people.'

I bought her four tickets. Three of them were blanks. The fourth had a number which fitted a bottle of vodka.

'I don't like it much,' she said, holding it dubiously.

'Nor do I.'

'I'll give it to the first person who's nice to you.'

'You might have to drink it yourself.'

We went slowly back down the aisle, not talking.

A thin woman sprang up from her chair as we approached her table and in spite of the embarrassed holding-back clutches of her party managed to force her way out into our path. We couldn't pass her without pushing. We stopped.

'You're Roberta Cranfield, aren't you?' she said. She had a strong-boned face, no lipstick, angry eyes, and stiffly regimented greying hair. She looked as if she'd had far too much to drink.

'Excuse us,' I said gently, trying to go past.

'Oh no you don't,' she said. 'Not until I've had my say.'

'Grace!' wailed a man across the table. I looked at him more closely. Edwin Byler's trainer, Jack Roxford. 'Grace, dear, leave it. Sit down, dear,' he said.

Grace dear had no such intentions. Grace dear's feelings were far too strong.

'Your father's got exactly what he deserves, my lass, and I can tell you I'm glad about it. Glad.' She thrust her face towards Roberta's, glaring like a mad woman. Roberta looked down her nose at her, which I would have found as infuriating as Grace did.

'I'd dance on his grave,' she said furiously. 'That I would.'

'Why?' I said flatly.

She didn't look at me. She said to Roberta, 'He's a bloody snob, your father. A bloody snob. And he's got what he deserved. So there. You tell him that.'

'Excuse me,' Roberta said coldly, and tried to go forward.

'Oh no you don't,' Grace clutched at her arm. Roberta shook her hand off angrily. 'Your bloody snob of a father was trying to get Edwin Byler's horses away from us. Did you know that? Did you know that? All those grand ways of his. Thought Edwin would do better in a bigger stable, did he? Oh, I heard what he said. Trying to persuade Edwin he needed a grand top drawer trainer now, not poor little folk like us, who've won just rows of races for him. Well, I could have laughed my head off when I heard he'd been had up. I'll tell you. Serves him right, I said. What a laugh.'

'Grace,' said Jack Roxford despairingly. 'I'm sorry, Miss Cranfield. She isn't really like this.'

He looked acutely embarrassed. I thought that probably Grace Roxford was all too often like this. He had the haunted expression of the forever apologizing husband.

'Cheer up then, Mrs. Roxford,' I said loudly. 'You've got what you want. You're laughing. So why the fury?'

'Eh?' She twisted her head round at me, staggering a fraction. 'As for you, Kelly Hughes, you just asked for what you got, and don't give me any of that crap we've been hearing this evening that you were framed, because you know bloody well you weren't. People like you and Cranfield, you think you can get away with murder, people like you. But there's justice somewhere in this world sometimes and you won't forget that in a hurry, will you now, Mr Clever Dick.'

One of the women of the party stood up and tried to persuade her to quieten down, as every ear for six tables around was stretched in her direction. She was oblivious to them. I wasn't.

Roberta said under her breath, 'Oh God.'

'So you go home and tell your bloody snob of a father,' Grace said to her, 'That it's a great big laugh him being found out. That's what it is, a great big laugh.'

The acutely embarrassed woman friend pulled her arm, and Grace swung angrily round from us to her. We took the brief opportunity and edged away round her back, and as we retreated we could hear her shouting after us, her words indistinct above the music except for 'laugh' and 'bloody snob'.

'She's *awful*,' Roberta said.

'Not much help to poor old Jack,' I agreed.

'I do hate scenes. They're so messy.'

'Do you think all strong emotions are messy?'

'That's not the same thing,' she said. 'You can have strong emotions without making scenes. Scenes are disgusting.'

I sighed. 'That one was.'

'Yes.'

She was walking, I noticed, with her neck stretched very tall, the classic signal to anyone watching that she was not responsible or bowed down or amused at being involved in noise and nastiness. Rosalind, I reflected nostalgically, would probably have sympathetically agreed with dear disturbed Grace, led her off to some quiet mollifying corner, and reappeared with her eating out of her hand. Rosalind had been tempestuous herself and understood uncontrollable feelings.

Unfortunately at the end of the aisle we almost literally bumped into Kessel, who came in for the murderous glance from Roberta which had been earned by dear Grace. Kessel naturally misinterpreted her expression and spat first.

'You can tell your father that I had been thinking for some time of sending my horses to Pat Nikita, and that this business has made me regret that I didn't do it a long time ago. Pat has always wanted to train for me. I stayed with your father out of a mistaken sense of loyalty, and just look how he repaid me.'

'Father has won a great many races for you,' Roberta said coldly. 'And if Squelch had been good enough to win the Lemonfizz Cup, he would have done.'

Kessel's mouth sneered. It didn't suit him.

'As for you, Hughes, it's a disgrace you being here tonight and I cannot think why you were allowed in. And don't think you can fool me by spreading rumours that you are innocent and on the point of proving it. That's all piffle, and you know it, and if you have any ideas you can reinstate yourself with me that way, you are very much mistaken.'

He turned his back on us and bristled off, pausing triumphantly to pat Pat Nikita on the shoulder, and looking back to make sure we had noticed. Very small of him.

'There goes Squelch,' I said resignedly.

'He'll soon be apologizing and sending him back,' she said with certainty.

'Not a hope. Kessel's not the humble pie kind. And Pat Nikita will never let go of that horse. Not to see him go back to your father. He'd break him down first.'

'Why are people so jealous of each other,' she exclaimed.

'Born in them,' I said. 'And almost universal.'

'You have a very poor opinion of human nature.' She disapproved.

'An objective opinion. There's as much good as bad.'

'You can't be objective about being warned off,' she protested.

'Er . . . no,' I conceded. 'How about a drink?'

She looked instinctively towards Bobbie's table and I shook my head. 'In the bar.'

'Oh . . . still looking for someone?'

'That's right. We haven't tried the bar yet.'

'Is there going to be another scene?'

'I shouldn't think so.'

'All right, then.'

We made our way slowly through the crowd. By then the fact that we were there must have been known to almost everyone in the place. Certainly the heads no longer turned in open surprise, but the eyes did, sliding into corners, giving us a surreptitious once-over, probing and hurtful. Roberta held herself almost defiantly straight.

The bar was heavily populated, with cigar smoke lying in a haze over the well-groomed heads and the noise level doing justice to a discotheque. Almost at once through a narrow gap in the cluster I saw him, standing against the far wall, talking vehemently. He turned his head suddenly and looked straight at me, meeting my eyes briefly before the groups between us shifted and closed the line of sight. In those two seconds, how-ever, I had seen his mouth tighten and his whole face compress into annoyance; and he had known I was at the dance, because there was no surprise.

'You've seen him,' Roberta said.

'Yes.'

'Well . . . who is it?'

'Lord Gowery.'

She gasped. 'Oh no, Kelly.'

'I want to talk to him.'

'It can't do any good.'

'You never know.'

'Annoying Lord Gowery is the last, positively the last way of getting your licence back. Surely you can see that?'

'Yes . . . He's not going to be kind, I don't think. So would you mind very much if I took you back to Bobbie first?'

She looked troubled. 'You won't say anything silly? It's Father's licence as well, remember.'

'I'll bear it in mind,' I said flippantly. She gave me a sharp, suspicious glance, but turned easily enough to go back to Bobbie.

Almost immediately outside the bar we were stopped by Jack Roxford, who was hurrying towards us through the throng.

'Kelly,' he said, half panting with the exertion. 'I just wanted to catch you . . . to say how sorry I am that Grace went off the deep end like that. She's not herself, poor girl . . . Miss Cranfield, I do apologize.'

Roberta unbent a little. 'That's all right, Mr Roxford.'

'I wouldn't like you to believe that what Grace said . . . all those things about your father . . . is what I think too.' He looked from her to me, and back again, the hesitant worry furrowing his forehead. A slight, unaggressive man of about forty-five; bald crown, nervous eyes, permanently worried expression. He was a reasonably good trainer but not enough of a man of the world to have achieved much personal stature. To me, though I had never ridden for him, he had always been friendly, but his restless anxiety-state made him tiring to be with.

'Kelly,' he said, 'if it's really true that you were both framed, I do sincerely hope that you get your licences back. I mean, I know there's a risk that Edwin will take his horses to your father, Miss Cranfield, but he did tell me this evening that he won't do so now, even if he could . . . But please believe me, I hold no dreadful grudge against either of you, like poor Grace . . . I do hope you'll forgive her.'

'Of course, Mr Roxford,' said Roberta, entirely placated. 'Please don't give it another thought. And oh!' she added impulsively, 'I think you've earned this!' and into his astonished hands she thrust the bottle of vodka.

CHAPTER NINE

WHEN I WENT BACK towards the bar I found Lord Gowery had come out of it. He was standing shoulder to shoulder with Lord Ferth, both of them watching me walk towards them with faces like thunder.

I stopped four feet away, and waited.

'Hughes,' said Lord Gowery for openers, 'You shouldn't be here.'

'My Lord,' I said politely. 'This isn't Newmarket Heath.'

It went down badly. They were both affronted. They closed their ranks.

'Insolence will get you nowhere,' Lord Ferth said, and Lord Gowery added, 'You'll never get your licence back, if you behave like this.'

I said without heat, 'Does justice depend on good manners?'

They looked as if they couldn't believe their ears. From their point of view I was cutting my own throat, though I had always myself doubted that excessive meekness got licences restored any quicker than they would have been without it. Meekness in the accused brought out leniency in some judges, but severity in others. To achieve a minimum sentence, the guilty should always bone up on the character of their judge, a sound maxim which I hadn't had the sense to see applied even more to the innocent.

'I would have thought some sense of shame would have kept you away,' Lord Ferth said.

'It took a bit of an effort to come,' I agreed.

His eyes narrowed and opened again quickly.

Gowery said, 'As to spreading these rumours . . . I say categorically that you are not only not on the point of being given your licence back, but that your suspension will be all the longer in consequence of your present behaviour.'

I gave him a level stare and Lord Ferth opened his mouth and shut it again.

'It is no rumour that Mr Cranfield and I are not guilty,' I said at length. 'It is no rumour that two at least of the witnesses were lying. Those are facts.'

'Nonsense,' Gowery said vehemently.

'What you believe, sir,' I said, 'Doesn't alter the truth.'

'You are doing yourself no good, Hughes.' Under his heavy authoritative exterior he was exceedingly angry. All I needed was a bore hole, and I'd get a gusher.

I said, 'Would you be good enough to tell me who suggested to you or the other Stewards that you should seek out and question Mr Newtonnards?'

There was the tiniest shift in his eyes. Enough for me to be certain.

'Certainly not.'

'Then will you tell me upon whose instructions the enquiry agent David Oakley visited my flat?'

'I will not.' His voice was loud, and for the first time, alarmed.

Ferth looked in growing doubt from one of us to the other.

'What is all this about?' he said.

'Mr Cranfield and I were indeed wrongly warned off,' I said. 'Someone sent David Oakley to my flat to fake that photograph. And I believe Lord Gowery knows who it was.'

'I most certainly do not,' he said furiously. 'Do you want to be sued for slander?'

'I have not slandered you, sir.'

'You said . . .'

'I said you knew who sent David Oakley. I did not say that you knew the photograph was a fake.'

'And it wasn't,' he insisted fiercely.

'Well,' I said. 'It was.'

There was a loaded, glaring silence. Then Lord Gowery said heavily, 'I'm not going to listen to this,' and turned on his heel and dived back into the bar.

Lord Ferth, looking troubled, took a step after him.

I said, 'My Lord, may I talk to you?' And he stopped and turned back to me and said, 'Yes, I think you'd better.'

He gestured towards the supper room next door and we went through the archway into the brighter light. Nearly everyone had eaten and gone. The buffet table bore shambled remains and all but two of the small tables were unoccupied. He sat down at one of these and pointed to the chair opposite. I took it, facing him.

'Now,' he said, 'Explain.'

I spoke in a flat calm voice, because emotion was going to repel him where reason might get through. 'My Lord, if you could look at the Enquiry from my point of view for a minute, it is quite simple. I know that I never had any five hundred pounds or any note from Mr Cranfield, therefore I am obviously aware that David Oakley was lying. It's unbelievable that the Stewards should have sent him, since the evidence he produced was faked. So someone else did. I thought Lord Gowery might know who. So I asked him.'

'He said he didn't know.'

'I don't altogether believe him.'

'Hughes, that's preposterous.'

'Are you intending to say, sir, that men in power positions are infallibly truthful?'

He looked at me without expression in a lengthening silence. Finally he said, as Roberta had done, 'Where did you go to school?'

In the usual course of things I kept dead quiet about the type of education I'd had because it was not likely to endear me to either owners or trainers. Still, there was a time for everything, so I told him.

'Coedlant Primary, Tenby Grammar, and L.S.E.'

'L.S.E. . . . you don't mean . . . the London School of Economics?' He looked astonished.

'Yes.'

'My God . . .'

I watched him while he thought it over. 'What did you read there?'

'Politics, philosophy and economics.'

'Then what on earth made you become a jockey?'

'It was almost an accident,' I said. 'I didn't plan it. When I'd finished my final exams I was mentally tired, so I thought I'd take a sort of paid holiday working on the land . . . I knew how to do that, my father's a farm hand. I worked at harvesting for a farmer in Devon and every morning I used to ride his 'chasers out at exercise, because I'd ridden most of my life, you see. He had a permit, and he was dead keen. And then his brother, who raced them for him, broke his shoulder at one of the early Devon meetings, and he put me up instead, and almost at once I started winning . . . and then it took hold of me . . . so I didn't get around to being a Civil Servant, as I'd always vaguely intended, and . . . well . . . I've never regretted it.'

'Not even now?' he said with irony.

I shook my head. 'Not even now.'

'Hughes . . .' His face crinkled dubiously. 'I don't know what to think. At first I was sure you were not the type to have stopped Squelch deliberately . . . and then there was all that damning evidence. Charlie West saying you had definitely pulled back . . .'

I looked down at the table. I didn't after all want an eye for an eye, when it came to the point.

'Charlie was mistaken,' I said. 'He got two races muddled up. I did pull back in another race at about that time . . . riding a novice 'chaser with no chance, well back in the field. I wanted to give it a good schooling race. That was what Charlie remembered.'

He said doubtfully, 'It didn't sound like it.'

'No,' I agreed. 'I've had it out with Charlie since. He might be prepared to admit now that he was talking about the wrong race. If you will ask the Oxford Stewards, you'll find that Charlie said nothing to them directly after the Lemonfizz, when they made their first enquiries, about me not trying. He only said it later, at the Enquiry in Portman Square.' Because in between some beguiling seducer had offered him five hundred pounds for the service.

'I see.' He frowned. 'And what was it that you asked Lord Gowery about Newtonnards?'

'Newtonnards didn't volunteer the information to the Stewards about Mr Cranfield backing Cherry Pie, but he did tell several bookmaker colleagues. Someone told the Stewards. I wanted to know who.'

'Are you suggesting that it was the same person who sent Oakley to your flat?'

'It might be. But not necessarily.' I hesitated, looking at him doubtfully.

'What is it?' he said.

'Sir, I don't want to offend you, but would you mind telling me why you sat in at the Enquiry? Why there were four of you instead of three, when Lord Gowery, if you'll forgive me saying so, was obviously not too pleased at the arrangement.'

His lips tightened. 'You're being uncommonly tactful all of a sudden.'

'Yes, sir.'

He looked at me steadily. A tall thin man with high cheek-bones, strong black hair, hot fiery eyes. A man whose force of character reached out and hit you, so that you'd never forget meeting him. The best ally in the whole 'chasing set up, if I could only reach him.

'I cannot give you my reasons for attending,' he said with some reproof.

'Then you had some . . . reservations . . . about how the Enquiry would be conducted?'

'I didn't say that,' he protested. But he had meant it.

'Lord Gowery chose Andrew Tring to sit with him at the hearing, and Andrew Tring wants a very big concession from him just now. And he chose Lord Plimborne as the third Steward, and Lord Plimborne continually fell asleep.'

'Do you realize what you're saying?' He was truly shocked.

'I want to know how Lord Gowery acquired all that evidence against us. I want to know why the Stewards' Secretaries sent for the wrong film. I want to know why Lord Gowery was so biased, so deaf to our denials, so determined to warn us off.'

'That's slanderous . . .'

'I want you to ask him,' I finished flatly.

He simply stared.

I said, 'He might tell you. He might just possibly tell you. But he'd never in a million years tell *me*.'

'Hughes . . . You surely don't expect . . .'

'That wasn't a straight trial, and he knows it. I'm just asking you to tackle him with it, to see if he will explain.'

'You are talking about a much respected man,' he said coldly.

'Yes, sir. He's a baron, a rich man, a Steward of long standing. I know all that.'

'And you *still* maintain . . . ?'

'Yes.'

His hot eyes brooded. 'He'll have you in Court for this.'

'Only if I'm wrong.'

'I can't possibly do it,' he said, with decision.

'And please, if you have one, use a tape recorder.'

'I told you . . .'

'Yes, sir, I know you did.'

He got up from the table, paused as if about to say something, changed his mind, and as I stood up also, turned abruptly and walked sharply away. When he had gone I found that my hands were trembling, and I followed him slowly out of the supper room feeling a battered wreck.

I had either resurrected our licences or driven the nails into them, and only time would tell which.

Bobbie said, 'Have a drink, my dear fellow. You look as though you've been clobbered by a steam roller.'

I took a mouthful of champagne and thanked him, and watched Roberta swing her body to a compelling rhythm with someone else. The ringlets bounced against her neck. I wondered without disparagement how long it had taken her to pin them on.

'Not the best of evenings for you, old pal,' Bobbie observed.

'You never know.'

He raised his eyebrows, drawling down his nose, 'Mission accomplished?'

'A fuse lit, rather.'

He lifted his glass. 'To a successful detonation.'

'You are most kind,' I said formally.

The music changed gear and Roberta's partner brought her back to the table.

I stood up. 'I came to say goodbye,' I said. 'I'll be going now.'

'Oh not yet,' she exclaimed. 'The worst is over. No one's staring any more. Have some fun.'

'Dance with the dear girl,' Bobbie said, and Roberta put out a long arm and pulled mine, and so I went and danced with her.

'Lord Gowery didn't eat you then?'

'He's scrunching the bones at this minute.'

'Kelly! If you've done any damage . . .'

'No omelets without smashing eggs, love.'

The chin went up. I grinned. She brought it down again. Getting quite human, Miss Cranfield.

After a while the hot rhythm changed to a slow smooch, and couples around us went into clinches. Bodies to bodies, heads to heads, eyes shut, swaying in the dimming light. Roberta eyed them coolly and prickled when I put my arms up to gather her in. She danced very straight, with four inches of air between us. Not human enough.

We ambled around in that frigid fashion through three separate wodges of glutinous music. She didn't come any closer, and I did nothing to persuade her, but equally she seemed to be in no hurry to break it up. Composed, cool, off-puttingly gracious, she looked as flawless in the small hours as she had when I'd arrived.

'I'm glad you were here,' I said.

She moved her head in surprise. 'It hasn't been exactly the best Jockeys' Fund dance of my life . . . but I'm glad I came.'

'Next year this will be all over, and everyone will have forgotten.'

'I'll dance with you again next year,' she said.

'It's a pact.'

She smiled, and just for a second a stray beam of light shimmered on some expression in her eyes which I didn't understand.

She was aware of it. She turned her head away, and then detached herself altogether, and gestured that she wanted to go back to the table. I delivered her to Bobbie, and she sat down immediately and began powdering a non-shiny nose.

'Good night,' I said to Bobbie. 'And thank you.'

'My dear fellow. Any time.'

'Good night, Roberta.'

She looked up. Nothing in the eyes. Her voice was collected. 'Good night, Kelly.'

I lowered myself into the low slung burnt orange car in the park and drove away thinking about her. Roberta Cranfield. Not my idea of a cuddly bed mate. Too cold, too controlled, too proud. And it didn't go with that copper hair, all that rigidity. Or maybe she was only rigid to me because I was a farm labourer's son. Only that, and only a jockey . . . and her father had taught her that jockeys were the lower classes dear and don't get your fingers dirty . . .

Kelly, I said to myself, you've a fair sized chip on your shoulder, old son. Maybe she does think like that, but why should it bother you? And even if she does, she spent most of the evening with you . . . although she was really quite careful not to touch you too much. Well . . . maybe that was because so many people were watching . . . and maybe it was simply that she didn't like the thought of it.

I was on the short cut home that led round the south of Reading, streaking down deserted back roads, going fast for no reason except that speed had become a habit. This car was easily the best I'd ever had, the only one I had felt proud of. Mechanically a masterpiece and with looks to match. Even thirty thousand miles in the past year hadn't dulled the pleasure I got from driving it. Its only fault was that like so many other sports cars it had a totally inefficient heater, which in spite of coaxing and overhauls stubbornly refused to do more than demist the windscreen and raise my toes one degree above frostbite. If kicked, it retaliated with a smell of exhaust.

I had gone to the dance without a coat, and the night was frosty. I shivered and switched on the heater to maximum. As usual, damn all.

There was a radio in the car, which I seldom listened to, and a spare crash helmet, and my five pound racing saddle which I'd been going to take to Wetherby Races.

Depression flooded back. Fierce though the evening had been, in many ways I had forgotten for a while the dreariness of being banned. It could be a long slog now, after what I had said to the Lords Gowery and Ferth. A very long slog indeed. Cranfield wouldn't like the gamble. I wasn't too sure that I could face telling him, if it didn't come off.

Lord Ferth . . . would he or wouldn't he? He'd be torn between loyalty to an equal and a concept of justice. I didn't know him well enough to be sure which would win. And maybe anyway he would shut everything I'd said clean out of his mind, as too far-fetched and preposterous to bother about.

Bobbie had been great, I thought. I wondered who he was. Maybe one day I'd ask Roberta.

Mrs Roxford . . . poor dear Grace. What a life Jack must lead . . . Hope he liked vodka . . .

I took an unexpectedly sharp bend far too fast. The wheels screeched when I wrenched the nose round and the car went weaving and skidding for a hundred yards before I had it in control again. I put my foot gingerly back on the accelerator and still had in my mind's eye the solid trunks of the row of trees I had just missed by centimetres.

God, I thought, how could I be so careless. It rocked me. I was a careful driver, even if fast, and I'd never had an accident. I could feel myself sweating. It was something to sweat about.

How stupid I was, thinking about the dance, not concentrating on driving, and going too fast for these small roads. I rubbed my forehead, which felt tense and tight, and kept my speed down to forty.

Roberta had looked beautiful ... keep your mind on the road Kelly, for God's sake ... Usually I drove semi-automatically, without having to concentrate every yard of the way. I found myself going slower still, because both my reactions and my thoughts were growing sluggish. I'd drunk a total of about half a glass of champagne all evening, so it couldn't be that.

I was simply going to sleep.

I stopped the car, got out, and stamped about to wake myself up. People who went to sleep at the wheels of sports cars on the way home from dances were not a good risk.

Too many sleepless nights, grinding over my sorry state. Insulting the lions seemed to have released the worst of that. I felt I could now fall unconscious for a month.

I considered sleeping there and then, in the car. But the car was cold and couldn't be heated. I would drive on, I decided, and stop for good if I felt really dozy again. The fresh air had done the trick; I was wide awake and irritated with myself.

The beam of my headlights on the cats' eyes down the empty road was soon hypnotic. I switched on the radio to see if that would hold my attention, but it was all soft and sweet late night music. Lullaby. I switched if off.

Pity I didn't smoke. That would have helped.

It was a star clear night with a bright full moon. Ice crystals sparkled like diamond dust on the grass verges, now that I'd left the wooded part behind. Beautiful but unwelcome, because a hard frost would mean no racing tomorrow at Sandown ... With a jerk I realized that that didn't matter to me any more.

I glanced at the speedometer. Forty. It seemed very fast. I slowed down still further to thirty-five, and nodded owlishly to myself. Any one would be safe at thirty-five.

The tightness across my forehead slowly developed into a headache. Never mind, only an hour to home, then sleep ... sleep ... sleep ...

It's no good, I thought fuzzily. I'll have to stop and black out for a bit, even if I do wake up freezing, or I'll black out without stopping first, and that will be that.

The next layby, or something like that . . .

I began looking, forgot what I was looking for, took my foot still further off the accelerator and reckoned that thirty miles an hour was quite safe. Maybe twenty-five . . . would be better.

A little further on there were some sudden bumps in the road surface and my foot slipped of the accelerator altogether. The engine stalled. Car stopped.

Oh well, I thought. That settles it. Ought to move over to the side though. Couldn't see the side. Very odd.

The headache was pressing on my temples, and now that the engine had stopped I could hear a faint ringing in my ears.

Never mind. Never mind. Best to go to sleep. Leave the lights on . . . no one came along that road much . . . not at two in the morning . . . but have to leave the lights on just in case.

Ought to pull in to the side.

Ought to . . .

Too much trouble. Couldn't move my arms properly, anyway, so couldn't possibly do it.

Deep deep in my head a tiny instinct switched itself to emergency.

Something was wrong. Something was distinctly but appallingly **wrong**.

Sleep. Must sleep.

Get out, the flickering instinct said. Get out of the car.

Ridiculous.

Get out of the car.

Unwillingly, because it was such an effort, I struggled weakly with the handle. The door swung open. I put one leg out and tried to pull myself up, and was swept by a wave of dizziness. My head was throbbing. This wasn't . . . it couldn't be . . . just ordinary sleep.

Get out of the car . . .

My arms and legs belonged to someone else. They had me on my feet . . . I was standing up . . . didn't remember how I got there. But I was out.

Out.

Now what?

I took three tottering steps towards the back of the car and leant against the rear wing. Funny, I thought, the moonlight wasn't so bright any more.

The earth was trembling.

Stupid. Quite stupid. The earth didn't tremble.

Trembling. And the air was wailing. And the moon was falling on me. Come down from the sky and rushing towards me . . .

Not the moon. A great roaring wailing monster with a blinding moon eye. A monster making the earth tremble. A monster racing to gobble me up, huge and dark and faster than the wind and unimaginably terrifying . . .

I didn't move. Couldn't.

The one thirty mail express from Paddington to Plymouth ploughed into my sturdy little car and carried its crumpled remains half a mile down the track.

CHAPTER TEN

I DIDN'T KNOW what had happened. Didn't understand. There was a tremendous noise of tearing metal and a hundred mile an hour whirl of ninety ton diesel engine one inch away from me, and a thudding catapulting scrunch which lifted me up like a rag doll and toppled me somersaulting through the air in a kaleidoscopic black arc.

My head crashed against a concrete post. The rest of my body felt mangled beyond repair. There were rainbows in my brain, blue, purple, flaming pink, with diamond bright pin stars. Interesting while it lasted. Didn't last very long. Dissolved into an embracing inferno in which colours got lost in pain.

Up the line the train had screeched to a stop. Lights and voices were coming back that way.

The earth was cold, hard, and damp. A warm stream ran down my face. I knew it was blood. Didn't care much. Couldn't think properly, either. And didn't really want to.

More lights. Lots of lights. Lots of people. Voices.

A voice I knew.

'Roberta, my dear girl, don't look.'

'It's Kelly!' she said. Shock. Wicked, unforgettable shock. 'It's Kelly.' The second time, despair.

'Come away, my dear girl.'

She didn't go. She was kneeling beside me. I could smell her scent, and feel her hand on my hair. I was lying on my side, face down. After a while I could see a segment of honey silk dress. There was blood on it.

I said, 'You're ruining . . . your dress.'

'It doesn't matter.'

It helped somehow to have her there. I was grateful that she had stayed. I wanted to tell her that. I tried . . . and meant to say 'Roberta'. What in fact I said was . . . 'Rosalind'.

'Oh Kelly . . .' Her voice held a mixture of pity and distress.

I thought groggily that she would go away, now that I'd made such a silly mistake, but she stayed, saying small things like, 'You'll be all right soon,' and sometimes not talking at all, but just being there. I didn't know why I wanted her to stay. I remembered that I didn't even like the girl.

All the people who arrive after accidents duly arrived. Police with blue flashing lights. Ambulance waking the neighbourhood with its siren. Bobbie took Roberta away, telling her there was no more she could do. The ambulance men scooped me unceremoniously on to a stretcher and if I thought them rough it was only because every movement brought a scream up as far as my teeth and heaven knows whether any of them got any further.

By the time I reached the hospital the mists had cleared. I knew what had happened to my car. I knew that I wasn't dying. I knew that Bobbie and Roberta had taken the back roads detour like I had, and had reached the level crossing not long after me.

What I didn't understand was how I had come to stop on the railway. That crossing had drop-down-fringe gates, and they hadn't been shut.

A young dark haired doctor with tired dark-ringed eyes came to look at me, talking to the ambulance men.

'He'd just come from a dance,' they said. 'The police want a blood test.'

'Drunk?' said the doctor.

The ambulance men shrugged. They thought it possible.

'No,' I said. 'It wasn't drink. At least . . .'

They didn't pay much attention. The young doctor stooped over my lower half, feeling the damage with slender, gentle fingers. 'That hurts? Yes.' He parted my hair, looking at my head. 'Nothing much up there. More blood than damage.' He stood back. 'We'll get your pelvis X-rayed. And that leg. Can't tell what's what until after that.'

A nurse tried to take my shoes off. I said very loudly, 'Don't.'

She jumped. The doctor signed to her to stop. 'We'll do it under an anaesthetic. Just leave him for now.'

She came instead and wiped my forehead.

'Sorry,' she said.

The doctor took my pulse. 'Why ever did you stop on a level crossing?' he said conversationally. 'Silly thing to do.'

'I felt . . . sleepy. Had a headache.' It didn't sound very sensible.

'Had a bit to drink?'

'Almost nothing.'

'At a dance?' He sounded sceptical.

'Really,' I said weakly. 'I didn't.'

He put my hand down. I was still wearing my dinner jacket, though someone had taken off my tie. There were bright scarlet blotches down my white shirt and an unmendable tear down the right side of my black trousers.

I shut my eyes. Didn't do much good. The screaming pain showed no signs of giving up. It had localized into my right side from armpit to toes, with repercussions up and down my spine. I'd broken a good many bones racing, but this was much worse. Much. It was impossible.

'It won't be long now,' the doctor said comfortingly. 'We'll have you under.'

'The train didn't hit me,' I said. 'I got out of the car . . . I was leaning against the back of it . . . the train hit the car . . . not me.'

I felt sick. How long . . . ?

'If it had hit you, you wouldn't be here.'

'I suppose not . . . I had this thumping headache . . . needed air . . .' Why couldn't I pass out I thought. People always passed out when it became unbearable. Or so I'd always believed.

'Have you still got the headache?' he asked clinically.

'It's gone off a bit. Just sore now.' My mouth was dry. Always like that, after injuries. The least of my troubles.

Two porters came to wheel me away, and I protested more than was stoical about the jolts. I felt grey. Looked at my hands. They were quite surprisingly red.

X-ray department. Very smooth, very quick. Didn't try to move me except for cutting the zip out of my trousers. Quite enough.

'Sorry,' they said.

'Do you work all night?' I asked.

They smiled. On duty, if called.

'Thanks,' I said.

Another journey. People in green overalls and white masks, making soothing remarks. Could I face taking my coat off? No? Never mind then. Needle into vein in back of hand. Marvellous. Oblivion rolled through me in grey and black and I greeted it with a sob of welcome.

The world shuffled back in the usual way, bit by uncomfortable bit, with a middle-aged nurse patting my hand and telling me to wake up dear, it was all over.

I had to admit that my wildest fears were not realized. I still had two legs. One I could move. The other had plaster on. Inside the plaster it gently ached. The scream had died to a whisper. I sighed with relief.

What was the time? Five o'clock, dear.

Where was I? In the recovery ward, dear. Now go to sleep again and when you wake up you'll be feeling much better, you'll see.

I did as she said, and she was quite right.

Mid morning, a doctor came. Not the same one as the night before. Older, heavier, but just as tired looking.

'You had a lucky escape,' he said.

'Yes, I did.'

'Luckier than you imagine. We took a blood test. Actually, we took two blood tests. The first one for alcohol. With practically negative results. Now this interested us, because who except a drunk would stop a car on a level crossing and get out and lean against it? The casualty doctor told us you swore you hadn't been drinking and that anyway you seemed sober enough to him . . . but that you'd had a bad headache which was now better . . . We gave you a bit of thought, and we looked at those very bright scarlet stains on your shirt . . . and tested your blood again . . . and there it was!' He paused triumphantly.

'What?'

'Carboxyhaemoglobin.'

'What?'

'Carbon monoxide, my dear chap. Carbon monoxide poisoning. Explains everything, don't you see?'

'Oh . . . but I thought . . . with carbon monoxide . . . one simply blacked out.'

'It depends. If you got a large dose all at once that would happen, like it does to people who get stuck in snow drifts and leave their engines running. But a trickle, that would affect you more slowly. But it would all be the same in the end, of course. The haemoglobin in the red corpuscles has a greater affinity for carbon monoxide than for oxygen, so it mops up any carbon monoxide you breathe in, and oxygen is disregarded. If the level of carbon monoxide in your blood builds up gradually . . . you get gradual symptoms. Very insidious they are too. The trouble is that it seems that when people feel sleepy they light a cigarette to keep themselves awake, and tobacco smoke itself introduces significant quantities of carbon monoxide into the body, so the cigarette may be the final knock out. Er . . . do you smoke?'

'No.' And to think I'd regretted it.

'Just as well. You obviously had quite a dangerous concentration of C.O. in any case.'

'I must have been driving for half an hour . . . maybe forty minutes. I don't really know.'

'It's a wonder you stopped safely at all. Much more likely to have crashed into something.'

'I nearly did . . . on a corner.'

He nodded. 'Didn't you smell exhaust fumes?'

'I didn't notice. I had too much on my mind. And the heater burps out exhaust smells sometimes. So I wouldn't take much heed, if it wasn't strong.' I looked down at myself under the sheets. 'What's the damage?'

'Not much now,' he said cheerfully. 'You were lucky there too. You had multiple dislocations . . . hip, knee and ankle. Never seen all three before. Very interesting. We reduced them all successfully. No crushing or fractures, no severed tendons. We don't even think there will be a recurring tendency to dislocate. One or two frayed ligaments round your knee, that's all.'

'It's a miracle.'

'Interesting case, yes. Unique sort of accident, of course. No direct force involved. We think it might have been air impact . . . that it sort of blew or stretched you apart. Like being on the rack, eh?' He chuckled. 'We put plaster on your knee and ankle, to give them a chance to settle, but it can come off in three or four weeks. We don't want you to put weight on your hip yet, either. You can have some physiotherapy. But take it easy for a while when you leave here. There was a lot of spasm in the muscles, and all your ligaments and so on were badly stretched. Give everything time to subside properly before you run a mile.' He smiled, which turned half way through into a yawn. He smothered it apologetically. 'It's been a long night . . .'

'Yes,' I said.

I went home on Tuesday afternoon in an ambulance with a pair of crutches and instructions to spend most of my time horizontal.

Poppy was still sick. Tony followed my slow progress up the stairs apologizing that she couldn't manage to have me stay, the kids were exhausting her to distraction.

'I'm fine on my own.'

He saw me into the bedroom, where I lay down in my clothes on top of the bedspread, as per instructions. Then he made for the whisky and refreshed himself after my labours.

'Do you want anything? I'll fetch you some food, later.'

'Thanks,' I said. 'Could you bring the telephone in here?'

He brought it in and plugged the lead into the socket beside my bed.

'O.K.?'

'Fine,' I said.

'That's it, then.' He tossed off his drink quickly and made for the door, showing far more haste than usual and edging away from me as though embarrassed.

'Is anything wrong?' I said.

He jumped. 'No. Absolutely nothing. Got to get the kids their tea before evening stables. See you later, pal. With the odd crust.' He smiled sketchily and disappeared.

I shrugged. Whatever it was that was wrong, he would tell me in time, if he wanted to.

I picked up the telephone and dialled the number of the local garage. Its best mechanic answered.

'Mr Hughes . . . I heard . . . Your beautiful car.' He commiserated genuinely for half a minute.

'Yes,' I said. 'Look, Derek, is there any way that exhaust gas could get into the car through the heater?'

He was affronted. 'Not the way I looked after it. Certainly not.'

'I apparently breathed in great dollops of carbon monoxide,' I said.

'Not through the heater . . . I can't understand it.' He paused, thinking. 'They take special care not to let that happen, see? At the design stage. You could only get exhaust gas through the heater if there was a loose or worn gasket on the exhaust manifold *and* a crack or break in the heater tubing *and* a tube connecting the two together, and you can take it from me, Mr Hughes, there was nothing at all like that on your car. Maintained perfect, it is.'

'The heater does sometimes smell of exhaust. If you remember, I did mention it, some time ago.'

'I give the whole system a thorough check then, too. There wasn't a thing wrong. Only thing I could think of was the exhaust might have eddied forward from the back of the car when you slowed down, sort of, and got whirled in through the fresh air intake, the one down beside the heater.'

'Could you possibly go and look at my car? At what's left of it . . . ?'

'There's a good bit to do here,' he said dubiously.

'The police have given me the name of the garage where it is now. Apparently all the bits have to stay there until the insurance people have seen them. But you know the car . . . it would be easier for you to spot anything different with it from when you last serviced it. Could you go?'

'D'you mean,' he paused. 'You don't mean . . . there might be something . . . well . . . *wrong* with it?'

'I don't know,' I said. 'But I'd like to find out.'

'It would cost you,' he said warningly. 'It would be working hours.'

'Never mind. If you can go, it will be worth it.'

'Hang on, then.' He departed to consult. Came back. 'Yes, all right. The Guvnor says I can go first thing in the morning.'

'That's great,' I said. 'Call me when you get back.'

'It couldn't have been a gasket,' he said suddenly.

'Why not?'

'You'd have heard it. Very noisy. Unless you had the radio on?'

'No.'

'You'd have heard a blown gasket,' he said positively. 'But there again, if the exhaust was being somehow fed straight into the heater . . . perhaps not. The heater would damp the noise, same as a silencer . . . but I don't see how it could have happened. Well . . . all I can do is take a look.'

I would have liked to have gone with him. I put down the receiver and looked gloomily at my right leg. The neat plaster casing stretched from well up my thigh down to the base of my toes, which were currently invisible inside a white hospital theatre sock. A pair of Tony's slacks, though too long by six inches, had slid up easily enough over the plaster, decently hiding it, and as far as looks went, things were passable.

I sighed. The plaster was a bore. They'd designed it somehow so that I found sitting in a chair uncomfortable. Standing and lying down were both better. It wasn't going to stay on a minute longer than I could help, either. The muscles inside it were doing themselves no good in immobility. They would be getting flabby, unfit, wasting away. It would be just too ironic if I got my licence back and was too feeble to ride.

Tony came back at eight with half a chicken. He didn't want to stay, not even for a drink.

'Can you manage?' he said.

'Sure. No trouble.'

'Your leg doesn't hurt, does it?'

'Not a flicker,' I said. 'Can't feel a thing.'

'That's all right then.' He was relieved: wouldn't look at me squarely: went away.

Next morning, Roberta Cranfield came.

'Kelly?' she called. 'Are you in?'

'In the bedroom.'

She walked across the sitting-room and stopped in the doorway. Wearing the black and white striped fur coat, hanging open. Underneath it, black pants and a stagnant pond coloured sweater.

'Hullo,' she said. 'I've brought you some food. Shall I put it in the kitchen?'

'That's pretty good of you.'

She looked me over. I was lying, dressed, on top of the bedspread, reading the morning paper. 'You look comfortable enough.'

'I am. Just bored. Er . . . not now you've come, of course.'

'Of course,' she agreed. 'Shall I make some coffee?'

'Yes, do.'

She brought it back in mugs, shed her fur, and sat loose limbed in my bedroom armchair.

'You look a bit better today,' she observed.

'Can you get that blood off your dress?'

She shrugged. 'I chucked it at the cleaners. They're trying.'

'I'm sorry about that . . .'

'Think nothing of it.' She sipped her coffee. 'I rang the hospital on Saturday. They said you were O.K.'

'Thanks.'

'Why on earth did you stop on the railway?'

'I didn't know it was the railway, until too late.'

'But how did you get there, anyway, with the gates down?'

'The gates weren't down.'

'They were when we came along,' she said. 'There were all those lights and people shouting and screaming and we got out of the car to see what it was all about, and someone said the train had hit a car . . . and then I saw you, lying spark out with your face all covered in blood, about ten feet up the line. Nasty. Very nasty. It was, really.'

'I'm sorry . . . I'd had a couple of lungfuls of carbon monoxide. What you might call diminished responsibility.'

She grinned. 'You're some moron.'

The gates must have shut after I'd stopped on the line. I hadn't heard them or seen them. I must, I supposed, have been more affected by the gas than I remembered.

'I called you Rosalind,' I said apologetically.

'I know.' She made a face. 'Did you think I was her?'

'No . . . It just came out. I meant to say Roberta.'

She unrolled herself from the chair, took a few steps, and stood looking at Rosalind's picture. 'She'd have been glad . . . knowing she still came first with you after all this time.'

The telephone rang sharply beside me and interrupted my surprise. I picked up the receiver.

'Is that Kelly Hughes?' The voice was cultivated, authoritative, loaded indefinably with power. 'This is Wykeham Ferth speaking. I read about your accident in the papers . . . a report this morning says you are now home. I hope . . . you are well?'

'Yes, thank you, my Lord.'

It was ridiculous, the way my heart had bumped. Sweating palms, too.

'Are you in any shape to come to London?'

'I'm . . . I've got plaster on my leg . . . I can't sit in a car very easily, I'm afraid.'

'Hm.' A pause. 'Very well, I will drive down to Corrie instead. It's Harringay's old place, isn't it?'

'That's right. I live in a flat over the yard. If you walk into the yard from the drive, you'll see a green door with a brass letter box in the far corner. It won't be locked. There are some stairs inside. I live up there.'

'Right,' he said briskly. 'This afternoon? Good. Expect me at . . . er . . . four o'clock. Right?'

'Sir . . .' I began.

'Not now, Hughes. This afternoon.'

I put the receiver down slowly. Six hours' suspense. Damn him.

'What an absolutely heartless letter,' Roberta exclaimed.

I looked at her. She was holding the letter from my parents, which had been under Rosalind's photograph.

'I dare say I shouldn't have been so nosy as to read it,' she said unrepentantly.

'I dare say not.'

'How *can* they be so beastly?'

'They're not really.'

'This sort of thing always happens when you get one bright son in a family of twits,' she said disgustedly.

'Not always. Some bright sons handle things better than others.'

'Stop clobbering yourself.'

'Yes ma'am.'

'Are you going to stop sending them money?'

'No. All they can do about that is not spend it . . . or give it to the local cats' and dogs' home.'

'At least they had the decency to see they couldn't take your money *and* call you names.'

'Rigidly moral man, my father,' I said. 'Honest to the last farthing. Honest for its own sake. He taught me a lot that I'm grateful for.'

'And that's why this business hurts him so much?'

'Yes.'

'I've never . . . Well, I know you'll despise me for saying it . . . but I've never thought about people like your father before as . . . well . . . *people*.'

'If you're not careful,' I said, 'those chains will drop right off.'

She turned away and put the letter back under Rosalind's picture.

'Which university did you go to?'

'London. Starved in a garret on a grant. Great stuff.'

'I wish . . . how odd . . . I wish I'd trained for something. Learned a job.'

'It's hardly too late,' I said, smiling.

'I'm nearly twenty. I didn't bother much at school with exams . . . no one made us. Then I went to Switzerland for a year, to a finishing school . . . and since then I've just lived at home . . . What a waste!'

'The daughters of the rich are always at a disadvantage,' I said solemnly.

'Sarcastic beast.'

She sat down again in the armchair and told me that her father really seemed to have snapped out of it at last, and had finally accepted a dinner invitation the night before. All the lads had stayed on. They spent most of their time playing cards and football, as the only horses left in the yard were four half broken two year olds and three old 'chasers recovering from injuries. Most of the owners had promised to bring their horses back at once, if Cranfield had his licence restored in the next few weeks.

'What's really upsetting Father now is hope. With the big Cheltenham meeting only a fortnight away, he's biting his nails about whether he'll get Breadwinner back in time for him to run in his name in the Gold Cup.'

'Pity Breadwinner isn't entered in the Grand National. That would give us a bit more leeway.'

'Would your leg be right in time for the Gold Cup?'

'If I had my licence, I'd saw the plaster off myself.'

'Are you any nearer . . . with the licences?'

'Don't know.'

She sighed. 'It was a great dream while it lasted. And you won't be able to do much about it now.'

She stood up and came over and picked up the crutches which were lying beside the bed. They were black tubular metal with elbow supports and hand grips.

'These are much better than those old fashioned under-the-shoulder affairs,' she said. She fitted the crutches round her arms and swung around the room a bit with one foot off the floor. 'Pretty hard on your hands, though.'

She looked unselfconscious and intent. I watched her. I remembered the revelation it had been in my childhood when I first wondered what it was like to be someone else.

Into this calm sea Tony appeared with a wretched face and a folded paper in his hand.

'Hi,' he said, seeing Roberta. A very gloomy greeting.

He sat down in the armchair and looked at Roberta standing balanced on the crutches with one knee bent. His thoughts were not where his eyes were.

'What is it, then?' I said. 'Out with it.'

'This letter . . . came yesterday,' he said heavily.

'It was obvious last night that something was the matter.'

'I couldn't show it to you then, not straight out of hospital. And I don't know what to do, Kelly pal, sure enough I don't.'

'Let's see, then.'

He handed me the paper worriedly. I opened it up. A brief letter from the racing authorities. Bang bang, both barrels.

'Dear Sir,

It has been brought to our attention that a person warned off Newmarket Heath is living as a tenant in your stable yard. This is contrary to the regulations, and you should remedy the situation as soon as possible. It is perhaps not necessary to warn you that your own training licence might have to be reviewed if you should fail to take the steps suggested.'

'Sods,' Tony said forcefully. 'Bloody sods.'

CHAPTER ELEVEN

DEREK from the garage came while Roberta was clearing away the lunch she had stayed to cook. When he rang the door bell she went downstairs to let him in.

He walked hesitatingly across the sitting-room looking behind him to see if his shoes were leaving dirty marks and out of habit wiped his hands down his trousers before taking the one I held out to him.

'Sit down,' I suggested. He looked doubtfully at the khaki velvet armchair, but in the end lowered himself gingerly into it. He looked perfectly clean. No grease, no filthy overalls, just ordinary slacks and sports jacket. He wasn't used to it.

'You all right?' he said.

'Absolutely.'

'If you'd been in that car . . .' He looked sick at what he was thinking, and his vivid imagination was one of the things which made him a reliable mechanic. He didn't want death on his conscience. Young, fair haired, diffident, he kept most of his brains in his fingertips and outside of cars used the upstairs lot sparingly.

'You've never seen nothing like it,' he said. 'You wouldn't know it was a car, you wouldn't straight. It's all in little bits . . . I mean, like, bits of metal that don't look as if they were ever part of anything. Honestly. It's like twisted shreds of stuff.' He swallowed. 'They've got it collected up in tin baths.'

'The engine too?'

'Yeah. Smashed into fragments. Still, I had a look. Took me a long time, though, because everything is all jumbled up, and honest you can't tell what anything used to be. I mean, I didn't think it was a bit of exhaust manifold that I'd picked up, not at first, because it wasn't any shape that you'd think of.'

'You found something?'

'Here.' He fished in his trouser pocket. 'This is what it was all like. This is a bit of the exhaust manifold. Cast iron, that is, you see, so of course it was brittle, sort of, and it had shattered into bits. I mean, it wasn't sort of crumpled up like all the aluminium and so on. It wasn't bent, see, it was just in bits.'

'Yes, I do see,' I said. The anxious lines on his forehead dissolved when he saw that he had managed to tell me what he meant. He came over and put the small black jagged edged lump into my hands. Heavy for its size. About three inches long. Asymmetrically curved. Part of the side wall of a huge tube.

'As far as I can make out, see,' Derek said, pointing, 'It came from about where the manifold narrows down to the exhaust pipe, but really it might be anywhere. There were quite a few bits of manifold, when I looked, but I couldn't see the bit that fits into this, and I dare say it's still rusting away somewhere along the railway line. Anyway, see this bit here . . .' He pointed a stubby finger at a round dent in part of one edge. 'That's one side of a hole that was bored in the manifold wall. Now don't get me wrong, there's quite a few holes might have been drilled through the wall. I mean, some people have exhaust gas temperature gauges stuck into the manifold . . . and other gauges too. Things like that. Only, see, there weren't no gauges in your manifold, now were there?'

'You tell me,' I said.

'There weren't, then. Now you couldn't really say what the hole was for, not for certain you couldn't. But as far as I know, there weren't any holes in your manifold last time I did the service.'

I fingered the little semi-circular dent. No more than a quarter of an inch across.

'However did you spot something so small?' I asked.

'Dunno, really. Mind you, I was there a good couple of hours, picking through those tubs. Did it methodical, like. Since you were paying for it and all.'

'Is it a big job . . . drilling a hole this size through an exhaust manifold. Would it take long?'

'Half a minute, I should think.'

'With an electric drill?' I asked.

'Oh yeah, sure. If you did it with a hand drill, then it would take five minutes. Say nearer eight or ten, to be on the safe side.'

'How many people carry drills around in their tool kits?'

'That, see, it depends on the chap. Now some of them carry all sorts of stuff in their cars. Proper work benches, some of them. And then others, the tool kit stays strapped up fresh from the factory until the car's dropping to bits.'

'People do carry drills, then?'

'Oh yeah, sure. Quite a lot do. Hand drills, of course. You wouldn't have much call for an electric drill, not in a tool kit, not unless you did a lot of repairs, like, say on racing cars.'

He went and sat down again. Carefully, as before.

'If someone drilled a hole this size through the manifold, what would happen?'

'Well, honestly, nothing much. You'd get exhaust gas out through the engine, and you'd hear a good lot of noise, and you might smell it in the car, but it would sort of blow away, see, it wouldn't come in through the heater. To do that, like I said before, you'd have to put some tubing into the hole there and then stick the other end of the tubing into the heater. Mind you that would be pretty easy, you wouldn't need a drill. Some heater tubes are really only cardboard.'

'Rubber tubing from one end to the other?' I suggested.

He shook his head. 'No. Have to be metal. Exhaust gas, that's very hot. It'd melt anything but metal.'

'Do you think anyone could do all that on the spur of the moment?'

He put his head on one side, considering. 'Oh sure, yeah. If he'd got a drill. Like, say the first other thing he needs is some tubing. Well, he's only got to look around for that. Lots lying about, if you look. The other day, I used a bit of a kiddy's old cycle frame, just the job it was. Right, you get the tube ready first and then you fit a drill nearest the right size, to match. And Bob's your uncle.'

'How long, from start to finish?'

'Fixing the manifold to the heater? Say, from scratch, including maybe having to cast around for a bit of tube, well, at the outside half an hour. A quarter, if you had something all ready handy. Only the drilling would take any time, see? The rest would be like stealing candy from a baby.'

Roberta appeared in the doorway shrugging herself into the stripy coat. Derek stood up awkwardly and didn't know where to put his hands.

She smiled at him sweetly and unseeingly and said to me, 'Is there anything else you want, Kelly?'

'No. Thank you very much.'

'Think nothing of it. I'll see . . . I might come over again tomorrow.'

'Fine,' I said.

'Right.'

She nodded, smiled temperately, and made her usual poised exit. Derek's comment approached, 'Cor.'

'I suppose you didn't see any likely pieces of tube in the wreckage?' I asked.

'Huh?' He tore his eyes away with an effort from the direction Roberta had gone. 'No, like, it was real bad. Lots of bits, you couldn't have told what they were. I never seen anything

like it. Sure, I seen crashes, stands to reason. Different, this was.'
He shivered.

'Did you have any difficulty with being allowed to search?'

'No, none. They didn't seem all that interested in what I did.
Just said to help myself. 'Course, I told them it was my car,
like. I mean, that I looked after it. Mind you, they were right
casual about it anyway, because when I came away they were
letting this other chap have a good look too.'

'Which other chap?'

'Some fellow. Said he was an insurance man, but he didn't
have a notebook.'

I felt like saying Huh? too. I said, 'Notebook?'

'Yeah, sure, insurance men, they're always crawling round
our place looking at wrecks and never one without a notebook.
Write down every blessed detail, they do. But this other chap,
looking at your car, he didn't have any notebook.'

'What did he look like?'

He thought.

'That's difficult, see. He didn't look like anything, really.
Medium, sort of. Not young and not old really either. A nobody
sort of person, really.'

'Did he wear sun glasses?'

'No. He had a hat on, but I don't know if he had ordinary
glasses. I can't actually remember. I didn't notice that much.'

'Was he looking through the wreckage as if he knew what he
wanted?'

'Uh . . . don't know, really. Strikes me he was a bit flummoxed,
like, finding it was all in such small bits.'

'He didn't have a girl with him?'

'Nope.' He brightened. 'He came in a Volkswagen, an oldish
grey one.'

'Thousands of those about,' I said.

'Oh yeah, sure. Er . . . was this chap important?'

'Only if he was looking for what you found.'

He worked it out.

'Cripes,' he said.

Lord Ferth arrived twenty minutes after he'd said, which meant
that I'd been hopping round the flat on my crutches for half an
hour, unable to keep still.

He stood in the doorway into the sitting-room holding a briefcase and bowler hat in one hand and unbuttoning his short fawn
overcoat with the other.

'Well, Hughes,' he said. 'Good afternoon.'

'Good afternoon, my Lord.'

He came right in, shut the door behind him, and put his hat and case on the oak chest beside him.

'How's the leg?'

'Stagnating,' I said. 'Can I get you some tea . . . coffee . . . or a drink?'

'Nothing just now . . .' He laid his coat on the chest and picked up the briefcase again, looking around him with the air of surprise I was used to in visitors. I offered him the green armchair with a small table beside it. He asked where I was going to sit.

'I'll stand,' I said. 'Sitting's difficult.'

'But you don't stand all day!'

'No. Lie on my bed, mostly.'

'Then we'll talk in your bedroom.'

We went through the door at the end of the sitting-room and this time he murmured aloud.

'Whose flat is this?' he asked.

'Mine.'

He glanced at my face, hearing the dryness in my voice. 'You resent surprise?'

'It amuses me.'

'Hughes . . . it's a pity you didn't join the Civil Service. You'd have gone all the way.'

I laughed. 'There's still time . . . Do they take in warned off jockeys at the Administrative Grade?'

'So you can joke about it?'

'It's taken nine days. But yes, just about.'

He gave me a long straight assessing look, and there was a subtle shift somewhere in both his manner to me and in basic approach, and when I shortly understood what it was I was shaken, because he was taking me on level terms, level in power and understanding and experience: and I wasn't level.

Few men in his position would have thought that this course was viable, let alone chosen it. I understood the compliment. He saw, too, that I did, and I knew later that had there not been this fundamental change of ground, this cancellation of the Steward-jockey relationship, he would not have said to me all that he did. It wouldn't have happened if he hadn't been in my flat.

He sat down in the khaki velvet armchair, putting the briefcase carefully on the floor beside him. I took the weight off my crutches and let the bed springs have a go.

'I went to see Lord Gowery,' he said neutrally. 'And I can see

no reason not to tell you straight away that you and Dexter
Cranfield will have your warning off rescinded within the next few
days.'

'Do you mean it?' I exclaimed. I tried to sit up. The plaster
intervened.

Lord Ferth smiled. 'As I see it, there is no alternative. There
will be a quiet notice to that effect in next week's Calendar.'

'That is, of course,' I said, 'All you need to tell me.'

He looked at me levelly. 'True. But not all you want to know.'

'No.'

'No one has a better right . . . and yet you will have to use
your discretion about whether you tell Dexter Cranfield.'

'All right.'

He sighed, reached down to open the briefcase, and pulled
out a neat little tape recorder.

'I did try to ignore your suggestion. Succeeded, too, for a
while. However . . .' He paused, his fingers hovering over the
controls. 'This conversation took place late on Monday afternoon, in the sitting-room of Lord Gowery's flat near Sloane
Square. We were alone . . . you will see that we were alone.
He knew, though, that I was making a recording.' He still
hesitated. 'Compassion. That's what you need. I believe you
have it.'

'Don't con me,' I said.

He grimaced. 'Very well.'

The recording began with the selfconscious platitudes
customary in front of microphones, especially when no one
wants to take the first dive into the deep end. Lord Ferth had
leapt, eventually.

'Norman, I explained why we must take a good look at this
Enquiry.'

'Hughes is being ridiculous. Not only ridiculous, but downright slanderous. I don't understand why you should take him
seriously.' Gowery sounded impatient.

'We have to, even if only to shut him up.' Lord Ferth looked
across the room, his hot eyes gleaming ironically. The recording
ploughed on, his voice like honey. 'You know perfectly well,
Norman, that it will be better all round if we can show there
is nothing whatever in these allegations he is spreading around.
Then we can emphatically confirm the suspension and squash
all the rumours.'

Subtle stuff. Lord Gowery's voice grew easier, assured now
that Ferth was still an ally. As perhaps he was. 'I do assure you

Wykeham, that if I had not sincerely believed that Hughes and Dexter Cranfield were guilty, I would not have warned them off.'

There was something odd about that. Both Ferth and Gowery had thought so too, as there were several seconds of silence on the tape.

'But you do still believe it?' Ferth said eventually.

'Of course.' He was emphatic. 'Of course I do.' Much too emphatic.

'Then . . . er . . . taking one of Hughes' questions first . . . How did it come about that Newtonnards was called to the Enquiry?'

'I was informed that Cranfield had backed Cherry Pie with him.'

'Yes . . . but who informed you?'

Gowery didn't reply.

Ferth's voice came next, with absolutely no pressure in it.

'Um . . . Have you any idea how we managed to show the wrong film of Hughes racing at Reading?'

Gowery was on much surer ground. 'My fault, I'm afraid. I asked the Secretaries to write off for the film of the last race. Didn't realize there were seven races. Careless of me, I'll admit. But of course, as it was the wrong film, it was irrelevant to the case.'

'Er . . .' said Lord Ferth. But he hadn't yet been ready to argue. He cleared his throat and said, 'I suppose you thought it would be relevant to see how Hughes had ridden Squelch last time out.'

After another long pause, Gowery said, 'Yes.'

'But in the event we didn't show it.'

'No.'

'Would we have shown it if, after having sent for it, we found that the Reading race bore out entirely Hughes' assertion that he rode Squelch in the Lemonfizz in exactly the same way as he always did?'

More silence. Then he said quietly, 'Yes,' and he sounded very troubled.

'Hughes asked at the Enquiry that we should show the right film,' Ferth said.

'I'm sure he didn't.'

'I've been reading the transcript. Norman, I've been reading and re-reading that transcript all week-end and frankly, that is why I'm here. Hughes did in fact suggest that we should show the right film, presumably because he knew it would support his case . . .'

'Hughes was guilty!' Gowery broke in vehemently. 'Hughes was guilty. I had no option but to warn him off.'

Lord Ferth pressed the stop button on the tape recorder.

'Tell me,' he said, 'What you think of that last statement?'

'I think,' I said slowly, 'That he did believe it. Both from that statement and from what I remember of the Enquiry. His certainty that day shook me. He believed me guilty so strongly that he was stone deaf to anything which looked even remotely likely to assault his opinion.'

'That was your impression?'

'Overpowering,' I said.

Lord Ferth took his lower lip between his teeth and shook his head, but I gathered it was at the general situation, not at me. He pressed the start button again. His voice came through, precise, carefully without emotion, gentle as vaseline.

'Norman, about the composition of the Enquiry . . . the members of the Disciplinary Committee who sat with you . . . What guided you to choose Andrew Tring and old Plimborne?'

'What guided me?' He sounded astonished at the question. 'I haven't any idea.'

'I wish you'd cast back.'

'I can't see that it has any relevance . . . but let's see . . . I suppose I had Tring in my mind anyway, as I'm in the middle of some business negotiations with him. And Plimborne . . . well, I just saw him snoozing away in the Club. I was talking to him later in the lobby, and I asked him just on the spur of the moment to sit with me. I don't see the point of your asking.'

'Never mind. It doesn't matter. Now . . . about Charlie West. I can see that of course you would call the rider of the third horse to give evidence. And it is clear from the transcript that you knew what the evidence would be. However, at the preliminary enquiry at Oxford West said nothing at all about Hughes having pulled his horse back. I've consulted all three of the Oxford Stewards this morning. They confirm that West did not suggest it at the time. He asserted it, however, at the Enquiry, and you knew what he was going to say, so . . . er . . . how did you know?'

More silence.

Ferth's voice went on a shade anxiously. 'Norman, if you instructed a Stipendiary Steward to interview West privately and question him further, for heaven's sake say so. These jockeys stick together. It is perfectly reasonable to believe that West wouldn't speak up against Hughes to begin with, but might do so if pressed with questions. Did you send a Stipendiary?'

Gower said faintly, 'No.'

'Then how did you know what West was going to say?'

Gowery didn't answer. He said instead, 'I did instruct a Stipendiary to look up all the races in which Cranfield had run two horses and compile me a list of all the occasions when the lesser-backed had won. And as you know, it is the accepted practice to bring up everything in a jockey's past history at an Enquiry. It was a perfectly normal procedure.'

'I'm not saying it wasn't,' Ferth's voice said, puzzled.

Ferth stopped the recorder and raised his eyebrows at me.

'What d'you make of *that*?'

'He's grabbing for a rock in a quicksand.'

He sighed, pressed the starter again and Gowery's voice came back.

'It was all there in black and white . . . It was quite true . . . they'd been doing it again and again.'

'What do you mean, it was quite true? Did someone *tell* you they'd been doing it again and again?'

More silence. Gowery's rock was crumbling.

Again Ferth didn't press him. Instead he said in the same unaccusing way, 'How about David Oakley?'

'Who?'

'David Oakley. The enquiry agent who photographed the money in Hughes's flat. Who suggested that he should go there?'

No answer.

Ferth said with the first faint note of insistence, 'Norman, you really must give some explanation. Can't you see that all this silence just won't do? We *have* to have some answers if we are going to squash Hughes's rumours.'

Gowery reacted with defence in his voice. 'The evidence against Cranfield and Hughes was collected. What does it matter who collected it?'

'It matters because Hughes asserts that much of it was false.'

'No,' he said fiercely. 'It was not false.'

'Norman,' Ferth said, 'Is that what you believe . . . or what you *want* to believe?'

'Oh . . .' Gowery's exclamation was more of anguish than surprise. I looked sharply across at Ferth. His dark eyes were steady on my face. His voice went on, softer again. Persuasive.

'Norman, was there any reason why you *wanted* Cranfield and Hughes warned off?'

'No.' Half a shout. Definitely a lie.

'Any reason why you should go so far as to manufacture evidence against them, if none existed?'

'Wykeham!' He was outraged. 'How can you say that! You are suggesting . . . You are suggesting . . . something so dishonourable . . .'

Ferth pressed the stop button. 'Well?' he said challengingly.

'That was genuine,' I said. 'He didn't manufacture it himself. But then I never thought he did. I just wanted to know where he got it from.'

Ferth nodded. Pressed the start again.

His voice. 'My dear Norman, you lay yourself open to such suggestions if you will not say how you came by all the evidence. Do you not see? If you will not explain how you came by it, you cannot be too surprised if you are thought to have procured it yourself.'

'The evidence was genuine!' he asserted. A rearguard action.

'You are still trying to convince yourself that it was.'

'No! It was.'

'Then where did it come from?'

Gowery's back was against the wall. I could see from the remembered emotion twisting Ferth's face that this had been a saddening and perhaps embarrassing moment.

'I was sent,' said Gowery with difficulty, 'A package. It contained . . . various statements . . . and six copies of the photograph taken in Hughes' flat.'

'Who sent it to you?'

Gowery's voice was very low. 'I don't know.'

'You don't know?' Ferth was incredulous. 'You warned two men off on the strength of it, and you don't know where it came from?'

A miserable assenting silence.

'You just accepted all that so-called evidence on its face value?'

'It was all true.' He clung to it.

'Have you still got that package?'

'Yes.'

'I'd like to see it.' A touch of iron in Ferth's voice.

Gowery hadn't argued. There were sounds of moving about, a drawer opening and closing, a rustling of papers.

'I see,' Ferth said slowly. 'These papers do, in fact, look very convincing.'

'Then you see why I acted on them,' Gowery said eagerly, with a little too much relief.

'I can see why you should consider doing so . . . after making a careful check.'

'I did check.'

'To what extent?'

'Well . . . the package only came four days before the Enquiry. On the Thursday before. I had the Secretaries send out the summonses to Newtonnards, Oakley and West immediately. They were asked to confirm by telegram that they would be attending, and they all did so. Newtonnards was asked to bring his records for the Lemonfizz Cup. And then of course I asked a Stipendiary to ask the Totalisator people if anyone had backed Cherry Pie substantially, and he collected those affidavits . . . the ones we produced at the Enquiry. There was absolutely no doubt whatsoever that Cranfield had backed Cherry Pie. He lied about it at the Enquiry. That made it quite conclusive. He was entirely guilty, and there was no reason why I should not warn him off.'

Ferth stopped the recorder. 'What do you say to that?' he asked.

I shrugged. 'Cranfield did back Cherry Pie. He was stupid to deny it, but admitting it was, as he saw it, cutting his own throat. He told me that he backed him—through this unidentified friend —with Newtonnards and on the Tote, and not with his normal bookmaker, because he didn't want Kessel to know, as Kessel and the bookmaker are tattle-swapping buddies. He in fact put a hundred pounds on Cherry Pie because he thought the horse might be warming up to give everyone a surprise. He also put two hundred and fifty pounds on Squelch, because reason suggested that *he* would win. And where is the villainy in that?'

Ferth looked at me levelly. 'You didn't know he had backed Cherry Pie, not at the Enquiry.'

'I tackled him with it afterwards. It had struck me by then that that had to be true, however hard he had denied it. Newtonnards might have lied or altered his books, but no one can argue against Tote tickets.'

'That was one of the things which convinced me, too,' he admitted.

He started the recorder. He himself was speaking and now there was a distinct flavour in his voice of cross examination. The whole interview moved suddenly into the shape of an Enquiry of its own. 'This photograph . . . didn't it seem at all odd to you?'

'Why should it?' Gowery said sharply.

'Didn't you ask yourself how it came to be taken?'

'No.'

'Hughes says Oakley took the money and the note with him and simply photographed them in his flat.'

'No.'

'How can you be sure?' Ferth pounced on him.

'No!' Gowery said again. There was a rising note in his voice, the sound of pressure approaching blow-up.

'Who sent Oakley to Hughes' flat?'

'I've told you, I don't know.'

'But you're sure that is a genuine photograph?'

'Yes. Yes it is.'

'You are sure beyond doubt?' Ferth insisted.

'Yes!' The voice was high, the anxiety plain, the panic growing. Into this screwed up moment Ferth dropped one intense word, like a bomb.

'Why?'

CHAPTER TWELVE

THE TAPE RAN ON for nearly a minute. When Gowery finally answered his voice was quite different. Low, broken up, distressed to the soul.

'It had . . . to be true. I said at first . . . I couldn't warn them off if they weren't guilty . . . and then the package came . . . and it was such a relief . . . they really were guilty . . . I could warn them off . . . and everything would be all right.'

My mouth opened. Ferth watched me steadily, his eyes narrowed with the pity of it.

Gowery went on compulsively. Once started, he needed to confess.

'If I tell you . . . from the beginning . . . perhaps you will understand. It began the day after I was appointed to substitute for the Disciplinary Steward at the Cranfield-Hughes Enquiry. It's ironic to think of it now, but I was quite pleased to be going to do it . . . and then . . . and then . . .' He paused and took an effortful control of his voice. 'Then, I had a telephone call.' Another pause. 'This man said . . . said . . . I must warn Cranfield off.' He cleared his throat. 'I told him I would do no such thing, unless Cranfield was guilty. Then he said . . . then he said . . . that he knew things about me . . . and he would tell everyone . . . if I didn't warn Cranfield off. I told him I couldn't warn him off if he wasn't guilty . . . and you see I didn't think he *was* guilty.

I mean, race-horses are so unpredictable, and I saw the Lemonfizz myself and although after the crowd demonstration it was obvious the Stewards would have Cranfield and Hughes in, I was surprised when they referred it to the Disciplinary Committee . . . I thought that there must have been circumstances that I didn't know of . . . and then I was asked to take the Enquiry . . . and I had an open mind . . . I told the man on the telephone that no threats could move me from giving Cranfield a fair judgement.'

Less jelly in his voice while he remembered that first strength. It didn't last.

'He said . . . in that case . . . I could expect . . . after the Enquiry . . . if Cranfield got off . . . that my life wouldn't be worth living . . . I would have to resign from the Jockey Club . . . and everyone would know . . . And I said again that I would not warn Cranfield off unless I was convinced of his guilt, and that I would not be blackmailed, and I put down the receiver and cut him off.'

'And then,' Ferth suggested, 'you began to worry?'

'Yes.' Little more than a whisper.

'What exactly did he threaten to publish?'

'I can't . . . can't tell you. Not criminal . . . not a matter for the police . . . but . . .'

'But enough to ruin you socially?'

'Yes . . . I'm afraid so . . . yes, completely.'

'But you stuck to your guns?'

'I was desperately worried . . . I couldn't . . . how could I . . . ? take away Cranfield's livelihood just to save myself . . . It would have been dishonourable . . . and I couldn't see myself living with it . . . and in any case I couldn't just warn him off, just like that, if there was no proof he was guilty . . . So I did worry . . . couldn't sleep . . . or eat . . .'

'Why didn't you ask to be relieved of the Enquiry?'

'Because he told me . . . if I backed out . . . it would count the same with him as letting Cranfield off . . . so I had to go on, just in case some proof turned up.'

'Which it did,' Ferth said dryly. 'Conveniently.'

'Oh . . .' Again the anguish. 'I didn't realize . . . I didn't indeed . . . that it might have been the blackmailer who had sent the package. I didn't wonder very much who had sent it. It was release . . . that's all I could see . . . it was a heaven-sent release from the most unbearable . . . I didn't question . . . I just believed it . . . believed it absolutely . . . and I was so grateful . . . so grateful . . .'

Four days before the Enquiry, that package had come. He must have been sweating for a whole week, taking a long bleak look at the wilderness. Send a St Bernard to a dying mountaineer and he's unlikely to ask for the dog licence.

'When did you begin to doubt?' Ferth said calmly.

'Not until afterwards. Not for days. It was Hughes . . . at the dance. You told me he was insisting he'd been framed and was going to find out who . . . and then he asked me directly who had sent Oakley to his flat . . . and it . . . Wykeham it was *terrible*. I realized . . . what I'd done. Inside, I did know . . . but I couldn't admit to it myself . . . I shut it away . . . they *had* to be guilty . . .'

There was another long silence. Then Gowery said, 'You'll see to it . . . that they get their licences back?'

'Yes,' Ferth said.

'I'll resign . . .' He sounded desolate.

'From the Disciplinary Committee, I agree,' Ferth said reasonably. 'As to the rest . . . we will see.'

'Do you think the . . . the blackmailer . . . will tell . . . everyone . . . anyway, when Cranfield has his licence back?'

'He would have nothing to gain.'

'No, but . . .'

'There are laws to protect you.'

'They couldn't.'

'What does he in fact have over you?'

'I . . . I . . . oh God.' The tape stopped abruptly, cutting off words that were disintegrating into gulps.

Ferth said, 'I switched it off. He was breaking down. One couldn't record that.'

'No.'

'He told me what it was he was being blackmailed about. I think I am prepared to tell you also, although he would hate it if he knew. But you only.'

'Only,' I said. 'I won't repeat it.'

'He told me . . .' His nose wrinkled in distaste. 'He told me that he has . . . he suffers from . . . unacceptable sexual appetites. Not homosexual. Perhaps that would have been better . . . simpler . . . he wouldn't nowadays have been much reviled for that. No. He says he belongs to a sort of club where people like him can gratify themselves fairly harmlessly, as they are all there because they enjoy . . . in varying forms . . . the same thing.' He stopped. He was embarrassed.

'Which is what?' I said matter-of-factly.

He said, as if putting a good yard of clean air between himself and the world, 'Flagellation.'

'That old thing!' I said.

'What?'

'The English disease. Shades of Fanny Hill. Sex tangled up with self-inflicted pain, like nuns with their little disciplines and sober citizens paying a pound a lash to be whipped.'

'Kelly!'

'You must have read their coy little advertisements? "Correction given." That's what it's all about. More widespread than most people imagine. Starts with husbands spanking their wives regularly before they bed them, and carries right on up to the parties where they all dress up in leather and have a right old orgy. I don't actually understand why anyone should get fixated on leather or rubber or hair, or on those instead of anything else. Why not coal, for instance . . . or silk? But they do, apparently.'

'In this case . . . leather.'

'Boots and whips and naked bosoms?'

Ferth shook his head in disbelief. 'You take it so coolly.'

'Live and let live,' I said. 'If that's what they feel compelled to do . . . why stop them? As he said, they're not harming anyone, if they're in a club where everyone else is the same.'

'But for a Steward,' he protested. 'A member of the Disciplinary Committee!'

'Gives you pause,' I agreed.

He looked horrified. 'But there would be nothing sexual in his judgement on racing matters.'

'Of course not. Nothing on earth as unsexual as racing.'

'But one can see . . . he would be finished in the racing world, if this got out. Even I . . . I cannot think of him now without this . . . this perversion . . . coming into my mind. It would be the same with everyone. One can't respect him any more. One can't like him.'

'Difficult,' I agreed.

'It's . . . horrible.' In his voice, all the revulsion of the normal for the deviation. Most racing men were normal. The deviation would be cast out. Ferth felt it. Gowery knew it. And so did someone else . . .

'Don't they wear masks at this club?' I asked.

Ferth looked surprised. 'Why, yes, they do. I asked him who could know about him . . . in order to blackmail him . . . and he said he didn't know, they all wore masks. Hoods, actually, was the word he used. Hoods . . . and aprons . . .' He was revolted.

'All leather?'

He nodded. 'How can they?'

'They do less harm than the ones who go out and rape small children.'

'I'm glad I . . .' he said passionately.

'Me too,' I said. 'But it's just luck.' Gowery had been unlucky, in more ways than one. 'Someone may have seen him going in, or leaving afterwards.'

'That's what he thinks. But he says he doesn't know the real names of any of his fellow members. They all call each other by fanciful made up names, apparently.'

'There must be a secretary . . . with a list of members?'

Ferth shook his head. 'I asked him that. He said he'd never given his own name to anyone there. It wasn't expected. There's no annual subscription, just ten pounds in cash every time he attends. He says he goes about once a month, on average.'

'How many other members are there?'

'He didn't know the total number. He says there are never fewer than ten, and sometimes thirty or thirty-five. More men than women, usually. The club isn't open every day; only Mondays and Thursdays.'

'Where is it?'

'In London. He wouldn't tell me exactly where.'

'He wants . . . needs . . . to keep on going,' I said.

'You don't think he will!'

'After a while. Yes.'

'Oh no . . .'

'Who introduced him to the club, do you know?'

'He said it couldn't be the person who introduced him to the club. She was a prostitute . . . he'd never told her his real name.'

'But she understood his needs.'

He sighed. 'It would seem so.'

'Some of those girls make more money out of whipping men than sleeping with them.'

'How on earth do you know?'

'I had digs once in the next room to one. She told me.'

'Good Lord.' He looked as if he'd turned over a stone and found creepy-crawlies underneath. He had plainly no inkling of what it was like to *be* a creepy-crawly. His loss.

'Anyway,' he said slowly, 'You will understand why he accepted that package at its face value.'

'And why he chose Lord Plimborne and Andy Tring.'

Lord Ferth nodded. 'At the end, when he'd recovered a little, he understood that he'd chosen them for the reasons you said, but he believed at the time that they were impulsive choices. And he is now, as you would expect, a very worried and troubled man.'

'Was he,' I asked, 'Responsible for this?'

I held out to him the letter Tony had received from the Steward's Secretaries. He stood up, came to take it, and read its brief contents with exasperation.

'I don't know,' he said explosively. 'I really don't know. When did this arrive?'

'Tuesday. Post-marked noon on Monday.'

'Before I saw him . . . He didn't mention it.'

'Could you find out if it was his doing?'

'Do you mean . . . it will be all the more impossible to forgive him?'

'No. Nothing like that. I was just wondering if it was our little framer-blackmailer at work again. See those words "It has been brought to our attention" . . . ? What I'd like to know is who brought it.'

'I'll find out,' he agreed positively. 'That shouldn't be difficult. And of course, disregard the letter. There won't be any question now of your having to move.'

'How are you going to work it? Giving our licences back. How are you going to explain it?'

He raised his eyebrows. 'We never have to give reasons for our decisions.'

I smothered a laugh. The system had its uses.

Lord Ferth sat down in the chair again and put the letter in his briefcase. Then he packed up the tape recorder and tucked that away too. Then with an air of delicately choosing his words he said, 'A scandal of this sort would do racing a great deal of harm.'

'So you want me to take my licence back and shut up?'

'Er . . . yes.'

'And not chase after the blackmailer, in case he blows the gaff?'

'Exactly.' He was relieved that I understood.

'No.' I said.

'Why not?' Persuasion in his voice.

'Because he tried to kill me.'

'What?'

I showed him the chunk of exhaust manifold, and explained. 'Someone at the dance,' I said. 'That means that our blackmailer is one of about six hundred people, and from there it shouldn't be too hard. You can more or less rule out the women, because few of them would drill through cast iron wearing an evening dress. Much too conspicuous, if anyone saw them. That leaves three hundred men.'

'Someone who knew your car,' he said. 'Surely that would narrow it down considerably.'

'It might not. Anyone could have seen me getting out of it at the races. It was a noticeable car, I'm afraid. But I arrived late at the dance. The car was parked right at the back.'

'Have you . . .' he cleared his throat. 'Are the police involved in this?'

'If you mean are they at present investigating an attempted murder, then no, they are not. If you mean, am I going to ask them to investigate, etc., then I haven't decided.'

'Once you start the police on something, you can't stop them.'

'On the other hand if I don't start them the blackmailer might have another go at me, with just a fraction of an inch more success. Which would be quite enough.'

'Um.' He thought it over. 'But if you made it clear to everyone now that you are not any longer trying to find out who framed you . . . he might not try again.'

I said curiously, 'Do you really think it would be best for racing if we just leave this blackmailing murderer romping around free?'

'Better than a full-blown scandal.'

The voice of Establishment diplomacy.

'And if he doesn't follow your line of reasoning . . . and he does kill me . . . how would that do for a scandal?'

He didn't answer. Just looked at me levelly with the hot eyes.

'All right, then,' I said. 'No police.'

'Thank you.'

'Us, though. We'll have to do it ourselves. Find him and deal with him.'

'How do you mean?'

'I'll find him. You deal with him.'

'To your satisfaction, I suppose,' he said ironically.

'Absolutely.'

'And Lord Gowery?'

'He's yours entirely. I shan't tell Dexter Cranfield anything at all.'

'Very well.' He stood up, and I struggled off the bed on to the crutches.

'Just one thing,' I said. 'Could you arrange to have that package of Lord Gowery's sent to me here?'

'I have it with me.' Without hesitation he took a large Manila
envelope out of the briefcase and put it on the bed. 'You'll understand how he fell on it with relief.'

'Things being as they were,' I agreed. He walked across the
sitting-room to the way out, stopping by the chest to put on
his coat.

'Can Cranfield tell his owners to shovel their horses back?'
I said. 'The sooner the better, you see, if they're to come back
in time for Cheltenham.'

'Give me until tomorrow morning. There are several other
people who must know first.'

'All right.'

He held out his hand. I transferred the right crutch to the
left, and shook it.

He said, 'Perhaps one day soon . . . when this is over . . . you
will dine with me?'

'I'd like to,' I said.

'Good.' He picked up his bowler and his briefcase, swept a last
considering glance round my flat, nodded to me as if finalising
a decision, and quietly went away.

I telephoned to the orthopod who regularly patched me up
after falls.

'I want this plaster off.'

He went into a long spiel of which the gist was two or three
more weeks.

'Monday,' I said.

'I'll give you up.'

'Tuesday I start getting it off with a chisel.'

I always slept in shirt-and-shorts pyjamas, which had come in
very handy in the present circs. Bedtime that day I struggled into
a lime green and white checked lot I had bought in an off moment
at Liverpool the year before with my mind more on the imminent
Grand National than on what they would do to my yellow complexion at six on a winter's morning.

Tony had gloomily brought me some casseroled beef and had
stayed to celebrate when I told him I wouldn't have to leave.
I was out of whisky again in consequence.

When he'd gone I went to bed and read the pages which had
sent me to limbo. And they were, indeed, convincing. Neatly
typed, well set out, written in authoritative language. Not at
first, second, or even third sight the product of malevolence.
Emotionless. Cool. Damaging.

'Charles Richard West is prepared to testify that during the course of the race, and in particular at a spot six furlongs from the winning post on the second circuit, he heard Hughes say that he (Hughes) was about to ease his horse so that it should be in no subsequent position to win. Hughes's precise words were, "O.K. Brakes on, chaps".'

The four other sheets were equally brief, equally to the point. One said that through an intermediary Dexter Cranfield had backed Cherry Pie with Newtonnards. The second pointed out that an investigation of past form would show that on several other occasions Cranfield's second string had beaten his favourite. The third suggested watching the discrepancies in Hughes's riding in the Lemonfizz and in the last race at Reading . . . and there it was in black and white, 'the last race at Reading.' Gowery hadn't questioned it or checked; had simply sent for the last race at Reading. If he had shown it privately to Plimborne and Tring only, and not to me as well, no one might ever have realized it was the wrong race. This deliberate piece of misleading had in fact gone astray, but only just. And the rest hadn't. Page four stated categorically that Cranfield had bribed Hughes not to win, and photographic evidence to prove it was hereby attached.

There was also a short covering note of explanation.

'These few facts have come to my notice. They should clearly be laid before the appropriate authorities, and I am therefore sending them to you, sir, as Steward in command of the forthcoming Enquiry.'

The typewriting itself was unremarkable, the paper medium quality quarto. The paper clip holding the sheets together was sold by the hundred million, and the buff envelope in which they'd been sent cost a penny or two in any stationer's in the country.

There were two copies only of the photograph. On the back, no identifications.

I slid them all back into the envelope, and put it in the drawer of the table beside my bed. Switched out the light. Lay thinking of riding races again with a swelling feeling of relief and excitement. Wondered how poor old Gowery was making out, going fifteen rounds with his conscience. Thought of Archie and his mortgage . . . Kessel having to admit he'd been wrong . . . Roberta stepping off her dignity . . . the blackmailer biting his nails in apprehension . . . sweet dreams everyone . . . slid into the first easy sleep since the Enquiry.

I woke with a jolt, knowing I'd heard a sound which had no business to be there.

A pen-sized flashlight was flickering round the inside of one of the top drawers of the dressing-chest. A dark shape blocked off half of its beam as an arm went into the drawer to feel around. Cautious. Very, quiet, now.

I lay watching through slit-shut eyes, wondering how close I was this time to the pearly gates. Inconveniently my pulse started bashing against my eardrums as fear stirred up the adrenals, and inside the plaster all the hairs on my leg fought to stand on end.

Trying to keep my breathing even and make no rustle with the sheets I very cautiously slid one arm over the side of the bed and reached down to the floor for a crutch. Any weapon handy was better than none.

No crutches.

I felt around, knowing exactly where I'd laid them beside me, feeling nothing but carpet under my fingers.

The flashlight moved out of the drawer and swung in a small arc while the second top drawer was opened, making the same tiny crack as it loosened which had woken me with the other. The scrap of light shone fractionally on my two crutches propped up against the wall by the door.

I drew the arm very slowly back into bed and lay still. If he'd meant just to kill me, he would have done it by now: and whatever he intended I had little chance of avoiding. The plaster felt like a ton, chaining me immobile.

A clammy crawling feeling all over my skin. Jaw tight clenched with tension. Dryness in the mouth. Head feeling as if it were swelling. I lay and tried to beat the physical sensations, tried to will them away.

No noticeable success.

He finished with the drawers. The flashlight swung over the khaki chair and steadied on the polished oak chest behind it, against the wall. He moved over there soundlessly and lifted the lid. I almost cried out to him not to, it would wake me. The lid always creaked loudly. I really didn't want him to wake me, it was much too dangerous.

The lid creaked sharply. He stopped dead with it six inches up. Lowered it back into place. It creaked even louder.

He stood there, considering. Then there were quick soft steps on the carpet, a hand fastening in my hair and yanking my head back, and the flashlight beam full in my eyes.

'Right, mate. You're awake. So you'll answer some questions.'

I knew the voice. I shut my eyes against the light and spoke in as bored a drawl as I could manage.

'Mr Oakley, I presume?'

'Clever Mr Hughes.'

He let go of my hair and stripped the bedclothes off with one flick. The flashlight swung away and fell on top of them. I felt his grip on my neck and the front of my shirt as he wrenched me off the bed and on to the floor. I fell with a crash.

'That's for starters,' he said.

CHAPTER THIRTEEN

HE WAS FAST, to give him his due. Also strong and ruthless and used to this sort of thing.

'Where is it?' he said.

'What?'

'A chunk of metal with a hole in it.'

'I don't know what you're talking about.'

He swung his arm and hit me with something hard and knobbly. When it followed through to the tiny light I could see what it was. One of my own crutches. Delightful.

I tried to disentagle my legs and roll over and stand up. He shone the light on me to watch. When I was half up he knocked me down again.

'Where is it?'

'I told you . . .'

'We both know, chum, that you have this chunk of metal. I want it. I have a customer for it. And you're going to hand it over like a good little warned off crook.'

'Go scratch yourself.'

I rolled fast and almost missed the next swipe. It landed on the plaster. Some flakes came off. Less work for Tuesday.

'You haven't a hope,' he said. 'Face facts.'

The facts were that if I yelled for help only the horses would hear.

Pity.

I considered giving him the chunk of metal with the hole in it. Correction, half a hole. He didn't know it was only half a hole. I wondered whether I should tell him. Perhaps he'd be only half as savage.

'Who wants it?' I said.

'Be your age.' He swung the crutch.

Contact.

I cursed.

'Save yourself, chum. Don't be stupid.'

'What is this chunk of metal?'

'Just hand it over.'

'I don't know what you're looking for?'

'Chunk of metal with a hole in it.'

'What chunk of metal?'

'Look, chum, what does it matter what chunk of metal? The one you've got.'

'I haven't.'

'Stop playing games.' He swung the crutch. I grunted. 'Hand it over.'

'I haven't . . . got . . . any chunk of metal.'

'Look chum, my instructions are as clear as glass. You've got some lump of metal and I've come to fetch it. Understand? Simple. So save yourself, you stupid crumb.'

'What is he paying for it?'

'You still offering more?'

'Worth a try.'

'So you said before. But nothing doing.'

'Pity.'

'Where's the chunk . . . ?'

I didn't answer, heard the crutch coming, rolled at the right instant, and heard it thud on the carpet, roughly where my nose had been.

The little flashlight sought me out. He didn't miss the second time, but it was only my arm, not my face.

'Didn't you ask what it was?' I said.

'None of your bloody business. You just tell me . . .' bash . . . 'where' . . . bash . . . 'it is.'

I'd had about enough. Too much, in fact. And I'd found out all I was likely to, except how far he was prepared to go, which was information I could do without.

I'd been trying to roll towards the door. Finally made it near enough. Stretched backwards over my head and felt my fingers curl round the bottom of the other crutch still propped against the wall.

The rubber knob came into my hand, and with one scything movement I swept the business end round viciously at knee level.

It caught him square and unexpected on the back of the legs just as he himself was in mid swing, and he overbalanced and

crashed down half on top of me. I reached out and caught something, part of his coat, and gripped and pulled, and tried to
swing my plaster leg over his body to hold him down.

He wasn't having any. We scrambled around on the floor, him
trying to get up and me trying to stop him, both of us scratching
and punching and gouging in a thoroughly unsportsmanlike
manner. The flashlight had fallen away across the far side of the
room and shone only on the wall. Not enough light to be much
good. Too much for total evasion of his efficient fists.

The bedside table fell over with a crash and the lamp smashed.
Oakley somehow reached into the ruins and picked up a piece
of glass, and I just saw the light shimmer on it as he slashed
it towards my eyes. I dodged it by a millimetre in the last half
second.

'You bugger,' I said bitterly.

We were both gasping for breath. I loosed the grip I had
on his coat in order to have both hands free to deal with the
glass, and as soon as he felt me leave go he was heaving himself
back on to his feet.

'Now,' he said, panting heavily, 'Where bloody is it?'

I didn't answer. He'd got hold of a crutch again. Back to
square one. On the thigh, that time.

I was lying on the other crutch. The elbow supports were
digging into my back. I twisted my arm underneath me and
pulled out the crutch, hand swung it at him just as he was having
a second go. The crutches met and crashed together in the air. I
held on to mine for dear life and rolled towards the bed.

'Give . . . up . . .' he said.

'Get . . . stuffed.'

I made it to the bed and lay in the angle between it and the
floor. He couldn't get a good swing at me there. I turned the
crutch round, and held it by the elbow and hand grips with both
of my own. To hit me where I was lying he had to come nearer.

He came. His dark shadow was above me, exaggerated by the
dim torchlight. He leant over, swinging. I shoved the stick end of
the crutch hard upwards. It went into him solidly and he
screeched sharply. The crutch he had been swinging dropped
harmlessly on top of me as he reeled away, clutching at his groin.

'I'll . . . kill you . . . for that . . .' His voice was high with pain.
He groaned, hugging himself.

'Serves . . . you . . . right.' I said breathlessly.

I pulled myself across the floor, dragging the plaster, aiming
for the telephone which had crashed on to the floor with the little

table. Found the receiver. Pulled the cord. The telephone bumped over the carpet into my hand.

Put my finger on the button. Small ting. Dialling tone. Found the numbers. Three . . . nine . . . one . . .

'Yeah?' Tony's voice, thick with sleep.

Dead careless, I was. Didn't hear a thing. The crutch swung wickedly down on the back of my head and I fell over the telephone and never told him to gallop to the rescue.

I woke where Oakley had left me, still lying on the floor over the telephone, the receiver half in and half out of my hand.

It was daylight, just. Grey and raw and raining. I was stiff. Cold. Had a headache.

Remembered bit by bit what had happened. Set about scraping myself off the carpet.

First stop, back on to the bed, accompanied by bedclothes. Lay there feeling terrible and looking at the mess he had made of my room.

After he'd knocked me out, he had nothing to be quiet about. Everything had been pulled out of the closet and drawers and flung on the floor. Everything smashable was smashed. The sleeves of some of my suits were ripped and lying in tatters. Rosalind's picture had been torn into four pieces and the silver frame twisted and snapped. It had been revenge more than a search. A bad loser, David Oakley.

What I could see of the sitting-room through the open door seemed to have received the same treatment.

I lay and ached in most places you could think of.

Didn't look to see if Oakley had found the piece of manifold because I knew he wouldn't have. Thought about him coming, and about what he'd said.

Thought about Cranfield.

Thought about Gowery.

Once I got the plaster off and could move about again, it shouldn't take me too long now to dig out the enemy. A bit of leg work. Needed two legs.

Oakley would shortly be reporting no success from the night's work. I wondered if he would be sent to try again. Didn't like that idea particularly.

I shifted on the bed, trying to get comfortable. I'd been concussed twice in five days once before, and got over it. I'd been kicked along the ground by a large field of hurdlers, which had been a lot worse than the crutches. I'd broken enough bones to stock a cemetery and this time they were all whole. But all the same I felt sicker than after racing falls, and in the end realized my unease was revulsion against being hurt by another man. Horses, hard ground, even express trains, were impersonal. Oakley had been a different type of invasion. The amount you were mentally affected by a pain always depended on how you got it.

I felt terrible. Had no energy at all to get up and tidy the mess. Shut my eyes to blot it out. Blotted myself out, too. Went to sleep.

A voice said above my head, 'Won't you ever learn to keep your door shut?'

I smiled feebly. 'Not if you're coming through it.'

'Finding you flat out is becoming a habit.'

'Try to break it.'

I opened my eyes. Broad daylight. Still raining.

Roberta was standing a foot from the bed wearing a blinding yellow raincoat covered in trickling drops. The copper hair was tied up in a pony tail and she was looking around her with disgust.

'Do you realize it's half past ten?' she said.

'No.'

'Do you always drop your clothes all over the place when you go to bed?'

'Only on Wednesdays.'

'Coffee?' she said abruptly, looking down at me.

'Yes, please.'

She picked her way through the mess to the door, and then across the sitting-room until she was out of sight. I rubbed my hand over my chin. Bristly. And there was a tender lump on the back of my skull and a sore patch all down one side of my jaw, where I hadn't dodged fast enough. Bruises in other places set up a morning chorus. I didn't listen.

She came back minus the raincoat and carrying two steaming mugs which she put carefully on the floor. Then she picked up the bedside table and transferred the mugs to its top.

The drawer had fallen out of the table, and the envelope had fallen out of the drawer. But Oakley hadn't apparently looked into it: hadn't known it was there to find.

Roberta picked up the scattered crutches and brought them over to the bed.

'Thanks,' I said.

'You take it very calmly.'

'I've seen it before,' I pointed out.

'And you just went to sleep?'

'Opted out,' I agreed.

She looked more closely at my face and rolled my head over on the pillow. I winced. She took her hand away.

'Did you get the same treatment as the flat?'

'More or less.'

'What for?'

'For being stubborn.'

'Do you mean,' she said incredulously, 'That you could have avoided all this . . . and didn't?'

'If there's a good reason for backing down, you back down. If there isn't, you don't.'

'And all this . . . isn't a good enough reason?'

'No.'

'You're crazy,' she said.

'You're so right.' I sighed, pushed myself up a bit, and reached for the coffee.

'Have you called the police?' she asked.

I shook my head. 'Not their quarrel.'

'Who did it, then?'

I smiled at her. 'Your father and I have got our licences back.'

'*What?*'

'It'll be official sometime today.'

'Does Father know? How did it happen? Did you do it?'

'No, he doesn't know yet. Ring him up. Tell him to get on to all the owners. It'll be confirmed in the papers soon, either today's evening editions, or tomorrow's dailies.'

She picked the telephone off the floor and sat on the edge of my bed, and telephoned to her father with real joy and sparkling eyes. He wouldn't believe it at first.

'Kelly says it's true,' she said.

He argued again, and she handed the telephone to me.

'You tell him.'

Cranfield said, 'Who told you?'

'Lord Ferth.'

'Did he say why?'

'No,' I lied. 'Just that the sentences had been reviewed . . . and reversed. We're back, as from today. The official notice will be in next week's Calendar.'

'No explanation at all?' he insisted.

'They don't have to give one,' I pointed out.

'All the same . . .'

'Who cares why?' I said. 'The fact that we're back . . . that's all that matters.'

'Did you find out who framed us?'

'No.'

'Will you go on trying?'

'I might do,' I said. 'We'll see.'

He had lost interest in that. He bounded into a stream of plans for the horses, once they were back. 'And it will give me great pleasure to tell Henry Kessel . . .'

'I'd like to see his face,' I agreed. But Pat Nikita would never part with Squelch, nor with Kessel, now. If Cranfield thought Kessel would come crawling apologetically back, he didn't know his man. 'Concentrate on getting Breadwinner back,' I suggested. 'I'll be fit to ride in the Gold Cup.'

'Old Strepson promised Breadwinner would come back at once . . . and Pound Postage of his . . . that's entered in the National, don't forget.'

'I haven't,' I assured him, 'forgotten.'

He ran down eventually and disconnected, and I could imagine him sitting at the other end still wondering whether to trust me.

Roberta stood up with a spring, as if the news had filled her with energy .

'Shall I tidy up for you?'

'I'd love some help.'

She bent down and picked up Rosalind's torn picture.

'They didn't have to do that,' she said in disgust.

'I'll get the bits stuck together and rephotographed.'

'You'd hate to lose her . . .'

I didn't answer at once. She looked at me curiously, her eyes dark with some unreadable expression.

'I lost her,' I said slowly. 'Rosalind . . . Roberta . . . you are so unalike.'

She turned away abruptly and put the pieces on the chest of drawers where they had always stood.

'Who wants to be a carbon copy?' she said, and her voice was high and cracking. 'Get dressed . . . while I start on the sitting-room.' She disappeared fast and shut the door behind her.

I lay there looking at it.

Roberta Cranfield. I'd never liked her.

Roberta Cranfield. I couldn't bear it . . . I was beginning to love her.

She stayed most of the day, helping me clear up the mess.

Oakley had left little to chance: the bathroom and kitchen both looked as if they'd been gutted by a whirlwind. He'd searched everywhere a good enquiry agent could think of, including the lavatory cistern and the refrigerator; and everywhere he'd searched he'd left his trail of damage.

After midday, which was punctuated by some scrambled eggs, the telephone started ringing. Was it true, asked the *Daily Witness* in the shape of Daddy Leeman, that Cranfield and I . . .? 'Check with the Jockey Club,' I said.

The other papers had checked first. 'May we have your comments?' they asked.

'Thrilled to bits,' I said gravely. 'You can quote me.'

A lot of real chums rang to congratulate, and a lot of pseudo chums rang to say they'd never believed me guilty anyway.

For most of the afternoon I lay flat on the sitting-room floor with my head on a cushion talking down the telephone while Roberta stepped around and over me nonchalantly, putting everything back into place.

Finally she dusted her hands off on the seat of her black pants, and said she thought that that would do. The flat looked almost as good as ever. I agreed gratefully that it would do very well.

'Would you consider coming down to my level?' I asked.

She said calmly, 'Are you speaking literally, metaphorically, intellectually, financially or socially?'

'I was suggesting you might sit on the floor.'

'In that case,' she said collectedly, 'Yes.' And she sank gracefully into a cross legged sprawl.

I couldn't help grinning. She grinned companionably back.

'I was scared stiff of you when I came here last week,' she said.

'You were *what*?'

'You always seemed so aloof. Unapproachable.'

'Are we talking about me . . . or you?'

'You, of course,' she said in surprise. 'You always made me nervous. I always get sort of . . . strung up . . . when I'm nervous. Put on a bit of an act, to hide it, I suppose.'

'I see,' I said slowly.

'You're still a pretty good cactus, if you want to know . . . but . . . well, you see people differently when they've been bleeding all over your best dress and looking pretty vulnerable . . .'

I began to say that in that case I would be prepared to bleed on her any time she liked, but the telephone interrupted me at half way. And it was old Strepson, settling down for a long cosy chat about Breadwinner and Pound Postage.

Roberta wrinkled her nose and got to her feet.

'Don't go,' I said, with my hand over the mouthpiece.

'Must. I'm late already.'

'Wait,' I said. But she shook her head, fetched the yellow rain-coat from the bath, where she'd put it, and edged herself into it.

' 'Bye,' she said.

'Wait . . .'

She waved briefly and let herself out of the door. I struggled up on to my feet, and said, 'Sir . . . could you hold on a minute . . .' into the telephone, and hopped without the crutches over to the window. She looked up when I opened it. She was standing in the yard, tying on a headscarf. The rain had eased to drizzle.

'Will you come tomorrow?' I shouted down.

'Can't tomorrow. Got to go to London.'

'Saturday?'

'Do you want me to?'

'Yes.'

'I'll try, then.'

'Please come.'

'Oh . . .' She suddenly smiled in a way I'd never seen before. 'All right.'

Careless I might be about locking my front door, but in truth I left little about worth stealing. Five hundred pounds would never have been lying around on my chest of drawers for enquiry agents to photograph.

When I'd converted the flat from an old hay loft I'd built in more than mod cons. Behind the cabinet in the kitchen which housed things like fly killer and soap powder, and tucked into a crafty piece of brickwork, lay a maximum security safe. It was operated not by keys or combinations, but by electronics. The manufacturers had handed over the safe itself and also the tiny ultrasonic transmitter which sent out the special series of radio waves which alone would release the lock mechanism, and I'd installed them myself: the safe in the wall and the transmitter in a false bottom to the cabinet. Even if anyone found the trans-mitter, they had still to find the safe and to know the sequence of frequencies which unlocked it.

A right touch of the Open Sesame. I'd always liked gadgets.

Inside the safe there were, besides money and some racing trophies, several pieces of antique silver, three paintings by Houthuesen, two Chelsea figures, a Meissen cup and saucer, a Louis XIV snuff box, and four uncut diamonds totalling twenty-eight carats. My retirement pension, all wrapped in green baize and appreciating nicely. Retirement for a steeplechase jockey could lurk in the very next fall: and the ripe age of forty, if one lasted that long, was about the limit.

There was also a valueless lump of cast iron, with a semi-circular dent in it. To these various treasures I added the envelope which Ferth had given me, because it wouldn't help if I lost that either.

Bolting my front door meant a hazardous trip down the stairs, and another in the morning to open it. I decided it could stay unlocked as usual. Wedged a chair under the door into my sitting-room instead.

During the evening I telephoned to Newtonnards in his pink washed house in Mill Hill.

'Hallo,' he said. 'You've got your licence back then. Talk of the meeting it was at Wincanton today, soon as the Press Association chaps heard about it.'

'Yes, it's great news.'

'What made their Lordships change their minds?'

'I've no idea . . . Look, I wondered if you'd seen that man again yet, the one who backed Cherry Pie with you.'

'Funny thing,' he said. 'But I saw him today. Just after I'd heard you were back in favour, though, so I didn't think you'd be interested any more.'

'Did you by any chance find out who he is?'

'I did, as a matter of fact. More to satisfy my own curiosity, really. He's the Honourable Peter Foxcroft. Mean anything to you?'

'He's a brother of Lord Middleburg.'

'Yeah. So I'm told.'

I laughed inwardly. Nothing sinister about Cranfield refusing to name his mysterious pal. Just another bit of ladder climbing. He might be one rung up being in a position to use the Hon. P. Foxcroft as a runner: but he would certainly be five rungs down involving him in a messy Enquiry.

'There's one other thing . . .' I hesitated. 'Would you . . . could you . . . do me a considerable favour?'

'Depends what it is.' He sounded cautious but not truculent. A smooth, experienced character.

'I can't offer much in return.'

He chuckled. 'Warning me not to expect tip offs when you're on a hot number?'

'Something like that,' I admitted.

'O.K. then. You want something for strictly nothing. Just as well to know where we are. So shoot.'

'Can you remember who you told about Cranfield backing Cherry Pie?'

'Before the Enquiry, you mean?'

'Yes. Those bookmaker colleagues you mentioned.'

'Well . . .' he sounded doubtful.

'If you can,' I said, 'could you ask *them* who *they* told?'

'Phew.' He half breathed, half whistled down the receiver. 'That's some favour.'

'I'm sorry. Just forget it.'

'Hang on, hang on, I didn't say I wouldn't do it. It's a bit of a tall order, though, expecting them to remember.'

'I know. Very long shot. But I still want to know who told the Stewards about the bet with you.'

'You've got your licence back. Why don't you let it rest?'

'Would you?'

He sighed. 'I don't know. All right then, I'll see what I can do. No promises, mind. Oh, and by the way, it can be just as useful to know when one of your mounts is *not* fit or likely to win. If you take my meaning.'

'I take it,' I said smiling. 'It's a deal.'

I put down the receiver reflecting that only a minority of bookmakers were villains, and that most of them were more generous than they got credit for. The whole tribe were reviled for the image of the few. Like students.

CHAPTER FOURTEEN

OAKLEY DIDN'T COME. No one came. I took the chair from under the door knob to let the world in with the morning. Not much of the world accepted the invitation.

Made some coffee. Tony came while I was standing in the kitchen drinking it and put whisky into a mug of it for himself by way of breakfast. He'd been out with one lot of horses at exercise and was waiting to go out with the other, and spent the interval discussing their prospects as if nothing had ever happened. For him the warning off was past history, forgotten. His creed was that of newspapers; today is important, tomorrow more so, but yesterday is nothing.

He finished the coffee and left, clapping me cheerfully on the shoulder and setting up a protest from an Oakley bruise. I spent most of the rest of the day lying flat on my bed, answering the telephone, staring at the ceiling, letting Nature get on with repairing a few ravages, and thinking.

Another quiet night. I had two names in my mind, juggling them. Two to work on. Better than three hundred. But both could be wrong.

Saturday morning the postman brought the letters right upstairs, as he'd been doing since the era of plaster. I thanked him, sorted through them, dropped a crutch, and had the usual awkward fumble picking it up. When I opened one of the letters I dropped both the crutches again in surprise.

Left the crutches on the floor. Leant against the wall and read.

Dear Kelly Hughes,

I have seen in the papers that you have had your licence restored, so perhaps this information will be too late to be of any use to you. I am sending it anyway because the friend who collected it is considerably out of pocket over it, and would be glad if you could reimburse him. I append also his list of expenses.

As you will see he went to a good deal of trouble over this, though to be fair he also told me that he had enjoyed doing it. I hope it is what you wanted.

> Sincerely,
> Teddy Dewar.
> Great Stag Hotel, Birmingham.

Clipped behind the letter were several other sheets of varying sizes. The top one was a schematic presentation of names which looked at first glance like an inverted family tree. There were clumps of three or four names inside two-inch circles. The circles led via arrows to other circles below and sometimes beside them, but the eye was led downwards continually until all the arrows had converged to three circles, and then to two, and finally to one. And the single name in the bottom circle was David Oakley.

Behind the page was an explanatory note.

'I knew one contact, the J. L. Jones underlined in the third row of circles. From him I worked in all directions, checking people who knew of David Oakley. Each clump of people heard about him from one of the people in the next clump. Everyone on the page, I guarantee, has heard either directly or indirectly that Oakley is the man to go to if one is in trouble. I posed as a man in trouble, as you suggested, and nearly all that I talked to either mentioned him of their own accord, or agreed when I brought him up as a possibility.

I only hope that one at least of these names has some significance for you, as I'm afraid the expenses were rather high. Most of the investigation was conducted in pubs or hotels, and it was sometimes necessary to get the contact tight before he would divulge.'

Faithfully,
B. R. S. Timieson.

The expense list was high enough to make me whistle. I turned back to the circled names, and read them carefully through.

Looking for one of two.

One was there.

Perhaps I should have rejoiced. Perhaps I should have been angry. Instead, I felt sad.

I doubled the expenses and wrote out a cheque with an accompanying note:

'This is really magnificent. Cannot thank you enough. One of the names has great significance, well worth all your perseverance. My eternal thanks.

I wrote also a grateful letter to Teddy Dewar saying the information couldn't have been better timed, and enclosing the envelope for his friend Timieson.

As I was sticking on the stamp the telephone rang. I hopped over to it and lifted the receiver.

George Newtonnards.

'Spent all last evening on the blower. Astronomical phone bill, I'm going to have.'

'Send me the account,' I said resignedly.

'Better wait to see if I've got results,' he suggested. 'Got a pencil handy?'

'Just a sec.' I fetched a writing pad and ballpoint. 'O.K. Go ahead.'

'Right then. First, here are the chaps *I* told.' He dictated five names. 'The last one, Pelican Jobberson, is the one who holds a fierce grudge against you for that bum steer you gave him, but as it happens he didn't tell the Stewards or anyone else because he went off to Casablanca the next day for a holiday. Well . . . here are the people Harry Ingram told . . .' He read out three names. 'And these are the people Herbie Subbing told . . .' Four names. 'These are the people Dimmie Ovens told . . .' Five names.

'And Clobber Mackintosh, he really spread it around . . .' Eight
names. 'That's all they can remember. They wouldn't swear there
was no one else. And, of course, all those people they've mentioned could have passed the info on to someone else . . . I mean,
things like this spread out in ripples.'

'Thanks anyway,' I said sincerely. 'Thank you very much
indeed for taking so much trouble.'

'Has it been any help?'

'Oh yes, I think so. I'll let you know, sometime.'

'And don't forget. The obvious non winner . . . give me the
wink.'

'I'll do that,' I promised. 'If you'll risk it, after Pelican Jobberson's experience.'

'He's got no sense,' he said. 'But I have.'

He rang off, and I studied his list of names. Several were
familiar and belonged to well known racing people: the bookmakers' clients, I supposed. None of the names were the same as
those on Timieson's list of Oakley contacts, but there was something . . .

For ten minutes I stood looking at the paper wondering what
was hovering around the edge of consciousness, and finally, with
a thud, the association clicked.

One of the men Herbie Subbing had told was the brother-in-
law of the person I had found among the Oakley contacts.

I thought for a while, and then opened the newspaper and
studied the programme for the day's racing, which was at
Reading. Then I telephoned to Lord Ferth at his London house,
and reached him via a plummy-voiced manservant.

'Well, Kelly . . . ?' There was something left of Wednesday's
relationship. Not all, but something.

'Sir,' I said. 'Are you going to Reading races?'

'Yes, I am.'

'I haven't yet had any official notice of my licence being
restored . . . Will it be all right for me to turn up there? I would
particularly like to talk to you.'

'I'll make sure you have no difficulty, if it's important.' There
was a faint question in his tone, which I answered.

'I know,' I said, 'who engineered things.'

'Ah . . . Yes. Then come. Unless the journey would be too uncomfortable for you? I could, you know, come on to Corrie after
the races. I have no engagements tonight.'

'You're very thoughtful. But I think our engineer will be at
the races too . . . or at least there's a very good chance of it.'

'As you like,' he agreed. 'I'll look out for you.'

Tony had two runners at the meeting and I could ask him to take me. But there was also Roberta . . . she was coming over, probably, and she too might take me. I smiled wryly to myself. She might take me anywhere. Roberta Cranfield. Of all people.

As if by telepathy the telephone rang, and it was Roberta herself on the other end. She sounded breathless and worried.

'Kelly! I can't come just yet. In fact . . .' The words came in a rush. 'Can you come over here?'

'What's the matter?'

'Well . . . I don't really know if *anything*'s the matter . . . seriously, that is. But Grace Roxford has turned up here.'

'Dear Grace?'

'Yes . . . look, Kelly, she's just sitting in her car outside the house sort of glaring at it. Honestly, she looks a bit mad. We don't know quite what to do. Mother wants to call the police, but, I mean, one *can't* . . . Supposing the poor woman has come to apologize or something, and is just screwing herself up?'

'She's still sitting in the car?'

'Yes. I can see her from here. Can you come? I mean . . . Mother's useless and you know how dear Grace feels about *me* . . . She looks pretty odd, Kelly.' Definite alarm in her voice.

'Where's your father?'

'Out on the gallops with Breadwinner. He won't be back for about an hour.'

'All right then. I'll get Tony or someone to drive me over. As soon as I can.'

'That's great,' she said with relief. 'I'll try and stall her till you come.'

It would take half an hour to get there. More, probably. By then dear Grace might not still be sitting in her car . . .

I dialled three nine one.

'Tony,' I said urgently. 'Can you drop everything instantly and drive me to Cranfield's? Grace Roxford has turned up there and I don't like the sound of it.'

'I've got to go to Reading,' he protested.

'You can go on from Cranfield's when we've sorted Grace out . . . and anyway, I want to go to Reading too, to talk to Lord Ferth. So be a pal, Tony. Please.'

'Oh all right. If you want it that much. Give me five minutes.'

He took ten. I spent some of them telephoning to Jack Roxford. He was surprised I should be calling him.

'Look, Jack,' I said, 'I'm sorry to be upsetting you like this, but have you any idea where your wife has gone?'

'Grace?' More surprise, but also anxiety. 'Down to the village, she said.'

The village in question was roughly forty miles from Cranfield's house.

'She must have gone some time ago,' I said.

'I suppose so . . . what's all this about?' The worry was sharp in his voice.

'Roberta Cranfield has just telephoned to say that your wife is outside their house, just sitting in her car.'

'Oh God,' he said. 'She can't be.'

'I'm afraid she is.'

'Oh *no* . . .' he wailed. 'She seemed better this morning . . . quite her old self . . . it seemed safe to let her go and do the shopping . . . she's been so upset, you see . . . and then you and Dexter got your licences back . . . it's affected her . . . it's all been so awful for her.'

'I'm just going over there to see if I can help,' I said. 'But . . . can you come down and collect her?'

'Oh *yes*,' he said. 'I'll start at once. Oh poor dear Grace . . . Take care of her, till I come.'

'Yes,' I said reassuringly, and disconnected.

I made it without mishap down the stairs and found Tony had commandeered Poppy's estate car for the journey. The back seat lay flat so that I could lie instead of sit, and there were even cushions for my shoulders and head.

'Poppy's idea,' Tony said briefly, helping me climb in through the rear door. 'Great girl.'

'She sure is,' I said gratefully, hauling in the crutches behind me. 'Lose no time, now, friend.'

'You sound worried.' He shut the doors, switched on and drove away with minimum waste of time.

'I am, rather. Grace Roxford is unbalanced.'

'But surely not dangerous?'

'I hope not.'

I must have sounded doubtful because Tony's foot went heavily down on the accelerator. 'Hold on to something,' he said. We rocked round corners. I couldn't find any good anchorage: had to wedge my useful foot against the rear door and push myself off the swaying walls with my hands.

'O.K.?' he shouted.

'Uh . . . yes,' I said breathlessly.

'Good bit of road just coming up.' We left all the other traffic at a standstill. 'Tell me if you see any cops.'

We saw no cops. Tony covered the eighteen miles through Berkshire in twenty-three minutes. We jerked to a stop outside Cranfield's house, and the first thing I saw was that there was no one in the small grey Volkswagen standing near the front door.

Tony opened the back of the car with a crash and unceremoniously tugged me out.

'She's probably sitting down cosily having a quiet cup of tea,' he said.

She wasn't.

Tony rang the front door bell and after a lengthy interval Mrs Cranfield herself opened it.

Not her usual swift wide-opening fling. She looked at us through a nervous six inches.

'Hughes. What are you doing here? Go away.'

'Roberta asked me to come. To see Grace Roxford.'

'Mrs Roxford is no longer here.' Mrs Cranfield's voice was as strung up as her behaviour.

'Isn't that her car?' I pointed to the Volkswagen.

'No,' she said sharply.

'Whose is it, then?'

'The gardener's. Now Hughes, go away at once. Go away.'

'Very well,' I said, shrugging. And she instantly shut the door.

'Help me back into the car,' I said to Tony.

'Surely you're not just *going*?'

'Don't argue,' I said. 'Get me into the car, drive away out through the gates, then go round and come back in through the stable entrance.'

'That's better.' He shuffled me in, threw in the crutches, slammed the door and hustled round to the driving seat.

'Don't rush so,' I said. 'Scratch your head a bit. Look disgusted.'

'You think she's watching?' He didn't start the car: looked at me over his shoulder.

'I think Mrs Cranfield would never this side of doomsday allow her gardener to park outside her front door. Mrs Cranfield was doing her best to ask for help.'

'Which means,' he added slowly, 'That Grace Roxford is very dangerous indeed.'

I nodded with a dry mouth. 'Drive away, now.'

He went slowly. Rolled round into the back drive, accelerated along that, and stopped with a jerk beside the stables. Yet again he helped me out.

'There's a telephone in the small office in the yard,' I said. 'Next to the tackroom. Look up in the classified directory and find a local doctor. Tell him to come smartish. Then wait here until Dexter Cranfield comes back with the horses, and stop him going into the house.'

'Kelly, couldn't you be exaggerating . . . ?'

'I could. Better to be on the safe side, though.'

'I'll never be able to stop Cranfield.'

'Tell him no one ever believes anything tragic will happen until it has.'

He looked at me for two seconds, then wheeled away into the yard.

I peg-legged up the back drive and tried the back door. Open. It would be. For Cranfield to walk easily through it. And to what?

I went silently along into the main hall, and listened. There was no sound in the house.

Tried the library first, juggling the crutches to get a good grip on the door handle, sweating lest I should drop one with a crash. Turned the handle, pressed the door quietly inwards.

The library was uninhabited. A large clock on the mantel ticked loudly. Out of time with my heart.

I left the door open. Went slowly, silently, towards the small sitting-room beside the front door. Again the meticulously careful drill with the handle. If they'd seen me come, they would most probably be in this room.

The door swung inwards. Well oiled. No creaks. I saw the worn chintz covers on the armchairs, the elderly rugs, the debris of living, scattered newspapers, a pair of spectacles on some letters, a headscarf and a flower basket. No people.

On the other side of the hall there were the double doors into the large formal drawing-room, and at the back, beyond the staircase, the doors to the dining-room and to Dexter Cranfield's own study, where he kept his racing books and did all his paper work.

I swung across to the study, and opened the door. It was quiet in there. Dust slowly gravitated. Nothing else moved.

That left only the two large rooms downstairs, and the whole of upstairs. I looked at the long broad flight uneasily. Wished it were an escalator.

The dining-room was empty. I shifted back through the hall to the double doors of the drawing-room. Went through the crutch routine with more difficulty, because if I were going in there I would need both doors open, and to open both doors took both hands. I managed it in the end by hooking both crutches over my left arm like walking sticks, and standing on one leg.

The doors parted and I pushed them wide. The quarter acre of drawing-room contained chairs of gold brocade upholstery, a pale cream Chinese carpet and long soft blue curtains. A delicate, elegant, class-conscious room designed for Cranfield's glossiest aspirations.

Everything in there was motionless. A tableau.

I hitched the crutches into place, and walked forward. Stopped after a very few paces. Stopped because I had to.

Mrs Cranfield was there. And Roberta. And Grace Roxford. Mrs Cranfield was standing by the fireplace, hanging on to the shoulder-high mantel as if needing support. Roberta sat upright in an armless wooden chair set out of its usual place in a large clear area of carpet. Behind her and slightly to one side, and with one hand firmly grasping Roberta's shoulder, stood Grace Roxford.

Grace Roxford held the sort of knife used by fishmongers. Nearly a foot long, razor sharp, with a point like a needle. She was resting the lethal end of it against Roberta's neck.

'Kelly!' Roberta said. Her voice was high and a trifle wavery, but the relief in it was overwhelming. I feared it might be misplaced.

Grace Roxford had a bright colour over her taut cheekbones and a piercing glitter in her eyes. Her body was rigid with tension. The hand holding the knife trembled in uneven spasms. She was as unstable as wet gelignite; but she still knew what she was doing.

'You went away, Kelly Hughes,' she said. 'You went away.'

'Yes, Grace,' I agreed. 'But I came back to talk to Roberta.'

'You come another step,' she said, 'and I'll cut her throat.'

Mrs Cranfield drew a breath like a sob, but Roberta's expression didn't change. Grace had made that threat already. Several times, probably. Especially when Tony and I had arrived at the front door.

She was desperately determined. Neither I nor the Cranfields had room to doubt that she wouldn't do as she said. And I was twenty feet away from her and a cripple besides.

'What do you want, Grace?' I said, as calmly as possible.

'Want? Want?' Her eyes flickered. She seemed to be trying to remember what she wanted. Then her rage sharpened on me like twin darts, and her purpose came flooding back.

'Dexter Cranfield . . . bloody snob . . . I'll see he doesn't get those horses . . . I'm going to kill him, see, kill him . . . then he can't get them, can he? No . . . he can't.'

Again there was no surprise either in Roberta or her mother. Grace had told them already what she'd come for.

'Grace, killing Mr Cranfield won't help your husband.'

'Yes. Yes. Yes. Yes.' She nodded sharply between each yes, and the knife jumped against Roberta's neck. Roberta shut her eyes for a while and swayed on the chair.

I said, 'How do you hope to kill him, Grace?'

She laughed. It got out of control at halfway and ended in a maniacal high-pitched giggle. 'He'll come here, won't he? He'll come here and stand beside me, because he'll do just what I say, won't he? Won't he?'

I looked at the steel blade beside Roberta's pearly skin and knew that he would indeed do as she said. As I would.

'And then, see,' she said, 'I'll just stick the knife into *him*, not into her. See? See?'

'I see,' I said.

She nodded extravagantly and her hand shook.

'And then what?' I asked.

'Then what?' She looked puzzled. She hadn't got any further than killing Cranfield. Beyond that lay only darkness and confusion. Her vision didn't extend to consequences.

'Edwin Byler could send his horses away to someone else,' I said.

'No. No. Only Dexter Cranfield. Only him. Telling him he ought to have a more snobbish trainer. Taking him away from us. I'm going to kill him. Then he can't have those horses.' The words tumbled out in a vehement monotone, all the more frightening for being clearly automatic. These were thoughts she'd had in her head for a very long time.

'It would have been all right, of course,' I said slowly, 'if Mr Cranfield hadn't got his licence back.'

'Yes!' It was a bitterly angry shriek.

'I got it back for him,' I said.

'They just gave it back. They just gave it back. They shouldn't have done that. They shouldn't.'

'They didn't just give it back,' I said. 'They gave it back because I made them.'

'You couldn't . . .'

'I told everyone I was going to. And I did.'

'No. No. No.'

'Yes,' I said flatly.

Her expression slowly changed, and highly frightening it was too. I waited while it sank into her disorganized brain that if Byler sent his horses to Cranfield after all it was me alone she had to thank for it. I watched the intention to kill widen to embrace me too. The semi-cautious restraint in her manner towards me was transforming itself into a vicious glare of hate.

I swallowed. I said again, 'If I hadn't made the Stewards give Mr Cranfield's licence back, he would still be warned off.'

Roberta said in horror, 'No, Kelly. Don't. Don't do it.'

'Shut up,' I said. 'Me or your father . . . which has more chance? And run, when you can.'

Grace wasn't listening. Grace was grasping the essentials and deciding on a course of action.

There was a lot of white showing round her eyes.

'I'll kill you,' she said. 'I'll kill you.'

I stood still. I waited. The seconds stretched like centuries.

'Come here,' she said. 'Come here, or I'll cut her throat.'

CHAPTER FIFTEEN

I TOOK MYSELF crutch by crutch towards her. When I was half way there Mrs Cranfield gave a moaning sigh and fainted, falling awkwardly on the rug and scattering the brass fire irons with a nerve-shattering crash.

Grace jumped. The knife snicked into Roberta's skin and she cried out. I stood half unbalanced, freezing into immobility, trying to will Grace not to disintegrate into panic, not to go over the edge, not to lose the last tiny grip she had on her reason. She wasn't far off stabbing everything in sight.

'Sit still,' I said to Roberta with dreadful urgency, and she gave me a terrified look and did her best not to move. She was trembling violently. I had never thought I could pray. I prayed.

Grace was moving her head in sharp birdlike jerks. The knife was still against Roberta's neck. Grace's other hand still grasped Roberta's shoulder. A thread of blood trickled down Roberta's skin and was blotted up in a scarlet patch by her white jersey.

No one went to help Roberta's mother. I didn't even dare to look at her, because it meant turning my eyes away from Grace.

'Come here,' Grace said. 'Come here.'

Her voice was husky, little more than a loud whisper. And although she was watching me come with unswerving murder in

her eyes, I was inexpressibly thankful that she could still speak
at all, still think, still hold a purpose.

During the last few steps I wondered how I was going to dodge,
since I couldn't jump, couldn't bend my knees, and hadn't even
my hands free. A bit late to start worrying. I took the last step
short so that she would have to move to reach me, and at the
same time eased my elbow out of the right-hand crutch.

She was almost too fast. She struck at me instantly, in a flashing
thrust directed at my throat, and although I managed to twist
the two inches needed to avoid it, the hissing knife came close
enough, through the collar of my coat. I brought my right arm
up and across, crashing crutch against her as she prepared to
try again.

Out of the corner of my eye I saw Roberta wrench herself out
of Grace's clutching grasp, and half stumble, half fall as she got
away from the chair.

'Kill you,' Grace said. The words were distorted. The meaning
clear. She had no thought of self defence. No thought at all, as
far as I could see. Just one single burning obsessive intention.

I brought up the left-hand crutch like a pole to push her
away. She dived round it and tried to plunge her knife through
my ribs, and in throwing myself away from that I overbalanced
and half fell down, and she was standing over me with her arm
raised like a priest at a human sacrifice.

I dropped one crutch altogether. Useless warding off a knife
with a bare hand. I tried to shove the other crutch round into
her face, but got it tangled up against an armchair.

Grace brought her arm down. I fell right to the floor as soon
as I saw her move and the knife followed me harmlessly, all the
impetus gone by the time it reached me. Another tear in my coat.

She came down on her knees beside me, her arm going up again.

From nowhere my lost crutch whistled through the air and
smashed into the hand which held the knife. Grace hissed like a
snake and dropped it, and it fell point down on to my plaster.
She twisted round to see who had hit her and spread out her
hands towards the crutch that Roberta was aiming at her again.

She caught hold of it and tugged. I wriggled round on the
floor, stretched until I had my fingers round the handle of the
knife, and threw it as hard as I could towards the open door into
the hall.

Grace was too much for Roberta. Too much for me. She was
appallingly, insanely, strong. I heaved myself up on to my left
knee and clasped my arms tight round her chest from behind,

trying to pin her arms down to her sides. She shook me around like a sack of feathers, struggling to get to her feet.

She managed it, lifting me with her, plaster and all. She knew where I'd thrown the knife. She started to go that way, dragging me with her still fastened to her back like a leech.

'Get that knife and run to the stables,' I gasped to Roberta. A girl in a million. She simply ran and picked up the knife and went on running, out into the hall and out of the house.

Grace started yelling unintelligibly and began trying to unclamp the fingers I had laced together over her thin breastbone. I hung on for everyone's dear life, and when she couldn't dislodge them she began pinching wherever she could reach with fierce hurting spite.

The hair which she usually wore screwed into a fold up the back of her neck had come undone and was falling into my face. I could see less and less of what was going on. I knew only that she was still headed towards the doorway, still unimaginably violent, and mumbling now in a continuous flow of senseless words interspersed with sudden shrieks.

She reached the doorway and started trying to get free of me by crashing me against the jamb. She had a hard job of it, but she managed it in the end, and when she felt my weight fall off her she turned in a flash, sticking out her hands with rigid fingers towards my neck.

Her face was a dark congested crimson. Her eyes were stretched wide in a stark screaming stare. Her lips were drawn back in a tight line from her teeth.

I had never in all my life seen anything so terrifying. Hadn't imagined a human could look like that, had never visualized homicidal madness.

She would certainly have killed me if it hadn't been for Tony, because her strength made a joke of mine. He came tearing into the hall from the kitchen and brought her down with a rugger tackle about the knees, and I fell too, on top of her, because she was trying to tear my throat out in handfuls, and she didn't leave go.

It took all Tony could do, all Archie could do, all three other lads could do to unlatch her from me and hold her down on the floor. They sat on her arms and legs and chest and head, and she threshed about convulsively underneath them.

Roberta had tears streaming down her face and I hadn't any breath left to tell her to cheer up, there was no more danger, no more . . . no more . . . . I leant weakly against the wall and thought it would be too damned silly to pass out now. Took three deep breaths instead. Everything steadied again, reluctantly.

Tony said, 'There's a doctor on his way. Don't think he's expecting this, though.'

'He'll know what to do.'

'Mother!' exclaimed Roberta suddenly. 'I'd forgotten about her.' She hurried past me into the drawing-room and I heard her mother's voice rising in a disturbed, disorientated question.

Grace was crying out, but her voice sounded like seagulls and nothing she said made sense. One of the lads said sympathetically, 'Poor thing, oughtn't we let her get up?' and Tony answered fiercely, 'Only under a tiger net.'

'She doesn't know what's happening,' I said wearily. 'She can't control what she does. So don't for God's sake let go of her.'

Except for Tony's resolute six foot they all sat on her gingerly and twice she nearly had them off. Finally and at long last the front door bell rang, and I hopped across the hall to answer it.

It was the local doctor, looking tentative, wondering no doubt if it were a hoax. But he took one look at Grace and was opening his case while he came across the hall. Into her arm he pushed a hypodermic needle and soon the convulsive threshing slackened, and the high pitched crying dulled to murmurs and to silence.

The five men slowly stood up and stepped away from her, and she lay there looking shrunk and crumpled, her greying hair falling in streaks away from her flaccidly relaxing face. It seemed incredible that such thin limbs, such a meagre body, could have put out such strength. We all stood looking down at her with more awe than pity, watching while the last twitches shook her and she sank into unconscious peace.

Half an hour later Grace still lay on the floor in the hall, but with a pillow under her head and a rug keeping her warm.

Dexter Cranfield had come back from watching the horses work and walked unprepared into the aftermath of drama. His wife's semi-hysterical explanations hadn't helped him much.

Roberta told him that Grace had come to kill him because he had his licence back and that she was the cause of his losing it in the first place, and he stamped around in a fury which I gathered was mostly because the source of our troubles was a woman. He basically didn't like women. She should have been locked up years ago, he said. Spiteful, petty minded, scheming, interfering . . . just like a woman, he said. I listened to him gravely and concluded he had suffered from a bossy nanny.

The doctor had done some intensive telephoning, and presently an ambulance arrived with two compassionate looking men and a good deal of special equipment. The front door stood wide open and the prospect of Grace's imminent departure was a relief to everyone.

Into this active bustling scene drove Jack Roxford.

He scrambled out of his car, took a horrified look at the ambulance, and ploughed in through the front door. When he saw Grace lying there, with the ambulance men preparing to lift her on to a stretcher, he went down on his knees beside her.

'Grace dear . . .' He looked at her more closely. She was still unconscious, very pale now, looking wizened and sixty. 'Grace dear!' There was anguish in his voice. 'What's the matter with her?'

The doctor started to break it to him. Cranfield interrupted the gentle words and said brutally, 'She's raving mad. She came here trying to kill me, and she could have killed my wife and daughter. It's absolutely disgraceful that she should have been running around free in that state. I'm going to see my solicitors about it.'

Jack Roxford only heard the first part. His eyes went to the cut on Roberta's neck and the bloodstain on her jersey, and he put his hand over his mouth and looked sick.

'Grace,' he said. 'Oh Grace . . .'

There was no doubt he loved her. He leant over her, stroking the hair away from her forehead, murmuring to her, and when he finally looked up there were tears in his eyes and on his cheeks.

'She'll be all right, won't she?'

The doctor shifted uncomfortably and said one would have to see, only time would tell, there were marvellous treatments nowadays . . .

The ambulance men loaded her gently on to the stretcher and picked it up.

'Let me go with her,' Jack Roxford said. 'Where are you taking her? Let me go with her.'

One of the ambulance men told him the name of the hospital and advised him not to come.

'Better try this evening, sir. No use you waiting all day, now, is it?' And the doctor added that Grace would be unconscious for some time yet and under heavy sedation after that, and it was true, it would be better if Roxford didn't go with her.

The uniformed men carried Grace out into the sunshine and loaded her into the ambulance, and we all followed them out into the drive. Jack Roxford stood there looking utterly forlorn as they shut the doors, consulted finally with the doctor who, with the minimum of fuss, drove away.

Roberta touched his arm. 'Can't I get you a drink, Mr Roxford?'

He looked at her vaguely, and then his whole face crumpled and he couldn't speak.

'Don't, Mr Roxford,' Roberta said with pity. 'She isn't in any pain or anything.'

He shook his head. Roberta put her arm across his shoulders and steered him back into the house.

'Now what?' Tony said. 'I've really got to get to Reading, pal. Those runners of mine have to be declared for the second race.'

I looked at my watch. 'You could spare another quarter of an hour. I think we should take Jack Roxford with us. He's got a runner too, incidentally, though I imagine he doesn't much care about that . . . Except that it's one of Edwin Byler's. But he's not fit to drive anywhere himself, and the races would help to keep him from brooding too much about Grace.'

'Yeah. A passable idea.' Tony grinned.

'Go into the house and see if you can persuade him to let you take him.'

'O.K.' He went off amiably, and I passed the time swinging around the drive on my crutches and peering into the cars parked there. I'd be needing a new one . . . probably choose the same again, though.

I leant against Tony's car and thought about Grace. She'd left on me a fair legacy of bruises from her pinches to add to the crop grown by Oakley. Also my coat would cost a fortune at the invisible menders, and my throat felt like a well developed case of septic tonsils. I looked gloomily down at my plastered leg. The dangers of detection seemed to be twice as high as steeplechasing. With luck, I thought with a sigh, I could now go back to the usual but less frequent form of battery.

Tony came out of the house with Roberta and Jack Roxford. Jack looked dazed, and let Tony help him into the front of the estate car as if his thoughts were miles away. As indeed they probably were.

I scrunched across the gravel towards Roberta.

'Is your neck all right?' I asked.

'Is yours?'

I investigated her cut more closely. It wasn't deep. Little more than an inch long.

'There won't be much of a scar,' I said.

'No,' she agreed.

Her face was close to mine. Her eyes were amber with dark flecks.

'Stay here,' she said abruptly. 'You don't have to go to the races.'

'I've an appointment with Lord Ferth . . . Best to get this business thoroughly wrapped up.'

'I suppose so.' She looked suddenly very tired. She'd had a wearing Saturday morning.

'If you've nothing better to do,' I suggested, 'would you come over tomorrow . . . and cook me some lunch?'

A small smile tugged at her mouth and wrinkled her eyes.

'I fell hopelessly in love with you,' she said, 'when I was twelve.'

'And then it wore off?'

'Yes.'

'Pity,' I said.

Her smile broadened.

'Who is Bobbie?' I asked.

'Bobbie? Oh . . . he's Lord Iceland's son.

'He would be.'

She laughed. 'Father wants me to marry him.'

'That figures.'

'But Father is going to be disappointed.'

'Good,' I said.

'Kelly,' yelled Tony. 'Come on, for Hell's sakes, or I'll be late.'

'Goodbye,' she said calmly. 'See you tomorrow.'

Tony drove to Reading races with due care and attention and Jack Roxford sat sunk in gloomy silence from start to finish. When we stopped in the car park he stepped out of the car and walked dazedly away towards the entrance without a word of thanks or explanation.

Tony watched him go and clicked his tongue. 'That woman isn't worth it.'

'She is, to him,' I said.

Tony hurried off to declare his horses, and I went more slowly through the gate looking out for Lord Ferth.

It felt extraordinary being back on a racecourse. Like being let out of prison. The same people who had looked sideways at me at the Jockeys' Fund dance now slapped me familiarly on the back and said they were delighted to see me. Oh yeah, I thought ungratefully. Never kick a man once he's up.

Lord Ferth was standing outside the weighing room in a knot of people from which he detached himself when he saw me coming.

'Come along to the Stewards' dining-room,' he said. 'We can find a quiet corner there.'

'Can we postpone it until after the third race?' I asked. 'I want my cousin Tony to be there as well, and he has some runners . . .'

'Of course,' he agreed. 'Later would be best for me too, as it happens. After the third, then.'

I watched the first three races with the hunger of an exile returned. Tony's horse, my sometime mount, finished a fast fourth, which augured well for next time out, and Byler's horse won the third. As I hurried round to see how Jack Roxford would make out in the winner's enclosure I almost crashed into Kessel. He looked me over, took in the plaster and crutches, and said nothing at all. I watched his cold expressionless face with one to match. After ramming home the point that he had no intention of apologizing he turned brusquely on his heel and walked away.

'Get that,' Tony said in my ear. 'You could sue him for defamation.'

'He's not worth the effort.'

From Charlie West, too, I'd had much the same reaction. Defiance, slightly sullen variety. I shrugged resignedly. That was my own fault, and only time would tell.

Tony walked with me to the winner's enclosure. Byler was there, beaming. Jack Roxford still looked lost. We watched Byler suggest a celebration drink, and Jack shake his head vaguely as if he hadn't understood.

'Go and fish Jack out,' I said to Tony. 'Tell him you're still looking after him.'

'If you say so, pal.' He obligingly edged through the crowd, took Jack by the elbow, said a few explanatory words to Byler, and steered Jack out.

I joined them and said neutrally, 'This way,' and led them along towards the Stewards' dining-room. They both went through the door, taking off their hats and hanging them on the pegs inside.

The long tables in the Stewards' dining-room had been cleared from lunch and laid for tea, but there was no one in there except Lord Ferth. He shook hands with Tony and Jack and invited them to sit down around one end of a table.

'Kelly . . . ?' he suggested.

'I'll stand,' I said. 'Easier.'

'Well now,' Ferth said, glancing curiously at Tony and Jack, 'You told me, Kelly, that you knew who had framed you and Dexter Cranfield.'

I nodded.

Tony said regretfully, 'Grace Roxford. Jack's wife.'

Jack looked vaguely down at the table cloth and said nothing at all.

Tony explained to Lord Ferth just what had happened at Cranfield's and he looked more and more upset.

'My dear Roxford,' he said uncomfortably, 'I'm so sorry. So very sorry.' He looked up at me. 'One could never have imagined that she . . . that Grace Roxford of all people . . . could have framed you.'

'That's right,' I said mildly. 'She didn't.'

CHAPTER SIXTEEN

BOTH TONY AND JACK sat up as if electrified.

Lord Ferth said, 'But you said . . .' And Tony answered, 'I thought there was no doubt . . . She tried to kill Kelly . . . she was going to kill Cranfield too.'

'She tried to kill me this time,' I agreed. 'But not the time before. It wasn't she who fiddled with my car.'

'Then *who*?' Lord Ferth demanded .

'Her husband.'

Jack stood up. He looked a lot less lost.

I poked Tony on the shoulder with my crutch and he took the hint and stood up too. He was sitting between Jack and the door.

'Sit down, Mr Roxford,' Ferth said authoritatively, and after a pause, slowly, he obeyed.

'That's nonsense,' he said protestingly. 'I didn't touch Kelly's car. No one could have arranged that accident.'

'You couldn't have imagined I would be hit by a train,' I agreed. 'But some sort of smash, yes, definitely.'

'But Grace . . .' began Tony, still bewildered.

'Grace,' I said prosaically, 'Has in most respects displayed exactly opposite qualities to the person who engineered Cranfield's and my suspension. Grace has been wild, accusing, uncontrolled and emotional. The planning which went into getting us warned off was cool, careful, efficient and brutal.'

'Mad people are very cunning,' Tony said doubtfully.

'It wasn't Grace,' I said positively. 'It was Jack.'

There was a pause. Then Jack said in a rising wail, 'Why ever did she have to go to Cranfield's this morning? Why ever couldn't she leave things alone?'

'It wouldn't have done any good,' I said. 'I already knew it was you.'

'That's impossible.'

Ferth cleared his throat. 'I think . . . er . . . you'd better tell us, Kelly, what your grounds are for making this serious accusation.'

'It began,' I said, 'When Dexter Cranfield persuaded Edwin Byler to take his horses away from Roxford and send them to him. Cranfield did no doubt persuade Byler, as Grace maintained, that he was a more highly regarded trainer socially than Roxford. Social standing means a great deal to Mr Cranfield, and he is apt to expect that it does to everyone else. And in Edwin Byler's case, he was very likely right. But Jack had trained Byler's horses from the day he bought his first, and as Byler's fortune and string grew, so did Jack's prosperity and prestige. To lose Byler was to him a total disaster. A return to obscurity. The end of everything. Jack isn't a bad trainer, but he hasn't the personality to make the top ranks. Not without an accident . . . a gift from Heaven . . . like Byler. And you don't find two Bylers in your yard in one lifetime. So almost from the start I wondered about Jack; from as soon as Cranfield told me, two days after the Enquiry, that Byler had been going to transfer his horses. Because I felt such a wrench of regret, you see, that I was not going to ride them . . . and I realized that that was nothing compared to what Jack would have felt if he'd lost them.'

'I didn't feel so bad as that,' said Jack dully.

'I had an open mind,' I said, 'because Pat Nikita had much the same motive, only the other way round. He and Cranfield detest each other. He had been trying to coax Kessel away from Cranfield for years, and getting Cranfield warned off was one way of clinching things. Then there were various people with smaller motives, like Charlie West, who might have hoped to ride Squelch for Nikita if I were out of the way. And there was a big possibility that it was someone else altogether, someone I hadn't come across, whose motive I couldn't even suspect.'

'So why must it be Mr Roxford?' Ferth said.

I took the paper Teddy Dewar had sent me out of my pocket and handed it to him, explaining what it meant.

'That shows a direct link between Oakley and the people in the circles. One of those people is Jack Roxford. He did, you see, know of Oakley's existence. He knew Oakley would agree to provide faked evidence.'

'But . . .' Lord Ferth began.

'Yes, I know,' I said. 'Circumstantial. Then there's this list of people from George Newtonnards.' I gave him the list, and pointed. 'These are the people who definitely knew that Cranfield had backed Cherry Pie with Newtonnards. Again this is not conclusive, because other people might have known, who are not on this list. But that man,' I pointed to the name in Herbie Subbings' list of contacts, 'that man is Grace Roxford's brother, Jack's brother-in-law.'

Ferth looked at me levelly. 'You've taken a lot of trouble.'

'It was taken for me,' I said, 'by Teddy Dewar and his friend, and by George Newtonnards.'

'They acted on your suggestions, though.'

'Yes.'

'Anything else?'

'Well,' I said. 'There are those neatly typed sheets of accusations which were sent to Lord Gowery. So untypical, by the way, of Grace. We could compare the typewriter with Jack's . . . Typewriters are about as distinctive as fingerprints. I haven't had an opportunity to do that yet.'

Jack looked up wildly. The typewriter made sense to him. He hadn't followed the significance of the lists.

Ferth said slowly, 'I obtained from the Stewards' Secretaries the letter which pointed out to them that a disqualified person was living in a racing stable. As far as I remember, the typing is the same as in the original accusations.'

'Very catty, that,' I said. 'More like Grace. Revengeful, and without much point.'

'I never wrote to the Stewards' Secretaries,' Jack said.

'Did Grace?'

He shook his head. I thought perhaps he didn't know. It didn't seem to be of any great importance. I said instead: 'I looked inside the boot of Jack's car this morning, while he was in Mr Cranfield's house. He carries a great big tool kit, including a hand drill.'

'No,' Jack said.

'Yes indeed. Also you have an old grey Volkswagen, the one Grace drove today. That car was seen by the mechanic from my garage when you went to pick over the remains of my car

I imagine you were hoping to remove any tell-tale drill holes which might have led the insurance company to suspect attempted murder, but Derek was there before you. And you either followed him or asked the garage whether he'd taken anything from the wreckage, because you sent David Oakley to my flat to get it back. Oakley didn't know the significance of what he was looking for: A chunk of metal with a hole in it. That was all he knew. He was there to earn a fee.'

'Did he find it?' Ferth asked.

'No. I still have it. Can one prove that a certain drill made a certain hole?'

Ferth didn't know. Jack didn't speak.

'When you heard, at the dance,' I said, 'That I was trying to find out who had framed Cranfield and me, you thought you would get rid of me, in case I managed it. Because if I managed it, you'd lose far more than Byler's horses . . . so while I was talking to Lord Ferth and dancing with Roberta, you were out at the back of the car park rigging up your booby trap. Which,' I added calmly, remembering the blazing hell of the dislocations, 'I find hard to forgive.'

'I'll strangle him,' Tony said forcefully.

'What happens to him,' I shook my head, 'depends on Lord Ferth.'

Ferth regarded me squarely. 'You find him. I deal with him.'

'That was the agreement.'

'To your satisfaction.'

'Yes.'

'And what *is* your satisfaction?'

I didn't know.

Tony moved restlessly, looking at his watch. 'Lord Ferth, Kelly, look, I'm sorry, but I've got a horse to saddle for the last race . . . I'll have to go now.'

'Yes, of course,' said Lord Ferth. 'But we'd all be obliged if you wouldn't talk about what you've learned in here.'

Tony looked startled. 'Sure. If you say so. Not a word.' He stood up and went over to the door. 'See you after,' he said to me. 'You secretive so-and-so.'

As he went out a bunch of Stewards and their wives came in chattering for their tea. Lord Ferth went over to them and exerted the flashing eyes, and they all went into reverse. A waiter who had materialized behind them was stationed outside the door with instructions to send all customers along to the members' tea room.

While this was going on Jack looked steadfastly down at the tablecloth and said not a word. I didn't feel like chatting to him idly either. He'd cost me too much.

Lord Ferth came briskly back and sat down.

'Now then, Roxford,' he said in his most businesslike way, 'We've heard Kelly's accusations. It's your turn now to speak up in your defence.'

Jack slowly lifted his head. The deep habitual lines of worry were running with sweat.

'It was someone else.' His voice was dead.

'It certainly wasn't Grace,' I said, 'Because Lord Gowery was quite clear that the person who tried to blackmail him on the telephone was a man.' So was the person who had got at Charlie West a man, or so he'd said.

Jack Roxford jerked.

'Yes, Roxford, we know about Lord Gowery.' Ferth said.

'You *can't* . . .'

'You belong to the same club,' I said assertively, as if I knew.

For Jack Roxford, too, the thought of that club was the lever which opened the floodgates. Like Gowery before him he broke into wretched pieces.

'You don't understand . . .'

'Tell us then,' Ferth said. 'And we'll try.'

'Grace . . . we . . . I . . . Grace didn't like . . .' He petered out.

I gave him a shove. 'Grace liked her sex natural and wouldn't stand for what you wanted.'

He gulped. 'Soon after we were married we were having rows all the time, and I hated that. I loved her, really I did. I've always loved her. And I felt . . . all tangled up . . . she didn't understand that when I beat her it was because of love . . . she said she'd leave me and divorce me for cruelty . . . so I asked a girl I'd known . . . a street girl, who didn't mind . . . I mean . . . she let you, if you paid well enough . . . if I could go on seeing her . . . but she said she'd given that up now . . . but there was a club in London . . . and I went there . . . and it was a terrific relief . . . and then I was all right with Grace . . . but of course we didn't . . . well, hardly ever . . . but somehow . . . we could go on being married.'

Lord Ferth looked revolted.

'I couldn't believe it at first,' Jack said more coherently, 'When I saw Lord Gowery there. I saw him in the street, just outside. I thought it was just a coincidence. But then, one night, inside the club, I was sure it was him, and I saw him again in the street another time . . . but I didn't say anything. I mean, how could I? And anyway, I knew how he felt . . . you don't go there unless you must . . . and you can't keep away.'

'How long have you known that Lord Gowery went to the same club?' I asked.

'Oh . . . two or three years. A long time. I don't know exactly.'

'Did he know you were a member?'

'No. He hadn't a clue. I spoke to him once or twice on the racecourse about official things . . . He didn't have any idea.'

'And then,' Ferth said thoughtfully, 'You read that he had been appointed in Colonel Midgley's place to officiate at the Cranfield-Hughes Enquiry, and you saw what you thought was a good chance of getting Cranfield out of racing, and keeping Byler's horses yourself.'

Jack sat huddled in his chair, not denying it.

'And when Lord Gowery declined to be blackmailed, you couldn't bear to give up the idea, and you set about faking evidence that would achieve your ends.'

A long silence. Then Jack said in a thick disjointed voice, 'Grace minded so much . . . about Cranfield taking our horses. She went on and on about it . . . morning, noon and night. Couldn't stop. Talk, talk, talk. All the time. Saying she'd like to kill Cranfield . . . and things like that. I mean . . . she's always been a bit nervy . . . a bit strung up . . . but Cranfield was upsetting her . . . I got a bit frightened for her sometimes, she was that violent about him . . . Well, it was really because of that that I tried to get Cranfield warned off . . . I mean, he was better warned off than Grace trying to kill him.'

'Did you truly believe she would?' I asked.

'She was ranting about it all the time . . . I didn't know if she really would . . . but I was so afraid . . . I didn't want her to get into trouble . . . dear dear Grace . . . I wanted to help her . . . and make things right again . . . so I set about it . . . and it wasn't too difficult really, not once I'd set my mind to it.'

Ferth gave me a twisted smile. I gave him a similar one back and reflected that marriage could be a deadly institution. Grace's strung up state would have been aggravated by the strain of living with a sexually odd man, and Jack would have felt guilty about it and wanted to make it up to her. Neither of them had been rationally inclined, and the whole situation had boiled up claustrophobically inside their agonized private world. Having dear Grace harping on endlessly would have driven many a stronger man to explosive action: but Jack couldn't desert her, because he had to stay with his horses, and he couldn't drive her away because he loved her. The only way he'd seen of silencing his wife had been to ruin Cranfield.

'Why me?' I said, trying to keep out the bitterness. 'Why me too?'

'Eh?' He squinted at me, half focusing. 'You . . . well . . . I haven't anything against you personally . . . But I thought it was the only way to make it a certainty . . . Cranfield couldn't have swindled that race without Squelch's jockey being in the know.'

'That race was no swindle,' I said.

'Oh . . . I know that. Those stupid Oxford Stewards . . . still, they gave me such an opportunity . . . when I heard about Lord Gowery being in charge. And then, when I'd fixed up with Charlie West and Oakley . . . Grace's brother told me, just told me casually, mind you, that his bookmaker had told him that Cranfield had backed Cherry Pie, and do you know what, I couldn't stop laughing. Just like Grace, I felt . . . dead funny, it was, that he really had backed Cherry Pie . . .'

'What was that about Charlie West?' Ferth said sharply.

'I paid him . . . to say Kelly pulled Squelch back. I telephoned and asked him . . . if Kelly ever did anything like that . . . and he said once, in a novice 'chase, Kelly had said, "O.K. Brakes on, chaps," and I told him to say Kelly had said that in the Lemonfizz Cup, because it sounded so convincing, didn't it, saying something Kelly really had said . . .'

Ferth looked at me accusingly. 'You shielded West.'

I shrugged ruefully. Jack paid no attention: didn't hear.

He went on miserably: 'Grace was all right before the dance. She was wonderfully calm again, after Cranfield was warned off. And then Edwin Byler said that we would be keeping his horses for always . . . and we were happy . . . in our way . . . and then we heard . . . that Kelly was at the dance . . . saying he'd been framed . . . and was just on the point of finding out who . . . and Grace saw Cranfield's daughter and just boiled over all over again, nearly as bad as before . . . and I thought . . . if Kelly was dead . . . it would be all right again . . .'

Ferth slowly shook his head. The reasoning which had led Jack Roxford step by step from misfortune to crime defeated him.

'I thought he wouldn't feel anything,' Jack said. 'I thought that you just blacked out suddenly from carbon monoxide. I thought it would be like going to sleep . . . he wouldn't know about it. Just wouldn't wake up.'

'You didn't drill a big enough hole,' I said without irony. 'Not enough gas came through at once to knock me out.'

'I couldn't find a large enough tube,' he said with macabre sense. 'Had to use a piece I had. It was a bit narrow. That was why.'

'I see,' I said gravely. So close. Not a few inches from the express train. One eighth of an inch extra in the tube's diameter would have done it.

'And you went to look for the piece of manifold, afterwards?'

'Yes . . . but you know about that. I was furious with Oakley for not finding it . . . he said he tried to make you tell, but you wouldn't . . . and I said it didn't surprise me . . .'

'Why didn't you ask *him* to kill me?' I said matter-of-factly.

'Oh, I did. He said he didn't kill. He said he would dispose of the body if I did it, but he never did the job himself. Not worth it, he said.'

That sounded like the authentic Oakley. Straight from the agent's mouth.

'But you couldn't risk it?' I suggested.

'I didn't have any chance. I mean . . . I didn't like to leave Grace alone much . . . she was so upset . . . and then, you were in hospital . . . and then you went back to your flat . . . and I did try to shift you out into the open somewhere . . .'

'You did write to the Stewards' Secretaries,' Ferth exclaimed. 'After all.'

'Yes . . . but it was too late . . . wasn't it . . . She really meant it . . . poor Grace, poor Grace . . . why did I let her go out . . . But she seemed so much better this morning . . . and now . . . and now . . .' His face screwed up and turned red as he tried not to cry. The thought of Grace as he'd last seen her was too much for him. The tears rolled. He sniffed into a handkerchief.

I wondered how he would have felt if he'd seen Grace as I'd seen her. But probably the uncritical love he had would have survived even that.

'Just sit here quietly a moment, Roxford,' Lord Ferth directed, and he himself stood up and signed for me to walk with him over to the door. 'So what do we do with him?' he said.

'It's gone too far now,' I said reluctantly, 'To be entirely hushed up. And he's if anything more dangerous than Grace . . . She will live, and he will very likely see everything for ever in terms of her happiness. Anyone who treats her badly in any way could end up as a victim of his scheming. End up ruined

... or dead. People like nurses ... or relations ... or even people like me, who did her no harm at all. Anybody ...'

Ferth said, 'You seem to understand his mind. I must say that I don't. But what you say makes sense. We cannot just take away his licence and leave it at that ... It isn't a racing matter any more. But Lord Gowery ...'

'Lord Gowery will have to take his chance,' I said without satisfaction. 'Very likely you can avoid busting open his reputation ... but it's much more important to stop Jack Roxford doing the same sort of thing again.'

'Yes.' He said. 'It is.' He spread out his hands sideways in a pushing gesture as if wanting to step away from the decision. 'All this is so *distressing*.'

I looked down the room at Jack, a huddled defeated figure with nervous eyes and an anxious forehead. He was picking at the tablecloth with his fingers, folding it into senseless little pleats. He didn't look like a villain. No hardened criminal. Just a tenacious little man with a fixed idea, to make up to dear Grace for being what he was.

Nothing was more useless than sending him to prison, and nothing could do him more harm: yet that, I imagined, was where he would go. Putting his body in a little cage wouldn't straighten the kinks in his mind. The system, for men like him, was screwy.

He stood up slowly and walked unsteadily towards us.

'I suppose,' he said without much emotion, 'That you are going to get the police. I was wondering ... please ... don't tell them about the club ... I won't say Lord Gowery goes there ... I won't tell anybody ever ... I never really wanted to ... it wouldn't have done any good, would it? I mean, it wouldn't have kept those horses in my yard ... wouldn't have made a scrap of difference ... So do you think anyone need know about ... the club?'

'No,' said Ferth with well disguised relief. 'They need not.'

A faint smile set up a rival set of creases to the lines of anxiety. 'Thank you.' The smile faded away. The lost look deepened. 'How long ... do you think I'll get?'

Ferth moved uncomfortably. 'No point in worrying about that until you have to.'

'You could probably halve it,' I said.

'How?' He was pathetically hopeful. I flung him the rope.

'By giving evidence at another trial I have in mind, and taking David Oakley down with you.'

PART THREE

MARCH EPILOGUE

YESTERDAY I rode Breadwinner in the Cheltenham Gold
Cup.

A horse of raw talent with more future than past. A shambling
washy chestnut carrying his head low. No one's idea of equine
beauty.

Old Strepson watched him slop round the parade ring and
said with a sigh, 'He looks half asleep.'

'Hughes will wake him up,' Cranfield said condescendingly.

Cranfield stood in the chill March sunshine making his usual
good stab at arrogance. The mean calculating lines round his
mouth seemed to have deepened during the past month, and
his manner to me was if anything more distant, more master-
servant, than ever before. Roberta said she had told him that I
had in some way managed to get our licences back, but he saw
no reason to believe her and preferred the thought of divine
intervention.

Old Strepson said conversationally, 'Kelly says Breadwinner
was a late foal and a late developer, and won't reach his true
strength until about this time next year.'

Cranfield gave me a mouth-tightening mind-your-own-business
glare, and didn't seem to realize that I'd given him an alibi if
the horse didn't win and built him up into one heck of a good
trainer if it did. Whatever low opinion Cranfield held of me, I
reciprocated it in full.

Farther along the parade ring stood a silent little group of
Kessel, Pat Nikita, and their stable jockey, Al Roach. They
were engaged in running poor old Squelch, and their interest
lay not so fiercely in winning as in finishing at all costs in
front of Breadwinner. Kessel himself radiated so much hatred
that I thought it was probably giving him a headache. Hating
did that. The day I found it out, I gave up hating.

Grace's hatred-headache must have been unbearable. . . .

Grace's recovery was still uncertain. Ferth had somehow
wangled the best available psychiatrist on to her case, and had
also arranged for him to see Jack. Outside the weighing room

when I had arrived, he had jerked his head for me to join him, and told me what the psychiatrist had reported.

'He says Jack is sane according to legal standards, and will have to stand trial. He wouldn't commit himself about Grace's chances. He did say, though, that from all points of view their enforced separation was a godsend. He said he thought their only chance of leading fairly normal lives in the future was to make the separation total and permanent. He said a return to the same circumstances could mean a repeat of the whole cycle.'

I looked at Ferth gloomily. 'What a cold, sad, depressing solution.'

'You never know,' he said optimistically. 'Once they get over it, they might both feel . . . well . . . released.'

I smiled at him. He said abruptly, 'Your outlook is catching, dammit . . . How about that dinner?'

'Any time,' I said.

'Tomorrow, then? Eight o'clock. The Caprice, round the corner from the Ritz . . . The food's better there than at my club.'

'Fine,' I said.

'And you can tell me how the police are getting on with David Oakley . . .'

I'd had the Birmingham police on my telephone and doorstep for much of the past week. They had almost fallen on my neck and sobbed when I first went to them with enough to make an accusation stick, and had later promised to deliver to me, framed, one of the first fruits of their search warrant: a note from Cranfield to Jack Roxford dated two years earlier, thanking him for not bidding him up at an auction after a selling race and enclosing a cheque for fifty pounds. Across the bottom of the page Cranfield had written:

'As agreed. Thanks. D.C.'

It was the note Oakley had photographed in my flat.

Supplied by Roxford, who had suggested the photograph.

Kept by Oakley, as a hold over Roxford.

The police also told me that Jack Roxford had drawn six hundred pounds in new notes out of his bank during the two weeks before the Enquiry, and David Oakley had paid three hundred of the same notes into his own account five days later.

Clever, slippery Mr Oakley had been heard to remark that he regretted not having slaughtered Kelly Hughes.

The bell rang for the jockeys to mount, and Cranfield and old Strepson and I walked over to where Breadwinner waited.

The one jockey missing from the day's proceedings was Charlie West, whose licence had been suspended for the rest of the season. And it was only thanks to Hughes's intervention, Ferth had told him forcefully, that he hadn't got his deserts and been warned off for life. Whether Charlie West would feel an atom of gratitude was another matter.

I swung up easily on to Breadwinner and fitted my right foot carefully into the stirrup. A compromise between me and the orthopod had seen the plaster off seven days previously, but the great surgeon's kind parting words had been, 'You haven't given that leg enough time and if it dislocates again it's your own bloody fault.'

I had told him that I couldn't afford to have Cranfield engage another jockey for Breadwinner with all the horse's future races at stake. Old Strepson was the grateful type who didn't dislodge a jockey who had won for him, and if some other jockey won the Gold Cup on Breadwinner I would lose the mount for life: and it was only this argument which had grudgingly brought out the saw.

I gathered up the reins and walked the horse quietly round the ring while everyone sorted themselves out into the right order for the parade down the course. Apart from the Grand National, the Cheltenham Gold Cup was the biggest steeplechase of the year. In prestige, probably the greatest of all. All the stars turned out for it, meeting each other on level terms. Bad horses hadn't a hope.

There were nine runners. Breadwinner was the youngest, Squelch the most experienced, and a bad tempered grey called Ironclad the favourite.

Al Roach, uninfected by Kessel, lined up beside me at the start and gave me his usual wide friendly Irish grin. 'Now Kelly my bhoy,' he said, 'tell me how you ride this little fellow, now.'

'You want to be warned off?' I said.

He chuckled. 'What's the owner got against you, Kelly me bhoy?'

'I was right and he was wrong, and he can't forgive that.'

'Peculiar fellow, he is, that Kessel . . .'

The tapes went up and we were away. Three and a quarter miles, twenty-one jumps, two whole circuits of the course.

Nothing much happened on the first circuit. No horses fell and no jockeys got excited, and going past the stands and outward bound for the second time a fair sized sheet would have covered the lot. The next mile sorted the men from the boys, and the bunch flattened out into a relentless, thundering, muscle-straining procession in which hope and sweat and tactics merged into a rushing private world of conflict. Speed . . . jumping at near disaster rate . . . gambling on the horse's co-ordination . . . stretching your own . . . a race like the Gold Cup showed you what you were made of . . .

Coming to the second last fence, Ironclad was leading Squelch by three lengths which could have been ten, and he set himself right with all the time in the world. Squelch followed him over, and, four lengths behind, Breadwinner strained forward to be third.

Between the last two fences the status quo was unchanged, Breadwinner making no impression on Squelch, nor Squelch on Ironclad. Oh well, I thought resignedly. Third. That wasn't really too bad for such a young horse. One couldn't have everything. And there was always Pound Postage in the Grand National, two weeks on Saturday . . .

Ironclad set himself right for the last fence, launched himself muscularly into the air, crossed the birch with a good foot of air beneath him . . . and pitched forward on to his nose on landing.

I couldn't believe it. Shook up Breadwinner with a bang of renewed hope and drove him into the last fence for the jump of his young life.

Squelch was over it first, of course. Squelch the sure-footed trained-to-the-minute familiar old rascal . . . Irony of ironies, to be beaten to the Gold Cup by Squelch.

Breadwinner did the best he could to catch him, and I saw that as in the Lemonfizz, Squelch was dying from tiredness. Length by length my gangling chestnut pegged back the gap, straining, stretching, quivering to get past . . . but the winning post was too near . . . it was no good . . . there wasn't time . . .

Al Roach looked round to see who was pressing him. Saw me. Knew that Breadwinner was of all others the one he had to beat. Was seized with panic. If he had sat still, he would have won by two lengths. Instead, he picked up his whip and hit Squelch twice down the flank.

You stupid ass, I thought breathlessly. He hates that. He'll stop. He always stops if you hit him . . .

Squelch's tail swished in fury. His rhythmic stride broke up into bumps. He shook his head violently from side to side.

I saw Al's desperate face as Breadwinner caught him . . . and the winning post was there and gone in a flash . . . and neither of us knew even then which had won.

The photograph gave it to Breadwinner by a nostril. And if I got booed by the crowd after the Lemonfizz they made up for it after the Gold Cup.

Kessel, predictably, was purple with fury, and he seemed on the brink of explosion when someone remarked loudly that Squelch would have won if Hughes had been riding him. I laughed. Kessel looked almost as murderous as Grace.

Old Strepson was pale with emotion but even the Gold Cup did not raise much observable joy in Cranfield; and I found out later that Edwin Byler had just told him he wouldn't be sending him his horses after all. Grace's psychiatrist had written to say that Grace's ultimate sanity might depend on Cranfield not having the horses, and Byler said he felt he owed the Roxfords something . . . sorry and all that, but there it was.

Roberta with her mother had been there patting Breadwinner in the winner's enclosure, and when I came out of the weighing room twenty minutes later after changing into street clothes, she was leaning against the rails there, waiting.

'You're limping,' she said calmly.

'Unfit, that's all.'

'Coffee?' she suggested.

'Yes,' I said.

She walked sedately ahead of me into the coffee room. Her copper hair still shone after she'd stepped out of the sunshine, and I liked the simple string-coloured coat which went underneath it.

I bought her some coffee and we sat at a little plastic topped table and looked at the litter left by the last occupants; empty coffee cups, plates with crumbs, cigarette butts, and a froth-lined beer glass. Roberta packed them coolly to one side and ignored them.

'Winning and losing,' she said. 'That's what it's all about.'

'Racing?'

'Life.'

I looked at her.

She said, 'Today is marvellous, and being warned off was terrible. I suppose everything goes on like that . . . up and down . . . always.'

'I suppose so,' I agreed.

'I've learned a lot, since the Enquiry.'

'So have I . . . about you.'

'Father says I must remember your background . . .'

'That's true,' I said. 'You must.'

'Father's mind has chains on. Iron bars in his soul. His head's chock-a-block with ideas half a century out of date.' She mimicked my own words with pompous mischief.

I laughed. 'Roberta . . .'

'Please tell me . . .' She hesitated. '. . . At the level crossing . . . when you called me Rosalind . . . was it her you wanted?'

'No,' I said slowly. 'It was you . . . in her place.'

She sighed contentedly.

'That's all right, then,' she said. 'Isn't it?'

THE INNOCENT BYSTANDERS

James Munro

*'The Innocent Bystanders' is published
by Herbert Jenkins Ltd.*

CHAPTER ONE

IT WAS TIME TO GO, and two by two the men embraced, looking in wonder into each other's faces, trying to read there what they felt: tension, fear, and an overwhelming joy. Zhelkov went first, in his hand the little packet of poison that Goldfarb and Kaplan had prepared. His task was dangerous, because when he fed the dogs a guard watched him, careful to see that he stole none of their food. But Zhelkov was dexterous, and the poison found its way into both food and water. He was very gentle with the dogs that night, fondling them, calling them by name, till the guard ordered him out and slouched off to his hut, and Zhelkov sat by himself and watched the dogs slump down and sleep. They always did, after their meal, but this time they did not finish their food.

Klein, Goldfarb, and Kaplan came next. They had the wire-cutters Zimma had made, and the skill to use them. Over and over they had practised on baling wire tougher than the obstacle in front of them. They sat by the wire and waited as the sky darkened. Then Moskowitz and Avramov brought out their mattresses and began to beat them. This was a common enough sight in the camp, where fleas and bedbugs abounded, but this time there was a special reason. The mattresses would protect them against the wire. Next it was Daniel, followed by Asimov and Gabrilovich. They were the rearguard, and in their pockets were the knives Zimma had made for them. Daniel had picked the other two because they were the fittest and hardest of the ten, and he had trained them well. They left the hut and moved, past the power-house and the guardroom towards their huts. The sky was dark now, and as they passed the stables the light came on, ponies stamped, and there was the chink of harness. In another five minutes the signal would sound for them to go inside their huts, and a guard would go to release the dogs. Daniel stepped out quicker. When the lights went out each man had to be as near a guard as he could, without causing suspicion. Without the guards' carbines they would have no chance at all, and this work mustn't be wasted, he thought. *Must not. And yet I feel it. Something is wrong. Where is Zimma?*

Zimma had prayed once more, alone, and God had heard him and clearly answered. When Zimma had heard all that God had

341

to say, he rose, picked up the axe that was in the toolshed, and limped towards the power-house. As he did so, Moskowitz and Avramov rolled up their mattresses and walked towards the wire, hanging on the outskirts of the crowd that was already moving towards the huts. Zimma kept on walking, a man who had been sent to chop wood and was returning his axe, and nobody noticed, or cared. When he reached the guard, Zimma went straight up to him, mumbling a question. The guard motioned him forward impatiently, and Zimma advanced two more steps, then swung the axe, and the blade bit deep into his head, severing the back of the skull. Zimma picked up the guard's carbine and turned. After a moment of incredulous quiet, prisoners were running, yelling, to their huts, away from the power-house to which the guards were racing. Zimma shot the first two guards and stepped into the power-house, a prayer on his lips. He was very happy. Quickly he found what he wanted, and limped forward. Hear ye, Israel, he said aloud, and swung the axe for the last time.

The darkness when it came was total, but already the men with the wire-cutters had moved into position, the men with the mattresses close behind. The pandemonium around them was so complete that men had eyes only for their own huts, thought only of the terrible revenge that would be taken for the power-house sentry. When Zimma fired, Daniel attacked his guard, who was trying to push his way through a crowd of prisoners to reach the source of the shots. Asimov and Gabrilovich followed his lead. Zimma had given them a wonderful opportunity, and they took it. Daniel's hands snapped the life from the guard as if it were thread. Gabrilovich and Asimov used their knives. All three men killed quickly, but without pity. The one Asimov killed had been his lover.

They took the carbines and ammunition pouches and grouped together. No one stopped them; every face they saw was filled with incredulous horror. Then the lights died and they raced to the wire, the mattresses went down and they were through, running, Daniel in the lead, feeling his way along the track that he had memorized, eyes closed, for the last three weeks. They found the clearing in the forest and lay panting as Daniel called out their names. Asimov, Avramov, Daniel, Gabrilovich, Goldfarb, Klein, Moskowitz, Zhelkov. Of Kaplan there was no sign.

Goldfarb said at last, 'I think he knew he had no chance. He did this to help us.'

Daniel heaved up the great stone that covered their hoarded food.

'I hope so,' he said, 'but there is something wrong. I know it.'

Quickly he gave each man his share of the food, then put into each hand a nugget of gold.

'We split up now?' Moskowitz asked.

Daniel said, 'In a moment. First let me have the weapons.'

He distributed them carefully. The best shot in each team got a carbine, the rest had knives. Gabrilovich led a team, and so did Klein. Daniel's team of four was reduced to two: Zimma dead, Kaplan missing.

'Go now,' said Daniel. 'Asimov and I will be the rearguard.'

They said no word, and it was dark still, but their silence was filled with meaning. Then Gabrilovich and Klein left, and the others followed.

'What do we do?' Asimov asked.

'We move north,' said Daniel.

'North? But that's the wrong way.'

Daniel said nothing for a moment, then: 'We'll draw off the pursuit,' he said, and smiled.

'You're a good man,' Asimov said.

Daniel remembered the jingle of harness in the stable. The ponies had been saddled and ready even before the break-out. No point in going into all that with Asimov; not now. The boy admired him too much.

A squadron of guards, mounted on ponies, overtook Gabrilovich's team before dawn and killed them all at a loss of a man and two ponies. It took them longer to find Klein's team, because they had lost their route, and when they did, Klein's team fought hard. The guards wanted one prisoner at least, but in the end only Zhelkov was left alive, and he died of wounds on the way back. The guards lost two more men. Shortly afterwards the Uzbhek commandant was shot by firing squad, and his second-in-command, who had led the pursuit, was promoted in his place. For six months Kaplan, Daniel, and Asimov were posted missing: after that they were presumed dead.

To die in Volochanka is not perhaps such a terrible thing: to survive is infinitely worse. Volochanka is special. It is designed, as Hell was, for the fallen angels, and like Hell's its final torture is despair. The achievement of the ten was that they faced despair, and did not let it defeat them. Gabrilovich began it, with the kind of accident that only later they learned to recognize as the hand of God. Gabrilovich had been a mining engineer, and worked in the coal-mine. It was part of his rehabilitation; learning how the miners themselves lived and worked and suffered, so that if society again found him acceptable, he, the intellectual, would know what workers must endure as a result of his decisions. His rehabilitation consisted of hauling a truck loaded with coal for fourteen hours a day from the face to the shaft. Zimma helped him. Zimma had been a doctor, specializing in survival techniques. For three years he had worked on the training of astronauts. They had hauled the trucks together for days, collapsed like exhausted animals in their rest periods, wolfed their appalling food at noonday, and talked hardly at all. Talk was dangerous, it led to nostalgia, and nostalgia only increased the just-bearable weight of suffering that each man bore. Then one night Gabrilovich had a dream: it re-created vividly the new suit his father had bought him for his bar-mitzvah, and the smells of the food his mother had cooked, the delicate dry flavour of Crimean wine. Gabrilovich wanted very much to share the weight of that dream. It was too much to carry alone. He had looked at Zimma that noon, gulping his luke-warm soup, dividing up his bread—Zimma always saved some of his bread, and Gabrilovich hated him for it—then he had spoken the words.

'Zimma, forgive my asking, but are you Jewish?'

Zimma stared at him, incredulous. He was transported back immediately to an Embassy party in Stockholm. He had worn a suit he had bought that morning, he remembered, a dark rich blue that exactly matched the pattern on his tie. A silk tie made in Italy. There was a young Swede there, called Nils, who had been to Washington and told American stories in English. And one of them had been about the millionaire who had lost all his money in the depression. His wife had left him, his children disowned him, his house and cars were taken away, and he had nothing. One day he stood in the breadline waiting for a hand-out. It was a bitter day in February and he had no overcoat, so to keep himself warm he, who had had millions, wrapped himself in old newspapers, picked up at random from trash bins, and one of them was the *Jewish Chronicle*. As he stood waiting, in line, a Cadillac drew up by the kerb and its chauffeur opened the door to a Jewish lady, snug in chinchilla, secure in diamonds, who walked down the line and gave each man a quarter. When she got to the former millionaire she saw the *Jewish Chronicle* wrapped across his chest and:

'Forgive me for asking,' she said, 'but are you Jewish?'

'Jesus,' the former millionaire said. 'That's all I needed.'

And Zimma had remembered, totally, completely, the party,

his suit, his tie, the young Swede and his story: and he had laughed. It was the first time anybody had laughed in that coal-mine, except a guard. It was a beginning.

At first it had been enough that there were two of them. They had begun by exchanging biographies, but from the start the nostalgia was carefully rationed. They had concentrated more on the fact of their Jewishness, and how much it had contributed to their being in the camp, even after the terrify-ing old madman had died in Moscow, convinced till the last that Jewish doctors were poisoning him. Then Avramov began to eat with them, and he too began to talk. Avramov had lectured on political science in Riga. It had been Zimma who brought in Moskovitz, and then Avramov reported that Daniel, who lived in his hut, would like to join, but Daniel worked in the forest. He could not come and talk in the mine. Daniel was also the camp's millionaire. He had been a soldier, and had risen to the rank of major. He was strong and ruthless, and had somehow stored away a little hoard of gold. One day Avramov brought word that Daniel would donate some of his gold to hiring a meeting-place. Moskovitz, a former lawyer, sought an interview with the com-mandant of his sector of the camp. The commandant had first beaten Moskovitz, who expected it. The commandant, an Uzbhek, always beat prisoners who asked for interviews. But in the end he agreed. They could meet for an hour once a week. The place they were given was a toolshed: the entirely unofficial rent a hundred roubles a month. The limit of their membership was to be ten: a number Moskovitz accepted at once. It was the number of the Minyan. But they said nothing of religion. Not then.

Daniel brought a young poet with him, and the poet, Asimov, suggested Kaplan, an agronomist. Zimma produced Goldfarb, another doctor, and then Klein the singer and Zhelkov the psycho-logist appeared. That closed the list. By then other Jews in the camp had heard about them, and begged to join, but they would accept no more. It was the other Jews who called them the Minyan: the minimum number of Jewish men who must meet together before a service can be held. The ten.

At their first meetings they talked about Communism. Avramov lectured, and the rest asked questions, dialectically pure questions about the dangerous fallacy of Israel and the gratifying decline in Judaic religion; questions one could address to the hidden microphone that Gabrilovich found within minutes of entering the hut. After four weeks the microphone was withdrawn: the Uzbhek had found the tapes both boring and pathetic. Obviously these men hoped to have their sentences reduced by proving how deserving of rehabilitation they were. But the Uzbhek knew they would never be released.

So did they. When the microphone went they talked about the world as it should be: not as it was. Avramov told them how the world need never hunger, Zhelkov told them how the human mind could develop into an instrument beyond their comprehension; Kaplan how the desert in Israel could blossom, quite literally, like a rose. Asimov told them stories, Klein sang. Without books or writing materials they created something new with their voices: part seminar, part magazine. Then Gabrilovich told them about survival, their own: how to hoard their food, their sleep, their strength, to give them the best possible chance to avoid the terror of the hospital and a slow but certain death. It was Daniel, always the bravest, who asked the question: How many of us want to survive? To their surprise, their joy, they found they all did, so long as they could meet together, and that night Klein prayed. He alone was Orthodox, he alone knew the words, but that night when Klein prayed they all prayed with him, and from him took lessons in their own religion.

Daniel let two more weeks go by before he talked of escape. He had never spoken before, and at first they did not want to hear him, but Daniel had two persuasive arguments: his gold rented their meeting-place, now, inevitably, nicknamed the synagogue, and on escape he was the expert, and a rule of their society was always to listen to the expert. He disarmed them at once by saying that it was inevitable that most of them would fail, but even they would achieve the reward of a quick death. For the others, the successful ones, there would be a chance to get out of the country, and if they succeeded in that, too, they could tell of their suffering and contribute to the arrival of the world as it should be. That was a debt they would owe to God. Asimov agreed at once: he was by far the youngest, and the enormous odds frightened him least. With the others it took time, but in the end they all agreed, even Kaplan, who at fifty had no chance at all. Two things persuaded them: the fact that it was a moral—even a religious—duty, and the fact that if they failed, as most of them would, death was their only punishment, and death, so long as it came quickly, was the only release that would ease them once the Minyan was disbanded.

Even so, the magnitude of their task, when they began to examine it, appalled them. The camp was at Volochanka, two hundred miles inside the Arctic circle. In its bitter winter no human being could survive outside the camp, in summer the guards were doubled, dogs roamed the spaces between the huts all night, and searchlights played at random: without predictable patterns. There were, besides, two tangles of barbed wire and machine-guns mounted at each corner of the camp's perimeter. The guards, armed with tommy-guns and clubs, used skis in winter and mongolian ponies in summer. And it was all waste; all display. Until the ten men began plotting together, none of the prisoners, even the crazy ones, had even thought of escaping. There was nowhere to escape to.

They began by nourishing and training their bodies. Daniel taught them how to exercise, Klein how to develop their breathing, Gabrilovich how to work their muscles to the utmost limit of their capacity. They pooled all their possessions except Daniel's gold: that would be needed after their escape—and used then to buy food. They were ruthless about this: when food could not be bought it was stolen, and to steal prisoners' food at Volochanka meant agonizing death at the hands of other prisoners, if they were caught. Here too the Mosaic law operated. A life for a life. To take a man's food *was* to take his life. But they succeeded, and grew strong. Goldfarb taught them hygiene, and they survived the wave of typhus that swept the camp in the spring. Chance alone had kept them alive as a group through the January influenza epidemic, and they thanked God for it. Asimov developed into a bold and cunning thief, and stole worn-out tools, hinges, screws, that Zimma patiently transformed into wire-cutters and weapons. That winter too a guard fell in love with him, and Asimov submitted and brought his presents into the common pool to buy food. The doctors sold their skill, and that too brought in money. Kaplan found a patch of ground and grew flowers in it and the camp thought he was crazy as the summer slowly waned, the nights grew shorter, and almost disappeared.

The break was planned for July. There were only two hours of darkness in Siberia then, and Kaplan's flowers had reached the state they needed. Nightshade, most of it, but there were other ingredients. One day he picked them all, as the camp jeered, and let them wither, then he and Goldfarb set to work extracting the poison that would deal with the dogs. It was Zhelkov who fed the dogs. They loved him. Whatever he fed them, they would eat . . . Zimma had his own plans to deal with the power cable. They might work, and they might not—insulation was impossible even to steal, but Zimma had agreed to tackle the job, and the risks were his own. God might yet let him live. They had their escape route planned, their rallying point in the forest that Daniel had mapped out for them already memorized, their hopes and prayers centred on a boat that might yet take them to Vaaso, in Norway, eight hundred miles away. Then Zimma cut his leg in the mine, and he knew that he, who by his laughter had started the movement, would not see it through to the end. The cut was not serious, but it turned septic and there were no medicines. It grew worse and he found it harder to work, his strength faded. But every day until the escape he staggered to work. On the last three days he gave the others his food. And he was happy. God had been generous. Even if He had decided not to let Zimma live, at least he had simplified the problem of cutting the power supply.

On the night of the break nine of them had assembled in the hut and waited for Kaplan, whose job it was to bring the poison for the dogs. This they needed desperately, but even more they needed his presence. Without him they were not ten: there could be no ritual prayer. It was strange how important prayer was to them. Zhelkov had lectured on it once, not stating a theory, but verbalizing the question that nagged in all their minds, except the orthodox Klein's: why do we need the prayers when we none of us believe in God? They had decided at last that the answer was in their Jewishness, which the ritual, the prayers, the Hebrew tongue, all made manifest. But there was more than that, and they knew it, though what that 'more' was they never could define. To the end the question nagged at some of them, though Zimma, Klein, and Daniel joined Kaplan in his faith. But now, all alike, believer and non-believer, waited for Kaplan and their prayers.

He came in at last and they moved towards him in a wave of impatience and relief. What had delayed him? Was anything wrong? Why did he have to be late on this night of all nights? It was Daniel who called them to order. Daniel was leader now. He took Kaplan to the window and examined him in its light. Beside Daniel's huge, slab-muscled body, Kaplan's wiry toughness looked frail. His face was grey and there was a bruise already darkening his cheekbone.

'Tell it,' said Daniel.

'I was bringing the poison,' Kaplan said, ' and a guard stopped me.'

'He found it?' Klein asked. Daniel motioned him to silence.

'He wanted me to fetch water. I was too slow for him. He

hit me—and kicked me. Here.' He pressed his hands to his stomach. 'Daniel—I don't think I can do it.'

'You must,' said Daniel. 'Each man has his place. You know that. Without you we cannot go.'

'I can stay behind and help Zimma,' Kaplan said.

'Then you will die.'

'Of course,' said Kaplan.

Daniel turned to Goldfarb. 'Look at his stomach,' he said.

Goldfarb's hands were deft and tender as he looked. The bruise was enormous and they had nothing for it.

'It hurts,' Kaplan whimpered.

'Does it hurt too much to pray?' Daniel asked, and Kaplan stood then, and Klein led them in prayer.

When they had done, Daniel sat down beside the older man, and his voice was gentle. 'Kaplan,' he said, 'it must be tonight. We are ready *now*. Tomorrow and every day that follows, little by little our courage will go. Our food will be found, our tools will be discovered. It has to be tonight. And please do not stay behind with Zimma. It is brave, but it is also foolish. If you want to die, volunteer for the wire.' Kaplan bent his head.

'Please do not hate me,' he said.

'How can I hate you? How can any of us? We need you, Kaplan.'

Then Kaplan said, 'Very well. I will come,' and the others crowded round to thank, to praise, and Daniel gave him some vodka, the only painkiller they had, from his carefully hoarded store. Kaplan raised his glass, and drank to their endeavour. Six hours later he, Daniel, and Asimov were declared missing: the rest were dead.

CHAPTER TWO

CRAIG accepted his third drink and watched as Thomson put in the ice, added whisky, and then ginger ale. His quantities were generous. At one time Craig would have hesitated when the third drink was offered, needing the assurance that it was safe to accept: that his mind and body would not be called upon to work for him with a speed and certainty that a third large Scotch could impair, perhaps with fatal results. But now Craig ran no risks, and so he accepted the third drink without hesitation. It was easier, too. Thomson was an over-forceful host. But then Thomson was an over-forceful everything. He had the flat above Craig's in the elegant block in Regent's Park, and that, Craig thought, was the only possible reason why he'd been invited to the party. The best way to keep the neighbours happy was to invite them too. He didn't mind: parties were boring, but then he was always bored. At least at a party you had company.

Thomson produced films for television. He had noisy friends who did noisy things, and a seemingly endless supply of young actresses who looked intense and called Craig 'darling' and were nice because Craig might turn out to be in the business, and if they weren't nice he wouldn't offer them a job. Craig knew that in television terms this passed as logic, so he played fair most of the time and admitted he didn't do anything. Only with the very pretty ones did he linger for a while, make them wonder, before the shocking truth came out. He was nothing, not even an ad-man, and not even ashamed . . . He sipped his Scotch and looked from a very pretty one to the bracket clock on Thomson's not quite Regency table. It was seven-thirty. Time to go out to dinner. After he had dined Loomis wanted to see him, but he wouldn't care if Craig were late, not any more. Loomis saved his anger for the important ones, and Craig was no longer important. The thought was consoling. Craig had known another man whom Loomis had considered important, and that man was incurably insane. He shook the ice in his drink and put it down on a coaster, dead centre. The girl he was talking to—Angela, was it? Virginia? Caroline?—noticed the power in the hand, the ridges of hard skin across the knuckles, along the edge of the hand from wrist to finger-tip. And because she was a sensitive girl, she noticed, too, the boredom of the man, and resented it. A man who stood six feet tall, a wide-shouldered lean-hipped man with mahogany-coloured hair and grey eyes that made her think of Scandinavian seas, had no right to be bored. Not when she was talking to him.

Suddenly he smiled at her, and the face, that had been only strong before, was suddenly handsome.

'You're very nice,' he said. 'Very nice indeed.' The words distressed her, though they were kindly meant. 'Look,' he said. 'Why don't I introduce you to those people over there? Two of them are producers, and one's a casting director.'

'You don't have to be so bloody polite,' said the girl. 'I'm not a hag yet.'

She left him in a flurry of anger, her mini-skirt riding over impeccable thighs, and Craig went to say goodbye to his host.

Thomson was hurt. He said so noisily, and at great length. The whole idea of the party, he explained, was for Craig and a few kindred spirits to get together. Have fun, enjoy themselves, talk to a few girls.

'I've done all that,' said Craig. 'It's time I was off.'

Thomson wouldn't hear of it. There was a second, and very exciting, reason why a favoured few had been asked along. He'd hoped to explain it later over a few sandwiches and a mouthful of champagne. As a matter of fact that girl he'd been talking to would be staying. Wouldn't Craig like that?

'Very much,' said Craig. 'But I really have to go. You know. Business.'

The word was one which Thomson had never taken lightly, and he responded to it at once.

'Just give me five minutes, old man. That's isn't too much to ask, is it?' And Craig agreed that it was not.

He found himself hustled into a room called a study, which was mostly Morocco leather, on books, on the writing desk and chair, even on the wastepaper basket. Thomson shut the door on him, disappeared, then re-entered almost at once with a short, squat young man and a trayful of Scotch. The squat young man, it seemed, had written a play, and Thomson needed a backer . . . Craig discovered it was even later than he had thought. He said so, and turned to the door.

The squat young man said, 'I'm an artist. I create things. Surely I have a right to a hearing?'

His voice was unbelievably harsh. Nothing it could say, not even 'I love you', would sound like anything but a threat.

'Some other time,' said Craig. 'I have enjoyed meeting you.'

The squat young man put a hand on his arm.

'Look,' he said. 'I used to be a wrestler. I've done bird for assault. You're going to hear me now.'

Craig looked at Thomson, who had the baffled look of a conjuror suddenly realizing that his best trick is about to misfire.

'Is he sober?' he asked.

'He's had a few,' said Thomson.

Craig looked at the hand on his arm.

'A year or two ago if you'd done that I'd have broken your arm,' he said.

The hand slid up the muscle of Craig's arm, and fell at once to his side.

'Some other time, when I'm not so busy,' Craig said, and left.

Thomson downed a drink quickly, looked in scorn at the wrestler turned playwright.

'And you thought he was a fairy,' he said.

Craig dined on salad, sole véronique, and a half-bottle of Chablis, and as he dined he thought of the squat young man. The violence of his own reaction surprised him. Their tactics, after all, had been perfectly reasonable in terms of the world they lived in. He'd made no passes at girls, therefore he was queer, and because he was queer the squat young man had put his hand on him. There were better ways to handle that situation than to talk of breaking arms. And yet it had happened at once: the flat threat thrusting at them both, escaping his conscious control. He could have done it too, even now. Without disarranging his tie he could have broken both their arms; or their necks. Craig shivered. He didn't want that feeling, not any more. Nor did he want to see Loomis, but he went. The fat man was power: irresistible power to those who had worked for him, and Craig had served him for five violent years.

Queen Anne's Gate looked well by night. The street lights softened the clean lines of the buildings to a pretty romanticism that made the street remember its elegant past with nostalgia, but Craig's thoughts were with the present. He ignored the row of brass plates: Dr H. B. Cunnington-Low, Lady Brett, Major Fuller, the Right Reverend Hugh Bean. They were precisely the sort of names that belonged in Queen Anne's Gate—but they didn't exist. Craig pressed the bell marked 'Caretaker' and waited till the door was opened by a muscular man in overalls. Somewhere about him, Craig knew, he carried a Smith and Wesson .38 revolver and a commando knife. The caretaker held his job because he could use them.

'You're expected, Mr Craig,' he said. 'You're to go straight up.'

Craig climbed the stairs to the flat marked 'Lady Brett', and went inside. The caretaker watched him go in. Lady Brett's flat was Craig's office, and Craig had no business there when Loomis had summoned him at once, but the caretaker made no move to interfere. Craig might be slowing up and drinking a bit too much, but he had a judo black belt and an expert's knowledge of karate, and the caretaker had to practise unarmed combat with him once a month. He never antagonized Mr Craig if he could help it.

The office was neat and tidy, the way his secretary, Mrs McNab, always left it. And anyway, there wasn't much work sent to him now. The place wasn't all that hard to keep in order. He looked through his 'In' tray, but nothing had been added since he left: there was no helpful memo from Mrs McNab. Whatever Loomis had in store for him would come as a surprise. The fat man liked surprises, when he delivered them. Craig went along the corridor and tapped on the door that was of panelled mahogany, polished silken smooth. There was an indeterminate growl from behind it, and Craig went inside, into a perfect establishment set-piece with a superb stucco ceiling, sash windows, and over-stuffed furniture covered in flowered chintz. Behind a Chippendale desk Loomis sat in a buttoned leather armchair that was the biggest piece of furniture Craig had ever seen, and yet it fitted the big man so exactly that a Savile Row tailor might have measured him for it. Loomis was vast: a figure of enormous power that had slopped over into fat, with pale, manic eyes, an arrogant nose, and white hair clipped close to his skull. When Craig first met Loomis the white hair had been dusted with red, but now the red had gone.

'Pour coffee,' said Loomis, 'and sit down.' For Loomis the invitation was cordial.

Craig poured coffee from a vacuum flask: it was black, bitter, scalding hot, then sat on the arm of one of the chairs. It was bad enough facing Loomis, even if he were in a good mood, without being three feet below him.

'I've been thinking about you,' said Loomis. 'Thinking a lot. I'm beginning to wonder if you still fit in here, son.' Craig waited: there was a lot more to come.

'You've done some nice jobs for us,' Loomis said, 'and I don't deny it. You kill people nice and tidy, and you got a few brains as well. But the last job spoiled you—or at least I think so. Do you still dream about it?'

'No,' said Craig, and it was true. The best and most expensive psychiatrist in the country had laboured for weeks to stop those dreams.

'Think about it?'

'No,' Craig said again, and this time it was a lie. When you have been tortured by having electric shocks run through your penis there are times when you think about it, no matter how hard you try not to.

'I don't believe you,' said Loomis, 'but it doesn't matter. You finished that job and I'm grateful to you, but I don't think you're ready for another one.'

'Nor do I,' said Craig. He put his cup down quickly before his hand began to shake.

'You do nice paper-work, but I got too many fellers for that already.' He paused. 'Experts,' he said, making the word an insult. 'I'm beginning to wonder if I can use you at all.'

'You can hardly just let me go,' said Craig.

'No,' Loomis agreed. 'I can hardly do that. Nobody ever leaves my department—once they sign on.'

Craig waited again.

'I been thinking of sending you to the school,' Loomis said. 'Training the young hopefuls. You're the kind of feller they'll be up against, once they get into the field—or you were. But I dunno. You're not exactly cut out to be a schoolmaster, are you? On the other hand, I got nothing else to offer. We better make it the school. I tell you what,' he said. 'I'll make you a sort of graduation exercise. Go down there tomorrow, have a look around, but don't let the students see you. Pascoe will pick out the ones who are ready, and you can set up test situations for them. See if they're any good. See if you're any good come to that. Like the idea?'

'No,' said Craig.

'I didn't think you would. You can go down there tomorrow. I'll tell Pascoe to expect you.'

The school was in Sussex, an isolated Elizabethan manor house in fifty acres of grounds enclosed by an eight-foot granite wall. There were always two men at the gates, and they were armed. Closed-circuit television warned them of every approaching car, and day and night Alsatians roamed the grounds. They were good dogs: Pascoe had trained them himself. The nearest village was seven miles away, and the villagers had kept well away from the manor-house ever since the dogs had caught a poacher ten years ago. The villagers believed that the manor-house was a nursing-home for wealthy, dangerous maniacs, and Pascoe did all he could to encourage that belief. Once he'd even faked an escape: a red-bearded schizoid armed with a crowbar, trapped in the snug of the Black Bull just before opening time; dogs and strait-jackets and a tremendous smashing of glass. It had cost Pascoe fifty pounds in breakages, and the village had never forgotten.

His pupils were driven hard. They had to be: there was a great deal to learn. The school existed only for the benefit of Department K, and those who worked for Department K were specialists of the highest order. Their business was destruction: of plans, of aspirations, of life when the need arose. And those who wished to serve Department K had first to master many trades. In the school Pascoe had a language laboratory, a small-arms range, a unit dealing with arson and sabotage, a gymnasium, and a garage. There were daily sessions in unarmed combat, there were visiting lecturers who taught safebreaking, the extraction of information, the use of the knife, the improvisation of weapons, the picking of pockets, on every conceivable subject from desert survival to everyday life in the Soviet Union. There was a course on how to resist methodically applied pain to the limits of physical and mental strength. At the end of each course—and courses were held only when there were a sufficient number of likely candidates —the school turned over to Loomis a handful of men and women who were afraid of nothing but their master's power. If they disobeyed, defected or used their skills against anyone but the targets Loomis selected he could have them killed, and they knew it.

They had been deviously recruited, those who served Loomis: from the Intelligence Services some of them, or the Special Branch of CID: from the armed forces, the universities, the business desk, and the factory floor. Some, not many, from prison. One of Loomis's experts spent his whole working life reading photostated personnel files acquired via his cover as director for the Unit of Psychological and Statistical Research. Likely candidates were spotted, observed, trailed, unknowingly interviewed, and tested. Loomis's expert was good. Of the candidates he spotted, perhaps four per cent reached the school, and after that they belonged to Department K for ever, whether they reached the standard of field operative or not. Loomis's security was absolute. No one who knew about the department ever left it alive.

Craig waited at the gate while one of the men on duty examined his pass. The other one wasn't in sight, but he'd be there, Craig knew, with a gun on him. The man he could see handed back the pass and said, 'Straight on up to the house, please, sir. And don't get out of the car till Mr Pascoe comes to fetch you. There's dogs about.' He went back to the gatehouse, pressed a button, and the gates swung open. Craig drove the Lamborghini through and at once the gates were closed. As he drove slowly up the drive, the car whispering, Craig spotted the dogs. They used cover like leopards, and they followed him all the time. He reached the main doors of the house, switched off the engine, pulled up the hand brake, and waited. The six dogs settled in a great arc round the car, ears back, the hair on their necks bristling. If he left the car they would kill him, for all his skill, and Pascoe wasn't there to meet him; Pascoe was enjoying the fact that Craig was helpless in the face of something that he, Pascoe, had created.

He appeared at last, and whistled to the dogs. At once they moved off back into the grounds and their endless patrol. Craig got out of the Lamborghini and moved up the steps, not hurrying, to where Pascoe waited. Pascoe had been a colonel in military intelligence and a liaison officer with the maquis, and had survived three months in a Gestapo prison. He was tall, thin, whipcord hard, and proud of his school. The people he turned out were the best there were, except that Craig had been better than any of them. Craig was the only Department K operator who had never attended the school. Pascoe detested him.

'You do yourself well,' he said, and looked at the Lamborghini, its insolent scarlet blaring at a bed of soft May flowers. Craig walked past him into a hall that held a Shiraz rug, a Jacobean chest, an oil by Stubbs.

'You don't do too badly yourself,' he said. 'For a schoolmaster.'

Pascoe's hands clenched. Soon or later they always did, when Craig appeared. He had never met the man who could beat him, until he met Craig. The thought was bitter to him. Then he remembered what Loomis had said to him over the scrambler phone. Craig was getting past it. The fists loosened, became hands again.

'Can I get you something?' he said. 'A drink?'

Craig looked at his watch.

'I'm not quite that far gone,' he said. 'Eleven o'clock in the morning is a shade too early, even for old dipsos like me. Where are all the pupils?'

'At a lecture,' Pascoe said. 'They won't know you've been here.'

'Can I see them?' Craig asked.

'Of course,' said Pascoe. 'They're watched all the time.' He took a key from his pocket, inserted it into the back of a television set.

and switched on. As its picture formed Craig saw five men and two
women listening to a doctor. He was explaining how to set a
broken arm. Craig thought he had never seen such an intensity
of concentration.

'No one-way glass?' he asked.

'Certainly—if you prefer it,' Pascoe said.

He took the key from the set, then led the way towards the
lecture room. Set in one wall of it was a mirror, and behind it
Craig stood. From his side the mirror became a window, and he
looked at the seven faces, the set of their bodies, the way they
used their hands. After the lecture they went to the target-range,
and again Craig watched, unseen. Then it was unarmed combat,
and he watched them on the dojo mat. Lunch then, with Pascoe
presiding, the meal conducted with the formal stiffness of an
embassy reception, butler and footman wary for mistakes with
glasses, forks, knives, as Craig spied on them. After lunch Pascoe
held his class in situations. You have to get information out of a
man, but you must make no noise. What do you do? . . . You
pretend to speak no Russian, and the KGB have trapped you into
showing a knowledge of Russian. What do you do? . . . You have
a message which must be delivered; a live drop. The courier who
turns up seems impeccable—and yet you are not quite sure. What
do you do? . . . Craig eavesdropped, and ate sandwiches. By the
end of the class he had made his choice. He went to Pascoe's
office, and Pascoe joined him.

'They're in the language lab for half an hour,' he said. 'After
that I really should turn them loose for a bit or they'll start to
wonder.'

'The one you called David,' said Craig. 'David Branch. I'd
like a copy of his file. And the fair lad—Andrew Royce.' He
paused, and Pascoe said:

'You were asked to pick three.'

At last Craig said, 'The rest of the men were pretty average.'

'And the girls?'

Slowly, reluctantly, Craig said, 'The tall one had possibilities.'

'Joanna Benson? I quite agree,' said Pascoe. 'They're the three
I'd have picked myself.'

He went to a cabinet and took out three files. Craig signed
for them.

'How do you propose to organize these tests?'

'You tell these three they've graduated. I'll take David first,
then Joanna, then Andrew. Loomis will see them at the department—and give them their first briefing. For them it'll be the

real thing. That way we'll know what they'd really be like—if and when.'

They walked back to the hall, and then on to the sun-warmed steps. At once the dogs appeared, then waited as Pascoe walked with Craig and saw him to his car. Craig slammed the door and Pascoe whistled; the dogs clustered round him.

'I'll keep them here till the gates close,' Pascoe said.

Craig switched on and the engine exploded with life, then muted at once to murmured power.

'I hope you won't hurt my students too much,' Pascoe said.

'I hope they won't hurt me,' said Craig.

CHAPTER THREE

LOOMIS gave the American lunch at his club. Years ago Loomis had decided that that was what Americans liked: the secret places of the Establishment, the by-ways that led to the corridors of power, the shabby leather of libraries, the mahogany bar, and pink gins before lunch with a man who had once been an admiral on the China Station. Then a traditional lunch; smoked salmon, roast beef and Yorkshire pudding, gooseberry fool, washed down with draught bitter. The American was a gourmet, and the food at Loomis's club was appalling, but Loomis had allowed for this. It made the American defensive. He had come to ask a favour after all. Loomis ordered the beef underdone, then asked for an extra portion of sprouts. Even the waiter was awed by this: the sprouts at Loomis's club were notorious.

Throughout the meal they talked of horses. Loomis had once served in a cavalry regiment and had hunted at Melton Mowbray: the American owned a ranch in Arizona and bred quarter horses. Their talk was detailed, impassioned, and very boring to others, as it was meant to be, and the American was grateful for it. It helped distract his mind from the appalling food. When they had finished the meal, Loomis said, 'If I were you I wouldn't try the coffee here. It isn't all that good,' and to the end of his days the American couldn't decide if he were serious.

'Tell you what,' said Loomis. 'Come into the little library. I got a picture of Jumbo there. Horse I rode with the Quorn in '33. Seventeen hands and jumped stone walls.'

The American said carefully, 'If you're sure it's all right?'

'It's perfect,' said Loomis. 'Nobody can disturb us there.'

They got up, and the head-waiter bowed as they left.

'I hope you enjoyed your meal, sir,' he said.

'Amazing,' the American said. 'Absolutely amazing.'

'You don't get grub like that in the States,' said Loomis.

The American shuddered.

The little library was drab and oppressively hot. It was also safe. Loomis began talking at once.

'We got your request,' he said, 'and I've been looking around. You want some pretty talented lads.'

'We do,' the American said.

'I thought you had some,' said Loomis. 'The ones I met seemed to know what they were doing.'

'We've had trouble in the Middle East,' the American said. 'Big trouble. There's a leak somewhere and we haven't plugged it yet. Anybody we sent could get blown.'

'We've had trouble, too,' said Loomis. 'We've fixed it for now, but we can't use anybody that's known there. It would have to be a new face.

'That's perfectly OK,' the American said. 'Provided it's somebody you have faith in.'

'I have faith in them all,' said Loomis. 'I made them. But I made them my way. Trouble is they don't understand your system. As a matter of fact, neither do I.'

The American hesitated. What he had to say now was painful to him, but it was an order. It had to be said.

'We would take it as a favour if your department would handle the whole operation,' he said at last.

'Ah now, wait a minute. This is a biggish exercise,' said Loomis, 'and I'm a bit short-handed, d'you see.'

They began to bargain and the American discovered that Loomis had the ethical standards of a horse-trader.

At last he said, 'Sir, I realize that we're asking you to mount a big operation, but what you're asking is far too much. After all, you can't give us any guarantee of success, now can you?'

'I think I can,' said Loomis. 'You can pay for the whole bag of tricks COD.'

'Would you care to amplify that, sir?'

Loomis said genially, 'Oh, I forgot. You used to be a lawyer, didn't you? Put it this way, cock. If we fail, you give me nothing. If we succeed, you give me the lot. That do you?'

'You guarantee success?'

'I guarantee it,' said Loomis. 'You want to draw up a contract?'

'Your word is acceptable,' the American said.

'So's yours,' said Loomis. 'When d'you want us to start?'

'Just as soon as you can. This one's urgent.'

'It'll take a week or two. I'm running some tests, d'you see. I got to find the right operators.'

'You think you'll need more than one?'

'Bound to,' Loomis said. "I gave you a guarantee, didn't I? You got stuff I need, son. I got to have it. That means using a decoy.'

'An expendable decoy?'

'We're all expendable in this business,' Loomis said, surprised. 'Surely you know that by now.'

This time the American was sure Loomis was not joking. He

got up, took a framed photograph from the wall, and passed it to the American. It was of an enormous and very handsome horse.

'That's Jumbo,' he said.

'Don't you have one with you up?' the American asked.

Loomis grinned, a vast and evil grin. 'Certainly not,' he said. 'Security burned 'em all. Want to stay for tea?'

'I'm sorry, I can't,' the American said. 'I have to be in Paris this evening.'

'Paris,' said Loomis. 'I pop over there myself now and again. Nice place. But you can't trust the grub.'

He saw the American out, went back to the main library, spread the *Financial Times* over his face, and sprawled out motionless. Around him the sleepers whinnied and snorted. They reminded him of Jumbo . . . The Americans would pay if they had to, but only if. The information he had asked in payment was too high a price to be paid willingly. That meant two sets of risks—the operation itself and the chance of the Americans snatching the prize at the last minute. The men who brought this off would have to be good. So would the decoy . . . and the decoy was expendable . . . Pity, that . . . Loomis slept, and his snore was thunder.

David Branch had not expected to like his first assignment. He had imagined himself being too much aware of the danger, too much *afraid*, if one were honest, to be able to enjoy applying the skills he had learned with so much labour; but it wasn't like that at all. He'd met Loomis and the task had been explained to him, and of course he'd chosen to be taken on as Craig's secretary. That was pretty good, too. A nice room in an enormous flat, delicious meals, excellent wine, and not too much to do. Craig had made a disreputable fortune, and he got his money's worth in the way of comfort. He also had a secret. Something to do with Morocco, and some shady French manoeuvres of ten years ago, when the sultan abdicated. Loomis wanted that secret: Branch had to get it.

At first, the job looked easy. Craig had nothing in safe-deposits, nothing—except money—at his bank, and no safe in the flat. Moreover, Craig was a man who was easily bored, and hence always involved in small, trivial expeditions: to picture galleries, to the cinema, the theatre, new bars, new restaurants. Branch should have had all the time he needed, but he never did. Too often Craig forgot things and telephoned him to fetch them, or asked his cook to come in early and prepare a special dish, or simply got bored with what he was doing and left the cinema half-way through the movie. He moved very quietly, too, and he was big. The hell of a size. Branch found consolation in the thoroughness of his training, but as the days slipped by and the deadline drew near the feeling of enjoyment left him. He began to worry if he would ever find that damn piece of paper.

Then one day his luck was in. Craig took him out to dinner and proceeded to get quietly, unobtrusively drunk. It was hard for Branch to stay sober, but his terror of Loomis helped, and he managed at last to get Craig talking about Tangier in the old days. Craig talked at length.

'Used to be a smuggler,' he said. 'Used to do all kinds of jobs. Made a bit of money—went into shipping. Did I tell you I was in shipping?'

'Yes, sir,' said Branch. 'You did. But I never knew you were in Tangier.'

'Ought to do a book about it,' said Craig. 'You could write it for me.'

'I couldn't do it without the facts.'

'Gotemallathome,' said Craig. 'Show you. Gemme taxi.'

Branch got one, and Craig fell asleep in it. He woke him up and got him into the flat—he was hell to carry—and talked about Tangier and the book. Craig's hands flopped aimlessly towards his pockets. 'Must find my keys,' he said. 'Drunk. Make me a cup of coffee, will you?'

Branch made it and came back carrying the cup, to find Craig on his feet, holding his keys.

'That's better,' Craig said. 'I must have had too much to drink. You shouldn't let me drink too much, David. It isn't good for me.'

'I'm sorry, sir,' said Branch. Craig lurched towards him, took the coffee and sipped, then scowled. 'Lousy coffee,' he said.

'I'm sorry, sir,' Branch said again. 'I made it just the way you like it.'

'I don't like this,' said Craig. 'Here, you taste it.' He held out the cup. 'Go on.'

He gestured again, and Branch took the cup and sipped warily. As he did so, Craig stumbled on the carpet and finished up behind him, then his right hand struck at the nerve in Branch's upper arm, paralysing it, his left clamped on the cup, pushing the lip across Branch's mouth so that his head tilted back and he had to swallow. Had to. The pain was so much. And when the coffee was down it was too late to struggle, and anyway Craig held him in a hammer-lock, and even breathing was agony.

'I'm sorry,' said Craig. 'You're just not up to it, old son. Four times you left signs you searched the place. And the way you ask questions is far too clumsy. You were wrong about the coffee, too. You shouldn't have drugged me till you knew which key to use.'

He could have said more, but Branch was asleep. Craig waited. Branch had a lot to tell him before he telephoned Loomis.

'I'm sorry to bother you like this,' Joanna Benson said.

'That's perfectly all right,' said Craig. He opened the door and stood aside. 'Come in, won't you?'

Her entrance was pleasing. She wore a ranch mink and a Balmain dress, her diamonds were real, and she handled her height with confidence. Craig led her to the sitting-room and she stood, uncertain. She looked beautiful in her uncertainty.

'Please sit down,' he said.

'Oh no. I couldn't possibly. I mean it's very late, isn't it?'

'Nearly one o'clock,' he said. She was doing much better than Branch.

'Oh dear,' said Joanna.

'How can I help you, Miss——?'

'Benson. Joanna Benson. Oh gosh—you do know who I am, don't you?'

'You're my next-door neighbour but one.'

'That's right. We've met in the lift, haven't we?'

'I'm flattered you should have remembered,' said Craig.

'You're very nice,' said Joanna. 'The thing is I've lost my key. I'm locked out. And I wondered if you could help me?'

'Gladly,' said Craig. 'Are you sure you won't sit down?'

This time she did so, and loosed her coat, and her body was there, decked and jewelled, the merest hint of a promise. Really, thought Craig, she's awfully good.

He went to the telephone.

'What are you doing?' she asked.

'Calling the hall porter. He has spare sets of keys.' He put the phone down. 'No. Wait a minute.' He walked towards her, and her eyes were wary.

'Are you sure you didn't overlook it?'

'Certain,' she said.

'It might be in your bag,' he said. 'Just as well to make sure.'

She took the bag—it was a small thing of crocodile skin, with diamond clasps—and tipped it on to the table beside her. Lip-

stick, make-up, lighter, cigarettes, change-purse, and wallet. No
key. And no pockets in the mink. She was very thorough.

'I'll ring for the porter,' he said, and did so.

'You've been awfully kind,' said Joanna. 'I'm sure I'm keeping
you up. Only you see I did see your light on as I came in, and
the people next door to me seem to be asleep.'

Very nicely done. Very nice indeed.

'It's no trouble,' he said.

'I don't want you to think I'm as stupid as this all the time,'
said Joanna. 'But at least it means we've got to know each other.'

'But we haven't. Not really. My name is——'

'John Craig,' she said, and added hastily, 'It's on your door.'

Then the porter came up with the pass-key, and she stood
up to leave. She left the mink open and it swirled round her,
making her very rich, very desirable. Craig walked with her to
the door, shut it, came back, and poured himself a drink.

This one was streets ahead of Branch. Everything she'd done so
far proved it. She'd handled the whole thing with just the right
amount of reserve—and of promise. If he'd been a normal man
he'd have lain awake all night working out ways of meeting
Joanna Benson next day, but he wasn't normal. He'd never be
normal again, after what they had done to him. Women were an
irrelevance now, or worse. An inconvenience. He looked and
acted so male, and they expected him to do something about it.
Their instincts were stronger than the squat young man's. They
knew he had no time for men. What they didn't understand was
that he had no time for anybody, not any more. A woman had
betrayed him, and a man had almost destroyed him in one of the
most agonizing ways anyone had yet devised. After that, it was
better to be on your own, except that on your own life was so
lonely and so boring.

He made no attempt to find her, and she left him alone for
two days, but on the third she came to call on him again. It was
four o'clock in the afternoon and she was dressed in jodhpurs and
hacking-jacket, and she held her key in her hand. Not one woman
in a thousand looks well in jodhpurs. Joanna Benson was the
one. The gamine effect was there, as it should be, but she looked
invincibly feminine. The best of both worlds.

'I'm not in trouble this time,' she said. 'I came to ask you to
dinner. Tomorrow.'

Damn Loomis, he thought, and his postgraduate exercises.
And damn this girl who was so sure he would accept because
her legs were long and her breasts were rounded. You were only

safe on your own. Once you let them get near, hurt inevitably followed.

'I'm afraid I haven't been too well,' said Craig, and hesitated. 'But it's very sweet of you. I'd be delighted.'

They dined with well-drilled friends: a rising young barrister and his wife, whom Joanna had been at school with. The wife, Rosemary, had obviously been carefully briefed by Joanna. They were there simply as window-dressing, and behaved accordingly. Craig was the target, the victim. There could be no doubt that Rosemary approved. She did everything but wink at Joanna from the moment Craig entered the room. The husband, too, was impressed, and left it to Craig to pour the drinks, test the temperature of the wine. Joanna had no talent for cookery, and said so at once. The food had been ordered, and was excellent. The wine she had attended to herself. It was superb, as was the brandy that followed. Joanna wore a short evening dress of black chiffon and looked very lovely, and, after the brandy, very slightly drunk. At midnight, the barrister remembered the baby-sitter, and Craig, too, got up to leave. He felt no surprise when he did not succeed. This time Rosemary all but winked at him.

Joanna poured more brandy and Craig realized that she was nervous as well as drunk, but she moved well even so, the short skirt swirling round her long, beautiful legs . . . And how, Craig wondered, do we get back to my flat? Why don't we just stay here, or are we saving my place for next time? Joanna moved about, stacking dishes and glasses, and as she moved she talked, about how lovely London was at this time of year, and how Regent's Park was the loveliest thing in London.

'To see it by moonlight,' Joanna said. 'It really excites me.'

'There's a moon tonight,' said Craig.

'But we can't see the park from here.'

'We can from my flat,' said Craig.

'So we can,' said Joanna. 'Darling, would you mind?'

Craig didn't mind, and Joanna loaded glasses and cups on a tray, Craig carried the coffee-pot and brandy bottle, and they moved with exaggerated stealth to his door, went quickly inside. The 'darling' was a fact now, the business of carrying the coffee and brandy a small intimacy, a game for lovers. Craig switched off the lights and pulled the curtains wide. Below them the park was a vast silver-point, elegant yet shadowed. Joanna sighed.

'I know it's trite,' she said, 'but it makes me think of Hermia and Helena and that ridiculous mix-up in the wood. Don't you think so, darling.'

'I think it's beautiful,' said Craig. And dangerous. Those pools of shadow are always dangerous.

The girl made a slight, inevitable movement, and she was in his arms. Her lips on his, the touch of her lightly clad body, were meaningless to him, but he returned her kiss with a simulated passion that the strength of his arms underlined. She gasped as he held her.

'You're very strong,' she said. Her body wriggled as she spoke. He sensed her fingers unhook, ungrip, and the black chiffon drifted downwards like a black cloud. She wore fashionably little beneath it. Mechanically his hands stroked the cool softness of her back, but his mouth could kiss no more.

'Don't you like me?' asked the girl.

Craig said, 'I'm sorry. I'm afraid I don't feel very——'

He allowed himself to sway on his feet. She grabbed him. It took all her strength to get him to a chair, but at last she did so, and he collapsed into it, and she looked down at him. In the moonlight, it was hard to read her face.

'Pills,' Craig whispered. 'In my pocket.'

He fell back, and at once she took his wrist, felt for his pulse, but the benzedrine he had taken took care of that. It was racing. For a long moment she looked at him, then drew the curtains together and switched on the lights: Craig made no move. She put on her dress and began systematically to search the flat.

Craig let her look for three minutes. She was quick, methodical, and sure, and wary always of him lying in the chair. She held her handbag with her, too, wherever she went . . . In time, this one would be deadly. At last she found it necessary to get his keys. They were in his right-hand trouser pocket, and she had to move him. She came up to him, wary as a cat, but he lay quite motionless. Reluctantly she put down her handbag, grasped his shoulders, and heaved. He was too heavy for her. She swore, and heaved again, and this time he came up in a quick surge of power, and one splayed hand pushed under her chin, one held her right arm away from her bag. Joanna found that movement, any movement, brought instant agony. She stayed still.

'You did very well,' said Craig. 'Very well indeed. But you should have checked to see where my pills were first . . . I haven't got any.' The hand under her throat moved, brought her to her knees. He let her numbed arm go, reached for her bag, took out the little Beretta automatic. 'And you should have kept hold of this,' he said. 'All the time. It was the only chance you had.'

Andrew Royce made no attempt to reach him at all. No dinner invitations, no call to read the gas-meter or chat in a bar. Instead, Royce studied the outside of Craig's flat, then worked in the gym every day, and with one of the experts who had visited the school. The expert's field was burglary, and he was a master. Loomis observed his plans and said nothing to Craig. Royce's choice of methods was his own.

He chose a night when Craig went to bed early. Patiently he waited for the lights in the flat to die, then climbed, steadily, not hurrying, his body protected by shadow from the dying moon. He found the window of the spare bedroom and felt for burglar alarms. There were none. No wires, no photo-electric cells. The tools the expert had taught him to use worked admirably, and the window catch yielded to him in minutes. Cautiously then, he greased the side of the window, let it slide open, and was inside. Once in, he pulled a mask over his face and moved silently to the door of Craig's bedroom. Royce had considered the problem of the sleeper from the beginning. Loomis had impressed on him how important the document was. Inevitably, it would be hidden. That meant either a long search or forcing Craig into telling him where it was. In either case Craig would have to be put out of action first. Royce looked at the cold chisel he'd used on the window, then dropped it into his pocket. The chisel was dangerous: he might hit too hard. For a job like this it was better to use the hands.

An accident saved Craig. As Royce opened his bedroom door and eased, slowly, noiselessly round it, his phone rang. Craig woke up at once and Royce saw him stir. He leaped for Craig, and his hand, held like an axe-blade, struck down with controlled force. (On no account must the man be killed, Loomis had said.) But Craig had flung the covers aside already and the blow was smothered in bedclothes. Royce followed it up with his fist, and the punch caught Craig on the side of the neck, the impact an immediate eruption of pain. Craig groaned, fell back, and Royce leaped for him, but Craig's fall became a spin that took him out of the bed and on to the floor. He scrambled to his feet and the pain stabbed at him, slowing him so that Royce too had time to roll free.

Royce was younger and faster than Craig, and he had not been hit. He was wide awake, and Craig had been asleep. He leaped in again, anxious to get it over, but Craig swayed away from the three-finger strike he aimed at him, and counted with a chop that smashed just below his ribs. Royce groaned and lashed out with a karate kick aimed at the groin. Again Craig swayed, and the shoe scored along the edge of his thigh, but his hand smacked under the heel even so. He levered and pulled, and Royce spun like a top in the air, then his arms smashed down, absorbing the impact of his fall. But Craig still held on to his foot, and any attempt at movement was agony. Craig looked at the masked face on the floor. This was Andrew, he had no doubt, and Andrew was fast and young and tricky—and mad because he'd been beaten. If he let him go, Andrew would immediately start again, and Craig had taken two blows already. Still holding the foot, he limped forward, then his own bare foot flicked, the hard edge seeking the nerve at the base of the neck, and Royce's body stiffened, then relaxed. The phone rang again. Craig picked it up.

'Is that the Mercury Mini Cab Service?' said a voice that would stand no nonsense. 'I rang you a minute ago and nobody answered.'

'You see it's a bit difficult,' said Craig. 'We're not on the phone.' He hung up. He hadn't finished yet.

Craig rang the bell at Queen Anne's Gate and the porter answered.

'You're expected,' he said, then watched Craig climb the stairs. It was some satisfaction to know that he was limping. Loomis made no mention of it, but for once Craig was glad to sink into an over-stuffed armchair and watched the red, eagle-beaked face glower down at him.

'Branch won't do?' he asked.

'Not at maximum risk,' said Craig. 'He gets excited. It makes him obvious.'

'And the girl? This Benson person?'

'Good,' said Craig. 'Subtle. And she doesn't overdo it. She'd have made it with another man.'

Loomis nodded. 'And Royce?' he said.

'Excellent,' said Craig. 'Strong and fast. Tough minded. A good brain too. He worked it all out.'

'Worked *what* all out?'

'The exercise,' said Craig. 'He knew there was a good chance this was a test, so he came in from outside—when I was asleep . . . I like that. And he knew he'd have to clobber me. Hurt me maybe. That didn't bother him. Even if I turned out to be on his side. He'll do well.'

'Weaknesses?'

'He hates being beaten,' Craig said. 'It makes him angry . . .

But it won't happen often. He'd have beaten me—if it hadn't been for that phone call.'

'You think I could use those two then?'

'I know it,' said Craig. Loomis sighed, and Craig thought of whales wallowing.

'Would they break easy?' he asked.

'Ask the psychiatrists,' Craig said.

'Oh I will, son. Over and over I'll ask them. But just now I'm asking you. You've had what you might call first-hand experience.'

'They'll break eventually,' said Craig. 'Everybody does. But they'll last as long as most.'

'Good,' said Loomis. 'They can be your assistants then. I got a job for you.'

'A month ago you said I was finished,' said Craig.

'I was wrong,' said Loomis. 'It's happened before. Twice. You showed I was wrong the way you handled those three. Royce in particular. And the Benson person. Women can't get at you, son. Not any more.'

'Royce and I won't get on all that well,' said Craig. 'Not after what I did to him. And the girl—she's bright. Maybe she knows about me. I couldn't work with her if she knew.'

'They won't work with you,' said Loomis. 'They'll assist you by being decoys. If they see you in the street they won't look at you twice.'

'What's the job?' said Craig.

'You're going to Turkey to pick up a feller,' Loomis said. 'And when you've got him you're going to take him to Israel. But first you're going to New York. There's people in New York can tell you all about this feller. Name of Kaplan. The Russians want him too.'

'That's why you're setting up decoys?'

'That's why,' said Loomis. 'They got him in one of their "Most Urgent" files. You know what that means.'

'It means he's going to die,' said Craig.

'That's not our business—provided we get him to Israel first. And that's your job. I'll send you the file we got on him. Work on it in your office. It doesn't leave here . . . You fly to New York on Thursday. That's all on file too . . . You better get on with it, son.'

Craig levered himself out of the chair and limped to the door. He felt old and battered and very tired. Three days in the gym would help, but not enough. The savage concentration of strength he had once summoned at will, was gone, perhaps for **ever.**

'Why me, Loomis?' he asked.

'You're not what you were,' said Loomis, 'but you're still the best I've got for this sort of caper.'

'The KGB are after him. "Most Urgent." That means they'll be after me too.'

'Not if we use decoys,' said Loomis.

'They're just out of school. What chance will they have?' said Craig.

'Very little,' said Loomis. 'But that isn't your business, cock.'

CHAPTER FOUR

THE KAPLAN FILE was thin. Aaron Israel Kaplan had been
born in Riga in 1915, the son of a rabbi, and the family had
moved to Moscow just before the Revolution. By 1932 he was a
komsomol leader and a biology student at Moscow University,
and had broken with his family: by 1936 he was researching in
agricultural method at the Lenin Institute, and had begun a
crash course in water-engineering. His over-riding interest was
the cultivation of crops in dry areas, and papers he had written
on this had gone as far as the Central Committee when the war
came. In 1938 his father had died, but Kaplan had not been
present at the funeral. During the war Kaplan had fought with
distinction as a political commissar attached to an infantry regiment that had finished up in East Germany. After it he had gone
back to his work at the Lenin Institute, at first with success. He
had survived the Lysenko scandal, and once again the Central
Committee had read his papers. There was talk of financing a
scheme of his: a capital investment of seven million roubles. He
had nine assistants, limitless opportunity for research, and access
to all the Institute's papers, no matter how highly classified.
Then, quite suddenly, he had crashed. His scheme was dropped,
his research team broken up. Then his membership of the
Institute was revoked, his car and dacha taken from him. For
three months he worked as a factory hand, then he was arrested,
tried, and sentenced to Siberia. His sentence was 'indeterminate'
which meant he stayed there till he died. The camp he went to,
Volochanka, was the hardest of them all. His sentence had never
been revoked, and yet he had been reported in Turkey. He was
one of three brothers. One had been killed at Stalingrad and the
other had left Russia with an uncle in 1922, and was living in
New York: Marcus Kaplan, 189 West 95th Street. The most
recent photograph of Kaplan had been taken in 1939 and had
all the fuzziness to be expected of a black and white print taken
with a box camera, ineptly handled. It suggested that Kaplan
was tall, scholarly, and thin, but his features were anonymous.

Craig turned the page. There followed a note in Loomis's
small, neat writing: 'For further information on Kaplan consult his brother and Laurie S. Fisher, the Graydon Arms, 145
East 56th Street.' On the next page was a description of Volochanka. Craig wondered how any man could possibly escape from

such a place. After that there came key information about Turkey: the sort of stuff he would need to get Kaplan out without the Russians knowing, but no information about where he was. Even Loomis didn't know that. That had to wait until he got to New York, and then Laurie S. Fisher would tell him, if he thought him good enough. The file didn't tell him why Kaplan was important, either, but that wasn't Craig's business. Craig's business was to get him to Israel. He telephoned Sanuki Hakagawa at the house in Kensington, and made an appointment for that evening, then went back to the file and read it through again and again. Gradually the information it contained began to stick. In two days he would never need it again.

The Hakagawas had the ground floor and basement of a house off Church Street, one of a series of Edwardian monsters of salmon-pink brick relieved with stone painted a glittering white. The exterior was fussy, ornate, blatantly opulent, the interior furnished with the spare elegance of Japanese who still lived in the traditional style so far as London would let them. Sanuki opened the door to him, slim and ageless in a sweater and jeans.

'Please go down to the gymnasium,' she said. 'Shinju is waiting for you.'

Craig went down the steps to the changing-rooms. There was a judo costume waiting for him, and a black belt. He changed slowly, allowing his mind to achieve the state of wary relaxation essential before a fight with Shinju Hakagawa. When he went in the Japanese was already waiting for him, on the dojo mat. Craig too went on the mat, and the two men bowed in the ritual of greeting.

'What style shall we fight?' Hakagawa asked.

'We'll just fight,' said Craig.

It was like very fast chess, every move played out to the limits of strength, every throw a potential opening to the checkmate that could end your life if you didn't get up, or counter, in time. At the end of twenty minutes Hakagawa signalled a halt, and both men were streaming with sweat. Hakagawa produced towels, and they dabbed at their sweating bodies, then knelt, facing each other, on the mat.

'You have been drinking too much,' said Hakagawa. 'You are slow. This time I could have killed you.'

'I'm old, Hak,' Craig said.

'Not as old as me. I am fifty-four years old.' Craig looked at the squat, bullet-headed Japanese. His face was astonishingly beautiful and almost unlined.

'Show me your hands.'

Craig held out his hands and Hakagawa very carefully examined the lines of hard skin along their edges, and across the knuckles.

'You have neglected them,' said Hakagawa. 'Suppose I asked you to punch the board.'

'I couldn't do it,' said Craig.

'It will take you two weeks to get your hands right. You will practise here every day.'

'I can't,' said Craig. 'I go to New York in three days.'

'I will give you the address of a master there,' said Hakagawa. 'You must become right again—or karate is finished for you.'

'Become right?'

'You do not mean it any more,' Hakagawa said. 'It is in your hands, but not in your mind. You are becoming what boxers call a gym fighter.' He paused, and looked at Craig in affection. 'Until your mind changes you will never beat me again. When it changes, you will beat me every time. Shower now. You drink too much.'

Each evening until he left, Craig fought with Hakagawa. His hands began to harden and his speed and stamina increased as he sweated the alcohol out of his system, but his mind remained the same. He could not beat Hakagawa. After the second defeat he went back to the department and booked a session on the firing range. He used the gun he'd always preferred, a Smith and Wesson ·38, and that skill at least had not deserted him. Over and over he aimed and fired, and each time he scored a bull. The PSI who ran the place, an ex-gunman himself, looked on and was happy. Craig never gave him any problems. Craig too began to relax, until the thought hit him: no matter what you do to a target, you cannot make it feel.

He went back to his flat and worked doggedly on his hands, punching and striking at the thin bags of hard sand. When he had had enough, he went to the phone and called Sir Matthew Chinn. Sir Matthew was the very eminent psychiatrist who had treated him after he had been tortured. Craig spoke to a housemaid, a butler, and a secretary. They were unanimous. Sir Matthew was unavailable for at least six weeks. Craig wondered if Sir Matthew's unavailability were Loomis's idea. Sir Matthew had not wanted Craig to work for the department ever again, but Loomis had insisted. He was insisting now. From time to time Craig hated Loomis, but there was no sense in it really, he thought. There was nowhere else for him to go.

New York began in the Boeing 707, and Craig was grateful for it. There was a hell of a lot of New York to get used to. The flight was all dry martinis and chicken à la king and the toasted cigarettes he could never learn to enjoy. There was a movie, too. Hollywood money, Spanish location. All about the war in Greece. It was bold, noisy, and totally inaccurate. Craig calculated that if the hero had behaved in reality as he did on the screen he would have been shot dead twenty-three times. He enjoyed the movie. It was right that he should. According to his cover, he was an advertising man sent over to study American Techniques; not the ulcer-gnarled, thwarted genius advertising man, the extrovert, jolly kind, the kind that actually likes war movies that gross six million. After the movie he read a paperback about rape in Streatham, then abandoned that for the *New York Times*. The race-riots were going to be late this year on account of the cool weather; the President needed another hundred million dollars for Vietnam; the longshoremen were going to strike after all, and baseball would never be the same without Mickey Mantle. Craig slept till Boston.

The run-in was slow and easy, the way Craig liked it, the tyres settled gingerly on the tarmac like a fat man in a hot bath. Craig remained seated and refrained from smoking as the signs and hostess told him to do, then queued, briefcase in hand, to be smiled at, wished a pleasant stay, and walk into the humid, infrequent sunshine of Kennedy Airport, the quickfire politeness of immigration and the ultimate, grudging acceptance of the world's worst customs officers that he was not carrying heroin, marijuana, or fresh fruit. He joined another queue then, for the helicopter, and the lazy, clattering journey through the concrete canyons of Manhattan, to look down at the cars like beetles, the human beings like ants, except that these ants, these beetles, scurried only in the predestined straight lines that the avenues and streets laid down for them. The helicopter waltzed slowly down the sky and Craig marvelled at the great ranks of skyscrapers, tall, thin giants that were sometimes elegant, sometimes ugly, sometimes—so quickly you grow blasé in New York—just dull. Then the clattering died and he was on the roof of the Pan-Am Building, and down or up New York was all around him as far as the Hudson River, and only the sky was closed to the scurrying ants below.

He took a cab to his hotel, an ant himself now, alive and

scurrying inside a beetle. The taxi-driver talked about the humidity, only fifty but still climbing and what the figure would have to be before the race riots started. Seventy? Seventy-five? Eighty? Meteorology and social science welded together to form an irrefragable law.

'What this city needs,' said the taxi-driver, 'is one hundred per cent air-conditioning. Just one big unit all the way to Queens. Then we might have some peace in the summer.'

Craig, sweating in the back seat, agreed with him.

They had found him a hotel in the East Forties, and it was the kind he liked; old, with a lot of leather, and pictures on the walls that related to people who had actually lived, actually achieved something in the hotel. There was a man waiting for him too, a single unit committee of welcome, A. J. Scott-Saunders of the British Embassy. A. J. Scott-Saunders was lean and exquisite, his tie was Old Harrovian and his manner distant, which impressed the desk clerk and overawed the bellboy who took Craig's bags to the elevator, opened the door of his suite, and demonstrated lights, taps, and air-conditioning like a saint performing all his miracles at once. Craig handed over money, and A. J. Scott-Saunders sighed.

'I'd like some ice,' said Craig, 'soda water and ginger-ale.' The bellboy went, and until he returned Craig kept up an uninterrupted flow of conversation about his trip, the food, the movie, and as he talked searched the suite for the kind of bugs unobtrusive enough to be smuggled into an exclusive hotel in the East Forties. There weren't any. When the bellboy returned he handed over more money and poured drinks from his duty-free bottle.

'You do yourself well,' said Scott-Saunders.

'When you're in the advertising game you have to,' said Craig.

Scott-Saunders looked disgusted and opened his briefcase.

'I have here fifty thousand dollars emergency money,' he said. 'The money is to be used at your discretion.' The thought obviously caused him pain, and the pain intensified as Craig counted it.

'All there,' said Craig, and waited. Scott-Saunders sipped Scotch and water.

'Have you got anything else for me?'

'Isn't that enough?'

'I didn't mean money,' said Craig.

Scott-Saunders looked surprised: his best yet.

'What else could I bring you?' he asked.

'Equipment,' said Craig. 'You know. Machinery.'

'I'm very much afraid I don't know,' Scott-Saunders said. 'Money was all I was told to bring. Money—and two requests. One: spend no more of those dollars than you have to. Two— keep away from the British Embassy. I trust I make myself clear?'

'Transparent,' said Craig, and Scott-Saunders flushed, finished his drink, and made for the door. Somehow Craig was in his way, which was strange. Scott-Saunders could swear that he had scarcely moved.

'I've done this sort of thing before,' Craig said. 'Have you?'

'Never,' Scott-Saunders said.

'You have a regular man for this job?'

'We do,' Scott-Saunders said. 'He was busy today.'

Craig let him go. The regular man was busy, so they'd sent him an idiot with the right accent who knew nothing about equipment or machinery. That meant no gun. Loomis had always been very anti-guns in the presence of allies, but this was carrying a prejudice too far. Admittedly a gun was no good unless you were prepared to use it, but then he, Craig, was prepared, and Loomis knew it. It would seem, Craig thought, that the fat man doesn't trust me any more.

He called Laurie S. Fisher and got no answer, then tried Victor Kaplan. A voice like that of a method actor playing Bertie Wooster told him that Mr Kaplan never returned to his apartment before seven. Craig showered and changed, and there were still three hours to kill before Kaplan got home. He sealed the fifty thousand dollars in its manilla envelope, took it down to the desk, deposited it, asked how to get to Brooklyn, and discovered for himself the blood and iron realities of New York's subway system, even when it wasn't rush hour. Even the damp heat of Brooklyn was preferable to it, but even so he walked slowly, cautious not to sweat too much, to the old brownstone house with the wide stoop, and grudged the effort needed to try to push his way past the throng of men sheltering on it.

They were all large men, large enough to make Craig's six feet and hundred and ninety pounds look skimpy. It took Craig some time to realize that, like him, they were waiting to get in. In England they would have formed a queue. At last one of them, who wore a single gold loop earring and hair dyed pink, put a hand on his chest.

'They're not hiring light heavies today,' he said.

Craig looked around him. On all sides, giants towered. It was like being lost in a primeval forest.

'I came to see Thadeus Cooke,' he said. 'I think he's expecting me.'

At once the giants opened up and let him through, then resumed their restless milling. Craig wandered down a corridor lined with open doors. In each room that he passed, giants were wrestling: in pairs, in tag teams, in groups, and with each set of wrestlers was a smaller man screaming directions: part referee, part choreographer. Craig walked on till he came to a door on which the name 'Thadeus Cooke' was painted, and below, in the same neat lettering: 'Keep Out. This Means You.' He went inside.

The man behind the desk was sleeping peacefully, feet up, thumbs hooked into his belt. He was tall, slender, and apparently ageless: his hair, close-cropped and bristling, could have been pale gold, could have been white, the lines on his dark skin the result of weather, or of age. He slept soundlessly, but woke almost at once as Craig walked into the room. Very blue eyes looked into Craig's, but the man didn't move: only there was a wariness, even in his relaxation, that told Craig at once: This one is good.

'Got a good business,' the man said suddenly. 'Wrestlers. I train 'em. Book 'em. Promote 'em. Branch out on the coast. Same deal. Only there we do stunt men and fight arrangements too. Doin' well. TV helped. You know what I grossed last year?'

'No,' said Craig.

'Hundred and fifty thousand dollars. It's not Standard Oil—but it's enough. For me anyway. I've got a hobby—now I can afford it. Know what it is?'

'No,' said Craig.

'Sleepin'. That's why I put that notice on the door. Maybe you can't read?'

Craig said, 'I can read.'

The man sighed and put his feet down, stood up. He wore a rumpled silk-tussore suit from Saks that must have cost three hundred dollars: his dirty unpolished shoes were hand sewn, English imported. The tie twisted almost to one ear was one Craig recognized as that restricted to former pupils of Eton College.

'I better throw you out,' he said. 'It'll hurt you, son, but we all have to learn some time.'

He moved forward slowly, easily, and for a moment Craig decided to let him do it—or try to. It would be the best practice he could buy. But it would also be noisy, and very noticeable. He backed off.

'Shinju Hakagawa sent me, Mr Cooke,' he said.

The easy movement stopped, and Cooke became once more a tired and happy tycoon.

'You're Craig?' he said. Craig nodded. Cooke's eyes moved over him warily. 'John Craig. He says you're maybe going to beat him one of these days . . . You know, I always thought I was the one who'd do that. Come into the gym.'

Craig moved back to the door, but the other man shook his head.

'No,' said Cooke. 'Not in public, son. One of us is going to find this embarrassing.'

Cooke's gym was a small, square room, its one article of furniture a dojo mat. Craig and Cooke changed and faced each other across it, bowing in the ritual way as Craig noticed the strength in the other's slimness. He was pared down to undiluted power, and, with it, a dancer's speed and precision. Craig moved warily forward and, as he did so, Cooke leaped at once into the air, aiming a snap kick that would have ended the fight then and there if it had landed. But Craig dived beneath it and whirled round, ready, as Cooke landed and aimed a fist-strike at his belly. Craig grabbed his wrist and threw him, and Cooke landed in a perfect break-fall, rolling over to avoid the kick of Craig's follow-up, his grab for Craig's foot just missing as Craig pirouetted away. Time and again they attacked each other and ran into a counter-move that just, and only just, prevented success. They fought, each of them, in silence and speed, and with all their skill: and they fought a draw. After twenty minutes Cooke signalled a halt.

'You're not ready for Shinju—not yet,' he said. 'But one day you're going to be—if you go on improving.'

Craig said nothing: his exhaustion was total.

'Bet I know what you're thinking,' said Cooke. Craig looked up. 'If I'd gone on for another two minutes I'd have licked you. That what you were thinking?'

'Yes,' said Craig. 'I was.'

'Know why I didn't? . . . Because I couldn't, son. You're the best I ever saw. What kind of business you in?'

'Advertising,' said Craig.

Cooke stared at him. 'Figured you were,' he said.

'Did you?' said Craig.

'Sure. You talk so damn much—what other business could you be in? Tell you something else.' Craig waited. 'If you ever decided you didn't like me—you'd kill me. D'you hate much?'

'Not often,' said Craig.

'Come in when you like, son. Any time. I ain't saying I'll teach you much, but I ain't too proud to learn.'

He walked with Craig back through the gym and paused near a mountainous Negro who appeared to be disembowelling a fat Greek with his bare hands. The Greek's yells were piteous to hear. Suddenly the Greek brought up his knee, and the Negro hit the canvas like a house collapsing.

'Constantine,' said Cooke severely, 'that wasn't nice. You want me to take Blossom's place?'

The Greek broke at once into a babble of broken English, all of it apologetic.

'You just watch it, that's all,' said Cooke. 'You too, Blossom.'

The Negro twitched in response, and Cooke walked on.

'Sometimes they mean it,' said Cooke. 'I can't let 'em fight if they mean it.'

'Why not?' asked Craig.

'Why,' Cooke said. 'They're valuable, son. Can't let 'em go damaging each other. They cost too much money.'

At five-thirty Craig reached the Graydon Arms. It was an apartment building, neat, unobtrusive, and wealthy, its air-conditioning Arctic, or at least Siberian, Craig thought, as the sweat congealed on his body. Kaplan's Siberia had not been so elegant: maplewood desk with ivory telephones, a desk-clerk out of a Frank Capra movie, dark blue carpet, pale blue walls. In front of Craig three matrons and what appeared to be two life-guards with clothes on—so bronzed they were, so golden their glinting hair—talked of vodka martinis as they walked to the lift. Craig told himself he was disguised as a lifeguard, and followed, and the desk-clerk looked on and sighed, but made no move to stop him. Perhaps, thought Craig, he wants a vodka martini too —or a matron.

The lift whispered its way to the ninth floor, and by the time they arrived Craig found that vodka martinis and matrons alike were at his disposal, but he stayed on, and went up to the pent-house, and Laurie S. Fisher.

The door to the penthouse was of mahogany, and polished till it glowed. A splendid door, a door belonging to a Georgian house; craftsmanship and artistry nicely blended. It made Craig feel good, even patriotic—just to look at it. Except that it was very slightly ajar. Laurie S. Fisher of the Graydon Arms was a wealthy man. He had to be, if he owned the penthouse—and wealthy men in New York don't leave their doors ajar: not even slightly ajar.

Craig examined the door and the gap between slowly, with extreme care. No wires, no bugs. Just a door that should not have been open. He pushed it gently, using his knuckles, and it swung wide. Craig took a deep breath and jumped inside, swinging in the air as he moved, hands clawing for whoever hid behind it. There was no one. He pushed the door shut and looked around the apartment. An empty hall, an empty drawing-room, an empty dining-room, all furnished with a deliberate, conscious good taste, a neat blend of modern and Georgian pieces that had cost Laurie S. Fisher a great deal of money. Craig moved on to an empty bedroom. Its occupant was a devotee of science-fiction, stock car racing, and bull-fighting. About seventeen, Craig thought, with a preference for English clothes conceived in Carnaby Street. Away—to judge by the books lying about—at one of those schools Americans call private, and the English, with a subtler, sharper irony—public. He passed on to the master bedroom. Fitted cupboards, pictures of horses, wall to wall carpet, a TV set high in one wall so that a man could lie down, relax, and look at his leisure. Or a woman.

A young woman, about twenty-eight, well-nourished, a mole on her right hip, once operated on for appendicitis. Not visibly pregnant. Blonde. Blue eyes. Probably of Scandinavian origin. And beautiful. Very beautiful. And dead.

Craig looked at the naked body without ruttishness or embarrassment. There was a faint stirring of pity, no more. In a sense she had been lucky. One shattering blow to the nape of the neck and—nothing. Oblivion. Everything finished. No more worries about beauty parlours, Italian shoes, Lord and Taylor dresses. He touched one slender foot—it was still warm—then turned to the small heap of clothes on the bed. Her purse was there, and it was empty. He left her and went into the bathroom.

Laurie S. Fisher hadn't died nearly so quickly. He had been tortured by experts, and they'd been in a hurry, but even so it must have taken an hour, maybe more. Craig marvelled that a man could hold out for an hour, even a man as strong as Fisher had undoubtedly been. And handsome too. They hadn't touched his face. He'd been gagged with a hand towel while they—while they—Craig turned away to the toilet basin and was violently sick, his body shuddering, then methodically cleaned and flushed the basin, ran the tap till the water was cold, washed his face and drank from his cupped hands. In the end, Fisher had talked, then they'd killed him as they'd killed his girl. One sudden, longed-for blow. The boy in the private school would be a man very soon, he thought, and turned his mind to the problem of leaving. But no one stopped him, no one came back to make sure that Fisher and his woman were dead. Why should they? They were experts, technicians. The man who had killed knew that Fisher and the woman were dead the moment he unleashed his hand.

Craig stood in the hall, recalled each movement he had made. The door pushed with his knuckles, the toilet flushed, the tap turned with his handkerchief. Nothing else. He used the handkerchief on the door again, and left it as he had found it, very slightly ajar, then ran down three flights of stairs and took the elevator to the mezzanine floor, where there was a cocktail lounge and Scotch whisky.

He drank two, taking his time, making himself look relaxed, even bored, and grateful that the lounge was busy. Grateful, too, that it had a separate door to the street . . . He should have left after one, but his whole body screamed for the stuff. Things had been done to Fisher that had once been done to him, and Craig needed to drink for a long, long time if he were to forget what he had seen. But he couldn't forget.

After the second drink it was six-thirty, and at seven Marcus Kaplan might be home, so the method actor had said. And at his home there might be experts, technicians, waiting to do to Kaplan what they had already done to Fisher and the girl.

Craig walked out, not hurrying, into Fifth Avenue. It was hotter than ever, and there were no empty cabs. (That's a thing to remember about New York, Loomis had said. They don't have empty cabs. Only full ones.) But he needed to walk anyway. And there was time.

Kaplan's apartment house too was smart and well-kept, but then Kaplan was in furs, and men who do well in furs tend to do very well indeed. Craig reached the building at five to seven. Nobody seemed interested in it except its Negro doorman. There were no waiting cars, no loiterers: but the window across the street could conceal a sniper, if they wanted Kaplan dead: if Fisher had told them all they needed to know. The roofs too. There was good cover, and too much of it. Suddenly Craig shivered, in spite of the damp, unrelenting heat. His face was known. He too had been in a Most Urgent file. Maybe they'd made it active again. He looked in a shop-window next to the apartment house. It held a display of hunting clothes, with pump-action shotguns and rifles brutally arranged to underline the masculinity of those who bought such very expensive clothes. The rifles were the best of their kind: telescopic sights, light action, a trigger you squeezed so that it didn't jar your aim. Craig felt as if he had a target painted on his back. From across the street you couldn't miss—but at least he could use the window as a mirror, and watch what was happening.

At seven five a Lincoln Continental drew up and the door-keeper sprang into action. Craig turned and moved slowly forward. The car contained a Puerto Rican chauffeur and a fat passenger, already dismounting. The fat passenger was exactly like his brother, plus fifty pounds weight. Craig moved faster. As Kaplan left the Lincoln, he was completely masked from across the street, Craig on one side of him, the doorman on the other.

'Mr Kaplan?' Craig said.

'That's right,' said Kaplan, and looked up at Craig. His eyes were bright, alert, and, Craig thought, wary.

'I've got a message for you,' Craig said. 'From Aaron.'

The wariness in the eyes intensified.

'You better come in,' he said without enthusiasm.

Another crowded elevator, fast, air-conditioned, careful not to let the stomach lag. Kaplan got out at the nineteenth floor. (No New Yorker lives lower than the seventeenth floor, Loomis had said. They only have sex when there's a power cut.) Kaplan stood by the elevator and looked down the carpeted corridor. There was no one else there.

'What's Aaron's full name?' he asked.

'Aaron Israel Kaplan. Last heard of in Volochanka.'

'OK,' Kaplan said, less enthusiastically than ever. 'We'll go to my apartment.'

He led, Craig a half-step behind him, and almost too late Craig remembered his trade.

'Mr Kaplan,' he said, 'are any of these apartments to let?'

'No,' Kaplan said at once. 'There's a waiting-list. Very desirable apartments.' He frowned. 'Maybe you're thinking of the Boldinis.'

'Am I?' said Craig.

'Number 37,' Kaplan said. 'But they're in Maine. They go there every summer. Lucky——'

By this time they had reached Number 33, and Kaplan thought that Craig had gone mad, for the deferential but very strong Britisher promptly knocked him down, a deft, efficient trip, and leaped over his body, hit the door of Number 37 just as it had begun to open. There was a sound like that of a large, wet sack hit with a paddle, and Craig was through the door. Kaplan,

bewildered but courageous, groaned himself upright and followed. Inside the Boldinis' apartment Craig was grappling with
a man who held a gun. As Kaplan entered the gun went off, and
Kaplan observed a vase he had detested for years shatter to
fragments inches from his hand, but instead of the dull boom of
the explosion there was a small, soft plop. Craig struck at the
gunman and he groaned. Kaplan moved into the room, noting
that Craig was gathering his strength to finish the fight. It was
suddenly important that he observe just how this was done. He
moved clumsily, and Craig saw him, his concentration weakened.
The gunman wriggled from Craig's arms and through a window,
then leaped crazily down the stairs of the fire-escape. Kaplan still
watched attentively as Craig scooped up the gun and ran to the
window. From below came the fading sounds of shoe-leather on
metal.

'I'm sorry,' Kaplan said.

Craig leaned in from the window and turned.

'It's all right,' he said.

'I didn't think I would put you off——'

'You wouldn't have,' said Craig, 'except that there's another
one behind you—and it's you they came for, after all.'

Kaplan spun round. There was a man lying on the floor, and
he had a gun in his hand. Right there in the Boldinis' apartment,
a gunman lay flat on his back, automatic in hand, and he, Kaplan,
stood amid the ruins of that damn ugly vase. That was as fantastic
as the gunman. The Boldinis had worshipped that vase. Paid
over a hundred dollars to have it shipped from Hong Kong, and
now here was this Englishman crunching over it, bending down
to look at this—gangster I guess you'd call him. Craig's face told
him nothing at all—but when he turned the gunman over, suddenly Kaplan knew he was dead, even before he looked up and
saw the set of teak shelves near the door, with their hard, sharp
edges, one of them just the height of a standing man, and that
one covered in what looked like jam. Kaplan turned away.

'Well well,' said Craig. 'How very careless of him.'

He went quickly through the man's pockets. Money, a packet
of Marlboroughs, book matches, a dirty and much-used handkerchief. And on the floor a Browning Hi-Power automatic with a
silencer. Thirteen shot. His unlucky day.

'You killed him,' said Kaplan. There was amazement rather
than accusation in his voice.

'That's right,' said Craig. He unscrewed the silencer from the
gun he'd picked up, then stuffed the silencer into his pocket, the

gun into his pants' waistband, and opened the door, using his
fingernails only. The corridor was still empty.

'At least you haven't got nosey neighbours,' said Craig. 'Did
you touch anything?'

Kaplan shook his head. Craig jerked his head at the door and
Kaplan left, Craig followed, still a little behind, and to the right.
The way the bodyguards walk on television, thought Kaplan.
The only crazy thing was he still wasn't scared. He still couldn't
believe it was happening.

Inside Kaplan's door the man-servant waited to take Kaplan's
hat and tell him that madam was having a cocktail in the
drawing-room. Craig looked the man over. The voice was
phoney, but a splendid phoney; rich and plummy as fruitcake.
The man himself, lean and rangy in his white mess-jacket, with
cold, expressionless eyes that noticed the bulge at Craig's middle,
and became more expressionless than ever.

'Cocktail?' said Kaplan. 'Sounds like a good idea. We'll have
one too.'

He led the way and Craig found himself shaking hands with a
plump and hennaed matron who took one look at her lord, and
blamed it all, whatever *it* was, on Craig.

She thinks I've had him out drinking, thought Craig, and
waited for the introductions.

'This is Mr Craig, honey,' said Kaplan. *So he knew I was on
my way here.*

'How d'you do?' said Mrs Kaplan, uncaring. 'Hetherton, mix
the drinks will you?'

Craig looked over his shoulder. Hetherton had exchanged the
mess-jacket for a swallow-tail coat that fitted badly on the left-
hand side. Craig asked for Scotch on the rocks, and Hetherton
mixed it and passed it to Craig with his left hand. When Craig
took it with his right, Hetherton began to look happy. Kaplan
accepted a modest vodka-martini and at once said, 'Business, Ida.
I'll take Mr Craig to the study.' This was the merest routine, and
yet, Craig thought, she still hates me. She knows there's something wrong.

'Will you be needing me, sir?' Hetherton said. His right hand,
Craig noticed, was adjusting an already impeccable tie, six inches
away from his gun-butt.

'No no,' said Kaplan. 'Mr Craig and I are old friends. We'll
look after ourselves.'

Hetherton bowed and relaxed still further. Craig assumed he
had the place bugged.

The study was small, untidy, and masculine, more den than study, full of small cups that Marcus and Ida Kaplan had won at bridge tournaments, and larger cups that Marcus Kaplan had won at skeet-shooting. There were also two huge and highly functional lamps. Kaplan tossed off his martini and promptly refilled it from a bottle in the base of one of them.

'Scotch is in that one,' said Kaplan, pointing. 'Help yourself.'

Craig twisted the base and pulled, as Kaplan had done. Inside the lamp was a bottle of Red Hackle. He freshened his drink.

'The trouble with Ida is she worries too much,' he said, then began to shake as the fear hit him, and from his mouth came a travesty of laughter. 'No that's not right—is it Mr Craig? The trouble with Ida is she doesn't worry half enough.' The laughter resumed then, shrill and crazy. Craig leaned forward politely. 'You can stop if you want to,' he said, but the laughter went on. Craig reached out and his fingers touched, very lightly, Kaplan's forearm, found the place he needed, and pressed. Pain seared across Kaplan's arm, terrible pain that stopped at once as his laughter died.

'You see?' said Craig.

Kaplan said, 'I see, all right.' His body still shook, but his voice was steady. 'You really got a message from Aaron?'

'Mr Kaplan, you know I haven't,' said Craig. 'I've come for your information.'

'Again?' said Kaplan. Somehow Craig's body stayed immobile.

'Again,' he said.

'But I gave it to the other two.'

'Which other two, Mr Kaplan?'

'Mr Royce,' said Kaplan. 'And that nice Miss Benson. They took me on a trip in a motor-launch. Taped the whole thing.'

'So they did,' said Craig. 'Now tell it all to me.'

Kaplan told it and Craig listened, and remembered. When he had done, Craig said:

'Thank you. You've been very helpful.'

Kaplan said. 'Helpful. Yeah. Is it going to find my brother?'

'It's possible,' said Craig.

'I'm fifty-nine,' said Kaplan. 'I haven't seen him since I was twelve years old—and he was seven. But he's my brother. I want him found.'

Craig said, 'So do a lot of people. Friends and enemies. If the friends find him first—you'll see him.' Before Kaplan could speak, Craig said, 'Do you know a man called Laurie S. Fisher?'

'Sure,' said Kaplan. 'He's the guy who got me into this thing

—whatever it is. Flew me out to his ranch in Arizona. And that reminds me—what in hell are we going to do about the Bol——'

Craig's voice cut across his. 'Mr Kaplan, I met you on your doorstep, you invited me in, and we talked. I'm grateful for the time you spared me, but that's all that happened.'

Kaplan looked down at the arm Craig had touched, where the memory of pain still throbbed.

'Jesus,' he said. 'You're a cold-blooded bastard.'

'If I'm to find your brother I'll have to be.' Craig put down his glass. 'Thanks for the drink,' he said. 'I never drank from a table-lamp before. It was delicious.'

'OK,' said Kaplan. 'I get it. Keep my mouth shut or you'll tell Ida.'

'Is it really so important?' said Craig.

'It is to me,' said Kaplan. 'And to her too. Looking after me— all that. You don't care about all that crap. Right?'

Craig said, 'You've had a shock, and I handled you roughly. I'm sorry.'

'Where I was brought up we used to have a saying,' said Kaplan. 'With you for a friend, who needs enemies?'

'Not you, Mr Kaplan,' said Craig. 'You've already got them.'

He left quietly. Sounds from another room told him that Thadeus Cooke's corps-de-ballet were performing on television, and that Mrs Kaplan approved. Craig kept on going and met Hetherton in the hall without surprise.

'How long have you been with him?' Craig asked.

'Three weeks, sir,' said Hetherton. 'May I ask——'

'Department K,' said Craig. 'MI6.'

'Ah,' said Hetherton.

'Ah, is right,' said Craig. 'Stay on a while, Hethers, old top. He needs you.'

Hetherton said in quite a different voice, 'There's been nothing out of line so far.'

'Number thirty-seven,' said Craig. 'The Boldinis. They're away in Maine. Somebody broke in and smashed a vase. Then somebody else broke in and smashed somebody's head. And somebody had a gun. With a silencer. Like this.' His hand dipped into his pocket, showed the silencer, replaced it. 'It's a good silencer, and Kaplan's a hell of a target. If I were you, old top, I'd put him on a diet.'

He went back to his hotel room, and wrote down what Kaplan had told him. He was hungry and tired, but that didn't matter. The hunger sharpened his memory and the tiredness could be ignored. It was all a matter of will. When he'd finished he read it through three times then repeated it back to himself. Twice his memory failed him, so he read it three times more. When he'd got it right he lay down on the bed and slept at once, waking two hours later as he'd willed himself to do. Again he repeated Kaplan's message. It came back word-perfect. The only thing wrong with it was it didn't tell him enough. One picture post-card sent from Kutsk, in Turkey, and a message about a rabbi they'd both known as children. And Kaplan had lost the postcard. Craig screwed the paper into a twist, set fire to it, and dropped the pieces into a metal trash-bucket. When they had burned out he flushed the pieces down the toilet and went out to eat.

By now it was close to midnight and New York was much too quiet. (If Cinderella had lost her glass slipper in New York, Loomis had said, her foot would have been in it at the time.) He found a place that sold him clams, steak and beer, and a piece of apple-pie that reminded him of Tyneside. When he asked for coffee with caffein in it, the waiter reacted as if he were a junkie. He walked back through the silent canyons, glittering with light, their only occupants in pools of shadow, men, always in groups, waiting, watching: men inhibited by his size and the way he walked, the suggestion of power to be used at once and to the limit if they tried to hurt him.

Craig went back to his hotel room and remembered that Loomis, detestable as he was, was invariably right. The thought reminded him of the equipment that hadn't been supplied, and Benson and Royce's visit to Kaplan. But he'd got equipment, anyway, a Smith and Wesson and four rounds, and a Browning Hi-Power. And Benson and Royce were problems he could do nothing about . . . Craig slept.

CHAPTER FIVE

THEY CAME FOR HIM at four in the morning, the dead hour when reactions are slowest and sleep at its most profound. They were good men, there were enough of them, and they didn't get too close. Craig, worn out as he was, heard them coming just three seconds too late. By then they were in his bedroom and one of them had flicked on a torch, its brilliant bar of light hitting him full in the eyes. Craig flung up one arm, and in the dazzling silence heard the click of a safety-catch. A voice said, 'You know what I'm holding, Mr Craig?' He nodded. 'Just keep looking this way and maybe I won't use it.'

He looked into the light. Behind him someone was moving very softly, someone poised for a blow. At the last possible second Craig swerved round .The hand shielding his face shot out in a fist strike. He felt muscle and flesh give under his hand, then a second man struck, a single blow behind the ear with a life-preserver of plaited leather, and Craig collapsed at once. The lights went on then, and three men dressed as ambulance attendants set up a stretcher, loaded him on to it. A fourth man clung to the bedrail, his fingers solicitous where Craig's fist had smashed into his belly. He was a young, strong, fit man. Had one of those prerequisites been missing, Craig's blow would have crippled him, or killed him. When Craig was on the stretcher, one of the men gave him an injection of paraldehyde. It was vital that he shouldn't move for twenty minutes. After that, two of them carried out Craig; the third supported the one he had struck. It would be an hour at least before he could walk by himself.

Craig woke up in a bed that was five feet from the floor, a hard bed on an iron-frame that was the only thing in the room except for a chair. He wore a nightshirt of some kind of coarse linen, his wrists and feet were tied to the bed by canvas straps, and there was a bandage round his forearm. His head ached vilely, the drug made his stomach heave, and his wrists and ankles were already sore. He had no doubt that shortly he would regard his present position as one of luxury, and shut his eyes at once, trying to buy time, to prepare his body and mind to resist what was going to be done to him. That he would tell what he knew eventually was inevitable: any man can be broken, and if you've been broken once before it's that much easier the second time. But it was Craig's business to escape if he could, and hold out if escape were impossible. Desperately he tried to drive his mind and body away from what was coming, but the memory of Laurie S. Fisher was too strong. Beneath the bandage gauges recorded the sudden spurt of his pulse, the increase of perspiration, and in the next room a doctor saw these things recorded on instrument dials, and nodded to the man beside him. Craig was ready.

The man who came into Craig's room was tall and lean. His clothes were elegant, his face at once weather-beaten and scholarly. He stood looking down at Craig for twenty seconds, and Craig remained immobile, though the dials in the next room leaped as he waited.

The tall man said at last, 'I think we should have a talk, Mr Craig.'

Craig opened his eyes then and looked at him: perhaps the most difficult thing he had ever done.

The tall man said, 'I think we can dispense with the formalities of outraged innocence, don't you? Your name is John Craig, you work for Loomis in Department K of MI6, and you're here to find out about a man called Kaplan.'

Craig said, 'My name is John Craig—yes, but I'm an account-executive for Baldwin-Hicks. I'm here on advertising business. I never heard of Department K. Or Kaplan.'

Believe your cover story all the way, they had taught him. Know it. Feel it. Belong to it. Even when they begin to hurt you. Especially then. Even if the other side knows you're lying, it'll help you to hold out.

'Yes of course,' said the tall man. 'And you didn't go to see Kaplan's brother today?'

'Of course not,' said Craig. 'I never heard of Kaplan.'

The tall man pressed a buzzer and two other men came into the room. They wore the white smocks of hospital orderlies, but Craig knew them at once for what they were.

In the next room, the dials on the instrument panel moved up farther.

'You went to an apartment block on West 53rd Street,' said the tall man. 'Kaplan lives there. Don't waste our time, Mr Craig. We *know*.'

'I went to see an advertising man,' said Craig.

The two men in white moved closer to the bed.

'And did you go to the Graydon to see another advertising man?' the tall man asked.

Craig said, 'I don't know what you're talking about. I don't know what you're doing here.'

One of the men in white took his arm, held it firmly, and the other moved up close. Something flashed in the room's hard light, and Craig whimpered at a brief stab of pain, before his mind told him they had injected him again. Pentathol, he thought. Truth serum. The only way was to blank out your mind, think of nothing that would make sense to your questioners. Methodically he began to recite the days of the week in Arabic, over and over again, saying them harder and harder as the tall man's questions came. It would be so easy to answer the questions, and such a pleasure to talk about the terrible thing he had seen. But his business was to recite the days of the week in Arabic. He went on doing so.

Suddenly the tall man had gone, and in his place was another, chubby and benign, with hexagonal rimless glasses that made him look like a cherubic gnome.

'Hi,' he said. The seven words went on and on in Craig's mind. He said nothing.

'What you doing?' said the chubby man, and settled down in the chair. The dials had told him all he needed to know. This one was terrified. 'Counting sheep? Reciting poetry? French irregular verbs? They try all kinds,' the chubby man said, then rose suddenly and stood over Craig, the chubbiness gone, and in its place a squat power, as he noticed the tension in Craig's hands.

'You're not comfortable,' he said. 'Let me tuck you up properly.'

His hands stripped away the sheets, and Craig gabbled his seven words as the other man lifted the smock and looked at the marks on his body, the sweat soaking from him so that the bed sheets were wet.

'My my,' said the man. 'Somebody certainly didn't like you. Somebody certainly hurt you all right. You must be a very brave man. And a strong one too. I admire you, sport, I really do.'

The voice continued, softly, gently, and Craig saw him grow chubby again, fat and well-meaning and anxious to help as he told Craig how brave he was, and asked him how he managed to withstand such terrible pain. Slowly, inevitably Craig listened, and answered, the seven words falling like pierced armour from his memory. The chubby man knew all about pain—and cared. On and on Craig talked, and gradually the chubby man's questions moved from Craig's agony to Laurie S. Fisher's, and Craig wept as he remembered what had been done to him.

'And you really didn't see who did it, John?'

'No,' said Craig. 'I thought it was the KGB, but——'

'But what? Go on. You can tell me.'

'You're the KGB, aren't you?'

'Just a research team, John. Asking questions about the problems of pain. Kaplan now. We heard there were two hoods in the Boldinis' apartment. Were they going to hurt Kaplan?'

'They were going to kill him,' said Craig. 'Only I killed one of them instead.'

'And the other one got away, right? You should have killed him too, don't you think so?'

'Noise,' said Craig. 'People.' Suddenly he felt very weary.

'Please, John,' said the chubby man. 'Don't go to sleep just yet.'

Craig said, 'They weren't—executives. Not like the ones who got Fisher. *They* were your best people. The two I met were just hired guns. Not worth killing.'

'Or hurting, John?'

Craig said, 'I don't like hurting people. I don't like being hurt.'

'John,' said the chubby man, 'I think you're in the wrong business.'

'That too,' said Craig, and slept.

The tall man came out of the shadows and looked at Craig as the two orderlies left. 'Well, well,' he said. 'The best in the business.'

'You take a blade, you sharpen it and sharpen it till it'll split a silk scarf drawn across it. Then one day you drop it on a stone floor. After that it'll still cut bread, but the silk scarves are safe. They stay in one piece.'

'Damn your parables,' said the tall man. 'What about Fisher?'

'He didn't do that to Fisher. He couldn't. Anyway, he told us the truth. He found him.'

'And the girl too?'

'And the girl. She was a Scandinavian type, just like he said. Mai Olsen. Fisher met her——'

'I know all that,' the tall man said, and turned back to Craig. 'What do you think?'

'Of John? He can still fight, still kill if he has to—but he can't cut silk scarves.'

The tall man turned away.

'Get rid of him,' he said.

There were rats. He could hear them scuttering about the floor, running up the legs of the bed, ducking beneath the bedclothes every time he turned his head to see them. He'd never actually seen one, but they were there all right. He could feel them. From time to time they bit him in the arms. Not that it mattered. The bites didn't hurt: they were just reminders that the rats were there. And there was another one—probably a baby he thought—that hid behind the pillow and bit him behind the ear. A baby rat. Brown fur, naked tail, scrabbling paws. He could imagine it perfectly, but it didn't disgust him —only it *was* a nuisance. Biting like that. The trouble was he couldn't stop it, because his hands were tied. Better to sleep, if the rats would let him.

Suddenly a bell sounded, deferential but insistent. A telephone, he thought, an American telephone. Only there weren't any telephones, not in that room where they'd talked about the pain. The ringing went on, and Craig woke, the rats disappeared, their scrabbling the hum of air conditioning, their bites the ache in his arms and head. As he woke he noticed that his arms and legs were stretched out as if he were still strapped down. Cautiously he reached for the telephone at his bedside, and pain stabbed behind his ear.

'Noon, Mr Craig,' said the voice of the girl at the switchboard.

'I beg your pardon?'

'It's noon,' said the voice again, acidly patient. 'Twelve o'clock. You left word for a call.'

'Oh yes,' said Craig. 'Thank you.'

'You're welcome,' said the girl. The words meant, 'Jesus. Another lush.'

He rang room service for breakfast and a bowl of ice, and spent a long time bathing, showering, soaking the pain from his body. The mark of the thing they'd clipped to his arm was red and angry, but it would soon go. The one behind his ear was another matter: purple, exotic, and with a lot of life left. He'd have to tell absurd lies about backing into a shelf, or something. Then he remembered the gunman he'd slammed against the wall with the door. The lie wasn't so absurd.

The waiter came and he tipped him, wrapped ice in a towel, and put it on the bruise, then ate his breakfast. He found it strange that he could be so hungry, when his life was finished. He was no danger at all, so far as they were concerned. So much so that they hadn't even bothered to kill him. To them, he wasn't even a joke. Doggedly he tried to remember the questions they had asked, but all he could remember was pain, and Laurie S. Fisher, and a fat little man looking at where he too had been hurt. He remembered a tall man too, but that was all. Craig finished his coffee and began to dress and pack. If he really was finished, Loomis would have to know. He booked a seat on a plane for the next night, the first flight he could get, and went back to bed. No rats, no dreams, no arms and legs in a Saint Andrew's cross. When he woke up he felt better, remembering the man he'd hit in the stomach, the way he'd saved Kaplan's life. He remembered, too, the information Kaplan had given him, word for word. There might after all be some point in staying on, in order to find out who had decided that Craig was finished. In tracking them down. After all, the night clerk at the hotel should be able to give him some sort of a lead.

But the night clerk, when he came on duty, knew nothing, except that Craig had come back very late with two friends, and he'd had a little—difficulty in getting up to bed. In fact the two friends had helped. That would be around six in the morning. Must have been some party, Mr Craig. Sure he remembered the ambulance, but that had been for another guest, two floors below Craig. The way the clerk had heard it, he'd called a doctor, and the doctor had diagnosed a perforated appendix and called a hospital. He didn't know what hospital. No. But the ambulance looked classy. Craig thanked him and gave him ten dollars in hard currency, taxpayers' money, then went back to his problem. The yellow pages told him just how full of hospitals and nursing homes New York is. Moreover, there was Loomis to be considered. He'd got Kaplan's information, and Loomis would want to know about that, as well as the fact that he, Craig, was a failure. Craig ate dinner in the hotel and slept for twelve hours.

Next morning he felt better than ever, and had found a way to solve his problem. He would call on Thadeus Cooke, and have another fight. If he won, he would stay on. If he lost, he would report back to Loomis.

Cooke beat him three times in seven minutes, and looked almost as horrified as Craig.

'Mr Craig,' he said, 'you must have got problems since I saw you last. Why, man, I tell you, they've even got down into your feet. You got to solve them, Mr Craig, or you ain't goin' to be no good at this game any more. I tell you honest, the way

you're doing now, you couldn't even lick Blossom. At least'—
he thought it over, and made one concession—'not if Blossom
was set for you. You go on home—get those problems licked.
Or take up golf.'

Craig went. Not home, not immediately. There was plenty
of time for the plane. But he had to see the Kaplans again.
There was a good man looking after them, and there'd be
others backing up and all that, but the Kaplans didn't *know*. It
was true that Marcus Kaplan had seen a man killed in the
Boldinis' apartment, but they didn't, either of them, know
Fisher was dead, or what had been done to him before he died.
It was up to Craig to tell them that these things happened:
that people got hurt, or were even destroyed, and yet were
allowed to go on living.

The doorman was off duty when Craig arrived, but the
apartment building seemed quiet enough, not at all the kind of
place where a man had been killed. No cops, no spectators, no
crowds of sightseers. Perhaps that was just the heat. (If Lady
Godiva rode down Fifth Avenue in July nobody would watch,
said Loomis. The sight of that poor horse sweating would kill
them.) He went up to the Kaplans' floor. The Boldinis' door
was unguarded, but Craig moved on more quickly and rang
the Kaplans' bell. Nothing happened, so he kept on ringing,
over and over. Hetherton wasn't going to keep him out.

But it wasn't Hetherton who stood there. It was a girl. A
small girl, long-legged, brown-eyed, swathed in the most
enormous sable coat Craig had ever seen. Just to look at her
made Craig melt in sweat, but she looked happy enough about
it and hugged the coat to her body with her arms. What she
was not happy about was Craig, whom she apparently cast as
an intruder, maybe even a prowler.

'I called to see Mr Kaplan,' said Craig. 'My name's Craig.'

'I'm sorry,' the girl said, 'he's not at home right now.'

She made to close the door, and Craig did not try to stop
her, but said quickly: 'When will he be back?' The girl hesitated.

'Three weeks—maybe a month,' she said. 'He and Aunt Ida
are on a vacation trip.' So that was all right. The CIA could
move when they had to. They'd taken the Kaplans away.

'Thanks,' said Craig, and turned to leave. He'd taken three
steps down the corridor when the girl called out: 'Just a minute.'
He went back to her.

'You've hurt yourself,' the girl said. 'Behind your ear.'

'Miss——?'

'Loman,' said the girl.

'Miss Loman—I know it.'

'Sort of a crazy place to hurt yourself.'

'It happens,' said Craig. 'I stumbled and banged my head on a shelf.'

The brown eyes looked puzzled and faintly amused, nothing more.

'You'd better come in for a minute,' she said. 'You look awful.'

She led the way to the Kaplans' living-room and sat, still wearing the coat. The air-conditioning wasn't on; Craig looked at her again, and began sweating seriously.

'You know why I asked you in?' she asked. 'I figured you couldn't be a prowler. You have a British accent. So it's O.K. Can I get you something?'

'No thanks,' said Craig. 'But I'd like to ask a question. Two questions.'

'Go ahead,' the girl said.

'Is Mrs Kaplan your aunt?'

'No,' said the girl. 'Just an old friend of the family—so I call her Aunt Ida. What's the other one?'

'Why are you wearing a fur coat?'

Miss Loman blushed a fierce, unpleasing pink. As Craig watched, she got up, looked in the mirror and brushed at her face with one hand, still clutching her coat with the other.

'Oh, shoot,' she said. 'I hate doing that. You see, Mr Craig —the Kaplans went away just this morning, and they asked me to close the apartment up for them. And Marcus is in furs. You know, so Aunt Ida has the most fan*tas*tic furs, so when I found a new one——'

'You just had to try it on,' said Craig. 'But aren't you hot?'

'I'm dying,' Miss Loman said. 'If you'll excuse me, I'll hang it up.'

She rose, still clutching the coat, tripped over a footstool, and flung up her hands to steady herself, and the coat swung open. Beneath it she was quite naked, and very pretty. She whirled round from Craig, and he remembered another girl in swirling fur, a very bright girl, and pretty too. As pretty as this one. When Miss Loman had finished swirling she held the coat in place, one-handed. The other one held the telephone. Craig hadn't moved from his chair.

'You're absolutely right,' he said. 'Much too hot to try on fur coats. How fortunate I'm not a prowler.'

Miss Loman laughed and put the telephone back on its cradle. 'You British,' she said. 'How do you get to be so diplomatic?'

'Practice, I suppose,' said Craig, and got to his feet unhurried. 'When you write to the Kaplans, tell them I said they should take care of themselves.'

'I will,' she said, and followed him to the door. When he reached it, she called out:

'What's your first name?'

'John,' he said.

'Mine's Miriam. Tell me, John—did you think I was pretty?'

'Delightful,' said Craig. 'Absolutely delightful.'

When he left she was blushing again.

He went back to London on an Air India Boeing 707. Curry, and hostesses in saris, and breakfast served an hour before landing, and when the plane touched down it was lunch time. He hadn't slept at all and felt bone-weary! Passport control and customs were separate purgatories. His world was finished, and waiting for him now was Loomis, with a thousand questions, and after them one fact: Loomis could hardly just let him go. It was conceivable that Loomis would have him killed. But even so, he had to call him. Loomis would know he was back anyway. He took a taxi from the airport to a pub he knew. It was not a very nice pub, but it had one valuable asset: from it you could see Queen Anne's Gate. He bought a drink, and went to a phone booth. First he got Loomis's secretary, then the fat man came on.

'That was quick. Get what you wanted?'

'Most of it,' said Craig. It was true enough.

'What's that supposed to mean?' Loomis said.

'I saw the Kaplans. And a young friend of theirs. A girl called Miriam Loman. Not Fisher. He was dead when I reached him.'

'Ah,' said Loomis. 'You better come and see me. Tomorrow morning.'

'Can't it be today?'

'No. I got a lot on today. Tomorrow morning. Ten sharp.'

Loomis hung up. At six o'clock Joanna Benson left Department K. Ten minutes later, Royce left too.

He went back to his flat, taking his time, but nobody was watching it. Craig, it seemed, was past all that. You just pointed him in whatever direction was necessary, wound him up, and off he went. When the job was over he just sat around waiting till the next time—or until he was thrown away. Craig discovered that he was very angry, and the anger surprised him. There was no fear in it: only rage. If Benson and Royce were so bloody marvellous, let them get on with it. *He* wasn't going to sit around while Loomis made up his mind whether he should live or not. And yet what else could he do? If he bolted, Loomis would be after him in earnest. For Loomis there was no such thing as an ex-agent, only a defector waiting for a new master. The new master might be offering money, or merely a cessation of pain, but sooner or later he would appear, Craig knew, if Loomis didn't act first. But Loomis always had acted first, in the five times it had happened, and Craig knew it well. He had executed one of them himself. The anger yielded to despair.

The only logical way out was suicide. A lot of whisky and a massive dose of chloral hydrate, painfully hoarded over weeks of sleeplessness. That would be easy, painless, almost desirable. His life was finished anyway: his ability as an agent gone, his zest in women gone, the booze he despised his only pleasure. It was right that it should help to kill him. Even if Loomis let him live it would kill him anyway. He looked at the whisky decanter then went into the kitchen and found a fresh bottle. The chloral hydrate tablets were in the bathroom. They could wait . . .

When the phone rang the bottle was a quarter empty and Craig was in the bathroom, counting the tablets. Twenty-three, that was more than enough. He poured the tablets back into their bottle and noticed that his hand was still steady. The discovery didn't please him: he wanted to be really drunk before he swallowed the damn things: so drunk that he couldn't change his mind even if he wanted to. He put the tablets in his pocket and went back to the drawing-room and the view of the park Benson had liked so much. The phone shrilled at him still. He picked up first his glass, then the phone.

'Craig,' he said, and swallowed.

'Where you been?' said Loomis.

'The loo,' said Craig. 'I'm allowed to. You gave me the night off.'

The words came out with the right insolence, but he was terrified.

'You drinking?' Loomis asked.

'I've had a couple.'

'Don't have any more. Come here instead. I want to talk to you.'

'But you said——'

'I changed my mind,' Loomis snarled. 'I'm allowed to. I'm the boss.'

He hung up then, and Craig finished his drink reflexively, without thought, then realized what he had done and put the glass down, very deliberately, still looking at the park. Benson had really liked that view, he thought. But then she was young and healthy and quite sure she wasn't going to die: that kind could afford to like things. He went back to the bathroom, and noticed on the way what a big mistake the last drink had been. He was staggering. He ran the water cold, stuck his head under it, and thought. The tablets were out now. If he took them, Loomis might send a man round—they'd find him and have him pumped out before they had a chance to work, and Craig had no intention of being as vulnerable as that to Loomis, if Loomis were going to let him live. He had to get away, have time to think—but in London Loomis was the master. There was nowhere to hide from him. And out of London? The seaports were watched, and the airports too. Always. And the men who watched them knew Craig. They'd know at once which ship, which plane—and at the other end Loomis's men would be waiting. Men who'd spot him at once, though he'd never seen them before.

'Sods,' Craig said aloud. 'Bloody *sods*.' And the words came out in the hard, flat accent of his childhood. And as he said them, he remembered. There was a way.

Getting there involved two tubes, a taxi, and three buses, and time was important. But even more important was to know you weren't followed, and by the time he reached the boatyard he was sure. It was in Wapping, behind a dirty back wall and a sagging door that waited in crumbling patience for the demolition squad. But inside it was neat, tidy, craftsmanlike, filled with every kind of pleasure craft from dinghies to trimarans, and every one built with patient skill. Arthur Candlish did well out of sailing-boats, and paid his taxes on them. His other incomes were all tax-free. He listened in silence, a slow, big-boned man of fifty, as Craig talked. Candlish's slowness was not stupidity, but it helped when others thought it was. Craig told him his life was in danger, and he had to get away.

'Who's after you?' Candlish asked. 'The coppers?'

'No,' said Craig. 'Not the coppers. These lads mean it.' And Candlish smiled.

'You brought a feller here once,' he said. 'Big fat feller. I did a job for you. Is that him?'

Craig nodded, and Candlish sighed. 'I'll charge you nowt, John,' he said. 'But there'll be others, and it'll cost money to beat him.'

'How much?' asked Craig.

'A thousand quid.'

'Fifteen hundred,' said Craig. 'I'll pay in dollars. You're entitled to your share.'

'I couldn't take money off ye,' said Candlish. 'I knew your da.' He paused, and Craig marvelled for the hundredth time that twenty years of London hadn't modified Candlish's voice in the slightest, so that he had only to speak to carry Craig back at once to his childhood: the cobbled streets, the gulls and docks, the cold, grey-glittering sea.

'Where?' Candlish asked, and Craig had dreaded the question.

'Ireland,' he said.

Candlish went out and Craig saw him dismissing his men, then at the telephone. There was no other way. He'd realized it there in Regent's Park, when he looked at Joanna Benson's view. He couldn't kill himself. Not now. Maybe if he'd been left alone and got drunk enough he'd have done it *then*. Maybe. But he couldn't try again. And he couldn't just drift, waiting for Loomis to find him. All he could do was finish the job, and do it well enough for Loomis to lay off him till the next time. That meant going back to the States and finding Marcus Kaplan—and getting more information. There had to be more. That was why the Americans had him, but he could be found.

Candlish came back. 'We'd better make a start,' he said.

He rose and put on a bowler hat of antique design that made him look like a bookmaker with a taste for religion.

'That fat friend of yours won't have forgotten me,' he said.

Loomis missed him by seven minutes. When he arrived the boatyard was locked up tight, and a sign outside said CLOSED TILL FURTHER NOTICE. Nobody had seen Craig, nobody had seen Candlish. The staff—three men and a lad—were on holiday, and Mr Candlish had probably gone up North to see his relatives . . .

Mr Candlish, in fact, was driving to Holyhead in a fish-lorry, and Craig went with him as his mate. They stopped in the suburbs for Craig to have his photograph taken, and were met outside Holyhead by a young man in an Aston Martin DB6 who had Craig's new passport—not too new, not too blank, the American visa exactly as it should be. Craig found that his name was John Adams, and that he was a general dealer.

'Useful that,' said the young man. 'You can deal in anything you like. Early Picassos or army surplus. Two hundred and fifty quid please.'

'Send me the bill,' Candlish said.

'Anything you say, Mr Candlish.'

The Aston Martin roared and disappeared, nervous at being so far from London, and Candlish drove on down to the docks. In place of the fishing-boat Craig had expected there was an elegant power-launch complete with owners: a thin Manchester cotton-broker and his fat Salford wife—Craig and Candlish were the crew.

'Six hundred quid they want—and a hundred and fifty for the lorry,' said Candlish. 'It's a bloody scandal.'

There was satisfaction in the thought that A. J. Scott-Saunders had provided the money.

They sailed at once, and made for Cork. There was relief in handling a boat again, the relief of knowing that one skill at least had not deserted him—and the realisation of what waited for him in the States killed his need for alcohol. The fat lady from Salford could cook, too, and the weather was clear and bright. The trip at least was bearable, and more than bearable when Arthur started to talk about the old days, about the father Craig could scarcely remember. He took the wheel while Arthur slept, and when it was his turn, found that he too could sleep. Four healing hours that left him alert, ready, as the boat ran into a small, empty cove and Candlish and Craig prepared to go ashore in the dinghy. The thin man and fat woman said nothing, but their eyes on Craig were hungry. Money was going ashore. A lot of money.

Craig took the oars and Candlish cast off. The sea gleamed in the morning sunlight, bright and diamond-hard, without the Mediterranean tenderness Craig knew so well.

'You'll have to watch those two,' said Craig.

'I'll watch them.' Candlish's voice showed no trace of worry. 'They're a bit scared of me, John.'

Craig was still laughing as the dinghy beached. They walked ashore dry shod.

'Straight up to those cliffs,' said Candlish. 'Get to the top and you'll find a bit of a path. Follow that and you'll come to a farmhouse. There'll be a Volkswagen there. Take it.'

'Stolen?'

Candlish chuckled. 'Your own car, lad. All in order. There's papers to prove it. Just leave it where you want. When the police find it—you'll be miles away.' It wasn't a question. He had no doubts of Craig's ability. 'Good luck, John.'

Craig scrambled ashore. 'Thanks,' he said. 'So long.'

Candlish watched as Craig went up the beach to the cliff. A good lad. A hard one to get on the wrong side of. He touched the inside of his jacket, and the hundred dollar bills crackled like music. That fat bitch would be happy when he paid her. Slow and easy he rowed back to the launch.

Craig found the Volkswagen waiting, a road map open on the front seat, and drove at once to Cork, and breakfast in a hotel. Bacon and eggs and tea, and a waiter who talked because he felt like it, because it was a beautiful morning. Craig went next to a travel agency, and then bought clothes, a suitcase, shoes, and set off for Shannon across the cheerful Irish landscape, the improbable green grass and whitewashed cabins unreal as a film set. And why not? The Irish were all actors anyway. That didn't make them any less efficient when they wanted to be, Craig thought, and drove the Volkswagen with care. He daren't risk an accident.

At Shannon, Ireland stopped and Mid Atlantica began. Even the tea tasted different, at one with the plastic and insurance machines and flight calls. Craig boarded an Aer Lingus Boeing at five o'clock. Nine hours later he was in Chicago, and it was eight p.m. Two hours after that he was at Kennedy, and it was nine p.m. He went into New York by bus, and found a hotel in the West Forties in downtown Manhattan, and slept for fourteen hours. When he awoke it was time to find Miss Loman.

He rang Marcus Kaplan Inc. and asked for him by name. When a secretary's voice told him he was on holiday, he said:

'My name is Adams. John Adams. I had rather hoped to see Mr Kaplan.'

'I'm sorry, Mr Adams. We have no way of contacting him right now.'

'Oh dear,' said Craig, very British. 'It's about clay-pigeon shooting. What I believe you call skeet-shooting over here.'

'That's right,' said the girl, and the voice was weary now, long-suffering: a secretary too often involved in her boss's obsession. Skeet-shooting to Kaplan was like a fix to a junkie. She didn't dare get in the way. Get off the hook, her instincts said. Fast.

'You might try Miss Loman, sir,' she said. It was that easy.

She lived in Greenwich Village, on the ground floor of a house in Grove Street, with a small brick yard where a maple tree somehow survived and even gave shade. When Craig called she had been sun-bathing, and had to put on a robe to answer the bell's ring. When she saw who it was, she blushed again.

'I'm sorry,' said Craig. 'Did I disturb you?'

'No,' she said. 'I was in the yard. Do you want to come out?'

He followed her, thinking how young she was, how easy her movements, with the ease that comes from knowing, really *knowing*, that nothing can ever go wrong, nothing can really hurt all that much. There was a chair under the tree, and she waved him to it. She sat on a li-lo that lay in the full glare of the sun. She was still blushing.

Craig said, 'What's wrong?'

'It's ridiculous,' Miss Loman said. 'Every time I see you I'm like this. Maybe you think I don't *have* any clothes . . . I was sunbathing.'

'Go ahead and sunbathe,' said Craig. She hesitated. 'Look, Miss Loman, I can't be a prowler. I'm British.'

She giggled then, took off the robe, and lay down. She wore a tiny bikini and her body was sleek with sun-tan lotion. A small, luscious body that would one day be fat, but that day was yet to come. A woman's body, thought Craig, who had never subscribed to the theory that women were failed men and ought to look like it.

'I've come to ask about your uncle,' he said.

Miss Loman pouted. 'He's fine,' she said. 'But he's not my uncle.'

'I'm sorry, I'd forgotten that,' said Craig. 'Just an old family friend, isn't he?'

'That's right.'

'Is your father in the fur business too?'

'My father's dead, Mr Craig. So's my mother. Marcus brought me up. Supported me.' She hesitated. 'He still does sometimes. When I get bored with being a secretary.'

'You know where he is?'

She swung round to look at him, her body's movements forgotten. She was wary of him now.

'I can't tell you,' she said.

'He's in danger,' said Craig. 'He could be hurt.'

She got up and backed away. Craig sat on, under the tree.

'Just who are you?' she said.

'You weren't surprised at what I said. You knew it already,' said Craig.

'And how did you know I was here?' She hesitated, then—

'Adams. You rang up Marcus's firm, didn't you? Called yourself Adams.' She took a step backwards, then another. 'I want you out of here.'

Craig sat on, and she retreated further.

'Marcus knows where his brother is,' Craig said. 'Maybe you know it too.'

The words stopped her.

'His brother's dead,' she said. 'He died in Volochanka prison.'

'He's alive,' said Craig. 'He escaped from prison—God knows how. The story is he's in Turkey.'

She began to move again, and Craig, still slouched in his chair, suddenly had a gun in his hand. It moved up slowly from her waist to a point between her eyes.

'Look at it, Miss Loman,' said Craig.

'I'm looking,' she said. 'You'd never dare——'

'Miss Loman, you don't believe that,' said Craig. 'Come and sit down.'

Slowly, her eyes fixed on the gun's black mouth, she obeyed. Craig still didn't move.

'There's a question you missed,' he said. 'You should have said, "Who the hell are you, anyway?" '

'Who the hell are you, anyway?'

'British Intelligence. MI6. Department K.' said Craig.

'You'll have to leave here some time. I'll call the police——'

She stopped. Craig was shaking his head.

'Why wouldn't I?'

'All sorts of reasons. If you did that—I'd kill your uncle. Or you. Or both.'

'But that's crazy.'

'Miss Loman, you're up to your neck in a very crazy business. There's another reason. Your uncle wants to see his brother.' Her eyes looked into his then, for the first time ignoring the gun. 'You know that's true, Miss Loman.' She nodded. 'I'm the only one who can find him.'

'You think you're so good?'

Craig said wearily, 'I have to be. If I don't, I'm a dead man myself.'

He stood up then, and the gun disappeared in a blur of speed. She looked up into flat grey eyes that told her nothing at all.

'Where's your uncle, Miss Loman?'

'Miami Beach,' she said. 'The Portland Arms.'

'Any skeet-shooting there?'

'Yes,' she said. 'But nobody goes there now.'

'We will,' said Craig.

He moved then, and took her arm. She could sense the power, carefully controlled, in his hard hands. There was something else too. He was trembling, but her body meant nothing to him. She was sure of it.

'I meant what I told you,' he said. 'If I don't get Kaplan, I'm dead. And if I die, Miss Loman, I'm going to have company.' He paused. 'I'm sorry,' he said, 'but I'll have to watch you dress.'

To her amazement, she realised the apology was genuine.

CHAPTER SIX

HE WOULDN'T let her pack. She wore the new dress Marcus had bought for her birthday—a drip-dry thing in glittering yellow, and her handbag was big enough to contain a spare pair of stockings, bra, and pants. He let her take them, but that was all, then they walked together down the street, the pretty girl and the attentive beau who was taking her out to lunch.

'Nothing's more conspicuous than a suitcase,' he said. 'Even if your neighbours aren't nosey.'

They took a cab to the Air Terminal and a bus to Kennedy. He paid for everything in cash, and seemed to have plenty. All the way he was polite and attentive, and she realized that in other circumstances this man would have been attractive to her, tremendously attractive, in spite of the threat of cruelty behind the politeness. Perhaps even because of it. But he was unaware of her as a woman, she knew, and the thought irked her, even then.

Only once did she almost panic and try to get away. They were in the departure lounge, waiting for their flight call, and a cop walked by, the kind of cop you needed in a situation like this. A big one, big and mean, not the kind who helps old ladies across streets. She stirred in her seat, ready to run, to scream maybe, but Craig was as fast and as sensitive as a cat. His left hand reached out and touched her arm, and pain scalded through her. He let it go, and she saw that his right hand was inside his coat.

'No,' he said. 'Not yet.' She sat very still. 'I had to do that to your uncle once,' he said. 'You're a hard family to convince.'

Then the flight call came, and they went out to the 727 and he was polite and attentive all over again as he sat by her side. It should have felt like a nightmare, she thought, but it wasn't. She knew that everything he had told her was true, and she was very frightened. For the first time in her twenty-three years of life, death was real to her. She did exactly what he told her, and the smiling, polite man watched her as intently as ever. When they touched down at Miami he bought her a meal, then took her to the car-rental firm that tries harder, and watched as she hired a Chevrolet coupé with the money he had given her. She drove, and he made her pull up on the road into town, slipped something into her hand.

'Here,' he said. 'Put it on.'

It was a wedding ring. Slowly, hating him, she put it on her finger.

'Don't be sentimental,' Craig said. 'That's a luxury, believe me—and we can't afford luxuries. You're alive, Miss Loman. Be thankful.'

She drove on, and he made her pull up at a supermarket. They went inside and he bought whisky, sandals, a shirt and jeans for her, and for himself, tooth brushes and a zipper travelling bag. They went to a motel then, and he booked them in for the night, saying little and sounding, when he did speak, like a New Yorker. The woman at reception hardly looked at him, at her not at all. The unending soap-opera on the transistor radio had all her attention. Craig thanked her even so, and they drove past the dusty palms, the minute swimming pool to Cabin Seven. She switched on the air-conditioning at once as Craig carried in the bag.

The plastic and vinyl room was as glittering and unreal as a television ad, but the chairs were comfortable and the twin-beds still had springs. Craig opened the bag, took out the whisky, and mixed two drinks, offered one to her. She shook her head.

'Suit yourself,' he said, and took off his coat and sprawled on a bed. She saw for the first time the supple leather harness of his shoulder holster, the gun-butt that looked like an obscene extension of his body. Her eyes misted with tears.

'Not yet,' said Craig. 'You can cry later. Drink your drink.'

'I hate you,' she said.

'I know. Drink your drink.'

The whisky was strong, and she choked on it, but the tears left her.

'Get your uncle on the phone,' he said, 'and tell him exactly what I say. Tell him you're with me—and he's not to worry about you if he does as he's told. Then tell him to meet us at the skeet-shooting place—does he know where it is?'

She nodded. 'He was at the championship here five years ago,' she said.

'Tell him to be there in an hour.'

She looked up the Portland Arms in the phone-book, and did just as he said. Aunt Ida was at the beauty shop, and that made it easier. Her uncle took a lot of convincing.

'Craig?' he said. 'That tough Englishman?'

'You're to meet him at the skeet-shoot—in an hour,' she said.

'Honey—you know I can't do that.'

She said quickly, 'Marcus, you've got to. If you don't—I'm all right now. But if you don't—maybe I won't be. I'm not fooling, Marcus.'

'He's with you?'

'Yes,' she said. 'He's with me. Marcus—please do as I say.'

Craig took the phone from her.

'That's good advice, Mr Kaplan,' he said.

'If you harm that girl——'

'It'll be because you didn't turn up,' said Craig. 'Drive carefully.'

He hung up. She was looking at him in loathing.

'I don't believe it,' she said. 'The first time I met you—I liked you.'

'It doesn't matter,' he said. 'Get changed.'

'Here?'

'In the bathroom, if you're shy,' he said. 'Just do it. And hurry.'

When she came back she wore the shirt and jeans. The gun lay on the bed, near her hand, and her eyes went to it at once.

'Go on,' said Craig. 'Pick it up. Shoot me.' She didn't move. 'Go on. Get the gun.'

She leaped for it then, and the speed of his reaction was terrifying. He came at her like a diver, and a hard shoulder slammed her into the bed as one hand pinioned her gun-hand, the other splayed beneath her chin, thumb and fore-finger pressing. She forgot the pain that made her drop the gun, forgot the pain in her breast where his shoulder had caught her, and thought only of the agony the thumb and finger made, crushing nerves, choking out breath.

'Please,' she gasped. 'Oh, please.'

He let her go, and the intake of air was an unavoidable agony to her. He picked up the gun and dropped it near her hand.

'Want to try again?' he said. She shook her head. 'Poor Miss Loman,' said Craig. 'But I had to do it, you know.'

'Why?' she said. 'Why?'

'To show you you can't win. Look at my hands, Miss Loman.'

He held them up in front of her, and she saw the hard ridges of skin from finger-tip to wrist, and across the knuckles.

'I can break wooden boards with these. With my feet, too. It's called karate. I'm a Seventh Dan black belt. There are only five men outside Japan who can beat me—and they're not in Miami. Miss Loman, we're not taking the gun.' He moved his hands closer to her. 'Just these.'

'You're hell on women,' she said.

'And middle-aged furriers. I want you to remember that.'

She drove him to the skeet-shoot club, through downtown Miami, past the resort hotels and the restaurants and the pastel blue Atlantic. Traffic was light, the tourist season was over, and they made good time. Craig sat back easy and relaxed, drinking in the wealth of the place. There was so much of it, and it went on for so long. They left it at last, and got into country-club land, golf-club land, where shaven grass was as obvious a sign of wealth as a Cadillac or a Chinchilla coat, and stopped at last before a building of glittering white stone, of the kind that she had called Hispaniola Baroque that time she had kidded Marcus about it, when he'd shot there five years ago: a glittering white building with pillars and pilasters and mullioned windows, and miniature cannon on its embrasured roof. All it needed, she'd said, was Long John Silver limping down the stairs, a parrot on his shoulder. Marcus had laughed then. He wasn't laughing now.

They left the car to a Negro attendant in white, a scarlet cummerbund round his waist, and walked up the steps towards him, Craig on her right. When they reached him Craig's left arm went round her waist, his right hand held out to Marcus, who hesitated.

'Take it,' said Craig, 'or I'll hurt her.'

His fingers moved, and the girl gasped. At once Marcus's hand came out to him.

'Great to see you again,' Marcus said. 'How are you?'

'Fine,' said Craig. 'Everything's fine. So far. Let's get on with the match, shall we?'

They went inside the building then, through a low, cool bar to the gun-room, where Kaplan signed for two guns and ammunition, then picked up one gun as Craig took up the other. With the gun in his hands, Kaplan changed at once. The gun was something he knew; it gave him confidence, even courage.

Craig said, 'You walk ahead, Miriam. Lead the way while Marcus and I talk.'

She did as he bade her at once, without question, and Craig followed, the shotgun under his arm, English style, the muzzle aimed at a point behind her feet, but Marcus knew, capable of tilting to her back in less than a second. He had been warned about shotgun wounds, knew what they could do to her at such close range. His courage receded.

'Guns are useless things,' Craig said, 'unless we're prepared to shoot. Don't you agree, Mr Kaplan?'

'What do you want me to do, Craig?'

'Tell me where your brother is.'

'I don't *know*.'

They reached the shooting-range then, and Miriam waited till they came up, ready to work the treadle that would fire the skeet.

'That's a pity,' said Craig.

'For you it certainly is.'

'For all of us. You see I know you're lying, Mr Kaplan. And if you go on lying, I'm going to kill Miriam here.'

'You're crazy,' Kaplan said.

Craig said, 'I'm desperate certainly. And I mean it.'

His hand moved on to the safety catch of the shotgun, the barrel came up.

'I'll kill *you*,' said Marcus.

'Maybe,' said Craig. 'You've never done it before . . . And even if you did, she'd still be dead.'

Kaplan didn't move.

Craig said, 'Mr Kaplan—if I don't find your brother, I'm dead anyway.' His finger moved to the trigger.

'Marcus,' said the girl, 'he means it. For God's sake tell him.'

'Outside Kutsk,' Kaplan said. 'In Turkey. He sent me a post-card from there eight months ago. That's the first time I heard from Aaron in twenty-five years. I told you that.'

The gun-barrel dropped.

'You told Miss Benson and Mr Royce too?'

'Yes,' said Kaplan. 'A man from the CIA asked me to.'

'What else did you tell them?'

'Things,' said Kaplan. 'Family things. You know. About my father, my uncle—all that. The way things were in Russia. So Aaron would know they came from me.'

'Does Miss Loman know these family things?' Kaplan nodded. 'Then I won't bother you about them,' Craig said.

Kaplan looked up. 'You mean you're not going to let her go?'

'How could I?' said Craig. 'You'd tell the CIA.' He raised the gun again. 'Just be quiet and everything will be fine.'

Kaplan stood immobile, his hands clenched round the shotgun. The CIA had warned him so carefully: no one but Royce and Miss Benson must be told the things he knew about his brother. To tell anyone else would be to betray his country, and Kaplan loved his country, not because of what it was, but for what it would become. His was a questioning, suspicious, and demanding love, but it was real; real enough for him to die for it. He had seen this, in his day-dreams: Major Kaplan, USAAF, in a dogfight with Messerschmitts; Commander Kaplan, USN, steering his tin-can to intercept a Jap cruiser. In the reality of his warehouse he had acknowledged the silliness of his day-dreams, but not his right to the dreams themselves. Only he had never daydreamed Miriam's death. His hands loosed their grip.

'This CIA man, Laurie Fisher——' said Craig.

Kaplan looked up. 'You know him?' he said.

'I've seen him once,' said Craig. 'He was the one who told you to take a vacation?'

'Yes,' said Kaplan.

'It was good advice,' said Craig, 'but from now on stay in a crowd. If you think I'm rough, Mr Kaplan, you should try the KGB—like your brother.' He paused, then added: 'Let's see you shoot, Mr Kaplan. That's what we came for, wasn't it?'

Miriam worked the treadle, and the skeet balls shot out, small and travelling fast. Kaplan fired, pumped the gun, fired, pumped the gun, over and over. The first two missed, the next eight were smack on the target.

'You're brilliant, Mr Kaplan,' said Craig. 'If you could keep emotion out of your shooting you'd be deadly. Me, please.'

Miriam worked the treadle, and Craig shot: the first two misses, then eight hits. He grinned at Kaplan.

'We must have a play off some time,' he said.

'So you're just brilliant, like me?' Kaplan said.

'No,' said Craig. 'I'm deadly. But I've never shot skeet before.'

They left Kaplan at the clubhouse, and she drove back to the motel. On the way they were picked up by a blue Buick sedan that followed them decorously through the Miami traffic. It was still with them when they turned off for the motel. Craig sighed.

'Drive on a bit,' he said. 'Make this thing go.'

The Chevrolet moved from fifty to seventy, then on to eighty, and the Buick was still there. When the girl slowed down, so did the Buick's driver. Craig sighed again.

'That Buick's following us,' said the girl. Her incredulity was touching.

'Start to slow down,' said Craig. 'Wait till we get near a layby, then cut your motor and coast in.'

She did as he said, and the Buick slowed too. When they went into the lay-by, the Buick slowed even more, then entered it in front of them. By that time Craig had got out of the car and was looking at its offside rear tyre. The man who got out of the Buick was young, broad-shouldered, Florida brown. He walked back to the Chevrolet and smiled at Miriam, a warm and friendly smile.

'Having trouble, folks?' he asked.

Before she could answer, Craig said, 'Yeah. Look here,' and the tall young man leaned towards the tyre.

Craig's body uncurled like a spring, and the tall young man went down to a back-handed strike. On the way down he met Craig's knee, and after that the concrete, then Craig went through his pockets, hefted him into the boot of the Buick, and threw its ignition keys into the bushes.

Miriam stared at him, her mouth open in a silent scream.

'Let's go home,' said Craig.

She fought for words that refused to come, and at last gasped out,' You killed him.'

'No,' said Craig. 'He'll live. And he's out of the way for a while. Drive on.'

She obeyed at last, and they made for the motel.

'Who was he?' she asked.

'No card,' said Craig. 'Licence said Harry Bigelow. Just fifty dollars cash, a big smile and a Colt .38. Harry Bigelow, CIA.'

'You're so sure?'

'We're lucky it was,' said Craig. 'The KGB wouldn't play it like that. And neither will Harry—not any more. To start with there'd probably be two of them—tailing your uncle. When we left they'd split up. The better one would take Kaplan. I got the apprentice, poor kid. It all looked easy, didn't it?'

'Horribly easy.'

Craig chuckled. 'It isn't usually. But your Uncle Marcus was routine—so they thought. So they gave some of it to a new boy. It won't happen again. The CIA knows its stuff.'

And so does Loomis, Craig thought: yet he's risking a new boy.

'What now?' said the girl.

'We go back to the motel,' said Craig, 'and ask for a nine o'clock call tomorrow morning. But that's because we're sneaky. Actually we leave tonight.'

'Where to?' Miriam asked. 'Back to New York?'

'Eventually,' said Craig. 'First we go to Caracas, Venezuela, then the Azores, then Rome, then Istanbul, then—if you're a good girl, back to New York.'

'But you can't,' Miriam said.

'I'm doing it.'

'But I haven't got my passport.'

'I looked it out for you,' said Craig. 'While you were dressing.'

Suddenly she started to blush again.

'What's the matter?' he asked.

'I've got to go to the john,' said Miriam.

CHAPTER SEVEN

THE TALL MAN'S NAME was Lederer. His cover was that of investment counsellor in the firm of Shoesmith, Lederer, and Fine. The chubby man with hexagonal glasses was called Mankowitz. His cover was that of consultant psychologist, and was worth a hundred thousand dollars a year. Some of those dollars he invested on Lederer's advice. It was an excuse for meeting, and Lederer's advice was good. They met in Lederer's office as Craig and Miss Loman landed in Caracas. Both men liked Lederer's office. It was in Wall Street, on the eighteenth floor of an ageing skyscraper, it had a kind of brown leathered, New England dignity, and it was not bugged. The last, negative virtue was the most desirable of all, but the others also had charm. For Lederer they represented a continuity of life: prep school in New England, Harvard, a home in Long Island, a summer place in Maine. For Mankowitz they had all the charm of novelty. Enormous leather chairs, Hogarth prints, period furniture: there was even a humidor, and the cigars it contained were Havana, and quite illegal in the States, no matter where your allegiance lay. He took one and pierced it with a device that might have been used for extracting confessions. Lighting it was a ritual that occupied two minutes and three matches. When it was drawing Lederer said:

'Craig got to Marcus Kaplan.' The chubby man looked up, surprised. 'He took the girl with him. Miriam Loman. They met at some skeet club Kaplan uses. It seems likely that Kaplan told Craig all he wanted to know.'

Mankowitz sucked on his cigar like a fat child with a lollipop.

'You gave us the wrong advice,' Lederer said. Mankowitz pouted.

'I didn't give you any advice,' he said. 'I gave you facts. Craig as an agent was finished. That was a fact. He's too scared of pain. That was a fact. He'd lost his drive—another fact. And the way Fisher was handled threw him—also a fact.'

'In Miami he put through a nice, smooth operation. He wasn't scared and he didn't panic.'

'Then something's happened to him,' Mankowitz said.

'What?'

The fat man's shoulders heaved in a comprehensive shrug.

'How do I know? For that sort of guessing I need a crystal ball.'

'I'd be obliged if you'd use it,' said Lederer, and Mankowitz pouted again.

'I can tell you a possibility,' he said. 'But that's all it is.'

'Tell me a possibility.'

'Somewhere Craig's got the idea that he's got nothing else to lose. He's so far down he can only go out—or up. Craig isn't the type to go out. So he's started to hit back.'

'But you saw him a couple of days ago. What could have happened since then?'

'He went back to London,' the fat man said. 'It's possible he saw Loomis.'

'Inevitable,' Lederer said.

'Maybe Loomis rejected him. The archetypal father-figure rejected him. That means he's absolutely alone.'

'Except for the girl.'

'The girl is expendable. For Craig, now, everyone may be expendable. And he is expendable to everyone. Hence his need for a hostage. Nobody loves him any more.'

'That's why I let him take the girl,' Lederer said. 'The way he is now, he might just do the job for us.'

'You can keep track of him?'

'Oh yes. He's booked through to Rome. He stops over at the Azores. If he makes Rome, he goes on to Turkey. We've got plenty of chances to pull Loman out if we have to.'

'It might be wiser not to take them,' Mankowitz said. 'If Craig's recovered his skill as a result of—whatever has happened, he'll need the Loman girl to find Aaron Kaplan. Then we can take over.'

'Not in Turkey. Turkey's a little difficult for us at the moment.'

'Then get him out of Turkey. Surely there are ways?'

Lederer thought for a moment, watching the thick coil of cigar smoke plume into nothingness as the air-conditioning got it.

'There's a man called Royce and a girl called Benson. They're after Kaplan too. Craig won't want to meet them. Perhaps we could use that. I'd like to. It would make the whole thing so much neater.'

'It would make Loomis mad too.'

Lederer smiled. 'There's that too, of course. And when Loomis is angry he's at his most vulnerable. Yes. That's the way we'll play it.'

One of Lederer's phones rang. He had three on his desk and one on a side-table, an old fashioned piece of ivory, inlaid with gilt, that belonged to Paris in the naughtiest nineties. Most people thought of it as decoration, but it worked, though its number was unlisted. He walked to it now, and picked it up.

'Yes?' he said. The phone squawked briskly, then went dead. He hung up and turned to Mankowitz.

'Craig's recovered remarkably,' he said. 'Yesterday he clobbered a CIA man.'

The journey was a gruelling one, and by the end of it the yellow Orlon dress had lost its glitter. Beside her, Craig looked as indestructible as ever, in his crumpled suit, the shirt that had stopped being white the day before. Rome was behind them now, and they were on an Al Italia Caravelle, headed for Istanbul. She had a confused memory of meals that were always breakfast, of Tannoy systems that shouted first in Portuguese, or Spanish, or Italian, then in English: of uneasy sleep and only half-awake wakefulness as one plane or another screamed across the Atlantic, Spain, the Mediterranean, Italy, and now the Middle East. All the way he had been kind to her, considerate for her comfort, easing the strain of travel that seemed to touch him not at all, so that in the end she had slept against him, her head resting on the hard muscle of his shoulder, and he had sat unmoving, hour after hour. Once she had awakened, and found him looking down at her. There had, she thought, been a kind of pity in his face, but it had disappeared at once, the blank mask taking its place as he settled her down again, put his arm across her shoulders, the most impersonal arm she had ever felt. It was there now as the plane strung islands like jewels below them: Limnos, Imroz, Samothraki, before the long ride down to Gallipoli, Marmara, Istanbul. He shook out one of his rare cigarettes and lit it left handed.

'Are we nearly there?' she asked.

'Soon,' said Craig.

'Boy, could I use a shower,' she said. The arm quivered, she looked up and saw that he was laughing.

'What did I say?' she asked.

'Miss Loman, Miss Loman, how American you are.'

'Well of course I'm American,' she said, 'and anyway, I wish you'd stop calling me Miss Loman.'

'Never spoil a professional relationship for the sake of a little politeness,' said Craig.

She looked up at him, but his face as usual told her nothing. He concentrated on the pleasure the cigarette gave him.

'Professional relationship?'

'We're colleagues,' he said. 'We may not want to be, but we are.'

The No Smoking sign came on then, and it was time to fasten seat-belts.

The customs, she thought, were disappointed in them. They carried so little luggage, but Currency Control cheered up appreciably when they saw the dollars he carried. They walked through the bright impersonality of the arrival lounge, and already she felt bewilderment, even resentment. The Middle East resembled the Middle West far too much. He guided her out to a clouded sunlight that added to her resentment—they had better weather in Chicago—and took her to a long line of taxi-cabs. This too was Middle Western, but twenty years too late. An unending line of museum pieces: Fords, Chevvies, Oldsmobiles, even a salmon-pink Cadillac that reminded her of the pictures Marcus had in his album: the kind of cars they made when Detroit started rolling again, just after the war, before she was a year old, battered now, their paint peeling, the shark's grin of chromium turned yellow, or non-existent, but as American, she thought bitterly, as Mom's apple pie. Only the drivers were different, but there the difference was so marked it almost compensated for the rest. Miriam had never seen taxi-drivers before who promised so much in so many different languages.

Craig let his glance move across them, taking his time. To her they all seemed alike, swarthy, noisy, not very clean, but Craig found one at least who was different, and walked towards him, a tubby and excitable man with an ancient Packard that smelled of nothing more terrible than coarse soap, recently used. Craig spoke to him in a language she didn't recognize, but which she presumed to be Turkish, and the taxi-driver grinned and answered him in a speech that lasted until they drove away from the cab-rank and were on the highway to the city. From time to time Craig butted in for a word or two, and once they both exploded with laughter, then the driver gave up at last and concentrated on passing everything else on the road. As he did so, he twiddled with the radio, and station after station wailed out the music of the Middle East.

For some reason this annoyed the driver, who twiddled even harder, but the radio was obstinate.

'So you speak Turkish too?' she said.

'No,' said Craig. 'That was Greek. There are thousands of Greeks in Istanbul.'

'You've—worked in Greece?' she asked.

'During the war,' he said. 'My war. You weren't even born then.'

'You're still fighting,' she said, and yawned. She couldn't help it. 'Where are you taking me?'

'This fellow knows a place,' he said, and she remembered the laughter, and willed herself not to blush. 'It's quiet and it's clean, and the food's good,' he said. 'I'll wake you when we get there.'

But in fact she woke long before, as they drove into the racket of the new suburbs, and the even worse racket of the old city: old cars, even older buses, horse-drawn carts, mules, and people, once even a small, bunchy herd of sheep that threaded their way through streets that grew narrower and narrower, past tall, shuttered houses, with now and again a glimpse of the dome and minaret of a mosque, until at last they turned a corner, and in front of them was the Golden Horn, blue and gleaming, the ships bobbing on it like birds. She looked and cried out, 'My God, it's marvellous.'

'You should have brought your camera,' said Craig.

The driver abandoned his war with the radio and turned to grin at her, then flung out a hand as if offering the blue water, the purple-hazed hills beyond, white houses embedded in them like pearls. He spoke again, and again Craig laughed.

'He says it was a Greek city first,' he said. 'And in many ways it still is.'

He settled back as the car just scraped through a narrow cobbled street, turned a corner, and stopped at last in a tiny square, one side of which was a long building of wood, that seemed to have emerged at the whim of generations of owners. Parts of it seemed wholly isolated from others. There were three roofs and four entrances, and everywhere tiny, shuttered windows. It was painted a fading green, but the white of its balconies still dazzled. There was a charm about the place that she found hard to define. It certainly didn't lie in its design or proportions— only there was a rightness about it; it belonged there, opposite the tiny Orthodox church and alongside the great warehouse that looked like a Sultan's palace. Their driver picked up the canvas bag and led them through an entrance, past a sign that said, in Turkish and Latin script, Hotel Akropolis.

They were in a cool room then, low, dim, marble-tiled, with a battered desk and a fat woman behind it who could only have been the driver's sister. Craig signed the register, and handed over his passport. Nobody asked for Miriam's and the fact annoyed her even as it consoled. Then an aged crone appeared, and led them through a maze of corridors, and flung open a door with a flourish. Inside was a huge room with an enormous canopied bed, more marble flooring, and a vast wooden fan like the paddle of a steamer that stirred the sluggish air when the crone pressed the switch. Off the bedroom was a bathroom with a copper bath built on the same scale as the bed, and a huge copper shower suspended above it. The crone looked at it in wonder that people should waste so much time in being clean, then went back to the bedroom again, prodded the mattress, and grinned. Here at least was luxury that made sense, and she said so to Craig. It cost him a quarter to get rid of her.

Miriam watched him take off his coat. The gun harness was still there, but the gun was in the waistband of his trousers. He took it out, checked it, laid it on the bedside table. The time was four-thirty, and she was dizzy with fatigue.

'You want to bathe first?' he asked.

She nodded.

'Go ahead.'

'Are we sleeping together?' she asked.

He looked at the bed. 'Looks like it,' he said. 'Don't worry, Miss Loman. I'll control my bestial desires.'

She flinched at that and went into the bathroom. When she came back, she wore a towel tied round her like a Hawaiian pareu, covering her from shoulder to thigh.

'Very pretty,' he said.

'I've washed my dress.'

'Tomorrow I'll buy you a new one. Which side of the bed d'you want?'

She got in on the left. The gun was close to her hand.

'I'll bet it isn't loaded,' she said.

'You'd win,' said Craig. 'Little girls shouldn't play with loaded guns. They go off.'

'Please,' she said. 'I'm not a child. Don't treat me like one. It's bad enough being here——'

'You're on your honeymoon,' he said. 'That's what I told them downstairs. You're nervous and shy, and you might try to run away. Don't try it, Miss Loman. Nobody speaks any English for miles around. They'd just bring you back and embarrass you.'

She began to cry then and, still crying, fell asleep.

When she woke it was daylight, and she was alone. She got up quickly, and the towel fell from her. She ran to the door—it was locked—and then to the bathroom. Her dress was dry, and she put on bra, panties, and dress with clumsy haste, then prowled the room. There was no sign of the gun, no sign that Craig had ever been there. She had no memory of him in the bed. The thought should have been a comfort to her. She wondered what Ida would say if she knew how her Miriam had spent the night, and the thought made her smile, until she remembered Marcus, and the look on his face when Craig had taken her away. She loved Marcus as he loved her, unquestioningly, without reservations. A fat, middle-aged furrier had no business to possess such a capacity for love. It was a wonderful thing, no doubt, but one day it would destroy him.

She went out on to the tiny balcony and looked down. The Bosphorus was below her, the ships tied up to the stone quays, the racket of the port unending: stevedores, lorry-drivers, even policemen milling about, and not one she could talk to, not one who could understand a word she said, even if she could escape from the hotel. She picked up her handbag and looked in the change-purse. A five dollar bill, three dollar bills, two quarters, and seven pennies. And Craig must be carrying thousands of dollars. Suddenly there was the sound of music, American music, below her. She leaned over the balcony and looked down. A small, dark man was washing the windows of the floor below. There was a transistor radio hooked to his ladder, and it was playing 'Stardust' very loud. It had to be loud to compete with the racket of the port, but the volume couldn't mar the clean drive of the trumpet. She began to feel better.

When he came back, his arms were filled with parcels. She lay on the bed, not sleeping, and he looked so like Hollywood's version of the wholesome American husband at Christmas time that she smiled.

'There should be a sound track playing Jingle Bells,' she said.

'I bought you some clothes,' he said.

She sat up then, angry.

'Did it ever occur to you I might like to choose my own?' she asked.

'Perhaps you'll like these, Miss Loman,' he said. 'It's possible.'

She opened the parcels then, and adored everything he'd bought her, and hated him even more.

'I'm hungry,' she said.

'Lunch is on its way up,' he said.

The feeling of frustration grew inside her. She had never known anything as hateful as this massive and very British competence.

Lunch was moussaka, grilled sword-fish, salad and cheese, and a white wine she decided she detested, then drank three glasses of it. After it, she felt well and wide awake for the first time since she'd left the aircraft.

'You're looking well,' said Craig, and again the intuitive competence enraged her. She watched in silence as the crone poured Turkish coffee from a battered brass pot and left them.

'This food will probably make me ill,' she said. 'You know what we Americans are like—if the food's not flown in from home we go down with a bug.'

'Ah,' he said. 'I'm glad you reminded me. I bought you some pills for that.'

She slammed down her coffee-cup.

'I hate you,' she said.

'That's obvious—but it doesn't matter, so long as we don't let it get in the way. You ready to go?'

'Now?'

'We haven't a lot of time,' he said. 'And Kutsk is five hundred miles away. Are you frightened?'

'Horribly,' she said. He nodded.

'Me too,' he said, and caught her look of surprise. 'No matter how often I do it, I'm always frightened. So are all the others—except the nuts, and they don't last very long. Being frightened's part of the game, Miss Loman.'

'This isn't my game,' she said.

'Poor little innocent bystander,' said Craig. 'Get your things together.'

The Greek taxi-driver had found Craig a Mercedes, a battered 200S that had nothing to recommend it except its engine, but that was astonishing. He drove Craig to the outskirts of the city, and again the girl had glimpses of the other Istanbul, the five star dream world of the tourist—Haggia Sophia, the Blue Mosque, the Dolmabace Palace, that gave way too soon to the narrow caverns of streets, first shops, then houses, then the dusty wastelands that fence in all big cities: abandoned cars, billboards, the first ploughed field. The driver pulled up at last by a bus-stop and made another speech. At the end of it, he shook hands with Craig then got out.

'He hopes we'll be very happy,' said Craig.

'That's nice of him,' the girl said. 'He's not to know it's impossible, is he?'

When she looked back, the driver was waving to them, teeth flashing.

Turkey turned out to be mostly dry hills and plains, waiting for water. That, and terrible roads that the Merc took with more philosophy than she did. And mosques of course, mosques in every village and town, built of everything from mud to marble. There were almost as many mosques as sheep. The car ate up the miles to Ankara—this was Turkey's main highway, the one they kept repaired—and Craig drove quickly, yet with caution, saving his strength for what was to come. When darkness came the girl drowsed again, and woke to more street lights, and Istanbul was nearly two hundred miles away. Craig drove slowly now, following the directions the Greek had given him, and stopped in a wide avenue, lined with olive-trees that whispered softly even in that still night. He led the drowsy girl to the doorway, rang the bell, and again there was the babble of Greek, another crone, another vast bed with cool, white sheets. Then supper came: olives, lamb kebab, rice and fruit, and a dark, acrid wine that Craig drank freely. The whisky stayed in his bag untouched. Then after supper came Turkish coffee, and the sound of the crone running a bath. She took the first bath without asking. This time there were bath salts, the talc he had brought her, and a dressing gown, a scarlet kimono he had chosen that did a lot for the plumpness of her body, made her taller, more elegant. She went back to the bedroom.

He was standing, half turned away from her, practising with the gun, drawing it, aiming, the muzzle a pointed, accusing finger, then putting it back in the holster, repeating the process over and over, then switching, the gun in the waistband of his pants, pulling it, aiming: and the whole thing so fast that the gun seemed to unfold in his hands into the hardness of death. He saw her, but didn't stop until he was satisfied, the sweat glistening on his face, pasting his skirt to his body. The girl thought of boxing champions she had seen on television, the endless training sessions devoted to just such a skill in hurting the man who faced you.

'You work so hard at it,' she said.

'I'm still alive.'

He left her then, and this time took the gun with him to the bathroom.

He'd bought her a nightgown, yellow like her dress. It lay

on the bed, and she picked it up, looked at it. Pretty. She pulled
the cord of her kimono, felt the smooth silk slide from her, felt her
naked body react to the coolness of the room. She was sleepy
again, but sleep was a luxury and her world was poor. Her world
was two hard hands and a terrifying speed with a lightweight
Smith and Wesson .38. And beyond that the certainty of danger,
probable pain, the possibility of death.

'I'm twenty-three years old,' she thought. 'It can't happen to
me. It mustn't.'

She turned, and the mirror on the wardrobe showed her a
pretty, plump girl, her nude body in a showgirl's pose, holding a
splash of yellow to bring out the honey gold of her skin. She
jutted one hip and admired the result. In twenty years she would
be fat—maybe in ten—but now she was, not beautiful maybe, but
pretty. And desirable. Surely she was desirable? She put a hand
to her breast that was firm and rounded—and cold. The cold was
fear.

He came in from the bathroom wearing pyjamas, carrying his
clothes. This time the gun went under his pillow.

'Who can hurt us tonight?' she asked.

'The Russians,' he said. 'My people. Yours.'

'Mine?'

'Not the CIA,' he said. 'They're not bad, but they're not up
to this one. For this, your side will use Force Three.' He frowned,
trying to explain it to her. 'Look, the Russians have the KGB.
But for really nasty jobs—like this one—they use the Executive.
That's blokes like me. And Force Three—that's me too, ten
years younger, in a Brook's Brothers Suit.'

'All to find Marcus's brother?'

'You know what he did,' said Craig.

She pulled the sheet more tightly around her.

'Betrayed the Revolution,' she said. 'They sent him to Volochanka. But he escaped, so they want him dead.'

'They have the easy job,' said Craig, and she shivered. 'Your
people want him alive.'

'*Marcus* wants him alive.'

'Because he's his brother. The Americans want him alive
because he can perform one miracle.'

'Only one?'

'It's a good one,' he said. 'He can turn sea-water to rain-water.
Cheap. He can make the desert blossom. He's America's present
to the under-privileged world.'

'And why do you want him alive?'

'So that I can stay alive too,' said Craig. 'If I've got him, everybody will be my chum.'

'With all that opposition—you think you can do it?'

'It's not much of a chance, but it's the only one I've got.'

He put the light off and got into bed. Before he could turn from her, her arms came round him, her body eased against his. He put up his hands and found that she was naked.

'Miss Loman,' he said, 'you're making a big mistake.'

Her mouth found his, her hands tore at his pyjama jacket, then she found herself pulled away from him. He was gentle about it, but his strength was too much for her.

'Please,' she said. 'Please, Craig.'

He got out of bed, switched on the light again, and looked down on her, her bare breasts tight with love, then he lit a cigarette and his hands were shaking.

'Miss Loman,' he said. 'What the hell are you playing at?'

'I don't love you,' she said. 'I never could love you. But I may die tomorrow. That scares me—it scares us both.' She wriggled out of the sheets, her body supple in youth, but the logic she offered was ageless. 'We need each other. Now,' she said. 'It's all there is.' He turned away from her. 'Am I that hard to take?'

'No, Miss Loman, you're not,' he said. 'But my interest in women ended a year ago. They have a machine that does that. All very modern. It gives you electric shocks.'

'Oh, my God,' she said.

'Maybe I'm wasting my time staying alive, Miss Loman.'

'Who did it to you?'

'A man who hated me. In our business, we stir up a lot of hatred. I nearly died. They tell me I was crazy for a while. Then they patched me together—the surgeons and psycho-experts— and sent me after the man who did it.'

'Did you kill him?'

'No,' he said. 'He had to live. But he wanted to die. Very much.' He came to her then, and he looked at her body and smiled. His hand reached out, smoothed the hair from her brow.

'I'm sorry, Miss Loman,' he said.

'Couldn't you just hold me?' she said. 'I'm so alone, Craig.'

He put the light off. She heard the rustle of cloth as he removed his pyjamas, then he lay on the bed beside her, took her in his arms, kissed her gently. Her hands moved across him, and her finger-tips told her of what he had suffered, the knife wound, the two gun shots, the flogging. His body was marked for life, but the strength inside him had overcome everything that had been done, until the last, most appalling pain had left him alone, uncaring, with only one emotion left, the fear of death. Her hands moved down, over the hard belly. Her body rubbed soft and luscious against him.

'I'll make you,' she said. 'I'll make you want me.'

There was a compassion in her hands and lips that went beyond the ruttishness of fear, a gentle understanding a million miles away from the game without rules he'd played for far too long. This girl was on the side of life, of tenderness, of friendship, even now. Every touch of her body told him that. Suddenly Craig decided that, whatever happened, Miriam Loman wouldn't die. Sweetly, persistently, her hands moved, on and on as she whispered to him, until he realised at last his need for her, and with that came the strength, the ability to love. His hands were strong on her now, and she rolled back then pushed up to meet him, brave in her passion.

'There, my darling, you see?' she said, then 'Yes. Oh, please. Please.'

When they had done, they bathed together, then lay down cool on the rumpled sheets. She smiled at him then, a grin of triumph.

'You didn't believe it was possible, did you?' she said. 'And I made you.'

'You made me.'

'That's something isn't it? After what they did to you? You ought to say Thank you, Miss Loman.'

'Thank you, Miss Loman.'

'That's a good boy.' She kissed his mouth. 'A *very* good boy. You can call me Miriam.'

She stretched out, feeling the hardness of his leg against hers. She felt marvellous: relaxed, fulfilled, yet still engrossed in her body's responses to his. There was just one thing——

'I don't want you to think I do this sort of thing all that often,' she said.

'I don't.'

'You mean I wasn't much good?'

She made a joke of it, but the anxiety to please was there, would always be there.

'You were perfect,' he said. 'That's how I know you didn't do it often.'

'Just one man,' she said. 'One nice Jewish boy. I adored him. And he went to Israel.'

'Does Marcus know?'

'I hope not,' she said. 'I never told him. He'll never know about you either. You bastard. You drag me here, kidnap me, then let me rape you. And tomorrow you'll probably get me killed.'

'No,' said Craig. 'You won't die, and it wasn't rape—or kidnapping either.'

She said quickly, 'I feel great—but I'm still scared.'

He turned to her then, and his hands were gentle on her, coaxing yet slow, as she had been to him, till the girl cried out aloud, her arms came round him, taking him to her.

CHAPTER EIGHT

THEY DROVE through Kirrikale, then on to Kayseri, climbing the foothills of the Taurus Mountains. The road was bad now, the metal giving out for long stretches, but the Mercedes took all it was given, and came back for more. They passed hamlets of mud and stone, tiny fields wherever there was water, and where there was not—scrubland, goats, and sheep. Petrol stations were a rarity, and whenever he passed one Craig filled up the tank, paying in Turkish lire this time.

Once a police car followed them, then shot past them, waving them down. The girl was frightened, but Craig was unhurried, and wound down his window as the two policemen came up to him, thin and hard and dark as gypsies. One of them spoke a little French, and asked them if they were lost. Craig said they were not. They were going to Iskenderun to consider the possibility of making a film there. The policeman was impressed, and gabbled to the other man in Turkish, then asked if Craig had ever met Brigitte Bardot, and Craig said no, but he'd met a man who had. The policeman asked if they were American, and Craig said they were. His partner then took a deep breath and said 'Hey, Joe. Gimme some whisky and a broad.' Craig applauded then, and scowled at Miriam till she applauded too. The French-speaking policeman then explained that his partner had fought in Korea, Craig handed round Chesterfields and they were free to go.

They drove on sedately to the next bend, then Craig put his foot down.

'My God,' said the girl.

'Take it easy. They were bored and they wanted cigarettes. When trouble comes, it won't be wearing a uniform.'

It came at Volukari, eighty miles further on. Craig had stopped yet again for petrol and the girl had gone into the fly-festooned shack beyond it that said café. He sat and waited, looking at the town that seemed to be in training for its next famine. Tired houses, unpaved streets, people who owned nothing but time, but in time they were millionaires. The women, he supposed, were bored at home; it was a crowd of men and boys who watched his tank fill up; the big excitement of the day. And then they had another excitement: the peremptory blast of a horn, the squeal of tyres that longed for tarmac and met only dirt, then an

E-type Jaguar went by, and the crowd exploded into comment. Four foreigners in one day. If things kept up at this rate they'd have to organise a festival. Miriam came back, and the crowd settled down to watch again, careful not to miss a single detail, the flick of her skirts, the glimpse of knee before the door closed. Craig's mind was elsewhere: he was thinking of the E-type. The man driving it was Andrew Royce, the girl beside him Joanna Benson.

'I've just seen two more film producers,' he said, 'and we're both after the same property.'

He had no doubt that Royce and Benson had seen him.

They drove on into the evening, through Iskenderun, on past a little beach where somebody optimistic had built a little white hotel, with beach umbrellas and fairy lights and a couple of discouraged palm trees like thin old ladies. It seemed like a good place to stop if you drove an E-type, but there was no sign of it. Instead they picked up an elderly Fiat truck that rattled along behind them, then dropped slowly back as they drove round the bay and came at last to Kutsk, a gaggle of fishermen's huts huddled round a mosque, with one larger building, just as dirty, just as decrepit as the others, coffee-shop, bar, and restaurant combined. With any luck, it would be the hotel, too.

'Welcome to the Kutsk Hilton,' said Craig.

He got out and stretched stiffly, near exhaustion, not daring to yield to it. The E-type could cover a hell of a lot of country, even this country. He took the girl's arm and led her inside the coffee-shop.

She found herself in a world of men. In Turkey, she realized, a man's business was to drink coffee: a woman's was to make it. The silence that greeted her was absolute, and she moved closer to Craig. The room was long and narrow, with deal tables and chairs. One unshaded lamp-bulb competed unsuccessfully with cigarette-smoke and flies. The room smelled—had smelled for twenty years, of cigarette smoke, sweat, and coffee. It reeked of coffee. The proprietor, a chunky man who smelled like his property, came up and stood in front of them without enthusiasm. Around him his customers looked on, like men pleased with themselves at being in on something good. Craig tried him in Arabic, French, and Greek, with no reaction. In the end he resorted to pantomime, and the patron nodded his understanding and relaxed enough to jerk a thumb at a table. The villagers relaxed then: the show was over. Someone switched on a radio, and they began at once to shout over it as a woman brought plates of fish stew, bread, and water to Craig's table. The girl looked at it dubiously.

'Eat,' said Craig. 'It'll be good.'

It was, and Miriam discovered how hungry she was. Craig ate left-handed, and watched the door. When the stew was gone, the woman brought coffee, and with it an ageing man who smelled of fish, walked up to Craig and bowed, then began making noises with his mouth. At first the girl thought he was singing, then realised, incredulously, that he was speaking English, but English of a kind she had never heard before. Craig pulled over a chair and signed to the woman to bring more coffee. The ageing man went on talking English with a combined Turkish and Australian accent.

He had fought in Arabia in the First World War and been captured by Australian Cavalry. Was Craig an American, he asked, and when Craig said he was English he was delighted, or so Craig deduced. Good on you, cobber, were the words he used. He went on to make it clear that what trouble Russia hadn't made, America had, and asked how he could serve Craig. A room? Of course. His son owned this appalling coffee-house, but it had one room for Craig and his wife. A good room. Almost an English room.

He led them to it. It was behind the coffee-room and the racket was appalling, but it was clean. Craig remembered where he was, and made a long speech in praise of the room. The ageing man was delighted.

'You know your manners, sport. My oath you do,' he said, then bowed again. 'My name is Omar.'

'John Craig.'

Still remembering his manners, Craig made no move to introduce Miriam as his wife or anything else, and Omar, remembering his, didn't look at her.

'Sorry I wasn't around when you came in,' Omar said. 'I was sleeping.' He yawned. 'You come far?'

'Ankara,' said Craig, and Omar's eyes widened. Craig might have said the moon.

'You have business here?' he asked.

'Maybe,' said Craig. 'Perhaps we can talk tomorrow?'

'Too right,' said Omar, and turned to the door.

'D'you get many English here?' Craig asked.

The ageing man giggled.

'Before today I hadn't set eyes on a Pommy for fifty years,' he said, and left them.

Craig locked the door. When he turned round she was removing her dress, but her eyes were angry.

'Why do I have to be British?' she said.

'You don't like us?'

Again the blush came. 'Oh you,' she said, then the anger came back. 'I love my country.'

Americans, he thought. With their passion for precision. Love is a pure word: colour it red, white, and blue. When would they get away from primary colours?

'Usually I'm quite fond of the old place, sometimes I adore it, sometimes I absolutely loathe it.' Was it possible to be as ambivalent as that to a fact as enormous as America?

'If you love it you want to help it,' he said. 'And you can help it best by letting Omar think you're British.'

'You're treating me like a child again.'

'No—an innocent American,' he said. 'I'm a wise European.'

'And decadent too?'

'You tell me,' said Craig.

'Henry James would have loved this one,' said Miriam.

'Who?'

She sighed, came up to him, put her arms round his neck and kissed him. 'Would a wise European help an innocent American take off her bra?'

They came at three o'clock in the morning, soundlessly, surely, the way they had been taught—the man at the window, the girl at the door. The man carried a nine millimetre Walther automatic, thirteen shot, a stopper. The girl had a ·32 revolver, a neat little job with a cross-checked butt. Nobody ever stopped anything with a ·32. The girl was a dead shot. They stood holding the bed in their crossfire, waiting for their eyes to adjust to the dark, picking out the masses of the shapes on the beds, ears strained for the faint sound of breathing in the most profound sleep of the night. Suddenly the light came on, and behind them a voice they knew and detested said, 'Pascoe would have been proud of you.'

Joanna Benson froze, Andrew Royce began to turn.

'No,' said Craig, and Benson stayed still. Miriam Loman sat up in the bed, frightened, bewildered, and pushed away the bolster she had lain against.

'Guns on the bed,' said Craig. The armed man and woman made no move to obey, and Craig, by the light switched, risked a quick look at Miriam. The terror was still there.

Omar's voice said, 'Your gun on the bed, Mr Craig.'

He stood in the doorway; in his hands was a single-barrelled shotgun. It was old, but serviceable, and it pointed straight at Miriam.

'I'll drop your Sheila, Mr Craig,' Omar said.

The Smith and Wesson landed at Miriam's feet, and Royce scooped it up, slipped it into his pocket and turned to Craig.

'Thanks, Omar,' he said. 'Come and join us, Craig.' He gestured with the Walther. 'Come on.'

Warily, ready for a blow, Craig moved forward. The shotgun still pointed at Miriam's breast.

'You lied to me, Omar,' he said. 'You disappoint me.'

'No,' Omar said. 'I told you that before today I hadn't seen a Pommy for fifty years. That was the truth, Mr Craig.'

Royce stepped back out of Craig's line of vision, but the barrel of Joanna Benson's gun was aimed steadily at his heart.

'Why did you do it?' Miriam asked. 'I thought you liked us?'

'I do like you,' said Omar, and his voice was indignant, 'but I like money more.'

Royce struck then, using the edge of his hand with a careful economy of strength. Craig fell across the foot of the bed.

'You're right,' Royce said. 'Pascoe will be proud of us.'

He came back to consciousness in a stone shed that smelled of animals. He was lying on straw, and the straw stank. The shed was lit by an oil-lamp hung high on the wall. His hands were tied behind him, and his neck ached vilely where Royce had hit him. His wrists, too, ached to the constriction of the wire that was cutting into him, but he lay still, not moving, eyes closed, letting his mind and body regain strength.

Joanna Benson's voice said, 'I think he's conscious.'

The toe of a shoe crashed into his ribs, and he gasped with the pain. Pain he could see coming he could control, but pain from nowhere made the body's reaction inevitable.

Royce said, 'He's conscious.'

Hard hands grabbed him, propped him against the wall of the shed. His head lolled forward. He needed time to recruit his strength.

'We brought your girl, too,' said Joanna Benson, and his head came up then. Royce chuckled. Miriam sat in the straw a few feet from him, and before them Royce and Benson stood. Royce's gun wasn't showing, but Benson still held her ·32. They looked relaxed, strong in the arrogant beauty of youth. The weight of Craig's years had never been so heavy.

'You're an innocent American,' Royce said. 'I'm a wise European.'

'And decadent too?' Joanna Benson asked.

'You tell me,' said Royce.

'Would a wise European help an innocent American to take her bra off?' Joanna Benson said. She even got the accent right. Miriam stood up, screaming.

'Stop it,' she yelled. 'Stop it. Stop it. *Stop it.*'

'Sit down, darling,' said Benson. 'You're not being dignified.'

'You have no right to do this,' Miriam sobbed. 'No *right.*'

'Tell her, Craig,' said Benson. 'Treat her like a child again.'

No, Craig thought. Not even a child. Any kid over there could follow the logic of their situation.

'Sit down, Miriam,' he said wearily. 'Sit down and be quiet. She's got the gun.'

Miriam slid down into the straw, pressed her hands to her face. Benson looked at her. The look was that of one fighter appraising another before the bell went for the first round.

'You must do something very special, darling,' she said. 'I got absolutely nowhere.'

Royce said, 'I think we'd better get on with it,' and Benson shrugged.

'Loomis is very angry with you,' Royce said. 'He told us to kill you.'

'In certain circumstances,' said Benson, and Royce nodded agreement.

'In certain circumstances. Those circumstances are almost fulfilled.'

'But you can't,' said Miriam. 'He's on our side.'

'No, darling,' Benson said, 'he's on your side. *We,*'—the ·32 flicked to Royce and herself—'*we* are on our side.'

Miriam's body tensed in the straw and Craig snarled at her, 'For God's sake sit still.'

Benson laughed, a husky, very feminine laugh.

'You really picked an innocent, Craig,' she said. 'I don't believe she's worked it out yet.'

Royce said to him, 'Perhaps you'd better tell her. She'd take it better from you.'

Craig turned to her then, and for the first time Miriam could read emotion in his eyes, a vast and weary compassion. 'If they kill me,' Craig said, 'they won't leave any witnesses . . . I'm sorry.'

The girl swerved round, staring at him.

'I don't believe it,' she said. 'I simply don't believe it.'

'But you will,' Benson said. 'When it happens—you'll believe it all right. Won't she, Craig?'

He made no answer. Whether she was enjoying herself or simply softening him up, there was no need to help her. Royce took a quick step forward, his foot moved, finding the place he'd hit before. But this time Craig saw it coming. He made no sound.

'Answer the lady,' said Royce.

Craig shrugged.

'She'll know nothing,' he said. 'She'll be dead. Like me. Like both of you, in all probability.'

'Loomis said you never gave up,' said Joanna Benson. 'Let's go on about your death.' She waited a moment. 'It's the best offer we can give you, you know . . . Death. Once you've told us where Kaplan is.'

'But you know where he is,' said Craig.

'Kutsk,' said Royce. 'That's all we got. We reckon you have more.'

'Why should I?' Craig asked.

'Because you went to see Marcus Kaplan,' Joanna Benson said. 'Because she's here with you. There has to be more, Craig.'

Craig said, 'That's all I got.' Royce's shoe came back. 'I came here looking for you.'

The leather cracked again on his rib cage. Once more, and the ribs would break.

'Wait,' Benson said. 'We'll have time for all that.' She came closer to Craig. 'Look, darling,' she said, 'if this place was all you had, why did you bother coming? You knew we'd be ahead of you.'

'At Volukari you were behind me.'

'We were looking for you,' Royce said. 'We got a tip off you were coming. You weren't all that hard to find.'

'You switched cars, didn't you? Followed us in a Fiat van?'

'Yes,' Benson said. 'Don't waste time, Craig. If all you knew was the town, why did you come?'

'To hi-jack him from you,' said Craig.

Royce drew back his foot again, but Benson spoke quickly, stopping him.

'It makes sense,' she said. 'You know what he's like—the middle-aged wonder boy.'

'But Loomis said——' Royce began.

'Loomis said somebody knew where Kaplan is, and somebody does.' She turned to Miriam. 'Right, Miss Loman?'

Craig said, 'You're completely wrong. She doesn't know a thing. I made her come here.'

'How?' Joanna Benson asked. 'By stealing her bra? Come on, darling. We know you're not that stupid.' She moved closer to Miriam. 'Force Three sent you, didn't they? They told you to let Craig pick you up. They told you to let him take you to Turkey. Help him get Kaplan out. Let him kill us, or the Russians if they were handy, and then let their boys take over.' Her dark eyes burned into Craig. 'You knew that all the time, didn't you, darling? But once you'd got Kaplan—you thought you could bargain.'

Miriam said, 'It isn't true. He did force me——'

'The innocent American,' Joanna Benson said.

'That was later. It just happened. I was scared. I——'

'No True Confessions,' said Benson. 'Just tell me where Kaplan is.'

'But I don't know. I honestly don't *know*.'

Benson said, 'Let me tell you about this place—and him.' She nodded at Royce. 'It's a barn. Part of a farm. The farmer and his family are away. There isn't another human being in five miles. You can scream pretty loud I should think, darling—you've got the build for it—but you can't scream five miles' worth. Now, our friend here. Where we trained, he did the interrogators' course. I gather he has a talent for it—and with talent there usually goes a certain amount of enthusiasm. He'll hurt you, darling. Later on you'll be amazed how very much he did hurt you. You wouldn't believe your body could stand so much pain. You'll hate him, of course, but you'll hate yourself more. Because you'll have told him, you see. All that pain will have been for nothing.' She looked down at Miriam. 'Now tell me, darling. Honestly, you'll do it anyway. Won't she, Craig?'

'Yes,' said Craig. 'She'll tell you.' He began to curse them both, a measured stream of the filthiest invective his mind remembered. Benson and Royce ignored him. Their whole concentration was on the girl.

'But I don't know,' Miriam said. 'Honestly I don't.'

Royce hit her, a hard right that left her sprawling in the straw. His hands went to his pockets and came out with a noose of wire. Quickly he twisted her hands behind her back, drew the noose around them till the girl screamed in pain as he twisted the wire to a spike in the wall.

'Sh, darling,' said Benson. 'He hasn't started yet.'

Royce sat on her legs, pulled the golden zipper of the dress, let it split open down her body. His hands moved again, and Craig turned away, tasting the horror of it, knowing what was to come. Suddenly Miriam screamed again, but not as she had screamed before. A blow hurts and you yell, but the pain is not so strong, and diminishes all the time: but this, this is appalling, degrading, unbearable, and its rhythm intensifies, this terrible, scalding thing he's doing: it never stops, it goes on, gets worse. Her screams ceased to be human, became an animal bellow of agony, continuing even after he'd stopped, he hurt her so much, so that in the end he had to strike her across the face, a savage left and right to bring her back to the awareness of the room, the man's weight on her legs, the woman looking down at her. The screams choked to sobs: the terror stayed in her eyes.

'Tell us where Kaplan is, Miss Loman,' Benson said.

'Please,' Miriam begged, 'please believe me. I don't know.' The man's hand moved and she screamed out, 'I want to tell you. Honestly I do. But I just don't know.'

Then the hand moved, the noises began again: the pain grew worse and worse, settled at a high peak of unbearable intensity, then again the blows on her face brought her back to reality.

'Three minutes,' said Miss Benson. 'He's only done it for three minutes . . . We've got all day, Miss Loman. How long have you got?'

'Don't know,' Miriam said, over and over. 'Don't know . . . Please.'

Craig said, 'Can I suggest something?' Benson nodded. 'Give me ten minutes with her. Alone . . . She'll tell you.'

'Royce is the expert,' Benson said.

'I don't need to hurt her,' said Craig.

'What then?'

'Talk to her.' The disbelief in her face was clear. 'What does it matter what I do, if I gave you what you want? Ten minutes,' he went on. 'Suppose I fail. You said yourself—you've got all day.'

'Why bother, Craig?'

'I don't want her to be hurt any more.'

'You'll recall that once she tells us you'll die?'

'I recall that very well. I still don't want her to be hurt.'

Again the dark eyes looked into his. She examined him as if he were a member of an alien species; one she'd been briefed on.

'Ten minutes,' she said.

'And my hands free?'

Royce wanted to protest at that, but she moved behind Craig and her hands found the slip-knot, eased him free. The release was agony: the renewed insulation of blood so painful he had to exert all his strength not to yell. He looked at Royce.

'You did this,' he said.

'My pleasure,' said Royce, and got up from Miriam, looked down at Craig, eager for the word that could unleash the power to hurt. Craig looked at him empty-eyed.

'I don't like this,' Royce said. 'It's better to use the girl. With his hands free——'

'If he tries anything I'll kill him,' said Benson. 'He knows that.'

'I don't trust him,' Royce said.

'You like hurting people,' said Benson. 'Miss Loman just warmed you up. But we didn't come here to get you your kicks, Andrew.'

'We came here for Kaplan,' Royce said. 'There's only one way to get him.'

Benson looked down at the gun in her hand. It pointed between Craig and Royce, an impersonal menace.

'You can have ten minutes' rest,' she said. 'You go first.' Royce hesitated for a moment, then left. Benson looked down at Craig.

'There's a bucket and towel over there,' she said. 'Clean her up if you want to, darling. Andrew can always do it again.'

She left then, and Craig unhooked the wire round Miriam's wrists, soaked the towel in water, placed it on her. Even the touch of the towel made her cry out. He held it against her, and gradually the agony on her face faded.

'Oh, my God, that's good,' she whispered. Then the fear came back. 'But he'll do it all again, won't he?' She began to cry, dry, racking sobs, and he took her in his arms, drew the dress around her.

'You really don't know where Kaplan is?'

She shook her head. 'If I did—I'd try to hold out against him. But I don't think I could. Not much longer. As it is—I guess it's all for nothing. What he did to me.'

'The postcard,' Craig said. 'Marcus didn't lose it, did he? He left it with you. What was on the postcard? Can you remember?'

'What's the use, John?' she said. 'I don't know where he is.'

He held her more tightly.

'Ten minutes isn't long,' he said. 'Just answer my questions.'

'It had a picture on it,' she said. 'A flock of sheep and a shepherd leading them.'

'What sort of shepherd?'

'Just an old man with a walking-stick.'

'Traditional sort of clothes?' She shook her head. 'What was the message?'

'He'd written it in Hebrew. It meant something like—"This is a lovely place. The old man reminds me of old Rabbi Eleazar. Do you remember how he used to read the psalms to us? He was a good shepherd to us, wasn't he? I miss him very much, and you too, Marcus. Be happy. Aaron." That was all.'

'Nothing else?' said Craig. 'You're sure?'

'Just the postmark, Kutsk. Marcus hired a private-detective from Istanbul to come down. Nobody had ever even heard of him. But he must have been here, mustn't he?'

'You're sure there was nothing else?'

She was silent for a moment, examining the postcard in her mind.

'Just the date,' she said. 'That was funny, too. He'd written it the Jewish way.'

'How is that?'

'We're in the year 5725. Aaron wrote 2.23.5725. Some lousy postal service.'

'Why,' asked Craig.

'Two must be February,' she said. 'The postmark on the card was April. Marcus got it in May.'

Craig said, 'When were you supposed to tell me all this?' He felt her body stiffen. and went on. 'You were, weren't you? Force Three set you up for me, didn't they? Just as Benson said.'

She nodded. 'They told me what to tell you—but when you made me come with you they said that was all right, too. I phoned them you know. When I went to the john.'

'Of course you did,' said Craig. 'Sometimes I thought you were never going to ask.'

'But when did you know?'

'Right from the start,' he said. 'It was all too easy. A girl in a fur coat—and almost out of it——'

'I hated that,' said Miriam.

'It's not a thing you forget,' said Craig. 'I was supposed to follow it up. Tell Loomis. Force Three knew he'd send somebody. It turned out to be me instead.'

'But you knew it was a trap.'

'There was nothing but traps,' Craig said. 'Yours was the prettiest. And it got me nearer Kaplan.' He looked at his watch. 'What did they tell you to tell me?'

'About the postcard,' she said. 'It seemed so stupid.'

'Not stupid at all,' said Craig. 'I'm surprised Marcus didn't see it.'

'See what?'

'Where his brother is.'

Cautious not to hurt her, he zipped up her dress. When Benson and Royce came back, they were sitting apart. This time, both the man and the woman carried guns.

Benson said, 'I hope you've got good news, darling.'

'Me, too,' said Craig. 'But at least I can tell you where he's been.'

'Get on with it, then,' said Royce.

'Marcus Kaplan got a postcard. There was a picture of a shepherd on it, leading his flock. The message was signed Aaron —his brother. The text had a reference to a rabbi they'd both known as children—that proved it came from Aaron. The rabbi had taught them the psalms. The whole thing was written in Hebrew—even the date: 2.23.5725.'

'So?' said Royce.

'2.23,' said Craig. 'It could be February twenty-third—except the card was postmarked April. On the other hand, if we remember the shepherd on the front of the card, it could be the twenty-third psalm—second verse.'

'Go on,' said Benson.

'Do you happen to know what that is?'

'He maketh me to lie down in green pastures: he leadeth me beside the still waters,' Benson said, and added: 'I once had to write it all out ten times. So *useful*, being taught by nuns.'

'Then there was the date—5725,' said Craig.

'That's a distance in yards, do you think?'

'No,' said Craig. 'Kaplan's a Russian. My guess is it means metres.'

'Green fields and a lake,' said Benson. 'About six thousand metres from here. Which direction?'

'You'll need a map,' Craig said. 'That's all she knows. She didn't even realize she knew that—till I got it out of her.'

'Maestro,' said Benson, and bowed. Royce raised his automatic.

'What a fool you are, maestro,' he said. 'You're going to die.'

'Well, actually, darling, not quite yet,' said Benson. 'We do have to be sure he's telling the truth.' She turned to Miss Loman. 'And that she told him the truth.'

'Do we leave them here?'

'They'll be safe for a little while,' Benson said. 'Get the car.'

'What about tying them up?'

'I'll do that,' Benson said. 'Give me the wire.' He handed it to her. 'On your tummies, darlings,' said Benson.

Royce watched as she drew the wire over Miriam's hands, heard the sharp gasp of pain, then went outside. Minutes later he came back, holding a large-scale map of the area. Craig and Miriam lay face down, wrists bound behind them, feet tied to staples in the wall. He grinned. 'Not even love could find a way,' he said.

'You've hardly made it worthwhile to try,' said Benson. 'Any luck?'

'Three possibles,' Royce said. 'It shouldn't take long.'

Benson crouched down by Craig. 'We'll do the whole thing in a couple of hours,' she said. 'Then we'll kill you, Craig. Sorry and all that, darling—but you know what Loomis is like.' She got up then, and left them.

Miriam lay in the straw, biting her lip to stop herself from crying out. The pressure of her body was bringing back the pain. Beside her she could hear the movements of Craig's body as he fought against the wire that held him. The fool, she thought. The poor, brilliant, stupid fool. To stop me being tortured he gets himself killed, and now he's trying to burst his bonds like a comic strip hero. The movement of his hands must be agony, she thought. Even lying still was almost more than she could bear.

'Save it, John,' she said. 'We're going to die. Accept it.'

The writhing movements went on beside her.

'Look,' she said. 'You did it to stop me being hurt any more. All right. I couldn't take any more. I wanted to die. I really did. All right. I got what I wanted. I don't blame you for it. Only please will you stop fighting? It's just no use.'

The writhing stopped at last, and then he was bending over her, untwisting the wire at her ankles and wrists. She sat up cautiously, and he rubbed her wrists and ankles, chafing back the circulation.

'I don't believe it,' she said. 'It isn't possible.'

'No,' he said. 'It's impossible. Unless the girl who tied you up did it wrong.'

'You mean that man-eating debutante made a mistake?' Miriam asked. 'Oh, I like that very much. I love it.'

'No,' said Craig. 'Benson doesn't make mistakes. She meant it.'

'But why?'

'We'll find out later. She also meant it when she said we had just two hours to get out of here. Otherwise Royce will kill us.'

'She didn't say that.'

'She meant it. She handled Royce as well as anyone could

handle him, but there are limits with his kind. Believe me, I know.'

He looked round the shed as he talked. The door was four great slabs of wood, hard and old, and bolted on the outside. The windows were too tiny even for Miriam to squeeze through. Patiently, he sought the straw for some kind of tool, but there was nothing. He went to the door again, tested its heavy strength. It could have stood up against a charging bull.

'She was only teasing us,' said Miriam. 'Making it worse.'

'There's a way,' said Craig. 'There has to be.'

He grubbed in the straw again and found a couple of horse-blankets, heavy, ancient things that stank to heaven. Quickly he began to pile the straw up round the door, working with care, clearing the rest of the dirt floor, then threw a blanket to her, took one himself, and moved the bucket of water back to the window.

'Get over here,' he said.

She obeyed him, and he lifted the oil lamp from its hook, hefted it in his hand, then moved back to join her.

'Benson doesn't make mistakes,' he said. 'But Royce does. He left the lamp burning—and it's daylight.' He soaked the blankets with the water, then flicked his wrist. The lamp spun through the air, then burst like a bomb against the door. She had never believed that a fire could take place so quickly. There was a bang, as the lamp burst, and the blazing oil streamed down into the straw, tongues of flame reared up like waves, searing the side of the door, and the blast of heat made her throw up her hands to cover her face. Even pressed against the furthest wall, the temperature was almost unbearable. Pieces of burning straw spiralled up in the warm air then drifted down on them. Craig pushed closer to the window as the room filled with stifling smoke. She stood there, whimpering softly, convinced that he'd gone crazy, that they'd burn to death.

Streaming-eyed, coughing, he watched the fire take hold of the door, reduce its weathered hardness to flame. At last, before the smoke made him unconscious, he went to the door, hands wrapped in the towel, holding the blanket in front of him like a shield, but even so the heat seared him through the heavy cloth. He drew up his knee, then kicked flat-footed at the burning door, aiming for the bolt, using every ounce of the karate skill. The flames bit into his leg, and he drew back his foot and kicked again, feeling the door yield slightly but not enough. Another kick was needed, delivering it a task almost beyond his powers.

Sobbing, he went closer, bent his knee, kicked, and the bolt gave, the door swung open.

He turned to Miriam. 'Put the blanket round yourself,' he yelled. 'Come on.'

But she stared at the flames and stayed, motionless. Her nerve had gone. Craig went back to her, wrapped one blanket round her, swathed the other over them both. When she realized what he was going to do she struggled, till he swore at her, threatening, and she was still. He took a last gasp of air at the window, then charged at the half-open door. Again flame leaped round him, then his shoulder hit the door, it opened wider, and he was through, running into the coolness of the morning, stopping at last, releasing her from the blanket as if she were a parcel.

'Gift-wrapped,' he said. 'That's nice.' He slapped at his trousers, charred from the flames, then sat down wearily, pulled up the trouser-legs, looked for the mark of the flames. Scorched, no more. He'd been lucky.

'I thought we hadn't a chance,' she said.

'We had the chance Benson gave us.' He looked at his watch. 'There's an hour and three-quarters before they get back. We'd better use them.'

He turned and looked back. The fire was dying now, the straw spent, only the wood still smouldering. Behind their prison was a derelict farmhouse and a corrugated-iron shed. He got up and went towards the shed. Somehow Miriam got to her feet and staggered after him.

Inside the shed was the Fiat van. He went over it carefully, wary of booby-traps. There were none. He opened the door, got into the van. The keys were in the lock. He drove it out, and Miriam got in beside him, picked up something lying at her feet, something heavy and metallic, wrapped in cloth. She handed it to Craig, and he uncovered his Smith and Wesson .38. He broke it, examined the magazine. It was loaded, but even so he took out each cartridge, checking that the shell was there intact, before he snapped it together, stuck it into his waistband. He turned to her and smiled.

'Nice, kind Miss Benson. Let's go and see Omar and give him a big surprise,' he said.

She shook her head.

'Look, darling,' he said. 'He likes money, remember I bet he's liking mine right this minute.'

Miriam said, 'He's got a lot coming all right. But we can't give it to him. Not yet, anyway.'

'Why the hell not?' asked Craig. 'I've got to get you out of here, and that'll take money.'

'There was something else on the card. Something I didn't tell you. The picture.'

'An old shepherd with a flock of sheep.'

'It was sunset, John, and he was walking towards it.'

'So the place is west of Kutsk,' said Craig.

'That's right. And there's a chance they'll leave it till the last. We could still be there first.'

'Look,' he said, 'you're scared. You know you are. You've been knocked stupid, tortured, hauled through a fire. A very efficient sadist wants to kill you. If we stay here, he probably will—when he's finished playing.'

'I know it,' she said, 'but we've got to do this. It's what we came for.'

Craig's shoulders began to shake, weird sounds came from his throat. He was laughing.

'You innocent Americans,' he said. 'When will I ever understand you?'

A jolting track led from the farm to the road, and from there they moved on to Kutsk. There was no way of skirting the place, and Craig drove through it fast, hoping that if Omar saw them he would think they were Benson and Royce. The west road was smooth and easy till they reached a cross-roads, and there Craig stopped. There were three roads to choose from. Two of them were at least metalled, the third was a potholed disaster. The girl chose it instinctively.

'That old shepherd looked as if he'd never even seen a high-way,' he said.

Gingerly he eased the van on to its pock-marked surface, and they bounced along for a couple of miles in second gear. At last they rounded a curve, and before them they could see a sheet of water, rolling green hills, dotted with the puff-ball shapes of sheep. Craig drew to a halt and the girl rolled down the window, absorbing the scene.

'I think so, John,' she said. 'I think this is it.'

He moved on again, hurrying now, feeling the holes in the road menace his axle, till at last they reached the lake-shore and a clump of olive-trees. A mile beyond them was a hut, and from its chimney soft feathers of smoke drifted up in the still air.

Craig drove past the trees, then backed the van in behind them. If anything, the ground seemed easier than the road. He got out, walked back to the road, and stared intently. The van was perfectly hidden. As the girl climbed stiffly out of the cab, he went back into cover, opened his coat and drew the gun, replaced it, drew it again, over and over, till hand and fingers felt right and the gun's movement was smooth, inevitable. Next, the terrain. The hills were small, undulating, deficient in cover, but a man could hide there if he had to. And if a man were hidden there, and had a rifle, he could pick the two of them off with no trouble at all. On the other hand, it was early yet, even for a shepherd, and there was smoke coming from the cottage. He looked at the ground that separated them from it, working out a line of approach. When he'd got it he said:

'We can get there—but it won't be easy. If he's out there on the hill, he can kill us as soon as we're in range. Maybe I'd better go in first by myself.'

'No,' she said. 'This is what I came for, too.'

'You always do what Force Three tells you?'

'I do what Marcus asks me,' she said.

'All right,' said Craig. 'But take your time. Do exactly what I do—and nothing else. Understand?'

She nodded and he moved at a running crouch to the shelter of some bushes, then began a slow and agonizing crawl towards the cottage. Again the sleeping pain awoke inside her, but she gritted her teeth and crept on after him. Despite the blows he had taken, the exhaustion, the frantic escape from the shed, he moved easily, deftly, with the tiniest whisper of sound. When at last her strength gave out, he led her to the shelter of a boulder and made her lie behind it, flat on her back, legs and arms outstretched, then did the same himself. No recrimination, no argument, only an acceptance of physical limitations, but those limitations were pushed as far as they could go.

After five minutes her legs had ceased to tremble, and he made her go on again, till at last they reached the end of the grass, bush, and stone, and found themselves among rows of vines. Beyond the vines was a neat kitchen garden, with orderly lines of melons, pumpkins and tomatoes, and beyond that, the blank wall of the cottage. Craig very cautiously rose to his feet, and motioned her to absolute silence. A dog lay sleeping under a vine. Carefully, a step at a time, Craig moved towards it. As he moved, she watched his hands. They were both held out straight, the little fingers rigid.

The dog awoke to complete alertness and changed at once from a cuddly chum to something very like a wolf, teeth bared, mouth opened to snarl, as Craig flung himself forward, taking his weight on his left hand, the right hand thudding into its neck like an axe-blade. The noise of breaking bone was the only sound she heard, and she knew at once that the dog was dead. His body pivoted on his left hand, and when he came up he was holding the gun. He moved off at once, not looking back, and she saw for the first time the Craig who had existed before he was tortured: a man who reminded her very much of Royce. Poor Marcus, she thought. Poor Miriam. What chance do we have?

She followed him round the blank wall of the cottage, waited at his signal as he moved round the corner, peered through a window, ducked down, and moved to the door. He never looked back at her, offered her comfort. He was an automaton now, programmed and set in motion, and it would be stupid on her part to regret it. She had done the programming. He reached the door, and contemplated its problem. It was flimsy enough, and its simple latch was rusted. He breathed deeply and evenly, then his foot came back once more, his body exploded into activity. The sole of his foot crashed against the latch, then his shoulder hit the opening door, he was inside the cottage in a dive that took him to the hard earth floor, looking up over the sights of the Smith and Wesson at a man trying to lift a rifle mounted on pegs in the wall.

'Shalom,' said Craig, and the man was still. Craig got up and moved to him, his left hand moved over the other's body, came away with a knife. He stepped back, the left hand flicked, and the knife spun away, stuck high in the wall. The man's eyes ignored everything but the gun.

'Miriam,' Craig shouted, and the girl came running, then stared at the man who faced her. He was taller than Marcus, and that was right. Thinner too, bone thin, but then Marcus had said that Aaron favoured his father's side of the family, who were beanpoles. It was Marcus and his mother who'd had weight problems. The face was OK too, in a way. In it there were echoes of things she knew and loved in Marcus: the boldness of a splendidly semitic nose, a sensitivity about the mouth, a chin she had always wished were a little more determined, especially when Marcus tried to persuade Ida it would be nice to have another cocktail before dinner. He was a Kaplan. She was sure of it: and yet he couldn't be. Aaron was supposed to be fifty-three years old; five years younger than Marcus. The man in front of her looked seventy at least. A tough seventy: the stringy body looked durable enough—but the deeply etched lines on his face, the wrinkled, work-worn hands—seemed to belong to Marcus's father, not his brother.

'Well?' said Craig.

'He looks right,' Miriam said. 'But he's too old.'

'Should he speak English?' Craig asked. She nodded.

'How old are you?' asked Craig.

The man stayed silent.

'Try him in Hebrew,' Craig said.

She spoke to him, first in Hebrew, then in Yiddish. The old man gave no sign of comprehension.

Craig waited, immobile, till she'd finished, then moved, suddenly, appallingly, so that the girl cried out. One stride took him to the old man, then the gun-barrel swung, smashed into his neck, slapping him to the floor, and Craig's voice bellowed orders in a language she did not understand. At once, agonizedly, the old man scrambled to his feet, lurched to the wall, and put his hands against it in the classic pose of the prisoner waiting to be searched.

'We'll take him,' said Craig. He walked to the wall of the cottage, tucked the revolver in the waistband of his trousers and took down the rifle, slung it over his shoulder, then again orders streamed from him in that language she did not know, yet which seemed familiar. The man moved forward at once, and out of the cottage, Craig behind him. There was a weariness in the old man's movements, an acceptance of ultimate defeat that sickened the girl. No human being deserved to be so crushed by another.

Outside, Craig looked at his watch then walked the old man and the girl ahead of him, up into the hills, in a line parallel to the path. They found a dip in the hills near the olive-trees, and he pushed them into its cover, then settled down to wait. The old man gave no least sign of resistance. His whole being was concentrated on Craig's hands, watching them test the rifle, examine its sights and magazine with care, before Craig lay sprawled on the ground, eyes on the road, sights set at a hundred metres. Again orders streamed from him, and the old man bowed his head in submission.

They waited thirty-five minutes before they heard the engine, then the Jaguar streamed effortlessly round the bend in the road, the engine whispering its contempt at the speed it was held to. The girl was driving. Royce sat beside her, looking angry. Craig waited till the car came past them, then the rifle came up, his finger squeezed on the trigger. The rear off-side tyre blew like an echo of the shot, and the girl fought the car to a standstill. As she did so, Royce was already moving, gauging his leap from the car, rolling out of it to the roadside before it had stopped.

'Good boy,' said Craig, and fired again. Royce went down as if his legs had been swept from under him. Benson stopped the car and left it, using it for cover as she too made for the cover of the road. Craig fired a third time, into the petrol tank, and the car exploded in a roaring whoosh of flame that sent Royce scuttling like a wounded snake from the shelter of the ditch. Craig got to his feet then, and led them down to the Fiat, ordered the old man into the back of the van and got in after him, then handed the keys to Miriam.

'You drive,' he said. 'Back towards the village. Stop when I tell you.'

They found a place a mile out of Kutsk—a track that led to a deserted quarry. Craig told her to stop, and she got out. The rifle still in his hands, he ordered the old man out, then followed. The hard words of that elusive language were still in her ears when he switched to English.

'This woman does not speak Russian,' he said.

Russian, thought Miriam. Of course.

'We will talk English. First, your name.'

'Imares,' said the man. 'Mohammed Imares.'

'Profession?'

'Shepherd . . . I used to be a business man, but I made a little money, you understand . . . I thought it was best to get away from the wickedness of life in Istanbul.'

'Of course,' said Craig. 'Your age?'

'Sixty. Perhaps I should explain that I have been very ill. I know I look older.'

'You talk too much,' said Craig. The man was instantly silent.

Craig transferred the rifle to his left hand then, almost casually, knocked the man down with a back-handed blow. He fell, heavily, but scrambled at once to his feet as Craig yelled at him in Russian. Miriam ran between them.

'Stop it,' she said. 'For God's sake, stop it.'

'Get out of the way,' said Craig. 'There isn't time for all that.'

'No,' she said.

His hand moved again, pushing her to one side, and he moved up to Imares, who stood swaying on his feet.

'I'm in a hurry,' said Craig. 'Don't waste my time.'

'I told you the truth,' said Imares.

'I thought Volochanka had better teachers,' said Craig.

Imares' face seemed to disintegrate. Suddenly and silently, he began to cry.

'Kaplan,' said Craig. 'Tell me your full name.'

'Aaron Israel Kaplan.'

'Age?'

'Fifty-three.'

'Profession?'

'Agronomist.' Kaplan sobbed out the word, and covered his face with his hands. Craig let him weep for a moment, then turned to the girl.

'You see,' he said. 'There was only one way to handle it. It didn't take long.'

'But how could you be so sure?' she asked.

'You spotted him straight off,' Craig said, 'apart from his age. And you've never seen anybody who's been in Siberia. I have. If they age only twenty years—they're lucky. So I tried him with Russian. Talked like a KGB executive——'

'And acted like one.'

'No,' said Craig. 'For a KGB executive I treated him soft. But he's broken already. And scared out of his mind. Two blows and a few Russian curses and I had him back in Siberia. After that, he couldn't help telling the truth.'

'What happens now?' she asked.

'I'm going to see Omar. Get my money back.'

'And go back to the States?'

'Eventually,' said Craig. 'First of all I want to get away from Benson and Royce. I bet they don't love us at all.'

'You didn't kill them,' she said. 'You could have done.'

'Disappointed?' he asked.

'No. Surprised.'

'I haven't finished with them yet,' said Craig. 'It isn't their time to die.'

They drove back to the road, and on towards Kutsk. When they reached the outskirts of the village Craig made her stop and, climbing a nearby hill, stared down into the village. There were only a handful of boats bobbing in the harbour: the quay-side was deserted, apart from three old men mending nets. It was a good time to call on Omar.

CHAPTER NINE

MIRIAM drove the Fiat up to the coffee-shop door. Inside the van Kaplan lay trussed like an oven-ready bird with handkerchiefs and ties. Craig had done it himself: the knots would hold. As the van stopped, Craig stepped out soundlessly, moved from the morning heat to the coolness inside. In the gloom he could discern one man sitting at a table, his head on his arms. An old man, having a good rest, conscious of a night's work well done. Soundlessly Craig moved up to him, his hand moved, the Smith and Wesson appeared. On Omar's table was an empty coffee cup and a glass of water half-full. Craig picked up the water-glass, emptied it over the sleeping man, and Omar shot up at once, shocked into awareness. The gun was the first thing he saw.

'How are you, digger?' said Craig.

Omar stared into the gun's barrel.

'Looks like I made a mistake,' he said.

'Looks like it.'

'The other girl—that tall sheila—and that young bloke——'

'They had an accident,' said Craig, and Omar sighed. 'Come to that, sport, you might have one too.'

'You don't have to get violent,' Omar said.

'Maybe I do,' said Craig. 'They were going to kill me, Omar. I don't like that. And you had a gun on my girl. You took my money and my luggage. I think you deserve an accident.'

'I'll give you your money back—and your luggage.'

'Of course,' said Craig.

'Look, mister,' Omar said, speaking more loudly. 'I know I done you no good, but——'

'Omar,' Craig interrupted, 'your family are all asleep, aren't they? And you're trying to wake them. But ask yourself one question first: Is it wise?'

'I don't understand,' said Omar.

'Then put it this way,' said Craig. 'If anybody else comes in, I'll blow your head off.'

Omar looked again into the Smith and Wesson's barrel.

'Do you believe me?'

'Yes,' said Omar. 'Jesus, yes.'

'Let's take care of your family,' said Craig.

Omar's son and his wife snored happily on top of a bed. Craig locked them in their room. Two old women snored happily in the kitchen. He locked them in too. In the guest bedroom he picked up the valise, his and Miriam's clothes. That left the money. Back in the coffee-shop, Omar disgorged it, reluctantly, from his person. It smelled a little more than it had done, but it was all there.

'You see?' Omar said. 'You got it all back. You don't have to shoot me, mister.'

'Maybe,' said Craig. 'How many boats have you got?'

'Three,' said Omar, then stopped, angry. 'I'm not all that rich, mister.'

'I don't want your money,' said Craig. 'I'm not even going to touch the money you got from the other two for helping them. I'm going to be nice to you, Omar.'

The old man looked wary.

'You take me for a cruise and I'll let you live. Isn't that nice of me?'

'Where d'you want to go, mister?'

'Cyprus,' said Craig. 'Now.' He raised the gun, tapped the old man's forehead with the barrel.

'Think about it,' he said. The old man sighed.

'You're the boss, mister,' he said.

'Remember that,' said Craig.

Before they left he drained the petrol tank of the Fiat, tore out its wires, unscrewed its steering wheel. Royce and Benson needed the exercise, he thought, and Craig needed time. They walked down to the quay then, and Craig's luck held. The three old men had finished mending their nets. The place was deserted. They walked in pairs, Omar and Kaplan leading. Kaplan, still groggy from the beating and tying up, seemed the older of the two. Behind them Craig and Miriam, he with a hand in his coat pocket, she limping along, carrying the rifle wrapped in sacking.

Two of Omar's boats were out on charter, fishing, but the third, the pride of his fleet, lay tied up at the quay-side. It was a big and beamy craft with a diesel engine and a lateen sail, very like the caiques Craig remembered from twenty years ago. He helped Omar cast off and made him go out under sail, moving easily before a following wind until they were out of the harbour. Only then would he let him fire the engine, and then they moved off at a steady, pop-popping six knots, watching the land diminish behind them from a toy village to a picture postcard to a grey smudge against the intense blue of the sea. At last, even the smudge disappeared, and Craig lay back, content. Omar heard the sigh, and risked speech.

'It's not good for a Turk in Cyprus, mister,' he said.

'It's not good for a Turk in Kutsk. Not when he robs me and nearly gets me killed,' said Craig.

He turned to Miriam and Kaplan, motioned them to the prow of the boat. From there Omar was clearly visible, but he couldn't hear them.

'Why Cyprus?' Miriam asked.

Craig said, 'I know a man there who'll help me.'

'All we have to do is find Force Three,' said Miriam.

'And how do you propose to do that?'

'They told me how.'

He saw the obstinate set of her mouth, and smiled.

'And you promised you wouldn't tell, is that it? All right. I don't want to know. To tell you the truth, I don't want to go near them.'

'But they'll help you,' she said.

'No,' said Craig. 'They'll help you, love. They'll give me back to a man called Loomis.'

'The one Royce said had condemned you to death?'

'That's right,' said Craig. 'But he can't now that I've got him.' He looked at Kaplan appraisingly.

'You'd be amazed how popular you are,' he said. 'Everybody wants you—and I've got you.'

'That's not strictly true,' Miriam said. '*We've* got him.'

'You forget so easily,' said Craig. 'Don't you remember when you told Royce and Benson we were all on the same side?'

'But you wouldn't hand him back to the Russians?'

'He's up for auction,' said Craig. 'Let's see what I'm bid.'

'But you've got no right to do this.'

Craig said, 'Force Three told you to use me. Right?' She nodded. 'And that's exactly what you did. But there's something you don't realize. When you use somebody—you get what that person has to offer, and nothing else. I can only do this my way, love. If I did it your way, I'd lose.'

'You used me too,' said the girl.

'We used each other. It was the only good thing in the whole business.'

'And now it's over?'

Craig shrugged. 'We can't make decisions any more. We're lumbered.' He nodded at Kaplan. 'With him. The solid gold leg-iron.'

Kaplan felt Craig's eyes on him and looked away. Craig spoke in Russian again, and he nodded.

'I've told him you're going to interrogate him,' said Craig. 'Come here.'

He led her to the side of the boat, away from Kaplan. Utterly weary, she went with him.

'Don't try to explain who you are,' he said. 'Just ask questions. He's the one who has to answer. Talk in English—and if you think he's lying, switch languages on him. Try him in Hebrew— or Yiddish. If you still think he's lying, send for me.'

'Can't I even tell him about Marcus?' she asked, and he shook his head.

'Why not?'

'Because that would make him a person—give him an identity. At the moment he's nothing. So long as he stays nothing, we'll get the truth.' She wanted to argue, and he went on, 'Look. All he understands is fear. It's the only emotion that makes him react. Why do you think I speak Russian to him? For him, Russian's the language of fear.'

Suddenly Kaplan moved, scrambling towards the far side of the ship. Craig leaped from her and his hands grabbed for Kaplan as he went over the side, one gripping his shirt, the other holding his thick, white hair. Craig stood straddle-legged, and lifted Kaplan back aboard the boat as Kaplan screamed with pain. He released his grip on the shirt and tugged on the hair, lifting Kaplan to his toes, then the hands moved down, forcing him to his knees, and all the time he spoke to him in Russian. The fingers twisted, and Kaplan screamed again.

'You pig,' Craig said. 'You stupid, lying pig. Don't you ever learn? Don't you know you can't even die till we say so? You're still in Volochanka, Kaplan. You'll always be there.'

He pushed him sprawling, then picked up an end of rope, knotted his hands behind his back and tied the other end of the rope to the mast, then turned to Miriam.

'Ask your questions,' he said. 'He's ready.'

He went aft then, took the tiller, and sent Omar into the cabin to prepare a meal. Omar scuttled away and Craig lazed back against the strakes, giving his body ease and rest. He could hear the sound of Miriam's voice and Kaplan's responses, but not the words. It didn't matter. Miriam's interrogation was only a warm-up, anyway: the truth would come when he had Kaplan on shore, alone: when Royce and Benson were out of the way. He supposed that eventually he'd have to kill Royce. Maybe Benson too. But she'd let him escape: that made it harder to kill her. Why did she do it? Craig wondered. What was she trying to gain? He leaned forward and looked down into the cabin. Omar was old, but he was determined, and money acted on him as fear did on Kaplan. Omar had sliced bread and cheese and peeled fruit. The knife he had used was long and sharp, and he held it in his hand, looked at it with love.

'No,' said Craig.

Omar sighed and put down the knife, then fetched up the food and four bottles of water, gave some to Kaplan and Miriam, then came back to Craig, sat cross-legged beside him as they ate, and took the tiller.

'Effendi,' said Omar, 'you must be very rich.'

'Sometimes,' said Craig.

'One day you might need a partner.'

'Why?'

'A very small partner. One who could keep his eyes and ears open. Tell you things.'

'What things?'

'What the Americans and the Russians are doing. For money I could find out.'

'Why should I want to do that?'

'You are a spy,' Omar said. 'Just as Royce and Miss Benson are spies.' There was neither shock nor surprise in Omar's voice. He might have said: 'You're a grocer.'

'Who do you think I spy for?'

'Not the Russians or Americans. Not the British, either. You spy for yourself. For money. I could help you. Truly, I could.'

'You're still afraid I'll kill you,' said Craig.

'I'll always be afraid of that,' Omar said. 'But I want to show you I'll be more useful if you let me live.'

Craig ate bread and cheese left-handed. The bread was dry, the cheese old and tough, but he chewed on it stolidly. It was fuel.

'Always the left hand,' said Omar. 'You take care of yourself.'

'That's right,' said Craig. 'Show me how you can be useful.'

'That shepherd there. He was in hiding.'

'I found him,' said Craig. 'There's nothing for you in that.' He ate some grapes. 'Did you know Royce and Benson were looking for him?'

'No,' said Omar. 'The bastards didn't trust me.' Craig chuckled. 'But I guessed it.'

'How?'

'The Russians were looking for him too.'

Somehow Craig went on chuckling. 'I know that,' he said. Omar's face fell.

'You know who they are?' he asked.

'No,' said Craig. 'I don't know that.'

'I do,' Omar said. 'How much is it worth?'

'A thousand dollars,' Craig said.

'It should be worth much more,' said Omar. 'This is big news.'

'A thousand dollars,' Craig said again. 'You're lucky I feel lazy today. I could get it for nothing.'

'That isn't very nice,' said Omar.

'We're not in a nice business.'

'They call themselves Israelis,' Omar said. 'They came to Kutsk three weeks ago. They are Jews, I think, and they had Jewish names—Lindemann, Stein—but really they were Russians. I heard them speak.'

'You speak Russian?'

'I know how it sounds,' said Omar. 'All Turks do if they've got any sense.

'Go on.'

'First they tried to find the shepherd themselves. He was too well hidden. Then they asked me. I said there wasn't any such man. I should explain,' he continued, 'that the shepherd paid us money to say he wasn't there.'

'You'd have sold him out to me—or Royce and Benson.'

'You would have offered more money than the shepherd. The Russians wanted him for nothing.'

'Describe them,' said Craig.

'Lindemann is tall—about your height—heavy-shouldered, brown eyes, black hair. He is the younger. Stein is a head shorter than you, but a big body. Like a bear. A very strong man. His eyes are almost black. His hair was once black, now it is grey.'

'Their age?'

'Hard to say. They look older than they are, I think. The way you do, effendi. He hesitated. 'What I mean is they look good at their job. Like you.'

'Where did they go after Kutsk? Back to Israel?'

'That's what they said in the village. They lied. They came in a boat, and my sister's husband's nephew saw it two days later. It was headed for Famagusta, in Cyprus.'

'Many Israelis go to Cyprus.'

'Perhaps they were Israelis who couldn't go to Israel.' His eyes searched Craig's face. 'Is it worth a thousand dollars?'

'Yes,' said Craig. 'You'll get it when you go.'

'I believe you,' Omar said. 'You're the biggest bastard I ever met, but I don't think you tell lies if you can help it.'

'Try to be like me,' Craig said. 'Tell me about Royce and Benson.'

'They came to Kutsk about three or four days ago. They said they were—those people who are interested in old things.'

'Archaeologists?' Craig suggested.

'Some Greek work. They drove all over the place. They were looking for the shepherd. At first they weren't in too much of a bloody hurry. Then one day Royce got a telegram.'

'What did it say?'

'You think I could get hold of somebody else's telegram?'

'I'm sure of it,' said Craig.

'It was all numbers,' said Omar. 'A code. I couldn't read it. But I think it told them you were coming. They were worried after that. They came to me before you did.'

'Why should they do that?'

'I've got a reputation,' Omar said.

'You mean a police record?'

'No, no.' Omar sounded more surprised than offended. 'I'm not stupid, you know. But a lot of people know about me. I'll help in most things if the price is right.'

He squinted up at the sun, altered course a point, and continued: 'They wanted me to help them if you turned up. I said I would—and you know the rest. For such young people, I thought they did a pretty good job. The sheila——'

'Yes?' said Craig.

'She is very beautiful,' said Omar, 'and very dangerous. Even more dangerous than the man. I think they'll try to kill you. I don't want to be there when they try—not for just a thousand dollars.'

'You won't be,' said Craig.

He lay back again, relaxed and comfortable. Miriam and Kaplan talked on as they ate, and in the distance a long bight of land grew slowly visible.

'Cape Andreas,' said Omar. 'You want to make for there?'

'No,' said Craig. 'Famagusta.'

'For just a thousand dollars I don't want to see the Russians either.'

'You won't.'

'Famagusta's full of bleeding Greeks,' Omar said. 'Greeks don't like me, effendi.'

'What an old worry-guts you are,' said Craig. 'Just do as you're told. You'll be fine. I'll even pay you.'

'You promise that?'

'I promise.' said Craig.

Omar sighed again, and obeyed. The big Englishman's strength was frightening, but there was comfort in it too—if you thought he was going to use it to protect you. There was also the money.

Craig dozed in the sun and watched the land slip by, white sand and scattered rocks, and beyond it a lush green vegetation, sloping back into the island's gentle mountains. Omar stayed well away from land, and to any casual watcher they would be just one more unhurrying boat in a sea full of boats that never hurried. He would be safe in Cyprus, and so would Kaplan, until his purchase price came through.

Craig thought of slaves and auction-blocks, of men and women examined as if they were animals. He'd come down to that. And now he was a slave-trader. The thought disgusted him, but he made his mind accept it. Once weaken, once relent, and Craig would be dead. And if he died, Miriam would probably die too, and Omar. Only Kaplan would have a chance to survive: a chance he might not want. Craig thought of the things he had done for Department K: cruel, terrible things. He thought of the smashed bones, the pistol-beatings, the neat holes that a Smith and Wesson Airweight makes if you use it right. He thought of the things that had been done to him. He'd been shot, stabbed, knifed, clubbed, and tortured in a way that almost cost him his manhood. All for Department K. For the department and its chief, Loomis. He supposed that Loomis connected to other people, other places. To MI6 and the government, ultimately to the people and the country. To Loomis's own highly personal view of Great Britain. But Craig hadn't felt like that. His loyalty had gone as far as Loomis and the department, and there it had stopped. (Mostly his enemies had been Russians and Chinese, because that was the way the world functioned nowadays—in a duality of terror and detestation that sometimes got very close to love. Look at the bright kids. The ones in the west all wanted to be leftists: the ones in Russia all wanted to be Beatles.) But he hadn't ever had that depth of patriotism that rendered Loomis immune from pity or self-disgust whatever disgusting trick he'd played.

He'd gone into this thing because he was good at it. The fulfilment of each assignment had been the most complete satisfaction he could hope to know. And the enemy hadn't always been Russian or Chinese. There'd been Spaniards, Italians, Germans, Frenchmen: and more than one Englishman. He'd handled them all, just as efficiently. And now he was putting a middle-aged Jew on the auction block and forcing a young Jewess to keep him there. He wondered if Miriam would ever know just how terrible a price she was paying. I must want to live pretty desperately, he thought. When I get out of this I'll take a course in ethics and kill myself.

The girl came aft to sit beside him, moving clumsily against the movement of the ship.

'His arms are hurting him,' Miriam said.

'Has he answered all your questions yet?'

'Yes,' she said. 'But I think he's lying sometimes.'

'Go back and tell him I'll let him loose when he tells you the truth.'

Beside him, Omar cackled respectfully. The girl got up and went back to Kaplan. Despite her clumsy movements, her body was beautiful again.

'Not like the Benson sheila,' said Omar. 'A tigress and a deer, eh effendi?'

Craig grinned at him. 'The world's big enough for both kinds,' he said.

The darkness came in quickly, and Omar was worried about the lights. Craig took the tiller as he lit them. Slowly they slipped closer to the shore, and then, in the last rays of the sunlight, Craig could see the white line of foam that marked the sunken ruins of Salamis, the speckled gleam of Famagusta in the distance. Craig got to his feet, picked the rifle up from the deck, slipped out the magazine and put it in his pocket. Omar watched without speaking. Next Craig took out his money, counted it, put it back in his pocket, except for ten one hundred dollar bills. Still silent, Omar licked his lips, then cried out aloud as Craig tore the ten beautiful pieces of paper in half, dropped one half into his lap.

'Half in advance. I'm going ashore soon,' said Craig. 'You'll get the rest when I come back. If you behave.'

'Yes, effendi,' said Omar.

'Are you a good Muslim?' said Craig.

'Pretty good.'

'If I were you I would pray a lot while I'm gone. Pray that nobody comes here looking for the shepherd. If they do, they'll kill you. If you try to contact anybody and do a deal, I'll kill you. Staying alone is your only chance of staying alive. Believe that, Omar.'

'I do believe it,' Omar said.

Craig went forward to the girl then, where she stood beside Kaplan.

'Well?' he asked.

'I think he's telling the truth now.'

Craig untied the man's hands, but lashed his ankles together. In Russian he said, 'You're too fond of swimming,' then to Miriam in English, 'I'm going ashore. I shouldn't be long. When I come back I'll have help.'

'For him?' She nodded at Kaplan who sat on the deck, head on hands.

'It's possible,' said Craig, 'but don't count on it.'

He told Omar to heave to, and together they manhandled over the side the stone that served as an anchor, then he disappeared into the cabin. When he came back he was naked, his clothes and shoes wrapped in a piece of waterproof and strapped to his head like a turban. The others turned away as he lowered himself into the water, swam in a steady breast-stroke towards the lights of the town. The sea was calm and warm, tangy with salt, as placid as a bath, but the feel of it round him was refreshing, shook off his drowsiness. Too soon he reached shallow water and waded ashore to dry himself on a scrap of sailcloth, the only towel on the boat, and dress quickly, in the darkness. He walked along the beach, staying out of reach of the villas' lights, the sight of holiday-makers having one last outdoor drink before dinner, then reached a path that led up to a road, and walked along the road till he found a café with one car parked beside it.

He went into the café and ordered ouzo. The language he spoke was Greek, but with a Cretan accent, very different from Cypriot. The barman who served him showed a flicker of surprise.

'I thought you Greeks were supposed to wear uniform,' he said.

'I'm not in the army,' said Craig, and looked round the bar. Its only occupants were three men playing xeri under a portrait of Archbishop Makarios. The barman watched him nervously.

'Things are quiet in Cyprus now,' he said. 'Most people like them like that.'

'I like it,' said Craig. 'I haven't come for trouble. Just visiting friends.'

He put an English pound note on the counter, and the barman gave him his change in Cypriot mils.

'Which is the taxi-driver?' Craig asked.

The barman called out 'Stephanou', and a fat man sighed,

put down his cards and gathered up his winnings, then walked out to the cab, the inevitable Mercedes.

Craig finished his ouzo.

'There are lots of UNO patrols now,' the barman said. 'The civil war is over.'

'I won't start it again,' said Craig. 'I promise.'

He went out to the cab, and in his mind he cursed himself, thoroughly and obscenely. It had been a mistake to speak Greek; a bad one. English was a far more natural tongue for Cyprus than the Cretan dialect that was the only Greek he knew. But Greek to him was the language of friendship: when first he'd been a fighting man, most of his comrades were Greeks. He'd lived with them and learned their skills. In the islands still there were men and women who regarded Craig as their brother. So out of his loneliness he'd spoken Greek, and like a damned fool forgotten that Cypriots regarded Greeks from Greece sometimes as heroes, more often as a dangerous nuisance, who took to the mountains and slaughtered in the name of Enosis.

And at one time Cypriots too had gone into the mountains, killed British troops and been killed by them. That had been a bad time for Craig. But the British had gone now, and UNO troops had replaced them: Irish, Canadians, unlikely Swedes, and highly improbable Finns on the island of Verus, drinking brandy at five shillings a bottle and persuading Cypriot Greeks and Cypriot Turks to stop killing each other. Enosis—union with Greece—was somehow forgotten: the island was prosperous, not least because UNO paid its bills so promptly. The Greek and Turkish troops billeted on the island to protect their own nationals were already resented as a threat of war, a threat to prosperity. And Greek civilians were resented even more. They hinted that the days of terror might still come back.

Craig told the driver to head towards the port, which was the Turkish quarter.

'Greeks can't go there,' the driver said.

'I'm not a Greek,' said Craig. 'I'm an American. My father came from Heraklion.'

'Oh, an *American*.' The driver was delighted, and all at once relaxed. 'Why do you want to go to the port? Whisky—girls? We got plenty in our own bars.'

'I want to look at it,' said Craig. The driver shrugged, a comprehensive movement involving his whole torso, completely Hellene, that said more clearly than words that Americans made their own rules as they went along. Craig watched as they drove through the new town, Varosha, past the smart bars, tavernas, souvenir shops, then into the older town of cheap bars and night-clubs, to the oldest Famagusta of all.

'This'll do,' he said, and remembering he was an American, gave the driver too much money. When he got out the driver roared off at once—to his favourite café, Craig hoped, to tell a worried barman to stop worrying.

He looked at the dark bastion in front of him. The Venetians had built that, more than four hundred years before: a stag-gering achievement in military architecture, massive yet shapely towers and walls built to keep the Turks out of Cyprus. For Cyprus was rich, and Venice had needed the money: but the Turks had got in even so, and flayed the Venetian commander alive. Craig thought that Omar would have been proud of his ancestors. Their descendants, huddled and restricted inside the walls, he would have had no time for. Every single one of them was poor.

Craig turned his back on history, and walked towards the bars and night-clubs. The place he wanted was small and intimate, and famous for its bouzouki music. Angelos, the man who owned it, had been a waiter in London when the Second World War began, and had joined the navy. In 1945 he and Craig had been part of a Special Boat Service Group that had landed on the island of Cos. It was Craig's eighteenth birthday, and he had saved Angelos' life.

Craig walked in and spoke English to the waiter who led him to a table. It was early, but already the place was filling up, the air-conditioning inadequate to counteract the heat of too many bodies. The waiter led him to a table near the back of the room, and Craig was quite happy about it. He refused the local cham-pagne, and ordered a bottle of Arsinoe, a dry, delicate wine, and a plateful of the delicious Cyprus sausage called seftalies, and the chipped potatoes that are different from the chipped potatoes anywhere else in the world. The waiter brought the wine at once, and Craig sipped and smiled, and asked to speak to Angelos.

As he waited, the show began, and Craig found that the days of originality were not yet over. A girl came on and started to strip to bouzouki music, while Canadians, Swedes, Irishmen, and Finns looked on and cheered. He watched, intrigued. Two cultures met and ignored each other completely. The girl was preparing for love or, at any rate, sex—in a brisk, mid-Atlantic sort of way: the bouzouki was telling of death and sacrifice in a mountain battle a hundred and fifty years ago. But nobody else seemed to find it displeasing, except the bouzouki player. He became aware of a man moving towards him, a tubby man, sleek with success, in a black sharkskin suit and a Hardy Amies tie: a man who carried a plateful of seftalies and chipped potatoes because he chose to, to oblige a friend. He put the food down in front of Craig.

'Hallo, John,' he said, and sat at the table, snapped his fingers. A waiter seemed to grow out of the ground like a speeded-up flower.

'Bring another glass,' said Craig.

'And another bottle,' Angelos added, and Craig remembered that Cypriots always drink as if all the alcohol in the world is due to disappear next day.

'You recognized me, then?' he asked.

'Of course,' said Angelos, and poured wine, motioning to Craig to eat his food. 'You haven't changed, John. Not like me. See how fat I'm getting.'

'Prosperity,' said Craig.

'I have money, yes. If you need any——'

'No,' said Craig. 'I've got money too.'

'What, then?' Angelos asked.

'Does it have to be anything?'

Angelos emptied his glass, poured more wine, and smiled at Craig.

'Yes, John. With you it has to be something.'

'You're right,' said Craig. 'But do me a favour first. Tell me how you knew.'

'That day in Cos,' Angelos said. 'In a way, it was the most important day of my life—the day I should have died—and didn't. You were the reason I didn't die. I have thought about it many times. On bad nights I still dream about it. Mostly I dream about the fat German—the one you got with the knife.'

'I thought I shot him,' said Craig.

'No. You shot the young one, the one who had hit me with the gun-butt. The fat one you knifed—in the throat. He bled all over me.'

'I'd forgotten that,' said Craig.

'That's the kind of man you are,' Angelos said. 'I'm not like that. I can't forget.'

'Maybe you're the lucky one,' Craig said. 'Go on about why you know I want something.'

'You are a very loyal person,' Angelos said, 'but you have no talent for friendship.'

'Now, wait a minute,' Craig said. 'If you don't want to help me, say so.'

'Of course I want to help you,' Angelos said. 'I *have* to help you.'

Craig looked at him across the table, expressionless grey eyes telling nothing. Angelos shook like a man in terror, but that was stupid. What was there to fear?

'I came back for you,' said Craig. 'I killed those two Jerries for you.'

'You killed them for the group,' Angelos said. 'That was where your loyalty was. For me—Angelos—you did nothing. You cared nothing. What did you do after that fat German died, John?'

Craig thought back hard. It had been in an olive-grove, he remembered. One of so many running fights, scrambling, terrifying, escstatic. They'd got back to a caique, and the pursuing Germans had run into a blast of Bren gun fire. But the details had gone.

'I can't remember,' he said.

'I'll tell you. You wiped your knife on the German, put it back in its sheath, then carried me back to the caique. The young German had hit me and broken my ribs. I couldn't walk. You carried me for half a mile, and you never said a word.'

'I was busy.'

'Not then, or afterwards. I was in hospital for a month, then I came back to the group. You never even mentioned what had happened. You have no talent for friendship, John.'

Craig said, 'Are you saying you hate me?'

'No.'

'What, then?'

'You'll never understand. You *can't* understand,' Angelos shouted, then lowered his voice as customers turned to stare. 'Almost everyone needs the friendship of others. They need it as they need food and drink. You—don't. All you need is a group to belong to—but for you the group is an abstraction, not people. Never people. Shall I tell you something. We've been talking for some while——'

'You've done most of it,' said Craig.

'—And you've never even spoken my name. After twenty-three years.'

'And yet you say you'll help me.'

'Of course I'll help you. I must. I've been waiting to do so ever since that night.'

'Do you mind telling me why?'

'I want to be free of you,' said Angelos.

Craig said, 'What I want—it isn't a small thing.'

'I'm glad of that,' Angelos said.

'There's risk.' He looked at the fat man. He was smiling. 'That makes you happy?'

'Very happy.'

'I want you to help pick up three people from a boat, then hide them, and me. Then I want you to act as messenger boy.'

'Who are these people?'

'An American girl, a Russian man, and a Turk.'

'A Turk,' said Angelos. 'That's all it needed. All right. I'll do it.'

'There's a risk in all of it,' said Craig. 'Being messenger boy is the worst.'

'It's a kidnapping?' Craig nodded.

'Yes,' Angelos said. 'It would be. Crime was inevitable for you, just as this'—he gestured to the club—'is inevitable for me.' He finished his wine. 'Shall we go now?'

'Two more questions,' said Craig. 'And one request—I want all the British and American papers you can get here. Next—are you married?'

'No,' said Angelos. 'There are plenty of girls available. I shan't marry for another few years. And the other question?'

'There are two men in Famagusta—supposed to be Israelis. One's called Lindemann. About my height. Big shoulders. Brown eyes. Black hair. The other one's called Stein. Stocky. Built like a barrel. Black eyes. Black hair going grey. Do you know them?'

'Very well,' said Angelos. 'They're sitting five tables away. Behind you.'

Craig's hands moved on the table, and Angelos watched them. They were weapons still, he thought. In twenty-three years Craig had only become more himself.

'They come in here very often,' he continued. 'They have what seems to be an inexhaustible passion for cabaret girls who don't cost too much. The girls usually find it flattering. I take it they are—business rivals?' Craig nodded. 'Do they know you?'

'I hope not,' said Craig. 'Otherwise the risk would be so big you'd be ecstatic. Can we go now?'

'Yes,' said Angelos. 'My car is outside. I have a boat, too. That will be useful.'

'Very,' said Craig. 'Where can you hide us?'

'In the mountains. I have a little place where I take a girl sometimes. It's very quiet. But I don't suppose you'll mind that.'

'Not a bit,' said Craig. 'Do you have only one car?'

'Two,' said Angelos.

'I want to borrow one of them,' said Craig. 'You won't refuse me?'

Angelos sighed. 'I forgot how clever you are,' he said. 'That was a mistake. I told you too much, didn't I? You aren't the kind of man to refuse an advantage just because it's unfair.'

He got up then and led the way to the door. When he'd reached it, Craig looked back. Lindemann and Stein looked just as Omar had described them. They were talking hard to the bouzouki stripper and another girl off the same assembly line. There were two bottles of brandy and four glasses on the table. They didn't look like men who were in a hurry to move.

Angelos' two cars were a Volkswagen and an MGB. Craig chose the Volkswagen. It hadn't the sports car's speed, but it was built for the mountains. They parked the cars near the beach and boarded Angelos' boat, a neat little outboard job that would just about hold five. Craig steered it towards Omar's sailing-boat, another problem.

'Can you put that somewhere inconspicuous?' he asked.

Angelos thought. 'I could take it to Melos,' he said at last. 'My brother has a boat-building business there. I could say it's due for overhaul.'

'How far is Melos?'

'Just a few miles. Or better still I could get my brother to come and collect it. Now if you like.'

'That would be fine,' said Craig, 'if your brother keeps his mouth shut.'

'He will,' said Angelos. 'He owes me money.' He hesitated, then said, 'Craig, do I have to hide a Turk?'

'Either that or kill him,' said Craig. Angelos said no more.

CHAPTER TEN

THE HOUSE in the mountains was the best accommodation Miriam had seen since her night in Ankara. It had comfortable beds, a bathroom, and a workman-like kitchen well stocked with food. It was the man who owned it who puzzled her. He behaved to Craig as if he detested him, yet obeyed his every word, and accepted all that Craig had done without question. When Craig had cut Kaplan loose for instance the fat man had accepted it without a blink; as if he expected violence from Craig, and cruelty, and a complete disregard for the comfort and dignity of others. The fat man wasn't like that, Miriam knew, yet he found it fascinating in Craig, as well as hateful. For his part, Craig simply issued orders, certain that the fat man would obey, and he did.

When the fat man had gone, Craig led her to the kitchen and made her cook a meal for Omar, Kaplan, and herself. They ate it in silence. When they had finished Craig took Kaplan to the bathroom, then to his bed. He looked at him in silence, then spoke in Russian.

'You've told the girl the truth?' he asked.

'Yes. I swear it,' said Kaplan.

'I hope so. Tomorrow you will tell the truth to me. Let's hope it's the same truth.' He turned away.

'Please,' said Kaplan. Craig turned back to him.

'Please. What are you doing to me? Why am I here? I thought I was going to be left in peace.'

'Tomorrow,' said Craig. He went out and locked the door.

In the kitchen, Omar was washing dishes, Miriam drying. Omar, Craig was pleased to see, looked very worried.

'Effendi,' he said, 'how long do I have to stay here?'

'A thousand dollars' worth,' said Craig. 'And maybe a bonus.' He sniffed. 'Take a bath, Omar, then go to bed.'

Omar left them. He still looked worried.

'Aren't you going to lock him in?' the girl asked. Craig shook his head. 'You trust him?'

'Nobody trusts Omar,' said Craig. 'But he's in Cyprus. The toughest part. The Greek part. A Turk out here alone wouldn't have a chance, and Omar knows it. He won't leave us.'

The girl slumped forward in her chair. She looked exhausted.

'It's just as well I've got you and your friends to arrange things,' she said. He said nothing. 'Are you sure you can trust your friend?'

'Yes,' said Craig. 'I can trust him. He's all alone. No woman to find out his secrets.'

She sat up then. 'Why do you have to hurt people all the time?' she asked.

'Do I? That wasn't supposed to be hurtful. I just said what I meant to say. Maybe that's what hurts.' He hesitated. 'I'm not cruel like Royce, you know.'

'But you are,' Miriam said. 'The way you treated Kaplan.'

'Cruelty's the key to Kaplan,' Craig said. 'All I did was use it. I didn't enjoy it.'

'The fact that you used it at all——'

'It's what we all use,' he said. 'Force Three, the KGB, Department K. We use it because it works.' He looked at her again, saw how tired she was. 'I wanted to hear what Kaplan told you,' he said, 'but it'll keep till tomorrow. Go to bed.'

'Are you coming with me?' she asked, and the question whipped the blood into her face.

'Suppose you get pregnant?'

'Would you care?'

He didn't answer. She would never believe that she was the only one he would look out for in the whole sorry mess. Better for them both that she wouldn't. He went with her to the bedroom and she came into his arms fierce and demanding, the body's needs drowning the questions her mind feared. But their bodies at least achieved a dialogue, a question and answer that at last achieved solution. When they had done, she fell asleep at once, and he kissed her as she slept, then fell asleep beside her; as relaxed as a cat, and as wary.

In the morning, as she put on her clothes, she put on her doubts, her fears, her wariness. It was early, but Omar was already in the kitchen, making omelettes. He looked cleaned and rested, and his omelettes were delicious. Craig took the girl on to a verandah that looked straight across the valley to the mountains of Troodos, rich, sweet mountains, green with vine and olive and pine-tree, swift tumbling snow-streams, houses perched like birds wherever a ridge made it possible.

'It's beautiful here,' Miriam said.

'And safe,' said Craig. 'What did Kaplan tell you?'

'Weren't you happy last night?' she said. 'Wasn't your body happy? Because if it was—that was thanks to me, wasn't it?'

'I was happy.'

'Then shouldn't you be grateful to me? Be nice to me? Or is it you just don't know *how* to be nice to people?'

Ask Angelos, Craig thought. He's the expert on my talents for friendship. He waited.

'Oh hell,' the girl said at last. 'Hell! *Hell!*

She sat down opposite Craig, and her voice became cold, impersonal.

'First of all, I'm sure that Kaplan is Kaplan. I ran all the checks Marcus told me about, and he didn't fluff one. He told me about his work in Russia——'

'What about it?'

'How he was a successful scientist. Then he fell out with the Politburo and finished up in Volochanka. Craig, he escaped from there!'

'We know that,' said Craig.

'But you don't know how. There were ten of them—all Jews. It was like a miracle.'

She told him about the Minyan, and the slow evolution of their plan to escape. ('Angelos should hear this too,' said Craig. 'He'd tell you all about my loyalty to groups as abstract concepts.') She told him of the break-out and how he got separated from the others: the long, agonized trek alone to freedom. How he'd wandered alone until he'd almost died, would have died if some Lapps hadn't found him and smuggled him over the border into Sweden, hundreds of miles away. Sweden was lucky for him. He had money in Stockholm. He'd got to the bank and taken out the money, but the Swedes were too interested in him. They wanted him to ask for political asylum, but he was afraid the publicity would betray him to the KGB. He'd had to get away. The money had bought him forged papers and a passage on a ship for Hamburg. From Hamburg he'd flown to Rome, from Rome to Ankara, and from there he'd drifted south, to settle finally at Kutsk.

'Why choose Turkey?' Craig asked.

'Because the Turks hated the Russians,' she told him. 'They'd give him asylum if ever he needed it. And it was remote. The kind of place nobody ever went to. When he bought the flock of sheep he'd learned something else too. He was happy there, a hermit, alone. He hadn't been happy for as long as he could remember.

'Isn't it wonderful?' said Miriam.

'Fantastic,' he said. 'What else is there?'

'He's afraid,' she said, 'of you and others like you.'

'Did you tell him about going to America?'

'You told me not to.'

'Did he say anything about our knowing his real name?'

'Yes,' she said. 'I don't understand that. He said Kaplan was supposed to be dead and buried. He said your people promised. I guess he meant the Russians.'

'I'm sure he did.'

Craig got up then and walked round the garden that encircled Angelos' house. He'd done it before, when they arrived the preceding night, but it was better to do it by daylight. The house was set in a fold in the hills, encircled by pine-trees. A stream supplied its water, a turbine generator its power. A mud track was the only approach to it, and the nearest neighbour was seven miles away. He went back into the house and called Omar and Miriam, led them into the living-room, where a big picture window looked out on the track that led to the house. For the last four hundred feet there was no cover at all.

'I want you to watch this place,' said Craig. 'If anybody comes up that road, call me at once.'

'You want both of us to watch?' Omar asked.

'Both of you. All the time, Omar.' The Turk looked up at him. 'It's possible the lady may want to leave this room. See that she doesn't.'

'Too right,' said Omar.

'What are you going to do?' the girl asked.

'Find out the truth,' said Craig. 'I'm sick of fairy stories.'

He left them, and she sat watching the path. After a few minutes she heard Kaplan cry out, and jumped to her feet. At once Omar also rose, standing between her and the door. He was an old man, but he was strong, she knew. She'd be helpless against him. Then Kaplan cried out again, and she ran at Omar, trying to get past him. But he picked her up, held her in his gaunt, work-worn hands, and looked at her with eyes that were curiously gentle, almost compassionate.

'It's no use, miss,' he said. 'We've got to do what the boss says. Now you sit down and watch the road. It's what we're here for.'

But she went on struggling until there was neither fight nor breath left in her, even when Kaplan yelled a third time. After that she sat down as Omar bade her, and there was no more noise.

Craig came back into the room forty minutes later, and Kaplan followed him. There was a bruise over his left eye and he

was limping. Miriam got up at once and led him to a chair. Craig
fetched water and gave it to Kaplan, who drank it eagerly.

'The shepherd's got a new statement to make,' said Craig.

'Looks like a pretty important shepherd,' Omar said.

'He is,' said Craig. 'A man could get killed just knowing what
his real name is. Do you want to know it?'

'No, thank you,' said Omar. 'I think I'd sooner cook lunch.'

Craig watched him go, then said, 'I roughed him up a bit.'

'I heard you,' Miriam said.

'It was nothing like you got,' said Craig. 'That's work for
experts. But this poor bastard's scared silly. He's got nothing
left.'

He turned to Kaplan, and this time he spoke in English.

'Now tell this woman what you told me,' said Craig. 'Unless
you want to change your story again.'

'I told you the truth,' said Kaplan.

'Now tell it to her.'

Kaplan looked at her, but his whole body was concentrated on
Craig, standing beside him.

'I'm sorry,' he said, 'but most of what I told you yesterday was
lies. There were no friendly Lapps, no smuggling across the
border to Sweden.'

'You didn't escape?' Miriam asked.

'No. The other nine did—that is true. But I did not.'

'Tell her what you did, Kaplan,' said Craig.

The agony on his face was unbearable.

'I betrayed them,' he said, 'to the commandant of the camp.
The price of my betrayal was a pardon.'

'Get on with it,' said Craig.

'I told the commandant the night we—we were ready to go.
You have to be in Volochanka to know how it was. Slow death in
the camp, quick death outside. The commandant was drunk all
the time. He was drunk when I came to warn him. He beat me.
Threw me out. Went back to his vodka. Then it happened. We
made our break. Only I didn't go. I went to the deputy-
commander instead, told them where to pick up the others. He
got seven of them. All the time I had to hide in his hut. If I'd
come out, the other prisoners would have killed me. Then the
commandant was shot, and the deputy took over. He put in a
word for me: got my pardon. I was allowed to live. They gave
me new papers, sent me to work in the Crimea. On a collective.
I was happy there.' He paused till Craig raised his head, then
went on immediately. 'Then a man came to see me from the

Central Scientific Bureau. They'd opened up my dossier again, run some tests on my theory. He said I was to be pardoned.'

'But what had you *done?*' the girl asked.

'Slept with a man's wife and been found out,' he said. 'The man was a close friend of Lavrenti Beria. The charge was moral degeneracy.' He looked at Miriam. 'It wasn't that. I swear it. I loved the woman very much. It was the second time in all my life I had known what love was and——'

'Tell us about your theory,' said Craig.

'It's a way to bring water to desert places. It's part engineering —using atomic plant to make sea-water into fresh water, and part agriculture—the growth of certain crops intermingled to help each other—catching the dew and so on. The Central Scientific Bureau said it ought to be tried out in a limited experiment. They were going to rehabilitate me. I couldn't stand it. I ran away.'

'You couldn't stand what?' Craig asked.

'Coming back to life. Beria was dead by that time, but his friend—the man whose wife I loved—he's still alive. Doing well. His wife is still with him. I'd have had to meet them again, go to receptions, parties—as if nothing had ever happened. And he knows I betrayed my friends. I couldn't face them—not with that. I ran away, stole money, crossed the Turkish border. It wasn't easy, but I'd been trained how to do it in Volochanka. In Turkey, I robbed again—it seems I have a talent for that, too, and bought papers. When I had enough money, I settled down, paid those peasants to keep their mouths shut. I had a life of my own then. It was a good life, but the peasants betrayed me. I should have expected it. It's what I did myself.'

'You felt safe?' Miriam asked.

'I'll never be safe. But the ones I feared were all Russian. If they knew I was alive, they'd kill me. The knowledge I have is too important to be taken out of Russia.'

'They know you're alive,' said Craig. 'They're looking for you now.'

'You won't give me to them?'

'Not if we can get a better offer,' Craig said. 'I'm pretty sure we can. The Americans want you, Kaplan.'

'They don't need my skills.'

'A gift to underdeveloped countries. A nice gesture from Uncle Sam.'

'Well, it is,' said Miriam.

'Of course it is,' said Craig. 'If they can keep him alive.'

CHAPTER ELEVEN

LATE THAT AFTERNOON, Angelos came back. Omar was watching the window and called out to Craig, who brought the rifle, held the MGB in its sights until Angelos stopped the car and walked up the path, a wad of newspapers under his arm. Craig left Omar on duty by the window, and let Angelos in. The rifle made him smile.

'I expected a Bren gun at least,' he said.

'I could use it,' said Craig, and led him to the kitchen. 'What's happening?' he asked.

'Nothing. The two Israelis got very drunk, but they made love to my girls first.'

'Nobody followed you here?'

'Nobody as far as I know. I haven't your skill in these matters. I brought you your papers. And came for my instructions.'

'I'll have to read the papers first,' said Craig.

He began to read through the small ad columns of the *New York Times,* the *Christian Science Monitor,* the Continental *Daily Mail, The Times,* and the *Daily Telegraph.* It was a long and boring process, but in the end he found what he wanted.

'Tell the girl to come here,' he said.

Angelos stiffened to attention, the parody of a soldier.

'Jawohl Herr Oberst,' he said.

He went out, and Miriam came in.

'There are a lot of messages for you. I've marked them,' said Craig. 'Look.'

He handed her the European edition of the *New York Times.* An advertisement read: 'Darling, Won't you listen to Stardust just once more? Marcus misses you.' A box number in Paris followed.

'It's in every paper,' Craig said. 'Crude—but they are in a hurry—and worried about you. So they make you worry about Marcus.'

'They shouldn't have mentioned him,' she said. 'That gave it away.'

'Only to me,' said Craig. 'And they know you're with me anyway. So they mention Marcus—and tell it to me too. Stardust was your code name, I suppose?'

'Yes,' she said.

'How many times did they reach you?'

'Only once. In Istanbul. Our people aren't too strong in Turkey. They were blown—that's the word, isn't it?—six months ago.'

'That's why they hired Loomis,' said Craig.

'What do we do now?'

'Write to the box number. Tell them our terms.'

'*Our* terms?'

'Mine, then. They can have him for me—if they'll get Department K off my back. Otherwise he goes to the Russians.'

'Can *they* get Department K off your back?'

'If they want Kaplan badly enough, yes. But with the Yanks it's easier.'

'You can trust us, you mean?'

'Of course not,' said Craig. 'But you spend more money.'

He found a piece of paper and an envelope, wrote an answer to the box number in the *New York Times*, and gave it to Angelos to post, watched the MGB back down the path to the road, then went to bed and slept for four hours.

That night, he and Omar took it in turns to watch the road, patrol the grounds. He trusted Angelos—all his instincts told him that he was right to do so, but he had no faith in his competence. For this kind of operation he needed a Royce and a Benson: what he'd got was a moralist, a female idealist, and an old man.

Next day, Angelos came back at dusk. Again Craig followed the drill in admitting him, and again Angelos grinned at the sight of the rifle, this time in Omar's hands.

'I have some news you should know,' he said. 'There are two English people in Famagusta asking for you. Or at least for someone who could be you. They are asking for a tall, well-built Englishman and his American wife, believed to be travelling with the girl's uncle and an elderly Turkish servant. The Turk is causing a great deal of excitement.'

'I believe you,' said Craig.

'They are saying the Englishman has come into a great deal of money, that is why he must be found.'

'Who are they?'

'A solicitor and his secretary. The secretary is very beautiful. The solicitor has a limp.'

'Benson and Royce,' Craig said.

'They say the senior partner is flying out today.'

'Who are they saying it to?'

'Anyone who'll listen. They want the word to get around, it seems.

Craig thought hard for a minute.

'Where are they staying?'

'The Esperia Tower.'

'I want you to stay here for a while,' Craig said. 'Keep an eye on my guests.'

'Very well.'

Craig hesitated, then took out the Smith and Wesson, offered it to the other.

'Are they such reluctant guests?' Angelos asked.

'They have enemies,' said Craig.

'And so have you, no doubt. I have a gun, John. It's in the car.'

'I won't be gone long,' Craig said. 'You shouldn't have any trouble.'

He called for Omar then and gave him precise instructions. When the old man agreed, Craig took out ten more hundred dollar bills, tore them in half and gave one half to him. That left Miriam. He called her into the kitchen.

'Department K's caught up with us,' he said.

'But how could they?'

'By knowing their job,' said Craig. 'I told you they're good. They're offering a deal.'

'What kind of a deal?'

'That's what I've got to go and find out.'

'Go to them? That's crazy.'

'No,' he said. 'It's sane enough. I've got Kaplan. They won't hurt me if I can hurt him.' She winced. 'This could be the end of it,' he said. 'You should be glad.'

'I want my people to have him,' Miriam said. 'They're the ones who'll help him to do what he should be doing.'

'We'll listen to their offer too,' said Craig.

Angelos walked back with him to his MGB, and took from the boot an old Webley ·45 revolver.

'Who are you going to shoot?' Craig asked. 'Elephants?'

'I hope nothing,' said Angelos. 'But if I use this, I make sure the man I hit stays down.'

'If you hit anything at all. That damn thing kicks like a mule.'

'How much you forget,' said Angelos. 'In the old days I always used one of these. I didn't miss very often.'

Craig drove the MGB back that night. It was fast, and he didn't have to use the mountain tracks. The new road from Troodos to Nicosia was finished now, a smooth-metalled highway that seemed especially designed for testing out an MGB. It was an eager, thrusting little car, and Craig enjoyed it as he swung into the road's wide, planing curves, easing down at last as he came into Nicosia. The town was noisy with people promenading in the whisp of a breeze that sometimes stirred at evening. There were taxis and buses with vast overhangs and donkeys pulling carts, and pedestrians who walked as if the internal combustion engine had yet to be invented. He was glad to thread his way through the town and get on to the highway to Famagusta.

This is a curious road. Once it had been a railway line, and when the railway was abandoned the track was pulled up, the road put in its place. It ran arrow-straight for almost all of its fifty miles, and the MGB liked this one too: rev-counter and speedometer climbed up and over in steady power. He kept going at speed till the last possible moment. If the senior partner of Royce's firm had arrived he would try anything, and the best way to combat him on a lonely highway was to keep moving, fast. At last the lights of Famagusta grew bigger and brighter, and Craig eased off his speed and drove with finicking care through the old town to Varosha suburb. He drove past the hotel and found space to park. This seemed to be one of the few places left in the world where you could still find space to park, Craig thought.

He went into the lobby and asked for Mr Royce. He was in the bar, the desk clerk said, with his secretary and another gentleman.

'A fat man?' Craig asked. 'Red face and white hair?'

The desk clerk said austerely, 'Mr Royce's friend is rather fat.' Craig moved to the lift.

'Is your name Craig, sir?' the desk clerk asked. Craig said it was. 'You're to go straight up. Mr Royce and the others are expecting you. They've ordered dinner at nine, sir.'

Whatever you did to Loomis he always bounced right back up, Craig thought. Dinner at nine, for instance. That was for his own benefit, not Craig's, designed to show Craig that he wasn't important enough to make Loomis miss his dinner.

He went into the bar. It was long and dark and cool, the air-conditioning muted to a murmur. At the bar itself, a group of wealthy Cypriots drank Keo beer, deplored the price of oranges, and tried not to be caught looking at Joanna Benson's legs. She, Royce, and Loomis were sitting on low chairs round a table. A fourth chair waited for Craig. Loomis didn't look as if he were enjoying it much. He never did enjoy sitting on chairs that weren't specially made for him. Craig moved towards them. The girl's face was impassive. Royce's glance told him that Royce hated him. Loomis raised his massive head and gave him a two-inch nod.

'Ah, Craig,' he said. 'Good of you to look us up. What'll you have?'

'Same as you,' said Craig.

'Ouzo,' Loomis said, and they sat in silence till the barman brought it.

'Nice here?' Craig said at last.

'Too nice for you,' said Loomis. 'Where the hell d'you get your clothes these days?'

'Savile Row,' said Craig.

'Have your suit cleaned, then. It's disgusting.'

'One of the nice things about being retired is you don't have to worry about looking smart all the time,' Craig said. As he spoke, he watched Royce's hands. The left one clasped his drink, the right one fiddled nervously with the lapel of his jacket. Craig turned to him. 'Why bother?' he said. 'You can't start anything here.'

Loomis glowered at him. 'Sit still,' he snarled, then turned back to Craig. 'He could start something if I told him to. And so could this Benson person.'

'You're not that daft,' said Craig.

'I want you, son,' Loomis said. 'I want your hide in strips.'

'That's just self-indulgence,' said Craig. 'I've wanted to put you on a diet for years, but I know I'm never going to get the chance. Anyway, I heard I'd come into money. That's why I'm here.'

'A bloke called John Adams has come into money,' Loomis said.

'You didn't give my name?' Craig asked.

'No,' said Loomis, and his voice was wistful. 'Not yet.'

'How much?'

'A hundred thousand pounds,' said Loomis. 'Any currency you want.'

Craig said, 'You're taking a risk, aren't you? Talking of sums like that in front of these impressionable young people?'

'No,' said Loomis.

'You aren't afraid that one day they may follow my example?'

'No, cock, I'm not. They got more sense.'

'And I've got a hundred thousand pounds. It's not enough, Loomis.'

'How much, then?'

'Oh, the money'll do,' Craig said, 'but I want something else as well. Security.'

Loomis laughed aloud, a roaring boom that seemed to bounce against the walls of the room.

'Oh, son,' he said. 'The things you say.'

Craig waited as he wiped his eyes.

'You want our friend, don't you?' he asked. 'That's the price. A hundred thousand quid I can enjoy in peace. Guaranteed.'

'And how could I guarantee a thing like that? Dammit, man, can't you see it's impossible?'

'You could give me a statement of what you did—and what these two did. What your orders were, how they carried them out. You could sign it and they could witness it. I'd call that a guarantee.'

'I'd call it bloody madness,' said Loomis.

'That's the price,' Craig said. He stood up.

'Wait,' Loomis said. 'Let's have dinner first.'

They went into the dining-room, Royce limping badly, and Craig enjoyed the food and wine; enjoyed even more Loomis's struggle to be polite. It had been so many years since Loomis had had to be polite to anyone. He spoke of Craig's abilities, and praised in particular the skill with which he'd outwitted Force Three.

'Good chaps,' he said. 'Very good chaps. But they have the American weakness—and you used it, cock.'

'What do you mean, sir?' Benson asked.

'They tend to think that patriotism compensates for skill,' said Loomis, 'so they used the Loman girl. Once Craig knew who she was, she had no chance.'

'How did you know Force Three was involved?'

'Those ads in the papers. "Marcus is worried." They must have been desperate to take a chance like that.'

Craig said, 'It's not that bad. They knew I'd see the papers—and it's me they want to talk to.'

For a moment, Loomis looked up from his plate; his angry eyes burned into Craig's.

'That's right,' said Craig.

'What about the Russians?' Joanna Benson asked. 'Are you open to offers from them, too?'

'I'm open to offers from Martians—if they've got the money and guarantees,' said Craig.

Loomis went on eating.

'There's something interests me,' Craig said. 'I wonder if I might ask about it.'

'We'll see.' Loomis's words were a growl.

Craig turned to Royce and smiled politely.

'What happened after I shot you?' he asked. There was a silence, then Joanna Benson giggled.

'What a bastard you are,' said Loomis. 'All right, Benson. You tell him.'

She pushed away her plate and sat back. Royce continued to eat, his eyes looking downwards. It was impossible to look at Craig: to see the mockery in his eyes. At least, Loomis hadn't made him answer. He was grateful for that.

'You were really rather kind to us,' Joanna Benson said. 'I can't think why. Blowing up the Jag was a bit strong, though, wasn't it? Such a lovely car.'

'Sorry about that,' Craig said. 'But I had to set you on foot.'

'Poor Andrew was hardly even that,' said the girl. 'It was hands and knees most of the time. You got him in the leg, you know. Nothing serious, but he bled quite a bit. I had to use tourniquets and things.' Royce went on eating. His tournedos Rossini absorbed him utterly. The girl went on: 'It was all a bit of a problem. I couldn't carry Andrew, and he needed a doctor. I walked back up the road and found a farm with a telephone and called the police. They produced an old boy who spoke a bit of German and I said we'd been attacked by bandits. You've never seen such excitement. Then I scurried back to Andrew and told him what to say, and the gendarmes arrived with an ambulance and took him off to hospital. After that it was all questions and statements and a big hunt for that mad shepherd. They patched Andrew up quite well, I think, and I said we had friends in Cyprus and we'd recuperate there, so they found us a boat and told us they'd let us know as soon as they'd found the mad shepherd. They thought he was running amok or something. His dog was dead, you see. They think he killed it.'

'No. I did that,' said Craig. He looked closely at Loomis. 'Why Cyprus?'

'Benson's a sensible young person,' said Loomis. It was as much praise as he ever offered a woman. 'She was in a spot of bother and she handled it well, then she reported back to me. When she phoned I had a look in your file, cock. Sending them here was my idea.'

'What made you do it?' asked Craig.

'Where else in this part of the world have you got friends? But

Angelos Kouprassi's your friend. He has to be. When you were a boy wonder in the SBS you saved his life.'

Loomis's passion had always been for detail, mountains of it. But he had an unerring ability to pick out the one fact that was significant, and use it.

'So I sent the two of them here,' he said, 'and damn if you're not here too. How's Angelos?'

'Well,' said Craig.

'Up in that little place of his in the mountains?' asked Loomis. He chuckled. 'Nice people these Greek Cypriots, but the biggest bloody chatterboxes I ever came across. Still, it's useful. Benson here's a good listener. She's sensible, Craig. Wouldn't you say?'

'She is.'

'Then how the hell did she come to let you get away once she'd tied you up?'

'I'm afraid that's my secret,' Craig said.

Joanna Benson gave no sign of relief.

'But I did it the way Pascoe showed me,' she said. 'It's impossible to—— No, that's ridiculous, isn't it? You're here, after all.'

'You'll have to show Pascoe that one,' said Loomis.

Craig shook his head. 'That's over,' he said.

Loomis turned to the other two. 'Go and take your coffee on the roof garden,' he said.

Royce left, still not looking at Craig, and limping heavily. The girl made no move to help him.

'He'd kill you for nothing,' said Loomis. 'You've beaten him twice. He hates you for it.'

'He hates too much. And he enjoys hurting people too much.'

'Yes. So I gather. And Benson?'

'She watched. I don't think she enjoyed it.'

'Tell me,' said Loomis. 'How d'you come to beat an upstanding young feller like Royce?'

'You made me angry. It was the best thing you could have done, Loomis. It gave me my skill back.'

'How on earth did I make you angry?'

'You used me for bait. All that stuff about how I had one more chance to prove myself. I had no chance at all. From the minute I got to New York I was the decoy, wasn't I? Money but no gun, no proper contacts—just a twit from the FO—and Royce and Benson ahead of me all the time. When I was picked up in New York I didn't have a chance.'

The fat man sat, impassive.

'Tell me about that,' he said.

'What do you care?' asked Craig. 'I got away and came back to London and you were too busy to see me. You weren't too busy to see Royce and Benson.'

'Ah,' said Loomis.

He struggled and wrestled with his own body to get a hand to an inside pocket. It came out holding a cigar. Loomis looked at it, sighed, and handed it to Craig, then wrestled himself again for another.

'Go on, son,' he said.

'You saw them that day. You didn't see me. And I knew why. Craig was out. Finished. If the KGB didn't get me, you would. So I got out of the country——'

'Your friend Candlish is a very resourceful feller.'

'"—went back to the States and got hold of Miriam Loman.'

'Royce and Benson should have got on to her,' said Loomis. 'Youth has its drawbacks.'

'They're not mine. The Loman girl took me right to Kaplan and I've got him.'

'In your friend's house in the mountains. Suppose we take him from you?'

'You can't,' said Craig.

Loomis clipped his cigar, lit it as if he were cauterising a wound.

'We're chums with the Cypriots now,' he said. 'We could tell them some yarn. They'd let us use force. There's a unit of the RAF Regiment not far from here.'

'Kaplan's no good to you dead. Or have you started subcontracting to the KGB?'

'I see,' said Loomis. 'You'd go that far, would you? But suppose I'd sent some of the boys along now—to pick him up while you and I were chatting?'

'He'd still be dead,' said Craig.

'Your friend Angelos? No, I don't think so. And not the Loman person. She's hardly appropriate for the role. Omar the terrible Turk, eh, Craig?'

'Never mind,' said Craig. 'Just believe what I told you. You only get Kaplan alive if you pay for him.'

'A hundred thousand,' said Loomis.

'And a written guarantee.'

'Even I can't give you that without authority.'

'Then get it. I have other offers, you know.'

For the first time since Craig had known him, Loomis became

angry in silence. No purple face, no outraged bull frog swellings of the chest, no pounded tables.

He said softly, 'I think you'd be very unwise.'

'The other offers have guarantees too,' said Craig.

'You'd still be unwise.'

Craig got up then and looked down at Loomis. The fat man was as still as a statue, and just about as hard.

'You know what we businessmen say,' said Craig. 'Buy now and avoid disappointment. Let me know when you've got your guarantee.'

He went down to the foyer and spoke to the desk clerk.

'Could you ring Miss Benson and Mr Royce?' he said. 'They're up in the roof garden. Tell them that Mr Loomis wants to see them in the restaurant.'

The clerk lifted a phone, spoke briefly, first in Greek, then in English, and turned to Craig.

'They're on their way, sir,' he said.

'Thanks,' said Craig.

At least now they wouldn't try to stop him reaching his car—and Loomis would have lots to say to them.

CHAPTER TWELVE

HE DROVE BACK to the mountains fast, alert for following cars. There were none. When he turned off on to the track to Angelos' house, he was quite alone. Up to Loomis now, he thought, unless the Yanks come up with a better offer. He sounded his horn as he drew to a halt, then deliberately stood in the glare of the headlights, making himself visible before he switched them off and walked up the path. The door opened as he approached it, and Angelos stood in the light, the Webley massive in his fist.

'You forget things, too,' said Craig. 'Don't you know better than to make yourself a target?'

They moved towards the living-room. From the kitchen there came a tinkle of glass, as Craig opened the living-room door. In the living-room Miriam, Omar, and Kaplan sat waiting. Craig raced into the room, tipped up the heavy chair Kaplan sat in, pushed him behind it.

'Angelos,' he yelled. 'The lights. Get the lights.'

Angelos reached for the switch and a shot boomed out behind him. His body jerked to its impact, and he reeled into the room, took two stiff-legged strides and crashed down on to the floor. Craig fired into the hallway, and risked a look into the room. Omar had disappeared behind an upturned sofa, Miriam beside him.

From the darkness behind the living-room, a voice spoke.

'Mr Craig,' it said, 'all we want is Kaplan.'

Beside him a rifle went off, an appalling explosion of noise in the confined space of the room, then Omar said softly, 'If I have to kill people—that's extra, effendi.'

The voice spoke again.

'It's no use, Mr Craig. We've got all the advantages. Just send Kaplan out. That's all we want.'

Craig looked at Kaplan, who was whimpering with terror, then crouched lower behind the chair. The Russian was right. He had no chance at all, pinned down in the light. The chair and sofa they crouched behind were solid enough, but not solid enough to stop a heavy calibre bullet. There was no chance of shooting out the lights, either: there were lamps all over the room, and he had no extra ammo . . . Something stirred by the door, and he looked at Angelos. The fat man, unseen in the angle of the door, had stirred. Blood soaked from a hole in his side on to the floor, but he was still alive.

Craig said softly in Greek, 'Angelos, turn the lights off.'

The fat man stirred again, and moaned.

Craig spoke more urgently. 'Angelos, you can hear me. Turn the lights off.'

The voice outside spoke again. 'I shall count to ten. After that, we'll start firing into you. It will be your own fault, Craig. We only want Kaplan.' There was a silence, then—'One—Two—Three——'

Craig said, 'Turn the lights off, Angelos—and then we'll be even. You won't owe me a damn thing.'

The voice had reached eight when Angelos rose with the shambling uncertainty of a drunk, lurched to the wall, and staggered into the doorway, his hand on the light switch. A second shot smashed into him, and it was the weight of his body falling that plunged the room into darkness.

Craig yelled to Omar not to fire, and swerved over the chair, wriggled on his belly to the door angle, waiting for a gun flash. When it came, he snapped off an answering shot and rolled behind the door. Another gun banged, and Craig noted its direction. In the darkness of the corridor a man was cursing—perhaps he'd hurt one of them, and he waited, tense, his hand stretched out in front of him, till he felt the softness of Angelos' body. He followed the outline of shoulder and arm, till at last he found the massive shape of the Webley, hefted it in his hands.

'All right, Omar,' he whispered. 'Give him three rounds then cease fire.'

'Three rounds,' said Omar. 'A hundred dollars a round.'

The sound of the rifle was like blows from a giant hammer smashing the room, and after the third Craig leaped crouching into the doorway, sensed movement to his right and dropped flat. A gun banged, a shot cut the air where he'd been, and behind him, he could hear Miriam screaming. He fired the Webley, and the kick from it brought up the barrel until it pointed at the ceiling. The noise it made was scarcely less than the rifle's. He fired again, rolled to a new position. There was a sound of scuffling feet, the heavy thud of a falling body, then silence. Craig lay still in the darkness. One man was certainly out of it, and his guess was that there had only been two, and that the second one was hurt. But even so, there was no point in taking chances: if he miscalculated now they would all be dead. He waited a minute, two minutes. In the living-room behind him he could hear Omar fidgeting restlessly with the rifle. At last, the voice spoke again. It sounded weak.

'There were only two of us, Mr Craig,' it said, 'and you have killed my partner and wounded me. I would like to surrender.' Craig willed himself to stay silent. 'I'm going to put my gun down,' the voice said. There was a scraping sound and a heavy object scraped along the corridor. Noiselessly, an inch at a time, he stretched out his left hand until he touched it: a gun all right, an automatic; nine millimetre by the feel of it. Three gun Craig.

'I'm now going to stand up,' said the voice, and Craig became aware of a dark shape in the darkness before him. In the living-room Omar's rifle clicked.

'Don't shoot yet, Omar,' Craig shouted.

'Thank you, Mr Craig,' said the voice.

Craig rose to a crouch and moved to the light switch in the hall, pushed it up with the barrel of the automatic while the Webley covered the corridor. A tall, heavy-shouldered man stood swaying in front of him. Farther back, in the kitchen doorway, an older man, squat, barrel-chested, built like a bear, lay flat on his back. He was dead.

'Come forward slowly,' said Craig. 'Let's have a look at you, Mr Lindemann.'

The young man's eyes flickered up at him as he lurched into the living-room, one hand pressed to his shoulder. In front of him Miriam, Kaplan, and Omar faced him. Miriam had both hands pressed to her face, stifling the screams that had muted now to sobs, Omar's hands were claw-like on the rifle, his face alight with excitement. Kaplan looked once at Lindemann, then away, his face ageing even more as Craig watched. Lindemann spoke in Russian.

'All that can wait,' said Craig, and led Lindemann to a chair, opened his coat, and looked at the wound.

'Get me some hot water,' he said. Omar moved, still holding the rifle. 'Not you,' said Craig. 'You stay here. Miriam.'

The girl's hands fell from her face and she moved slowly to the door. Angelos' body was in the way.

'Move him, Omar,' said Craig.

The old man slung the rifle over his shoulder and dragged Angelos out. Craig looked at the wound, a clean puncture through the right shoulder, a neat, purple-ringed hole back and front.

'You were lucky,' he said.

'In a sense,' said Lindemann.

Miriam brought hot water, and linen cloth torn into strips, then watched as Craig bandaged the wounded man, his hands deft and sure. Once he hurt Lindemann, making him cry out, but Craig went on as if nothing had happened, as if there were no blood on the carpet, no reek of cordite in the room, no ache in the ears from the crash of the rifle: as if Lindemann were a perfectly ordinary young man who'd had minor injuries in a car crash. When he'd finished he gave him a cigarette and a drink.

'So all you wanted was Kaplan,' Craig said. Lindemann was silent. 'Only you didn't get him,' said Craig. 'You got a mate of mine instead.' Again silence. 'Nice chap. Quiet. Ran a nice little business. You and your friend used to go there, didn't you? Chat up the girls. Is that why you killed him? So he couldn't identify you?'

'Stein killed him.'

'You didn't work all that hard to stop him. And now we can identify you. The girl, the old man, and me. Are you going to kill us if you get the chance?'

'The question is academic,' Lindemann said.

'Not to me . . . Maybe not to you, either.'

'All we wanted was Kaplan. Angelos—it was an accident. I am sorry for it.'

'Me too,' said Craig. 'He didn't have to die at all. You could have bought Kaplan. He's for sale.'

'Bought him?'

'A million roubles COD.'

'We are Israelis,' Lindemann said.

Craig looked over to Kaplan. 'Is that right?' he asked.

Kaplan said, 'I don't know. I've never seen them before.'

'But you spoke in Russian,' Miriam said. 'They're Russian, aren't they? KGB?'

'Russians, yes. KGB, no,' said Craig. 'They're in your file,' he told Kaplan. 'They're the ones who survived the break-out from Volochanka. Their names are Daniel and Asimov. Daniel's the dead one. Right?' The young man looked away again. 'You wanted Kaplan because he betrayed you. Isn't that right, Kaplan?'

Kaplan said, 'I have never—have never—' Then his voice choked. He turned away.

'You've wanted him dead ever since you got out of Volochanka.'

'One year, three weeks, and four days,' said Asimov. 'It was the only thought in our minds.'

'Tell us about it,' said Craig.

'He's sick,' the girl said. 'He should be in a hospital.'

'No,' Asimov said. 'That isn't important. What Kaplan did —that is important. I want you to know.'

'We do know,' said Craig.

'Not all. I am sure Kaplan did not tell you all.'

Asimov looked at Kaplan then, with a hunger of hate such as Craig had rarely seen, an almost sensual appraising of the older man's body, as if Asimov were calculating how much he could endure before he broke.

'Please. I want to get out of here,' Kaplan said.

'No,' said Craig, and at once Omar moved in on Kaplan, who sat down and turned his face from them. He was willing himself not to listen, Craig knew, but his will was not strong enough.

'He told you about the Minyan, no doubt,' said Asimov. Craig nodded. 'And about our plan to escape? It was a good plan. A beautiful plan. Daniel made it.' He looked up then, facing Craig. 'There is something you must realize. I worshipped Daniel.'

'Go on,' said Craig.

'The plan worked perfectly, as Daniel had promised it would. Only—when we got out, Kaplan was missing. I thought he had been unfortunate, but even then Daniel knew better. He knew that Kaplan had betrayed us—and because he knew it, I am still alive. When we split up, you see, we took a different route— not the one we had discussed when Kaplan was present—and so we got out alive. We learned later that the others did not. The guards caught them and killed them, every single one.'

'What happened to you?'

'We should have died then. I mean—there was no real possibility that we could survive. And yet somehow we did. Fishing. Trapping animals. Digging up roots. We lived like beasts, and like beasts we survived, and got away to the West. The filthy capitalist West. A place called Vardo, up in the north of Norway. By then it was winter, and we got a job on the railway. We told the boss we were Finns and we'd lost our passports. He didn't believe us, but he didn't do anything about it either. Labour's scarce up there in the winter. We worked through till spring, then took off. It was time for him to tell the police about it. We got to Oslo. That wasn't easy, but after Volochanka, nothing was too difficult.'

'You could have told the Norwegians who you were,' said Craig. 'They'd look after you.'

'On their terms,' said Asimov. 'We wanted our freedom—to find out about Kaplan.'

'What happened in Oslo?' Craig asked.

'Daniel knew of a man there who could forge papers for us if we paid him.'

'Where did you get the money?' asked Miriam.

'We stole it. Stealing isn't difficult—not if you're taught by experts. There were many thieves in Volochanka. We got the money and the man gave us our papers. We became Israelis. Lindemann and Stein. Then we flew to Cyprus.'

He stopped then, as if the recital were finished. Craig thought otherwise.

'You didn't stay here,' he said.

Asimov looked at Miriam.

'I really am tired now,' he said. The girl moved closer to them, her eyes fixed on Asimov, glowing with admiration. Behind her Kaplan sat like a stone man, but he had heard every word.

'Can't he rest for a while?' Miriam asked.

'No,' said Craig. 'He has to finish it. Then we can decide what to do with him.'

'He's been through so much.'

'More than you realize,' said Craig, and turned to the Russian. 'Tell us about when the KGB found you.'

Asimov's good hand clenched on his lap. He said nothing.

'Was it the man who forged your papers?' Craig asked. 'Is that how they found out?' He waited a moment, looking at Asimov. He was white now, exhausted, the onset of shock catching up with him at last.

'I've got all night,' Craig said. 'I don't think you have. But the KGB found you, didn't they? They even offered to help you. Weapons—money—information. And you took them all.'

Kaplan said, 'That can't be true. You know that can't be true.'

Craig looked at him. His face trembling, Kaplan walked over to Asimov, looked down at him, and spoke, his voice a scream. 'Is it true?'

Asimov lay back and closed his eyes, and Kaplan grabbed for him, shook him.

'You must tell me now,' he screamed.

Miriam went to him, pulled his hands from Asimov and pushed him into a chair.

'Let him rest,' she said.

'You will never know how important this is,' he told her.

'I know,' said Craig. He bent closer to Asimov. 'All right

you're tired, so I won't make you talk. All you have to do is listen. But you'd better do that Asimov, or I'll leave you with Kaplan.'

'Talk, then,' said Asimov. 'It's all foolishness anyway.'

'The KGB reached you,' said Craig, 'and they told you what you already knew—that Kaplan had betrayed you. They said they'd help you to find him, because they wanted him dead too. They gave you money, and sent you to New York.' The girl turned to him, wide-eyed. 'You had to get information from Marcus Kaplan, I should think, but when you got there you found the Americans were ahead of you. Marcus already had a bodyguard. So then you went to see the man who'd interrogated Kaplan, a man called Laurie S. Fisher—at an apartment building called the Graydon Hotel.'

Asimov leaned back further in the chair.

'Don't go to sleep now,' said Craig. 'This is where it gets interesting. You found Fisher all right. The way you found him must have been perfect for you. He was in bed with a woman. You killed the woman, then tortured him until he told you all you needed to know. Then you killed him.' He hurried on, not looking at Miriam. 'Then your KGB contact found out I was in town and sent a couple of blokes to kill me. They tried, when I was with Marcus Kaplan—and they made a mess of it. But that wasn't too important, was it? Fisher had told you Kaplan was in Kutsk, and you went there looking for him. You made a mistake at Kutsk, Asimov. That place is full of Omar's relatives. The only language they understand is money . . . But your luck held anyway. You stayed on in Famagusta, waiting. It's nice and handy for Turkey, and your cover was good. A lot of Israelis stay here. Then damn me if I didn't walk right in on you at Angelos' night club. And the girl who takes them off while the bouzouki plays said: "I can't understand Angelos. He's never at the club these days." So you followed him, didn't you, mate? And you did a spot of mountaineering and climbed in through the kitchen window and brought your score up to three.'

'How can you know this is true?' Kaplan asked.

'I saw Fisher and his girl,' said Craig. 'I saw what was done to him. And that's the only way our intrepid hero could have found out how to reach you, Kaplan.' He turned to Miriam. 'You think I'm rough,' he said. 'You should see this fellow's work. Even Royce wouldn't be ashamed of it.'

Asimov said in a whisper, 'That was Daniel.'

'You should record that and save your voice,' said Craig.

'I don't mean to excuse myself. I was there and saw it happen and did nothing to prevent it. I did nothing to stop him killing your friend, either. And Angelos had been very kind to us.'

'And this is the man you worshipped?' Miriam said.

'He saved my life so many times I almost lost count. Even in the camp, he helped me. Looked after me. He showed me how to survive—and how to hit back. If it hadn't been for Daniel, I'd still be an animal in the cage of Volochanka. When we got out —in Norway, in Sweden, then here—he taught me how to be a man again, and not just an animal.' He looked at Kaplan. 'Also he taught me how to hate properly. In this world, existence is hopeless unless you can hate. And I hate you, Kaplan. I will hate you till Craig kills me.'

'Maybe I'll let him do it,' said Craig. 'Maybe I won't do it at all. You puzzle me, friend. You really do.'

'I did what had to be done to kill Kaplan,' said Asimov. 'Why is that puzzling?'

'Can you tell him, Omar?' Craig asked.

'You don't have to tell a Turk anything about hating,' Omar said. 'We've been doing it for years. Greeks mostly. And Arabs. Almost anybody who isn't a Turk—and quite a few that are. But when we hate—we hate a man and his family. Not strangers. We don't torture strangers or kill a woman making love because she's in the way, or a fat man who has been kind to us, even if he is a Greek.'

Asimov said, 'Killing Kaplan was our whole world. Nothing else mattered.'

'I hate your world,' said Miriam.

'I spit on it,' said Omar. 'I spit on you.'

'Hate it, spit on it, my world exists,' said Asimov, and looked at Kaplan.

'Let the old Jew kill the young one, effendi,' Omar said. 'It's the worst punishment you could think of for the young one, and the old one will enjoy it.'

'No,' said Kaplan. 'I don't want to kill him.'

'He wants you to live,' said Craig. 'To remind him there's somebody else as bad as he is. After all that wonderful talk in the camp, you wound up working for the KGB.'

'Are you going to kill me, then?'

'Why should I?'

'I let Angelos die.'

'And I killed Daniel—the one you worshipped. Just how

good a hater are you? Suppose I let you live—do I go on your list too? And Omar and the girl? They stood by and let me do it.'

'Please,' Asimov said. 'Please, I really am tired.' His lips curled up for a moment. 'Dead tired.'

His body slumped forward. Craig caught him and carried him into a bedroom, then came out and looked at the body of Daniel. Omar came up beside him.

'It's hot here, boss. Even up in the mountains. This one and the Greek—they won't keep long.'

Craig looked down at the dead face. It was strong and hard as a weapon, the face of a man with an overwhelming drive to the achievement of one objective at a time: a man who would feel neither pity nor remorse for what had to be done to achieve that objective. Asimov didn't look like that. Not yet.

'Put them in the garage,' Craig said. 'Take the air-conditioning unit out of your bedroom and plug it in.'

'Air-conditioning, boss?'

Craig did it for him.

CHAPTER THIRTEEN

THEY LAY TOGETHER in the coolness of the room, and she could sense his relaxation in the tenderness of his hands as he embraced her, the sigh of content when he lit a cigarette after they had made love. In the darkness her fingers explored the scars on his body.

'There was a time when I thought you were the most hateful man in the world,' she said.

'You had a remarkable way of showing it.'

She dug an elbow into his stomach and he grunted with pain.

'It was partly cracks like that that made me think it,' she said. 'But now I know you're only Little League stuff—compared with Kaplan, Daniel, Asimov. You're just an amateur.'

'I was never in Volochanka,' he said.

'You've had things done to you——'

'And I've hit back.'

'Sure—at your enemies. Not people who haven't harmed you. And you didn't betray—like Kaplan.' She put an arm round his chest. 'I hate that man,' she said. 'Liar. Betrayer. And now he's happy—just as you said—because somebody else is as bad as he is. What a credit to my people. He's like a cartoon Jew in a Nazi comic-strip.'

'He's what other people made him,' said Craig.

'He could have done so much.'

'He will.'

Suddenly the girl's body moved away from his. He put out his hand, felt the tender weight of a breast, then his fingers moved up her throat to her face. She was crying.

'I say, look here. Dash it, old girl. What?' he said.

She giggled for a moment, but her tears continued. He gathered her into his arms and held her gently, whispering to her as the tears spilled on to his shoulder. She was weeping for a world of illusions wrecked, of values destroyed, and for Kaplan too. Soon and late, Miriam would shed a lot of tears for Kaplan. Craig got up and dressed. It was his turn to keep watch.

As he entered the living-room he knew at once that something was wrong. Omar sat in the chair, as he should—but he was too still, too relaxed. Craig went to him. The old man lay back in his chair, breathing in great snoring gasps. A bruise darkened the side of his head. The rifle was gone. Craig raced to Kaplan's bedroom, took the key from his pocket, unlocked the heavy door, and went in. Kaplan lay sleeping, and Craig raced back to Asimov's room. It was empty.

He roused Miriam and sent her to look after Omar, then went back to Kaplan, grateful for the solid doors in Angelos' house, and for the fact that he'd locked Kaplan in every night. He'd locked in Asimov, too, even though he'd looked so weak, and so defeated. But he'd found a way past the door. And now he was up in the mountains with a rifle. Craig woke up Kaplan and told him what had happened. The fear that was a part of his life came back to his face.

By the morning, Omar had recovered consciousness. His face looked grey, and very old, but his strength was astonishing. Craig marvelled at the hardness of the old man's head, and the stamina that had brought him round.

'I was a fool, effendi. A bloody fool—and at my age too,' he said. 'He asked me if he could go to the toilet.' He put a hand to his head. 'My oath, he can hit.'

'It wasn't your fault,' Craig said.

'He'll be up in the mountains.' Craig nodded. 'With a rifle. But he won't use it, boss. Not with that shoulder the way it is.'

'Why not?'

'It'll kill him.'

'I don't suppose he cares,' said Craig, and made for the door. Omar called out to him. 'Did he take my money, boss?'

'No,' Craig said. 'It's here.' He rummaged in a dressing-table drawer and produced the half bills, put them in Omar's hands.

'Thanks,' said Omar, and went to sleep holding his money.

Later that day a Land-Rover appeared on the path. Miriam was watching, and she called Craig at once. Joanna Benson was driving, and beside her Loomis sat, enormous, liquescent, and very angry.

Craig told Omar to stay out of sight, and left Miriam on watch, then he went into the kitchen, collected Kaplan, who was preparing lunch, and locked him in his room, warning him to stay away from the window. As Loomis waddled angrily to the open front door, Joanna following, Craig stood inside it, the Smith and Wesson in his hand. Loomis puffed past him without a word, and Craig let Joanna go by and took them into the kitchen. The smell of food made Loomis angrier than ever.

'All right,' he said. 'I accept your offer.'

Craig raised the Smith and Wesson.

'What the devil are you looking so coy about?' asked Loomis. 'And put that thing down.'

'I hardly know how to say this,' Craig said. 'Face the wall, please.'

'You really have gone potty,' Loomis yelled.

'Face the wall.' The gun, that had pointed between them, now concentrated on Loomis, and he obeyed.

'Handbag on the table, Miss Benson,' Craig said. She put it down. 'Now, turn around. Put your hands on the wall. Lean forward.'

In silence, they did as they were told. Joanna Benson's handbag yielded the .32 she had carried before: neither of them had weapons concealed on them.

'All right,' said Craig. 'You can turn around.'

'I bet you enjoyed that,' Joanna Benson said, and Loomis said only, 'There are limits, Craig. You've reached them.'

'It's a compliment, really,' said Craig. 'There's nothing you wouldn't try to do me down, and we both know it.'

'Balls,' said Loomis. 'I told you. I accept your offer.'

'Let's see the guarantee,' said Craig.

Loomis reached into his pocket and handed over a sheet of paper. It contained all that he had asked.

'The money,' said Craig.

'Ah,' Loomis said. 'We got conditions about the money, cock. Kaplan goes to New York—the Yanks insist on delivery—and you take him. When you get there you get a hundred thousand quid in dollars—less fifty thousand dollars you pinched from the emergency fund.'

'Why doesn't the department take him?'

'I want my hundred thousand quid's worth,' said Loomis.

'I may need a bit of help.'

'Why?'

'The KGB want Kaplan too. Let me have Royce and Benson here.'

'All right.'

'She can take you back in the Land-Rover, then come back to pick us up. Royce too.'

'His foot's still bad,' said Loomis.

'He doesn't shoot with his foot. She can also get a man's white wig, a man's yellow wig, a Cyprus stamp on Miriam Loman's passport—and mine. And air tickets to New York.'

Loomis glowered at him once more.

'Oh son, you like your pound of flesh, don't you?'

'That brings us to Omar,' Craig said. 'You'll have to smuggle him out or it's no deal. Well?'

'I'll find a feller to do it,' said Loomis.

'That's it, then,' Craig said.

He stuck the gun in his waistband. 'You're a pleasure to do business with, Mr Loomis.'

Loomis used three words. Craig had heard them all before. He put the .32 back in the handbag and gave it to Joanna Benson.

Miriam was delighted to be going home. Omar too was happy. He'd lost his boat—that was unfortunate—but instead he had a vast wad of hundred dollar bills. Craig found him a roll of transparent tape and Omar was happy. Kaplan alone made difficulties.

'I don't want to go to America,' he said. 'I was happy in Kutsk.'

'You can't go back there. Asimov will find you,' Miriam said. 'And anyway—what's wrong with going to America? Your brother's there.'

'I'd like to see Marcus. That's fine,' said Kaplan. 'But what will they make me do there?'

'Work,' said Craig. 'The kind of work you should be doing.'

'But the KGB will find out. They'll come after me again.'

'You'll be looked after,' Craig said.

'I was happy in Kutsk,' Kaplan said again.

'You had six months,' said Craig. 'You're lucky it lasted that long.'

The Land-Rover arrived, and in it were Royce, Benson and a taciturn sailor whose business was to take Omar back to Turkey. Craig sent them both off at once in the Volkswagen. The old man turned to Craig, his fingers counted the money for the last time.

'You made me rich, effendi,' he said. 'The only rich man in Kutsk,' He sighed. 'Now I'll have to buy my wife a fur coat.'

'Don't tell her,' said Craig.

'Boss,' Omar's voice was reproachful. 'She's a woman. How can I help it?' He bowed to Craig. 'Have a good journey. And come and look me up some time. Maybe we can do some more business together.'

Craig watched him go, then turned to Royce. 'How's the limp?' he asked.

'Fair,' Royce said.

'Let's see you walk.'

Royce braced himself, then moved across the room. For a short distance, at least, the limp was hardly noticeable.

'That's fine,' said Craig. 'Now you and Kaplan change clothes.'

'What is this?' said Royce.

'Didn't Loomis tell you who was boss? Go in the bedroom if you're shy.'

When they'd gone, Joanna Benson looked from Miriam to Craig.

'Isn't there someone missing?' she asked.

'Who?'

'Your friend Angelos. I thought he was with you.'

'He is,' said Craig. 'But it's better if you and he don't meet.'

'Fair enough,' said Joanna. 'Then there's the Israeli pair. I had a look for them, Craig. They've disappeared.' She hesitated. 'Is that why Andrew's changing clothes with Kaplan?' Craig didn't answer. 'Loomis was right. You really do like your pound of flesh.' She turned to Miriam. 'Doesn't he, darling?'

Royce and Kaplan came back and Craig fitted on the wigs Joanna had brought.

'These wouldn't fool anybody,' said Royce.

They'd fool a man on a mountainside, watching a moving car.

Asimov would soon be ill. He'd taken another look at his wound, seen how inflamed it was. His temperature was rising too, and soon he'd have fever. But there was food enough to keep him going—last night he'd robbed the kitchen—and water in the mountain streams. And he didn't have to hold out for long. He was certain of it. The Land-Rover would be coming back soon, with Kaplan in it, and no matter what precautions Craig took, he, Asimov, would then kill Kaplan. The likelihood was that he would then die, of exposure and weakness, up here in the mountains, or by execution, if they hanged murderers in Cyprus. He didn't know. It was funny. He was going to commit a murder and he didn't know what the penalty was. Life imprisonment, perhaps. The British had abolished hanging, and maybe the Cypriots had too. Life imprisonment he could face, so long as the prison wasn't Volochanka, and he'd even escaped from there.

Asimov lay on his back, nursing his strength as Daniel had taught him. He was weary now, utterly weary, with a tiredness of the will that exhausted him as completely as the mine at Volochanka. He thought of the ten of them, the plot to escape, the lectures, the preparation, the training. They had all meant hope for the future, and with hope even Siberia was bearable.

And when he and Daniel had escaped, they still had a reason to go on fighting life. Revenge, this time. An ignoble emotion, though the Elizabethans, he remembered, had made a whole literature out of it, with Hamlet as its finest flower. Love was better, the philosophers said, and he'd loved Daniel. He must have done, not to have stopped him that day in the Graydon. But revenge was better than nothing. It made you keep on living till you achieved what you set out to do. But it would be better if he could forget that day at the Graydon: the surprise on the girl's face just before she died: the man's agonized screams smothered by the gag. Daniel had been so skilful, and he'd stood by and watched. Maybe he'd enjoyed—— The thought was unbearable. If it were true, it made him everything that Turk had said. No better than the guards at Volochanka, no better than Kaplan.

He began to think of a poem he had written in prison. A pattern of ice on a birch tree, and the dull red disc of the sun. Since they'd got out, he hadn't written a line of poetry. Couldn't. He looked up into the darkness of the pine tree that sheltered him. Behind it were the mountains of Troodos, rich, fat mountains, alive with hares, birds, fruit. If it weren't for his shoulder, he could live here indefinitely. From the distance he could hear the growl of a heavy engine. Asimov rolled over on to his stomach. The rifle was by his side, the shoulder of his jacket stuffed with grass to take the impact of its recoil. He was as ready as he would ever be.

Craig had rehearsed the move to the Land-Rover carefully. First Joanna, going quickly into the driver's seat, backing it up to the door, then Miriam, then Kaplan, limping, wearing a blond wig, then Royce in a white wig, then Craig, Kaplan and Craig acting like bodyguards. Royce got into the Land-Rover next to Joanna, and Craig sat beside him. Miriam and Kaplan were in the back. Joanna let in the clutch and drove off at once, and the four-wheel drive tackled the mud track as if it were an autobahn. Mindful of his instructions, she hit a good pace and kept to it.

'Something's up,' Royce said at last. 'And you know what it is.'

Craig kept his eyes on the mountainside. Slopes and ridges, outcrops of rock; perfect sniper country.

'You've got no right to do this to me,' said Royce, then yelled at the silence: 'For God's sake, tell me what's happening.'

'It's possible there's a sniper out there,' said Craig.

Royce hunched down in his seat, and as he did so a bullet starred the window by Craig, smacked into Royce as they heard the report of a rifle. Joanna accelerated, and reached a corner in a burst of speed as Craig yelled instructions. The car skidded round the corner and stopped. Craig leaped out of it and raced up the side of the hill, rolled into cover behind a rock. From where he lay he could see Kaplan bending over Royce; Joanna getting out of the driving seat, examining the engine with what looked like frantic haste. He could see, too, a ripple of movement in the long grass on the mountain-side, the movement of a man who had been trained to move with caution and skill. Craig took out the 9-mm. automatic. It had nothing like the range of the rifle, but if Asimov came close enough, it would do.

The ripple of the grass came closer, and at last he could see Asimov's body as he wriggled his way between Craig and the Land-Rover. The group on the road didn't see him until he raised himself to his feet, the rifle held at the hip. Craig could see that he was swaying, very slightly.

Joanna and Miriam froze, as he had told them to do, but Kaplan panicked, turned and dived out of the car seat, racing across the road. And as he moved, Asimov saw him. He raised the rifle, his body swaying more than ever, though the gun was steady. Behind him, Craig got to his feet, his arms raised in the classic pistol-shooting position.

'Asimov!' he yelled, and the Russian checked, then started to turn, far too late. Craig fired once, then again, and the impact of the heavy bullets knocked Asimov sprawling, set him rolling over and over down the long, lush grass until he came to rest at last by the Land-Rover's front wheel. Joanna Benson looked down at him. Two wounds: one through the side of the head, one through the heart, fired from fifty feet away as he turned. Asimov had had no chance at all, and that was exactly as it should be.

Craig came slowly down to them, his eyes on Kaplan as he walked back across the road. Miriam, for the first time, saw emotion in his eyes, a boiling rage it took him all his strength to contain. He looked down at Royce, picked up a spent bullet embedded in the floorboard of the car.

'Is he dead?' he asked.

'No,' Kaplan said. 'The bullet hit him across the neck. Creased a nerve, I think.'

Craig pulled Royce upright. The bullet had furrowed a great gouge from his ear almost to his nape. He'd be marked for life, unless Loomis paid for plastic surgery, but he was alive. Joanna got a first-aid kit from the back of the Land-Rover, put lint on the wound and held it in place with tape.

'Poor Andrew,' she said. 'It's all I seem to do for him.'

Still looking at Kaplan, Craig said, 'Asimov wasn't so lucky. You damn fool, why couldn't you stay still and let me take him alive?'

'I was afraid,' Kaplan said. 'I can't help it, Craig. I'll always be afraid.'

'That's what makes you so dangerous,' Craig said. 'You get scared and somebody else gets killed.'

He bent, picked up the rifle, and dragged Asimov into a cleft behind a rock that hid him from the road. The face that looked up at him was suddenly ten years younger, smooth and untroubled. He'd lived through horror, and he'd seen and done terrible things, but he hadn't been irreclaimable, like Daniel. There had still been loyalty in him, and courage, and a zest for life. Something could have been done with Asimov, but not nearly as much as could be done with Kaplan. And so, thought Craig, he died. No. That was dishonest thinking. And so I killed him.

Royce recovered consciousness on the road to Nicosia. He looked up, and saw Craig beside him.

'You bastard,' he whispered.

'If it makes you any happier, the man who did it is dead,' said Craig.

'You set me up for this, didn't you? You wanted it to happen.'

'Rest,' said Craig. 'You're suffering from shock, poor boy.'

Joanna had their air-tickets and passports, luggage waited for them at Nicosia airport, and the fat man himself waited to see them off. The sight of Royce displeased him, and he said so. Royce closed his eyes as the great voice roared on. Craig took him to the bar.

'I had to do it that way,' he said. 'I knew Asimov was up in the hills with a rifle.'

'You get him?'

'Yes,' said Craig.

'That leaves Daniel.'

'No,' Craig said. 'He's dead too.'

'You *have* come back to life, cock,' Loomis said.

'My swan song. Anyway, I muffed it. I let Asimov get away. And Daniel killed Angelos.'

Loomis looked at him and said carefully, 'Rule Number One in our business. Never have any chums.'

'He wasn't my chum,' said Craig. 'He didn't like me at all.'

'What was he, then?'

'My debtor.'

'Not any more,' said Loomis. 'I reckon he's paid. Which reminds me—Royce is no good to you now either. D'you want me to send some people out from England?'

'We'll have to go to Athens to get to New York,' said Craig. 'Force Three could be waiting for us. I'll need a man there. A Greek if you've got one.'

Loomis downed a massive jolt of local brandy, and wrapped on the counter for another.

'We got a bloke in Athens already,' he said.

'I'll need him too,' said Craig, and began to explain. When he'd finished, Loomis thought for a moment, then said, 'It might work, cock. If you're as good as you think you are. But are you sure two men's enough? You don't want any help after that?'

'Benson's all I need,' said Craig.

'At least she's on your side,' said Loomis. Craig turned to him, wearily going through the motions of calm, hand steady as he lifted his glass, knowing he didn't fool Loomis for a second.

'What the hell does that mean?' he asked.

'She helped you get away, cock. And we both know it. That day they had you and the Loman person prisoner in the barn, she measured you against Royce and opted for you. Why?'

'Royce tortured Miriam,' said Craig.

'You're saying Benson's squeamish?'

'I'm saying she thinks ahead. Royce enjoyed his work—and it showed. And Benson saw it was a weakness. Look, Loomis—Benson talks like a deb and acts like an idiot with a daddy in the peerage, but she's as shrewd as you are. So she let me get away. It was her way of making a deal.'

'And very nice too,' said Loomis. 'Except I'm the one who pays the bill. I must have a word with her about that. Royce too.' He sighed. 'Pity about that. He was damn good at the school. Think I should send him to a psychiatrist?'

'You could try,' said Craig. 'A pity Asimov missed him, isn't it?'

'Tut tut,' said Loomis. 'The things you say.'

'Like a couple of weeks ago. I said, "You can hardly just let me go, can you?" And you said, "No. I can hardly do that."'

Loomis said, 'One of these fine days I'll drop dead of over-eating, and a nice little feller in a bowler hat and pin-striped underwear'll come and see you and offer you my job. What'll you do then, son?'

'Refuse.'

'That may not be easy.'

'I can always shoot myself,' said Craig.

The flight call came then, and they went out to the aircraft. For once Loomis had been generous, and they travelled first-class. Craig sat beside Kaplan, and they made the journey in silence. Joanna and Miriam didn't talk much either.

CHAPTER FOURTEEN

THEY HAD FOUR ROOMS in a hotel in Constitution Square. It was a pleasant hotel, big, shady, cool, with a fifty-year-old elegance that was already as valuable as an antique. The hotel was full of Americans just off to Delphi, Germans just back from Crete, Italians making a film, and Swedes absorbing sun and culture in such quantities that only the bar could save their sanity and their skins. Craig watched them as he waited for the lift. There were too many of them. Kaplan shouldn't stay here. And yet in America it could only be worse. When the lift doors opened, Craig watched approvingly as Joanna pushed Kaplan in ahead of her, her tall body covering him. Then Miriam went, and Craig last, his right hand inside his coat, ready, waiting.

The rooms were on the fifth floor, and the clang of contemporary Athens was muted below them. Athenians have never been an inhibited people: noise as an art form they find as convenient as any other, and cheap to practise. Craig sent Kaplan to his room, locked him in, and turned to the others.

'What do you want to do?' he asked.

'I want to go out,' said Miriam. 'I'm sick of being cooped up.'

'All right,' said Craig. 'I'll go with you.'

'If you want to,' she said. 'Wouldn't you sooner take a rest?'

'I would. Yes,' Craig said. 'I'm just worried about you, that's all.'

'Oh, I'll be just fine,' she said. 'All I want to do is be a tourist for a while. Go to the Acropolis, maybe.'

Joanna Benson opened her mouth, saw the look in Craig's eye and shut it again.

'Off you go, then,' said Craig. 'But don't be late. I'm waiting for a cancellation on a flight. If we get it, we leave at dawn.'

Before she left, Miriam kissed him. Then the door closed and Joanna Benson said, 'Darling, I know she sleeps with you and all that, but aren't you being a teeny bit self-indulgent?'

'No,' said Craig. 'She'll be followed. I set it up with Loomis before I left.'

The tall girl sighed her relief. 'Do you think there's much danger in Athens?'

'Some,' said Craig. 'The CIA did a deal with Loomis—information for Kaplan. Then they sub-contracted to Force Three. If Force Three picks up Kaplan here, Loomis doesn't get his information and I don't get my money.'

'So you let her take a walk,' said Joanna.

'I like to know who the opposition it,' said Craig.

It was pleasant to be out alone, to walk across the square, to feel the press of an anonymous crowd about you. That reminded her of New York, and the thought made her smile. She had always hated the crowds in New York. She crossed the street to a café in the middle of the square, and Maskouri, who was following her, hoped she would sit down and drink coffee. It was much too hot to walk very far. She chose a table in the shady part, and Maskouri was relieved. Too many Americans liked to sit in the sun. He found a table nearby and ordered beer, sipped first at the glass of cold water that came with it. The Loman girl ordered a large, and, to Maskouri's eyes, disgusting ice-cream, and spooned it up with enthusiasm. Then suddenly she hesitated. A tall American was approaching her. He was carrying a transistor radio, and it was playing a tune Maskouri recognized vaguely, and somehow associated with a sad-faced little man who played the piano. The American looked down at the girl, then said:

'Why, Miriam Loman! Well, for heaven's sakes. I was talking to Marcus just two days ago.'

The girl smiled at him, and said 'Hello,' and asked him to sit down. Maskouri doubted that she had seen the tall American before, and this might be important. And once he'd sat down, he wasn't talking loud enough for Maskouri to hear. He wondered whether he should report back or not, when the American rose, took the girl's hand and said, 'Great to see you, Miriam. Just great. Be sure to give my love to Marcus when you see him.'

'Oh, I certainly will,' said Miriam.

The tall American went off, and Miriam paid her bill, changing dollars with the waiter, then walked to the taxi-rank. Maskouri got up to follow, and was promptly knocked flat by a couple of Americans, who apologized profusely for not looking where they were going. They picked him up and the grip they had on him seemed friendly enough, but Maskouri was sensible. He knew enough not to struggle. When the taxi had gone, one of the Americans said, 'Sorry feller,' and offered him a cigar. Maskouri, being Athenian, was a philosopher. He accepted it.

'She's taking her time,' Joanna Benson said.

'So's the man Loomis sent to Athens,' said Craig. He looked at his watch. 'He should have rung in an hour ago. I think we'd better make arrangements.'

'Such as?'

'They'll come for Kaplan—alive. And to make sure of that, they'll immobilize us first.'

'Immobilize? Do you by any chance think they'll kill us?'

'Not if they can avoid it,' said Craig. 'But the bloke Maskouri saw talking to her will do it if he has to. He'd prefer to use knock-out drops or a bang on the head.'

'Neither's terribly pleasant.'

Craig grinned. 'Neither's going to happen,' he said. 'Listen.'

He began to talk; and first Joanna smiled, and then laughed aloud.

'But darling, it's positively kinky,' she said.

'Get the silencer.'

She produced it from her handbag and Craig screwed it on to the end of the Smith and Wesson, then broke the gun, looked into the magazine. Three shots left. But the silencer wouldn't last more than three shots anyway. After that he would have to fall back on the Webley, and an utter lack of privacy.

'You'd really use that thing on our allies?' the girl asked.

'I have no allies. I'm a free-lance,' said Craig.

'Yes, but even so——'

'Listen,' said Craig. 'These aren't nice, gentlemanly Ivy Leaguers from the CIA. These are professionals. The way you think you are.'

'You'll find out,' Joanna said.

'I always knew. Forgive the sarcasm,' said Craig. 'Just take my word for it. These are blokes the KGB would be proud of.'

The phone rang. Craig picked it up and listened, then turned to her.

'That was Loomis's man,' he said. 'Miriam met two more Americans at the Acropolis. He couldn't get close enough to hear.'

When Miriam returned, she found the others in Craig's room, having a meal of coffee and sandwiches.

'Aren't we dining downstairs?' she asked.

'No,' said Craig. 'Too risky. Have a sandwich. Joanna, pour Miriam some coffee.'

'Risky?'

'Yes,' said Craig. 'I've had a premonition. Do you ever have premonitions, Miriam?'

Joanna handed her a sandwich. The whole thing was as English as a Thirties farce: sandwiches and tinkling spoons, and the distinguished elderly foreigner who was about to upset his cup any minute. And there was farce in the way they were over-playing it, too. Farce or its nearest neighbour, violence.

'John,' Miriam said. 'What *is* all this?'

'An hour and a half ago I heard from a dark stranger,' said Craig. 'At least I expect he's dark. Most Greeks are. Chap called Maskouri. You didn't see him, by any chance?'

'I didn't see anybody—except a man who used to know Marcus. But I got rid of him. Then I had some ice-cream and went to the Acropolis.'

Craig turned to Joanna. 'Why should she lie to me? A nice girl like that.'

'*Do* have another sandwich,' Joanna said to Miriam, then to Craig, 'Patriotism, perhaps?'

'You mean the American she met told her it was in her country's best interests not to tell a soul that they had met?'

'He probably showed her a picture of Lyndon Johnson or Bugs Bunny or somebody.'

'More likely music. Music to remind her of happy days. Junior Proms and old films on TV and travelling in the elevator at the Hilton. I bet he played her "Stardust".'

Joanna's eyes had never left Miriam's face.

'Do you know,' she said. 'I believe he did.'

'You followed me,' said Miriam. 'But you got it wrong. He was a friend of Marcus.'

'Good heavens, we British chappies don't have to follow people,' said Craig. 'We get ruddy foreigners to do that. No, love. We deduced it.' He moved a step closer to her. 'I'm afraid you're going to have to tell us, you know.' She was silent. 'Ah, he said. 'I know what you're thinking. Royce isn't here, you tell yourself, and a decent chap like Craig wouldn't do things like that, and Miss Benson's an English gentlewoman after all. Sews Union Jacks on her panties. But that isn't the point love. The point is we know they're in Athens.'

'How could they be?' Miriam asked.

'Loomis sent a wire to that box number in Paris,' said Joanna. 'Told them the deal with Craig is off. And there's only three ways out of Cyprus, darling—Turkey, Israel, and Greece. They'll be watching them all. But it's the ones in Greece who'll get hurt.'

Craig said, 'We won't hurt you, Miriam, and I don't want to hurt them. You tell us what they're up to and we won't hurt them. If you don't—it might get a bit messy.'

'You're angry with me—for what I've done,' she said.

'If I am, I have no right to be.'

'It's my country, John. My people.'

He nodded. 'And it's your people who'll get hurt—if you don't tell me.'

'Don't you ever fight fair?' she asked.

'How can I?' said Craig. 'Now, drink your coffee and tell me all about it.' Suddenly the mockery had gone. She was aware that he wanted to be kind to her, kind and uncomplicated, and that he was finding it difficult.

Early morning, the dead hour, the hour of the ultimate spy. The one who will kill if he must. There were three of them. One stayed in the corridor, watching the rooms of Kaplan and Joanna, the others entered the room that Craig had given to Miriam. Her bed, they knew, was to the right of the room, facing the bathroom, and Craig would be in it. That had been Miriam's assignment, to get Craig into her bed, and she'd resisted it furiously at first. She'd taken a lot of convincing, but in the end she'd agreed. And having got him there, the team-leader reckoned, she'd keep him pretty busy. Craig was a tough one. Exhausted or not, their instructions were to keep out of range of his hands. Those hands of Craig's could batter like steel clubs.

The lock specialist took out his skeleton key and got on with it. Hotel locks, even the locks of good hotels, didn't keep him waiting long. He probed with the casual skill of a surgeon performing a routine operation. Two tiny clicks sounded, and the lock specialist withdrew the key, slipped it into an oil bottle and inserted it again. Next time he turned it, the door opened without a sound, and he and the team-leader entered in a whisper, the door drifted to behind them as they stayed still for a count of ten, their eyes grew used to the blackness.

At last, the leader touched the lock man. In the imperfect dark they could see the two shapes of bodies lying on the bed, one hunched over the other. The lock man moved to the wall, switched on the lights, and as he did so his right hand made an abrupt gesture, ended up holding a short-nosed Colt .45 fitted with a silencer. The leader stood six feet away from him, holding a similar gun, and one of the figures on the bed stirred and shot up indignantly.

For a moment the leader thought they'd gone into the wrong room—a mistake so elementary he wanted to kill himself—for the figure in front of him was that of a beautiful and very naked woman. He hesitated just a split second too long, and was already starting to turn when Craig's voice spoke behind him.

'Be sensible,' said Craig. 'You can't win them all. Guns on the bed, please.'

The lock expert waited until the leader's hand moved, then he too threw his gun down. The gorgeous broad moved as if she was wearing clothes up to her chin, and tucked the guns under her pillow. The lock expert began to sweat, then sweated harder as she got out of bed and put on a negligée. She moved like a stripper and her body was perfect. The last thing the lock expert saw before Craig hit him behind the ear was the splendid curve of one deep, full breast. Craig caught him before he fell, lowered him to the floor. The leader turned then, fast, but the gun was already on him. When he looked up, the dark girl held a gun too, his own, and the leader had no illusions about its accuracy. In the bed, Miriam Loman slept. She, too, was naked. The dark girl pulled the covers over her.

'You got one outside?' asked Craig. The leader nodded. 'Tell him to come in. You'll need some help with your friend.'

The leader hesitated, and Joanna said, 'I'd do what he says. Honestly I would.'

'Come on in, Harry,' the leader called, and Harry came in to see the team leader covered by Craig, and a broad in the kind of negligée they used to wear at Minsky's pointing a gun at him.

'Tell Harry what to do with his gun,' said Craig.

'On the bed,' said the leader, and Harry obeyed, and his gun went on the pillow.

'Sit down over there,' said Craig, and nodded towards two chairs in a corner of the room. The leader moved first. 'Stay away from the bed,' said Craig. 'This isn't a party.'

Carefully, the two men sat.

'What is this? A dyke affair?' Harry asked.

'No, darling. The girls' dorm,' Joanna said.

'Miss Loman seems a good sleeper,' the leader said.

'I put a little something in her coffee,' said Joanna. 'Poor darling, she needs her rest. She's had too much excitement lately.'

The leader nodded. Even with two guns pointed at him, he managed to look elegant enough for a whisky ad.

'You're looking better, Craig,' he said.

'I'm feeling it,' said Craig.

'No hard feelings, I hope?'

'None,' said Craig, and spoke to Joanna. 'This gentleman took me on a drug party in New York. I wound up telling him the story of my life.' He turned back to the leader. 'Do you have a name?'

'Lederer will do. Where's our mutual friend?'

'Dickens,' said Joanna. 'I adore intellectual conversation.'

'In the bathroom,' said Craig. 'Go and take a look—but mind how you walk.'

Lederer looked round the bathroom door. Kaplan sat strapped to the toilet, fast asleep.

'That's some coffee you serve,' said Lederer. 'I'll give you half a million dollars for him.'

'I've got half a million dollars.'

'A million—tax free.'

'You shouldn't talk in such vast sums. It's what makes you Americans so unpopular,' Joanna said.

'And guaranteed protection,' said Lederer.

'I've already got a deal—with Loomis,' said Craig.

'So has the CIA. He wants information. I'd sooner spend money.'

'I'm sorry,' said Craig. 'I really am.'

It was at that moment that Harry found it necessary to prove his manhood. A broad half-way through a burlesque routine seemed to him an insult to his maleness, even if she did hold a Colt .45. And anyway, he reasoned, a Colt is too big a gun for a broad. And with Lederer watching he'd be doing himself a whole lot of good. He'd been watching her, and sure enough the gun-barrel had sagged, her concentration was all on Lederer and Craig.

Harry swivelled slightly on his chair. She took no notice. Careful to show no evidence of tension on his face or body, Harry prepared himself the way they'd taught him and made his grab. What happened was like a nightmare in slow motion. She seemed to have all the time in the world to bring the gun up, to choose the spot where the bullet would go. There was no tension in her eyes, only a glittering excitement as she pulled the trigger, the gun popped, and Harry felt as if the room had fallen on his shoulder before he lost consciousness. And all the time, Craig's gun stayed on Lederer.

'He's a little over-excitable,' Lederer said.

Joanna went to him, opened his coat.

'He's lucky he's not a little dead,' she said. 'He didn't give me much time to choose a spot.'

She went into the bathroom and came back with a towel.

'First they make one shoot them, then they expect one to patch them up. It's no fun being a woman,' she said.

'No deal at all?' Lederer asked Craig. 'I could go up to a million five.'

'No deal,' said Craig. 'I'm sorry.'

'It's too bad we need that bastard,' said Lederer. 'He costs too much.'

Joanna looked up from Harry.

'What makes him so very expensive?' she asked.

'He can make the deserts blossom,' said Lederer. 'Put him down on sand and sea-water and he'll turn it into an orange grove. It takes money and it takes technology, but he can do it. So we'll work out the technique, and sell it round the world.'

'Sell it?'

'Not for money. As you say—we Americans have enough. For co-operation. For commitment.'

'You should start with Israel,' Craig said.

'We intend to.'

'He's not exactly a willing worker,' said Craig.

'He will be. Who else has he got but us?' He looked into Craig's eyes. 'You don't like him much, do you?'

'I don't like him at all. But he's needed. A lot of better men died because of him, but the world hadn't any use for them. They couldn't do his trick.'

'Give him a few years and he'll be just as friendly and lovable and integrated as any other millionaire,' said Lederer. The lock expert groaned and twitched feebly.

'I guess we better be going,' Lederer said. It sounded like a question.

'I think you had,' said Craig.

'Just one thing I want to ask. How on earth did you know we were coming?'

'We had her followed.'

'Sure. I know that. Your local guy. We blocked him off before he could get near.'

'We rather thought you would,' said Craig. 'You're very efficient. So we put another man on to her as well. Flew him in from England this morning.'

Lederer accepted it without regret. 'I guess we had it coming,' he said. 'One way and another, we gave you quite a run-around.' He looked at the sleeping figure on the bed. 'And Miss Loman.'

'If your own operators hadn't been blown, you'd have got him yourselves,' said Craig. 'You did all you could do—under the circumstances.'

'The circumstances were lousy,' Lederer said. 'But at least we've got Kaplan.'

'You will have, tomorrow,' said Craig.

'You're flying him back?'

'BOAC. It was funny how every American airline just happened to have four seats available.'

Lederer grinned. 'Can't blame us for trying, son,' he said. 'Next time, we'll block you off before the operation even gets started.'

'There won't be a next time,' said Craig.

The man on the floor groaned again. He should have been happy.

For the Americans, getting out of the hotel was easy. They used the same drunken party technique they'd used with Craig, a hundred drachma note to a night porter, and a waiting Buick. When they'd gone, Joanna put down the gun, stretched her arms and sighed. Translucent silk slid over her hips, stretched taut across her breasts.

'What a very exciting night,' she said.

'Stop being the middle pages of *Playboy*,' said Craig.

She moved towards him.

'I feel like the middle pages of *Playboy*,' she said. She stood very close to him, and kissed him. He made no response. 'Is it her?' she asked, and looked at the bed.

'No,' Craig said. 'That's over. In a way, it never even started. It was all loneliness and fear and'—he struggled for the word—'compassion. It almost got her killed. She deserves better than anything I could give her.'

'I don't,' Joanna said. 'I don't expect it. I don't want it. You're what I want.'

'Is that why you let me go free?'

'Of course it was.'

Craig laughed. 'And I thought it was because you thought you had a better chance with me than with Royce.'

Suddenly, she was laughing too. It made her more beautiful, more exciting than ever. Still laughing, she pressed herself against him once more.

'You and I will get on beautifully, darling. You've so much to teach me,' she said. Her arms came round him. 'And vice-versa, of course.'

CHAPTER FIFTEEN

THEY FLEW TO ROME, and then to New York. This time the movie was about sex in the deep South. Craig's sympathies were with the South. He had always understood it had problems enough without that. Back in time they went, eating the same plastic meals, drinking the exactly measured drinks; bored, restless, embalmed in space. Craig sat beside Miriam, and tried to think of ways of saying goodbye. There were none.

'I'm taking a holiday,' she said. 'I reckon I deserve it.'

'Send the bill to Force Three,' he said. 'The least they can do is pay.'

'I thought maybe you'd like to come along too.'

'You've had enough of me, and everybody like me.'

'Listen,' she said. 'Sometimes I hate you. Sometimes I could kill you for the way you can always get a rise out of me. The way you look at life—the things you do—it hurts me even when I think of them. The trouble is I love you.'

'The trouble is I make you unhappy.'

'I was happy for five nights,' Miriam said. 'Maybe I was lucky it lasted so long. You said something like that to Kaplan—that night in Troodos. Only he had six months.'

'Maybe he earned it,' Craig said.

'After what he did?'

'After what he suffered. You had it rough, Miriam, and most of it was my fault, and I'm sorry. But Kaplan—we can't even begin to guess the things they did to him.'

'What about the things he did to the Jews? His own people.'

'He's paid for some of them,' said Craig. 'He'll go on paying. Even more than he owes.'

'How?'

'The United States wants his knowledge—to help under-developed countries. They'll protect him, give him asylum, and in return he'll work on desert reclamation problems.'

'What's wrong with that?'

'The first place they'll send him to is Israel.'

'Israel?'

'Can you imagine the propaganda the Russians will make out of that? The things they'll say about him? What he did to the friends who trusted him?'

'Israel won't accept him,' Miriam said.

'Israel must,' said Craig. 'They need the water. But he'll never be one of them, love. He's alone now till he dies. You should pity him.'

'He deserves it,' the girl said. 'He deserves much more. Even a Jew couldn't pity him, after what he'd done.'

Craig leaned back in his seat. Maybe the best thing was silence, after all.

He'd hoped for a glimpse of Marcus Kaplan when they reached Kennedy, but instead they were whisked into a VIP lounge and a smart matronly person like a successful beautician took Miriam away as soon as they'd said goodbye. Three men waited for Kaplan. Two of them were Lederer and the lock expert, the third a scientist whom Kaplan recognized at once. The scientist began asking questions, and Kaplan's replies at first were hesitant, dredged up deep from the well of memory.

'It's been so long,' he said.

'Wait till we get to Utah,' the scientist said. 'We have everything set up there under test conditions. You'll soon catch up.'

He went on talking and, as they watched, Kaplan came to life.

'How's Harry?' Joanna asked.

'Mending,' said Lederer. 'But you've really shaken his faith in Western woman. If he doesn't watch it, he'll wind up a fag.'

A chauffeur and two more men appeared, and Lederer tapped Kaplan on the shoulder. He started, and for a moment the fear returned, then he relaxed. *He* was important now, with a bodyguard of his own. Gravely he waited as the big men surrounded him, walked him to the door. Craig wondered if he'd lied to Miriam after all: if the Kaplans of the world ever paid back a cent.

He and Joanna were alone now, except for a short, stumpy figure who had waited for them patiently. Now he came forward: a chubby, benign man wearing hexagonal rimless glasses.

'Hi there,' he said.

'Hi,' said Craig. 'How's the pentathol business?'

'That's what I came to see you about,' said the benign man. 'Oh, say. My name's Mankowitz. Excuse me, sugar.' He walked Craig away from Joanna. 'I came to ask if we could run some more tests on you.'

'Who's we?'

'Force Three. You know that,' Mankowitz said. 'Mind you, last time you thought I was KGB. That helped. They really scare you, don't they? Come and see me. If you pass, there's a chance we could use you.'

'Mr Mankowitz, do you know how old I am?' asked Craig.

'Know everything about you. We really could use you, feller. If the tests work out. Tell you the truth, I could stand to know what happened to you during the last ten days. Last time I saw you, you were finished.'

'I still am,' said Craig. 'Sorry.'

'Suit yourself,' Mankowitz said. 'You ever change your mind, I'm in the book. First name Joel. Psychiatrist. 1419 59th Street. That's in Manhattan.'

'Isn't everything?'

'Cynicism suits your age-group,' Mankowitz said. 'Work at it. And don't forget my address.' He clapped Craig on the shoulder and was gone.

Because he was rich Craig took a taxi to the hotel in the West Forties. He and Joanna had suites booked already, and letters awaited them both. Craig's was a statement from the First National Bank that two hundred and thirty-nine thousand dollars were at his disposal and they waited his instructions. His very truly. Joanna's was a brisk but cordial request from Loomis to get back as soon as she could. She handed it to Craig.

'How long have I got?' she asked.

'He'll usually hang on for two days. After that, he gets mad.'

'That isn't what I meant,' she said.

'I know it wasn't. Look, I've got to go out for a while.'

'Must you?'

'Yes,' said Craig. 'Just to make sure this money's OK. Wait for me, will you?'

'I'm glad you said that, John.' She began to loosen her coat. 'It sounded as if you really wanted me to.'

As he went down in the elevator, Craig thought it might be the last time he'd ever see her.

He came back two hours later with the beginning of a black eye and two inches of skin missing from his left elbow.

'Darling, what on earth did you do at the bank? Rob it?' she asked.

'The bank? No. The money's fine. I just beat hell out of a man called Thadeus Cooke,' said Craig.

She was still shaking with laughter as they began to make love. Later they rose, dressed, drank in the murky twilight of the cocktail bar, ate at the Four Seasons. They were asleep when the knocking began, but she, like Craig, was awake at once. Quickly they put on dressing gowns, and Craig slipped the .38 into the pocket of his as she reached for her handbag.

'What is it?' asked Craig.

'Telegram for Mr Craig.'

Craig moved into the lounge, unlatched the door.

'Bring it in,' he said. 'The door's not locked.'

He moved into the space behind the door. Suddenly it flew open, and Marcus Kaplan came into the room. In his hands was a skeet-gun. He seemed almost crazy with rage, but the hands on the gun were steady. If I give him half a chance he'll blast me, Craig thought. The only sane thing to do is put a bullet in him now. But he couldn't. It was impossible. The realization flicked through his mind as Marcus started to turn. Craig tossed his life up in the air like a coin, and took a long stride towards him, put the muzzle of the gun on Kaplan's neck.

'Just drop it,' he said.

Kaplan tensed, willing himself to turn and blast, and Craig found he couldn't even hit him.

Joanna's voice spoke from the bedroom door. 'I shouldn't, Mr Kaplan,' she said. 'You kill him and I'll kill you. You won't die quickly.'

Kaplan's hands opened; the skeet-gun thudded on the carpet. Craig grabbed it up and pushed on the safety catch, then went to the door. The corridor was empty, except for a long, soft leather bag. He brought it inside, and steered the other man to a chair. Marcus was crying. Craig opened the drinks cupboard and poured whisky.

'I'll have one too,' said Joanna.

Craig offered one to Marcus, who pushed it away. He waited till the man's sobs died, and offered it again.

'Murder doesn't come all that easy to you,' Craig said. 'Take a drink, you need it.'

Reluctantly, Marcus Kaplan accepted it, and choked it down. Craig poured him another.

'D'you want to tell me why, Marcus?' he asked.

'I've just finished talking to Miriam,' Marcus said. 'She told me—she told me——'

'She'd been to bed with me?'

'I hate you, Craig. I want you dead.'

Craig waited once more, and Joanna came to the room and poured herself a drink.

Suddenly Marcus sprang from the chair and hurled himself at Craig, a pathetically unskilful attack; the onslaught of a civilized man who doesn't know how to hurt. Gently, Craig took hold of the clumsy hands and forced him back into the chair.

510   THE INNOCENT BYSTANDERS

'Don't try it,' said Craig. 'You don't know how to.'

He increased his pressure a little, and Marcus was still.

'Did she tell you how we became lovers?' Craig asked, and Marcus nodded. 'And you can't forgive her for it?'

'Her? Of course I can,' Marcus said. 'I could have understood you, too. But you kicked her out, didn't you? For this—this——' He turned to Joanna.

'I did right,' said Craig. 'You know I did.'

'You left her when she was helpless.'

'It won't be for long,' said Joanna. 'And Craig has no future in the fur business.'

The words hit Kaplan like blows.

'Joanna, for God's sake,' said Craig.

'But he's jealous, darling. Surely you can see that.'

'I've never touched her,' said Kaplan.

'But you'd like to, wouldn't you, Marcus?'

'Lay off,' said Craig, and turned to Marcus once more. 'It happened. There's nothing anyone can do. Accept that.'

'No,' Kaplan said. 'One of these days I'll catch up with you. I swear it.'

'Marcus, you're no good at this. That telegram gag's archaic,' Craig said. 'You don't even know how to hate. Believe me. I've seen experts. Forget about me. She's the one you should be looking after——'

'It's easy for you,' said Kaplan. 'You do this to her and just walk away——'

'I did rather more than that,' said Craig. 'I got her father back.'

Joanna swirled round. The whisky slopped in her glass.

'She's your niece, isn't she?' Craig said. 'Aaron's daughter. You brought her out of Germany in 1946. You should have told her, Marcus.'

'I couldn't,' Kaplan said. 'By that time Russia was the enemy. I didn't want her to think her father was—one of them.'

'Before we set out to get him,' said Craig. 'She had a right to know then.'

'By that time she was virtually my daughter,' Kaplan said.

'What about your wife?' asked Joanna.

'Ida never knew,' said Kaplan. 'Aaron wrote to me just after the war—but it was to the office. He asked me to look out for a girl he'd met. He'd been ordered back to Russia, and the girl had moved out into the Western zone. I—I didn't like to tell Ida. I faked a business trip to Europe and went to see her. Brigitte, her name was. Brigitte Hahn. She was dying then—tuberculosis.

Aaron hadn't even known she was pregnant. I adopted the baby—it was easy then. She didn't look like Aaron at all.'

'What did Ida say?' Joanna asked.

'I told her I'd found her in a Jewish orphanage. That I couldn't resist her.'

'Ida loved her as soon as she saw her,' Kaplan said.

'Why Loman?' asked Craig.

'It was the name on her papers,' said Kaplan. 'Forged papers. They cost me seven hundred dollars. It was like investing in Paradise.' He sipped at his drink. 'How did you know, Craig?'

'I guessed it,' said Craig. 'It fitted so well it had to be true. Except—you still haven't told me why you kept quiet before we went to Turkey.'

'I wanted to find out if she loved him,' Kaplan said.

'And now you know. She hates him. What are you going to do, Marcus?'

'What can I do?'

'Keep quiet.'

'But she's his daughter.'

'He doesn't deserve a daughter like that—but you do,' said Craig.

'But I came here to kill you,' said Marcus.

'That's part of it. Go home, Marcus. Put your skeet-gun in its nice leather bag and go home.'

He watched, empty handed, as Marcus Kaplan picked up the gun and packed it into its container.

'You take some terrible chances, John,' Joanna said.

Marcus looked up, genuinely puzzled.

'Oh,' he said. 'The gun. Believe me, Miss Benson, I wouldn't—I mean, I'm very sorry, I——'

'Forget it,' Craig said. 'Just tell me how you knew I was here.'

'This was the thirty-fifth hotel I phoned,' said Kaplan. He picked up the bag. 'Well——' he said.

'Forgive me,' said Joanna, 'but didn't anybody ask you what was in your bag?'

'Why should they?' asked Kaplan. 'Some very important people shoot skeet.'

He left then, and Joanna snorted with laughter. This time Craig didn't join in.

'Darling,' she said. 'Wasn't he funny?'

'Hilarious,' said Craig. 'But he had to break his heart to do it.'

Next morning, Craig went through what he intended to be a

ritual for the rest of his life. After bathing, shaving, and ordering breakfast, he looked first at his bank statement, then at the letter Loomis had signed. The bank statement was fine: the letter was a blank page. Craig held it to the light, ran a finger over its surface. It was a blank paper and nothing more. He went into the bedroom and woke Joanna, held the paper out in front of her.

'You knew, didn't you?' he asked.

She shrugged. There was no sense in denial.

'Yes, darling. That's why we made you wait a day. Loomis didn't need authority. He needed the ink. It had to be flown out from London.'

'The bastard,' said Craig. 'The great, fat, cunning bastard.'

'You've still got two hundred and thirty-nine thousand dollars,' she said, then, 'He gave me a message for you.

'Well?'

'We can travel back together if we want to. Economy. If we go back first we pay the difference.'

Craig took off his coat, began to loosen his tie.

'What on earth are you doing?' she asked.

'I've got two days of freedom,' said Craig. 'I'm going to enjoy them.'

'But you said you'd show me New York.'

'You can begin with this ceiling,' said Craig.